To
Jody's-Joe

Love
Fred

FREDERICK MUNN

THE CROOKED *Olive Branch*

Love will find a way

novum pro

Printed in the European Union on environmentally friendly, chlorine- and acid-free paper.

ISBN 978-3-99107-667-4
Editing: Philip Kelly
Cover photos: Teresa Azevedo, Charles Mccarthy | Dreamstime.com
Cover design, layout & typesetting: novum publishing
Internal illustrations: Frederick Munn

The images provided by the author have been printed in the highest possible quality.

www.novum-publishing.co.uk

Dedication

Dedicated to the memory of 2337543 Sergeant Edgar Stanton (1919–2011) of The Royal Corps of Signals and colleagues of Station X, the British Forces personnel involved in Yugoslavia, Jani Kovac* and the Yugoslav partisans who are acknowledged for their work behind enemy lines providing 'ammunition' for the Bletchley Park code breakers. Also acknowledged is the part played by Italian partisans in the destruction of significant strategic Axis reserve supplies in the Caves of Postojna.

Edgar gave nothing away about his involvement before Government recognition over 60 years after the events and too little afterwards. This book was inspired by the author's conversations with Edgar following the issue of commemorative medals in the first decade of the 21st century. This acknowledgement by the U.K. Government was the first his family knew of these epic events in the Second World War, 1939–45.

Although following the chronological progress of the period, this novel is a fiction inspired by talks between Edgar and the author and the author's memories of those times.

* Jani Kovac was the train driver who helped rescue Edgar from discovery by the Nazis by hiding him in the overhead toolbox of his railway engine. The partisans took Edgar from hiding in Ljubljana moving him to the Kovac's home in north east Slovenia thus avoiding his capture by the Nazis and the inevitable execution of Edgar as an enemy spy.
Jani's and Edgar's families became friends after the war and keep in touch.

Acknowledgements

Coral Lynn Jackson	Edgar Stanton's Daughter
John Stanton	Edgar Stanton's Son

'The Lambeth Walk' from the West End show *Me and My Girl.* Lyrics by Douglas Furber and L Arthur Rose, (Music Noel Gay.) This was a huge dance 'craze' promoted by Lupino Lane.

Edgar Stanton

Edgar Stanton

Edgar Stanton. Born 26th December 1919 in Rotherham, South Yorkshire.

Parents, Percy and Polly Stanton.

Percy, a postman, worked 5 a.m. until mid-day/ 2 p.m. until his post round was complete.

Wireless Telegraphy was the early 20th century 'Smart 'Phone.

Percy taught himself and his children Nancy and Edgar, Morse code.

Polly and Percy took in lodgers, workers at the Post Offices (Wireless Telegraphers?)

This was the environment of Edgar's upbringing.

Even as a very young boy, he was proficient in sending and receiving Morse.

A talented raconteur, Edgar told of having 'secret' conversations, in Morse, with sister Nancy during lunch by tapping knives on their plates.

'Secret Conversations' subsequently took Edgar on an unusual and dangerous journey.

It was a journey about which he was prevented from speaking of for over 60 years.

Piecing together Edgar's story is akin to finding a sixty-year old jigsaw puzzle in a 'dusty attic,' with half the pieces missing. It is impossible to even approach the truth after so long, and after Edgar's death. The only options left being guesswork or fiction. Therefore, although using the background of Edgars' memories and my memories of the Second World War, The Crooked Olive Branch is perforce a total fiction.

In July 1995 on the evening of our son's wedding, Edgar and James Musty, a cousin, were talking on the terrace of the Avon

Gorge Hotel. James, a British Airways captain, had visited the Caves of Postojna in Slovenia. These hugely cavernous spaces had been used by the German Army to store massive quantities of munitions, vehicles and fuel during the war.

During this conversation Jim sensed that Edgar knew so much more about these caves and the area, that there must be a story there. He said as much to me. At a subsequent family event in Maidenhead, Jim and I compared notes.

Late one morning in the mid-1980s I was working in my office in Horsham, West Sussex, when I received an urgent telephone call from Edgar. He and his wife Rosa were at Gatwick Airport. Due to a mix-up between Edgar and the travel agent he should have been at Heathrow for the intended flight to Ljubljana. "Could I ferry them across to Heathrow in time to catch the 14:50 flight?"

This I achieved with seconds to spare. They were being met in Ljubljana by 'friends.'

Hearing this, Jim Musty was convinced there was a connection leading to a story.

Why Ljubljana? Why there and not a package holiday to Dubrovnik? Did Edgar know more than he was telling about the sabotage of the German reserve munitions, fuel and vehicles carried out by British Sappers aided by Italian Partisans?

Ten years passed until Gordon Brown, the Prime Minister, finally acknowledged the work carried out by Edgar and his colleagues in Yugoslavia behind the German lines.

Edgar and his colleagues of Station X and the Bletchley Park Code Breakers then were released from their oath to observe the Official Secrets Act and were given Citation Certificates and Medals.

THE GOVERNMENT CODE
AND CYPHER SCHOOL

Edgar Stanton

*The Government wishes to express
to you its deepest gratitude
for the vital service you performed
during World War II*

Gordon Brown

Rt Hon Gordon Brown MP
Prime Minister

July 2009

Certificate and Medal

Then and only then did Edgar acknowledge his service in S.O.E. (Special Operations Executive) and that it was he who sent the success of operation signal to headquarters of the destruction of the German reserves at Postojna. The signal code name "FLAMBO."

The 'friends' meeting Edgar and Rosa in Ljubljana Airport were Jani Kovac and his wife. Jani the son of the train driver who in the occupation was instrumental in helping Edgar escape the S.S. following FLAMBO, by hiding him in the overhead toolbox in his cabin. Transporting him from Ljubljana to his home in North East Slovenia. Edgar survived several weeks hidden in their home until the S.O.E. arranged his repatriation.

Edgar died in 2011. The full story died with him. I gleaned only the basics, these memories being clouded by time. Edgar's stock answer to my questions was, "it was all such a long time ago." As a result, I have resorted to a total fiction to alert the wider world to just how much is owed to Edgar and his colleagues at Station X and Bletchley Park.

COINCIDENCE OR THE HAND OF PROVIDENCE?

Many years had passed until Edgar retired. Whether or not he thought to himself 'What do I do now?' He clearly resolved to try and find Jani Kovac, the train driver who helped save his life.

This presented problems and not just with the passage of time.

As with Alan Turing, he was still held under oath by the Official Secrets Act as were all from Station X and Bletchley Park.

Under the sixty year rule he was bound to stay silent. How then would he explain to his wife Rosa and his family why he was compelled to try and find a Jani Kovac in Yugoslavia?

In addition, the name Kovac is common, maybe as common as Smith in England. There were probably thousands named Jani Kovac at the time. Edgar was also sparse of knowledge not knowing just where he was behind enemy lines. His only solid geographical reference point had been Ljubljana. The Yugoslavian partisans had hidden Edgar there following FLAMBO.

The Nazi search net closing in, he was moved by the partisans via Jani Kovac's train's toolbox into some small town or village where he remained for several weeks until the S.O.E arranged his repatriation.

Rosa was finally persuaded. She and Edgar booked on a flight to Ljubljana and into a hotel. This was either a massive leap of faith or maybe he just had to know that he had tried his best.

With so little hope and in order to keep faith with his oath Edgar probably took Rosa to the Caves of Postojna behaving as any tourist would.

One day they took the bus to Lake Bled. In the evening, tired and wishing to return to the hotel, hey needed to find the bus stop. Rosa saw a coach load of schoolchildren and their teacher obviously on an outing to the lakes. She asked the teacher where to find the bus stop for the hotel. Fortunately, the teacher spoke a little English. Asking the name of the hotel and where?

Immediately the teacher offered to take them there on the coach which had spare seats and it was on their way home anyway.

It was a very happy coach; the children were singing and the teacher practising her English.

Edgar noted the name of the teacher and the school's address.

On that coach, unbeknown to Edgar at the time, was Jani Kovac's granddaughter Sabina! They returned to Rotherham in ignorance of just how close they had been.

Edgar once home, wrote to the teacher at the school thanking her for the kindness and explaining why they were in the country and asked her if she or anyone knew of a Jani Kovac. Maybe he thought the school coach was travelling south west where he had been taken. Or maybe not.

The teacher took Edgar's letter to the school secretary, Cveta, a linguist, for translation.

Amazingly, Cveta happened to be Jani Kovac's daughter-in-law who was married to Jani Kovac Jnr, his son!

One very sad note to end this scarcely believable historyis that Edgar's saviour, Jani Kovac, died in 1947. Edgar never did get to thank him.

Cveta Kovac – Jani Kovac Jnr – Coral Lynn Jackson

The Crooked Olive Branch relies mainly upon the author's memory of a tumultuous decade from 1936 to 1946. The story, although complete fiction, is inspired by real events, experiences and histories.

Nine decades of learning colour the pages. Living long has taught that there are no absolutes in life and that action and interaction between people is mainly tempered and directed by experience. We can never be sure what is true. That which exists in the mind of each participant is at best subjective. This story contains elements of Edgar's memories and the best of my memory. Both experiences and recollections are wrapped up in the tinsel of a tale inspired by memories of the Second World War.

Allowing for vagaries of memory and perception of histories, first and second hand, I was persuaded by some seemingly inaccurate offerings via all forms of communication, that my memory might just contribute something worthwhile to the history of the Second World War.

If it does not and my story only entertains it is hopefully still worthwhile and it is my way of maintaining mental alertness and staving off the incoming tide of atrophic deterioration.

My thanks are extended to all readers for helping to indulge the fancies of an old man.

All characters in the following novel, other than the obvious historical, are fictitious, and any resemblance to real persons, living or dead, is purely coincidental.

The Fourth Dimension

Time, the fourth dimension,
has no beginnings and no ends,
The clock is man's invention, hours,
thoughts and all intention, time transcends.
This peg, to which we chain
our lives of ill forgiving minutes,
Restricts, like goats,
to trample in tight circles,
Which have small purpose
and few friends.
We cannot remember
true what has been,
Or know what might be seen.

Corinthians one,
verses twelve/thirteen.

Prologue

You might ask why I am attending a wedding in a small town in Connecticut U.S.A. in the year 2020. The marriage is of special interest to me. A typical human reaction would be to think that I am here to preen.

Sorry, I ought to introduce myself. I am Lot. No, not that Lot. I am just one of the many Lots from the tribe Naphtali.

Should you think that this takes some believing, then consider the issue from a cared one in my charge. One Miriam Kessler, about whom there are many stories. She is part, a big part of this story I am about to tell, and I am following at this wedding.

Who is Miriam Kessler and why is she important? To partly answer this question, I wind time forward to the year 2036. I am stood at the graveside of the said Miriam Kessler who has died, aged 101, in the village of St. Mary Upperford where she lived for most of her life. In the moment of her passing her issue numbered almost 100 including grandchildren, great grandchildren and their issue. All these and their stories would not have existed if Miriam Kessler had become one of the many victims of the Nazi authorities of Munich, Bavaria in 1938. As it is now, there are enough stones around her grave to build a small house. If you carry all issue and their procreation forward just a few hundred years, there are more people and stories than there are pebbles on Chesil Bank.

Back to the wedding. The bride and groom are connected to my assignment to be Charge Angel to Miriam Kessler. Why, how? To learn more, you will need to read the story.

My medium for the story is an old man who is using his instinct to write now because his mobility is such as to limit normal physical activity. Crossword and other puzzles have palled. I suspect that he is aware of my involvement but not the level. It is fortunate that it is only necessary to point him in the right direction and let him loose. This, incidentally, mirrors the allowed activity of we guardians in their clients' lives.

Having difficulty in believing? Try this: Imagine a web, similar to those built by spiders, constructed, as such a web is, in multiple sections all connected to a central point. Each section a parallelogram, some square, some rectangular, some irregular, bounded by unbreakable threads to the past. Imagine then each of these 'boxes' encompassing one person's connected life within a specified time scale. If you have got that, now imagine the little fugitive Miriam Kessler as the epicentre of this web. If Miriam had not been rescued from the Nazis, this 'web' would change in its entirety and every single connected life would be different, very different. Each life having a changed epicentre. Got it?

Now please read on.

Chapter 1

The beautiful August afternoon hummed with bees, wasps and sheer contentment.

Bluebirds trapesed in the cascading willows which fringed the river's edge while swallows skimmed the sparkling waters and the green outfield oblivious to the crack of willow on leather.

Gnats danced in the shadows under an arc of trees, dragonflies shot unexpectedly into the open, their jewelled bodies flashing, reflecting sunlight as they performed breathtaking acrobatic displays of speed, stop, turn and hover. The day stoked up a thirst for lemonade, cream teas and memories. Old men yawned and yarned in deckchairs while the scorer peered down from the score box window to record each dot ball, run, no ball and soaring six outside the white-lined and picket-fenced boundary which marked the extremes of success or contained failure. If ever there was a moment in the annals of man which exuded peace and tranquillity, this was it.

Yet, in the shadows three men were considering a very different scene. Their minds focused on an impending, probable conflict which, win or lose, could destroy such moments.

Perhaps never to return. A few yards away in the pavilion, consideration of another possible conflict was hovering just below the surface, restrained for the time being, within knowing glances and sly smiles.

Pen and Henry, unaware of any such attention, leaned on the rail of a footbridge which spanned the river alongside the old drover's ford.

Henry mused as he looked down at the sparkling waters as they bounced and gurgled over the pebbles at the edge.

"Minnehaha," he murmured.

Pen smiled happily. "Laughing water ... it does seem to, doesn't it?"

Their conversation flowed as easily as the river. Both were comfortable in the long pauses while they took in the beautiful scene. The river bent gently round to the left towards the next crossing a little over a mile further downstream. The banks of the river were dressed by weeping willow, flowering shrubs and occasional felled tree seats along a well-used river path between the village of St. Mary Upperford and the market town of Bendesbury.

Pen, wishing to impress Henry with her knowledge, broke the silence.

"Longfellow," she murmured just loud enough for Henry to hear.

After a short pause Henry replied, "Tall guy."

Pen began to giggle.

"Mini Ha Ha," said Henry to peals of laughter from Pen.

The Hon. Penelope Alice Amelia Bridge-Thompson felt as though she had freed from jail.

She understood now why Peter, normally reclusive, had made a friend of this American who was destined to become best man at their wedding. In his presence, she felt safe.

He exuded a quiet charm and warmth. Yet she perceived great strength. He was clearly comfortable in his own skin, in the presence of others, king or commoner, prince or pauper.

She smiled at the thought as they stood for a while in silence, just 'being'.

Henry Steading III was not however all that comfortable in Pen's presence. His upbringing would not allow for being remotely rude or dismissive. He was aware that she was sending out signals which were difficult to ignore. Sitting next to her outside the pavilion a short time ago had seemed not to be a good idea. At the first opportunity, he made an excuse to get away saying. "If you will excuse me, I will go and inspect the river. I'm sure drawn to water."

To be followed shortly after by the persistent Pen.

It was Henry who next broke silence, whispering. "I fit."

"What was that, Hank?"

"Call me Hal," Henry replied. "I prefer Hal. Hank the Yank was Cambridge speak. Peter and the crew."

"O.K. Hal." Pen tried copying Hal's Pennsylvanian brogue. "You fit."

Another pause followed. "Sure, I could live here." Henry sighed as he spoke.

"Don't you find that we British are a little quaint, slightly potty?"

"Potty?" Hal chuckled "I guess you mean eccentric. Potty, what a super word!"

"And quaint?"

"No, I guess not quaint. Quaint is one description of the Drovers. It is hot and cramped and if that is quaint, I'll take Potty."

"Yet you fit?"

"Sure, I could live here."

"You could?" exclaimed Pen, slightly surprised, secretly pleased. "But not in the Drovers?"

"No, I guess in one of those cottages around the Green." Hal smiled at the thought as he added:

"with a wife and a couple of kids."

Pen sighed. "You fit. You really mean that, don't you?"

"Sure, I do, but I guess that's just a dream." He paused and chuckled again. He was happy sharing his thoughts. "A guy can always dream."

"I fit. What a sweet way of putting it."

"My Ma and Pa would really get this place. I just know."

There followed a further pensive silence before Hal continued.

"Ma and Pa go up to New England each fall. Take a log cabin by the river. The first thing they do is to link little fingers and say, 'I fit', then they would recite a little verse. I guess it came from a Valentine."

Pen turned to face Hal whose gaze steadfastly remained on the tumbling waters.

"What verse was this?"

Hal sensed they were entering dangerous 'waters' and that he had better not carry through.

To be rude however, especially to a lady, was not in his nature. He smiled at his memories. It clearly meant so much to him. He began to recite softly with such meaning that it seemed he was back in New England with his family. Once more, a carefree child.

"If I could choose a world to be,
I'd begin at once with you and me,
Then we would paint a Sky of blue,
white fluffy clouds, just one or two.
Spring and Fall with their tints would
intermingle with their stints,
And by the river's sparkling flow
we'd go about our 'to and fro.'
Then raise our thanks to heaven above
for all the beauty and our love."

Hal's resolve to keep Pen at arm's length was immediately shattered. His reservations dissolved by his memories.

"That is beautiful."

"When me and my brothers came along, we insisted that we join in. Join hands in a circle."

"And you fit in St. Mary?"

"I guess I do. I really do."

Instinctively, Pen linked arms with Hal. Shocked by this sudden move of affection he pulled away sharply.

"Howzat!" came the cry from the cricket field. "Out!" The umpire replied lifting his finger.

Chapter 2

St. Mary Upperford had the usual complement of gossips, two of whom were helping prepare the pavilion tea under the close eye of Lady Amelia Bridge-Thompson.

Edna was preparing potted beef sandwiches and Freda the cream teas.

"You'd think she would have stayed to watch while Peter was batting." Freda whispered.

"And wandering off with that American fellah" came a 'stage whispered' reply from Edna.

Amelia Bridge-Thompson stiffened and turned to Pamela Avery.

"Pamela, take over will you please while I go to get Penelope to give a hand."

Without waiting for a reply, she swept out of the door and around the boundary of the cricket field towards the ford where Pen was last seen.

"There she goes, trying to save her investment," said Freda.

Edna chuckled. "Some chance, Freda. That Genie is out of the bottle and she'll not get that back in, no matter how."

"You reckon?"

"You were there Saturday. Saw as well as I did. Almost dropped her knickers at first sight of him." Edna gave another chuckle. "At her engagement do an' all."

Pamela Avery turned, pleading. "Ladies, please."

"Don't you get hoity-toity, Pamela Avery. You're only trying to protect your future.

If the Hon. Penelope Bridge Doo Dah doesn't marry money, you will all be out on the streets."

Pamela took a deep breath and paused to control her temper, to collect her thoughts before replying. When she did, she spoke quietly and firmly.

"Peter is a lovely young gentleman and Pen thinks the world of him."

Edna however was in full flow of 'informed' opinion. "Ask me; Lady Toffee Nose and Sir Surgeon Commander are stony. They are spent up. One step from the knacker's yard. Sending Penny Poo to be presented at court has scuppered them. They're boracic and the bank manager is in hot pursuit."

"Do be quiet Edna, you don't have the first idea."

"Don't I now! Well, I know this, they are a pair of jumped up nothings."

Pamela put down her knife and fixed Edna with a stare.

"You really do know nothing. Lady Amelia is the first born of a baronet."

"Who was that then? Baron Stoneybroke?" The pair fell about laughing.

Pamela tried again to regain control while looking round anxiously to see where Lady Amelia was.

"I don't see how anyone can know about another's financial affairs. How can you possibly know?"

"Well, that's where you are wrong. My cousin Stan is a postman and the number of letters marked private and confidential are legion."

"They are most probably just bank statements."

"Not every week."

"It's the bank manager ... he's behind you" shrieked Freda convulsed with laughter.

Pamela realised there was little she could say or do, so she recommenced buttering bread in silence.

"What's the matter, the cat got your tongue?" Edna, continued to taunt. "See, can't deny it!"

Pamela remained silent which only encouraged Edna who was now in full cry.

"Time all you high and mighties got your come-uppance. I for one will not be sorry."

"She's coming back," announced Freda, saving further embarrassment.

"Pen's in tow. Obedient to the last."

"Treats her like a puppet. Arranged marriages in this day and age! That's all it is you know."

"Really Edna, what nonsense you talk," said Pamela, although she was not entirely sure that it was.

Chapter 3

"Howzat?" "Out!" The umpire raised his finger.

"That's Peter's wicket. I'd better go," said Pen who at the same time could see her mother bearing down towards them. Pen hurried towards her.

Hal watched her go then returned to watching the bright waters bouncing over the pebbles and stones. "Mini Ha Ha," he whispered to himself then shrugged his shoulders trying to come to terms with his emotions.

Surgeon Commander Sir George William Bridge-Thompson had been in earnest conversation with Richard Barnes, Peter's father, and another gentleman, a Bryn Rhys James when he noticed that Peter was out.

"That's Peter gone. We'll have that word. Agreed?" The other two nodded. Richard Barnes saw Lady Amelia and Penelope coming around the boundary. He waited until they came within earshot to call out. "Pen, ask Peter if he can spare us a minute, please."

Peter was still unbuckling his pads as he arrived hot and perspiring. He looked at the stranger and nodded to him, wondering who this might be. He then acknowledged Sir George.

"Sorry sir, not the glorious day I envisaged."

He failed to add the reason which was lack of concentration caused by Pen's behaviour.

He then turned to his father "You wanted a word?" adding reluctantly, "sir".

Sir George interjected. "Shall we take a stroll around the boundary?"

Peter was desperate for a cold drink and an explanation from Pen. Reluctantly he accepted this as an order which it was."This is Bryn Rhys James." Sir George introduced the stranger.

Rhys James then without so much as acknowledging Peter's "how do you do, sir?" walked off into the shadows of the trees behind the sightscreen, assuming all would follow, which they did.

Lowering his voice, he took Peter's arm, saying. "Come."

He 'propelled' Peter into the shadows.

"Peter, we understand that you and your friend are going to the Oktoberfest in Munich next month?"

"Yes, sir" Peter replied, his mind whirling. He was confused by this sudden turn of events dominated by this stranger. He looked anxiously to his father, who nodded and put his finger to his ear then pointed at his son mouthing "Listen."

"Your father, Sir George and I have been wondering if it possible for you to go a little earlier stopping off at Bochum to attend the European Special Steel Conference."

"When is this conference, sir?" Peter avoided replying directly.

He had too many other things on his mind. This confusing, unwelcome question was the last thing he wished to consider. The perceived affair between his intended and his best friend was paramount. Stuck in the batting crease while watching them move out of sight had disrupted his concentration. He needed answers, not more problems.

"September 21st to 23rd," he replied. He looked to his father hoping for support or failing that, an explanation for this request from a stranger.

Richard Barnes, however, was offering little other than a look which suggested that he should acquiesce. Left without support, Peter answered.

"I suppose I could." Rhys James continued speaking, oblivious of Peter's discomfort.

"We know quite a lot about you. A first in modern languages, fluent in German plus others and a Cambridge blue no less."

"Rowing not cricket," interrupted Peter.

His father shot him another shut up and listen look, leaving him in no doubt that he was not going to get any support there.

Rhys James continued, "The Germans will not suspect for one moment that you are anything other than a representative of Barnes Tool and Special Steels."

"Why would they suspect me at all, sir?" Peter answered his mouth dryer than ever.

He was desperate to get away for a cooling drink.

Sir George took Peter's arm "Look around you, Peter. Isn't today and our way of life just wonderful? You must agree that it worth preserving. But this ..." He waved his arm towards the Bank Holiday scene, "our world, our lives, all that we hold dear are under threat."

"If you think as we do, then you will listen and listen well." Sir George paused for effect, then continued. "What Bryn is asking is of the utmost importance. We don't expect you to be a spy or anything like that. Just to listen and be aware of any new ventures and pass on all that is of interest."

Peter's memory 'rifled' back to an incident at school when as a young fresher. Surrounded by taunting bullies, his normal clear thinking deserted him. All he could think was "why me?" The 'why me' being unspoken. Confused, he found himself turning towards Rhys James as if someone else was speaking for him.

"Yes, sir."

"If you agree, we need you to observe and listen only. Try and note every piece of information about industrial developments in the steel industries, no matter how trivial. We can then determine its import."

This gave Peter a clue what this was about.

The 'why me,' resurfaced, this time as a studied thought. He could hear this man speaking, his mind now elsewhere trying to rationalise. He tried to find the real reason for his being involved but found none.

Rhys James's voice returned into focus. "You will be given a list of names, those to whom we hope you will meet and engage in conversation." Peter was now determined not to speak or nod. It being safer to avoid anything which remotely suggested that he agreed.

Rhys James continued in the manner of a man who was used to giving orders; for them to be obeyed and not accepting any deviation.

“Richard will arrange everything. Also, we think it would be good to take your friend Henry along with you. Having an American there will be of help. They might wish to impress. Be interested in what is new in special steels in the U.S.A.”

He turned to Richard Barnes. “You did say that you could get Steading approved Barnes?”

Peter was furious about Henry being included.

He realised that the only reason his father allowed this to go unchallenged was that there was some substantial gain to be had. What this could be was one question. Why Henry was another.

Bryn Rhys James continued speaking but Peter was no longer paying any attention.

His anger built up as this man droned on.

“There are a couple of chaps we wish you to pay close attention to.”

Peter interrupted. “Really Mr. Rhys James, I fail to see that Henry, or I can be of any use whatsoever.” Sir George, realising that Peter was getting angry, intervened.

“What say you put this to Henry? See what he thinks. May not produce anything.

It could be an interesting few days. I understand the Germans put on a good show.”

“Henry will say the same as me. Why us?”

“Tell you what, young man.” Rhys James took over. “We'll give you a moment to think about it.”

Signalling to the others he ushered them to the riverbank, leaving Peter to his thoughts.

Peter through the trees, could see them talking.

Rhys James was like an American coach calling time out. It was clear that this man, whoever he was, was nervous when either of the other two men interrupted.

His father and Sir George were almost standing to attention, receiving instructions.

This was so unlike his father. This suggested that Rhys James was a man of significance and not just to Richard Barnes.

Peter began to analyse.

He was involved because of his command of German but why Henry?

The political situation in Europe was a probable catalyst. Again, that didn't answer the why of Henry.

Peter decided to talk with him to get his view of this strange request.

The three conspirators returned, Rhys James leading the way.

"Well, young man?"

"I will speak with Henry first." Peter chose his words carefully.

"Good ... now who's for a cream tea?"

Rhys James marched away leaving Peter with the uncomfortable feeling that his message was being deliberately misinterpreted.

Peter, confused and angry with his father and Sir George, wondered how to retract this 'perceived agreement'.

The conspirators, although serious, gave him the impression of a gang of fourth formers who had just conjured up a wizard prank.

His father's continued association with Sir George was more to do with the search for a knighthood and government contracts, than genuine friendship. The arrival of this stranger had the same smell about it.

Peter followed the others back towards the pavilion in silence.

The question of Pen and Hank thrust brutally to the back of his mind for the last half hour, now returned with complications. The idyllic scene of a gentle pleasant bank holiday afternoon had been tainted by something more sinister than a flirtation between his fiancé and his best friend.

Even the desperately needed glass of lemonade tasted sour.

Chapter 4

"Tea, Peterkin?"

Until she spoke, Peter had not been aware of Pen who had been sent by her mother to mend fences.

Grateful for the tea, he was still in no mood to receive Pen's opening gambit at conciliation. "Thanks." He grunted before adding testily, "This is not Coral Island, Pen."

"Owl isn't pleased, and Pussy Cat is very, very sorry." Pen purred and took his arm.

"Nor are we setting sail in a pea green boat." Peter shrugged her away.

This 'slap in the face,' shocked Pen. "Sorry Peter, I am truly sorry."

A brooding silence followed, both unaware that all in the know were watching.

From the pavilion Lady Amelia looked on anxiously while Edna and Freda nudged each trying hard not to show their fascination with this real-life drama unfolding before them. Edna was salivating with thoughts of informing the Women's Guild with all the lurid detail.

"What's going on with you and Henry?" Peter's blunt question broke an awkward silence.

Pen was shocked even though she was expecting something of the sort.

"Peter, there's nothing." She swallowed.

"You have my promise, there's nothing between Hal and me."

"So, its Hal now, is it? What happened to Hank?"

"Henry prefers to be called Hal. He doesn't like Hank the Yank it being Cambridge speak, just the fun of the crew. I guess he wishes to drop it."

"You guess? You are even beginning to sound like an American."

"Look Peter, Hal is good fun I like him a lot but it's you I love. You I intend to marry." Peter didn't reply for some little while. When he did, he managed not to sound too aggrieved.

"Do you realise that walking off with Henry upset my concentration. Your father hoped that I would produce an innings to sink Bendesbury, and I failed."

Pen who had been up to this last remark, a model of contrition, was angry that this had degenerated into a discussion about a piddling little cricket match. Cricket she had little interest in and no wish to even try to understand it. Here she felt that she had something in common with Henry.

She, however, placed a conciliatory hand on Peter's.

"I am really sorry darling, truly I am. I will do better in future."

Peter did not reject this gesture entirely. They remained like that for what seemed an age. Peter broke the silence and the tension. "Where's Henry?"

"Down by the ford. Why?" Pen replied anxiously.

"There's something we need to discuss."

Pen caught her breath. "You'll not mention our little tiff to him, please."

Peter removed Pen's hand from his arm. "I'll not make promises that I may not keep. I suggest you do likewise." He turned to go, then relenting, offered her some comfort.

"Actually, it's to do with a little matter your father and mine have cooked up between them."

After a very short pause, he added, "Still no promises."

With these final words Peter headed towards the ford.

Lady Amelia, who had been watching, immediately set off to join her daughter.

"Off she goes on her fool's errand," sniggered Edna. "No chance there. You mark my words." Amelia wrapped her arm around her daughter. "Well?"

Pen was shocked by this seemingly unusual show of affection. She just shrugged and didn't answer.

"Humble pie, darling." Amelia continued. "Buckets of it, trust me."

"Please mummy, just leave me alone." Pen turned and walked away with Amelia following.

"All right darling, but please don't throw your life away."

'What life?' Pen thought. It's your life you're worrying about not mine. Fortunately, she did manage to keep these thoughts to herself.

Henry, meanwhile, was still trying to sort out his thoughts. It was clear from Lady Amelia's sortie to retrieve Pen, that his innocent little meander to soak up the glory of this unique scene had had some consequence. Just what, he did not have too much difficulty in imagining. Pen tagging along did not overly disturb him until she became too familiar. Whether to say anything or nothing to Peter was now the decision. He decided that he had nothing to explain.

Peter arrived at the ford to find Henry engrossed in thought.

"Ah! Henry there you are."

Hal turned around and leaned back on the handrail.

"Hey Pete, what a peach of a place you have here. Cambridge was great, but this is something else."

"Henry," Peter began, not acknowledging Hal's comment. "There is something we should discuss."

"Hal please, Henry is my Sunday name if you don't mind. No more Hank. That was Cambridge. As far as I'm concerned it should stay there."

Peter was completely thrown by Henry's relaxed attitude. "Hal, it is then."

"My Pa used to say, 'if you hear your Ma call me Henry, be sure and make yourself scarce, there's trouble a brewing.' He called it his Sunday name, only used when he was in the doghouse."

Why Sunday name, thought Peter.

Calmed by Henry's relaxed charm, Peter relaxed. It was the same at Cambridge when they first met. All perceived troubles seemed to melt in his presence.

This plus Henry's request to call him Hal convinced Peter that his fears were unfounded. There was nothing other than Pen's inattentiveness at the cricket to concern him.

Relieved, Peter turned to the other problem on his mind. "Henry." He began.

"Hal" Henry corrected, smiling. "Sure, old buddy, there's something you want to discuss?"

When Peter had finished telling of the afternoon's strange encounter Hal didn't say a word.

He continued looking into the distance along the river as if for inspiration.

Peter waited for his friend's deliberations. Hal thoughtfully considered.

"These guys seem to me to be a slippery bunch. Question number one, why me?

You Pete we can guess, except for the spying gig. That we get, maybe, but not the whys of involving two greenhorns. Why especially me? They sure would not give me the time of day without reason. We need to figure that one."

Hal continued looking into the distance, seemingly still trying to work out what this was about.

In the following silence Peter was content to wait for his friend to continue.

Suddenly Hal's mood changed. Turning, he leaned back once more on the handrail.

"Why not? It could turn out to be a spiffing lark. What say you, old bean?"

"Do you really think so?" Peter asked, ignoring his friend's attempt to impersonate former university undergraduate colleagues.

"Sure, let's accept a stake in this affair and give these slippery goats enough rope. They might recycle round to tread in their own shit. Meantime we work out what really gives."

Chapter 5

The train slowed to a halt and was immediately surrounded by armed soldiers.

Hal looked out of the window. "Not again." He moaned.

"What the heck are these stooges looking for?"

Peter shrugged. "This is another unscheduled stop. They are clearly after someone special."

Hal went to the compartment door and looked up and down the corridor, muttering.

"They have checked our papers three times already, once at boarding and on the train twice.

I thought this Hitler guy was making the trains run to time."

Peter, puzzled by this unusual show of bad temper, offered his opinion.

"You know Hal this really is a police state. We got the whiff of it last night at that reception.

I can't speak for you, but it made me uncomfortable. It is one thing reading about it but ..."

Peter hesitated and sighed before continuing. "This is sinister." He paused repeating:

"really sinister."

Hal stretched and yawned. He was fed up, travel sick and weary.

"What a waste of time and all as far as I'm concerned for nothing. What was that all that about yesterday Pete, you figured it yet?"

"No, not yet. I don't agree that it was a complete waste, Hal. In any case what happened to the spiffing lark?"

Hal was unhappy, not just with the visit to Bochum and the extra journey time involved.

He was aware that his relationship with Peter had not been the same since that August day.

He knew that he had been correct and had dealt with Pen's familiarity as well as he could, but it was impossible to deny that he remained disturbed by it.

No matter how he tried, his thoughts kept returning to that afternoon on the bridge.

Mini Ha Ha Bridge was how he thought of it.

A stream of memories returned defying attempts to dismiss them as irrational and dangerous.

Peter, initially, was more successful in dismissing any thoughts.

But the usual friendly camaraderie was missing.

Thoughts neither wished to voice, hung around like a pebble in a sandal.

Peter was more and more convinced that his friend was withholding something from him.

Hal was broody and far from the 'all-inclusive' confidant.

The reason he was not being entirely open, however, was not what Peter suspected.

Hal was struggling with an embarrassing situation. and seeking the best way to explain.

The question of the incident at Mini Ha Ha, whilst it did figure, was not the main source of discomfort.

Hal was first to speak following a long silence. "You must admit this is one heck of a train journey. Could we not have gotten an overnighter?"

Peter replied with forced jocularity. "Bear up old chap, we'll be in Munich by five at the latest."

Realising he sounded boorish, regretting this, Hal attempted to copy Peter choosing his words carefully in his response.

"Sorry Peter, you would expect a seasoned traveller like me would take this in his stride."

"You are beginning to sound like an Englishman Henry."

Hal seized upon this opening and replied in kind, relieved to take his mind away from troubled thoughts.

"That Peter, old buddy, is the very compliment I need. I would sure like to have the *savoir faire* of that guy last night, Sir Filton Fowlkes Browne. You will note the triple barrelled name.

I would sure like to be able to handle life as him. Now there's an Englishman I would love to emulate.

He seemed so with it. Even knew my name."

Peter smiled, relieved to change his mindset, and see that Hal was relaxing.

"I think Henry you should know that he was Scottish."

"Sounded very English to me."

"You'd be safer saying British as a coverall," Peter advised, then added:

"Now you know Sir Filton it would be a good idea to stay in touch. It could prove useful."

"You know this guy?"

"No, but he sounds really important. As you say, he knew your name."

Both friends were relieved to be speaking freely. The conversation began to flow more easily for the next few minutes. The tension lessened as they became more involved. Hal tried to speak less formally.

"Very well my dear old friend, I'll take particular note." Hal was clearly imitating Sir Filton.

In truth, he was becoming naturally indoctrinated. Then, he reverted to type as he continued.

"These two guys last night, I guess they were Nazis. They were beginning to get up my nose. I was starting to weigh up the consequences of starting the Second World War by punching one of them in the face, when this Sir Filton guy appeared like a guardian angel and says, 'I see you are entertaining Herr Braun and Herr Lietz, Henry.' I guess I was too dumbstruck at this stranger knowing little old Henry's name, I didn't answer. I figured he was someone important, that I ought to bow or do something special."

Hal paused. "Where did he come from? Were you told he was to be there?"

Peter shook his head "I didn't notice him. It was a large meeting. I was too busy feeling out of my depth I suppose."

The two were silent for a while, deep in thought.

Eventually, Peter broke the silence. "I think that we can safely assume that Fowlkes-Browne is a British agent. That the Sir Filtons of this world have a secretary who provides them with a complete dossier on all participants. This he will study. It will include photographs in addition to descriptions." Peter paused for a moment before continuing. "And we can guess that there is a connection between him and Rhys James."

"O.K. Fine, I get that, but it doesn't explain why we two greenhorns were there in addition to Sir Filton. For sure we are novices. We gave nothing to the scene."

Peter took a moment to consider before replying.

"Could it be that as innocents we might hear more?"

Hal sighed. "I can't speak for you Pete, but I had not one clue what I was about. What to look or listen for. I was off my base. If Sir Filton had not intervened, I could have started a Second World War."

"Hal, unfortunately, the war will happen without any help from you."

They broke off the conversation while their papers were checked for a fourth time.

The compartment door closed on the German officials. Neither spoke for almost a minute then Peter forced his eyes away from the door. "Hal, are you alright?"

"Jeez Pete, these Goons are something else, polite, efficient but somehow they give me the creeps. There is something just, just ..."

"Just what, Hal?"

"I can't figure, it was just something."

Peter took a breath, letting it out as he spoke. "Malevolent!"

"Yes Pete, you are so on it. I have never had much cause to use the word before. That was why I was fishing. You felt it too? They made me feel to be a victim. Kind o' scared even though I know they would not dare touch me. Now I feel angry, not just with them but myself for sitting there and taking it."

"I was like a rabbit mesmerised by ferrets. I feel dirty and impotent. Like you, a victim."

Neither spoke for some while. Peter was the first to gather his wits.

"You were about to start a second world war when Sir Filton appeared?" He prompted, trying to resume where they left off.

Hal was taken out of his thoughts by Peter's sudden return to the interrupted discussion.

They were thoughts not only about the German officials but another matter he was wrestling with.

The two had become strangely entwined. He made a big effort and picked up the story where he left off. "Sure, as I was saying. This Fowlkes-Browne arrives like the Lone Ranger and says:

'Ah Henry, I see you are entertaining Herr Braun and Herr Lietz'. He introduced himself.

It was then one of the goons began to simper and wheedle and claim kinship with him."

"Kinship?"

"Keep up Pete, Braun and Browne. This goon Braun says, 'are you aware Sir Filton that you and I share the same name?' Sir turns around and says, 'Really, Herr Braun do you really think that you and I could belong to the same tribe?' He sure did not dig the idea.

He managed to make it sound preposterous without using any words, just using that impolite dismissive manner born of centuries. He reduced this Braun guy to the size of a squeaking mouse." Hal chuckled at the memory. "I tell you Pete, it beats smacking the guy in the mouth.

Then he says to them 'please excuse us gentlemen while Henry and I mingle.' Away we sped.

Then he says to me. 'I don't know about you Henry, but I get somewhat irritated when something nasty is crawling in the hairs of my arse. I need a drink'. I tell you Pete that incident almost made this trip worthwhile."

"Wait a sec, Hal. Where was Fowlkes-Browne while you were talking to the Nazis?"

"Don't know he must have been nearby I guess."

"And he arrived just on cue?"

"So it seemed."

"What were you talking about?"

"Let me think. They had been bragging how they had gotten around the Treaty of Versailles, built this battleship Bismarck, which could outrun and outrange anything else afloat, equipped with gun turrets which swivelled independently and could engage any enemy on all sides."

"Did Fowlkes-Browne move in then?"

"No, let me think." Hal, realising that Peter was on to something, went over the conversations in his mind. Peter waited then, impatient for the answer, prompted.

"It was when you were thinking of hitting him. What upset you?"

Hal snapped his fingers as he remembered. "Some snide remark that the U. S. of A should not still behave as colonials as if we were England's puppets."

"They were trying to get under your skin. What exactly was said immediately before that?"

"It was something about a joint research project between Sheffield and Pittsburgh."

Peter nodded. "Makes sense. That's the venture my Father got you involved with?"

"Sure, they knew that I was a member of the research team. The co-operation between teams from the States and Great Britain."

He looked quizzically at Peter. "You're on to something aren't you?"

Peter did not reply immediately, instead he asked, "So, Sir Filton arrived when this came up?"

"Sure did, it was then this stooge made his comment about the States not dancing to a British tune and I was about to, you know."

"You said nothing about it; the research?"

"No, not a chance I wouldn't anyways."

"Oh, Hal!" Peter went red and threw his head back against the seat.

"What gives Pete?"

"We were not there to gather information. We were bait. At least you were."

Hal took a deep breath, thought for some seconds then let out a low whistle.

"The bastards. The slimy bastards."

Peter didn't answer. Hal looked concerned. "Sorry Pete I didn't mean ..."

Peter held his hand up. "Don't be sorry. My father and father-in-law are slimy bastards."

Peter awaited Hal's response but when he didn't, spoke his thoughts.

"Hal, you know something I don't. I am guessing the research project you were working on is the catalyst for this whole affair. Am I right?"

Hal still didn't answer. Peter continued. "My father is lurking in there somewhere."

He paused before engaging Hal forcefully. "TRUE?"

The compartment which had been empty for almost the whole of the journey was entered by a man who sat in the corner and began to read. He had no luggage. He carried only a book.

Peter looked across at Hal, pulled a face, then mouthed, 'not now, later'.

It was obvious to both that as there had been no recent scheduled stop, this man had moved from another part of the train after their passports had been checked.

Unable to pursue the conversation both Peter and Hal spent the rest of the journey thinking over events and trying to make sense of the happenings. Their thoughts were interrupted by the arrival in Munich.

Chapter 6

"At last," said Hal grabbing his luggage. "We are meeting this Dieter guy where?"

Peter put his finger to his lips and mouthed, 'Later.' Hal mouthed back, 'you're getting paranoid'.

Hal was clearly ill-tempered. Peter was worried that his friend would lose patience.

This could prove dangerous for his friend. Hal, on the other hand, an American in a very strange environment, was more than uncomfortable with the intrigue and the restrictions this placed upon them.

The station platform was an endless river of travellers. There were armed police everywhere, at every exit.

Peter looked around and whispered. "We meet at the news stand outside".

Hal replied in a louder than normal voice, "Speak up Pete, we've nothing to hide."

Irritated by his performance back on the train Hal decided enough was enough.

They picked their way through the teeming crowd to the newsstand.

The city centre was thronged with revellers, many dressed in traditional costume.

The men in Lederhosen, the women in blue and white, most wearing hats with feathers. Beer steins decorated almost every horizontal surface. Outside one bar a pig roasted on a spit.

"Just my take of the Fest, no joke. As I imagined."

"I'm not sure the pig roast is usual." Peter murmured, not really paying attention and looking round the square. "Where's Dieter? I can't see him."

"This Dieter guy reliable?"

Peter didn't answer and continued to search for his friend.

Conversation was proving difficult. They were surrounded by people laughing, talking loudly and jostling. A brass band marched into the square followed by a troop of Brownshirts singing loudly, raucously.

"Let's find a beer," Hal shouted in Peter's ear.

"We should wait for Dieter," Peter shouted back.

"I'm hot and travel weary and looking for a long cool drink. Let's get the hell out of here."

Peter was jostled by the crowds pouring out of the station. He felt someone place a small slip of paper into his hand. He turned around but saw no one he recognised. No one acknowledged him.

He unfolded the paper and read.

TAXI TO THE FAIRY GROTTO
IN THE ENGLISH GARDEN.

Peter passed the slip to Hal and shouted in his ear.

"Let's get out of here, take a taxi and get you that drink." Puzzled at the change of plan, Peter led the way to the taxi rank alongside the station. Just before they got there, one pulled alongside.

The driver alighted and asked. "Herr Barnes?"

"Ja das bin ich."

"Your taxi." The driver said in English and opened the rear door.

Hal and Peter climbed in without question, pleased at last that something positive was happening. The taxi driver picked his way slowly through the crowds towards the English Garden to be held up by the marching Brownshirts still singing.

"What's that song?" Hal asked.

"The tune is the Horst Wessel anthem, but they have changed the words. If I could hear clearly it would help. Suffice to say it sounds arrogant and aggressively anti-Semitic."

"It would be great if you could try and interpret, please, it will make good copy."

Peter turned and looked at Hal. "Good copy, what does that mean?"

Hal flushed. "Look Pete, I was going to tell you back on the train when the guy came into the compartment and you slammed me up."

"Tell me what and why did the guy make the problem? You had a couple of hours to say what you will."

"There is a connection. Pete I'm sorry. I am not joining your father's research and development team in Sheffield."

Peter began to speak and ask why.

Hal interrupted. "I've accepted the post of Europe correspondent for the East Coast Press Association. I've already got my press card. Got it two days ago. Just before we set off."

Peter didn't answer, he just sat wide eyed.

Hal continued. "This has bothered me ..." He hesitated then began once more. "I was looking for the best ..." He hesitated again. "No, I wasn't, I flunked it. I've been sat on the fence so long my butt aches. Pete, I am so sorry."

Peter still didn't answer, so Hal repeated. "I am sorry Pete, really sorry."

Peter found his voice. "Great so you had another reason to take this trip, including Bochum."

"I didn't know that at the time at the bridge."

"You must have known that it was on the cards."

"Sure, but I didn't expect to get the post."

"But you *were* short listed?"

"I guess this does look dodgy but there was so much going on and – and I flunked it. How to tell you and your father."

"Don't worry about him, he is all self-interest."

Peter felt betrayed. Now it seemed his best mate was becoming as devious as his father.

This was not Peter's major concern. This was the whereabouts of Dieter.

There was clearly a problem. This was so not like his German friend.

To Hal it appeared that Peter had got the hump.

"This is what I've always wanted, not metallurgy. Metallurgy and Cambridge was my family's idea. Please understand I didn't expect to be accepted when I applied, even when I was short listed."

Hal was tired and thirsty. His priority, however, was to explain his actions.

Peter took a while to try and sort his mind, eventually he asked.

"You said there was a connection, what did you mean?"

"When the guy entered the compartment, I was about to confess."

Peter thought that, confess was an interesting choice of words. "Why then?"

"I realised what all this Rhys James project was about and that my defection from Cambridge and your father would throw up more problems. It was then that I decided to come clean, when this guy turned up."

"Talk about it later, Hal, looks like we've arrived."

The taxi pulled in opposite the English Garden. The driver opened the doors.

"Follow me please, gentlemen." He took their luggage and headed for the bar.

The restaurant was clearly different from the one in Berlin. If this was now Helga's a clear attempt had been made to give it the appearance of an English venue. Peter, interested in the changes, looked around thinking this could be Helga's new venture. "I reckon this is Helga and Dieter's place."

"What gives Pete, are we staying here?"

"I don't know but at least we can eat." Peter was looking around, hoping that Dieter would be there to meet them. There was no sign of him. The fear that something was seriously wrong intensified.

"And get that beer," said Hal as they walked under the coloured lights into the foyer.

On cue, a waiter appeared.

"Good evening gentlemen, your luggage will be taken care of. I will show you to the washroom."

"Can we go straight to our rooms to freshen up?"

"Sorry, sir?"

"We are to lodge here?" Hal persisted.

"That I cannot say, sir. I am just your waiter. This is the washroom, please make yourselves comfortable. Do you prefer a table inside or out?"

"Out, I think. Agreed, Hal?"

Hal spread his arms and shrugged but didn't answer. Peter smiled at the waiter.

"Outside it is then."

Once the waiter had left, Hal sarcastically remarked, "Sure, how very English."

Peter realised that Hal was 'on the edge' since their arrival and in those few words guessed that there was seething anger about to explode.

Hal placed both hands on the wash basin and took several deep breaths before cupping his hands to drink some water.

"What's bugging me is that we have yet to meet this Dieter guy. Where is he and what's more to the point where are our promised lodgings?" He splashed water on his face.

"How well do you know this Dieter guy? Do you trust him?"

"I trust Dieter. It will work, please be patient. I'm sure he'll do something."

Peter was now certain there was a problem and was at pains not to convey his anxiety to his friend.

"You trust a guy who doesn't turn up as promised?"

Peter looked at his friend. He had never seen him like this before. He felt sure it would pass.

He was determined not to get into an argument. Turning his back,he replied. "implicitly!" and left the room.

Hal sighed, wiped his hands and followed.

Peter was tired and worried that plans had changed. That something had happened to Dieter.

Aware they were being manoeuvred without explanation, he approached the waiter. "Can we eat now, please?"

They were shown to a table set a little way out from the others in a very pleasant spot on the edge of the lawns looking out across the huge park.

"Beer, gentlemen or would you prefer the wine list?"

"Beer." They answered in chorus.

"Light or dark?" Gentlemen?"

"Light." Again, they spoke together.

Peter tried to lift the mood especially his own.

"Not very English or he would have offered bitter to match our mood."

Hal, who was in no mood to exchange small talk, didn't answer. They sat in silence until the beer was served and for a while afterwards. The beer and the ambience served to change their mood.

Hal queried Peter's association with Dieter. This time his tone was less aggressive.

"How well do you know Dieter?"

The question, reasonable given the circumstances, was tinged with suspicion.

Peter placed his beer back on the table and looked his friend in the eye.

"Very well indeed, in fact I would trust him with my life."

"How long have you known him?"

"Since thirty-two." Peter was glad of the opportunity to defend Dieter.

"That long? I figured you'd met at the Olympics."

"No, Dieter's mother owned a restaurant on a lake in Berlin. I went there each summer from 1932. Lodged with them. I earned my keep by waiting on at tables."

"You didn't meet him last year as I figured" Hal carefully removed his note pad and pencil from his pocket. Peter appeared not to notice.

"No, every year from 32 to 36 we spent the summers together."

Although more relaxed, he was still worrying what had happened to Dieter.

"And you didn't just come over last year for the Olympics?"

"No, but I hoped to go to the rowing. The restaurant was so busy it was difficult to get away.

Then there was an incident with the Brownshirts."

"Brownshirts, you mean the guys who we saw marching and singing ... who are they? What are they?" Hal at last got to the copy he was hoping for.

"Independent militia, illegal officially. Unofficially not only tolerated by some Nazis but encouraged; they are rude and arrogant and violent. They focused on the restaurant."

The waiter arrived to take their order.

"I see you are serving ham," Peter said, surprised.

The waiter answered in his normal voice to begin with then came closer and lowered his tone.

"Of course, sir, we cater for every taste." He looked across at a man sitting alone at a nearby table. "In today's harsh climate it is prudent to accommodate everyone."

Peter nodded. "Fillet steak for me. You, Henry?"

"Bring it on," was the reply from Hal, who was noting the waiter's comments.

Peter lowered his voice "Hal, there's a chap over on the next table. I do believe we are being watched."

"What the hell. Why is that?"

"Keep calm Hal, this is serious. It could be that he is a Nazi agent. They could be searching for Dieter. They could be following us, hoping we will lead them to him."

Peter was convinced that Dieter was evading the Nazi authorities.

Hal continued in a whisper. "Why Dieter?"

"This I believe is Helga's restaurant. Her place on a lake in Berlin was called Die Feen Grotten. That is The Fairies Grotto. You remember I was saying there was trouble in Berlin with Brownshirts that they targeted Jews and Jewish premises? Well, that morning Dieter, a couple of friends and I were out rowing on the lake when another boat containing several Brownshirts saw us and attacked us."

"Why did they attack you?"

"One of our friends was wearing a Kippah."

Hal raised his eyebrows. "A kipper?"

Peter smiled. "A skull cap, as good as saying we are Jewish. I was rowing and easily outpaced them. They followed us to the restaurant and wrecked it. Helga tried to carry on, but they targeted the place. The regular clients drifted away. Now here she probably is, in Munich, re-established and wiser. Even serving ham."

He looked out across the expanse of the park beyond the restaurant's gardens. A beautiful autumn evening contrasted sharply with the turmoil in his mind; not knowing where Dieter was or where they were to spend the night.

"So, you were in Berlin to improve your German language skills."

Hal's question shook Peter out of his thoughts.

"Yes, every summer for four years and it was a great place to visit. It was perfect. A lovely spot on the lake. There were many tourists, big tippers. 1936 changed all that. The best customers drifted away. The Jewish clientele were frightened off."

The beer and the ambience plus a greater understanding mellowed Hal's mood.

By the time the food arrived, he was feeling much more human. He sat back and took a long draught of beer and sighed.

"Beautiful here, like a scene from *A Midsummer Night's Dream.*"

The scene was superb. The sun had set but the sky was still light to the west.

To the east it was a deep blue with a crescent moon already showing low in the distance.

The coloured lights picked up the richness of the flower beds.

"Pete, what was the name of that restaurant in Berlin again?"

Peter sat back. "Die Feen Grotten," he replied thoughtfully spelling it out for Hal then continuing with his thoughts out loud. "This must be Helga's place, so, where is she? More to the point where's Dieter? I hope they are all right. They have done everything to fit in, adopting local customs and choosing German names, even moving home. I just hope this has not been in vain."

Although the friends appeared to be having a conversation, their minds were in different places. The waiter arrived with the 'check'.

Payment was politely refused via a written message presented in the cover as though it was the bill. 'Gentlemen, your taxi will be at the entrance in five minutes to take you to your rooms. Your luggage has gone ahead. Please leave as quietly as possible, thank you.'

Peter passed this to Hal.

"Hal don't show surprise. I'll leave a large tip. You go to the men's room. Leave in five minutes.

Be ready to join me then.

Chapter 7

Leaving the English Garden in a taxi. Hal nudged Peter and whispered.

"Different taxi but the same driver, in a hat."

The driver then spoke in English, maybe to advise Hal that he understood him.

"Your luggage has been sent ahead gentlemen."

Peter didn't comment, his thoughts racing, trying to make sense of everything.

Hal asked. "Why and where are we going?"

The driver didn't answer immediately. When he did it was in German and at length.

Peter acknowledged in German.

Hal was bemused and angry at his question being ignored. He tugged at Peter's sleeve Peter signalled him to keep quiet.

Hal was having none of this.

"What the heck is going on Pete?"

"Please Hal, I'll tell you later."

There was something about the urgency of his reply that persuaded Hal to be quiet.

The taxi drew up alongside a small hotel. Peter paid the driver.

Hal, under the impression that they had finally reached their destination, followed Peter into the hotel bursting with questions.

The lobby was crowded, they went through into a bar, which was also crowded.

To Hal's further confusion they carried on straight out through a fire exit into a yard behind the building.

Peter immediately climbed into a dark red car which was waiting with the engine running.

He signalled for Hal to follow.

Hal was furious, his hopes of a resting place snatched away. He stood rooted to the spot.

Peter leaned out of the car.

"Hal, please get in and hurry. I'll explain as we get under way."

This pleading and the look on Peter's face had the desired effect.

Hal climbed into the car which was being driven by a young woman who set off immediately driving steadily out into the streets and into the night.

Hal's subsequent furious volley of questions were directed at Peter. It was the young woman driver who answered speaking English.

"Sorry for the loss of your holiday, sir. Dieter has been arrested and the house for your occupation has been commanded."

"Commandeered," Peter corrected her.

"Also arrested Dr and Frau Kessler, your hosts for the Fest."

"Why?" asked Hal.

"They are Jewish." The girl answered, in a matter of fact manner.

Hal's anger melted as he took out his notebook and asked. "That is a reason?"

"In Nazi Germany. Yes."

Hal already knew this. having been briefed only days ago.

Peter asked the obvious question.

"Why Dieter?" he asked believing that Helga and Dieter had been at pains since moving to Munich to hide their heritage even with the restaurant menu.

"Dieter had arranged for you to stay with the Kesslers hoping that your presence would give them some protection. We needed time to obtain the necessary papers to get them out over the borders and into Switzerland. We planned to do this under cover of the Fest, but they were arrested three days ago."

"And Dieter?" Peter asked. "Was he arrested also?"

"No, not then."

"When and why?"

Hal struggled to make notes in the dark, hampered by the vibrations of the car.

The young woman turned into a long narrow straight country road away from the lights of the city.

It was too dark for Hal to continue. He put away his notebook, hoping to remember this young woman's dialogue.

The lane was straight but very narrow, lined by trees on both sides.

The yellow of the headlights picked up their dark outline as they flicked by with monotonous regularity adding to the tension in the small car.

She checked in the rear-view mirror.

"I think we are clear, gentlemen," she announced reducing speed to a safer level.

"Clear of what?"

"Of being followed."

"Why would they follow us?"

"They think you could lead them to Dieter's mother and the Kessler child."

Peter and Hal took some time to process this information.

The silence was filled by the hum of the motor as the tree shadows flicked by.

"So, they are looking for this Helga and a child? I don't quite understand." Hal asked.

"Frau Kessler and Helga, Dieter's mother, saw the police arrive. Frau Kessler passed Miriam their three-year old daughter to Helga while Dr Kessler was answering the door.

Dieter and Helga brought Miriam to us. They are now, both in a safe house over the border.

Dieter came back to meet you, it was then that he was arrested."

Hal was in the in middle of a dramatic story, copy that any reporter would normally kill for.

Yet he could not dismiss remembering the last words of his editor.

'Remember Hal, keep it light. You know the thing fairy stories and I don't mean trolls and hob goblins. Leave that to the heavies in Washington. The folk in Pittsburgh and Boston just don't wanna know.'

Hal questioned. "Why?"

Spoken out loud, the question was directed at his editor.

It was when he repeated it for the third time, Peter asked.

"You all right Hal?"

Peter's question jolted Hal out of his thoughts.

"What's happening to us Pete? Where are we heading? Why would they wish to arrest these guys? I mean they are looking for a three-year old kid?"

"Yes, why all this effort for a three-year old and Helga?"

The young woman didn't answer for some time. It was only when Peter started to repeat his question she finally did.

"Look, my name is Eva. The reason my colleagues and I are doing this is because the Kesslers are arrested for their religion and a three-year-old is thought to be an enemy of the Reich."

Hal offered an alternative argument.

"They are following us hoping that we will lead them to your outfit. They are not after the kid."

"We are sorry that you are troubled but in Munich at the Fest we were unable to find an alternative place for you at such short notice, less than twenty-four hours."

Peter and Hal didn't answer so Eva continued. "We are doing our best, our very best to help as we are helping those who are wrongfully deprived of their liberty, especially the little children."

Hal felt himself blushing with humiliation.

Peter was angry and confused. He was feeling badly about what was happening to his friend and muttered almost to himself. "This cannot be right."

Hal just wanted to get out of the car. He was cramped, tired and very, very angry.

"I need to pee," he snorted.

Peter began to explain in German, but Eva cut him off.

"I understood the first time. I will pull in shortly after we leave the main road in a kilometre or so.

"This is a main route?" Hal was shocked that such a narrow, metalled track could be referred to as a road, main or otherwise.

After a few minutes Eva turned into a side road, little more than a dirt track and drew to a halt.

This road was fringed by bushes which were ideal for Hal's purpose. He was first out of the car. He walked deeper into the bushes than was necessary and relieved himself of more than one pressure.

"Pete, has it occurred to you that we are foreign nationals? Yet here we are behaving like fugitives from the law? We are going along with this without question?"

"What options do we have?"

"I don't know but giving over complete control to these people cannot be right."

Peter studied for a short while. "You are right of course, Hal. This has gone on far too long without question. I don't think it's beyond the realms of possibilities for someone to have found a space for us, if only on the floor."

"Sure thing, and you know what? They need not have involved us at all. The danger of us leading the Nazis to this woman or the kid does not wash with me. There is another agenda, and we need to know this. Eva must come clean before we move another inch.

"We ask for more information."

"Such as?"

"How much longer and the real reason for this journey."

Hal agreed. "O.K. let's do that."

"Sorry, Hal." Peter apologised. "I should have dealt with this earlier but the shock of Dieter not turning up and his arrest upset me. Robbed me of all reason. You O.K?"

"Pete, I just need somewhere to lay my head. Anywhere."

Peter realised he needed to lift Hal's spirits.

"Have you thought Hal that this will make great copy for your first report?"

"I have thought, but I don't think my editor will accept it even if he believed me."

"Why ever not? I would back you up."

"Orders. Keep out of politics and controversy in notes on Europe."

Eva was waiting impatiently for their return. Her jumpy attitude plus the implied reprimand earlier was not helpful. When she pleaded with them to hurry Hal's reply was less than pleasant.

"Hey. Hey, sister watch it! Your internal squabbles are nothing to do with us, so just cool it."

Peter moved in quickly to calm down what could have been a nasty incident.

"Sorry, Eva but before we move on, we would appreciate learning the truth about today's events. Why we are being forced on this journey? Its been a long and difficult day. We deserve more openness. We would like to know the real reason for this. Where we are heading, how long it will take? In fact, why are we involved at all?"

Eva, agitated, repeated the excuse. "It was difficult finding for you, accommodation."

"Oh no! That will not wash," snorted Hal.

Eva turned to Peter "Will not wash?"

"It is not a believable reason. We do not believe you."

Eva pleaded. "Please I am only doing as asked."

"Which is and who's doing this asking?" Hal thrust his face into Eva's.

Peter had never seen his friend this angry and moved in between them.

"Just tell us, please, where you are taking us and why."

"I am to take you over the border to a meeting place." Eva spread her hands. "That's all I know." Neither friend moved. They stood and looked at each other neither knowing where to go next.

"Please," Eva pleaded. "It not so far and we are late."

"How far?"

"Fifty maybe sixty kilometres."

It was much further. Eva was lying.

Hal's tiredness, frustration and confusion exploded in temper. Peter had great difficulty persuading him back into the car explaining that they had no option but to go along with Eva.

What else could they do and at least they had an idea of what they faced, even if they had no idea why. More to the point they had little idea where they were.

Wearily they climbed back into the car. A kilometre or so later both exhausted travellers fell fast asleep.

They were jolted awake over three hours later with the car bouncing over rough ground and the tyres crunching over gravel.

In the gloom, it was difficult to make out where they were. They appeared to be in the grounds of a large building.

Shown into the house kitchen, they were offered supper by an old couple, speaking only German.

They accepted coffee only and asked to be shown to their rooms.

Taking the coffee with them, they were taken upstairs to a very large room and flopped on the two beds exhausted.

Chapter 8

Peter was the first to wake. Confused, he struggled to establish some understanding of where he was.

Thirsty, he sat up and looked around the room. A coffee mug stood on an oak side-cupboard, untouched. He took a sip and pulled a face.

Responding to the 'call of nature,' he staggered out of bed looking for a bathroom.

There were several doors serving a large, elegant room. Tall, beautifully draped windows let in streams of daylight on to a polished wooden floor and scattered Persian rugs.

Hal was fast asleep, fully dressed on the bed alongside. One of his shoes had fallen off and was lying upside down mirroring his sleeping position.

Their luggage had been placed neatly just inside a door. Peter's trousers and shirt were lying on the floor beside the bed. For the life of him, he could not remember undressing.

To his right one door stood slightly ajar. Sunlight streamed across the room picking out the colours in the rugs.

Peter pushed the door open to reveal a large bathroom furnished from another era.

It was like walking back into another world.

Over to the right a flowered wash basin beckoned. Peter emptied the contents of the coffee mug rinsed it and refilled with cold water from one of the gold taps, then drained it.

His head began to clear and the events of yesterday hit him like the seventh wave on a shingle beach. The import of yesterday's dramas, crowded out by confusion and fatigue, flooded back.

He looked around the room which would not have been out of place in the 19th century.

A flowered enamel 'sit-up and beg' hip bath, sited alongside the window wall, set the mood.

A matching wash hand basin and W.C. completed the picture.

Peter sat on the toilet taking in the scene. Broad polished wooden floorboards complete with Persian rugs and three-metre tall draped windows framed a picture of sartorial elegance.

Peter bent forward and rubbed his palms on the smooth wooden floor hollowed by polishing and the passage of many feet down the years. He was calmed by the thought of so many ghosts.

The early morning autumn sun streamed through the window catching dust particles dancing and sparkling in the light from an open window accompanied by the hum of dawn, the sound of a river, birdsong and a distant barking dog.

There being no way he could control events in this warm, friendly feeling house, he decided to let the next chapter unfold.

The smell of coffee drifted in on the breeze.

Back in the bedroom Hal was still asleep.

The contrast between the fury of last night and now was stark.

Peter now had to think how to explain yesterdays' drama and the loss of the Oktoberfest.

A victim himself, he still felt responsible.

He dressed and quietly left the room finding his way out on to a landing. Stairs, broad and elegant, led down into a large sitting room.

The furnishing at the far end of a large room covered by dust sheets suggested that the owners had either just arrived or were leaving. The near furniture being uncovered.

Tall windows faced the garden lawns stretching down to a river. In the centre French doors opened out on to a terrace.

Hearing sounds of activity over to his right he called out. "Hello."

The old woman who met them last night, appeared from the kitchen doorway and beckoned him through into a bright and cheerful breakfast room. On a large sideboard there was an array of cheeses, meats, breads, fruit and cakes.

Peter could not remember passing through this room in the early hours. Once more he had the feeling of being in the middle of a time slip.

The events of yesterday, a distant bad dream.

Some while later Hal joined him on the terrace, having breakfasted on veal, eggs and coffee.

"Hey Pete, is this place for real? What gives? Have we been transported into the nobility?"

He stretched and yawned. "Woke up starving, smelled the coffee couldn't wait. Didn't even shave. You been up long?"

Peter had been wondering how Hal would react to this massive change of scene and the loss of the planned holiday.

"Good morning, Hal. I haven't shaved either. I thought we could unpack later when we know how long we are here." He answered holding his breath, still unsure how to deal with the loss of the Fest. It was clear there was little chance of returning to Munich.

He need not have worried. His friend stretched and yawned.

"Strange not knowing. What about this place? Whose is this and why here? I hope we stay a while. Suits me. This house it's super and the cuisine is fantastic. A week or two of this will just do me fine."

Peter smiled. His friend's good humour had returned. Clearly, Hal was coming to terms with this strange situation. He felt the same.

There was a tranquillity, an air about this place.

Peter, used to being disappointed, was still aware that the real world with all its problems still existed. He added a word of caution.

"I don't wish to upset you Hal, but we could be away by lunchtime."

"I hope not, put in some central heating, I could put down roots and keep the staff, especially in the kitchen."

Peter didn't answer, he was still wondering what the day could possibly have in store.

Hal took a swig of coffee leaned back on the seat and sighed.

"This is great I can't wait to explore. Everything is so well cared for. It must take a huge staff but where are they and how do we fit in and why in this big place? Hey Pete, with God knows how many bedrooms, why did they fit us both into one?'

Peter deep in thought, didn't answer.

"Pete, you still there?"

Peter was startled to reply, "I haven't really thought about it. You are right, we appear the only ones here, also all that food at breakfast. Where are the owners and Eva? Did she stay the night?"

"No guesses Pete, and as for Eva no clues. Last night I just died."

"I didn't even undress at first."

"Me not at all, slept just as I was."

Peter stood up. "I ought to shave, change and unpack. Come to think of it, do we unpack?"

"Go shave and change? Who for? I'm for bumming it. Forget it Pete, let's go and explore."

The slow pace of life suited them. Peter hoped that they stayed, if only for a day or so. The sun shone from a cloudless sky and as it rose higher the day became very warm.

Hal headed for the riverbank where it was cooler and sat on the bank, his feet dangling over the water. "Sorry about yesterday Pete."

"Hal, you're sorry! I'm so sorry. I still can't come to terms with what happened to Dieter and what happened yesterday. What about the Fest? We didn't even have a chance to settle."

Peter sat down alongside his friend in silence.

There were so many unanswered questions, so much to think about.

Eventually Hal broke the silence.

"Forget the Fest, from what bit I saw of it, there was an undertow of evil. Maybe it was all the armed police. Then there was that band and marching Brownshirts. It was more a demonstration, not a celebration."

Peter just nodded agreement, still wondering what was to happen and how long they would be there.

"What a louse I was Pete. So sorry. I was feeling rotten. Ratting on you, not to mention your father." Peter didn't answer so Hal continued.

"I just could not bring myself to tell you. Think how to tell you."

Peter still didn't answer. Hal added. "I just couldn't turn down the offer, sorry."

Peter, still deep in thought, answered. "If you apologise just once more, I will push you in the river. Yesterday has gone now we need to decide what next? What we do now? Where do we go from here?"

Hal shrugged. "Just sit tight I guess." He lay back on the bank and sighed. "Suits me."

He was happy at last to have gotten his worries off his conscience and that normal relations with Peter had resumed.

Later that morning clouds gathered across the distant hills. Sheet and fork lightning flickered and cracked vividly against a darkening sky.

"Reckon we should get back to the house Pete. That storm could travel. Anyways it must be lunch time."

They strolled back to the house. The buildings, along with the trees and statues lost definition in the heat shimmer. They did not see a slight figure sitting in the shadows on the large seat encircling a tree in the middle of the lawn. As they approached, they were greeted by a lady with an Australian accent. "Nice to see you again Peter and to meet your friend. Oh! and so sorry about all the hoo-hah yesterday."

Peter started to run forward. "Lulu, is that you?"

"Who else, you tiny Limey."

"I thought you and Rolf were going to Australia after the Games." Peter hugged her.

He was relieved to see a familiar face.

"That was the line, Peter. We needed to disappear off the map and you don't need a nudge as to why."

Dieter, Peter, Rolf and Lulu were old friends from back in Berlin. Their last meeting was in the summer of 1936 at the time of the Games. Peter introduced Lulu to Hal.

"Hal, this is Lulu my old friend known to all as Peach Melbourne. Lulu, this is my friend Henry from university, known to all as Hal."

"Hi Hal, great to meet you."

Rolf Neuberger had married Louisa in 1935 and planned to emigrate to Australia but had difficulties in obtaining clearance. After the incident in Berlin on the lake they returned to Austria, his birthplace officially to await events. Subsequently they announced that they were at last on their way to the Antipodes. This was Peter's understanding. The truth was clearly somewhere else.

"Peter, Hal, there's something you need to know. Rolf and I have had a change of identity.

Rolf and I are now known as Johannes and Gerda Weismann."

"You've changed names. Why?"

"You didn't imagine that we would cop out with our tails between our legs, did you? And you don't need that university degree to figure why. So, you'd best be knowing that you are dealing with thieves and forgers."

Peter hugged her again. "Pleased to meet you Gerda Weisman and my best to Johannes."

Hal was still working out what was happening.

"O.K. let's be knowing what that hoo-hah yesterday was all about ..."

"I'm here because we need your help, please."

Gerda addressed them both but the 'please' was directed at Hal.

"What help is this and who are we?" Hal's question was tinged with caution.

"We," Gerda answered, "are a group who are assisting Jewish people who wish to leave the country. Escape the Nazis, especially the kids."

Hal thought for a moment. "Correct me if I am wrong. This is Austria we are speaking of, not Germany?"

"Both, Hal," Gerda answered. "That might have been a valid question once. No longer true, I am afraid. The oppression has moved south. It is violently active. The imperative is that we provide an urgent escape route for all who wish to leave."

"Why? Can't they just leave and cross the border, just normally?"

Gerda shook her head. "You don't understand. Not many do outside of the country."

"They are prevented from leaving?" Hal shocked, started taking notes. Determined to report all.

"Not only prevented but forcibly returned. This depending on who is on border guard. Some get through of course but more and more are being blocked, returned. It is why we are asking for your help."

Peter, who had been quietly listening, asked "Are you saying that Austria is no longer independent?"

"Officially yes, but the Nazis are gaining more and more support. The police and border guards seem to do whatever they please. Furthermore, the Anschluss could take place any day now.

It is gaining support everywhere."

Peter, aware of his responsibilities to Hal, persisted. "And the hoo-hah as you call it, yesterday?

Why were we shipped unceremoniously across the border and not bedded down in Munich?"

Hal repeated this question, the foremost in their minds.

"Yes, the hoo-hah as you called it, you still haven't explained. Don't you think we are due one?" Noticeably, Hal was not angry.

Gerda sat back down on the tree seat.

"You fellas best join me. This could take some time."

"Time, we have. If we are to help, we need to know everything."

"Everything is a big ask but I will do my best. You deserve an explanation for all that took place yesterday." Gerda folded her arms defensively across her chest.

Hal, then Peter took their places alongside her as she requested.

"You have no idea how sorry we are to have taken liberties," she sighed, "but needs must when the devil drives and the devil is truly driving events in Austria as well as Germany. We needed to arrange the evacuation of the Kessler family. Dieter arranged for you to lodge with them. This could have given them some protection by your presence. Also give us some time to arrange papers to transport them across into Switzerland. The Gestapo maybe knew of our plans. They arrested them three days before you were due to arrive."

"Yes! We have heard about that. Did our late arrival cause problems?"

"I would think not."

"Afterwards, they arrested Dieter. Why?" Peter still hoped something could be done about his friend.

"Not then, two days later, the day before you arrived."

Hal took over the questioning "The reason for these arrests being?"

"For the Kessler's they *have* given a reason. Often they arrest prominent Jews without any explanation."

"And the reason was?" Hal was determined to get all the detail even though he was aware his editor may not accept his copy.

"They were arrested and charged with subversive activity against the Third Reich."

"That is both Dr Kessler *and* his wife?"

"Yes. They intended to arrest the whole family, Dr Kessler, Frau Kessler and Miriam their three-year-old daughter."

Hal looked up from his note pad. "That's what Eva said. You're sure, a three-year-old kid?"

"It is their intent to take the complete family." Gerda looked to Hal making notes being aware of the need to spread this knowledge, particularly to the United States.

"Frau Kessler foiled the police by passing Miriam over the fence to her neighbour Helga while Dr Kessler was opening the front door. Helga and Dieter brought her across to us and we have her safe. When Dieter returned to meet you, he was arrested for aiding and abetting enemies of the state."

Peter interrupted. "It explains why Dieter wasn't there to meet us, not why we were shipped over the border?"

Hal was absorbed with getting the complete story. Partly he was excited to have stumbled upon what he deemed to be a major story; a perfect feature for his first submission yet horrified at what he was hearing.

"Helga asked us to watch out for you and to take you to the Fairy Grotto Bar for them to find you accommodation but on the way, we learned that you Hal, held a press card."

Peter and Hal looked at each other.

"The taxi driver, it figures." said Hal.

Peter nodded. "Why does Hal's press card make a difference?"

"We have a party of thirty or so children and five adults, including Helga and Miriam, awaiting their chance to cross over to Switzerland. As things stand, they may well be turned back at the border. The cover story is a day trip to Zurich from school. The Nazis however are wise to this and unless we meet unbiased border control, they are almost sure to be stopped. The presence of the American press may just make the difference. Observed by you they could be persuaded to allow them through. Miriam Kessler is too young to pass as a schoolgirl and we are sure that the border guards will be ordered to lookout for a three-year- old girl."

"So, you abducted us?" Peter still angry at events, called it as it was.

"Sorry Peter, Hal we had no time to plan. We had to make it up 'on the hoof,' as you say."

"And this house just happened to be available?"

"The house is the summer residence of a prominent financier. It is about to be closed for the winter.

He is presently in America on important business. His family are at another of their homes in Switzerland. It is possible they will not return."

"You have permission to use the house?"

Gerda nodded. "Until the end of the month."

"What will happen to the house?" asked Hal, "if they don't return?"

"They will try to sell it. If they are lucky, they might get a third of its true price."

"And if they are not?"

"After an Anschluss, the Nazis will just take it, just as they took the Kesslers."

"They do that?"

"They are already doing so in Germany and not just the house, contents, valuables, jewellery anything; it's theft, plain and simple, under the guise of authority."

Hal thought for a moment.

"So, you want us to turn up at the border the same time as your refugees?"

"If you will."

Hal looked to Peter. "I'm with you. Pete, what about you?"

Peter hesitated before nodding and saying. "Of course."

Gerda looked at her watch. "Lunch is ready I believe. I must be on my way."

She got up to go then sat down again. "There is another favour if you would oblige us further."

Hal was so pumped up and involved with the situation he was more than anxious to hear.

"What else can we do?"

"The little Kessler girl is distressed and hysterical. What she might do if she just sees any uniformed men at the border is anyone's guess. She could scupper the whole project. What is more she is only three and cannot possibly pass for a schoolgirl."

"That figures but what can we do?"

"When Frau Kessler handed Miriam over to Helga she said don't worry, my darling, Papa Yo will take care of you. I am leaving you in the safe hands of Papa Yo. Now Miriam is blaming Helga and us for not finding this Papa Yo. If we could separate her from the main party, it would be a big help.

We are already keeping her away from the others. They are distressed enough already."

Gerda looked to Hal who spread his hands in question. "So?"

"If you were to take Miriam across the border with you, say as your niece, would that work?"

Hal again thought then turned to Peter. "What do you think Pete?"

"Sounds as though it could work but we need to think this out."

"I pose as the girl's uncle taking her over to the States, is that what you mean?"

Hal ignored Peter's advice.

"That's about it, Hal," replied Gerda concentrating on Hal.

"What say if I pose as this Papa guy? The little girl would be then more settled."

"As Papa Yo? That, Hal is brilliant, would you?"

"Figure that would cover all bases."

Peter meanwhile abandoned his attempts to persuade his friend to take time out to think.

Gerda jumped up and embraced both men.

"Thanks fellas, you have no idea just what this means. I must be away, there's much to be arranged." Blowing each a kiss, she disappeared into the house through the kitchen out into the yard and into a dark red saloon.

"Let's away, Eva. Game on. Tell Ilsa, tonight, that for this operation only my name is Gerda Weismann."

"Was that wise?"

"Had to. The Englishman knows me from Berlin."

The driver started the engine and sped away. "Papa Yo? Everything?"

"*Everything*" Gerda replied leaning back and sighing.

Chapter 9

After lunch, there was little else the friends could do but to walk again in the garden and down to the river. The afternoon sun lit the distant hills which seemed to dance in the heat haze.

Hal began to sway to and fro as if mesmerised by the scene. This amused him.

Peter, still pre-occupied, sat down on the riverbank in silence.

A heron stalked the shallows, it froze loop necked, before spearing into an eddy. A fish flashed silver in the sunlight but only for a split second before disappearing into the bird.

"Jeepers Pete, did you see that? What a way to go, swimming happily one second then gone, never to be seen again."

Peter didn't answer or show any interest and continued staring at the river.

"Oh! Peter, I'm so sorry. That was crass of me. I wasn't thinking about Dieter."

After a short pause Peter replied. "Actually, I am thinking about the children. The little Kessler child, what is happening to her? Dieter knew he was swimming in pike-infested waters. The children what do they know? They are truly innocents."

Hal got up and went to sit beside his friend. "I'm at a loss to find a word for these people. Bastards is unfair to the illegitimate. There is no word for them."

"There is, Hal, it's Nazi." Peter murmured.

Hal nodded. "What are they doing to these countries and their people? How do they cope with losing all this? All they have built, their dreams, their family home, this great house. Why and for what?"

"I believe, Hal, that the owner of this house will be all right. Not only will they survive, they will survive well. It's the children, the poor, the ordinary folk and the Kesslers. What a terrible time for them." Peter stared into the river, which was much more turbulent than this morning.

The storm over the hills was already making its presence felt. The river level was building rapidly, driving debris which bounced along in the mainstream. To one side, in contrast, a gentle eddy circled carrying a single leaf round and round. Peter found this strangely calming.

He lay back and looked up into the sky at the clouds slowly changing shape as they moved across.

"You know, Hal." He began unsure himself what he was going to say. Confused and conflicting emotions, the sharp edges of recent events, dulled by the peaceful scene. When he did speak, it was as though someone else was dictating.

"Thinking about this drama that we are caught in the middle of, I feel untouched by it, unemotional. Does that sound stupid?"

"I guess not, I figure it's this place. It's like being in a bubble of contentment. We are looking out at the world as if protected by its skin."

Hal lay back and joined Peter staring at the clouds.

"You feel it too?" Peter was relieved to hear this.

"From the moment I woke. The world suddenly seemed right even though I know it's not."

"You are aware Hal just what we have let ourselves in for? That sometime soon, very soon, someone is going to prick this bubble?" Peter was fighting to keep their 'feet on the ground'.

He was trying to alert Hal to the serious elements of that already agreed to.

"Yep, so we soak it up while we can," Hal replied, seemingly unconcerned. "Forget what may be tomorrow and live for this moment. My conscience keeps saying to me, return to the house unpack, bathe and get shaved and changed. Then I think, why bother?"

Hal turned on to his stomach smiling reassuringly at Peter.

"What say Pete we shave and change for dinner? This afternoon let's just live it up."

Hal lay back down in the shade of a tree. "This is heaven." He sighed.

This attempt to calm Peter was met with a sullen silence.

Bathed, shaved and changed, they dined on venison, fresh vegetables, fruit, cheeses and fine wines then took Calvados and coffee out on to the terrace.

They had been assured that the owner had given permission for them to use the ample larder.

And take whatever they wished from the wine cellar and drinks cabinet. They were making the most of this generous offer.

It was a lovely evening, warm, balmy, soporific.

"Let's go sit under the tree and watch the stars come out," suggested Hal, aware that his friend was still brooding.

They walked across the lawn away from the lights of the house to the rustic seat where that afternoon they had met Lulu. The tree seemed to draw them into its shade.

Hal picked up a fallen leafed twig and swept the day's debris from the seat and sat down.

He looked out across the lawns over the river to the distant hills.

"This so, so beautiful, so peaceful. How could you cope with losing all this, all you have built and nurtured, your dreams, your family home with all its memories and for what?" He sighed again. "Envy, jealousy, greed, sadistic amusement, take your pick."

"Give it a rest, Hal, I thought we were here to watch the stars come out," said Peter, testily.

"Sorry Pete." Hal apologised.

As if on cue, the evening star pricked into sight as the sky darkened with the sun finally sinking behind the hills rimming the crests with a golden glow which fingered up into the sky.

"Sunset and evening star," Peter whispered.

"What's that Pete?" Hal was relieved that his friend showed some animation having been locked away in his thoughts all evening.

"And one clear call for us," said Peter as he connected with the day's events.

"What?" Hal asked, realising that Peter was speaking of the commitment made earlier.

"Take no notice, Hal. It's just a couple of lines from Tennyson which seem appropriate, that's all." Peter was clearly disturbed. This, despite his comment earlier about being untouched.

"O.K. Pete if you are in the mood. Give with the rest."

"Perhaps not, it goes downhill from there." Peter tried to close the topic.

"Why?" Hal countered, trying to keep him talking.

"It's about death. So best left." Peter, once more, clammed up tight.

That was as far as the conversation got. Gerda had quietly crept up behind the tree and was waiting for the right moment to announce her arrival. In the silence which followed, she took a deep breath and spoke out.

"Let there be no moaning at the Bar as we put out to sea."

The friends spun around looking. Gerda added quickly.

"The Pilot has been here all the while but in the dark, you did not see her."

Startled, Peter turned. "Lulu?"

"Gerda," she corrected.

"Sorry." Peter apologised.

"Pilot what Pilot?" Hal was confused.

"Take no notice Hal, Gerda was taking liberties with Alfred Lord Tennyson."

Peter could have added. 'She is also taking liberties with us.' Aware that one man's freedom can mean another man's 'incarceration'. That they had responsibilities however unwelcome.

"Chance would be a fine thing," Gerda replied. She took another deep breath and returned to her intrusive errand. "Fellas I'm sorry but I am here on serious business."

"Don't concern yourself, Gerda. It's this place, it brings out the whimsy in us, it is full of happy ghosts," Peter replied. "I hope you are not here to spoil it."

Gerda, anxious that her mission was being sabotaged, passed over the remark and turned to his friend.

"Hal, we have brought Miriam. Do you mind?"

"The Kessler girl, why tonight?"

"Yes. Big favour needed?" Gerda added anxiously.

"And that is?" Peter stood and walked into Gerda's vision determined not to let Hal be railroaded as he was earlier.

Gerda ignored Peter and addressed Hal. "Miriam is very distressed."

"Yes, you said so before." Peter was determined not to be ignored.

Gerda, however, did ignore him, speaking to Hal. "We've brought her along to you. To her *Papa Yo*, in the hope that it might settle her. If it does, can we leave her with you, probably until Friday when we hope to move?"

"What? A three-year-old girl?" Clearly the prospect now was scaring Hal. "You mean overnight?"

"Easy Hal, we have brought a carer with her. A nanny who will deal with all the necessary. Hopefully, she will sleep." Gerda added hoping to calm Hal.

Hal looked to Peter for inspiration. He received none.

"I suppose we could give it a go."

The reality of the commitment now struck home. Their discomfort was obvious.

Hal's answer gave Gerda the opening she was looking for. Aware of their reluctance, she took it immediately.

"Good. I'll go get her." Gerda turned on her heels and disappeared swiftly into the shadow of the house.

"Where's she gone?"

"To get the little girl, Hal. Are we sure about this? It's a huge commitment."

Three figures appeared out of the darkness, Gerda, another woman and a very small child.

"There she is now." Hal peered through the gloom trying picture the little girl.

Gerda called out, "Papa Yo." Then she repeated in German and English. "Papa Yo, Wo bist du?

Are you there?"

Hal cleared his throat. "Who calls?"

The tiny figure detached herself from the others ran and launched herself at Hal clinging on to his leg like a baby Lemur to its mother.

"Papa Yo, Papa Yo. Wo warren du? Wo warren du? Ich war gans alien."

Then burying her face in his leg, she sobbed and repeated.

"Gans alein."

Hal needed no translation. He bent and swept the tiny girl into his arms. Holding her tightly he shuddered with every trembling sob of this little child, his face against hers their tears mingling until her sobs subsided. Hal sat down on the seat then cradled and rocked this tiny lost child.

Slowly, gradually she settled. Her head fell back against his arm and she slept.

The other woman came forward, reached out with her arms and spoke in German.

Hal turned and looked at Peter. "What did she say Pete?"

"Thank God, I will take her now."

Hal handed her over. Immediately he felt bereft. Hal felt that he should say and do something more. The woman walked away taking Miriam into the house. Gerda came forward and embraced Hal.

"Thank you. Thank you, it worked."

Gerda then hurriedly followed the nanny back into the house leaving Hal literally 'holding the baby'. Hal, distraught, stood rock still. Sensing his distress Peter came forward. Finding it difficult to speak, he managed to croak.

"You all right Hal?"

Hal gathered himself.

"I think, old buddy, our bubble has just been burst."

Neither moved for quite some time and when they did it was aimlessly. Hal wandered in circles looking at the ground, but here there was no eddy, no calm.

Peter, finding this silence oppressive, felt compelled to speak.

"Hal, what on earth have we let ourselves in for?" He was thinking that this situation had arisen because of his father and his stupid ideas. He felt somehow responsible, the shock of the last few minutes still drumming in his brain.

Hal sat down on the seat and looked out towards the hills. After almost a minute he whispered.

"We must get that little girl out of this stinking country. This is personal now."

Peter, ever 'the Job's comforter' replied.

"Easier said than done. I don't think you understand the dangers. This is real. It is not really our problem. We never asked to get involved."

Peter waited for his friend to answer. When he didn't, he continued.

"Why can't this girl go through with the others? Think about it? This could be all a fit up. We need to work this out before we commit further."

Peter Barnes, used to being conned and manipulated, let down by others, was naturally suspicious. He did not make the same connection as his friend.

Hal suddenly stood up.

"What if she wakes up and asks where I am?" He started towards the house then he stopped and turned around. "Sorry Pete, see you later."

Peter began to move after Henry, then thinking better of it, sat down on a terrace seat to sort out the confusion in his head. Some while later he gave up and made his way upstairs to their room.

He reached up to switch on the lights then stopped. Hal was sat on the edge of his bed head in hands.

Moonlight streamed through the tall windows picking up his shadow across the white of the pillows and bed sheets.

"You all right Hal?"

Receiving no answer, Peter left the lights off and sat on his bed opposite his friend.

Hal didn't answer for some time. He just sat thinking before doing so.

"Sure! You are thinking we are being manoeuvred, Pete? I don't blame you. We *are*.

We know so little about this outfit. The little girl virtually dumped here without our consent. Fitted up by this Lulu/ Gerda woman who is probably just a front because she knows you and your friend Dieter. What do we have? Hearsay as to what has gone on so far. Kidnapped, brought here as you say, without our leave and a distressed child."

Hal let out a huge sigh.

"Whether or not they are pulling an emotional stunt, that kid is not acting. She is real."

He paused. "And she needs me."

"What happens now Hal?"

"We go along with it, old buddy. At least I do. I can't let the kid down. I just can't."

"If that's the way you feel, I'm with you."

Hal sighed and removed his shoes letting them drop striking the wooden floor echoing briefly in the silence. "I am bushed Pete. Time to hit the hay."

Chapter 10

The following morning just the two of them finished breakfast, in silence. The door opened and in ran Miriam who climbed up on Hal's knee, helping herself to the remains of a croissant from his plate. Crumbs spilled down his shirt as she pushed it into her mouth.

"Noch mal," she squeaked spitting more crumbs.

Hal, surprised and clearly delighted, brushed away the crumbs smiling. "Crumby business, kids." Miriam returned the smile and looked up to Hal's face.

Peter went to the side and collected cake, breads and preserves, placed the plate in front of them and sat down. Miriam claimed another croissant and scattered more flaky crumbs as she pushed it into her mouth. She forced some into Hal's mouth. Laughing, he accepted the offering showering the table and themselves with even more. Meantime the nanny had arrived and was watching from the door smiling at the scene, partly with relief. She went to the side, poured a glass of milk and added this to Hal's worries. He looked up at the nanny, smiled and said:

"Thank you."

"Ilsa," she replied with a little bob of a curtsy.

"Good morning Ilsa, kid been O. K.?"

It was Peter's turn to smile.

"If I didn't know Hal, I would assume you have done this before. It looks right."

"Feels kind o' right."

From that moment on all plans for the day, at least for Hal, disappeared. The day was controlled entirely by this little girl who demanded and got one hundred percent attention from Papa Yo. Not that this pleased Ilsa who was rebuffed by both Miriam and

Hal whenever she tried to intervene. Even when it was necessary for her to take over, she was assailed by a ferocious tantrum.

Peter, also not at all pleased, remained a worried spectator.

After dinner that evening Peter was able to voice his concerns.

Hal sat down on the lawn before lying flat and looking up at the stars.

"I'm bushed Pete," he groaned, "what is that expression of yours, jiggered? But I've rarely enjoyed myself so much. Reckon I was made for this."

Peter studied his hands thinking how to approach his worry without ruining Hal's day.

Quietly he spoke, he hoped gently.

"Have you thought what will happen if you succeed in getting Miriam through safely?"

"Whoa, whoa there, partner, how do you mean if? Miriam is going through, be sure of that buddy!" Hal sat up.

Peter looked at him and realised that he was agitated more than angry.

Sorry, yet satisfied he'd made the point. He took to thinking how to lighten the conversation, to regain the comfortable mood which disappeared with Miriam's arrival. He forced a chuckle.

"I wished I'd had my camera when you and Miriam were laid back kicking your legs in the air."

He chuckled again, this time the laughter was genuine.

Miriam and Hal had been on the lawn playing, facing each other when she fell on her back kicking her legs squealing 'Mach so.' It was a command which Hal obeyed without redress for a translation.

It was a good choice by Peter. Hal immediately engaged but clearly did not share Peter's amusement.

"Too right, Pete. I have a press camera. Will you carry it for me when we get to the border?"

"Why?" Peter sounded belligerent.

"Evidence, Pete. Faced with a camera the Goons will back off."

"You think so? Do you think it will be that simple?"

Peter's stance was making Hal uncomfortable. He stood up.

"They had better, Pete. Don't underestimate the power of the pen." He turned to walk away from Peter whose logical argument was making him uncomfortable. Peter also got up from the seat and went after him.

"Best not bond with the little girl, Hal."

Hal ignored his friend's remark. "I'm for hitting the hay."

"So soon?" Peter now knew he was getting through to Hal and was reluctant to let him go.

"Leave me Pete, just leave me. I need to think."

Hal left waving his arm as if wafting away Peter's logical arguments.

Peter, much troubled, sat alone with his thoughts and fears.

It seemed to him that the repatriation of Miriam had not been thought through properly. A Jewess would naturally be adopted by a Jewish family which would mean a forced separation from Hal and this would mean a new trauma for them both.

Peter was now certain that his friend had bonded with Miriam. That Miriam was replacing her family with her Papa Yo, with all the further heartache that this entailed.

All he could do now was hope that he had warned his friend of the pitfalls to come.

As for the little girl's future, he just dared not to think.

The following day followed much the same pattern at breakfast.

Miriam insisted Hal get up from breakfast to play out in the garden. Peter's anxiety was not being helped by this.

The old woman came in to clear the table and collected the crockery on a large wooden tray. Before leaving she stood and watched Hal and Miriam through the window. "Give a man a daughter he is her slave and guardian, give him a son he is his captain.

It was always so!" The old woman observed in German.

Peter was surprised by the woman's comment. She, having rarely spoken before.

"Miriam is not his daughter." He protested.

"Matters not." The woman replied leaving the kitchen.

Chapter 11

The following morning Ilsa woke early to find Miriam missing from her bed.

She did not panic, guessing at once just where she would be. Putting on her dressing gown she crept across to the men's bedroom.

She pushed open the door slightly and peered in to confirm that Miriam was fast asleep in Hal's bed. Carefully she closed the door and stood thinking for a few moments, then realising there was little she could do without embarrassment decided to go down for a coffee and await events.

Gerda was in the kitchen waiting for the house to awake. She greeted Ilsa as she placed the papers from the table back into a folder.

"Good morning, Ilsa. Miriam still asleep?"

"Yes, I've come down for a coffee."

Ilsa poured herself a cup and stood with her back to the stove.

"Can you have Miriam packed and ready to move by 10.30?"

"You've got the papers? Good, we will be ready."

"Not you Ilsa, just the little girl." Gerda had misread the extent to which Ilsa had bonded with Miriam.

Ilsa was shocked into silence.

Gerda aware of Ilsa's discomfort fought to deal with this.

"We don't have papers for you. It is better that the two men travel alone with Miriam. The rest of us will keep clear. We can't imagine that the Nazi S.S. have been idle. They will have their agents watching all exits."

"The border is between Austria and Switzerland?"

Gerda didn't answer. She gave Ilsa the look schoolteachers give when a pupil has said something silly.

"We are severing all connection with Miriam with effect from 10.30. That includes you.

That *is it*, Ilsa."

Ilsa still objected. "Who will look to Miriam? I mean a little girl with just two men?"

Gerda lapsed back into English in frustration.

"Good God, woman, we can't be bothered with your prissy protocol."

She then reverted to German speaking calmly.

"Just get her ready please." She paused repeating, "Please, Ilsa. You know how it works. We will have no more contact nor will they with us. Pegasus will take over once they get over the border."

Ilsa looked out of the window concentrating on the branches of the tree bouncing in a stiff breeze heralding the onset of autumn and a change in the weather.

She bit her bottom lip which was beginning to tremble.

Gerda noted this and changed to a much gentler tone.

"She will be fine, Ilsa, you know that this is the only solution. Also, we will be needing you again."

Ilsa didn't reply but turned on her heels and speedily left the room.

Much later Peter arrived in the kitchen closely followed by Hal and the little girl.

Gerda was getting anxious. "At last fellas, can you be ready to move at 10.30?"

Peter was shocked and stopped pouring the coffee. Then he gathered his wits and spoke calmly.

"Good morning, Gerda. Sorry, didn't see you. I was homing in on the coffee."

He looked around aware of a change in the atmosphere.

"No servants today?"

Gerda accepted Peter's implied reprimand. "Sorry, Peter. Good morning, can you be ready at 10, 30 please?"

"Ready for what?" Peter asked, playing for time.

Hal who had sized up the situation, spoke up.

"Sure, we can. Take no notice of Pete, he's been in another world for the last day or so. He does that sometimes."

Hal collected breads, croissants and meats and sat down with Miriam on his knee.

Peter was now even more panicky. "Can be ready for what, exactly?"

"Can what" Miriam repeated grabbing a croissant.

"See speaking English already. Sure, we are ready. Let's get this show on the road."

"Today?" Peter at last allowed himself to accept what was going on.

Hal smiled and shook his head "Too true it seems old buddy. Care to join us?"

Peter sat down at the table, his heart beating. "What is the plan?"

Gerda reached and placed a small leather solid briefcase on the table.

"Miriam's supplementary luggage," Gerda announced. She placed her hand on it.

"Don't open it until you get over the border and then only if you have to. Here is a key. Otherwise hand it over to the courier on the other side."

"How do we know when and if to open it? For that matter, know the courier?"

Peter now realising fully what was to happen was wanting more detail. Hal was content to listen.

"The courier is Pegasus."

"Pegasus, just Pegasus?"

"They will approach you and enquire if you are from the Mercury. You will answer:

'Barkis is willing'. From then on, they will take over. Here are Miriam's papers they are made out to a Sudeten Jewess who died in infancy."

Hal, making notes, butted in. "A Jewess, is that wise?"

"Think about it, Hal. The Nazis will be primed to look out for a three-year-old accompanied by a carer. Or they might expect her to be in a group. Whichever, they will be on the lookout for false papers. What they will not expect is that these papers will be those of a Jewess. They'll expect anything but Jew. Also, you three will not be the type of target they have been primed to investigate."

Hal looked up from his notes. "The Nazis will do all this just to arrest a little kid? That takes some swallowing!"

"No, Hal. They will pick her up if they can of course, but the real agenda is to get a bead on our outfit, our cell. The border guards will not have time to cross check on Sudeten nationals. If you are prepared to be Miriam's uncle. That, with the fact that you are American, we think will work."

"I will show my press card if it gets sticky," said Hal, adding, "I get the picture."

Gerda nodded continuing, "We will have no contact with you after Ilsa and I leave in a short while. That is the last you will see of us. You will be on your own. Can you cope with Miriam and all that it entails, toilet etc.?"

"I've seen guys back home take them into the men's toilets. Is that O.K. here?"

"Depends, but I see no option, you could ask a female for the favour, but I fear Miriam will panic and create. No, best try and cope yourself. Miriam is very capable. Take her to the men's or if you can manage until you are on the train, so much the better."

With this answer Gerda considered the matter closed and passed over a wallet.

"There are Schillings, Swiss Francs and some French Francs. If you miss the meet, you may need to go straight through to the ferry where they accept Sterling. I doubt you will need the French Franc. Otherwise the ferry reservations will be dealt with by the couriers. The tickets to and from Zurich to Calais are in this envelope, if needed."

Hal opened the wallet. "That's one heck of a lot of Schillings."

"For the hire car driver. This car will arrive from a local firm who are familiar with commissions from this house. It has been arranged already by phone. They are nothing to do with us and have only the instruction to deliver you to Landeck station for the Zurich train.

Treat them as a normal hire car, which they are. Pay in cash. If they query this, expecting to charge to the account, say the house is closing for the winter, which it does each year at this time."

Peter who had been listening to all this swallowed the lump in his throat and whispered:

"What if we are challenged?"

"We hope you won't be, just do your best whatever." Gerda stood up.

"I must go, there is much to do."

"Of course, are you seeing the others across the same time as us?"

"They left earlier. It is supposed to be a school day trip. They should be through shortly.

Fingers crossed they will be meeting you in time for the afternoon train from Zurich to Calais."

She embraced Peter. "Bon voyage" then embraced Hal.

"Thank you, Hal, you are a brick."

She bent down to Miriam who, immediately hid behind Hal's leg. "Bye sweetie."

Miriam hid her face in Hal's trousers. Gerda called upstairs.

"Ilsa come, we are away."

Ilsa came downstairs, ran through the kitchen and out into the yard.

Gerda turned to follow. "What few possessions Miriam has will be upstairs. Grab yourselves some food and drink from the larder. The caretaker/gardener will close up once you are away."

These final words were spoken while she hurried from the room.

Chapter 12

A limousine arrived promptly at 10.15. Their luggage loaded, complete with cheese, meats, bread rolls, water and cake, they climbed aboard.

"Landeck Bahn?" The driver sought confirmation of the destination.

"Correct," replied Peter, asking. "How long the journey?"

"Two and a half hours, sir."

"Another long trip, Hal. You O.K. with that?"

"In this limo I am fine, plenty of leg room," he closed the glass partition, "and privacy."

Miriam was soon fast asleep, her head on Hal's lap.

Peter, unable to relax, raised the subject bothering him.

"Have you worked out the real reason for using us and splitting Miriam from the main party?"

"No Pete. What's the beef?"

"She would be distressed that is for sure but that would apply to others also if I'm any judge."

He felt responsible for his friend's involvement in this mission. It had also destroyed the atmosphere which they just managed to recover from, following the Munich fiasco.

"You still don't go with them, do you?"

"No and I reckon it's possible that Gerda's group are aware that the Nazi S.S. are fingering Miriam who could lead them to the cell."

"And?" Hal paused adding, "Come on Pete, spill. There is an 'and' isn't there Pete?"

"I reckon we are being used as a decoy; divorcing us from the main group gives them a better chance of getting through."

"Which leaves us where?" Hal was both puzzled and irritated.

"Exposed and vulnerable? At the same time as giving them a better chance."

"Come off it, Pete! They wouldn't sacrifice a kid. If they were, why bring us and Miriam all this way? You are out of your tree. The very opposite will be the case if I am any judge."

Neither spoke for some time until Hal, sick of Peter's brooding paranoia, said:

"Pete, forget it. We are going to take Miriam through, and you are going to help. These suspicions don't help in any way. We need to be positive. Have that camera ready and get ready to punch your weight."

The driver's estimate of two and a half hours was good. They arrived at Landeck Station on time. The driver piled the luggage on the pavement. Hal thanked and paid him cash as instructed.

Miriam clung to his trousers. Whenever Hal had a free hand, he placed it on her head.

The journey had been uneventful, but Hal was uptight. He was keyed up anyway. Peter's nerves were getting to him. 'What now' he thought, 'trains for Zurich?'

Peter stood aside like a spare part obviously feeling out of it and moody.

A porter appeared. Without instruction from either Hal or Peter, he loaded their cases on to a trolley. Speaking good English, he explained that there was a thirty-minute wait for the train and suggested that he would look after their luggage while they had coffee at a nearby café.

Half an hour later this same porter escorted them to a compartment and loaded their luggage refusing Hal's offered tip. Hal breathed a sigh of relief as they took up reserved seats in a first-class carriage.

The First-Class compartment was a pleasant surprise.

Gerda with this and the limousine, had clearly demonstrated care and understanding.

Peter was no help, being uptight and pessimistic, still suspicious of motive.

Hal engaged with Miriam as he would any child, but more so.

Language proved not to be a barrier. Whatever Hal pointed out and named, be it a house, cow or sheep, Miriam repeated each word.

Eventually Hal was prefixing everything of interest by 'guckmal', copying Miriam.

Even using, 'guckmal was ist?' The little child was teaching Hal more German in half an hour than Peter had to date. This all helped to keep Hal's mind occupied. The journey passed reasonably well.

Peter, largely ignored, sat in one corner brooding.

This was made worse by Hal's preoccupation with the little girl.

Hal was aware of the problem but was unable to think of what he could do.

Every thought he came up with was countered with negativity.

When the train slowed to a stop at the border, they were forced into communicating.

"The camera Pete, get ready."

Peter took a deep breath. "Am I supposed to be with you or not?"

"Not the time to bring that up now."

Hal was irritated that Peter had waited until now to start a constructive discussion.

This in turn irritated Peter.

"Stow it! Hal. Am I of your party? We should have been sorting this on the way."

"Guckmal es gibt andere kind." Miriam announced pressing her face to the window.

Hal and Peter looked out of the window to where the little girl was pointing.

Hal understood what was said immediately.

The train had shunted into a siding across from which a line of barriers led to a custom post.

Beyond this a chain fenced area separated from the main route to the customs shed.

Corralled in this were the children and carers. Guarding the entrance, a lone sentry.

"What do you reckon Pete?" Hal was the first to comment. "I reckon that's the other party."

"I'm sure Hal, the taller woman is Helga, Dieter's mother," whispered Peter, his brain finally kicking into gear. "The bastards are stopping them Hal." He ran his hands through his hair.

"What can we do?"

Hal thought for a moment. "Get the camera ready and take your cue from me."

Peter gasped. "What will you do Hal if you have to hand Miriam over?"

Knowing his friend's attachment to Miriam, Peter imagined mayhem.

"Quit that Pete, you're freaking me out."

Hal succeeded in sounding calm although he was anything but.

Miriam had her head pressed to the window "freaking me" she repeated.

Peter was stood trembling. Hal looked from him to Miriam. Once he saw she was all right, he thought quickly what he could do. Clearly, he needed to settle Peter before the officials appeared.

"Pete it's O.K. so leave this to me," he assured. "I'll handle this. I will need your help."

Peter was still breathing heavily and shuddering.

In a flash of inspiration Hal began to recite rhythmically. "One out, two out, three out, four out."

Peter started to laugh even though he was short of breath.

"It's clear you were never stroke and you would never have made cox."

"Peter, seriously old buddy ease back, relax, you're O.K. I need your help and I need it now."

They could hear the officials moving down the corridor repeating at each door.

'Passports please' in English, French, Italian and German.

"Just sit down and relax Pete, act casual. Read a book or something."

They could see a line of passengers being shepherded through the barriers to the customs house. First-class passengers were being allowed to remain in their compartments.

The compartment door slid open. A policeman and a customs official appeared.

"Good afternoon gentlemen, please present your passports and luggage for inspection."

Chapter 13

Peter jumped up, almost standing to attention. He handed over his passport. "My papers."

He turned reached up and took down his luggage. "These are mine."

He was speaking English whereas, in similar non-stressful circumstances, he would have communicated in German.

Hal, shocked by Peter's response, was aching to do something. Say something to calm Peter down.

Miriam had hidden behind him and was clinging on so tightly he could feel her tiny fingers trembling. All this plus the memory of a similar event only a few days ago in which he was less than happy with his performance,allowing these bullies to strut their stuff without challenge.

The officials were homing in on nervousness.

'Never allow bullies to dictate. Face them down. Dictate events, take control'. Familiar advice from his father and teachers flooded into his mind. Hal picked Miriam up in his arms and looked at the two officials who were now crowding and intimidating Peter.

Hal needed to break this up.

Taking out his press card he tapped the policeman on the shoulder.

The man spun around. Hal fixed him with a stare which lasted but seconds shattering the control they had on Peter. The customs man turned to look what was happening.

Hal waited until he had their full attention to speak.

"Henry Steading, Eastern Coast Press, the United States of America. Can I ask, is it normal for police to accompany customs officials in Austria? For them to clear travellers and their luggage when they are leaving the country?"

He flicked open his note pad and posed, pencil poised. This 'performance' was as much for Peter as the officials.

The policeman ignored the question and looked Henry up and down, before asking to see his passport, speaking in German.

Hal took a step towards him and put his face uncomfortably close to the man.

"Do me the courtesy of speaking English. I know you can because you did so in the last compartment, and you understood this gentleman just now." The policeman found it difficult not to give ground and was rocking back on his heels, asking in English, "Yours and the child's papers please, sir."

Hal handed over his and Miriam's papers. The policeman's eyebrows lifted momentarily as he took a step back.

"Sudeten Jewess?" He looked closely at Miriam who buried her face in Hal's chest.

"That's right, my niece from the Czechoslovakia."

Hal's answer and his claim not to understand German, was already in question.

"The name is not the same as yours." The policeman watched for a reaction from Hal.

"My wife has a different name from her sister who is also married. Why expect my niece to have the same name as me?"

The police officer looked pointedly at Miriam for a while, took a step backwards, clicked his heels and said, "One moment please, Herr Steading."

He had a quick word with the customs officer, turned on his heels and left.

The customs officer cleared all the luggage including Miriam's additional case which Hal deliberately placed prominently and nodded politely.

"Thank you, gentlemen and thank you for visiting my country." He turned and left.

Peter breathed a sigh of relief. "Is that it, what do you think Hal?"

"Nope, I figure that cop's gone for reinforcements. When they come back and they will sit down, look unconcerned and leave the rest to me."

"Don't you think you are taking one hell of a risk?"

"I don't know, I've got my fighting irons on Pete, couldn't help myself. I just hope I know what I am doing. That policeman is dying to take me down a peg and would have done so if he had dared.

He has gone for advice and help."

Hal noted the customs had cleared their luggage and passed Miriam's smaller case to Peter.

"I guess the customs guy is Swiss and the cop is Austrian, strange set up. Look after this and if we get held up take it through with you. I guess it's important and could be incriminating. The other one just contains her clothes so that's O.K."

Peter looked shocked.

"Don't worry, Pete. If he brings the whole police force with him, they also dare not move for precisely the same reason as him. Leave everything to me. Trust me."

Peter began to feel calmer with this interaction with his friend. This intercourse had been missing over the last days. He sat down and tried reading a newspaper. Peter looked out of the window and noted that some of the adults and children had moved up to corral fence and were looking towards the train. Helga he could see clearly, even to the resigned look on her face.

"Hal, we must do something about Helga and those children." Peter pleaded although he had no thoughts as to how.

"One thing at a time old buddy, hopefully we will get an opportunity before it's too late."

"You have a plan?"

"Sure Pete, just have that camera handy and be prepared to use it."

Peter hesitated. On the one hand, he was desperate to save Helga and the kids. On the other he knew they would be risking Miriam's freedom.

"What about Miriam? Won't anything we do risk her being caught?"

Hal placed a reassuring hand on Peter's arm. He was pleased that his friend was thinking of her.

"Pete buddy, I have given this some thought."

He spread fingers and progressively pointed to them in turn with his right index finger.

"First base, the goons will expect us to cower and hide. Second base, they know full well what they are doing is illegal in Austrian law, which still is in force. Third base, they dare not risk alerting the now dormant American conscience to their nasty ways." Hal then spread both hands and smiled. His outward demeanour contrasted with his inner nerves.

"All things considered I reckon we can pencil in a home run. Don't worry, just do as I ask."

The door slid open to reveal an army captain.

"Herr Steading?"

Hal, now faced with an army officer, was momentarily shocked at the level of control at the border and realised just how accurate Gerda's assessment of the situation was.

"That's me."

Miriam was on his knee looking out of the window across at the other children.

The officer stepped inside the compartment and stood over Hal but at a respectful distance.

"Your papers and the Madchen papier, please sir."

Hal handed them over but otherwise did not move. He continued to concern himself with Miriam, who for a change did not feel threatened by this man. Maybe it was because of the officer's quiet polite manner or because she was looking out of the train window engrossed with the other children.

The captain looked casually at the papers.

"On business Herr Steading?"

"Yes, I am on an assignment to assess the political scene and cover social events in Austria."

Hal showed his press card. The officer returned the card and papers to Hal with a smile and a polite bow.

"We trust you have enjoyed our beautiful country, have a good trip."

He saluted, smiled again and with a slight bow left the compartment.

"Pete, I think we might have done it," Hal whispered.

"Now do we sit tight until we are across the border, or risk seeing what we can do about the other kids?" He raised his eyebrows in question to Peter.

"I know it's a risk Hal, I trust your judgement above all. We can't ignore them. We would always wonder. Never forgive ourselves."

"How long have we got before the train moves do you reckon Pete?"

"They'll be through the first class shortly. We must keep an eye on the queue over at the customs shed. I think we might have a little time, but for what?"

Miriam had her face pressed to the window watching the children across the way.

"Follow my lead, Pete."

Hal turned to Miriam bent forward and whispered in her ear.

"Shall we go and see the other kids?"

Miriam immediately jumped down and took Hal's hand.

"Ja Kommen."

Hal laughed. "Get this Pete. She understands me. Let's go."

The three alighted from the carriage. Hal handed down the little girl to Peter. As soon as her feet touched the trackside Miriam was running and skipping towards the other children, her hair blowing in the stiff breeze.

She stopped by the stock fence putting her fingers and nose through the mesh.

The lone sentry at the gate was startled by the sudden appearance of a small child on the outside of the fence and called out. "Verboten, raus."

Hal and Peter were following up.

"Hey fella, leave that kid alone. She's with me," Hal called out, then turning to his friend, added:

"Pete, get photos of the kids behind the fence while I deal with this guy."

Miriam ran to Hal and took up her usual position behind his leg.

Peter took a photograph of the scene then went to the fence to take another.

Hal picked up Miriam and walked towards the sentry.

"What are those kids doing in there?"

The guard, not understanding Hal but at the same time intimidated by his presence, left his post and ran to Peter putting his hand in front of the camera. "Verboten," he said almost apologetically, as if unsure just what his role should be.

The captain appeared from the train hurrying towards them. The sentry, relieved, went back to his post and stood to attention.

Hal thought that he would feel vulnerable with Miriam along. Somehow, he felt stronger.

Picking her up in his arms he turned to face the captain once more.

The officer however marched by him and went to Peter.

"Please sir, do not take photographs."

"Why not?" Hal asked, following the officer. "Have you got something to hide?"

"No sir. These people unfortunately have been left behind. We are awaiting transport to return them safely home."

Hal put Miriam down and took out his notebook. The little girl reattached herself to his right leg.

"How did they come to be left?"

The officer was more concerned about Peter who was asking questions of the captives and taking more photographs. Moving towards the fence the officer answered Hal.

"A foolish mistake, sir. Don't worry we will see that they are safely returned to their homes."

Hal followed him determined to stay in his line of sight.

A comical vision of Hal trying to keep up with Miriam firmly stuck to his leg would in other circumstances have been a source of amusement but here it only added to the sense of desperation.

Hal had written in his notes, LYING BASTARDS, underlining the block capitals.

"Ask them how long they've been stuck in there Pete."

"Wie lang," Peter began only to be interrupted by the captain.

"We've had problems arranging transport, sir."

"And you just did not think to allow them into the customs shed out of the wind and rain?"

Hal replied turning to Peter.

"Take a picture of the captain Pete with the children behind him please."

Hal continued making notes.

"What do you think the temperature is? A cool blustery showery day and outside, how long? Over five hours would you say?" Hal called to Peter.

"Gentlemen, you have been cleared to leave. Please return to the train."

The officer was now getting angry and his manner was becoming more threatening.

"Get this captain," said Hal in a quiet measured tone not looking up and continuing to make notes, "I think we understand each other. I am darned sure that my fellow countrymen back in the United States will get the picture." He looked up.

"Perhaps it would only fair to hear your side of the story. If you wish, you could be quoted acknowledging your name."

"I am just doing my job Herr Steading."

"Sure thing, captain. Obeying orders. I should have known that."

Hal fixed the officer with a prolonged stare.

There followed a long silence. The officer paced backwards and forwards slapping his thigh with his swagger stick.

The detainees who had gathered at the fence were following every nuance. Even though the exchange was entirely delivered in English, they understood exactly what was happening.

It was Hal who finally broke the impasse.

"It appears, Herr Capitan that we have choices to make. You can either allow these people here to leave with us on this train or I have the choice whether or not to splash this story across the newspapers of the United States of America. I could choose to write a different story.

Not sure I will if this party leave on this train. It would then have little impact."

The officer stopped in front of Hal legs apart still slapping his thigh with his stick.

Both sides of the fence held their breath.

After what seemed an age the captain stuck his swagger stick under his arm as if he was ramming it into Hal's guts, spun on his heels and issued a sharp order to the guard who opened the gate and stood back. The officer stood to one side and 'semi saluted' the adults by touching his cap with the stick as they left.

"Guten tag."

Peter made to go to Helga who was looking towards them mouthing 'Thank you.'

He was stopped by Hal. "Stow it, Pete. Behave like a professional. At least until we cross the border. It doesn't pay to get personal. The goon might smell a rat."

"You don't think they'll change their mind, do you?"

"I guess he's working a holding tack while he checks with his boss, whoever that may be. One thing for sure we know each other's game. They will not let those kids through if they can help it."

Hal picked Miriam up. He had been hanging on to her to prevent her going to the other children. This hadn't proved too difficult because the officer and sentry were between them and the group. They made their way back to their reserved seats.

"Move back slowly and make sure they all are aboard. Then Pete, make your way back through the train and get a shot of those kids on board. Then hang around to make sure the Goons don't pull a fast one."

Hal's thoughts were racing trying to figure out the captain's next move.

"What if they do?" asked Peter.

Hal had not the first idea.

"We'll figure that out, if and when. What we do know is that they have no legal basis to hold them, but they could cook one up."

Back on board, Peter made his way down the train to discover the children crammed in the bottom end of the last carriage. A sentry was moving the other passengers up into the next carriage. Peter took a photo of the scene and returned to speak to Hal.

"They are being isolated in the last carriage. The army are planning to uncouple this by the look of it."

"They may not be bluffing. We must figure out what to do."

Peter knew his friend well enough to await Hal's solution for as sure as hell he would do something.

Hal considered long and hard before consulting him.

"Pete, I daren't risk Miriam's future. She will not stay here without me.

What say you take the camera and camp in the last carriage with the kids until we are safely over the border? If they try and move you on, hang in there. Take photos of any official. Hopefully they will just give in and let them go."

Peter did not answer immediately so Hal continued.

"Unless you have a better idea."

Peter knew he could not leave Helga and the kids. He took a deep breath.

"Sounds good to me. If they do uncouple I will 'sweat it out' with them. You carry on. I will make my own way back if stranded."

He picked up the camera and nodded to his friend preparing to leave.

Hal took hold his arm and slipped a notebook into his pocket along with a pencil.

"Get as much information as you can. If the guards are watching, so much the better. Ask the name and question any goon. You're the guy to do this with the language. They'd pretend they didn't understand me. It doesn't matter whether or not they answer so long as they know you are watching them."

"Got it, Hal."

Peter quickly took Hal's hand and left. These last hours had put his concerns well and truly into perspective.

In determined mood he made his way back to the last carriage.

A guard stood at the entrance barring his way.

Peter thought at first just to take a photo then changed his mind.

"Excuse me please, I recognised a friend in this carriage. I am certain it is her, please let me through to have a word."

"Sorry sir, no one is to enter."

Peter had the feeling that from his apologetic manner, that he was a reluctant participant.

He took a photo of him before asking:

"Who gave this order and why?"

Notebook and pencil poised, and using the sentry's confusion then took a deliberate step out through the connecting door into the last carriage.

The guard was now aware that a situation was developing where an international incident could occur. "My orders are to isolate this coach. Please step back into the other carriage, sir."

Encouraged by this diffidence, Peter placed his hand on his shoulder.

"Don't worry my friend. I'll explain to the officer, just send him through to me."

Without looking back, he made his way into the carriage proper.

Helga, and the other carers, were dealing as best they could with the children. Some were wet, not just from the rain showers but from having soiled themselves. They had been trapped for hours without facilities. Fear and trepidation had taken a heavy toll. The others were huddled together for comfort and warmth. Peter looked for Helga at the same time taking more photos.

Helga stopped what she was doing and ran to him followed by others. Peter was surrounded at once by the adults and some children all clamouring to know what was happening.

Peter addressed them.

"I am not sure what is to happen. I intend to stay with you all until we are over the border."

"You got past the sentry? Is he still there?" Questions were fired at him from the anxious carers and children.

Peter had to consider his words, so he held up his hands, playing for time and at the same time trying to calm them by lowering his palms slowly downwards softly calling, "Sh ... sh ... shush."

When he had their attention, he spoke quietly but firmly.

"Try and stay calm and behave normally until we are into Switzerland. Hal, my friend and colleague is in control, dealing with the authorities. He is a journalist. He has the power to make things very difficult for these people. So, trust him."

If only that were true, he thought, being acutely aware that it was at best a distortion of the truth. But the power of the press had for now got them on board this train.

Even so, it was still not moving.

"Please, all of you, sit down and try to be patient," Peter pleaded.

To Peter's relief they sorted themselves into seats.

Helga remained by him.

"Do you think you could get me by the sentry into the toilet in the next carriage? I am getting desperate. The toilet here is occupied by children and is in a state. They have flushed down on to the sidings and the toilet stinks worse than this carriage."

Peter, aware that the atmosphere in the carriage was bad, was not surprised at this request. He was shocked to know that they had flushed on to the sidings. Perhaps this could give the Nazis an excuse to delay them. He went with Helga to the sentry who was not unsympathetic to the request.

Being unable leave his post the guard put Helga on trust to return.

"Please be quick and return to the carriage without delay."

Peter looked with fresh interest at the soldier.

"You definitely don't go along with this, do you?"

"I don't understand, sir. Please will you leave this carriage and return to your compartment."

Peter, now encouraged and feeling better about himself, smiled at the sentry.

"You are a good man and a good soldier."

He then added, "Grus Gott," before going back into the carriage to await Helga's return.

Everyone settled into their seats, a little calmer.

Peter looked out of the window. The queue at the customs shed had gone.

The last of the passengers had made their way back with their luggage.

The train should be leaving, crossing the border shortly.

Peter had not yet spoken to Helga about Dieter. Apart from not having the opportunity, he was diffident, nervous of the answers. He got to wondering whether Helga had anyone to turn to when and if she escaped. Helga returned looking for Peter. She sat down alongside him and took his arm. Peter could feel her trembling. His questions about Dieter died on his lips.

"What will they do, Peter? Will they keep us?"

Peter did not wish to answer.

"The guard still there?" he asked in return.

She nodded. Peter knew Helga was no one's fool and deserved a straight answer.

"They will probably uncouple this carriage at the last minute. Don't worry I'm not going anywhere. I will stick with you whatever."

The train jerked forward then stopped jolting their bodies and their nerves.

Peter was sure that the Nazis had uncoupled the carriage. Pulses began to race as Helga's grip on his arm dug into his flesh.

Slowly the train began to move and pick up speed.

Realisation dawned that the train was crossing over into Switzerland. All in the carriage collapsed into each other's arms. There was no celebration. Quietly the carers went among the children reassuring and settling them down. This took a little time.

Helga, apart from a hug and a brief heartfelt thanks, excused herself and joined in helping with the children.

Peter stood up and watched for a while trying to adjust his mind. He had expected cheers and wild celebrations. None of this happened. It felt more like he was intruding in a very private moment.

He felt a hand on his arm. Hal had come to check that the refugees were finally out of danger.

He just nodded his approval.

"Come on old buddy, let's go back to our compartment. We need to rest up, it will be some time before we reach Zurich."

Chapter 14

Peter and Hal looked out of the compartment window as the train pulled into Zurich station.

They quickly saw what they were looking for: A tweed-clad, brogue-shod, felt-hatted lady small in stature but large in personality.

There was no need to guess her nationality. If she had worn a placard announcing, 'British, aspiring upper class, don't mess with me' it could not have been clearer.

She commanded the platform.

Peter and Hal spoke together.

"There's our contact."

Hal added, "What's your bet that she has a double barrelled, hyphenated name?"

The lady, Daphne Wallace, so proved to be their contact.

Miriam was still asleep. By the time they had woken her and collected all their belongings.

The rest of the refugee children were already organised and provided with packed meals.

"I guess this is where we hand Miriam over Pete. I am not happy. I don't think Miriam will be either."

Hal picked up the little girl and held her close.

Two women were looking in their direction talking earnestly, obviously discussing them.

Helga and the other carers were ushering the children into a waiting room.

Daphne Wallace joined the other two. Oozing 'tweedy class' she failed to outshine one other lady, a lanky, chain smoking woman of middle years with a tanned, heavily lined complexion framed by short unruly dark hair flecked with grey.

When this woman smiled, which she did readily, her tobacco-stained over large teeth stood out even in the platform shadows.

The other lady, also of middle years, did not add much to the conversation other than to nod in agreement. She seemed to be a typical indispensable worker, a 'back room girl'. Probably the backbone of the team. After a short conversation, she left and the other two made their way over to them.

The small woman held out her hand, "Daphne Wallace." She announced then indicating the tall woman. "Peggy Firth."

"Hi." The tall woman removed the cigarette from her mouth and thrust out a hand to each.

"Pegs to my friends. Tussy if you qualify."

Then looking down at Miriam who was once more clinging to Hal's trousers she said:

"You must be Miriam."

She gave a big toothy grin. "I think I will call you Mim. You ..." She said emphasising the 'You.' "can call me Tussy."

Miriam took a short peek around Hal's leg then ducked back behind.

The woman dropped down into a squatting position and spoke in passable German.

"Hallo liebschon. Sind Sie hungrig?"

She held out a hand. Miriam disappeared behind Hal's other leg. Peggy dropped onto 'all fours' and peeked around Hal's leg at her. "Kommen sie mit Tussy, liebschon?" She held out her hand.

Mim sidled around Hal and looked at Pegs from the other side.

Daphne Wallace clearly disapproved of this performance.

"Pick her up Peggy, she'll be fine once assimilated into the group."

Hal bent down and picked up Miriam.

"Assimilated into the group, what the heck does that mean?"

Head and heart in conflict. The heart won. Hal couldn't bring himself to part with her.

Peter, watching this drama, found it difficult to comment or contribute anything sensible. Turning to Daphne, he introduced himself and Hal.

"So sorry, I'm Peter Barnes and this is my friend Henry Steading. Hal to his friends."

Hal seemed unaware of what else was happening. He was looking down at Peggy Firth who was retrieving the burning stub of a cigarette on one side on the platform while speaking to Miriam. Peggy Firth stood up, lit a fresh cigarette from the stub before flicking the failing tab on to the line.

She squinted at Hal, and the little girl clinging to his neck, through a haze of smoke.

"Tell you what Mim, why don't you and your Mr. Hal come with me and meet the other children?"

"Thank you," said Hal, seizing the opportunity. "I need to come with you, she has been through so much."

"Right-oh then," said Peggy, "follow me."

Peter made as if to join them only to be stopped by Daphne's curt suggestion.

"Shall we leave them to it?"

Back straight as a ramrod and head erect, Daphne fixed Peter with her gaze.

"Not very tall are we."

She smiled and added, "Still good stuff in small places, eh?"

Peter's mind was on Hal and how he would handle parting with Miriam. He forced a smile and nodded. He remained focused on the waiting room door where Miriam and Hal were last seen.

Daphne Wallace appearing oblivious to Peter's concern,continued:

"Miss Price told us of your magnificent effort in Austria Mr. Barnes, well done."

She looked down at her papers.

"We're in a bit of a pickle. The delay has forced us to change arrangements. We are now hoping to leave tomorrow morning instead of the night train." Barely pausing to breath, she continued.

"Miss Price, excellent woman, has managed to book the children into a small hotel for the night. Not very salubrious but beggars can't, etc.," She sighed, took breath and continued.

"Still it has bathrooms. Couldn't leave them on the platform all night. Could we?"

"No," Peter answered dutifully.

"No indeed not." Daphne continued her flow leaving Peter stunned by the torrent of information and her apparent inability to consider any contribution from him.

"You are not on our list so there is no provision for you three. The little girl of course we will cater for but not yourselves. The children will be sharing as it is. The little ones' top to tail four in a bed. We are fortunate that we have found an understanding hotelier and that it is in between seasons." She paused as she referred to her notes.

"Miriam Kessler came over with you. I wonder why she was not with the main party?"

Daphne looked to Peter for the answer.

Peter's mind was elsewhere and was only vaguely aware. He was trying to look serious thinking. 'I am not really needed. She could perfectly well have had this conversation by herself.'

"What I suggest Mr. Barnes." Daphne continued, "is that we all meet later at the hotel."

She looked again at her notes.

"The Seefeld, a couple of streets away to your left. What say sevenish, agreed?"

"Without question and I am certain that Hal will agree." Peter was making certain that this forceful woman was aware that his friend may have an opinion.

Chapter 15

The Seefeld could not accommodate Peter and Hal. The hotel across from the station had space and would exchange travellers' cheques and was only a short distance away. Peter booked them both in.

Dorothy brought Hal round later. He seemed more relaxed. Peter assumed that Miss Price had gone some way to persuading Hal to part with Miriam. He was about to ask when Miss Price took the two men to one side to ask.

"Please gentlemen can I be so forward as to suggest that you employ thrift. We have some way to travel and on limited funds." Dorothy blushed as she spoke.

"We have two nights' accommodation to cover because of the delay. Instead of the night train and the ferry to England, the only viable route available is train tomorrow to Paris then another overnight stay. All ferries are fully booked for the weekend. Peggy Firth is trying to arrange for us to stay in a hostel she knows. All of this is my fault for running too tight a schedule."

Hal seized upon this request. "Sure thing, Miss Price, we must pool resources, count on us."

Peter, aware of Hal's agenda, nodded.

"Certainly, we will. We have surplus from monies given to us by Gerda for Miriam."

That evening at the Seefeld the ladies busied themselves bathing and settling the children into their rooms. Miriam, delighted at last to be able to join in with the other children, went along happily in the charge of Peggy Firth, who she now accepted.

Dorothy arranged with the front desk to launder soiled garments and dry them overnight.

Most of the older children were exhausted, confused and fearful. They just wanted to go straight to bed. If there was any remaining who were travelling with the illusion that this was temporary, probably just an exciting adventure. This had been crushed out of them by the incident at the border. The hours corralled like cattle in the October wind and rain had drained their spirits.

That is if there was any left to drain.

The smaller children were more resilient. Daphne rolled up her sleeves along with Helga and the other two carers and bathed them in relays.

"You'll feel better for it, a big day tomorrow," she announced, in response to all protests.

On their way back to the Seefeld Hal and Peter were arguing.

"Looks like we are now included in the journey to England plan." Hal was pleased about this.

Peter voiced his concerns.

"I understood the plan was to hand Miriam over in Zurich and go our separate ways."

Hal didn't answer at once, so Peter prompted,. "What say you Hal?"

"Can we talk later?"

They carried on to the hotel in silence, Peter wondering what to do about his friend.

Miriam was taking over his life and common sense.

They arrived at the Seefeld for the agreed meeting in silence neither raising the subject again.

Miriam had got out of bed and found her way back downstairs looking for Papa Yo.

She had fallen asleep in one of the chairs. Peter was the first to notice. He spread his hands in a gesture of frustration.

"What shall we do? She should be in bed with the others. She must have sneaked out after she was put to bed."

"Leave her Pete until the others come then maybe I can stay with her until she is asleep."

"She ***is*** asleep Hal. You'll have to make the break Hal and the sooner the better."

Peter was losing patience.

Hal sat down in the chair alongside Miriam and put his face in his hands and gave a sigh before speaking through his fingers.

"If only I could start over. I didn't expect this when I agreed to be this Papa Yo."

He paused before continuing and looked up at Peter to explain.

"It was when I first picked her up. It hit me, like that fish in the river earlier that day. One moment, I was swimming free in calm waters, the next I was part of that little girl and she part of me.

Quicker than that heron that took the fish. I can't break free."

He sighed. "Nor do I want to."

Peter put his hand on Hal's shoulder, shaking him gently as he spoke.

"Hal, it can never work, you could not adopt even if you wanted to. There's no way you can maintain sensible contact at any level."

"Why not?" Hal's reply was more plaintive than defiant.

Peter sat down alongside his friend.

"You are not Jewish nor are you married. Even if you were married there's no guarantee of you gaining custody. Sorry old chap, it's a nonstarter."

Hal did not raise his head.

"I just can't part with her Pete. I just can't."

Neither spoke for some while until Hal finally looked up.

"Pete, can you imagine a three-year-old torn from her family. She then finds and bonds with me, her new Papa, only to be torn away again? Sorry I can't be a part of that. I will fight to avoid it if I can."

Daphne Wallace and Peggy Firth arriving heard most of this.

Neither noticed them, so engrossed were they with the discussion.

Peter turned finally noticing the ladies.

Daphne started to apologise for being late when she noticed Miriam asleep in the chair.

"Hello! Do we have an escapee in our midst?"

Peggy stubbed out her cigarette and blew smoke out of the side of her mouth to avoid Miriam as she picked her up out of the chair.

"Wrong choice of words, Daph."

Daphne pulled a face and held her breath to avoid taking in the fumes.

"I'll pop her back in now she's asleep," Peg added ignoring Daphne's unspoken criticism. Starting on her way back upstairs she stopped and turned to fire a parting shot at Daphne Wallace.

"By the way this little girl was not escaping from, she was running towards."

Looking at Hal, she added, "That's something we should be thinking about very seriously don't you think, Mr. Hal?

Peter broke the awkward silence.

"Have you ladies eaten?"

Daphne seemed, for the moment, to have lost her bounce.

"Err- no, we haven't had time."

"I reckon Hal we could run to some dinner. That is if the restaurant is still serving."

"Of course, it is not yet eight o' clock," said Daphne, recovering her character. "Most generous."

"What say we eat now when Peggy returns, then relieve the other four to eat later?"

Hal was still lost in thoughts triggered by Peggy Firth's remarks.

Peter nudged him back into the discussion. "That all right with you Hal?"

That evening was spent organising the tasks and a new routine for the following day.

Dorothy Price joined them later to take charge of these arrangements while the other ladies relieved the night watch. Peter and Hal left for their hotel before midnight tired, sapped by the day's events neither referred to the question of Hal's attachment to the little girl even though it was now the centre of both their thoughts.

Chapter 16

The following day Peter and Hal met up with the others on the station as arranged.

Miriam immediately tried to run to Hal screaming and fighting her carer when she tried to prevent her from leaving.

Hal made to go to her. Peter put a restraining hand on his arm.

Peggy Firth flicked her cigarette on to the floor, went to the carer, collected Miriam and took her over to Hal. Miriam burying her face in his chest.

"I understand you are holding Mim's travel tickets?"

It was Peter who answered. "Yes, I suppose Gerda thought it wise because they were unsure if all would get through."

"That's saves us a fare." said Peg looking at the distressed tiny girl.

"And by the look of things you'd best keep Mim until we get to Paris."

"Keep Mim." The little girl sobbed burying her head back into Hal's chest.

"This is like a small private lounge," said Peter, surprised. The tickets were for a first-class couchette open for any journey. They only noticed this morning at the station, not having looked at them properly before.

"Sure is. How come? It must have cost some."

Peter looked around "I don't know about you Hal, but I'm embarrassed. What say we offer this to the ladies?"

"Already did, Pete, I knew you would feel the same."

"And?" Peter prompted.

"They refused. Won't leave the kids I guess."

Peter nodded. "I saw you talking to Peg. What was that about?"

"The couchette and Helga."

"Helga? What about her?" Peter asked. "Where is she?"

"She has other arrangements. She is staying in Zurich."

Peter was shocked. "Strange she didn't say anything to me."

"She left early before breakfast on some errand or other, left a message that she would be in touch."

"That's all?"

Hal shrugged "I guess."

Miriam meanwhile had climbed from Hal's lap on to the seat was looking through the carriage window. Turning she took Hal's face in her tiny hands and pulled it towards her and away from Peter and their conversation. "Papa Yo, Wo ist unser zuhause?"

Hal turned to Peter who sighed and translated.

"She is asking where's your home?"

"God, Pete, what can I say?"

Peter shrugged but didn't answer. Hal just clasped the little girl in his arms.

"I don't know sweetie but be sure I will find somewhere for us, be sure of that."

Then looking at his friend. "I'm not giving her over Pete no matter what."

Peg, outside the compartment was about to knock on the door. Seeing the drama unfolding inside she stopped to witness this through the glass. She tapped firmly on the glass and slid the door open. "Can I come in?"

Immediately Mim hid behind Hal's back who looked for all the world as if he had been caught with his hand in the cookie jar. Peter, realising they had been overheard, started to explain.

Peg stopped him with a smile.

"It's O.K. chaps," peeking at Mim behind Hal's back.

"It's all right, my sweet, Tussy has not come for you."

"You heard our conversation?" Peter asked. This was a question not an accusation.

"I wasn't prying mon enfants. I was coming to ask a favour and couldn't help overhearing."

"I was hollering a bit. Please sit down and ask away for your favour."

Peg sat down. Mim came out from behind Hal and sat on his lap still clinging on to him.

Peg took a deep breath. "About this little girl." She paused. "Look Hal we can see where you are coming from, but you are going to have to face it, it probably is not going to happen."

"Why not?"

Peg smiled sadly. "You are not married, are you?"

"How can you know that?"

"Peter said so last night. He also pointed out that you are not Jewish. To which, I might add, that Mim is travelling on false papers. Any claims you have will be waived away by Immigration.

She will be passed on to the appropriate agencies, probably the Jewish Council. It will be then out of your and our hands." She reached out and put her hand on his shoulder. "Sorry."

After a short pause, she filled the stunned silence. "I apologise for eavesdropping, but you do tend to speak out. It was not intentional I assure you."

There followed another silence. This was broken by Mim. She stood up on Hal's lap put her arms around his neck and kissed him then taking his face once more between her tiny hands asking.

"Wie lange zu uns nach hause Papa?"

Peg sat stock still for a moment, shocked, then fumbled in her bag for her cigarettes.

Peter didn't speak or translate for Hal as usual, it being clear that he understood.

Peg was the next to speak. "Mind if I smoke?"

"Please go ahead and can I suggest that you take a big draw on that cigarette before replying to Mim's question because I'm fresh out of answers."

"I am not the architect of this situation Hal. I am just pointing out the truths."

Peg stood up and defended her position.

"Perhaps you should consider telling the truth to Mim before you continue this hopeless dream."

Peter was compelled to protest. "To a three-year-old?"

"Children are remarkably adaptable, gentlemen. You would be surprised."

This reply was not as convincing as Peg hoped but she had little else to offer.

Hal could have replied 'how do you expect *me* to adapt' but he remained silent.

Peg made as if to go.

"If I'd have known how this would play out, I wouldn't have gotten into this. I can't let Mim down. I can't just let her go." Hal's protest stopped Peg in her tracks.

"Now you know how we girls feel, once committed you can't turn the clock back no matter how much you wish you hadn't gone along. We live with the consequences. I guess you will too."

Peggy, edgy, was clearly disturbed by this exchange.

Hal, not wishing to be talked out of his argument, countered.

"Yes, but you can keep or choose whether or not to abort. Mim is being torn out of my life as if she doesn't matter."

Peter, anxiously listening, flushed bright red but was at a loss as to how to stop his friend from making any further comment.

"Not legally and never without scars, just as you Hal are going to be scarred," was Peggy's acrid reply.

Peter guessing something of the history knew that Hal had touched a nerve. This was not helping. Miriam sensed they were talking about her and picked up the atmosphere. She buried her face in Hal's chest. The clickety-clack of the wheels over the rails added to the drama.

All embarrassed. Wishing they were somewhere else.

Eventually Peter, more out of desperation to break the tension, said. "You came for a favour?"

"Yes." Peg, relieved, replied. "It seems almost trivial now, yet it is not."

Silent for a short while she took courage and another deep breath to regain control of her emotions she asked, "Have you any money we could borrow. Any spare cash?"

"I think so," Peter replied looking at Hal. "We agreed with Dorothy last night to pool resources."

Hal said nothing, not being in any shape to respond.

Peg also looked to him. She realised he was not going to answer. She remembered the details of her mission and began to explain, “I know you offered to help but the situation is worse than we thought. Helga has contacts in Zurich. She left before breakfast to raise some cash. We hoped she would be able to fund us before we left. Didn’t happen, solicitors and bankers even if they rose before nine, they would take a week to say no.”

‘Helga didn’t make it, so that’s why she didn’t say farewell.’ Peter thought. Pleased to learn why Helga left without a word.

“She is staying in Zurich anyway and didn’t get chance to speak with you before she left.”

Peg continued as if reading Peter’s mind. “We work on a shoestring. The delay has thrown our calculations out. Now we need to stay another night in Paris. I know of a hostel, but we are still a long way short to cover accommodation and food.”

“So, Helga was never coming to England?” Peter questioned, not answering Peg’s request for cash until he had Hal’s agreement.

“She left this note for you.” Peg handed over an envelope. “It could explain everything.”

Peter took the envelope. “Thank you.” He opened it and took out a single page note asking at the same time. “How short are you, of money I mean?”

“Some way it depends what the hostel will accept?”

“Leave that with us and we will see how much we can raise.”

Peter looked to Hal for confirmation.

“Sure, whatever.” was the disinterested reply. Hal had more to concern him than a request for money.

With a final look at Hal and Mim, Peg decided there was little else to say. In any case, she felt she had said too much, so she shrugged and left.

“That wasn’t the happiest of encounters,” Peter muttered as he read Helga’s note.

Peter, dearest Peter,

Sorry not to have spoken but I think you will now know why. I am sure that you will accept the responsibilities I ask you now to take. Dr and Frau Kessler in duress named me and Dieter as guardians and executors of the Kessler estate which now will no doubt pass to Miriam.
The detail of this is held by a firm of Zurich lawyers in conjunction with a partnership of solicitors, Joubert and Joubert of London.
Dieter's arrest allows me to name a replacement.
I know of no one better than you and I ask you to take this on.
You will be in England with Miriam. I believe Dr and Frau Kessler would approve were it possible to contact them.
The power of attorney lies in Zurich. In case of need, you will be able to contact them or me through these London solicitors. Copies of all necessary documents are in Miriam's attaché case (The one given to you by Gerda.) I will be in touch. Please do not try to contact me directly, only through the London solicitors. Your contacts, if you agree to my proposal, are Daniel Joubert, senior or junior (uncle and nephew).
I hope to see you and Miriam before too long but there is much now for me to do.
I need to sort out my own affairs in addition to those of the Kesslers. In any event who knows what the future holds.

Sincere and affectionate regards.

Helga

Peter folded the letter, pleased that Hal did not seem interested in its content. The implications of it could be disruptive. He needed time to think about his answer first. This he did, using the silence from Hal. A silence which had been triggered by the recent exchanges.

His first thought took him to Helga's phrase 'Guardians and Executors of the Kessler estate'.

This could only mean Miriam now. This in turn forced him to look beyond his resentment and previous logical assessment. Slowly, Peter jolted out of his previous mindset, now focused on parallels between himself and the little girl. Memories of a lost and lonely six-year-old flooded into these thoughts.

Hal sat staring out of the window, his mind changing. He was confused as the scenery flashed by as the train crossed into France. Mim, picking up on his mood, sat on his lap sucking her thumb her head lolling against Hal's chest as sleep overtook her. Hal laid the tiny girl down on the couch using his jacket as a pillow. He spent the next minutes just looking at her.

Peter could not help but feel distraught. He was sad about the inevitable consequences.

"Are you all right Hal?" he asked thinking to himself at the same time ... 'What a stupid question!'

"I'm sorry Pete about my mood but I can't think what to do. You and Peggy Firth are right I know. It's just that I can't accept it." Hal knew that that which he wished for was impossible.

It was then Peter handed Helga's letter to his friend.

Chapter 17

Peter concentrated on counting how much cash in all denominations they had.

"That's all we can muster Hal. We've only fifteen pounds left in travellers' cheques, some Deutsch Marks, a few Austrian Schillings even less in Swiss Francs. The travellers 'cheques will be useless because the banks will be closed when we arrive. This will leave us short of cash. Do you agree we hand the lot over?" Peter looked across at Hal, who didn't answer.

Hal was now sitting with Mim on his lap looking out of the train window. Mim had woken up and immediately scrambled back on to his knee. Peter watched them for a short while.

He did not repeat the question.

Mim's head was leant against Hal's chest and unusually for them they were not interacting.

They presented a picture of deep thought if not melancholy. Mim, sucking her thumb, had clearly continued to pick up Hal's mood.

Dorothy Price arrived outside the compartment, as Peg had done earlier. She watched Hal and Mim through the window. It did not take long to for her to work out the problem. Peg had summed up the troubles and advised her well. She took a deep breath, tapped on the glass and slid the door open.

"I'm not interrupting anything am I?"

Peter was surprised by yet another unexpected visit. "No of course not," he replied politely.

Hal turned from his window gazing. Miriam shot round his back and buried her face in his jacket. Dorothy feeling the tension and disturbed by it, realised it was up to her to dispel this if possible.

She opened a difficult conversation.

"I haven't had a chance to speak with you privately."

She indicated the seat next to Peter. "Mind if I sit down?"

Not having recovered their composure neither Hal nor Peter managed to answer immediately.

Time appeared to stand still for a very long second or two before Peter sprang to his feet.

"Sorry, of course please sit." Feeling awkward, he sat down in silence.

Hal and he had worked out last night that this woman was more in command than they first thought.

Hal detached himself from Mim and held out his hand. Hal managed 'Hi' before lapsing into silence. Both felt like school-boys up before the head. Dorothy smiled at each in turn.

Peter aware of the tension, tried to relieve this by handing her the currency.

"This is all we can muster. You are welcome to all."

He guessed that was why she was here.

Hal, with Mim still clinging to his arm added, "Sure, you can take the lot if it's of any use."

Dorothy smiled, took the money then took both their hands, Peter with her left and Hal with her right, to their surprise and consternation. "Thank you," she said and took another breath. "Peter, Hal, I know just how difficult this is for you." She paused again before continuing. "Little do you realise just how difficult this is for me."

Neither friend replied unsure still what this was all about. This over familiar woman suddenly appearing centre stage was overwhelming them.

Dorothy looked down at the floor. She took a little while before she continued.

Finally, she looked up, took another deep breath before saying quietly.

"I want to thank you both, you have been brilliant and need, no, deserve an apology."

She looked from one to the other as she did so, squeezing their hands as she said to each in turn. "We are so sorry."

"Sorry?" echoed the two men in unison sensing they were about to learn something.

"Yes, sincere apologies and explanations are in order. First, I need you to assure me that whatever is said does not leave this compartment. It may not matter if this is the last trip we make. We cannot be sure about that. If we can we must try and complete more rescue missions."

Dorothy looked at the two friends who didn't answer.

"Can we count on your cooperation to keep this confidential, repeat nothing?"

She asked again squeezing their hands.

Peter and Hal nodded. "Sure thing, we couldn't risk future trips." It was Hal who answered for both. "Where to start?" She thought for a moment before turning to Peter and continuing.

"Helga and Dieter were well known to you, that we knew. In fact, we know a lot about you Peter and all your histories."

She paused again, clearly finding this difficult. "Helga is a cousin of mine on my mother's side. A distant cousin nevertheless we have stayed in touch especially lately."

Peter was surprised. "You are Jewish?"

Dorothy smiled and nodded.

"There was I thinking you were Welsh, with the name Price," he added, still feeling a little awkward and confused.

Dorothy realised that it would be difficult to 'break the ice'. She was unsure how her explanation would be received after the gross liberties they had taken with their holiday plans particularly those with Henry Steading.

She released their hands which she had held on to for far too long, sat back and thought perhaps this was not such a good idea after all. She then began to explain the origin of her name, hoping to release the tension which was affecting all three.

"As a refugee I came to England with my parents, from Eastern Europe in 1901. Price is a name I adopted later."

Hal interrupted Dorothy. "Is this part of the explanation?"

"No. I was just answering Peter," Dorothy explained.

"I don't know about you Pete, but I would like to hear this explanation." Hal looked directly at Dorothy. Feeling uncomfortable with Hal's eyes on her, she turned to his friend.

"Peter, I promise you that all Dieter intended originally was for you to lodge with the Kesslers. They would have provided excellent accommodation for you both throughout your stay and your presence would afford some protection against their probable arrest."

"Arrested, why?" Hal although having heard the story at least in part was interested hoping to learn more.

"They are Jews and that is enough reason in Nazi Germany. Dr Kessler is a prominent figure, a lecturer at the university. He was outspoken, witty and clever mostly to the Nazis' discomfort."

"Not so very clever," Hal muttered after managing to clear himself from Mim's clutches. She was falling asleep sucking her thumb allowing him to reach for his notebook.

Dorothy clearly did not wish to be drawn into a question and answer session with Hal, so she continued to address her comments to Peter.

"We thought that your presence would give 'breathing space' while we arranged for the necessary papers to move them into Austria, then out to Switzerland. You could have gone about your holiday and returned home none the wiser. We are so sorry it didn't work out as we'd hoped."

She turned to Hal. "We are particularly sorry that this involved you Mr. Steading."

Hal and Peter looked at each other with a, 'now we are beginning to understand' look as Dorothy continued.

"When we learned you were coming, Mr. Steading we were elated. An American in the house might have made all the difference, an ace in the pack. The Nazis moved three days before you were due to arrive. I think the rest you either know or can work out. Dieter being arrested, Helga only just getting out. The rest we made up 'on the hoof'."

"Some hoof," muttered Hal who was no longer making notes. "And the house in Austria?"

"The summer residence was sheer chance. The Jewish owners leaving at the end of the season gave us full use till the end of the month. All the staff had left apart from two retainers, seasonal staff packing up for the winter."

"Very convenient." Henry was still not convinced. It seemed too pat to swallow.

"Mr. Steading." Sensing hostility, Dorothy began to speak.

Hal interrupted. "Look, drop the Mr. Steading." Realising he was sounding hostile, he added more gently, "Please, I am not hostile. I just need to figure this out."

"Hal," Dorothy started again, "we did use you shamelessly once we learned about your press card. Also, you were cajoled into being Papa Yo. This now turns out to be a serious miscalculation.

A sad and bad one on our part. We are so sorry."

Peter looked across at Hal wondering about his reaction to these revelations. Hal was looking down at Mim who was now fast asleep. He did not speak so Dorothy continued.

"These are desperate times and we are dealing with a ruthless enemy." She paused before adding:

"So sorry, but we also needed to be ruthless."

When Hal finally spoke, he did so quietly with so much emotion. "It served to get Mim and the other kids out. I guess we don't care that much what you did. Still, it was taking one hell of a liberty with our time. Then you dupe me into playing Papa to this little girl." He sighed.

"This is really messing me up."

The silence which followed weighed heavily on Dorothy until she felt compelled to make further explanation. "It was your press card which drove us. An American and a gentleman of the press. We couldn't have wished for a better protection. We knew the Nazi influence in Austria was gaining more and more ground in addition, they were desperate to discover our cell. They were frustrated that we had only to nip over the border from Bavaria. They started using this growing influence in Austria."

"You were using me. We'd figured that much. Why put Jewish on Mim's papers? Surely you could have used any nationality any religion but Jew."

"Yes," added Peter. "Surely that was risky?"

"Miriam's papers were done in a rush. Any diligent officer could have picked up on Austrian or German papers. Miriam speaking only German was even riskier. Choosing to use Czechoslovakian papers covered this risk. I disagree that putting Jew was risky. It was the last thing that they were looking for. Checking papers from Czechoslovakia would be difficult. Using Sudaten Juden helped divert them from the documents' validity. All they focused on was that, as we hoped. Not the forged papers. It worked even though we think the officer appeared to suspect something."

"What if it hadn't worked?"

"Again, we thought you would be all right. Being an American," Dorothy paused, "Well we hoped.

We were desperate. If that officer had read his newsletter to look for a fifty-year- old woman and a three-year- old little girl probably travelling separately, it could have scuppered us.

That one word, Jew, addled their brains and we got away with it. They may even have thought that Helga and Miriam were in the school party. That could have been why they held them up at the border."

"Did you also figure out what to do if they had arrested me?" Hal asked pointedly.

Dorothy was now feeling uncomfortable.

"I suppose that could have happened. We thought your press card would save that. We counted on it. Rightly, as it turned out. They wouldn't wish for their activities to be broadcast in the wider world, especially in America."

Hal recognised, even sympathised with and admired the motive and logic. Aware of Dorothy's discomfort, he attempted to lighten the atmosphere.

"My heart was beating so hard I figured the Goons might hear it. Fortunately, I was not thinking about being arrested at the time."

"My heart was thumping, I could scarcely breathe." Peter said, also relieved that the conversation had changed tack.

"And mine, it nearly jumped out of my chest." Dorothy picked up on the change of tone adding, "then when you tackled them about the other children I nearly collapsed."

Hal and Peter were shocked into speaking in unison.

"You were there? On the train?"

"You have not been out of our sight since Munich."

"You were in Munich?"

"No, I joined the train at the same station as you taking over surveillance when the hire car dropped you and the porter took your luggage." Dorothy explained.

This exchange disturbed Mim who slid down off Hal's lap and he took the opportunity to stand and stretch. Childlike, she held up her arms to be picked up again. Hal did so with the instinct of a parent. Mim put her arms around his neck and leant her head against his.

Dorothy noticed all this and realised that Peg was not exaggerating the bond that existed between the two. Back in Hal's arms Mim watched and listened to the exchanges being aware of her mentioned name. Hal's manner was natural, tolerant and loving yet matter of fact.

Dorothy noted the love and the ease of expectancy each had, one of the other.

"Were Peg and Daphne on the train with you?" Peter asked.

"No, they know nothing and must know nothing of anything other than their end of this operation, although I trust them implicitly. It is best not."

"So how is it you come to know each other?"

"Peg and I were at school together. We were best friends. We have stayed closely in touch even though she has lived in Paris since the war."

"And Daphne?" Peter persisted knowing that Hal at least needed to hear everything.

"She's great, she's resting. Modestly claims she is doing this for free travel, board and lodgings," Dorothy said, now relaxing having dealt with the awkward questions.

"Resting?" Hal asked.

"She's an actress," it was Peter who answered, "and a good one too, certainly fooled me."

"Tuss speaks French and passable German which is useful moving German-speaking children through Zurich and France."

"Tuss? You keep calling her Tuss?"

"She was not just my best friend from school, she was my only friend at first. We hoped to be called Dot and Peg but, kids being kids, we ended up as Soft Chuff and Tussy."

Peter winced. "How come?"

"My birth name phonetically in English sounds like Soft Chuff. It is Polish spelled S-A-W-C-Z-U-C." She spelled it out. "I pleaded with my father to change our name. He would have none of it and replied, 'we changed when the family moved into Poland centuries ago. Get used to it, this is a tolerant country. The English will understand.'

"I said I am sick of having to spell it out all the time. The truth was I was embarrassed at school. My father said it is the price we have to pay. So, as soon as I was old enough, I changed it to Price.

Tuss said that I had a new price tag."

"And Peg lives in Paris?"

"Yes, she has had liaisons there, lives over a shop in Montmartre. You can find her there most summers. Apart from teaching English in the evenings, she sells knick-knacks to the tourists. Usually at the top of the steps, that is unless the police have moved her on. It is where she gets the dark tan."

"She's glad to help out or do you run these ventures together?" Peter continued to question. Hal was content to make notes.

"Tuss likes to, she has issues, doesn't like inactivity, needs to help the children. Come September she's at a loose end."

Dorothy gave a huge sigh. "It is a massive relief to get this off my chest, thank you gentlemen."

She stood up to leave. "Thank you, we can't thank you both enough and thanks for the money."

Both friends stood up but once again it was Peter who answered.

"We thank you for the opportunity. We are proud to have been part of this."

He turned to Hal. "That goes for us both doesn't it Hal?" His friend did not speak he just nodded and as he did a single tear squeezed from his right eye and began to trickle down his cheek, Mim raised her head from Hal's shoulder watched for a second then stuck out her tiny forefinger, touched the tear then wiped it away with the palm.

Dorothy took in every move of this little drama then turned to go before turning back and speaking quietly. "Mr. Steading, Hal, we understand, but just think, Mim is a refugee and you a bachelor. How is it possible for you to be granted parentage let alone care for and raise this three-year-old little girl? She is Jewish. It's a non-starter." She turned to go.

"I promise you we will do all possible to see her safely settled. I give you my word to do all I can to ensure that you are kept in touch."

Dorothy registered the shock evident on Hal's face. She again turned to leave, uncertain how to deal with it. She stopped at the door and without turning added, "Miriam is not officially on our list. She is travelling separately and under separate papers. I suppose she will be dealt with by immigration as such."

Picking up on this comment, Peter took Helga's note from his pocket.

"Helga has appointed me as guardian for Mim. This to be confirmed when I meet her London solicitors." He passed the letter to Dorothy who read but did not comment directly.

"I'll be sending you back Miriam's attaché case then." Dorothy was referring to the case they handed over yesterday. Dorothy deliberated for some seconds before adding,"Which happens to have a false bottom."

Relieved to have completed a very difficult task, she hurried away.

"Why did she say that? Strange!"

Hal hadn't moved showing little interest.

"She knew, Hal. She knew." Peter, realising that Hal was struggling tried to divert his thoughts.

He tried again. "What do you think?"

"I guess. Then she could have set the whole scene. What do you think Pete?"

Peter didn't answer at once wondering where his friend was going.

Hal continued, "It gives us a get out. Don't you see? Letting us go our own way with Mim."

Peter looked at his friend, who was willing him to answer. He was getting the feeling that he was being trapped into a situation, not for the first time that week. He certainly didn't take kindly to the phrase 'it gives us a get out'.

Used to being constantly manipulated by his father, Peter was both cautious and scared of committing himself. Choosing his words carefully he said thoughtfully, "No. I believe that Helga gave me this responsibility because she knows me and trusts me to do the right thing for Miriam. That means seeing her settled into a good Jewish family and secure. I will be in England so she had little option but to choose me. There was no one else."

"But Mim wants to be with me. I know she does, she'll be heartbroken."

It was Peter's turn to be lost for words. Hal pushed harder.

"Look Pete, I didn't major in con-a-kid routines. I need some help."

Peter looked at his friend who was pleading desperately, thinking to himself. 'Am I just being jealous and obstructive?'

Mindful of his shameful behaviour over the last days he decided to sound constructive.

"If we do, and I say *if*, we decide to try and keep Mim, plans will be needed. First, to get through immigration. Then the Jewish Council or whoever deals with orphaned or displaced refugee children nowadays."

Hal lowered his voice. "Pete, please ship off the subject. The kid knows we are arguing about her. Imagine yourself in her place at three ... how- how ..." He then lost it. His voice trailed to a hoarse whisper. Hal took hold of Mim and held her close. Peter immediately recalled his own trauma as a six year old and in that split second fully understood.

Dorothy returned with the attaché case. Aware that she was interrupting something serious, she handed it in with a brief. "I'll leave you to sort this now." Without waiting for a reply, she left.

Peter was glad of the interruption giving him time to think. He seized upon it and began to search through the contents.

"You are darned right. We do need plans." Hal managed to answer. Ignoring the interruption, he didn't wish to let this discussion die. Not yet anyway.

Peter studiously ignored the remark and started to examine the attaché case. A small solid sided structure of the sort carried by solicitors and bankers. Inside were three folders neatly labelled, which he placed on the seat. Taking out a pocket-knife he felt around the edges of the case.

"It feels like there is a false bottom," he said, measuring the outside and the inside. "There's perhaps a half inch difference, but how do we get in there?"

"Can't be much room. Half an inch you say?" Despite his wish to continue the discussion about Mim, Hal was as eager as Peter to find out what was in the case.

"I guess Pete it can only be a thin card covered with the cloth lining. Get your knife and slit round the edges."

"I don't think we should do that Hal." Peter was clearly appalled at the thought.

Hal, however, was a little impatient to see what it contained.

"Pete, you are now official guardian of Mim's affairs."

Mim now more relaxed and curious as any child took her thumb out of her mouth and repeated, "Mim's affairs."

Peter, happy now the conversation had veered away from the custody of the little girl, looked up and smiled. "Yes, young lady I am the keeper of the keys to your estate."

He was beginning to understand Hal's attachment to this little girl.

"Although there are a couple of lawyers between us and absolute clearance. Still here goes,"

Peter said, reminding Hal that nothing was cut and dried. He examined the case while speaking. Then he decided to stick the penknife through the cloth and slit along three sides revealing a thin board loose insert. Removing this, he took out two envelopes and a small canvas bag.

One envelope was handwritten addressed to Verfehlen Miriam Kessler in copper plate handwriting along with a brief message in Gothic German.

The other envelope was neither sealed nor addressed and contained large denomination bank notes in Deutsch Marks, Swiss Francs and French Francs. Peter counted the money while Hal picked up the sealed envelope.

"Guess this one is from your Ma and Pa, Mim. What does this say underneath, Pete? This bit in fancy writing?"

Peter, counting the money and adding up the total in his head, looked up and took the envelope.

"It says something to the effect that this is to be opened up by Miriam at the time of her understanding to be determined by Helga or Dieter at their discretion. Or else by an appointed attorney at law should this be correct." He then returned to counting the money.

Hal meanwhile was stood holding Mim close. "God, Pete, how sad is that?"

"Hal," said Peter, "there must be upwards of two hundred pounds Sterling here, nearly one hundred in French Francs. We can use this to cover all costs. I can replace this when we get back."

This information jolted Hal out of his sad moment.

"How much?" he exclaimed.

"About eight hundred Dollars' worth. A bloody fortune." Peter was clearly astounded.

"What's in the canvas bag?" Hal asked. Peter was already opening it and emptying the contents. "Two rings, diamond I think and a jewelled brooch." He whispered in awe. "They look the real thing to me. Set in gold. Oh! Another smaller bag." He loosened the string and emptied several cut stones on to his palm. Neither spoke for a few seconds, they just stared, unable to take in the implications of this stash. It was Hal who spoke first.

"Pete, this could stop me from adopting."

"You can't anyway and even if you could, what difference does a bit of money make?"

"A bit of money. Jeepers. That is not a bit of money, as you exclaimed before we saw the jewels it's a bloody fortune. That my friend is the first time I've heard you swear since you were a Fresher at Cambridge. That's how impressed you were."

"How does this affect you Hal?" Peter was back arguing Mim's future logically.

"Folk will think I'm after her money."

"It is a lot of money not a fortune and you've got to accept that you were never in the hunt. This will not change anything Hal."

Hal sighed and looked down at the little girl who was looking from one to the other as they spoke. "Best watch what we say, she is taking in every word."

Peter continued to look through the first folder. "She'll need to know sooner or later."

Hal ignored this comment saying, "What have you there Pete?"

"Deeds to the Munich property. Useless now is my guess."

"Useless! You really think so?"

"Sadly, yes," Peter answered continuing, "all is not lost thanks to a very astute Dr Kessler. This second folder contains bonds and share certificates, also something which looks as though it is a bank reference for a bank in Zurich. No doubt the solicitors in London will fill in the gaps."

"What gaps?"

"There is much more to this story than we realise. We will probably never know the extent of or the value of the estate, but it is certainly substantial."

Peter tapped the third folder which was sealed and addressed to the lawyers in Zurich and London. "This, I assume, contains legal documents containing the transfer of executive authority pending Mim reaching her majority."

Mim on hearing her name went over to the folder and also tapped it with a finger, repeating "Mim."

Peter appeared to be thinking. Sh turned to look enquiringly at Hal, who smiled and said.

"Yes, Mim all yours." Then he continued to question his friend. "How does this affect you Pete?"

Peter did not answer, not being sure of his position. Knowing just why his friend was asking the question.

Hal persisted. "As her guardian in the U.K?"

Peter still did not answer this question directly.

"I suppose we could also use some cash to have lunch in the dining car and ask Dorothy to join us. There's some sorting out to do."

Hal immediately challenged him. "Why? It seems to me she gave us carte blanche to do as we please." "It seems," said Peter emphatically, "she knows a lot more than she is telling."

"And you think she will give with the rest? Well, I don't think she will. The only reason she has told us so much already was either because she was obliged to or out of necessity."

"Necessity?"

"The money, Pete. She knew it was there. They need it for tonight's accommodation for the kids. She thought twice about telling us about the false bottom. She only did so as she was leaving. *After* you showed her Helga's note naming you as guardian and executor."

Peter thought for some while before speaking.

"You are right, Hal. What do reckon she would have done about the cash if it were not for Helga's note? Would she have gone in anyway?"

"I figure she was in a fix, knowing it was there. Your guess is as good as mine whether she would feel justified in opening the attaché case or using the money. Your showing of the letter got her off the hook. She is sat back there right now hoping to hear from you with an offer to loan the cash."

“So, I take her the French Francs?” Peter looked at his friend.

“Your decision buddy, you’re the guy in charge hereon in.”

Peter left at once and was gone some time. As soon as the door had closed behind him, Mim stood on the seat, put her arms around Hal’s neck, kissed him then sat down at his side before sliding on to her back and his lap, looked up and smiled. Then she fell fast asleep secure in the knowledge that she was going ‘Nach hause mit Papa Yo.’

“I guess you didn’t get much sleep last night my little cookie. Mom used to put me down in the afternoons,” Hal whispered. He looked out of the window at the countryside sliding past, left alone with thoughts and the rhythm of the train.

Chapter 18

Peter returned with sandwiches, fruit and drink courtesy of Dorothy and the group.

"Problem solved as far the hostel is concerned?"

Hal was pleased to see Peter return. Being left alone with his thoughts was getting to him.

Peter raised the table, setting out the food. "That put paid to my thoughts of you and me lunching in the restaurant car now we don't need to watch the money." When Hal didn't answer, he added, "Using our cash not Miriam's, I mean."

"Did Dorothy know about the money, Pete?"

"I'm certain of it, but she didn't admit it."

"Sure, she knew. She's known all the time."

Peter took a bite of a sandwich. Hal watched him eat but made no attempt to have anything himself. "I'd like to know what else she knows. One thing's for sure she's no soft chuff. Do you think she knew Mim's Ma and Pa? Maybe helped them. They have certainly done all that's possible to provide for this little girl. She could have been part of that. Think about it."

"Except Hal," said Peter between mouthfuls, "Miriam's father could have been a bit more discreet. He must have known he was living dangerously."

The story in almost its entirety had been laid before them in the last hours. It was all becoming a little bit too much for Hal who began to mutter under his breath. Peter had noticed that he had been doing this on and off since yesterday and began to show concern.

"Hal, you're beginning to talk to yourself."

His friend didn't answer at once but gave a great shuddering sigh before speaking with great emotion and difficulty. "The bastards, those bastards, rotten stinking bastards."

Hal struggled with his feelings.

A tear squeezed out of one eye followed by another and his whole body began to shake. Peter was alarmed and did not know what to do at first. Mim woke up, stood and put her arms around Hal.

Peter found his voice.

"Hal, we'll cope. You are upsetting Mim. Come on old chap we need a plan."

Hal did not answer. He was clinging on to Mim silently weeping. The little girl climbed down from his lap and picked up Peter's pocket handkerchief which he had been using as a serviette, climbed back on Hal's knee then began to dry his tears.

"I would say you are truly an Anglophile. You were cursing like a navvy."

This forced a smile from his friend. Hal did not reply at once then gathered Mim to him and took a series of deep breaths before apologising.

"I'm sorry Pete, its all been a little too much these changes over the last week. I have been pitched into another world. I can't find my way back."

Then, seeing just how much Peter was concerned, Hal continued.

"Yet it is less than eight weeks since that beautiful day in St Mary. It was idyllic, I'd even gotten to like cricket."

"Really?'

"No." Hal replied. "Not really."

Peter smiled, Hal was back in control, or so he thought. Now more relaxed he sat back and finished his sandwich. In the meantime, he watched his friend closely. Hal was the closest he had ever had to an older sibling. Even though he had looked at Pen as a sibling from being small, she had always looked to him to lead, take decisions. Hal? He was different, he was the leader, more the older 'brother' he didn't have.

Hal, meantime, sat staring out of the window. Mim resumed sucking her thumb.

"You know Hal, I've been thinking. When Dorothy pointed out that we are travelling as a separate group then, afterwards, you said she was giving us the green light to go it alone?"

Peter was looking to raise Hal's spirits.

"So, what gives?"

"I must have some influence now, being appointed an executor, perhaps even guardian of Mim's affairs in the U.K. We need more than that though, we need a plan. A plan that will get us by the immigration authority. That won't be easy."

Hal looked at his friend, surprised by this sudden change of tack,thinking what had caused this?

A short while ago he was at best not interested. At times he was even hostile to the idea of retaining any contact with Mim. Peter had previously made it clear his hopes were to hand Mim over once clear of Austria then move on.

"Confirmation of my guardianship is in the lawyer's hands. I doubt that immigration will take any notice of Helga's letter. However, I have the germ of an idea." Peter paused.

"Give me time. I need to work on it."

Hal was confused, even suspicious of Peter's motive, surprised at his reaction yet unable to dispel his fears. This suspicion transferred to Mim who clung on to her Papa Yo, looking over her shoulder at Peter who either didn't notice or because the little girl had never accepted his presence, saw no change in her demeanour.

"Do I figure in this plan?"

"Not worked it through yet."

"Will I figure, or won't I?'

"I can't see how you can be involved, best leave it to me. At least I have some sort of delegated authority."

A plan really was beginning to form in Peter's mind. In a strange way it connected to the thoughts that had troubled him throughout the last weeks. The happenings of the last days had failed to dispel these suspicions, dramatic and dangerous though they were, so much so that if anyone asked him if he trusted both his fiancé and his friend, he would not be able to decide.

Or, if asked whether to choose between one or the other, he could not have done so.

It might have focused his mind. He had no such counsel which was not helpful.

Watching Hal closely Peter chose his words carefully.

"To adopt Miriam in English law you would have to be married."

At the mention of her name Mim stopped what she was doing and turned to look at Peter, who forced a smile and spoke to her in German.

"Yes Mim, we are talking about you and where you might live." Then he explained to Hal.

"I'm telling her that we are discussing where she might be living."

Hal picked Mim back on to his lap. "You'd best be telling me also because all this is confusing me."

"There is one possible solution."

"There is? Then give, Pete. Give."

"That Pen and I bring our wedding forward then *we* could then apply to adopt."

Peter paused and watched for his friend's reaction. He half expected a sharp response at the mention of his marriage to Pen, if only in Hal's body language.

Hal studied before answering, giving no indication of concern other than the adoption of the little girl. "Yes, but how do I fit in?"

Relieved, Peter continued. "As a reporter, you can work anywhere, am I right?"

"Sure can, so long as I am in easy reach of London."

Hal was beginning to believe that Peter could have a workable plan. "Where will Mim be?"

"With you." Peter replied without hesitation.

"Where? She can't travel with me, even just to London."

"Ah but she *could* stay with Pamela Avery, Hal. She was Pen's and my Nanny and what's more, Paul, Pamela's son, starts at Brunel this autumn. She will have a spare room which I am sure she will rent to you."

Peter was warming now to his idea, forgetting, that is if he ever knew, how the discussion all began.

"She will still be *your* daughter though. I won't figure legally." Hal stated the obvious.

Peter looked at his friend who was displaying a cross between pleading for and demanding a solution that could not be delivered. Peter was also aware that if Pen and he could, by some miracle, adopt Mim, it would add an opportunity to pursue an association with his fiancé.

Having noted earlier Hal's reaction and as their adopting was an unlikely outcome, he decided to humour Hal. It seemed that it was an impossible idea yet in a strange way it intrigued him.

Peter took seriously the responsibility of looking to his charge's affairs. He had no intention of letting Helga down.

"No." He answered Hal's question honestly. "But you could be there to watch over her and know that in Pamela, she is in good hands. Technically, Pen and I would be her guardians but that's all."

Hal studied for a while before asking. "What will your Pa and Pen's Ma and Pa think?"

Peter chuckled as if he was sharing a quiet joke. "Once they know the value of this little girl's estate it will be done and dusted."

"Done and dusted? I guess that means a home run?"

Peter nodded. "Nothing is certain but it's our best chance."

Hal liked Peter's use of 'our' and lapsed into his thoughts as did Peter.

Mim snuggled down into Hal's lap and went back to sleep.

After a while Hal spoke. "She feels safe with me Pete, don't let them take from her only Papa."

Peter didn't answer. Hal continued, thinking about the future of this little girl.

"Do you reckon there's a chance she could eventually be reunited with her family, with her real Ma and Pa?" Hal was indicating that the only people he would willingly hand Mim to would be her own parents.

Peter didn't know how to answer. From what they had learned from Gerda and others in the last week, the chances of the Nazis releasing the Kesslers were slim.

Why else would families separate themselves from their children except in the direst of circumstance? He could only guess what the real situation could be. His friend had become obsessively possessive over the last days. Peter could imagine that could be the reasoning behind the question. According to his father's opinion and many others in political circles, war with Germany was a probability even though the government was pursuing peaceful solutions.

Rearmament was already under way in the U.K.

The silence following was only broken by the rhythm of the wheels over the track as each retreated into their thoughts.

Peter shook off his darker thoughts and began to develop in his head the plan already partly formed. He felt the responsibility now of looking after Mim's welfare. Despite his recent attempts to break the bond between Hal and the little girl he now decided to try and include his friend.

Hal partly believed in Peter's plan, out of desperation. Part of him was not sure, thinking that he would still lose his grip even if it did work. Fatigue and the rhythmic drum of the wheels plus the warmth of the child asleep on his lap began to play on his mind forcing him to plead.

"I know I'm all screwed on this Pete but please I really need your help."

Peter looked at him wondering how to answer. He was getting irritated by Hal's refusal to accept the truth. "Hal, you need to come out from under the butterfly bush."

It was Hal's turn to be irritated. "That's no answer, what the heck does it mean anyway?"

"It means stop hiding in your dreams and come out into the real world."

"How come? This is not the first time you've used that butterfly bush crack. You never explain it. Sounds screwy to me."

Hal now wished to divert the discussion, not liking the way it was going. Peter, realising that they were on the cusp of a row, sat back and took deep breaths counting to ten. Once this exercise was completed and it had worked, he got back to thinking through the plan when Hal interrupted his muse.

"Are you going to give with this butterfly crap or not?" Hal asked. Refusing to be side-tracked.

Peter was shocked to realise his friend was still angry. It being ridiculous to get into an argument over such trivia, he quickly realised this was more to do with Hal's state of mind than the issue of an explanation.

"Pamela was my lifeline as a child, my only contact with humanity."

It was Hal's turn to be shocked. "No," he gasped, "what about your Ma and Pa?"

Peter looked down. "Never knew my mother."

"Not dead?"

Peter nodded then continued hurriedly, without comment.

"My father was always at work or somewhere else, rarely home. Even on those few occasions when he did come home, I was always in the way or a scratching post. Pamela was my refuge. Back then she was all there was, housekeeper, cook and nanny. In effect, she was my mother."

Hal was shocked, his anger melting into sympathy. He felt it prudent to avoid further questions about his friend's parentage. "And the butterfly bush?"

Peter, relieved to change the subject, began.

"You've not been to my father's house. It is quite big in its own grounds up a steep slope and reached by a steep drive and overlooking a valley. To one side are the moors and to the other a large coppice."

"A coppice? Remind me, what is this?"

"Managed woodland from the Middle Ages or earlier. This one was used for wood supply and charcoal, mainly it was to provide fuel."

"Nothing like that back home to my memory."

"You must come up and see the house, it's worth the visit. The frontage overlooks six broad terraces reaching almost to the road at the bottom of a steep hill. On the second terrace, up against the wood to one side, is a well-established butterfly bush, a buddleia. In the summer when I was small, Pamela would take me down to see the butterflies. We had to go right down to the third terrace to do so. The bush was right on the edge of the second terrace and curled down to the third.

The spear-like flowers touched the grass. Later when I was a little older, I discovered that I could get into a cavity between the bush and the terrace wall. It was where I would go to hide whenever my father was home."

"You were scared of him?"

"I suppose I was in a way, but the real reason was that it was my dream world where I could escape into my imagination, into my own little island."

"We all do that as kids I reckon."

Peter lapsed into silence and his memories. After a short while, Hal, interested to learn about his friend's history, asked, "Go on then Pete, give with the rest. How does this 'coming out', figure?" Thinking his friend could guess the rest Peter was reluctant.

"You're sure you wish to hear this? It's a long story.'

"Sure I do."

"All right but remember you asked for this." Peter, now intrigued by his friend's interest, continued. "Well, Pamela would read me one chapter of a story each night at bedtime. I became fascinated by one story. It was about some folk shipwrecked on a desert island surviving by their wits and available materials. Self-sufficient, away from civilisation. My favourite character was a boy called Peterkin."

Hal smiled at this and interrupted. "That figures."

"My little cave behind the bush became my island of refuge. When my father demanded my presence, Pamela knew exactly where to find me. She would come down to the edge of the second terrace to call 'Peterkin, tell Peter his father wants him.' I didn't always answer. Pretended I couldn't hear. This forced Pam to come down to the third terrace to look for me. I suppose she always knew I was there. She would come and pull the branches to one side and say, holding out a hand "Peter, my love, it's time to come out from under the butterfly bush."

Peter was almost crying as he spoke the last words with difficulty.

Hal was choked and unable to speak so he looked out from the carriage window at the passing scenery trying to gather his wits thinking that he should say something, but what?

Peter left the compartment and when he returned soon afterwards Hal was ready, having had time to come to terms with the sharp contrast between their upbringings. He had assumed that Peter was from a well-grounded family, as was his. That Peter's reticence in not referring to his background was just British class reserve.

Unable to stand up because Mim was still sleeping he held out a hand to his friend.

"O.K. Pete, let's get to grips with reality."

Chapter 19

It was turned 8:00 p.m. when the train arrived in Paris, much to relief of everyone. Only the smaller children who were able to sleep soundly on the train showed any sign of animation.

The journey had sapped the last dregs of courage from the rest.

Mim slept for the last hours but with that strange instinct of a child, woke when the train slowed into the station. She jumped up and went to the compartment door looking back at Hal.

"Look at Mim, she knows more about what is going on than I realised," said Peter.

Hal stretched and replaced the shoes he had taken off to lie down to sleep.

"I don't why I bothered. I barely slept at all."

Peter didn't answer but smiled to himself as he turned to reach down their cases.

Hal's snoring had told another story. While they were sleeping Peter had been able to refine his plans. First, to get Mim through customs and immigration, then to get everyone else on board especially Pen, his father and Sir George and Lady Amelia.

His thinking was to bring their wedding forward; a civil wedding to be followed by the church wedding on the original date. This he calculated could clear the way for them to apply to adopt Mim. He was more than confident that Pamela would agree to act as Nanny also that Sir George and Lady Amelia would agree. The problems would probably arrive via Pen and his father.

He had been careful not to leave out the human element from the equation. Pen he thought, would accept be it only via parental pressure. His father was the big worry. He would not take kindly to any change of plan.

The travellers made their way out into the city streets as a weary straggle. They were stiff, tired, fearful and hungry. The overwhelming emotion was the fear of the unknown.

The dim lighting of the station seemed to blanket them in foreboding. Peggy Firth did her best to rally their spirits. "Come on everyone just one stop on the Metro and we are there."

The line of children stopped almost as one, placing their luggage such as it was, on the pavement.

It was as if she had been met with a chorus of 'No, please Miss not another train journey.'

Peggy worried that her version of German was not understood, and was about to repeat it was only one stop. She saw the children looking towards the Metro entrance. Situated in the shadow of buildings and in the yellow streetlights it presented a sinister picture. The entrance? A black hole into the unknown. She watched as the children turned to look towards the bright lights of the main boulevard. Dorothy whispered to Peggy, "How far is it to walk to the hostel?"

"A little over a kilometre towards the east."

"Along the main street?"

"Yes," Peggy nodded, then raising her voice she addressed the group who were still looking towards the bright lights only two hundred metres away. After the dim lighting of the carriages and the station, this was 'fairyland'.

They could hear the lilting tune of an accordion and the sounds of Paris on a Saturday night.

Despite all their fears, it was a relief to be off the train, out into the open air.

The smaller children, those who had slept well on the journey were excited and inquisitive.

"Anyone prefer to walk to the hostel?"

There was a chorus of approval.

Dorothy said, "What about the luggage? We are all so tired and it is quite a long way."

Peggy did not answer but went immediately to the taxi rank alongside. Walking along the rank she opened one door and looked in. All were amazed when the driver got out and embraced her kissing her on both cheeks. Peggy then held a brief conversation before returning.

"Stack your luggage against the wall everyone please." Turning to Peter and Hal, she asked,"Are you joining us or making your own arrangements?"

It was Hal who answered on behalf of both. "We'll stick with you if you don't mind."

Peg replied. "Good, now place your cases with the others, that is unless you wish to carry them."

"Quite the school Ma'am," muttered Hal as they moved away.

Out on the main boulevard, Paris, dressed in her weekend best welcomed all. It was a warm, pleasant October evening. Trees graced the avenue into the distance. The many lights twinkled. Cafes, restaurants and hotel forecourts, thronged with happy diners.

Tables and chairs spilled out on to the pavement, buskers, violinists, accordionists, mime artists and puppeteers were everywhere. It became more and more difficult to get the younger children to move on especially away from the puppeteers.

The older children soon lost any interest, walking on ahead in a straggle of resignation, like children who after looking briefly in a sweet shop window,but havingno money, they moved on. Their hearts elsewhere, recent experiences having taught them acceptance without question.

Hal, Peter, Dorothy and Peggy remained behind with the younger children.

Shepherding the little ones was difficult. Dorothy looked up to see the older children now way up the avenue.

"I think bringing a mixed age group this time has been a problem. It was that which gave us away at the Austrian border but how could we leave any behind?"

Peter was about to say that it was more likely that they were looking to catch Helga and Miriam or smoke out the cell then thought better of it.

A sycamore seed detached from a tree and spiralled down to the pavement. Mim and two other children ran to catch it. Hal, anxious as a mother hen, ran to get between them and the traffic. Dorothy looked at Peg and smiled.

Shortly after they turned into a side road. In doing so this turned off the magic. The children's mood changed. Mim immediately ran to Hal raising her arms to be picked up. Thumb in mouth, she laid her head on his shoulder and closed her eyes. Peg had two others clinging to her skirts.

One hundred metres later they arrived.

The hostel was much better than they had imagined. They were met by motherly French women who took charge of the children. Daphne followed with Peter and Hal's luggage, delivered by taxi.

"There's supper in the dining room, please go through." She indicated an archway.

Peter, tired and hungry, was also aware that his friend was eager to stay at the hostel with Mim.

He decided to abandon thoughts of finding a hotel. He went through the archway into a large room set with long tables. Daphne who had followed them through, looked at the friends.

"I suppose you are staying, if so, do we take all your luggage up to the room?"

Hal looked at Peter. Peter answered for both. "Yes, please do."

Daphne indicated Mim's attaché case.

"I'll keep this if you don't mind. There are papers I might need."

"Find a seat, gentlemen, you'll be served shortly."

Almost at once they were served with bread rolls and spoons wrapped in cotton napkins by a lady who ghosted in and out of the room returning with bowls of vegetable soup. Meantime Hal had left the table looking for a menu. He had eaten little since early morning. He was feeling faint with hunger. He came back to the table to find the soup waiting.

"I didn't order this." His hopes of steak and eggs disappearing.

Peggy laughed. "Just eat your soup."

Peter, knowing his friend's moods, quickly added, "It's a set meal, Hal. No choice."

Dorothy joined them and sat opposite. "It will be an early start tomorrow I'm afraid. The only ferry we can book is the 11.00 a.m. There's a train at 7.45. Sorry, it's the best I can do. Later ones are full.

It's going to be hard on the children. I hoped for some respite for us all. No choice I'm afraid, Tuss, we are out of funds." Dorothy shrugged. Tired and emotionally stressed, the four sat in silence until Peter offered, "I am thinking if I can arrange some extra francs tomorrow. I doubt that I could contact my father, but my fiancé's father has a telephone at home."

This was as far as he got before Dorothy interrupted.

"Thank you, Peter. Forget it. We are speaking of the unknown. What we do have, is a ferry for the morning. Let's make one final push, get these children to England and settled. I doubt they can take much more of this."

Once more silence overtook them as they retreated each within their own thoughts.

The soup was excellent, the homemade bread delicious. This was followed by a simple plate of green beans dressed with olive oil and herbs. Peter and Hal cleaned their plates before Peter resumed the conversation.

"What do we owe for the ferry? At least we can pay for that."

"You don't have any French money, you gave all to me, remember?"

"We still have a few francs of our own and other currency. Maybe we can get that exchanged."

"On a Sunday?" Dorothy questioned. "In any case I guess it is mainly Mim's money."

Hal interrupted jumping up and looking round.

"Where's Mim?"

"In bed." Peggy answered. "I bet you can't remember her being taken from you. She was fast asleep."

"I do, sure I do," said Hal trying to remember and wondering if he was losing his mind.

Truth was that once Mim fell asleep, he could not remember anything except needing a bed himself. Peter then returned to the question of paying for their ferry crossing and the hostel protesting that they probably had enough other currency to cover that and themselves.

"Peter forget it, this was all pre-arranged. Mim's francs cover most of it. There are more important things to discuss."

"Such as?"

"Getting Mim through immigration for a start. She is travelling on false papers. Her official ones do not exist. She would normally be travelling on her parents. Unless you come with us you will need to plan, if not." Dorothy paused looking at Peter and Hal. She realised then that Hal was not engaging in the discussion.

"Hal, you all right?" she asked.

Hal did not respond.

Peg, who had been aware for some time that he was having problems, stood up.

"Best we discuss tomorrow, I'll see Henry to his room."

"Tuss we may not get chance tomorrow. It needs sorting now."

"Then sort it with Peter for God's sake. You seem to be doing quite well up to now."

She stubbed her cigarette out in the ash tray with excessive force. She looked from one to the other before switching from anger to concern. She took Henry by the arm and began to walk him out of the room.

"Come old pal, let's get you to your bed."

"Take no notice of Tuss. She has issues," said Dorothy. The pair of them watched them leave before she continued. "I must say he did look grey. I hope he will be all right."

"He's exhausted, not been sleeping too well, too much has happened in too short a time. He'll be O.K. He just needs time to adjust."

"That is our fault, so sorry."

Peter reached across the table. It was his turn to take Dorothy's hand and hold on. For a moment or two he didn't speak. Then gathering his emotions, he whispered.

"No, no, no, we both know who's responsible for this, this ..." He paused and swallowed, unable to find the words. For someone with a double first in languages, this was also a first. He kept hold of her hand until he found his way back.

"What the Nazis have done, are doing, is unspeakable.

What you have done, are doing is remarkable. No! This is certainly not your fault."

He took a deep breath and continued. "It is one thing reading about this. Living it drives the cruelty home with a force that is difficult to deal with. With Hal and me we were all right at the crisis points now we are through the worst. I think Hal has hit an emotional wall."

Both looked down at the table as if for inspiration until Peter finally let go of Dorothy's hand.

"You were saying?"

"Where was I?" Dorothy had trouble in retrieving her thoughts.

"Plan to get through immigration," Peter offered, "if not; you were going to say?"

"Miriam will need to through with us on our papers. This will result in her being handed over to the Home Office officials. Then, from there to the Jewish Council. which means weeks, maybe months, in limbo."

Peter nodded. "I do have an alternative plan but need to refine this and verify that it is possible."

He thought for a few seconds before asking.

"Do you think I can access a telephone line from here?"

"Not from this hostel, maybe from the big hotels. Ask Tuss, she's the one in the know."

She opened an envelope and took out some papers and began to study and sort them.

"This plan, has it got any chance?" she asked, without looking up.

Dorothy started making out immigration forms for the next day before continuing.

"Because, if not, Mim must be included on this form. Even if she is, I can't guarantee keeping in touch. It's the best chance of getting through. If she is separated from us, that could prove impossible."

"I will have executive powers as guardian, surely that will count for something."

Dorothy dismissed this. "Maybe, in the long term, but that is open to challenge. I mean a signed but unwitnessed letter from Helga won't carry any weight against a serious challenge. Face it, Peter, there's plenty of incentive to challenge. Once we lose track of her, which is very possible, anything can happen."

"You are forgetting the London solicitors."

"It will take months to resolve anything even if you are successful."

Dorothy was reluctant to encourage this line of thought.

She had little knowledge of what would happen to the children once they entered the U.K. Thinking of her previous rescues, once they had been safely delivered to the authorities, she lost track of most of them.

"Months in limbo," Peter murmured, "that would destroy Mim, Hal, and everything everyone have achieved."

"Then we'd best not fail," said Dorothy. "Now let's assume the best. First let me have a permanent address for Henry and yourself."

Not knowing exactly where either Hal or he could be at any time, Peter gave Greensleeves as a contact address for them both.

"This is the best contact address for the time being. If it changes, we'll let you know."

Dorothy handed over two cards. "You will be able to contact me at either of these two addresses," she replied as she noted Peter's address. She looked up surprised.

"Care of Sir George and Lady Bridge-Thompson." Dorothy raised her eyebrows. "Really?"

"Really," Peter answered.

"Well, Peter." Dorothy stood up and held out her hand. "I am convinced it will be safe to leave tomorrow in your hands. I think now we had best get to our beds."

Chapter 20

The following morning Peter entered the dining room before the agreed 7.00 am breakfast, hoping to find a cup of coffee. Dorothy and Peg were already there at the same table studying the immigration documents. Joining them, he asked, "Any chance of coffee?"

"Good morning Peter, you're early." Peg looked at her watch. "Nowhere near seven o'clock. Couldn't you sleep?"

"Anything wrong?" Dorothy asked.

"We are not coming with you today. Hal is not good."

Peter was using Hal's exhaustion to cover his real intentions. It being true, however, that Hal was under some strain and in need of a break.

"We intend to keep Miriam with us. Is that acceptable with you? We will need help with procedures and paperwork."

This suggestion was met with silence.

Peg got up to find some coffee, having seen movement in the kitchen.

"Give us time to think and sort things, please Peter. Is Hal ill?"

"No just tired, it's best we rest up for a while."

Peg returned with coffee. "Did I hear you say that you can't travel today?"

"Not today, it's Sunday."

Both ladies looked up. "Sunday what do you mean?"

"I'm not sure how immigration works at Dover, but I believe the main decision makers will be home for the weekend. The chances of getting Mim through against the lower ranks who will be unable or unwilling to make any decision are not good. They will go by the book. This would mean Mim ending up in the care of the local authority or whoever and we will lose control. Either way she could end up as ward of the Home Office."

"She can still come through with us and in that case, we might retain some control."

Dorothy offered. "Then I will do my best to keep track of the little girl."

"Thank you, can we use that as a fall back?"

Peter considered for a moment before deciding to explain his thinking.

"I need for Sir George, my future father-in-law, to be at his desk also for his Home Office colleagues to be in their offices. Therefore, I think we will take our chance on Monday. Also, it will give Hal a chance to recover."

"Sir George?" It was Peggy's turn to be surprised.

"Later, Peg," said Dorothy, now more interested in Peter's plan. "Are you sure Hal's all right?"

"Yes, it's just that he's not slept well for some days," Peter explained, adding, "the advent of instant parenthood has disturbed his rhythm. Before Mim, I would have put money on Hal getting his eight hours if he was to be shot at dawn; not now."

It was some seconds before he realised his gaffe. He held his hand up, "Sorry."

It was Peggy who, not knowing the full history, broke the silence with "Comes with the territory I'm afraid."

"Peg," Dorothy interrupted edgily.

Tuss lit another cigarette from the diminishing stub and grinned at Peter.

"She always calls me Peg when I irritate her."

Dorothy took a deep breath and sighed.

"Tuss, not now, this is too important. Pass me that supplementary."

Peg passed her one of the forms they had been dealing with. Dorothy tore the form in two.

"I like Peter's idea, can you come over on the ferry with us then wait to help Peter and Hal through immigration tomorrow?"

"Then what?" Tuss blew a huge smoke ring. "You still after me returning to London?"

"It would make sense. Think about it, please?" pleaded Dorothy. "You would be safer there."

"I live in Paris for God's sake. These tin pot bullies will probably take over in Austria, but do you really think they will take on France and England?"

"I'd feel happier if you at least come over to help. You could wait and see Peter and Hal through immigration and have a new form ready to fill in. Then if Peter's ploy fails, try and marry Miriam up to the main party. That way we can keep track of her."

Peg blew another smoke ring. "Does make a sort of sense."

She thought for a moment, sure that Dot had another agenda but after all, her argument had merit, so she agreed.

"O.K. then." She stood up and looked at her watch.

"7.00 breakfast time, more coffee." Peg headed off to the kitchen.

Dorothy smiled at Peter. "That's Tuss! Got her own way of dealing with things. It's her way of coping with life. I assure you that she is still focused and aware. She'll not let us down."

"I'd hoped you would come on board with my idea, thank you. Hal will then know that we tried everything."

"No Peter, thank you and Hal, it is *you* helping us, remember" Dorothy was quick to point out.

Rounding up the children after breakfast wasn't too difficult. Peter found it poignant the way they tolerated the hustle to get them to a coach waiting outside. They lined up with an acceptance, a resignation which tore at his heart strings. They appeared to accept events as prisoners rather than refugees being saved from a tyranny. Time was short. they had to make the early train in time for the ferry. Peg managed a toothy grin for Peter.

"See you in Dover tomorrow."

She ushered the final child aboard and hanging on to the coach step, shouted "Righty-oh." As the coach moved away, she shouted to Peter, "About the phone, Andre will be in touch."

Peter ran after the coach shouting, "Andre, who's Andre?"

It was of no avail, the coach was away.

Returning to the hostel Peter, looking for the receptionist, was met one of the kitchen women. “Petit-dejeuner pour le monsieur et la enfant?”

Peter suddenly realised that Mim would be left on her own. “Ou est la petite fille?” he asked.

“Avec l’ homme.”

“Merci.” Peter forgot his question to the reception and hurried to Hal’s room. Quietly he opened the door and peeked inside. The scene served to confirm everything he knew about the relationship between his friend and this tiny child. In turn, it reinforced his intention to succeed in his plan to try and adopt her. Returning to the dining room, he collected croissants and milk and took these up. Mim was just waking, sitting up and rubbing her eyes. Peter placed the tray on the side table and turned to pick up Mim. Peter was intending to take her downstairs so that Hal could sleep on, but she was already poking Hal in the cheek with her forefinger and he was stirring. Peter tried not to laugh as he spoke.

“See you two downstairs.”

Hal sat up and grunted. “Thanks, Pete.”

Downstairs in the reception area Peter was met by a young man.

“Ah! Mr. Barnes you wish to telephone to England?”

Andre had no trouble recognising Peter. Peter realised he was the taxi driver from last night.

“Yes please,” he answered realising that this must be Andre.

“You speak good English.”

“Today, Sunday it is not good. The telephone office is very busy. You will wait a long time for a connection.”

“It’s imperative that I telephone today. Is there no other way? Please, Andre.”

Andre considered this request while whistling tunefully and tossing a small coin from hand to hand in time to the whistled tune. He did this repeatedly catching the coin in the hand, palm downwards then returning it in the same manner to his other hand.

"You see ambidextrous," he said with a smile.

Despite Andre's charm, the performance annoyed Peter. Seeing Peter's frown, he said, "What I am meaning to say is there is always more than one way of progressing."

He continued tossing the coin while speaking. "You go to Calais tomorrow?"

"Yes, to catch the 11.00 a.m. ferry."

"You will be rushed then to catch this ferry. Like Miss Firth today. Not good."

He continued tossing the coin and resumed whistling. Suddenly he stopped and popped the coin into his pocket.

"Today I will drive you to Calais in my taxi. I know there a hotel where you can stay the night. They have a telephone service for their guests. They make and receive calls all the days, to and from England. If you wait for connections, it is better to wait in a bar."

He smiled. "You see, another way."

Without seeking Peter's agreement, he continued,"I'll meet you and the others here in just one hour."

He held out a hand. Peter didn't know whether this was a question or an order. This charming young man was irresistible. He had quickly dispelled his annoyance of his apparent casual manner, with a swift logical assessment of the problem. Equally, a swift presentation of an excellent solution. This covered most of the questions which had occupied him since waking.

Peter took his hand and answered. "We will be there, thank you Andre you are a star."

"I do twinkle sometimes," he chuckled, "See you in one hour."

Chapter 21

Travelling by car suited all three. Hal and Mim travelled in the back seat where they slept for the greater part of the journey. Peter rode in front with Andre.

He was intrigued by this charming Frenchman and wished to know more about him and his connection with Peggy Firth.

"How long have you known Miss Firth?" was Peter's first question.

"Since I was a boy, she was teaching English at a Moulin Academy."

"A schoolteacher, there's a surprise."

"Not with children with older people, mostly at nights in the academy. Also, in their houses, some days."

"You were only a boy."

"Yes. I did try and go to the night classes."

Andre, a taxi driver liked to talk, especially about himself.

"With the older pupils?" Peter's admiration for Andre was not in doubt.

"No, before that big class."

"Peg, Miss Firth, agreed to take you before the main class began?"

The opportunity to learn more about Peggy Firth was seized upon by Peter. Andre seemed not to mind Peter's constant questioning in fact he appeared to encourage him.

"I wanted to go with the others in the class, but they asked thirteen weeks' money in the first. This was too much money at one time." "How did Miss Firth know of this? About your problems I mean?"

"I waited outside the academy until after the lessons and asked to be taught at my home. To pay only for one lesson at one time."

"And she agreed?"

Peter already knew enough about Margaret Firth not to be surprised.

"Yes, but in her home not mine. She charged only ten centimes an hour. I thought that it was right and ran errands to earn it, not knowing that it was stupid money. I was only seven."

"Why did you wish to learn a foreign language at such a young age?"

"My uncle was a taxi driver and he earned much money, more than the others, because he spoke English. Rich American and English tourists would hire him for the day to show them Paris.

I wanted to be like him." Andre delivered his usual logical answer.

Peter was quiet for a little while. Andre had told him enough of his and Peggy Firth's story for the time being. He just sat and thought over the last week. He watched the countryside dressed in its autumn best slide by. Andre eventually interrupted his thoughts.

"The little girl, you speak to her in her language, yes?" he suddenly asked.

"Of course." Peter was a little surprised by the question.

"Don't, please don't. If she asks a question in German answer in English. Speak English to her always. She is three, an age where she will learn quickly. She understands more than you think."

Peter didn't answer, already aware of Mim's knack of picking up the language.

Andre continued. "She comes to England then she will learn quickly and good."

"Did Miss Firth ask you to say this?"

"No, it's how she taught me. I ask a question in French and she answers in English. I say what does this mean? She say, 'find out', in English. I say what is this? What is that? She say, 'find out'.

These are the first words I learned, find out. Miss Firth cooked me suppers all the time speaking in English. I say how can I find out? She sold me a little book, 'French/English-English/ French' for two centimes.' Stupid price two centimes. I owe much to Miss Firth. I look for her always."

"You look for her?" Why, how do you do this?"

"She smokes and drinks too much. When she is not working, she drinks the wine."

Peter was surprised, Andre seemed to be saying she is an alcoholic.

"I didn't realise that. Is the drinking bad?"

"It's why Miss Price finds things for her to do, I think."

"Miss Price does this often?"

Peter was wondering how many times they had rescued children together.

"She is too far away. Miss Price gives me money, says look for her. So, I do."

"Usually in a wine bar?"

"Yes. I take her home many nights." Andre gave a little sigh as he answered.

This didn't fit quite with Peter's impression of Peg.

"She seems to be all right now."

"When you are gone, I will look for her."

Andre's answer suggested that left alone, she did indeed drink. There had to be an explanation or so Peter thought. His impression of Peg was of a capable, reliable, caring woman.

That she was intelligent and dedicated was without question. He needed an answer.

"Do you know why she drinks?"

"I think one day she kill a child." Andre answered without hesitation.

Peter was too shocked to speak. Andre dropped into a higher gear and slowed down pulling slowly into the side of the road. Clearly, he was also shocked by his own words.

Thoughts which he had subjugated for years had been teased out by Peter.

Andre sat for a short while looking into the distance before continuing to whisper each word keeping time with Peter's beating heart.

"She said one night when I found her in a wine bar, very ill. 'You've saved me again Andre, you are always saving me.' I said to her, 'you saved me when I was a child.' She say to me, 'if I saved every child in creation it will not espound the memory of the one I killed'."

Neither spoke for a while as if nothing had happened. Andre started the engine. He put his hand into the glove compartment and took out a battered English/ French dictionary, which he handed to Peter. "I can't find espound." Then he pulled away as if the last minutes had not occurred.

None of this disturbed the two in the back seats.

Peter didn't try to answer Andre but thumbed aimlessly through the little book. All his questions had done was to give him a greater desire to find out more answers, which he doubted Andre would have.

"Expunge," Peter exclaimed.

Andre nodded. "Expungere. Was my thinking."

Whether Peg's drunken confessional was blurred by alcohol, was not further questioned. Neither spoke for the rest of the journey.

Chapter 22

The taxi finally pulled into a side road and stopped in front of a small hotel.

"Mr. Barnes, we have arrived. This is the hotel."

Peter took out his wallet to pay Andre, but he faced a problem; he had only one ten Franc note and one traveller's cheque.

"Andre, will the hotel change a traveller's cheque?"

Andre was already out of the car. He turned around and looked back in.

Peter was aware that the cost of the journey would far exceed his ability to pay.

Andre was thinking only of the night's bill.

"It is a small hotel, Mr. Barnes. They will accept your personal cheque against your passport."

He turned and went to the back to collect the luggage. Peter realising Andre had misunderstood hurriedly climbed out and joined him.

"I need to pay you for the journey," said Peter, looking at the same time for the attaché case.

He moved Mim's other case out of the way and picked it up.

Andre already had Peter's and Henry's cases, one in each hand. He stopped, looked pointedly at Peter as if to say something, then turned and walked into the hotel. Peter followed carrying just the small case. Andre placed the two cases in the foyer then went back to collect Mim's other case from the taxi. He returned to find Peter conversing with the owner.

"Do I wake your friend and the little girl? They are still sleeping."

"Sorry Andre, I'll go get them shortly but first we must discuss your fare. I can only pay you in foreign notes plus just ten francs, sorry."

"Ten francs will do."

Peter, unused to being without funds and knowing that ten francs was ridiculous, muttered.

"I can give you a cheque in sterling. Will that do?"

Peter had, as was his won't, shut off from reality and immersed himself in the problem of Hal and Mim. Not really taking the question of adoption seriously but originally as a kind of exercise.

As time progressed, he had come to realise that he was dealing with a potential tragedy and the high emotions attached to this nigh impossible task. This began his intention to try his best if only for the sake of appearances. Then there was the added complication of his responsibility as guardian to the little girl. With all these thoughts crowding his mind no matter how he tried to push them away.

The problem of paying Andre a reasonable fare for the journey from Paris caused him worry.

He thought of taking the Swiss francs from Mim's case to compensate. This was however in Peter's confused mind tantamount to stealing. He could think of no other solution. He took the Swiss francs from the case and handed the lot over to Andre.

"Take this please, Andre and continue to look for Miss Firth."

Andre took the notes picked out the ten franc note, returning the rest to Peter.

"Mr. Barnes, there's going to be another war."

He put his hand on Peter's arm "*Please* keep Miss Firth in England. She can be mother to the little girl and you can look for her. If she is mother to the little girl, then perhaps she will not get drunk." Peter was stunned by this sudden passionate plea from Andre and the return of the Swiss francs.

At first, he was lost for a reply until finally he whispered as much to himself rather than asking the question.

"You love her, don't you? You really do love her?"

Andre didn't answer. He put a hand in his pocket and took out a coin. He began to whistle and toss it from hand to hand. He turned away and walked up to the reception desk. He had a brief discussion with the proprietor before going into the bar and sitting down. Peter went out to the taxi and stood watching trying to gather his wits. He took a deep breath reached into the car and picked up the little girl who was lying on Hal's lap. This woke his friend.

"Come on fellas, just one last big push."

Peter returned to the foyer looking for Andre, who had disappeared.

He went to the door and the taxi was still outside. Returning he saw him leaving one of two small booths to one side of the bar. Peter went to him and took the hand of this young man who'd he known for less than one day.

"Andre, thank you for everything and I promise to do all I can to persuade Miss Firth to remain in England."

The young Frenchman didn't speak but the pressure of his hand said it all.

He then embraced Peter and 'spoke' again through the tears in his eyes and the urgent nodding of the head before turning and returning to the car. Peter watched him drive away and thought 'How little we know about Margaret Firth, Peggy, Peg, Tussy, Tuss. A woman of many names all of them respected and loved yet seemingly so frail and vulnerable.'

He had promised to give this woman, an alcoholic, the responsibility for a three-year old refugee girl. The thought of this was too much for his already overcrowded mind. Typically, Peter pushed it away and returned his thoughts to his master plan: The adoption of Mim. This was still hovering between an exercise in thwarting his father and gaining some control of his own destiny and also helping, or appearing to help, his friend. Returning to the hotel lounge he found Hal and the little girl tucking into tea, milk and biscuits.

"Shouldn't we be checking into our rooms first?"

"You're forgetting Pete we've not eaten since a very pushed breakfast."

Hal was aware that his mother would not have approved of his behaviour, neither the pushed breakfast nor a cookie snack mid-day.

"Stomach's all over the place as is the rest of our lives. The kid's coping well, better than me. I figure it's O. K. to give her a break."

"Chocolate biscuits, Hal? My thoughts are that we will regret the choice."

Peter looked to exert some control. Hal looked genuinely puzzled.

"Why so buddy?"

"Mim doesn't have a change of clothing."

"She's has another dress in the case, hasn't she?" Hal's answer sounded tetchy.

"Hal my old friend, that dress is already soiled. In any event, it is too big."

"You're sure? Why pack a dress that's too big?"

"Think about it, Hal, her mother didn't have time to pack a bag. I suppose she was passed over to Helga with what she was dressed in on the day. The dress in the case is one that Gerda or someone found for her. It probably belonged to one of the older children. Her smalls, the ladies washed and dried overnight."

Peter looked at his friend who was still looking blank.

"We don't have any ladies to see to her things tonight and we need her to look presentable tomorrow."

"We do?" Hal, now aware he was not making sense, seemed incapable of controlling his thoughts. Peter sighed.

"If immigration pass her on to local social services for opinion, she needs to appear cared for.

I don't think two chaps and a dirty appearance is going to help."

Peter replied, keeping up the pretence that they could be given control. At the same time, he was reminding Hal to be prepared to part with Miriam.

Meanwhile Mim, who would otherwise have taken notice of the conversation at the mention of her name, finished off the biscuits. Peter looked at the damage.

"See what I mean Hal?"

Hal did see what Peter meant.

"I'll try and clean this up, maybe we could buy another dress in Calais or find a laundry."

Peter picked up his case and Mim's attaché case.

"It *is* Sunday, Hal. Remember the Sabbath. See you down here in half an hour and maybe we can have lunch proper."

Later, after lunch, they were sitting in the bar with coffee when the receptionist called from the doorway.

"Your call to Bendesbury, England, Monsieur Barnes, Bureau one."

Peter left his coffee cup on the table, stood up and looked at his friend.

"This is it Hal, wish me luck."

Hal, still unsure of Peter's intentions, wanted to know more, beinguncertain of his role in this plan.

At least it was a plan.

"Sure Pete, do your best."

Hal was left wondering what it was that Peter really intended.

Mim, who had been playing make believe with a napkin wrapped around a bread stick, picked up on the importance of this exchange and climbed on to Papa Yo's lap. She sat there sucking her thumb as they watched Peter disappear into the booth.

Twenty minutes later Peter replaced the receiver in shock. Sir George's response to his suggestions had taken his breath away. It was almost as if his father-in-law had been sat waiting to hear this very proposal so immediate was his acceptance, to take over over the planning from Peter.

Peter, from a position of expecting a rejection of support from his future in-laws, and expecting to tell his friend, 'No deal.' now had to reassess the situation, stillunsure of the real reason why he had embarked on this unlikely venture when he picked up the telephone.

He was now left with having to think through the discussion of the last minutes as a probable outcome. Peter's suggestion of adopting a refugee child carried with it kudos to be seized upon.

That plus the fact that she was probably an heiress, was indeed manna from heaven to Sir George.

Well versed in the intrigues of government and the Civil Service, he took control.

Peter returned to the bar in a daze. Hal anxiously awaiting, picked up on this.

"Please Pete, don't pitch me a curve. Not now."

Peter didn't have an answer ready, at least one that he was prepared to give. He tried desperately to sort out his emotions. From a position of expecting to have acquired the credit for trying to sort out his friend's problem then failing and waiting for their relationship to return to where it had been for the last few years, he was now having to consider that his unlikely plan was far from dead.

"Well?" Hal prompted.

Mim, who in the meantime had returned to her game once more climbed on Hal's lap and stared at Peter. Another time, another day, Peter would have marvelled at her ability to pick up so easily on the importance of events. Today he just grappled with the need to reply intelligently.

"Plans are now in place but please Hal, don't expect too much."

Feeling pleased with this reply he did his best to appear in control. Peter was desperate to ignore the obvious import of the relationship, the bonding of Hal and this tiny refugee. He was keenly aware of the potential distress caused by the failure of this plan.

"The best laid plans ..."

Hal interrupted him. "Don't give me that Pete, just do your best. Please help us."

Peter didn't have an answer. Unable to cope with the following silence, he went outside the hotel to get some space and take time to think. Hours later he still hadn't returned. Tired of walking and of turning the problem over and over in his mind he was sitting in the waiting area of the ferry terminal.

He had tried to tell his friend that his hopes of adoption were just pipe dreams. He knew also that Sir George had powerful friends in Whitehall and that anything could happen. Alongside these thoughts was his own wish that the whole trauma could end. They could then return to where they were just one week ago.

"Hi there, Peter. Thank you."

A familiar voice penetrated his thoughts. He looked up at the familiar toothy smile shrouded in a blue haze.

"Thank you?"

"I guess you are here to save me the journey into Paris. Didn't Andre tell you?"

"Tell me what?"

Peg looked long and hard at Peter. "You all right?"

Peter at last gathered his wits. "You came back."

Peg realised that Peter was not there to meet her.

"We decided that it would be best if I came across with you. The immigration chaps will be more amenable if I am around as Mim's carer." Peggy Firth looked around.

"Where are Hal and the little girl? At Andre's uncle's place?"

Peter was still staring at the floor and trembling as he tried to recover his wits, not understanding what was happening to him, trying to control his limbs and failing. He wanted his old life back even though it was less than perfect. He wanted above all Hal back in his life. Peg realised that all was not well tossed her cigarette on the floor and blew a lung full of blue smoke away from Peter then began to waft the air around him as if to blow away any evil spirits. Peg didn't ask questions she just sat next to him and put her arm around his shoulders.

"Shall we go and find the other two?"

Peter was warmed and comforted by Peggy's presence. Surprised by his emotions, he was unable to speak and just nodded. Together they walked back to the hotel.

Chapter 23

After a restless night Peter changed from being ambivalent about his plan, to being totally committed. Whether or not this change of heart was about helping Hal was another matter.

Whatever he had imagined the Immigration office to be, this was not it. Both his and Sir George's plans were now defunct. He was 'funnelled' along with many others and shown straight from the ferry control into what appeared to be an adapted storage warehouse.

Canvas screens, identified by large capital letters, were placed throughout the length and breadth. Each unit was manned by one officer and tannoy broadcasts making regular announcements giving a number and a capital letter.

At the far end were several collapsible tables. These were manned by customs and police officers. Each screen was identified by these capitals.

At the far end of the warehouse, two armed military policemen presented a less than welcoming picture.

The presence of genteel ladies offering help and advice plus duplicated leaflets of contact addresses and telephone numbers, did little to lift the atmosphere.

The whole scene gave the impression of haste and improvisation.

Hal, trying to control his nerves, was making notes and taking photographs.

Peg made yet another attempt to make Mim look presentable.

All of which served to transfer tension to the little girl. She accepted all Peg's attentions like a rag doll.

They were given a number then asked to wait on the wooden benches until called. There was not enough seating for all who waited. Applicants were either standing or seated on the floor. The four of them had to wait for vacancies on the wooden forms in order to sit.

Tensions increased as they witnessed a distressing rejection and several referrals.

Hal controlled his anxiety by using his position as a reporter. He engaged with one of the lady helpers.

"What is happening? It seems they are blocking everyone, letting no one through."

"Standard procedure, sir for applicants with questionable papers or no papers. It doesn't mean they are being rejected. Its been like this for months and getting worse."

Hal was shocked, 'All these people without papers?' he thought looking round the hall.

His head was hurting. All he could think was that getting Mim through was hopeless.

Mim was being distracted by Peg. She had almost reverted to her former happy self, playing games.

Interview sections were anything but private. Although they couldn't hear, they were able to sense what was happening in many sites. Some officers appeared to be kind and helpful, others stern, obdurate and clinical. Refusals and referrals were common. Most accepted with resignation with few protests or tears.

All interviews were carried out in 'open tragic theatre.'

How long had passed Hal did not know.

Peter shook him out of his thoughts.

"Come on my friend we've been called." Peter whispered.

This was not planning out as Peter had hoped. It was worse than he had feared.

All the rehearsed interviews he had conducted in his imagination evaporated.

"Good day Mr. Barnes and Miriam is it?"

The immigration officer smiled at the little girl. Neither answered.

"And you are?" he asked looking at Hal.

"Henry Steading, sir, Eastern Coast Press Associates. U.S. of A. May I have your permission to stay?" Hal presented his press card.

The officer looking down at his papers did not even look up. "On what grounds?"

"As an observer."

The officer then turned his attention to Peg.

"And you Madame?"

"Margaret Firth, temporary nanny to Miriam Kessler." Peg was clearly used to the scene.

"U.K. citizen?" the officer asked. Peg nodded and handed over her passport which she had ready. The officer examined it and made some notes before speaking again.

"Miss Firth, please stay with your charge." He paused. "Mr. Steading please leave."

"Why?" Hal exclaimed.

"You are not required." Again, the officer did not even look up.

Peter, secretly pleased with this response, mouthed. "Leave this with me, Hal."

The officer continued to look at his papers and make notes.

Hal moved outside the screen, out of sight but not earshot.

The officer continued to read and make notes. "Miriam has no papers," he said looking up and asking, "Her parents were arrested, why?"

"Officer, I think you know. An official in your position and experience must know.

It is the same reason that we are seeking asylum for a three-year- old who would also have been arrested but for the intervention of some very brave people."

The officer made no further comment. Looking down he continued to read through the application.

Peg, sensing a growing anger, touched Peter's arm and put her finger to her lips.

Eventually the officer looked up and addressed Peter.

"You, Peter Richard Barnes, are the applicant on behalf of Miriam. How come you are involved in this application?"

This being an anticipated question Peter was ready with a prepared answer.

Handing over the note from Helga he replied. "Acceptance of my responsibilities. I am a long-standing friend of the family."

Peter was careful not to mention which family. He read the note without comment. The officer returned to the forms and made some notes then pressed a switch.

A middle-aged woman entered from behind the screen.

"All done, Reggie?"

The officer handed over a form.

"Six-month temp, rubber stamp confirmation I expect. The rest is down to you."

Peter, unsure what was happening, was about to ask when the woman who was reading the form spoke.

"You wish to adopt Miriam Kessler?"

Peter nodded but before he could speak the woman continued.

"We'll take account of that Mr. Barnes. We will need a contact address."

Peter guessed that she was a children's officer.

That she was preparing to take charge of Mim. They were probably about to lose control of the situation.

Peter, about to be relieved of his responsibilities, at least for now, replied with the St. Mary address. "You can contact us at Greensleeves, The Green, St. Mary Upperford, Hampshire, care of Sir George Bridge Thompson."

The mention of Sir George caused both the officer and the woman to look up sharply.

In a flash of inspiration Peter added, "He will be at his desk in Whitehall now should you wish to call him."

He searched through his mind for a more convincing argument.

Hal appeared by his friend's side. Mim shook free from Peg and ran to him to be picked up. This Hal did at once, preparing to fight for her.

The woman looked from Peter to Hal and back to Peter seemingly unable to comprehend what was happening.

"Whitehall, did you say Whitehall?"

"Yes, is that a problem?"

The woman thought for a moment before turning to the officer. "What do you think Reggie?"

The officer shrugged. "Your baby, literally. She is cleared as far as we are concerned."

The woman, clearly shocked by this reply, for a split second lost all semblance of authority. Peter was watching for clues as to whether they were to be allowed to keep Miriam or whether she was to become a ward of the local authority.

The children's officer made her decision.

"I think this case needs to be considered by my manager. Please come with me."

Mim clung to Hal with her face buried into his shoulder sucking hard on her thumb.

Hal clung to her with equal intensity. He was almost incapable of breathing let alone speaking. The shock of realising that the children's officer was about to take Mim away had hit hard.

Peter, doing his best to hold on to her, was Hal's only hope.

Peg, aware, was content to let things ride. At the same time, she was gasping for a fag.

She realising that lighting up would not give a good impression and refrained.

They followed the children's officer out of the hall and across the road towards an office building, the permanent offices of Immigration Control.

Peg suggested to Peter that she wasn't needed and could wait outside.

"No Peg, please stay with us."

Peter's reply persuaded Peg that she was really needed.

They were shown into an elegant, carpeted office tastefully furnished with an arranged bunch of flowers in the open-hearth unlit fireplace. It could have passed for an upper middle class, drawing room.

Behind a mahogany desk sat a middle-aged man in a pin-striped suit.

Behind him, in the corner, the obligatory bowler hat and furled umbrella on a wooden hat stand.

The contrast with the immigration reception hall could not have been more pointed.

Coffee and two telephone calls later the friends found themselves once more outside the offices. Peter, a temporary visa for Miriam in his pocket, waited for a taxi to take them to the railway station. He was still confused as to how this could have happened.

Hal was still in shock and yet to recover.

Mim, aware instinctively of the import of the last thirty minutes, still clung to him.

Peter was some place between triumph and resentment of the power that Sir George and his colleagues wielded, had now to think what the next move was.

Peg leaned back on the wall outside and lit a fag and blew an enormous smoke ring which hung long enough in the calm October afternoon air to be noticed.

She followed this with a huge, loud, prolonged, "Phewwww!"

"Who would have believed this just one hour ago, fellas? We made it! Or rather you did Peter. I reckon you're a genius."

She took an enormous drag on her cigarette and blew another even bigger smoke ring.

Peter basking in the warmth of this comment found his voice.

"You will stay with us, come home with us please Peg, as Mim's nanny of course."

Peg took another drag, replying through a blue haze as she shook head.

"Sorry Peter, I can't."

"Stay as little or as long as you wish." Peter persisted, mindful of his promise to Andre but forgetting the complications which would arrive via Pamela.

Peg looked at each one in turn as she spoke.

"Peter, Hal, Mim, I love you all and I love what you are doing but I must return to Paris."

"Why?" they asked.

"Whatever you think of me you would be wrong. It would be wrong of me to accept.

Thanks for your trust but sorry, you are wrong. Please let me go."

Without waiting for an answer Peg embraced each one in turn then lit another cigarette from the stub. Blowing each one a kiss through the customary haze, she turned and headed back towards the ferry terminal.

Peter started after her. Hal caught hold of his arm.

"Let her go, Pete."

Peter looked at him. A week ago, faced with the same situation, Hal would have been running after her.

Peter was pleased that she had not accepted his offer because of problems it might have thrown up, and also pleased to have honoured his pledge.

The taxi arrived at that moment to take them to the station.

Still in shock they climbed in mindful that they still needed to face the next episode of this drama.

Neither spoke during the journey to the railway station.

The wait for the next train to London was even more difficult.

Both remained acutely aware of the sea change in their relationship and Peter unsure of why he had embarked on his scheme or how it would play out.

Hal was concerned and equally unsure about what was to happen; just how much he was in control of events, if at all.

The arrival of the train broke the spell, to the relief of all.

Hal picked up the little girl leaving Peter to collect his luggage plus the small, all-important attaché case, which had never left his side. Other matters occupied Peter's mind.

"Sorry Pete, I was not thinking." Hal popped Mim on to the seat and returned to help his friend with the luggage.

"Do you realise Pete we escaped the attention of the Customs?"

The awkwardness in their relationship was obvious. He tried to lighten the atmosphere.

Peter's mind however was now on other matters. He didn't answer at once.

Mim, who was kneeling on the seat looking out of the window managed to amaze Peter and Hal by speaking in almost perfect English.

"Train, another train," she said pointing as it pulled in alongside.

Peter and Hal looked at each other. "How the hell!" Hal exclaimed.

Peter interrupted sharply. "Watch it Hal, she is picking everything up."

Hal was rebuked and angry. Was Peter letting him know that Mim was *his* responsibility? Predictably, Hal's natural good manners came to his rescue.

The growing rift between them, the feeling that he was being subtly being cut away from Mim, contrasted sharply with his realisation that without Peter's help the little girl would already be a ward of the local children's services.

"But where?" Hal asked spreading his hands, thinking how Mim could possibly learn so quickly.

"She is merely repeating what we are saying." Peter's answer was clipped and curt.

"But Pete, she clearly knows what is meant."

"Yes, I suppose that is spooky," Peter reluctantly offered, dismissing Hal's subsequent attempts to make conversation in a manner learned from, or inherited from his father.

It was a habit that Hal was familiar with and one which Peter exhibited when concentrating.

Peter was now faced with the responsibility of the little girl, it seemed almost on a whim. He needed time to think.

He had only the adoption plan to fall back on. This without the agreement of Pen or his father. His knowledge of Sir George's involvement or intentions were confined to a few instructions over the telephone yesterday. He could only guess what the thetelephone discussions were between Sir George and then Sir George's Home Office colleague and the immigration manager.

Then he had to deal with his father.

Hal tried again to lighten the atmosphere, saying, "Did you see that manager's face when Sir George rang him back?"

Peter didn't answer so Hal persisted.

"Then when the Home Office rang him, we could almost see him bowing."

Hal's voice fell away as he realised that Peter was not listening.

Silence became the norm as they both retreated into their thoughts.

The journey to London and from London to Fernborough remained difficult for both.

Peter 'escaped' between trains to make telephone calls to Pen. Then he retreated once more into his thoughts and plans.

Hal interacted with Mim while trying to subdue his fears which included Peter's unhealthy attachment to the little girl's attaché case.

The journey across London, then across to Fernborough seemed to take forever.

It was some relief when a taxi dropping off a passenger, accepted the fare to St. Mary.

Following a third and last telephone call to Pen, they set off on the last mile.

Chapter 24

The sun was about to drop behind the rooftops as they turned into The Green, casting an ethereal golden glow over the scene. The lengthening shadows of the houses accentuated the light. The sunbeams streaming through the garden's birch tree, creating a dapple effect over the grass in front of Greensleeves, taking the eye away from a small knot of welcoming neighbours standing in the shadows. Several of the others came to their garden gates to wave.

In front of the house a reporter and cameraman were waiting at the request of Sir George.

Sadly, for Sir George, they were only from *The Bugle*. The national newspapers approached by him, had failed to show any interest.

"Sir George has been hard at work," said Peter climbing out of the taxi clutching Mim's attaché case.

"Thank God, at last we are here," Then turning to the little girl he stretched his open hand towards the house while at the same time looking anxiously for Pen. He then announced, with just a hint of triumph, "Mim, this is your home."

Scrambling over Hal's lap she jumped down on to the path.

"Mein hause?"

"Your home," Peter repeated.

Hal felt bereft. His only semblance of reality was that he was losing his grip on this little girl.

Pamela had not been still since learning about the plight of this tiny refugee.

The nursery had been re-established. New clothes had been bought. A special diet planned. All this had kept her mind away from the ghastly thoughts of what had happened to Miriam and her family. How she might help repair and rebuild this shattered little life.

The drama had been amply 'embroidered' by Sir George to anyone and everyone willing to listen.

As soon as Pamela saw Miriam jump down from the taxi, she ran to The Green. She knelt on the grass holding out her arms. Mim instinctively ran to her.

Through the sunbeam curtain of multi-patterned light, Hal saw Pamela's arms enfold Mim. This vision was despatched by the flash of a camera, leaving Hal with black shadows across his eyes.

The press interview, conducted outside on The Green, was dominated by Sir George.

He gave the impression that he had orchestrated the whole affair. Sadly, this was witnessed by just the local newspaper and a small band of curious neighbours.

After the first photo shoot Hal, Peter and Pen left the scene to Sir George and Lady Amelia. They followed Pamela inside with the very tired little girl.

"The nursery is ready. I think milk, supper and a quick warm bath then bed is called for," Pamela announced, once again inhabiting the world she loved and understood.

"I'll go and run the bath," said Pen and turned quickly to Peter.

"You and I can say our hellos properly when all the fuss has died down."

She gave him a quick second kiss before disappearing upstairs.

Mim looked at Hal. "Unsere haus?"

"Yes." It was Peter who answered. "Your home."

"Und mit Papa Yo?" she asked, looking to Peter this time for an answer.

Peter, whilst acknowledging Miriam's ability to pick up on the vibes, didn't have the answer. Pamela looked questioningly at both friends who were looking very uncomfortable.

"What is she saying?"

The two looked at each other for some seconds before Peter broke the silence.

"Tell you all over dinner, meanwhile it is perhaps best if Hal helps you settle Mim in."

After a moment's hesitation, Pamela agreed.

"Where did *they* go to with that child?" Lady Amelia complained as she and her husband returned to the house.

"I suppose, Old Girl, Pamela is putting the little girl to bed. She must have been through Hell and back."

"Are you so sure we need to do this, George?"

Amelia was far from convinced that this was a good idea to take Miriam into their home.

She was only persuaded because she believed the whole thing to be exaggerated and that the child would be back with her family or the German authorities soon.

"Most certainly, old girl. Take my tip there will be thousands more like her before long," he assured her.

Amelia was still far from being convinced.

"How can you possibly know, George? You've been listening to Randolph's boy Winston.

You know what Jellicoe said about him at the Jutland Memorial dinner."

"No, what did he say?" Sir George asked, looking out of the window. He was deliberately showing disinterest in Amelia's argument and also noting that the curtain had now fallen on his moment in the spotlight.

"That he is a loose cannon on the poop deck."

Sir George sighed as he turned away from the window.

"I don't think so Old Girl. I heard that story. Lord Jellicoe wouldn't have said that and in any case, that was years ago, 1926 wasn't it? As far as I understand it there is not one shred of truth in it. Spread by his enemies no doubt."

At this point Peter came into the room closely followed by Pen.

"Good." exclaimed Amelia. "Now we can have dinner. You, Peter, can tell us all about your adventures."

"Shall we wait for Henry?" Peter suggested. "He'll be down shortly."

Amelia looked pained. "*Down*? You mean your American friend is up *my* stairs?"

Only Pen managed a smile. "Don't worry Mummy we've set for six."

Amelia froze and managed to impersonate a slow worm caught in the gaze of dog, much to the discomfort of Peter and, despite years of marriage, Sir George.

Chapter 25

The next morning in her new home, an excited Mim woke Pamela. Not that Pam was bothered because she was equally excited. They bathed together splashing water at each other. With every squeal of childish laughter Pam's spirit soared.

Paul, Pam's son, who was leaving for residence at Brunel for the autumn term, had left an aching void in her life. Giving her bungalow over to Peter and Hal and moving into Greensleeves to be Nanny to Mim, was an answer to her prayers.

Mim was dressed in all new, hair brushed and shining, ribbons tied, face flushed, but then no more than Pamela's. They arrived early in the morning room for breakfast.

Sir George looked up from his paper, folded it and moved it to one side.

Good morning Nanny." Then turning to the little girl. "And a very good morning to you, young lady. Don't you look beautiful?"

Pamela, glowing with pleasure, noted just how easily Sir George had reverted to the use of Nanny after a break of many years.

Mim read the 'tone' of Sir George's rhetorical question. She recognised a compliment was being tended. In a manner worthy of one of much more advanced years she studied Sir George for a few seconds before deciding that it was genuine and promptly climbed up on to his knee.

Sir George glowed. He hugged her and kissed her hair.

He looked across at Pamela, saying, "A ready-made granddaughter, Nanny. How lucky is that?"

Mim in turn picked up on the old man's mood and snuggled against him. In the words of her beloved Papa Yo, 'she fitted'.

In less than twenty-four hours, Mim had captivated Sir George. His disappointment at not making the national newspapers was forgotten.

By the end of the first week Mim had enthralled all the household including Lady Amelia.

She missed her Mummy and Daddy specially her Mummy.

A week was a long, long time for a three-year-old to be without the security of a loving home. Settling in was not a choice, it came naturally.

"Now I am living in again, Sir George. I will get your breakfast from now on."

"Good heavens Nanny, I'm quite capable of tea and toast."

He looked up and smiled, the sort of natural smile that had been missing for so long.

"No need for you to be getting up at 6 a.m. to see to me. Oh, and ask Peter not to contact his father until I have a word," he said, looking at his watch.

"Good heavens I must go, or I'll miss my train."

Pamela smiled and decided that she very much preferred this version of Sir George even if he did preface nearly every comment by 'Good Heavens.'

Before Sir George reached the front door, Pam had poured milk on cornflakes, buttered a soft roll, wiped Mim's mouth and dress from the residue of Sir George's toast and marmalade and made a mental note to buy bibs at the first opportunity.

"More milk?" said Mim.

"Please," prompted Pamela.

"More milk, please," Mim responded.

Pamela beamed.

By the end of the week, Hal had been frozen out of Greensleeves by Lady Amelia.

Now sure that Mim was settled and happy, he accepted the situation and returned to his London flat commuting into St. Mary on Mondays and Tuesdays. Peter defied his father's demand to return up north at once, busying himself with setting up Mim's future and using this as an excuse to avoid any unpleasantness.

Chapter 26

Laurence Greenberg alighted at the bus stop on The Green at St. Mary. Tuesday was not a busy day, nevertheless he was not enthusiastic about being summoned to a Gentile household.

If they were looking for favours, they should travel to meet him.

The only reason he had accepted this request, was that it almost certainly concerned the refugee child he had read about in *The Bendesbury Bugle*.

A thoughtful and cautious man, he was slightly early for the appointment.

He sat in the wooden bus shelter to think over all the possibilities.

One was they might wish to pass the tiny refugee over for him to find a Jewish family with a mind to adoption. In normal circumstances, this would not have been a problem but a recent flood of refugees of all ages had put a massive strain on available friends willing to house, adopt and employ refugees. Having been involved with many such distressed and homeless families, he was stressed and short of answers. The local Jewish community was already failing to deal with the demand for accommodation, care and employment.

He looked at his watch and muttered to himself. "Why, oh why was this problem not left with the Dover authorities and the Jewish Council?"

He stood and dusted himself down with a force akin to chastisement, saying firmly, "Rabbi Greenberg, you were appointed for the hard bits, not the easy."

Striding purposefully across The Green he stopped halfway and looked up to the sky and prayed. "Lord, I would really appreciate a little help with this one."

Hal, Peter, Pen and Pamela waited in the front room of Greensleeves, Peter looking out of the window across the Green.

"Mummy has taken Mim to the playground. I haven't seen her this, this ..." Pen began then stopped seemingly stuck for a word.

"Human?" offered Pam.

"I was," replied Pen with mock firmness, "about to say happy."

"Aye, pet. The little lass has filled this house with sunshine, that she has."

"Enough, quit," said Hal. He turned to his friend. "Peter, *you* asked to see the rabbi. Why?"

"Isn't this a little risky, Peter?" Pen added.

"As I see it, "Peter replied, "one possible objection to our adoption of Mim could come from the Jewish community. If we take the initiative by asking to register for the Schule in Bendesbury that could quell any objections. Approach them first I mean."

Hal considered this before observing, "Pete, it's your call but please get it right. Let's all get it right.

When exactly is the rabbi due?"

"Any time, he'll probably arrive on the next bus from Bendesbury."

A little over one hour later Lady Amelia arrived back at Greensleeves with Mim. She poked her head around the door in a most unlike 'Lady Bridge-Thompson' manner.

"I saw the rabbi leave. How did it go?"

"It appears that we were pushing at an open door." Pen replied.

Peter was glowing at the success of his plan.

"Mim is booked to attend the Schule with effect from next September. Pamela has agreed to deal with all the necessary when the time comes."

"They will not oppose Mim's adoption?" Amelia asked. Surprisingly, she was anxious.

"Not as far as he is concerned. In fact, he practically proposed it. Remember it will not be just up to them, there are others involved. The next step is to inform my father about the plan to adopt including our earlier marriage," Peter replied.

"Ah!" The real Lady Amelia reappeared.

"Sir George and I think there is no need to speak to Richard or anyone else for that matter other than those necessary to complete a civil ceremony."

Peter was shocked. "You mean not tell father?"

"Well, do we need to?" Lady Amelia replied forcefully.

Peter could not believe it. "I think we do."

Lady Amelia ignored Peter's protest and continued her argument.

"Sir George and I think you should proceed as if you were single. You Peter, living up north. Of course, you could visit Penelope on the odd week. Ultimately we proceed with the church wedding as planned."

Peter turned to his fiancé for support.

"What do you think, Pen?"

Pen looking distinctly uncomfortable, avoided Peter's gaze and struggled to answer.

Before she could, Lady Amelia took the initiative.

"Penelope, answer Peter's question." She paused. "Well, girl, what *do* you think?"

Pen shrugged her shoulders. "I don't mind."

Peter was so shocked by her response he ceased to think.

Hal, sensing everyone's discomfort particularly Peter's, pitched in.

"Let it all hang out guys. Live the truth, trust in the outcome. If Peter and Pen have a civil ceremony, it is still commitment. Let them commit totally I say."

Lady Amelia bridled. "If Richard opposes this, Peter could live to rue the day."

She retorted, adding 'acidly'.

"With respect Mr. Steading, this being a family matter, I suggest that you withdraw both that remark and your personage from my home."

Embarrassment and the last vestige of an otherwise happy day vanished.

Pen ran from the room followed by Pam, taking Mim with her.

Hal stood looking at first at Lady Amelia then, remembering his manners, said quietly "Sorry if I have caused any offence."

Lady Amelia turned her head, avoiding all eye contact.

After a short pause and when it was clear she was not going to reply, Hal placed a conciliatory hand on Peter's shoulder and left.

Later that evening Peter, after walking aimlessly around the cricket ground, sat on the veranda of the pavilion still trying to think what he should do next.

Hal had the common sense to leave Peter to sort his head out in his own time and took off to the Drovers. He had an absolute trust in his judgement and natural dignity.

Pamela retired to the nursery and did not reappear at dinner.

Once Sir George returned from Whitehall, he and Lady Amelia locked themselves away in his study coming out later to eat alone.

Pen was missing. No one knew of her whereabouts. Peter sat on the cold bench, shivering, not just from the cold night air. The day which promised earlier to be a triumph, had been soured.

The night was mostly clear with just a few clouds, a bright moon and a jewelled sky.

Clouds obscured the moon for a little while, deepening his depression.

He knew he had to sort out the problem with Pen. He knew also that he owed an explanation to his father and not just about not returning to Sheffield immediately following his return from Germany.

Repeating shivers began to consume his body invading his ability to sort out his mind.

He longed for Hal's comforting hand on his shoulder, his presence, his support.

One cold spring night at Cambridge he had stood by the river in a similar state of shiver.

He was angry and disappointed at being passed over as cox for the annual boat race when he felt the familiar friendly hand on his shoulder.

'Coffee in my room.' Hal had suggested. It was such a moment he now longed for.

He felt wretched and low. He was on the verge of tears when the clouds cleared the moon.

The cricket ground was flooded by its silver light. This was so sudden and unexpected.

Peter couldn't help being surprised out of his despair.

Across the lucent green he could see his footprints in the dew. This triggered a memory of their first night back from Germany.

Hal and Peter returned to Pam's bungalow exhausted. They flopped into opposing armchairs to sit in silence in the dark. The room was lit only by this same moonlight.

They sat in silencefor what seemed an age. Peter had expected his friend to fall into bed.

He didn't. He sat quietly, so quietly that Peter thought that he was sleeping.

Eventually Hal's thoughts escaped in the softest of whispers. "Footsteps," he said.

Peter thought Hal was talking in his sleep. In case he wasn't, he replied equally softly.

"What was that, Hal?"

"Thank providence." Hal raised his voice slightly.

Peter, now even more puzzled asked, "Thank who?"

"If it hadn't been for my agreement to join you on this venture, I would have missed it."

"Missed what?"

"Our chance, old buddy, to place our footprints in the sands of time."

Peter, stunned by this remark, felt he needed to be alone with his thoughts and replied:

"You are getting fanciful old chap. Time for bed."

Looking now at his footprints in the dew, this discussion took on a new perspective.

The picture postcard scene calmed his troubled thoughts.

He looked across to the trees on the far side of the ground marvelling at how beautiful and different everything looked in the moonlight.

A small shadowy shape on the footbridge caused him to jump to his feet.

"Pen," he called. His voice sounded eerily through the gathering mist from the river.

Pen turned, they ran towards each the other in a desperate reaching out, meeting in the middle of the field and holding tight on to one another.

Feeling Pen trembling with cold, Peter removed his coat and draped it around her shoulders. Gradually her trembling subsided dissolving into the occasional shuddering sob.

They took comfort in one another just as they had when they were children.

"I'm sorry Peterkin, so sorry," she gasped. "So sorry I was a funk."

"It's all right Pen, I know what to do. I should not have asked you."

"Whatever happens, promise me this. If this all goes wrong or even if it doesn't, that you will only marry me out of love."

Peter, still holding her shoulders, stood back at arm's length speaking with emphasis.

"And no other reason."

"I promise." Pen nodded, relieved.

"Where have you been?"

"The footbridge over the ford."

"In the dark?" Peter was shocked. "All this time?"

"I have been walking and thinking. I was ashamed. I just wished to hide."

"You all right now?"

Pen just shook her head.

"Pen, it's fine, we're fine. You know what we need to do. We must not be deflected by anyone or anything. You O.K. with that?"

This time Pen nodded. "You are beginning to sound like Hal."

This remark caused Peter to pause and think. Then he decided to push the negative thoughts to one side and continue.

"Then let us seek him out. Let him know we're all right. He'll be in the Drovers. For sure he will not be dining with Her Ladyship."

Pen slipped her arm through his and laid her head on his shoulder.

"Yes, let's go find him."

Pamela Avery watched from the nursery window overlooking the Drovers Lane as they passed arm in arm towards The Green. She smiled with relief and drew the curtains on a dramatic day.

She checked once more that Mim was sleeping soundly, then retired to her bed.

Hal was sitting in the bar with a pint and a half-eaten ham sandwich when they entered.

He gave no hint of his inner turmoil when he looked up and asked, casually, "You guys O.K.?"

"We're fine."

'When and what are you going to tell your Pa?" Hal asked. He avoided the subject matter which had sparked the trouble.

"Tomorrow, I am returning up north with the whole truth and nothing but," Peter answered.

Hal smiled in relief. "This calls for a celebration drink. What will it be?"

The two answered in unison, "Beer."

"Not champagne?"

Pen smiled. "Too bloody pretentious by half."

It was Peter's turn to smile. He knew Pen was all right.

Chapter 27

Peter left the train at Sheffield Midland and caught the bus to the village. From there it was just a short walk to Hilltop Barn, his father's house on a hill overlooking a vast valley.

The drive leading up to it was very steep, passing a series of terraces up to a final patio at the front. Even in his recent memory, the drive seemed steeper than ever. He needed to stop halfway to catch his breath.

May Sheppard, the housekeeper, watched from a side door as he did so. She stood wiping her hands on a cotton cloth waiting to greet him.

"Thaht 'ohem then," she said as he arrived stating the obvious.

Her manner of speech and thick dialect disturbed his father, but not Peter. He liked May Sheppard and her down to earth unique way of noticing the truth in every event.

She had the ability to include more subject matter into every sentence whilst adding to the confusion by substituting pronouns in place of the proper and either omitting or truncating some words.

The whole scene he found both amusing, but somehow comforting.

Maybe this was because it infuriated his father.

"Yes, Mrs Sheppard, I'm home." Breathing deeply, Peter smiled but offered no indication of his wish to embrace her or at least to shake hands. May Sheppard turned away and looked down the long winding drive. "'Av telled mester, that drives too steep, by t'way, beds not aired."

"I'll manage." Peter placed his case in the hall.

"Thahs best come in then. I'm alreet coming up but one o days going down in t' winter, I'll tipple headlong. 'Ave you 'ad yer tea?" Her speech was as busy as her hands as she straightened ornaments and the antimacassars.

May was glad to see Peter. Richard Barnes left early each morning. More often, than not, he came home after she had left for her cottage. Alone all afternoon with two cats, any company would have done, but Peter. Well, Peter was special.

Peter had already noted the delicious smell of new baked bread.

"No, but a sandwich will do," he said, answering May's question.

"There's brisket on t'cellar 'ed yu can 'av that but tha can't 'av new loaf cos it's only just out, cooling on t'slab."

Peter smiled, at one-time, May's speech confused him. Now he was proud to add it to his portmanteau of languages.

"That will be fine Mrs Sheppard, thank you."

May busied herself making a sandwich, filling the kettle moving in and out of the cold room, which she called t'celler 'ead. All the while, she conducted a one-sided conversation.

"I must say thaht easier dealt wi than yer lass's mam and dad. 'Ad caterers in when they cum, not that I mind, (fancy goings on). 'av yer finished yer gallivanting then?"

May as usual crammed three subjects into the one sentence.

Peter amused, replied to the last question using a metaphor that she would easily understand by referring to the winner of the Grand National steeplechase.

"Mrs Sheppard, if Royal Mail had been through what I have over the last weeks, it would not have cleared a single fence. It would have been in the knacker's yard." Peter was referring to the winner of that year.

"Sid ad a tanner on that un, 'e said at thirty-five, lying pig, I bet 'e got 'undred at least."

"I think it probably was thirty-five, Mrs Sheppard." Peter took Sid's side.

"Nay lad 'e bet anti by at least a three week, e'd get a 'undred, ne'er fret. Give me just two bob. Git." May placed a tray containing a china pot of tea, crockery, a daintily cut sandwich and a pristine white double damask dinner napkin on the table. "Pickled cabbage or mustard?" She asked the question whilst placing both items on the table without expecting an answer or taking a breath.

"Aye, yer lasses mam and dad, all la-di-dah, swanking an' showing off their money."

Peter stripped away the Bridge-Thompson façade.

"I think you will find, Mrs Sheppard, that they are broke. They have no money."

May looked aghast and was silent for a second.

"Dunt mek me laff; stoney-*stoney*," she repeated, "they dunt know t'meanin."

All this time she was walking in and out of the kitchen putting on her coat and hat.

"Am off, Sid'll be wanting 'is tea. *Stoney*, lerr'em try livin on thirty bob for a month or two and if them cats cum wowin' tak no notice, they've 'ad their teas. 'Tilt morning then, get your own brekky. Yu dad only 'as mi fo't 'alf day now?"

Peter was sorry she was going. "Good night, Mrs Sheppard."

May stopped halfway to the door.

"Oh, afore I forgets, yon natty tins empty. Mester owes mi fourpence for t' shop."

May looked a little embarrassed to mention this to Peter. She hadn't seen Richard Barnes since the weekend and four pence was badly needed if she was to last the week out.

Peter looked to his pocket change.

"Here's sixpence Mrs Sheppard, please take that."

He had the change but wanted to show his appreciation for the warm welcome. He liked May and knew that her existence was truly, hand to mouth, as was usual in these parts.

May however would have none of it.

"Nay lad let's be reet. I've getten tuppence." Looking in her purse she counted out three half pennies and two farthings.

"Do yer mind farthins? Peter lad. They waint tek 'em 'ere but I 'ear tell they still teks 'em in London, praps thah could change 'em when thaht theer next?"

"I'm sure I can Mrs Sheppard."

"Reet then I'm off. Sid 'll be feer clemmed."

May Sheppard's use of obscure dialect no longer bothered Peter. This was accepted as just another language to absorb.

Peter watched her move quickly down the drive towards the village.

Without May Sheppard's busy presence, the house seemed suddenly cold and empty.

Sat in the morning room he watched the sun disappear behind the hills to the west catching the edges of the distant hills in a golden rim. This faded quickly with the last vestige of natural light. Peter was shocked just how gloomy the house became.

This was his father's house, he never thought of it as home. He had loved the garden and the friendly gardener, now replaced by the new fashionable once a week travelling landscape artist.

The only regular daytime presence was May Sheppard. Richard stayed overnight, leaving early and coming home late. Even on a Sunday he left for 'who knows where', after lunch returning only to sleep, often in a drunken stupor.

Peter now felt liberated. He had been unsure of himself and still thinking how to deal with his father when he first arrived.

He was bolstered by May Sheppard and her simple outlook on everything.

Always sure of herself, she appeared to Peter, to know exactly what she needed to do in all situations.

Thrusting his hand into his pocket he brought out a handful of change.

Reaching up, he switched on the standard lamp and looked through to pick out the two farthings. "Nay lad let's be reet." He murmured. Placing the farthings into a small pocket in his wallet he resolved to keep them safe. If he ever lost faith in human nature, he resolved to take them out and remember May Sheppard. In which case, he would never be destitute, financially or morally.

It was just after nine o'clock when Richard Barnes arrived home.

Seeing the light on in the front of the house he didn't bother to garage the car. Parking it outside on the drive, he walked into the hall.

Taking off his hat and coat he noted Peter's suitcase. He shouted through to the morning room.

"You took your time, lad."

Peter took a deep breath preparing to fight.

He needn't have bothered because his father continued talking as he came through the door.

"I knew it was you home as soon as I saw the light. Good trip, lad? You did a first-class job. You both did. Rees James was delighted."

For a moment Peter was lost for words. He had not anticipated any of this. He gathered his thoughts whilst his father poured himself a whisky.

"We were duped, father. We were being used."

Richard Barnes downed the whisky in one. "Used? What do you mean?"

"We were stooges."

Richard Barnes paced the room, waving an arm airily.

"Whatever, it worked. Got exactly what we wanted."

"And that was?"

Richard stopped pacing and took a moment to look at his son. There is something different about him, he thought. Then he continued to pace and talk.

"Thanks to you two we managed to home in on our target."

"And the target was? I fail to understand this homed in. What was that about?" Peter asked sitting forward, his chin jutting.

Richard paused and thought. 'There *is* something different.' Then he resumed pacing as he continued. "You managed to flush out the chap we are interested in, a fellow by the name of Braun I believe. Anyway, Rhys James's chaps over there have moved sharpish and ..."

Here, Richard stopped pacing and faced Peter with a smile of triumph.

"I'm reliably told that they have located prototype drawings of advanced engineering projects and son, get this."

He stopped and leaning forward, placed his hands on the arms of the chair trapping Peter.

His face was so close Peter could smell the whisky on his breath.

Speaking very slowly and with dramatic emphasis, Richard whispered.

"Not a word of this to anyone son, *anyone* ..." He paused. "A copy of the Din specification for a prototype jet engine steel."

Peter tried to turn his face away to avoid his father's breath. Richard followed Peter's head continuing in his face. "Jet engine steel. Savvy!"

"So, what's different, father?"

To Peter's relief, Richard stood up and clapped his hands.

Peter thought 'He's had far too much to drink.'

"The Holy Grail, you know the high temperature, high stress material your friend Henry is working on and we are in on the ground floor. This could put us up there with the big boys in Sheffield," Richard replied. He was swaying backwards and spreading his arms.

Peter gulped. This was something else he had to cover: Hal's defection.

Then he thought again. 'I've got enough on my plate, leave that for Hal to cover.'

He decided just to tell his father of the changed wedding plans.

Richard, however, was in full flow. "That's why you are needed back here.

As soon as we get our hands on the spec. I need you to translate, tappy lappy."

'He *is* drunk,' thought Peter before blurting out, "Pen and I are getting married next January, registry office wedding."

He was going to add that the church wedding would take place later, as arranged and leaving the question of Mim's adoption until later.

Richard appeared not to hear. He continued as if he hadn't heard.

"Then there is as I understand, a furnace drawing to translate. It will be a busy time."

Richard carried on as if he was conducting a works meeting.

"We can talk terms. A new contract if you wish. Secrecy is the key."

Peter thought. 'I am your son, not some stranger. I have just told you of a major change of my wedding plans.'

Peter's news finally registered with his father who stopped pacing momentarily, looked at his son and winked.

"Don't worry about it, son. That sort of thing happens."

He stopped pacing appearing to think. Then he continued.

"Now, with regard to the next vital months."

Peter's jaw dropped. He just couldn't bear to hear any more. Angrily he announced, "There's brisket on t' celler 'ed, if thaht 'ungry. Oh, and t' natty tins empty."

Richard stopped at the sideboard and poured himself a drink, believing he was toasting a future grandchild.

"This calls for a double celebration," he said pausing and looking at Peter. "Whisky and splash?"

Peter was confused as to how to handle his father. Not knowing whether he was more intoxicated with the alcohol or recent events. Peter decided to play a 'holding tack'.

"No thanks, don't you think that you should eat something or have a coffee instead?"

Again, Richard appeared to ignore his son.

"What that you were mumbling just now?" Richard asked sitting down in the chair opposite and looking at Peter.

Peter had to guess the subject matter, thinking at the same time, how similar it seemed to be interpreting both May's and his father's language.

This version of Richard he had not met before. Drunk or not, he much preferred this 'version'.

"The petty cash tin in the kitchen cupboard is empty. May Sheppard had to spend four pence from her own money to pay for the shopping."

Richard didn't answer. Fumbling in his pocket for his wallet he took out a ten- shilling note.

"Put that in the tin for me please, son."

Peter was close to tears. He was getting glimpses of the father he'd always wished for.

"You trust May not to rip you off?"

"She was the first one ever not to. Until I got May, I didn't realise ten shillings could last over a week." He took a drink from his glass. "Here's to May Sheppard."

"How did you find her? She really is a diamond."

"At the cemetery in Sheffield she just buried her third little one." He slurred. "Diphtheria, polio, you name it." He took another drink. "Husband laid off from a coal mine somewhere in South Yorkshire, lungs shot, pnuemo' something. Sad story." Richard drained his glass. "What say have another?"

"You just hired her. With no checks?"

Richard was up pouring another drink. He returned and sat down with a sigh.

He didn't answer Peter's question but flopped back in his chair legs splayed.

Peter was now certain he was drunk. This was more like the father he always wished for but why, oh why, did he need to be inebriated.

"Why do you keep this house on? It's far too big for you and you spend so little time here."

Richard took another drink, looked at the glass, smiled then drained it.

"It's been a good day son, a really good day."

Peter thought his question was to remain unanswered. Richard spent some while staring into his whisky. Peter thought to himself 'there are never any sensible answers ever found in a glass.'

Richard jerked into action. Placing the glass on the table with a sharp rap, the drink slurring his speech, he answered Peter.

"Investment, my son. We own this and all the land down to the river at this side, including several properties, the Post Office, half a dozen stone cottages alongside, backing on to the river.

Think on my son, all this will be yours someday."

This was news to Peter, and he thought. 'I wonder if he would have told me this sober.'

Richard leaned back in the chair and gave a huge sigh.

"This *is* good, son. What say when you and Pen are wed, you settle, live up here with the little one. After all, this is meant to be a family home?"

Peter was shocked and took a few moments to gather his wits and courage.

"Sorry, dad." He began, surprising himself with the use of *dad* which would normally be as unfamiliar as the father figure presented to him this evening. "There *is* no baby on the way."

This revelation provoked no reaction. Richard Barnes was fast asleep.

Chapter 28

Richard Barnes's drunken enthusiasm proved so far misplaced that it was February the following year before he had access to a single drawing. This drawing and specification was for a specialised electric furnace. Hopes of having exclusive access to the jet alloy specification had been blocked by governmental edict.

One dark snowy morning Richard sat with his chief engineer, the works manager and Peter perusing the detailed drawing and specification alongside translations from the German.

His face was darker even than the weather.

"I refuse to accept this defeatism." He thumped the desk in frustration.

Walter Pegg, the chief engineer, looked to Peter for support.

"Mr. Peter, are you certain this demands a re-melt of Bloom stage steel in a totally sealed furnace?

Remelting in a vacuum?" Walter's tone was indicative of the scepticism he felt.

"Walter, this is written in technical language, outside my knowledge agreed. I assure you that is the case."

Walter then turned to Richard.

"In which case, sir, this is way outside our capabilities. We would need new departments of development engineers and research metallurgists, etc., This is going to be a problem for the big boys, let alone us. There is no such capability in this country or anywhere else to my knowledge."

Richard leaned forward across the table and moved his face inches away from Walter's.

"Then sort it or find another job," he said menacingly.

Peter who had so far avoided challenging his father felt compelled to support Walter.

"Mr. Pegg is right, sir. It *is* a massive undertaking. It will cost a fortune even if we *could* do it."

Richard banged the desk hissing.

"Government money laddie, *Government money*! This is a green field site, plenty of room. Away from the city and air attacks. Ask the big boys if *they can* match that."

It was Peter's turn for Richard's 'in the face' treatment.

"Sort it together or you can both look for another job."

With this parting shot Richard stormed out slamming the door.

They looked towards the door where he had left. Walter smiled.

"Don't you worry Mr. Peter he will see sense, or I *will* be looking for another job. He is the proverbial monkey with his hand in the sweetie jar. However, there is sense in looking for something to gain in this."

He read through Peter's translation.

"You are sure there has to be a first melt in a separate but exclusive regular furnace?"

"That is certainly the case."

"It is unusual, but I have heard of it," the works manager commented. "Maybe we could just do that."

Marian, Richards secretary, entered. "Sorry to interrupt Mr. Peter, your wife is on the 'phone. She says it is urgent." Peter jumped to his feet. "Excuse me please, gentlemen, I must take this."

Peter grasped the telephone as others might grab a lifeline.

"Hi Pen, is there a problem?"

"Nothing desperate just to check if you can make London tomorrow. Did I call at an awkward moment?"

"Fortuitous more like, it got me out of an awkward situation." Peter laughed. "I don't think I am cut out for this commercial life Pen."

"Your father giving you problems?"

"Who else! I will be glad to get away."

"Good, because we are needed at Mim's solicitors off the Euston Road tomorrow. Can you make it for 11 a.m.?"

"Easily, the Master Cutler gets into St Pancras station at 10.30 which should be perfect. Will Mim be there?"

“Not necessary, just you and I, the solicitors, a representative of the Jewish adoption society and a Swiss lawyer I understand. Oh! and Hal wants to come as well, is that all right darling?”

“Of course, see you tomorrow then Pen, ‘bye.”

“’Bye, darling. See you tomorrow. I love you.” Pen waited for a response which did not arrive.

Peter replaced the receiver feeling surprisingly uncomfortable, apparently incapable of returning his newlywed wife’s affection.

Marian returned to the office. “All finished Mr. Peter?”

“Yes, thank you Marian, I will be away in London tomorrow on urgent business.

Tell my father, please.”

“I would sooner you did so Mr. Peter. He is not in the best of moods. He’ll be furious and doubtless take it out on me.”

Peter hesitated for a moment before replying.

“Sorry, Marian, comes with the job I’m afraid,” then added almost speaking to himself:

“We’re best apart, at the moment.”

Marian thought to herself, ‘at least he’s got the I’m afraid bit right.’

Chapter 29

Peter left a smoky and cold Sheffield before first light to arrive to a bright sunny London February morning which seemed worlds away from the one he'd just left.

The day got better from the moment he stepped from the train.

It turned out to be full of surprises. The first was finding out that the representative of the Jewish adoption society waiting for them at Mim's solicitors was Dorothy Price.

He was able to introduce Dorothy to Pen while in the solicitors' waiting room.

Pen was delighted to meet this lady she had heard so much about.

Everything was well organised the formalities took little time. The Swiss lawyer was content to rubber stamp all decisions.

Shortly after noon, Peter and Pen were legally the nominated guardians of Miriam Kessler, all witnessed and approved by the Swiss lawyer and Dorothy Price.

Daniel Joubert Snr. shook both their hands.

"Congratulations that is ***it*** as far as we are concerned. Your marriage lines will be returned when all has been ratified by all authorities along with necessary certificates of citizenship, etc. This may take time, the current workload being enormous. However, it is just the formalities. You need have no worries."

"Herr Barnes, I believe you have the papers for the Kessler house in Munich, please to send them to Herr Joubert," The Swiss lawyer asked then bowed and shook hands.

"And the rest of the estate?" asked Peter.

"That remains in our control, you are to be awarded 18 pounds Sterling each calendar month for Frauline Kessler's keeping. If you require for anything other, we consider."

Peter could hardly believe this was so easy. "And the jewels?" he asked.

The lawyers looked at each other. It was Daniel Joubert Snr who replied.

"Jewels? There are jewels? Where are these?"

"In a strong box at the bank."

The lawyers looked at each other. Daniel Joubert Snr asked the Swiss lawyer, "Are they listed?"

"No, we have no knowledge," he replied. "Please excuse us." The two lawyers left the room to return minutes later. The Swiss lawyer smiled as he addressed Peter.

"Herr Barnes, please to list the items and have them valued for Herr Joubert. Also, please to continue to care for them. Is that a problem Herr Barnes?"

Peter astonished, agreed. The lawyers then excused themselves with a very polite thank you and good wishes.

A confused and delighted couple were shown from the offices.

Dorothy followed a few minutes later to find Peter and Pen outside on the street.

They had waited for Dorothy. As soon as she came out, Peter shook her hand warmly.

"Thank you, the formalities went so smoothly. We were just saying that you must have eased the way for us," Peter said, hoping to be congratulated in return.

Dorothy failed to respond to Peter's disappointment.

All three stood thinking what to say next.

Dorothy's body language worried Pen, who sensed there was something wrong.

Pen's first concern was that all was not as simple with Mim's adoption as they thought.

That there must be a 'catch'.

Pen took Dorothy's arm. "I am so pleased to meet you at last. I've heard so much about you from Peter and Hal. We'd best tell Hal the good news. He's waiting in the pub over the street. After that we can perhaps get to know one another."

They walked over on to the Euston Road, Pen seeking to confirm that her belief that all was not well with the adoption was correct. Dorothy's answers to questions were monosyllabic and vague.

She appeared aloof.

Pen was certain that this was not the 'real woman'.

Peter, unaware, was euphoric. Mim's adoption which began as an impossible scheme thought up on a whim and the boredom of a long train journey to encourage and impress his friend, had somehow become a reality. How? He had not the first idea. It had lifted him temporally out of the confusions of a life in which he struggled to find a place. Glowing with success, he could not wait to tell Hal. When they arrived at the pub, Hal leapt to his feet spilling his beer as he did so.

"Well?"

Peter raised his arms in triumph. "We did it." In his inner thoughts this translated as, 'I did it'.

Pen following on brought him swiftly to earth, adding, "with Dorothy's help."

Seeing Dorothy, Hal went to embrace her.

Dorothy almost turned away.

Hal picked up on this immediately. "What's this Dorothy? Something wrong?"

Dorothy staggered. Pen shot quickly forward and ushered Dorothy to a seat.

"Peter, get her a drink."

The haste of Pen's intervention was lost on Peter who stood transfixed.

Pen looked around at him. "Water preferably, then perhaps she can tell us what is troubling her."

"I've got it." Hal said taking over, returning with a glass of water.

"Another beer for me Pete and whatever for you and Pen," Hal said looking at his friend and nodding towards the bar.

Dorothy sat with her face in her hands, Pen's arm around her shoulders.

"What's the problem, Dorothy? How can we help?"

Dorothy looked up at last. It was to Pen she spoke, a young woman she had only just met.

"Tuss is probably dead." Dorothy's whisper was barely audible.

This whisper still thundered in the ears of all.

The silence which followed the noise of the traffic on the Euston Road seemed to amplify.

A taxi's honking horn seemed to Peter to be mocking his early euphoria.

Hal was the first to gather his wits. "Probably! How do you mean, probably?"

"I don't know. I just don't know," she whispered, her face back behind her hands.

Pen turned to face her kneeling to do so and took her hands gently away from her face.

"Do you wish to tell us about it?" she said gently.

Not getting an answer, Pen persisted.

"If it would help, you could come to St. Mary with us. That way you could meet Mim and Pamela."

Still not getting a response, Pen continued. "Then you could tell us, or not, in your own good time."

At this point Dorothy nodded and looked at Pen. "Could I?"

"Of course. Can we get you something stronger, a brandy?" Pen suggested.

Hal and Peter until that moment were still in shock.

Together they hurried to the bar appearing to compete with Hal finally returning with the brandy.

Meanwhile, Dorothy who had said little way to explain her short ambiguous announcement that her friend was probably dead, produced from her handbag a newspaper cutting which she handed to Pen. After reading it Pen passed it to Peter and Hal.

It was headed.

FERRY MYSTERY

The inquiry into the missing passenger from the cross-channel ferry has recorded an open verdict. This investigation is about the whereabouts of Miss Margaret Firth, formerly of London and currently living in Paris. A regular passenger well known to the crew.

She was last seen on the night of 9th. Oct 1937 aboard the last sailing to Calais. Miss Firth did not disembark at the port.

Her luggage and personal effects were found abandoned in the main saloon.

Enquiries on both sides of the channel proved fruitless.

In the absence of any conclusive evidence the Coroner, Justice Poppleton said he had no other option other than to record an open verdict. He did however make an appeal for anyone who has any pertinent information to contact their local police station.

Dorothy controlled her emotion and began to explain. She spoke at length, between shuddering breaths, quietly, so that they all needed to lean forward to hear.

"Andre contacted me when Tuss didn't turn up in Paris. I went to the police in Dover to discover that the ferry company had already been in contact, believing they had lost a passenger.

Andre made enquiries in Paris and Calais, but she had just disappeared.

The police have ruled out foul play. The Coroner agreed. He also said there seems to be only three possibilities, a tragic accident, suicide or a deliberate attempt to opt out of her present life."

She accepted Pen's offered handkerchief and blew her nose.

"I'm sorry but I couldn't think how to tell you. I have had no one to talk to. No one else who would understand."

"You *are* thinking what we are thinking though?" Hal put the question for everyone.

Dorothy nodded. "The police think so."

All four sat in silence until over a minute later Peter whispered, "Why?"

No one else spoke.

After a short pause, Peter continued.

"There was something that Andre said. He told me that she had killed a child."

"How was that? That is ridiculous." Hal retorted.

The ladies were silent. "I don't know the detail," Peter hastened to add. "From what Andre told me my guess is that she may have had an abortion and regretted it. Couldn't forgive herself."

Dorothy answered, this time a little more strongly.

"Some chap she was mixed up with ditched her when he found out that she was pregnant.

She took to the bottle, got drunk one night, fell down the steps and lost the baby.

We tried to keep a watch on her because I feared something of this sort could happen.

She *would* say that she killed the child. That was never true. It was an accident."

Dorothy began to cry, softly at first, then uncontrollably.

"Now there's no one to call me Dot, no friend to care for, talk to." She gasped between sobs.

"Best we return to St. Mary somewhere less public then," Hal suggested. "That O.K. with everyone?" "Then you can meet Pamela maybe the rabbi. Help sort Mim's future," said Pen taking out a fresh handkerchief and handing it to Dorothy.

"You will like Pamela she's a lovely lady about your age."

Dorothy dried her eyes and blew her nose. "Sorry and thank you."

Pen and Hal helped Dorothy to her feet. As they did a small white frilly handkerchief fell from her lap on to the floor under the table.

Peter taking Pen's hand explained. "I'm needed back at the works, returning to Sheffield. There is much still to sort out, sorry."

Pen who had been expecting Peter to return with them was a little surprised but nonetheless nodded. Concerned about Dorothy, she joined her and Hal out on the street.

She linked arms with Dorothy, stopped briefly, looked back over her shoulder and shouted to Peter against the noise of the traffic. "See you at the weekend then."

That was it. Peter was left standing on the Euston Road with the crowds jostling around him.

Chapter 30

With so much on his mind Peter was surprised how quickly the train arrived in Sheffield.

He had been sitting with the brightest of the two farthings in his hand. It had a pert little bird on the reverse side which attracted him. It was busy like May Sheppard. Of small value, but bright and optimistic. He longed to be able to talk to May.

Her adherence to the truth he longed for. That integrity, that was 'foreign' to his father or Sir George and Lady Amelia for all their so-called positions.

Peter found it fascinating that May appeared to revel in the difficulties of her life, even thrive despite her struggles. 'I dunt mind uphill but down, I'll likely tipple headlong' could be her motto. He lost count of how many times he had gone over the day's events without being able to clear his mind. The violent contrasts served to confuse.

He had been musing what May would say, if he were to ask her. There being so many unanswered questions, he seemed incapable of clear thought. Consequently, he almost missed the station.

He only recognised that his journey was over at the last minute and tumbled out of the train in confusion.

Dusk was falling, and the snow underfoot was already beginning to crunch as it froze.

He needed to take care that he didn't slip.

His flat was only a short distance away in the city centre, uphill from the station.

It was difficult walking. The day's footprint slush was freezing. Yet this helped his demeanour, taking his mind of his problems. He stopped to buy fish and chips on the way only to end up throwing most of them away.

Arrival at his flat did not bring any relief. It was cold and unwelcoming.

He switched on the electric fire and sat down still wearing his overcoat and shivered.

Losing track of time, he turned the day's events over and over in his mind.

Suddenly he was jolted out of his thoughts by the telephone.

It was Marian calling, Richard's secretary.

"Thank goodness I've found you Mr. Peter. Mrs Barnes said you should be back tonight."

"You rang Pen. Is there a problem, Marian?"

"Your father is incandescent, threatening to sack Walter and you. He's had me type memos to you both. They are vitriolic, threatening to fire you both. I don't want that to happen."

"Marian, I don't know how much you are aware of current developments, but can I say this, it is an empty threat. We know too much." Peter assured her (and himself).

"Are you sure Mr. Peter?"

"I'm sure and Marian thank you for your concern and for ringing Pen. I'll reimburse you with the cost of the call tomorrow."

"There's no need to do that Mr. Peter, I rang from work. Mr. Richard asked me to phone the account number to Mrs Avery, so I spoke to Mrs Barnes at the same time."

Peter didn't reply. Marian puzzled, asked. "Are you still there Mr. Peter?"

"What account is this, Marian?"

"For Master Paul, now he's at Brunel. You know, for his monthly allowance."

Again, the line went silent. Marian added, "I thought you'd best be knowing about the memo, Mr. Peter."

It was a very thoughtful Peter who answered. "Thank you, Marian. Good night."

Peter stood stock still in the dim light for a full minute. Blood flowed into his cheeks. He removed his overcoat, allowing it to drop to the floor and placed both hands over his face.

"You fool, you idiot," he muttered.

Chapter 31

After a restless night, Peter rose early and caught the tram to the terminus changing on to the Red Country bus to travel three stops up the valley to the works.

His presence caused amusement and interest from workers on the morning shift.

Entering the deserted office, he packed away all his personal effects then sat at his desk waiting for his father's arrival. His father often arrived before eight. He would have to pass Peter's office door on his way.

Peter sat tapping the unopened envelope marked 'Confidential' on the desk top.

He had no intention to open it, to play to his father's agenda. He knew he had unfinished business not only here but also in St. Mary. What to do after that he had no idea.

Never being financially independent, this would be his first hurdle whatever happened.

He was scared, so scared of that which he intended to do. He steeled himself against the fears and intermittent trembling of his limbs.

He muttered over and over. "Nay lad let's get it reet."

Richard Barnes drove into his parking spot behind the office block and smiled in triumph.

Looking up and seeing the light in Peter's office he thought. 'Peters in early.'

He climbed the stairs with unusual vigour and threw back the door of Peter's office.

Standing framed in the doorway, he almost shouted.

"Seen sense at last, laddie?"

Peter, holding the unopened memo between his index finger and thumb, skimmed it towards Richard. It landed at his feet.

"Yes father, I've seen sense at last!"

Peter managed to control his voice, giving no hint of his anger. Richard looked down at the envelope realising it was unopened.

He looked up at his son's silhouette against the pale February sky.

His mouth opened but no words issued.

It was Peter who spoke.

"I'm off, father. Don't try looking for me under the butterfly bush. I won't be there."

Picking up his belongings, he walked to the door.

"Excuse me please, father, I have a train to catch." Peter pushed forcibly by him.

"Where are you going?"

Richard found his voice at last. Reaching out to try and stop him, he added, "Son."

The last word was uttered as a desperate plea.

"To see the mother of the brother you didn't bother to tell me about."

Peter didn't look around, if he had it might have broken his resolve.

Out in the works yard he stood trembling, relieved that it was all over. He was now left with deciding how to return to St. Mary, not having thought beyond the moment.

He began to walk aimlessly towards the works entrance past the melting shop offices intending to cross the road towards the bus stop.

Walter Pegg was at that moment looking out of the office window for inspiration, Richard's memo on his desk. He saw Peter and ran out to intercept him.

"Mr. Peter, where are you going?"

Walter noted that Peter was walking out of the gate with his personal belongings and thought that he had been dismissed.

"He's never gone and sacked you, has he?"

"No, Walter, I have just quit. I won't be coming back," Peter replied as he tried to walk on.

A shocked Walter stood in front of him and spread his arms.

"Peter, be sensible you don't need to do that. Think about it, please. We'll talk about it together."

Peter just wanted away. He shook Walter's hand.

"Thanks, Walter but I am being sensible. I have thought about it. I don't belong here. I need to get back to Sheffield. I have a train to catch."

Walter realised that Peter was serious.

Accepting this, he said,"The morning bus has long gone Peter, lad. It will be over an hour 'till the next. Wait here, I'll get the works van and run you down the valley to the tram terminus."

Walter hoped to at least find out what had happened, if not, to try change Peter's mind.

Later that morning Richard Barnes sat with his head in his hands.

"What now Pegg?"

Walter, delighted to be consulted and not shouted at, took a big breath. He too had been thinking hard and had a fair bit to say.

"First, sir, we were never going to get the whole project. The fact is that the Government have only sent us the initial furnace specification. That says it all. We need to show them we can do that first. Then, maybe, we could be given the next step."

Richard nodded. "Without Peter to translate, what do we do to keep our secrets? The Department doesn't allow outside translations on these drawings, being top secret. We are responsible and answerable."

"Ask a rabbi," Walter answered.

Richard looked up sharply and resumed his normal belligerent posture.

"Why is everyone talking in riddles? First, Peter, now you. What the hell does 'ask a rabbi' mean?"

"Mr. Peter's suggestion, sir. I asked the same question this morning. He said the country is swarming with refugees looking for work. There must be a metallurgist or engineer out there who is a German- speaking national. A far better bet than a university graduate with no technical knowledge. If we ask a rabbi, any rabbi, they will find that man for us. It's how they work. Then we can have them checked by security."

"Peter said that?"

Richard thought for a moment before continuing.

"By God, Walter he is right, get on with it right away."

Richard Barnes now could see a way forward. He stood up, slapped the table and walked to the door with a new spring in his step. He stopped and asked Walter, "You don't know where Peter is, do you? I need to talk to him."

Walter knew that, although Richard Barnes had not commented, he had accepted his premise on how to proceed. To be addressed by his Christian name underlined this. Sympathetically, he replied, "No, sorry, sir. He just said that he had a train to catch."

Chapter 32

Returning to his city flat, Peter cleared out and packed his few belongings. He left a note and money for his landlord then hurried to catch the earliest possible train to London.

Meanwhile in St. Mary, Pamela Avery busied herself making scones and trying to control her nerves. The day, which had begun happily with her new-found friend Dorothy, had crashed.

They had been late going to bed the previous night.

Hitting it off immediately when they first met, they soon both knew they were destined to be more than casual acquaintances. They couldn't wait to carry on in the same vein but later that morning a telephone call from Richard Barnes had ruined everything.

Dorothy, understanding and considerate, used the excuse that she needed to see Rabbi Greenberg in Bendesbury. It gave space and time for her new friend to deal with a difficult moment.

Pamela had spent the early part of the afternoon looking anxiously for the arrival of each bus on the hour. She breathed a temporary sigh of relief when Peter didn't arrive. She decided that she needed to occupy her mind: Bake some scones to help calm her nerves. She was up to her elbows in scone mix when Peter did arrive, unannounced, in the kitchen.

Pamela sensed his presence. She did not look up and took a series of deep breaths before speaking. Peter, she knew, would not start a shouting match. That was not his style.

What Pamela feared most was that he would retreat into a sulk lasting for years.

Only in the very recent times had she been able to resume a semblance of their former relationship. She also knew that she would have to take the initiative.

Pam opened with, "You took long enough to work it out Peterkin, too long. I was surprised."

"Why didn't you tell me Pamela? Please I need to know."

Peter's questioning was studied with no hint of emotion.

Pamela, surprised at the calm manner of the question, wiped her hands and sat down.

"Peter, my love, I wanted to, but I wasn't allowed."

She motioned him to sit, which he did.

His reply was again calm and measured. "Why?"

"Think about it, pet. Who do you think funds me, my home and Paul's education?

I am here on a grace and favour ticket under the guise as housekeeper for Sir George whose excesses are funded by your father in exchange for favours and business access to Whitehall."

"So, we all dance to his tune?" Peter nodded, adding, "as normal."

"The hand which holds the purse strings rules the world," Pamela sighed then added:

"also, I was afraid."

"No more than me Pamela, you were ***all*** I had. I was packed off to boarding school. I was barely seven."

Peter's pain now showed in his eyes as he pleaded.

"I lost you and no one told me why."

This hurt Pamela so much that she could barely speak.

"I'm sorry, so sorry Peter. I was twenty years old, single and pregnant. No one wanted me either, not even my father who warned me not to return to Tyneside."

She paused and gathered herself.

"I was drowning in a sea of accusations and finger pointing. Your father was my only lifeline."

She wiped her face with the cloth.

"I didn't know what else to do."

"You could have married him. Did you think of that? That way we both could have stayed."

"Your father didn't want me. He just pushed me out of the way and out of his mind. He only began to visit after Paul was born."

The sudden look on Peter's face caused Pamela to catch her breath. She hastily added:

"We were told to keep quiet or he would have pulled the plug on everything."

Peter was quiet for a long, long time. Pamela willed him to speak.

He had done a whole lot of thinking since leaving Sheffield, including why he had not realised that Paul was his half-brother.

This was partly because he could not imagine a liaison between his father and Pamela.

This was partly because of his hurt, being cut away from Pamela without explanation and his jealousy of the new baby who had taken his place.

Being sent to St. Mary during the school holidays was no compensation. This was just his father shunting him out of the way.

The only good thing was finding Pen who was also lonely and in need of a friend.

After the long silence he asked, "Did Pen know?"

Pamela shrugged but didn't answer.

Peter looked around. "Where is she? Out with Mim?"

Pamela flushed. She had dreaded the second question, knowing that nothing but the truth would be acceptable.

Mim had run up into the nursery that morning full of excitement shouting.

'Nanny Pammy, I go to zoo mit Papa Yo und Mama Pen.'

Pam's ability to handle Mim was limited despite her experience. Once outside the nursery, Mim was 'Queen of the castle'. Defying Pamela's efforts to keep control, she knew the zoo trip was a bad idea given the delicate situation between Peter and Pen.

Knowing this question would probably be asked had not helped her peace of mind.

When Peter did ask, not even the Angels knew what went through her mind as she forced the answer through her lips, causing her to stammer.

"I, I am sorry Peter. Hal and Pen have taken Mim to the zoo."

Peter didn't move. He just sat slowly nodding.

This was another question which had occupied his thoughts on the journey here.

His reaction frightened Pamela, more so than if he had thrown a tantrum.

She began shaping the scones trying at the same time to think what to say.

This silence continued until in desperation she lined them up on the baking tray. She stood looking at Peter who still had not spoken or moved.

"I'd best get these in the oven, or they will not be ready pet, sorry."

She said this with as much confidence as she could muster. She left Peter sitting at the table.

When she returned, he had gone.

Pamela could feel the cold February air flowing through the house.

She walked through to the front and looked down The Green. Peter was nowhere in sight.

Closing the door, she walked slowly back to the kitchen, sat down at the table and the tears flowed.

Chapter 33

Peter sat in the shadows in the corner of the bus shelter and looked up the Fernborough Road trembling with nerves.

He would be waiting for the bus for a long time, if that why he was there. The one he came on had already returned to Fernborough.

Turning around it would carry on to Bendesbury to come back again before he could get away.

One thing for sure was he now believed that he didn't belong here in St. Mary, any more than he belonged in Sheffield. That is if he ever belonged anywhere; but where *could* he go?

His only thought was to head for the railway station.

One thing Peter hadn't thought about was money. After leaving some in the flat for the landlord, his cleaner, paying for his rail fares for two journeys to London, one a return, then on to Fernborough, funds were running out. He had changed his last note. Now he was leaving Pen and all security with very little money and no plan.

He had resolved in the last hours not to hide from the truth. The last time he had chickened out was on the cricket field when he had placed the responsibility on Pen.

He knew then that Hal and she belonged together.

The question in his mind was, must he now leave to give them a chance of happiness?

He took the farthing coin out of his wallet and turned it over in his hands. His heart said, 'please I want to stay with my friends', his head said, 'if you do it could all tipple downhill.'

Problem was he had nowhere left to go. He had little money. His luggage was still back in the hall at Greensleeves.

the farthing on his thumb with the bright little bird uppermost and flipped it.

Failing to catch it cleanly, it landed on the ground, in the dark corner. He was feeling around for it when the bus from Fernborough appeared, the headlights lighting up the shelter.

Peter shot back into the corner shadows. Just the three alighted as he expected.

They began to walk across The Green, Hal and Pen on each side of the tiny girl holding her hand.

He watched the shadowy figures move out of sight into the gloom until they disappeared into the dark background. Peter left the shelter and stood looking after them long after the sound of them died away. Returning to the shelter he searched for and found the coin but could not see which way it had landed. This no longer mattered, if it ever did. He carefully held its position until he could see and waited for the bus to return.

Once aboard he looked to see the result, it was heads. He nodded and turned the coin over to find the pert little bird covered in mud where he had trodden it into the soil.

Chapter 34

Peter peered out of the train window as it drew in to yet another stop. Tired and confused and for no reason at all, he opened the door, stepping out on to the station platform.

He did not move for some minutes until the train left, the last carriage slipping away into the night. The platform was now empty; the sound of the train echoing to silence. He was shuddering against the cold and loneliness. Nothing in the way of possessions, not even a toothbrush, he walked out into a town square.

The square was dimly lit by a few streetlights, diminished by the February evening mist.

Over to the right the light from a telephone box revealed a small knot of soldiers queuing to make calls.

To the left of the square, a pale-yellow shaft of light spilled on to the pavement from the door of the town hotel.

Peter's priority was to speak with Pen now that he was safely away from her persuasion.

He started towards the telephone box. An argument between the incumbent and the next in line stopped him in his tracks.

A woman, phone still in hand, fought to close the door, which was being held open forcibly by a soldier, the next in line.

The language which issued from her mouth Peter had heard often before at university but never with such vitriol and from a young woman. His mouth dropped open. Covering his ears, he ran in the opposite direction. Just why he had not the first idea.

Peter ran towards the light, into the foyer of the hotel.

Sam Partridge, the night porter, looked up from reading *The Times*.

He was used to sizing customers up quickly. Sam noted a small gent, neat suit, good shoes, no luggage and alone.

"Sorry sir, last orders nine o clock. The restaurant's closed." Sam assumed the visitor was hoping to dine.

Peter, confused, took some time to sort out his mind. He just stood wondering what to do. He waited a while, then resumed reading *The Times*.

Peter gathered himself at last.

"I would like a single room."

Sam looked up slowly. He fixed Peter with a long stare which suggested disdain.

His reply, however, came with studied politeness.

"You have luggage, sir? Do you need me to bring it in for you?"

Peter, answering, tried to sound confident.

"Been mislaid, which reminds me I should be grateful if you can supply a razor and toothbrush."

Sam took a deep breath and held it for a while whilst he made the decision.

Releasing it suddenly and noisily, he replied, "I don't know about the razor etc., but I will see what I can do."

He opened a ledger.

"That will be eight shillings and sixpence, *cash*, please sir."

He emphasised the word cash, adding. "Breakfast is extra."

"Will you not take a cheque?"

Peter was aware he had only about eight shillings and a few coppers in change.

He was trembling, struggling to keep control of his emotions.

"Sorry sir, casual business on the night is cash up front only."

He paused for emphasis. "Company policy."

Peter, now desperate, was finding it more and more difficult to hang on to his feelings.

"Can I make a telephone call?" Peter asked, adding hastily, "I can pay."

"Sorry sir, residents only." Sam resumed reading the newspaper.

Peter was now failing to hold himself together.

"Please!" He pleaded, shocked at the sound of his voice. His plea was like the squeal of a hurt animal.

Sam was also shocked and looked up sharply. He realised that Peter was distressed and in need of help.

"Please understand, sir, I can't. I could lose my job. There's a public telephone across the square," was the best answer Sam could think of.

"There's a long queue and it was getting nasty," Peter pleaded, even though he knew his argument was futile. He was once more a small boy frightened of the dark, scared of the unknown across the square.

"Often does, the squaddies come over from Aldershot 'cos the queues are even longer there.

Like as not they've got wives and girlfriends waiting outside a phone box somewhere.

That's no fun in February. If someone takes too long, the upset starts."

Sam looked at the hotel clock.

"The army lads will be clearing about now. They've got to be back in barracks by ten."

"Thank you." Peter hesitated then asked, whilst trying and failing to sound calm.

"I've nowhere to sleep tonight have you any suggestions?"

Sam sucked his teeth. "My Mam will be coming around soon with my supper, she'll know. Come back after you've made your call and wait."

He resumed reading the newspaper thinking, why did I say that. He hoped this would be the last of this incident. Knowing, full well, it would probably not be.

Peter finally got into the booth. Not having used one before, he didn't know what to do. He tried to read the instructions on the panel in the dim light. A tap on the glass caused him to look round.

A young woman was looking in at him. She opened the door.

"Having trouble, sweetheart?" she said, smiling. Without waiting for Peter to answer, she stepped inside with him.

She stood close, very close, embarrassingly so. He could smell her perfume, feel her warmth.

"I can't read the instructions," he explained trying in vain to back away.

She took the receiver from him.

"Easy peasy, darling. My pleasure. And the number, sweet-heart?"

"St. Mary Upperford 389." Peter, glad of any help, let her take charge.

"Got a shilling or a sixpence? Pennies will not do it."

Peter reached into his pocket. He was unable to avoid contact with the girl's body. This was an embarrassing struggle. Peter had the distinct impression she was standing closer than she needed.

He handed her a sixpenny coin.

The young woman dialled nought then answered.

"St. Mary Upperford 389."

Putting the sixpence in the slot she handed the receiver back, saying, "When they answers, press button A."

The girl smiled, stroked his face then left.

Peter was relieved to hear the telephone ringing. Fortunately, it was Pen who answered.

"Thank God, Pen I have been trying to call you all night."

"Peter, what's happening? Where are you?"

"I am in a 'phone box in some small town near Aldershot, I think. I don't know how much time I have."

Peter tried to read the name on the dial, but it was too dark.

"I will call again when I am settled."

"Come home, please? Then we can talk about this together. Hal was on his weekly visit and Mim wanted to go to the zoo. That's all there was to that."

Knowing that was not all there was to it, Peter ignored Pen's pleas.

"I just need to say sorry for being a coward and not facing up to the truth that night on the cricket field."

"Peter, my love, what do you mean?"

"I left it to you to decide whether we were to marry or not."

"I don't understand." Pen was genuinely confused.

"I knew our marriage was not right but left it to you to decide. You were under pressure from your parents."

Peter waited for an answer but when it didn't come he continued.

"I knew then it was not right. If it wasn't for letting Hal and Mim down, I think I would have called it off, then."

He paused, adding tearfully, "I should have done."

Peter could hear Pen crying as she said,"Peter, please come home. We can talk properly then."

This was too much for Peter and he almost agreed.

"I can't. I mustn't," stammering his answer in the effort it took.

He was as much talking to himself as to Pen. He banged his head in frustration on the side window.

"The money's running out, I'll be in touch." He lied and hurriedly replaced the receiver.

Peter's legs almost gave way as he left the telephone box.

Waiting outside, the young girl immediately linked arms.

"You all right, dearie. Had one too many have we?"

Peter stopped. "Please, leave me alone. *Please*." he repeated, tearfully.

The young woman looked at him wide eyed, surprised at his reaction.

"All right, dearie, keep your hair on," then added, "I'll be in the bar if you change your mind."

With a wiggle and a smile back over her shoulder she disappeared into the hotel.

Back in the hotel foyer Sam was still reading the paper when Peter returned.

He didn't look up. Aware of his presence, Sam spoke as if Peter hadn't been away.

"If you ask me that Hitler fella is bleeding mad. Says here he has designs on the Sudetenland wherever that is, and it could start another war."

He sucked his teeth. "Don't fancy ending up in the trenches like me dad."

He was silent for a while then he closed the paper and looked up. "Never knew him."

"He was killed?" asked Peter pleased to have something other than his problem to talk about.

"Missing, it amounts to the same thing. You can have the paper for what it is worth.

Then again you'll read anything when you are on nights."

He offered *The Times* to Peter. "Maizie propositioned you, did she?

I saw her follow you out. She was in the bar watching."

Peter took the paper and realised he was talking about the girl in the telephone box.

"She helped me telephone. I think I might have been rude to her. Is she still around?"

Sam smiled.

"I reckon you don't know what she was about, do you?"

Then, taking Peter's blush as confirmation, he continued.

"She buses in from somewhere, probably Pirbright or some area. Targets the squaddies. When they've gone back to the barracks, she hangs out in the bar looking for customers.

Made a mistake with you, I reckon."

Peter didn't answer but stood unsure what to say or do. With nowhere to lay his head his only hope was to hang around in the vague hope that the night porter's mother might help.

Sam, meanwhile, was answering a telephone call.

Peter sat and tried to read the newspaper wrestling with the sense of hopelessness engulfing him.

He had cut himself off from his father and his only friends without an idea of what to do next.

He started to read the opinion column. His eyes blurred. Unable to see the print, he began to tremble and shake violently.

"Can you stand up for me please, son?"

The words forced themselves into his consciousness.

"Sam, get along here and give me a hand to get him up on to this chair."

Peter became aware that he was being helped to his feet by Sam and a woman.

He heard the woman say, "A glass of water now, Sam, look sharp about it."

It was several minutes before he was able to stand. He allowed himself to be led out of the hotel by a motherly woman.

"That's the way my son, just a couple of streets."

The woman encouraged him, leading him by the arm for a short distance to a small, terraced house.

The front door opened directly on to the street and into a living kitchen.

A short step but the contrast was stark. Peter was transported out of his despair on this cold misty February night, into the bright warmth of a neat home.

A large black Yorkshire range dominated with its bright orange fire enveloping Peter in its warm glow.

Bessie Partridge pulled a chair from the table.

"Sit yourself down, son. When did you last eat?"

She was already serving a dish of broth as she asked. Bessie took a home baked loaf from an enamel bread bin and started cutting into it on a stone slab.

"I don't remember."

Peter heard his answer, his mind swirling, trying to comprehend yet realising how similar this woman's approach and mannerisms were to those of May Sheppard.

Later, replete with hot broth and homemade bread, Peter remembered his manners and found his voice.

"Thank you. How can I thank you?"

He wanted to hold this woman, weep on her shoulder.

Bessie Partridge, kneeling, busily closed off the dampers on the range. She didn't look round.

"Time you were in bed, son," she said standing and wiping her hands on a coarse cloth.

Taking Peter by the arm she propelled him towards the steep narrow stairs between the living kitchen and the scullery.

Chapter 35

An urgent call of nature woke Peter the next morning. He started to reach for his dressing gown when the shock of confusion hit him so unfamiliar were his surroundings.

A flush of embarrassment flooded his face as he remembered the happenings of the previous night. Anxiously he pulled on his trousers and found his way to the stairs which were so very narrow and steep. There was no bathroom upstairs, the only other room door was open revealing another bedroom.

It was cold, very cold and his feet ached on the cold, sparsely covered floor.

Returning, he put on his socks and shoes and crept downstairs.

To his right was the scullery with a copper boiler. A large stone sink in one corner predominated.

The small windowpanes were misty. Rubbing one of the panes to look out he was shocked to find the glass covered with a thin film of ice on the inside. There was no sign of a bathroom or toilet.

Hearing noises from the living kitchen Peter went through to find Bessie Partridge raking out the ashes and opening the flues on the Yorkshire range.

She looked up, a smile of understanding on her smudged face.

"Across the yard son, key's hanging behind the scullery door. No 21, same as the house."

Across the yard a line of doors faced him, all locked and numbered. Quickly, he found No. 21.

Inside it was clean and functional despite a thin crust of ice on the water closet defying the heat of a candle burning alongside.

This was a voyage of discovery for Peter; the realisation that these people could live like this and retain more integrity than his father and Sir George.

Bessie Partridge and May Sheppard were truly 'giants' alongside the Lady Amelias of this world.

Shuddering against the freezing morning, he hurried back into the house.

Bessie was washing her hands in the stone sink.

"Key back behind the door afore you forget, son."

"Oh sorry!" Peter ran back across the yard to collect the key from the toilet door.

He returned to receive more orders from Bessie.

"Up you go, son and get dressed. Make the bed. Sam will be needing it soon. Fire's building up nicely. The porridge is on the stove. We can have a nice chat over breakfast."

It would be someone to listen and perhaps help, possibly even sympathise. This luxury was a new experience. He ran upstairs.

Later while eating hot porridge and a slice of homemade bread and dripping, Peter was wondering how to broach the question of payment for the night's lodging.

Bessie was drinking tea from a large pint pot. She swirled the tea around the pot looking down into it as if she was reading his fortune in the leaves.

"I just hope you didn't leave in anger, son," Bessie said looking up, fixing Peter with unusually sad eyes.

Peter was shocked by the suddenness and relevance of the question.

"No, no, not with Pen." He stuttered in answer.

Bessie looked down once more into her pot and asked,"Then who?"

"No, you don't understand." Peter almost shouted. "I left because I love her."

Bessie continued to look down into her pot as if was the font of all knowledge.

"Strange, I sense much anger."

"My father," Peter got no further, his voice faltering and fading.

Bessie waited for Peter to continue. When he didn't, she asked "And your mother?"

Peter dropped his head sharply avoiding Bessie's gaze and looked down into his empty plate.

"Never knew her," he answered. His voice was barely a whisper.

"Ah!" Bessie carefully considered her words. "Died in childbirth?"

Peter didn't know whether or not this was a question.

"I don't know, my father won't speak about her."

"And you long to know."

Peter realised this was not a question from Bessie.

Bessie nodded. "You keep saying my father. I sense you don't call him dad or pops even pa, always "it's father or sir?"

Bessie looked into Peter's eyes, indicating this was a question, not just an observation.

Peter nodded. Tears began to run down his nose dripping into the plate.

Bessie reached across the table and took Peter's hand.

"One thing for sure, son, your dad loved your mum."

Peter stiffened, offended by this observation.

"How can you possible know that?" he protested.

"Happens a lot, son, seen it too many times."

She removed her hand because Peter was pulling away. She sat back and swilled the tea in her pot and took a drink.

"You see, son, I helps folk into this world, and I helps them out. In between, I help if I can. Meantime it is impossible not to notice things."

With barely a breath, she continued. "Incidentally, talking of such, Cissie Dodds started this morning. When she gets to every ten minutes, I will need to pop out, until it does, if you get my meaning."

"You do all that? I mean births and deaths. What about doctors and undertakers?"

Peter found all this difficult to accept.

"They cost money. If they've no money they're on their own. Doctors, need paying."

"And you don't need paying?"

"Well yes, they pay, as and when. When I tidy and lays out, there might be insurance. If not, I accept shoes or clothing anything that's not needed on the voyage. That is after I've laid them out in their best."

"What then?" Peter asked, knowing that funerals and interment were not cost free in his world. "The council buries them in a commune."

"A commune?"

"A communal grave. One open to all as can't pay or maybe pays a small charge."

Bessie nodded gravely. "I just try to give them some dignity."

The two of them were silent for a while. Bessie continued to swirl her tea in her pint pot.

Eventually Peter asked half a question.

"What makes you think my father?" His voice again faded as he failed to complete.

It didn't matter, Bessie understood.

"I've seen too much in my days. Women do die in childbirth. When they do the father is lost.

They are left with the little one. They need someone to blame. Even if they don't blame the little one, they find it difficult to bond."

She banged the pot down on the table, got up and walked to the window and began to wipe up the water which was running down the windows on to the window ledge and looked out onto the street. "Son, don't let the sun go down on your anger another day."

As she spoke, a little woman walked by and half looked in before turning away when she saw Bessie looking out. Shortly afterwards she walked back again.

Bessie went to the door and opened it.

"Are you going to come in Dolly Munton or not?" Bessie shouted.

Dolly Munton entered, a frail bony little woman whose bird-like eyes darted every which way, as if she was about to be attacked.

"Cissie started yet?" she asked taking in the scene especially Peter at the table.

Bessie closed the door.

"Dolly, you know as much as I do, probably more. That's not why you are here, is it?"

"I've nothing for the kids when they get home, and the welfare won't help."

Dolly eyed Peter up yet again.

"Is your stove lit?" Bessie asked Dolly.

"I've no coal." Dolly took every opportunity to look at Peter when Bessie wasn't looking.

Peter felt that he was being assessed like a prize bull at an agricultural show.

"Right," said Bessie, "go home bring a pan. Then call at Allsops Butchers on the High St."

She turned to Peter.

"Have you got a halfpenny, son?" she asked continuing, barely taking breath. "Ask Portly Bill not Stevie Longshanks for a bone for the dog. If he asks a penny Dolly, say you will give the rest next week. Mind that you do."

Bessie stayed Peter's hand.

"Just a halfpenny, son."

When Dolly had left Peter said, "Did you have to do that?"

"What? Give her just a halfpenny?"

"No, I mean buy a bone to feed her children. It was for them, wasn't it?"

Bessie did not have time to answer. She was interrupted by a hammering on the door which opened on a small boy.

"Me mam says can you come, please?" The little lad was gasping from running.

"Tell her I'll be there directly, son."

Bessie turned to Peter answering his question.

"It gives me a chance to feed the kids something a bit more nourishing than jam butties."

She went into the scullery and returned with a wicker basket from which she took two potatoes and a small onion. Stripping the outer leaves of a cabbage, she put it back in the basket. She then placed the leaves and the other items on the table. Without looking around she shouted to the boy still waiting outside.

"Off now and tell your mam I am coming."

She laughed.

"He's another one of mine. I am blessed if I can remember all their names.

No, Dolly got what she came for. All the rest was an excuse, which you probably guessed."

All this time Bessie was putting on a hat and coat. She reached up on to a shelf for a tin from which she spooned a black powder on to a paper which she screwed into a packet and placed on the table. "When Dolly comes back pop all this into her pan with a kettle of boiling water, stick it on the hob and wait till I come back. Oh, and tell Sam there's porridge on the stove. Well, he knows what's what. And don't take any nonsense from Dolly, she'll con you if she can. She's probably conning me now. Still with kiddies I can't take a chance. Peel those potatoes and the onion, chop them for the pan. Wash the peel and cabbage leaves chop them and add them with this screw of gravy salt. Got it?"

The latter part of the instructions was given as she went through the door.

Peter dutifully picked up a potato and began to peel while thinking that Bessie could get more subject matter and sentences into a single breath than May Sheppard.

Comfortable as he was, he knew he couldn't stay. He was thinking what he could do to establish a new life when Sam returned.

"Your mother has ..." Peter began.

"I know," Sam interrupted. "I just passed her." He flopped down in the chair.

"I'm for bed. Jiggered is what I am." "Here, there'll be nothing left of that 'tater, give it here."

Peter, glad to be relieved of this duty handed everything over.

"I can't see as how it matters, your mother said to peel them and put everything in the pot.

Why bother peeling at all?"

Sam didn't answer but peeled both potatoes and handed them back.

Peter, irritated by his incompetence and uncomfortable with the silence, then tried to deliver the rest of Bessie's message.

"Your mother says ..."

Sam interrupted. "I know; porridge is on the stove." He sounded tetchy.

Peter allowed him to eat and leave for his bed without further comment.

This reinforced his understanding that he could not stay.

Later with Dolly's pan simmering on the stove as instructed, Peter sat thinking what to do, unable to think forward, unable to rid himself of the feeling that he wished to stay.

For all the surface deprivation, this was a real home. He was still trying to sort his mind by the time that Bessie returned.

She 'busied' herself through the door. She swept through the kitchen talking as she checked everything on the stove. She passed through taking off her hat and coat while continuing a running commentary as if she had never left the house.

"Lovely, well done, son. A little boy this time, lovely little chap. No problems, being her fifth. It's mostly like shelling peas after the third."

She brewed a fresh pot of tea then came and sat opposite Peter.

"Have you thought what you are going to do yet, son?"

Fortunately, she didn't wait for an answer otherwise Peter would have been stuck.

Leaving the tea pot on the table she stood up and swept out into the scullery returning putting on a flowered overall.

"You'll need to be making your mind up."

She stopped at the table once again and poured tea into her pint pot.

"You realise you can't stay here, don't you, son?" Bessie said and sat down, waiting for Peter's response, which didn't come.

She swirled her pint pot then, looked into the resulting maelstrom.

"I'm going to ask you questions and I hope you will try and answer with just a yes or a no. Will you do that?"

Peter nodded.

"Will you be going back to your wife?"

Peter shook his head. "No."

"To your father?"

"No."

"Do you have a job?" Bessie continued with her check list.

"No," Peter continued to answer letting Bessie take charge.

"Little or no money?"

Peter nodded. He was now facing his predicament in stark detail.

"Nowhere to lay your head?"

Peter shook his head, waiting for the next question, which was a long time coming.

Eventually it did when Bessie looked up from her pint pot sat back and sighed.

"You are not going to last long then, are you?"

Peter didn't answer this last question. He remained with his eyes fixed on the empty space in front of him. A single tear ran down his nose. Dripping on to the oil cloth it sparkled in the February sun which had finally appeared over the opposite roofs.

Bessie ached to jump up and embrace him but resisted firmly. It crossed her mind that her mother would have given him a clip around the ear. That was not Bessie's style.

She looked down into the pot and swirled her tea yet again.

"Do you want me to say what I think?"

"Please." Peter's answer was barely a whisper.

Bessie continued to swirl her tea.

"As I see it you have two choices. One is to go home wherever that may be and the other ..."

She stopped speaking for a few seconds, then didn't continue the thought.

Instead, Bessie observed.

"Everything points to you having a nervous breakdown. You are running away from whatever it is that you can't handle. You have rejected your present life and you have nothing to replace it."

She swirled the tea yet again.

"You have bottled your feelings so long, that the pressure has blown the 'cork' out of the 'bottle'. There's no fizz left. You need to regain control, have a plan, a discipline."

Bessie paused for several seconds before adding with emphasis."And you have nothing!"

"So, what do I do?"

Peter was now pleading. It showed in his voice.

Bessie banged the pot down on the table.

"'You owe me a shilling for a night's bed and breakfast. I suggest the only thing you can do is join the army. There's a recruiting office on Aldershot Railway Station. The sergeant there will no doubt be glad to replace the cost of your night's lodgings with the King's shilling."

Perhaps my mother was right, Bessie thought, it would be better to give him a clip round the ear. Shocked by this sudden change of mood. Peter fumbled in his pocket then placed a shilling on the table. Confused and sad he left, closing the door quietly behind him.

Bessie's instinct was to run after him. Instead, she took a long swig of now cold tea, wiped her mouth and went over to rake out and refuel the range.

Chapter 36

The recruiting sergeant taking Peter's details, studied him for a few moments then looked up.

"I think sir, that I had better refer you. Give me a moment, please." He left the office.

Peter sat waiting still wondering what the future held. There was a relief now in having a purpose, if not a complete plan.

Captain Walton perused the enlistment form then addressed the sergeant.

"Has he been given the King's shilling?"

"No sir, I thought it best left to you."

The captain smiled.

"Thank you, sergeant, that was astute."

The sergeant sprang to attention.

"Sir. Do I show him in?"

The captain nodded.

"Yes. And sergeant. Well done."

The sergeant spun around and stamped his about turn with the enthusiasm born of this praise.

"Sir."

Captain Horace Walton reached for the telephone. He was still speaking when Peter knocked. "Captain Bailey still there? Try and catch him before he leaves."

He put his hand over the speaker. "Come."

He indicated to Peter to sit, then continued to speak on the phone.

"Barney, sorry to call late but remember that special request you made a couple of months ago? Well, I might I have him in my office right now." He listened for a moment then turned back to Peter and asked. "Academic German learned in situ, or both?"

The captain then left the phone on the desk so that their conversation could be overheard.

"Both. I waited on at a restaurant in Berlin for six summers plus technical and sales visits on behalf of the works."

"The works?" asked the captain. "Which works?"

"Barnes Special and Tool Steels."

The captain looked down at his papers.

"Barnes? Are you connected?"

"My father's company."

Captain Walton wanted to continue to question Peter, but he still had Captain Bailey holding on.

"Barney, it looks good. Would you care to have a word?"

He handed the telephone to Peter.

Captain Bailey opened with,"How do you do Mr. Barnes. Are you free this evening?"

"I can be," Peter answered, wondering what this was about.

"Pass me back to Captain Walton, please."

Peter did so.

Barney Bailey continued.

"Charlie, if this is a leg pull, I shall address you as Horace in the mess for the rest of creation."

"Genuine Barney, absolutely. Promise."

"Sounds damn near perfect. Have you enrolled him yet?"

"No, I would be obliged to place him in the Second Training Battalion. In which case he would be off the map for thirteen weeks or more."

"Can you hold off until tomorrow?"

"Can do, will do, Barney."

"If he agrees, bring him over to the mess tonight please, Charlie."

Captain Walton looked to Peter.

"May we defer your enlistment until tomorrow and, if you are free, would you care to join us for dinner this evening?"

Peter, speechless with disbelief, could only nod.

"Right Barney, we will be there. You'll be sending a staff car of course?"

"Don't push it Charlie if you don't like the 15cwt, catch the bus," Barney replied with a chuckle.

William 'Barney' Bailey slapped his thigh as he marched smartly across to the mess. He was feeling on top of the world.

"Corporal." He addressed the N.C.O. on the doorway. "Clear a civilian guest for dinner. In the anteroom if you can. We will be working. Oh, and check with the sergeants' mess and see if they can do a sleepover for one tonight.

That same hour Sir George was speaking on the telephone with Richard Barnes.

"Pen says that he was speaking from a telephone box in Aldershot."

Sir George was replying to Richard's question.

Richard Barnes, after a moment's' thought, ordered,"See if you can track him down. Sounds to me as if he is joining the army."

"My thoughts entirely. I will get on to it immediately," Sir George replied.

Chapter 37

That evening, Peter was perusing one of two blueprints spread out on the table.

"I can translate this, if that is what you wish." He looked up at Captain Bailey.

"Just tell me what you think of it," Captain Bailey asked, tapping the table with his pencil.

"You are familiar with drawings, or so I was given to understand?"

Peter understood that he was being assessed. He hadn't been told why.

He read carefully through the captions and instructions which gave no clues. After the second reading, he looked up enquiringly at the captain.

"What am I looking for?"

"What do you see, Mr. Barnes?" Captain Bailey countered.

"It's a drawing of a 500 kilogramme, bomb case."

Aware that the captain needed more, he looked again.

"Along with appendages, nose cone, spinner, fins, etc."

Peter continued looking up, hoping for approval.

The captain appeared to be expecting more.

This was a familiar scene for Peter. He had met this situation many times with his father.

He looked again.

"Anything unusual?" The captain prompted. He then added a clue.

"Anything missing?"

Peter again searched every inch of the drawing and every word of the instructions but to no avail.

He was about to say I give up. The drawing was of a bomb casing. A simple ovoid container, complete with detonating appendages and fins. He sensed an impatience by the captain.

This was a familiar scene, having experienced similar exercises conducted by his father; even to the tapping pencil. Knowing that there would be something obvious that he was missing, he checked again.

Suddenly he looked up. "There's no filler cap."

The captain sat back and smiled asking,"Why do you think that is?"

"Probably because it is both sophisticated and secret."

Peter sat back and smiled with relief.

"There is no 'probably' about it. If you look at the screw tapping in the filler hole you will see there is a tiny gap in the penultimate thread." He leaned forward tapping the drawing with his pencil.

Peter nodded. "What does that mean?"

The captain leaned back again in his chair.

"That is the concern of others. It is a visual clue. What we are lacking is someone capable of spotting verbal clues. Someone with language skill, to spot a minute clue in the text, maybe as small as that tiny notch in the screw thread."

He tapped with his pencil on the cloth.

"There is such a clue on the other drawing. This drawing states, in bolder print, 'Any malfunction of screwing in the filler cap shall be referred. NO attempt to rectify shall be made, no matter how small." Clues of that nature. Rarely so obvious.

He paused and again tapped the drawing with his pencil.

"This little gap is the dog that does not bark. The instruction, not shown here, is its 'kennel mate'. That specific drawing and instructions are for the filling operatives only. No other function is involved other than filling with the explosive material and screwing in the filler cap.

This is the nuance that we need to spot, but in German. Do you think you can do this?"

Peter was beginning to understand what his involvement was about.

"I suppose I am so qualified. Is the purpose of this interview to employ me?"

"Not immediately, it is likely that you pass through basic training, then move on to officer training. We will be making an application for your transfer to this unit." The captain, smiling held out his hand. "I hope you will join us."

The next morning outside the C.O.'s office, Barney Bailey adjusted his Sam Brown. "This has got to be about last night with Barnes, but why? We played everything by the book."

Charlie Walton did not answer. He was going over everything in his mind checking that they had. Captains Bailey and Walton had been summoned to attend C. O.'s orders with one slight adjustment. They had been ordered to be there at 8 a.m. and not the usual 9.30. This was confusing if not inconvenient.

Inside his office, Colonel Strong was in discussion with his adjutant.

"Go at once yourself, do not delegate this. Check his full name, address, next of kin and date of birth. I must have absolute confidentiality and accuracy, major."

Colonel Strong did not use the major's Christian name.

Accordingly, the adjutant sprang to attention. "Sir," he replied. while thinking to himself 'What the bloody hell is this all about.'

"Oh! and send those two in please, Jack." The colonel sought to mollify his tone.

He looked down at the War Office communication on his desk also wondering what it was all about.

The two captains marched in and stood to attention. The colonel acknowledged their salutes.

"At ease, gentlemen. This is a formal enquiry not a disciplinary measure although that may be an option, understood?"

"Yes sir." Both officers acknowledged.

There followed a detailed question and answer session regarding events of the previous day concerning Peter Richard Barnes.

"*Everything* by the book?" The colonel looked at each in turn.

"Yes, sir." They each answered.

"Good." A relieved Colonel Strong replied. Looking down once more at the War Office communicate. "Horace," he continued, once more attempting to mollify his attitude.

"If he is to enlist, book him into the second and keep a weather eye on him. I want regular reports on his progress. Arrange that with the training officer commanding. You know the drill."

Captain Bailey sprang to attention.

"Sir, on completion of his training I would like your support for the transfer of Peter Barnes to my unit. Sir."

Colonel Strong looked irritated.

"At ease, Barney. It will be possibly over a year before anything like that will happen and you know as well as I that Intelligence will have their hooks in him like as not."

"It is important, sir, if I am to carry out my remit successfully."

Barney persisted, knowing that it would play well if he failed.

"Sorry, Captain Bailey." The colonel, with resumed formality, knew full well what Barney was up to. He looked down yet again at the communicate.

"On this, I am not only outgunned, but outranged and way, way outranked.

Thank you, gentlemen, dismiss."

He watched the captains march out with mixed feelings.

However, his greatest emotion was one of triumph, that his was the unit, was the only unit to respond to the War Office's request. He knew nothing of what it was about.

What mattered was his command occupied the limelight.

He and his battalion would be shown to be efficient and reliable.

Chapter 38

1418586 Officer Cadet P R Barnes stepped from the train in Dover.

It was hard to believe that Margaret Firth had been missing for only the one year. So much had happened.

Peter was apprehensive. He would be seeing Pen and Hal for the first time since that evening when he watched them disappear into the February evening mist.

This was a meeting he was not looking forward to.

Ignoring their pleas for him to join Dorothy and them to remember the life of Peggy Firth would have been churlish. His first thought of 'how can I escape this?' he had dismissed as such.

One telephone call, plus two letters, stultified and curt, to his wife were unacceptable.

Pen deserved more.

The ease with which he obtained a compassionate 72-hour pass for a non-relative, removed his only viable excuse.

For several minutes, he stood on the platform summoning the will to take the first steps.

He knew that he could not hide forever. He needed to explain his actions; to apologise. Taking a deep breath, he set off for the ferry terminal.

Pen, Hal and Dorothy, were already in the building. He embraced each in turn, avoiding eye contact.

Pen and Hal behaved naturally, to Peter's relief. Maybe this was because Dorothy was there.

They had had some time to adjust to his sudden, unexplained defection.

Dorothy broke the awkward silence which followed by announcing,"Andre is coming over on the afternoon ferry, turning straight round and returning with us.

"We will be reflecting Margaret's last journey, saying our final 'goodbyes' and sharing our memories in mid-channel with a simple ceremony. We are booked into his uncle's hotel tonight where we will have dinner. We will stay overnight and return tomorrow."

Peter found the situation to be surreal. Being in the presence of the two people who meant the most to him yet being unable to interact normally and 'surmount' the invisible barrier between them. The discussions about Tuss hardly registered. Hardly helping was the current ambience on the ship.

The ferry was crammed with weekend revellers travelling to France to 'let their hair down'.

Last Thursday's announcement of Peace in our time was 'uncorking' an unprecedented rush to rejoice.

This was not the, hoped for atmosphere. There was no quietness. No silent reverence.

Dorothy's plan was to cast a wreath on the water; to say a few words in remembrance of her friend.

The little party eventually moved out of the saloon on to the open fore deck in search of a better scene.

The celebrations continued there also.

Avoiding the crowds was proving difficult.

They made their way down the side passage of the ship to the stern area which offered some semblance of order.

The idea now was for them all to hold the wreath over the side, for Dorothy to speak, then release the flowers to the elements and also have a minute's silence to pray and remember Tuss.

The noise of the revellers and the buffeting of the wind was dominating.

There was no other option but to adapt to the conditions. It was difficult to hear Dorothy speaking above the wind and noise.

They all reached out to try and hold the wreath over the side. This was impossible in the narrow space.

Dorothy picked a flower for each, then turned to say a few words.

A conga line of revellers danced down the side passage towards the stern singing loudly.

Any evening any day, once you get down Lambeth way, you'll find them all doing the Lambeth walk Oi.

The leader of this conga line was first to see the mourners.

He was aware of gossip, the reason for Dorothy, her friends' presence with the wreath.

Stopping, he raised both his hands.

"Cease your ranting folk," he shouted.

With his hands still raised, he yelled against the wind to the mourners.

"Sorry chaps, we are all a bit Lupino," referring to the star of the West End show, Lupino Lane.

He dropped his hands, spread them, shrugged and shouted, "Peace."

Whether or not this was a reference to Neville Chamberlain's declaration of 'Peace in our time.' was not clear.

He then he indicated to those following to turn around.

Returning towards the prow, they continued singing.

Everything's free and easy, do as you darn well pleasey. Why don't make your way there, go there, stay there ...

Dorothy, head bowed, waited for the singing to fade. She realised that the passage from psalms chosen, would not be heard. Trying not to shout but needing to be heard above the noise and wind, she repeated the word "Peace." Then she released the wreath which spun away into the darkness followed by the flowers. Dorothy looked out into the darkness, the wind whipping her hair against her face and sticking to her tears.

Chapter 39

The return journey on Sunday morning seemed endless.

Peter couldn't wait to dock. He leaned over the rail watching the dark swirling waters matching his mood. His mixed thoughts and emotions and the dark confusion which had blighted the weekend continued. Gone was the easy charm.

Even Hal was incapable of lifting the tension.

They had 'tip toed' around each other like bomb disposal operators removing a trembler switch.

Was this the price of honesty and openness? Peter ached to turn back the clock.

"Are you all right, Peter?"

The suddenness of the question took Peter unawares.

He turned to find Pen behind him holding out her hand which he took instinctively.

"Come home with us! Please, darling," Pen pleaded.

"I am truly sorry, Pen. I just want you and Hal to be happy."

Peter apologised, removing his hand and turning away as he spoke.

"I know. Please come home. Then we can really talk about it."

Peter, eyes steadfastly fixed on the swirling water, countered, knowing that his answer was a lie.

"I will come soon, but the truth is the truth. It will not change that."

Pen did not mean to be put off.

"We could at least try to return to something like normal."

Peter did not answer. He turned to look at her properly, probably for the first time that weekend.

This look was enough.

Pen dropped her gaze.

"Sorry," she whispered.

Peter turned back and looked once more into the swirling waters.

"Does Hal? ..." He didn't finish the question.

"He doesn't. He can't, not yet."

This understanding of the unspoken by Pen, spoke volumes.

Peter nodded. "I must go to Sheffield first. Unfinished business, then maybe I will come to St. Mary."

They both stood uncertain what to say or do.

Peter in a sudden movement, took her in his arms and said quietly, "Go now and tell Hal to come out from under the butterfly bush."

Shocked by this sudden show of affection, Pen looked at Peter through a vale of tears.

"The what?"

"I think, I hope Hal will know what I am asking."

It came as relief to all when the ferry docked.

Chapter 40

Peter changed trains for Derbyshire in Sheffield then decided to walk from the village station.

The sun picked out the purples, browns and greens of a hillside speckled with black rocks and the white blobs of grazing sheep.

He walked up towards the house.

In the sunshine, everywhere looked peaceful.

The evening was fresh with that sharpness that comes with sunlit early autumn evenings.

The sun, low to the west, picked out the rust and gold of the coppice and the bright red of the Virginia Creeper-clad house. The creeper a startling contrast to the white walls.

Peter stopped and looked unsure whether he was admiring the view or using it as an excuse not to confront his father.

At a bend in the lane there was a small wooden hut. This served as a bus shelter and other weekend 'pastimes'.

Peter had to pass this before he turned right up the drive. He didn't look into the hut in case it was occupied.

May Sheppard was sitting inside catching her breath before facing the driveway up to the house. She saw Peter and stood up.

"You've cum 'ohm then. Yer dad were reet, an' I didn't believe 'im."

May showed no other element of surprise.

Peter, delighted to see her, resisted the urge to embrace her. He simply answered, "Hello, Mrs Sheppard, I thought you would be home by now."

"Your dad cum back early for a Sundy an 'e warnt drunk. Sed yu might cum. Any road 'e's waiting fo' yu, an I've med dinner fo' two."

"I could be staying the night. Is that all right?" Peter wondered why May was there.

"Yu bed ull need changing, I'll get clean uns out o' airing cupboard."

"I can do that, there's no need for you to climb up the drive."

Peter didn't wish to be a cause of unnecessary work.

May set off up the hill, ignoring Peter's offer.

"We'd best get going, yu dad ull think I've got lost. By t' way am living in now Sid's gone."

"Sid's gone?" Peter was shocked. He was sad for May, but she showed little emotion.

"It were only a matter of time. Brought him aht 'ere fo t' fresh air, but he started spitting blood cum Easter last year, an' they found out it warnt thingy it were t'other."

"Sorry to hear that Mrs Sheppard. So, you are now living in?"

"Yo' dad give me a half crown extra, says I'm housekeeper and hires a daily fo' shopping and heavy work." May stopped to catch her breath.

"Good man yo' dad, extra money for less work and living in, can't believe it." She gasped.

Peter thought to himself yes and his father would now be getting a fat rent for May's cottage.

He took May's basket then her arm.

"Shall we help each other up Mrs Sheppard?"

May Sheppard's eyes glistened with tears.

"Aye, son that would be nice."

Halfway up the hill at the third tier May stopped again to catch her breath.

Peter looked across at the butterfly bush which was looking in need of attention and wondered about asking his father to place a seat adjacent to the terrace.

May watched him for a few seconds realising something was taking his attention.

"Give me a minute, son," she said leaning on the wall.

Peter put the basket down and went across to the bush and straightened some of the branches.

The 'cave' was much smaller than he remembered. He kicked some of the autumn debris back against the wall uncovering a dead mouse.

He hesitated before picking it up by the tail and slinging it over the wall into the coppice.

There remained not one shred of the warmth; the security of memory. It was just a dirty little hole.

He kicked back some more of the debris as he walked back to where May stood.

"Them gardeners are useless but yo dad dunt seem to mind."

Peter picked up the basket and took May's arm.

"Where does my father go each Sunday? Why does he drink?"

May stopped, took his face in both her hands, turning it towards hers.

"Yo' mun ask 'im son, yu'll learn nowt from sullen silence."

"You do know, don't you Mrs Sheppard?" Peter peered back into her eyes. "Don't you?"

May turned her head away.

"'appen," was all she said.

Peter knew it was useless questioning further, so he saved his breath for the climb.

The thought that she knew, and he didn't, took over in his brain diverting it from the impending meeting with his father. Reaching the side door, he handed May's basket back.

May looked at him. He was distant, as distant as the hills he seemed to be studying.

"Go now son an' talk to yo' dad."

With a final look, she walked through to the kitchen shaking her head.

Peter stood unmoving for over a minute.

"Cemetery," he muttered to himself then walked through into the front room.

In those few steps, he recalled Bessie Partridge's words. The chaos of the last months, of his life, began at last, to make some sort of sense.

Richard Barnes was sat with his back to the window. The *Sunday Times* in front of his face, perhaps a little higher than it should be. This suggested that he was hiding not reading.

Peter stopped in the doorway.

"Sorry, Dad." He announced his arrival with an apology.

Richard did not move for seconds. Long enough for Peter to see his silhouette through the paper against the setting sun. Slowly the paper lowered to reveal his face, dark and featureless against the light through the windows. He didn't answer.

Peter walked into the room and sat in the same chair opposite his father just as he had done so a one year ago. This time Richard was sober.

"Have you been to visit my mother's grave today?" Peter asked.

Richard nodded.

"Will you please take me tomorrow?"

Richard didn't answer immediately.

"Please?" Peter urged.

Richard again nodded, his silhouette appearing to shrink. An embarrassing silence followed. Neither found the words needed.

"Sorry!" Richard eventually whispered. His voice sounded strange and distant, so unlike him. Peter knew his father was struggling.

"Can I get you a drink, dad?" he asked hoping that a whisky might help.

Richard shook his head then began pouring out a torrent of information. His voice was devoid of the brash, loud, confident manner of which Peter was familiar.

So much so, that he had to lean forward to hear.

"It was your sixth birthday. I had been to Charlotte's grave as I do every ..."

Richard didn't finish the sentence. After a short pause he continued.

"Pamela was angry that I had not returned for your birthday party. I did promise to."

He paused again to gather his thoughts, then continued.

"I had a drink or two. No! I was drunk and came back late."

Richard struggled to continue against the memory.

"Too late. You were in bed. Pamela shouted at me 'your own son's birthday and you can't be bothered.' She smelled the drink on my breath. And you're drunk," she said.

She looked at me as though I had crawled from under a stone. I started to cry."

Peter was crying.

Richard struggled to continue.

"You see son, your birthday was also the day ..."

Richard stopped. Peter went to the sideboard and poured a large whisky.

This Richard accepted. Taking a drink, he managed to continue.

"Pamela hadn't realised where I'd been. When it dawned on her, she put her arms round me to comfort me."

Richard took another drink.

"Paul just happened." He paused again for some while.

Peter waited for Richard to continue which he eventually did, saying, "I was so ashamed. It wouldn't have happened but for the drink."

"And you go every Sunday? Also, on my birthday?" Peter did not intend this as a question. Richard nodded and continued.

"I *did* mean to come back for your birthday. I just lost track of time."

He paused giving Peter space to ask.

"Was it because I was alive and your wife, my mother had died giving me that life?"

Maybe this was the first time Richard faced this question.

"I don't know, son, what happened with Lottie, your mother. It was probably because of the war and lack of care and attention. I was at sea, so can only guess. I didn't get to her funeral.

Her parents interred her in their family plot. When I finally came home it was all over."

Richard again took time to gather his thoughts.

"I didn't come home again. I can't remember why. Then I was injured. When I finally got back to see you, I was a stranger. A strange man in a blue suit. You didn't understand."

"How old was I? When we first met, I mean."

"Two maybe going on three."

Peter had a vague memory of this man in a blue suit, people around trying to force him into his arms. "I didn't want to know you," he whispered.

Richard's nod was the only acknowledgement of Peter's comment. Richard paused then continued.

"Your granddad, you remember, brought you up in this house. He was busy at the works. He hired a wet nurse for you. This nurse had this daughter, Pamela. Well, you know the rest."

Richard sighed and drained his glass.

The sun sank behind the distant hill. The two sat in the gathering gloom in silence.

Peter spent the next moments thinking.

"Sorry, I didn't like you. It seemed to me that you were always shouting."

Peter apologised again, breaking the silence.

"You were always hiding," Richard countered.

This was an observation, not an accusation.

Peter realised this, nodding his agreement.

Richard was unable to see this reaction. He reached back and switched on the standard lamp. Father and son blinked, blinded by this sudden light. Peter who was facing the lamp put up a hand to shield his eyes.

"Why send Pamela so far away and me to boarding school?"

"I didn't know what to do to hide Pamela and me from the shame. It was George who came up with the idea."

"Why Sir George?" Peter asked, thinking, 'what had this to do with him?'

"George and I have been close for years. He is a confidant of mine."

Peter thought 'don't I know it. You are as thick as thieves.'

"Why was that? How did that begin?"

"You may not know this. George saved my life and that of others.

Even though wounded himself he stemmed the bleeding otherwise I would have bled to death. Later we convalesced together down in Surrey. It was then that we became friends."

When Peter didn't answer, Richard continued.

"George suggested Pamela could be nanny for Penelope who was just beginning to walk. Pamela went down as a live-in nanny and the rest you know."

"Why couldn't I go with her? Why not send me with Pamela?"

"We tried that one, but Amelia wouldn't have it at first."

It took some while for Peter to come to terms with the flood of information. Mostly it made sense yet part of him struggled to let go of his resentment.

Later, over dinner, he was still struggling even though most of his questions had been answered. They ate mostly in silence. The atmosphere was still tense. Attempting to lighten this, Peter asked about his father's injuries, Peter realising that he knew so little about his father.

"How did you come to be wounded?"

Richard stopped eating, moved his knife and fork back on the plate, wiped his mouth on his napkin, stood and turned from the table.

"People keep asking me that. I have not the first idea. I remember nothing. Nothing at all."

He walked to the dining room door then stopped and turned saying, "I will be in the front room. If you go to bed, I'll see you in the morning early to go to the cemetery. What time is your train?"

Peter was puzzled by this reaction. Realising that his father wished to be left alone, he answered:

"I have time enough. I am not due back until 23.59."

Chapter 41

At the cemetery the following morning, after his father had left Peter remained alongside his mother's family grave. Her name Charlotte had been added to the headstone with the birth and death dates, little more. Just one more marble headstone. 'Charlotte Barnes beloved Daughter of Charles and Anne Wilton 30th March 1895. Died 15th July 1916 aged 21.' That was it.

A few yards away against the path side there was the communal grave pointed out by his father saying 'This grave contains the remains of May Sheppard's 'last little one.'

Peter *was* drawn to this grave even though it had no headstone just a plain plot covered with a plant May called Snow-in-Summer. It was probably planted by her some time ago.

Peter stood looking at the brief record of his mother's life.

He kissed his hand and 'blew' the kiss to his mother's grave which he felt to be a fraud. knowing that this was only because he believed that he ought to. He failed to subdue the resentment welling up, drowning out all other emotion.

Picking his way back to the pathway he couldn't take his eyes from the clump of white flowers.

He stopped briefly by the communal grave and shed his first tear before turning and running from the cemetery.

Chapter 42

May 1940; In the distance a dark cloud of smoke lay in a pall across the Belgian town of Lille to the north east of the river crossing where 1418586 Lieutenant Barnes P.R. was assessing the situation. He climbed up the river embankment out from under a bridge in urgent discussion with his corporal. The flashes of many explosions, the scream of dive bombers and noise of the distant battle caused them to look back anxiously. Peter checked his watch yet again.

"I reckon the sappers aren't coming corporal. The battle is getting closer. We will need to improvise."

"How do we do that then sir?"

"By cadging or commandeering what explosives and ammo' off the chaps who will no doubt be passing through as they retreat."

Peter had little idea of exactly what he intended.

His remit was to meet up with sappers at the bridge then make a judgement as to when it was prudent to destroy this river crossing. The sappers failed to show. One.38 issue revolver and one.303 Lee Enfield rifle were not going to hold up any advancing units for long, if at all.

"Tall order that, sir."

The corporal's statement of the obvious did nothing for Peter's composure.

"Maybe corporal, but I'll be beggared if we've come all this way to fail, not to try."

He snapped, ending the discourse and creating an ominous silence.

Peter wheeled away back to the 15cwt truck and placed his hands on the still warm bonnet and began to wonder how they could block the bridge using the truck.

Just audible above the noise of the distant battle the spluttering chug of an almost defunct engine was heard.

Lt Barnes took out his side arm as another British 15cwt truck struggled into view.

Stopping several feet before the bridge, it was unable to negotiate even this, the slightest of slopes.

Peter looked up from checking the chambers of his Browning.38.

"Corporal, we confiscate that truck."

Peter shouted. The two converged on the stricken vehicle.

Sergeant Stevens climbed gingerly out of the driver's seat. A blood-soaked right trouser leg was evidence of the source of his discomfort. He winced as he raised the bonnet.

"In trouble, sergeant?"

Sgt Stevens straightened up painfully to find out who was asking, to discover that it was a British officer. His instinctive move to attention caused him to grimace.

"It's the engine, sir."

"At ease please, sergeant. What do you believe to be the problem?"

"Don't know, sir, it could be a fuel blockage as there's diesel enough in the tank."

Peter turned to the corporal.

"What do you think, corporal?"

The corporal looked under the bonnet.

"Not sure, sir, but I don't think it's a blockage. I think it's the engine."

He replied mindful that the lieutenant needed a good reason to confiscate a truck, stranding an injured N.C.O.

"I can't think of the technical term, but I reckon it begins with F and ends in D."

"Finished?" Peter suggested then he suppressed a smile when he noticed the look on the sergeant's face.

"Where are you heading, sergeant?" he asked, adopting a more serious tone.

"Field hospital, sir, that is if there is one, or the coast. I've got three more wounded in the back."

Peter walked around and looked in. The men in the back didn't look up or acknowledge his presence. To one side he noticed a Bren gun. He turned to the sergeant.

"Any ammo. For the Bren, sergeant?"

"Just the one magazine, sir."

"I'll take it, swap my wagon for yours and get you on your way. Move your wounded men over into my truck. The corporal will give you a hand."

Peter left his corporal and the sergeant to transfer the wounded. He checked the Bren gun.

It seemed to be in good condition with a full magazine.

He immediately took himself into a large house adjacent to the bridge. Peter looked in all rooms facing the river and the road to Lille. In one of these there was a full-sized billiards table.

"Perfect," he muttered. Placing the gun on the table he climbed on to it. He aligned the Bren gun to fire out of the window talking to himself all this time. "Plenty of room," he said settling himself into the firing position.

Satisfied, he sat up to slide off the table then stopped. He focused his field glasses and studied the road out of Lille for the barest of moments. Leaping off the table he 'rocketed' down the stairs, two and three steps at a time.

"Corporal Savage, to me at the double," Peter shouted, running towards the almost defunct truck, calling over his shoulder.

"Sergeant, I need you to join us. Hurry!"

Corporal Savage arrived followed by the limping Sergeant Stevens.

"Truck loaded and ready to go, sir."

"None of us will be going anywhere unless we get a move on. Sergeant, into the driving seat."

Peter helped the wounded sergeant and at the same time gave another order.

"Engage first gear and when I give the word, pull this wreck on to the centre of the bridge by the starter motor. Corporal, get behind with me and push like hell. Sergeant, you steer to the very middle of the bridge staying in first gear. When there, apply the hand brake."

"Move!" Peter ordered. The starter motor whined as Peter and the corporal pushed.

Minutes later, the truck was parked in the middle of the bridge. Peter helped the sergeant down.

"You chaps, leg it now for the coast. Follow the Ypres road north, corporal."

"What about you, sir?" the corporal protested.

"Get out NOW. That is an order." Peter almost snarled as he spoke.

Leaning into the cab he released the bonnet of the stricken wagon.

The two N.C.Os hurried to the other truck and left at speed.

Peter removed the dipstick and the oil filler cap and stuffed some paper into the open tube. Returning to the back of the 15cwt. he removed the diesel filler cap, took his pocket handkerchief, wiped it on the dipstick and stuffed it into the fuel tank. Striking a match, he lit both 'fuses' waiting just long enough to ensure they were well alight before racing back up the stairs of the house to the billiards room. He settled behind the Bren gun fixing the firing to single shot.

The German motorised column slid to a halt. The commander barked out an order and several men left the nearest personnel carrier and ran towards the truck on the bridge.

Peter fired a single round at the near stone parapet. The bullet ricocheted rattling and moaning over the heads of these men who instinctively dived for cover.

"Burn damn it, burn," Peter muttered before firing a second shot into the road keeping heads down. The truck still wasn't burning. He aimed again at the road, this time immediately before the front tyre of the leading car. This round hit the road, shredded the tyre and ricocheted off the metal wheel rim whining like a lost soul into the distance.

Both German officers and the driver ducked instinctively. Peter then turned his attention to the rear tyre with equal success. He then moved on to the second vehicle waiting to cross the bridge.

The commandant, Joachim Kollman straightened up and stepped from the vehicle.

He walked towards the truck on the bridge shouting out an order. This was barely audible under the rattle of returning small arms fire.

Peter fired a shot at the road in front of his feet.

Joachim barely faltered as he repeated the order, continuing to walk forward.

Several men followed crouching low as they did so.

Peter's position of advantage was being diminished as the Germans quickly worked out his position. Several rounds entered the room chipping the window ledge, partly destroying the ceiling.

The debris disturbed his field of vision. An anti-tank round struck just below the window destroying the wall.

Peter now blinded and choked by the dust, ears ringing, slid off the table with the gun.

He ran upstairs to the attic rooms only to find that he was too short to take effective aim through the window.

"You should have shot the officer when you had chance," Peter chided himself.

He ran back downstairs. Blinded by sweat and dust, he tripped and fell headlong to land winded at the bottom. He parted company with the Bren gun and it with its magazine.

He searched feverishly for both and found the gun, minus the magazine.

On the unlit stair amongst the rubble Peter could not see the magazine.

Taking his Browning.38 out, he released the safety catch and ran outside.

He took aim towards the truck on the bridge. Several men were attempting to move the truck.

A flash burst from under the bonnet and ran along the side of the truck.

With a dull thud the whole wagon ignited in a sheet of flame scattering the men.

Peter was stunned by the success. Inexplicably, he emptied his revolver at the stricken truck.

This was just as well because his vision was badly affected. All he could see was the flames of the truck. Peter walked out into the middle of the road in full view of the enemy and sank to his knees. Peter's head was banging, ears ringing and eyes streaming adding to his confusion.

The noise and black smoke combined to destroy any coherent thinking.

Joachim Kollman held up his hand.

"Cease fire, fire extinguishers at the double," was his shouted order.

Joachim's two I.C. approached. "Why did you stop us taking him out, Herr commandant?"

"More use to us alive Henrik and interesting."

He stood with his swagger stick held by both hands behind his head, nestled into the nape of his neck to steady his shaking hands. Thinking, 'small man, a very small man with a big tactical brain and he is waiting for us to kill him'.

He began to hum tunefully the *March Militaire,* breaking off to think. Why didn't he raise his hands in surrender?

Outwardly, to his men, Joachim appeared calm and fearless.

Inwardly, his heart beat time to the music while thinking. 'did not shoot to kill yet does more damage than if he had killed a thousand.' *Dum diddy dum diddy dum, dum dum.*

He turned to Henrik saying. "One very small man, half a dozen rounds plus a pea shooter and clearly a big brain. He expects, no, he wishes to die. Maybe he should because he's held us up for probably one and a half, maybe two hours." *Dum diddy dum diddy dum, dum dum.*

Joachim Kollman was about to make the worst decision of his illustrious military career.

He had his remit and understood the thinking behind this. Aware, mostly via rumours, that a German advance had split the French and British armies and a Panzer division was swinging north to the coast cutting off the B.E.F. His column was carrying out a similar exercise to cut off the British and French remnants to the south of Lille to prevent them escaping the trap and joining the British forces in the north.

Joachim had avoided all action to achieve this aim circumventing the main route and the battle for Lille along this minor road.

This little man, single handedly, was thwarting him. Killing him was pointless. Joachim admired the initiative and inventiveness. In addition, this little officer could have vital information.

Peter meanwhile was waiting for the *coup de grace* which never came. He thought at first that this was because he was obscured by the flaming truck and the smoke. He rose to his feet and pointed his Browning towards the officers on the other side of the river.

He clicked away at the empty chambers before falling flat on his face.

Joachim's two I.C. snorted. "The big brain doesn't know when his gun is empty."

Joachim looked at Henrik. "Just get that truck out of the way major, the quicker the better."

He returned to his car to find his driver had already changed wheels.

Joachim was calming down thinking to himself at least someone knows what the world at war is about.

"Well done, driver. If necessary, use the spare wheels from the second car.

I need this one to be in good order. Thank you."

Chapter 43

Forty-one exhausted and dispirited officers disembarked from the covered trucks.

The camp commandant turned to Colonel Strong, the senior British officer.

"This is an unusually large and unexpected intake, colonel." He looked at his watch.

"I have moved the Polish officers out of hut 6. You must do the best you can, and it is late."

Without another word, he turned and left.

"Is that it?" Major Etteridge whispered.

"Bloody hell, Frances. What now?" muttered Charlie Strong.

"This will take some sorting. One hut for 41. I hope our Polish friends left blankets."

"For sure there will not be enough beds. Also, sir, we have to tell them there is no food."

Frances Etteridge reminded him of this responsibility.

Charlie Strong stared at the group as they shuffled into a kind of order.

He cleared his throat and addressed the weary and demoralised men.

"I can hardly say welcome chaps or that I am pleased to meet you, because I am not."

He cleared his throat and continued.

"I will promise you this, I will do my damnedest to make you comfortable. Help you all I can."

Charlie Strong coughed. He was having difficulty in speaking, in keeping still.

He was desperate to give the impression of calmness and control while thinking to himself.

'Forty-one officers in one go implies a disastrous defeat.'

With a massive effort he forced further unwelcome news through his lips.

"Sorry chaps, there's no grub at this late hour, not even a hot drink."

The colonel swallowed, adding, "You must be tired. Our Polish colleagues have been persuaded to hand over one of their huts, a number of bunks, blankets, etc., Tomorrow we will do what we can to provide more stable accommodation."

He paused before asking, "Which of you is senior?"

An officer stepped forward. "Colonel Hargreaves, sir." he answered, springing to attention.

"Colonel Hargreaves, you will bunk with me. Just for the night," Charlie ordered. He hoped to learn more of what had occurred via this officer. He looked around. "The next senior?" he asked.

Another officer stepped forward to answer.

"Captain Simmonds, sir, substantive from October 39."

Charlie Strong took courage from the manner of these two gentlemen. Discipline clearly had been maintained.

"Take charge of the hut please, captain. My colleague Major Etteridge will show you where. Dismiss." Charlie performed a smart about turn to march away. Colonel Hargreaves followed.

Once out of sight Charlie shook hands with Hargreaves.

"Bloody hell, thank God that's over. Sorry, I'm Charlie Strong. What, in heaven's name has happened? I mean 41 of you?"

"Bill Hargreaves." The officer introduced himself. "I don't know. My guess is a massive outflank of the French. Anyway, the Hun got behind us and cut us off; The whole of the Fifth infantry and the Second armoured and others."

"You?" the major asked.

Charlie Strong took a moment to answer, but when he did, he gave the minimum of information. "Ditched in the Med. Picked up by the Italian navy."

"Why then a German camp?" the major asked.

Charlie Strong's jaw set. "Least said, soonest mended."

Charlie avoided any further words of speculation as did his new guest. They headed for their quarters in silence.

Chapter 44

The following morning, all 41 were interviewed and allocated huts and tasks.

Peter was one of the last to be called not being part of the majority who belonged to the same units.

Isolation was not a new experience to Peter. It was just more of the same.

Initially he had a brief interview with an officious major who irritated him by his dismissive attitude. Peter's background and knowledge being such, he was attached to the logistics section which covered geography and maps. Captain Tommy Davage was the officer in charge.

"Hello Peter. I'm Tom Davage. Welcome to our humble abode."

Tommy was watching for any sign of psychological damage as a routine.

Peter gave no clues other than an obvious disinterest. Tommy then proceeded with the standard induction spiel.

"I am supposed to tell you that you are still sworn in. Allegiance to King and country. King's rules and regulations and all that." He sat back and smiled, adding, "Can we consider that done?"

Peter realised that this was a serious question and answered, "Yes."

Tommy recorded this acknowledgement. "Pretty rotten welcome last night. Over forty of you in one smack. Caught us on the hop. Take it you were fed this morning and have now got a permanent bunk and hut?"

Peter replied, "Yes." His demeanour was lethargic and distant.

Tommy noted this and searched his mind to try and engage with this disturbed officer.

He asked a routine question. "Have you any idea where this camp might be situated?"

Peter immediately showed interest.

"Well sir, I do have a fair appreciation. If I can have a sheet of paper. I can show you what I mean."

This enthusiastic reply startled Tommy.

"Steady on old chap," Tommy smiled again. Still trying to settle this intense little officer down.

Tommy, familiar with these sudden mood swings, understood.

"I understand you have already tried to show the major. Got right up his nose."

"It was he who asked me," Peter replied.

"Know this Peter, ***he*** wanted to do the telling."

Tommy took a moment to reassess, before saying, "You are not great on people skill, are you?"

Tommy's routine smile was supposed to mollify the comment.

Peter felt rebuffed. His head dropped.

Tommy thought. 'Oh dear! We have a delicate flower. That was a stupid comment. I have probably lost him!'

Keeping his eyes on Peter, he smiled, trying to calm him.

Then he imagined Peter and Frances Etteridge together and the smile widened, then faded as his empathetic 'antennae' quivered into action.

His natural and intended optimistic and jocular approach did not work with every new P.O.W.

He reached quickly for a sheet of paper, saying, "Let's begin again. I understand you have a fair appreciation of this camp's position. It is vital we glean the maximum.

Give us your ideas please."

He pushed the paper and pencil across the table.

To Tommy's relief, Peter's demeanour changed.

Peter drew a large cross on the paper.

"Assuming the vertical is north to south and the horizontal west to east and we are here at the centre, the crux," Peter began.

Tommy Davage suppressed the smile of relief.

Peter looked up seeking acknowledgment to see Tommy looking interested.

Encouraged, he continued with his theorising.

Tommy Davage however was *not* listening, only appearing to do so.

Charlie Strong had transferred the induction of Lt Barnes from Major Etteridge to him realising that it was a bad match. The colonel knew this was the P. R. Barnes, the recruit he had been requested to monitor by the war office.

This monitoring had ceased once Barnes had moved on to Sandhurst and officer training.

Charlie Strong now planned to inform the War Office of this reconnection.

'Well, you never know' was his thinking.

Tommy was thinking. 'Why is Charlie Strong so involved with this particular incomer?'

He was about to ask Peter. 'Have yours and Colonel Strong's paths crossed before?'

when it dawned on him that Lieutenant Barnes perhaps really had some useful information and tuned in to Peter's theorising.

Peter was explaining. "We were travelling approximately 26 hours. That is actual travelling not counting stops."

Tommy interrupted. "Remind me, where were you travelling from?"

"A camp roughly around the border of central East Belgium and Holland, sorry I can't remember exactly where. I was in shock and didn't get my head together at first."

Tommy made a note. "Please carry on," he encouraged.

"We were travelling at speeds somewhere between 25 and 30 miles an hour in a south easterly direction. This works out at approximately 700 miles."

"How did you assess the average speed?" Tommy made a note.

"By counting and timing the expansion gaps in the rails."

Tommy looked up. "How?"

"The clicks as the wheels pass over them," Peter explained.

"Ah, the diddly dahs. Actually, I can never tell my diddly dahs from the diddly dees," Tommy acknowledged.

Tommy didn't intend to be flippant. It was how he remembered from his childhood listening to the sound of the trains wheels on the tracks when going to the seaside and singing in excited chorus with his sister ...'diddly- dah, diddly- dee, diddly- dah, diddly- dee, we're on our way to see the sea.'

Peter recognising this, answered.

"The dahs are the furthest pair of carriage wheels and the dees the nearest pair, or the other way around. It doesn't matter. Just the timing between the wheels hitting the expansion gaps."

"Right, so 700 miles 'ish!" Tommy made a note then asked. "Where does that leave us if your southeast direction is correct? How did you work that one out?"

Tommy now knew Peter had something useful.

Peter tapping his watch, answered the second question.

"By the sun and time."

"And you managed all this for 700 miles and 26 hours plus?"

"Yes, sir." Peter nodded then continued filling in place names on the sheet.

"That puts this camp somewhere in southeast Bavaria, possibly Czechoslovakia. The range of mountains we can see to the east, suggests the Bavarian Wald bordering Czechoslovakia.

If true it puts this camp north east of Munich tucked in just between the Czech and Austrian borders. Prague to the north east, say 180/200 miles. Salzburg to the south maybe 80. A major route direct to some port on the Danau a mere 40 or so miles at the most to the south, possibly even closer."

Tommy, surprised at this analysis, struggled to listen while trying to evaluate.

"Port? How can you know that there is a port?"

"This camp was clearly a logging camp which the Boche have taken over. The slope to the south away from the Alps foothills, leads to the river. To transport logs any distance you need a major route. The Danau, which you probably call the Danube, would be a main transport route.

The only road out of here is well worn, wide and metalled. Not a mountain trail,suggesting frequent and heavy traffic."

"Bugger me!" Tommy exclaimed realising that Peter's assessment was 'gold dust'.

He flicked his fingers. “May I have that sheet, Peter?”

Peter handed it over. Tommy looked at this little man.

“Beats me how you managed this.”

Peter shrugged. “Keeps me from thinking of other things and getting depressed.”

“But for 26 hours, strewth.”

Tommy Davage walked to the door.

“Peter, you will come to me with your problems and ideas, won’t you?”

A few minutes later Captain Davage was stood reporting to of the camp C.O.

Charlie Strong studied the map in front of him alongside Peter’s theoretical positioning of the camp.

“I do know Tommy that Lt. Barnes has a double first in modern languages. I had no idea about his other talents. This is remarkable. It not only concurs with our assessments. It’s tighter and adds much more detail and he has done this in 48 hours whereas we took weeks. He must have a photographic memory of maps. That is unless he has an atlas stuffed down his pants.”

The colonel sucked on an empty pipe then pointed it at Tommy.

“I do know his German is fluent. Put that to good use and keep me informed about his progress.”

Tommy Davage was well pleased with his day’s work.

“Will do, sir.” He saluted and left.

Chapter 45

The following afternoon Tommy sought out Peter with plans for his immediate future and to check that he was settling down.

Some did so quickly, this being a combination of relief of surviving traumatic weeks and moving into the calmer and structured routines of the camp. Boredom and the pain of separation from their families usually came after. Others took much longer, some never settling.

These few presented problems by upsetting the smooth running of the camp even to the extent of endangering their colleagues.

All P.O.W.'s needed to be handled carefully. The trick was to see them all fully occupied as early as possible. Tommy had worries about Peter. They needed to keep him interested and involved.

He intended to find out more about this introspective intelligence officer.

"Peter, tell me please, were you interrogated?"

Peter nodded, but didn't speak.

"By whom?"

Peter again didn't answer. He just shrugged.

Tommy realised he'd hit upon a dangerous spot. He searched his mind as to how to proceed eventually deciding to think further before pursuing the question. Quickly changing tack, he said, "Peter, I would like you to officiate in the game of Sevens."

Peter looked vague for several seconds before repeating. "Sevens?"

Tommy took this to be a question.

"It's a game, quite a good one actually. It's designed to occupy the empty hours. We only started a month ago. It has taken off a storm."

He waited patiently for Peter's answer. No answer came. It was as if Peter had not heard.

Tommy continued, "It consists of teams of seven players. A 'court' of two mats, each two metres by one, courtesy of the camp commandant. These mats are placed three metres apart.

The bats are made from bed slats, the balls from tightly wound string.

Each member of the team, in turn, stands on the bowling mat or the batting mat and bowls or bats seven balls. Each innings lasts just 49 balls."

Throughout this explanation Tommy watched closely Peter's body language.

There seemed to be little or no reaction. Undeterred, Tommy continued with his explanation. "Teams made up from each hut play home and away. Home games are played in front of the team's own hut. The rules are simple, the bowler and batter must not leave the mat otherwise they will give one point away. If the bowler hits the batter's leg below the knee, also one point away."

Tommy paused as much interested in Peter's reactions. Whether or not he was interested or even listening? Tommy could have been talking to a stuffed cat for all the reaction shown.

"This is why we need umpires to adjudicate and to allocate points. We hope that you will agree to be one," Tommy continued, undeterred.

Peter was not looking at Tommy but over the captain's shoulder.

At first Tommy thought he was looking out to the distant mountains and turned to see but Peter was just looking at a blank wall. Tommy turned back to Peter.

"About being an umpire. What do you say?"

Tommy was taking in as much body language as he could. There was no fidgeting, no trembling. Nothing. He could have been looking at a dummy.

The proposal he had just made was in no way challenging. The lack of response was beginning to worry Tommy when Peter replied.

"Yes." Peter then shook his head indicating refusal. Thinking, 'how ridiculous! Yet sadly, necessary.'

To Tommy, this was the answer of a man not fully in control.

"Thank you, Peter." Tommy quickly accepted the affirmative.

"You will come to understand the sense of this when you have been here a few weeks."

Peter did not respond.

Tommy thought for a moment then changed his manner. He decided to 'pull rank'.

"Lt Barnes, what is being asked of you is *not* trivial. I am now ordering you to comply fully."

Standing up he turned and marched out to report to Colonel Strong.

Charlie Strong tapped his huge yellow teeth with his pencil.

"Keep a weather eye on him Tommy please, that's all we can do. I'll ask the camp commandant to arrange for a doctor to assess him. I suppose that will come to nothing. So, we will have to cope."

He threw the pencil on to the table then picked up his pipe and began to fiddle with it.

"Could do with some tobacco."

He was so accustomed to the comfort of the pipe which helped him think. He forced his mind back to the problem. "Returning to Barnes. I asked Captain Simmonds to see what he could find out about his history; how he came to be captured, but little is known. Barnes arrived in the holding camp sometime after the others. This is hearsay. The German officer who brought him in said that they no longer needed him because the British army had been routed. Running scared.

Can't say I was delighted to hear that."

The colonel proceeded to scrape out his pipe bowl with a penknife even though it was pristine and had not seen any tobacco for weeks.

Tommy considered what to say next before offering, "One thing, sir, he seemed rational and in control when dealing with the question of the camp's position. He must have been, to record such detail of the journey here. That does not sound to me like he's not with it. Today he's not the same man."

"That's it, Tommy, find him a task. Something on which he can focus. Have you told him the real reason for the Sevens league?"

"No, sir," Tommy answered. "I thought to keep it between ourselves until we are fully operational."

"Do so. He's not going to give the plan away to a colleague even in confidence. He has no friends. That might be part of the problem. In any event it will be common knowledge soon enough."

Chapter 46

Peter was sitting in the shadow of the hut looking up to the snow-capped mountains to the northeast. It was warm in the sun, even warmer in the hut. Incongruous as it may seem, the sight of the snow caps was as cooling for Peter as it was calming.

He was feeling homesick, longing for news of his friends, even dreaming of walking up the path to his father's house to sit in the kitchen and talk with May Sheppard.

The was trapped here with no one to talk to. Surrounded by silly people. Being asked to take part in stupid games was unbearable.

'I lift up mine eyes unto the hills from whence commeth my faith, my faith commeth from the Lord who made Heaven and Earth.' This phrase circled round and around in his head.

In vain, Peter tried to think of Shakespeare, Gray or Milton. Verses he loved.

This psalm returned yet again.

Tommy Davage arrived interrupting his thoughts.

"Beautiful, isn't it?"

Tommy's sudden arrival, embarrassed Peter who did not know whether he was thinking of or speaking out loud the words of the psalm.

Peter shrivelled into a tight ball trembling with anger and frustration.

Hearing Tommy's comment 'Beautiful, isn't it?' Peter thought he was referring to the psalm.

Tommy was not. He was leaning back on the hut looking up towards the mountain tops.

"I hope I am not disturbing you, Peter?"

Peter wanted to reply with the truth. 'Yes, you are, please leave me alone I want no more of your patronising ideas." But of course, he lied.

"Not at all, sir."

Tommy warmed to his theme.

"I want to put on my walking boots and hike up there. Sadly, there is the small matter of two high fences, barbed wire, several watch towers, searchlights and machine guns."

Tommy was watching Peter closely for any reaction.

The impression he got was one of sullen anger and withdrawal.

Tommy continued, "Trapped for years. Only God knows for how many years."

Tommy walked towards the fence. As he did so, the guns in the two nearest watch towers swung round and followed him.

Peter sat up and watched. This was something he had thought of doing: rushing at the fence and climbing. The prospect of surmounting one let alone two fences was not in question.

It was a way out he had thought about.

Tommy turned around and strolled back kicking at the ground. The dusty soil of the hot dry summer rose around his legs. He stopped in front of Peter. He scraped some of this same dust together with his shoes into a little pile between his feet.

Peter had guessed what Tommy was up to. He was expecting the lecture about the effect of a bullet-ridden body hanging from the wire dripping blood on the remaining prisoners.

He was surprised by Tommy's comments.

Tommy looked down at the pile at his feet.

"Very noticeable little piles of dust or dirt especially if there are a lot of them appearing out of nowhere. Question is, how to get rid of them before anyone notices? One is easy."

He swept this pile away with his shoe as he spoke.

"Dozens of them? Now that is a problem."

He looked pointedly at Peter who was now showing some interest.

Encouraged, Tommy continued, "This is a small camp. Not enough room for football or cricket.

Then there's the risk of fetching balls from the fence. Bored guards with itchy trigger fingers looking on. It is a situation ripe for tragedy."

Tommy paused then asked, "Throughout these long waiting years how do we keep ourselves fit mentally and physically Peter?"

Illogically, Peter thought Tommy's performance was criticism of his indifference.

His restrained anger seized upon this. He stood up and the two faced each other like two gunfighters. Tommy was a relaxed *Doc Holliday* and Peter a, tense as a coiled spring, *Billy the Kid.*

Tommy, for once, didn't smile. He raised his eyebrows in question, bent down to dust off his trousers, turned and walked away.

"How did it go Tommy? Well, I hope. The last thing I need is a tragedy on my watch especially not Lt. Barnes."

"What is it that is special about Barnes, sir?"

"Don't know Tommy, but trust me, he really is. He is on the books in very high places.

If anything happens to him, it will look bad on my record. Not only that, he could be more than useful with his language skills." Charlie Strong, anxious to learn about Barnes, persisted.

"You still haven't said how it went."

"Difficult to say. I think I may have caught his attention."

Tommy, aware that he was dealing with a very tricky situation and possibly more, continued.

"I think we must tread carefully though. He clearly has association problems. Difficulty in making friends and trusting people. I intend to give him the night to think things over. I will try again tomorrow."

Charlie nodded. "You would make a good angler. Play him like a salmon. Do your best, Tommy."

Captain Davage smiled.

"I am pleased to have your understanding, sir."

He saluted and turned to go.

Colonel Strong sucked on his empty pipe. "Let me know when you have him in the net."

Tommy who was leaving, stopped and turned back.

"He's already netted, sir. As are we all. The trick is to persuade him there is a way out."

Chapter 47

Tommy visited the shadows of the hut the following afternoon knowing that Peter would be there. Expecting a bad reception, he took up position alongside him.

Making no attempt to speak, he just stood for almost five minutes then squatted alongside Peter. Squatting with his back to the wall was an unnatural position for a tall man.

Very quickly the back of his legs began to hurt.

The last thing Tommy wished to do was to fidget. After several minutes he just couldn't take any more. He painfully stretched each leg, then sat with them outstretched waiting for the pain to subside.

His intent was to maintain silence until Peter spoke. He found this more onerous than he'd imagined. After a while the challenge became one which grew to a determination not to give in.

How long passed he didn't know.

Tommy moved into a trance-like state. After some time, Peter spoke.

"Hal would do this at first," he suddenly said without preamble or other explanation.

Tommy resisted the temptation to ask who Hal was.

Instead, he asked, "Do what?"

"Just sit with me."

Tommy waited for a follow-up which didn't happen immediately.

Eventually Peter did speak again. "It hurts, doesn't it?"

"What hurts Peter?"

Tommy struck at the 'bobbing float', hoping this was a clean strike.

Peter didn't answer the question.

"The Goons didn't understand," he said instead, suppressing what Tommy could only perceive as the beginnings of a laugh.

"Hal used to call them Goons."

Tommy thought to himself, 'I've finally hooked him.'

He resisted the obvious questions, believing that he was achieving most by silence.

Goons he surmised were the German interrogators, S. S. or regular officers even Gestapo and wondered what exactly they didn't understand.

These questions occupied his mind for several minutes until Peter spoke again.

"So, you are digging an escape tunnel using this Sevens game to distribute the excavated soil." Tommy still didn't respond so Peter continued.

"The Goons could twig. One of us caught in possession will give the whole game away."

All this had been anticipated by them and plans laid. Tommy ignored all this and asked:

"What do you suggest we do?"

"Post scouts out before every event," Peter replied. Clearly, he had also thought the plan through. "Scouting for what?"

Peter stood up then turned to look down at Tommy.

"Look, what exactly *do* you want?"

Tommy spread his arms but didn't speak. Peter persisted.

"You have already a complete plan. What then do you want from me?"

"Your help, especially with language. Your knowledge of German."

Tommy was ready with his answer.

Peter thought about this. "Preparation of documents and the like?"

"Yes, but not *just* that."

Tommy didn't explain what more they might need and continued.

"Peter of course you are right. We've covered everything including the distance needed to travel between the inner and outer fence to ensure we are truly outside when we surface."

Tommy paused, then asked, "What then?"

Peter gave this only a moment's thought.

"So, maps of the immediate area are needed. How do we manage that?"

Tommy delighted with the 'we' in 'how do we,' replied.

"I think you with your knowledge you could make a start. We can take it from there."

He paused before adding, "Also, hut six faces the gate between the inner and the outer fences. Do you think you could observe the comings and goings of outsiders, electricians, carpenters, etc., to get clues as to the nearest town plus anything else useful? I will get you transferred to hut six. Whenever a Sevens is played outside this hut, try to station yourself as near to the gate as possible. Listen in on any conversations held between guards and incomers. We are keeping quiet about your knowledge of German."

Tommy got stiffly to his feet and offered a hand to Peter.

The offer was ignored so Tommy left to inform the colonel of significant progress.

Peter, having spent a night thinking over the possibilities, concluded his options were cooperate or vegetate. Knowing he was going to agree eventually, he decided not to do so until the following day. He waited for Captain Davage to repeat the request, but he didn't.

Tommy didn't speak about it, thinking he had the measure of this disturbed little man.

He made general enquiries as to Peter's welfare, stood up, dusted his trousers then smiled as he turned away saying, "See ya."

He didn't say where. He didn't say when.

The only thing missing was this and 'Pete'.

The same feeling of loss, of being incomplete, overtook Peter's emotions. The years fell away to that moment when Hal left him staring over the bridge into the river Cam with a 'see ya, Pete,' as he left.

The next afternoon Peter took up his now usual position behind the hut.

Now, with a sense of anticipation, he was feeling better. If he was honest the advent of Tommy with all the attendant irritation had rescued him from the 'pit'.

Tommy turned up at the same time as the days before taking up his usual position next to Peter. Nothing was said for a minute or so. Peter then passed a paper on to Tommy.

It was the surmised map of the area around the camp. Little had changed from Peter's first crude drawing other than to prognosticate on the position of cities and the positions of possible Danube docks.

This was just what Tommy needed. It confirmed that Peter was 'on board'.

That he was confident of his previous calculations.

Chapter 48

Over two years trapped in a 'Tantalus' presented Tommy with massive problems;keping Lt. P R Barnes sane was just one of them.

Peter was special. He became the source of vital information via his command of German.

This was also vital in the preparation of documents and the instruction of escapees in the basics.

Boredom was eased by the huge interest in the game of Sevens. The players became more skilful and involved in leagues with the rivalry between huts and the entry of the Polish officers into the game providing the impetus.

This plus information that the R.A.F. were hitting back at the German war machine helped morale particularly so when Peter reported that constant bombing of the marshalling yards at Hamm was causing food shortages in some major German cities. The resulting cheers could be heard by the guards.

The approach of a third winter in captivity was now giving Colonel Strong concern.

The tunnelling was behind schedule, roof falls and the shortage of timber for support, a constant concern. Time was running out for the tunnel to be useable before the winter snows.

Tommy was under pressure to provide information about the near geography.

They needed it quickly.

The September days were pleasantly warm although the nights were becoming distinctly chilly.

One afternoon Tommy appeared in his regular spot behind hut 6, alongside Peter.

"Peter, we desperately need more information about the nearest mountain village or town, and we need it more than quickly. We need it now."

Tommy waited for a response which did not come.

"Perhaps it's time to try and engage one of the guards in conversation."

Peter still didn't answer. He was thinking.

He was already very friendly with one of the regular guards on the inner gate.

Having broken camp orders, he could not mention this.

The regular army guards had been gradually replaced by older conscripts and recuperating wounded. One such was Walter, an older man in his late fifties and a reluctant conscript.

The guards' living quarters were less than ideal and the camp commandant's attention to his own comforts, irritated.

The arrival of a little old man to attend to and to update his shower and flush the toilet was one such irritation.

This tiny, ageing plumber arrived on a bike carrying his tools on the panier. He was wearing a long dark coat and a floppy broad brimmed hat. Ridiculous clothes for a cyclist in warm weather even though the mornings and evenings in autumn were chilly at altitude.

He entered the outer gate, took off his overcoat and hat and hung them up and parked his bicycle in a lean-to hut which was built into the watch tower alongside the inner gate guarded by Walter. The plumber entered the compound to go to the commandant's quarters which were part of the old accommodation block for the logging company at the head of the camp.

Peter realised that this old man could not have cycled a great distance and must live in a nearby community. A plumber would need clients within a short distance.

For this old man to cycle uphill carrying tools at his age, his base would not be that far away.

Questioning Walter had proved unproductive. Although friendly, he was no fool.

Peter had now to decide whether or not to pass on this information, such as it was to Tommy.

"How is the tunnel coming along?" Peter asked Tommy.

Tommy decided it was time to come clean, although economical with the truth.

Talking about progress was not the norm but it was safer than treating the subject as taboo.

Those involved in the operation knew of the problems, especially the shortage of suitable timber. Best to leave the camp with the impression that all work was on schedule and not destroy their hopes.

"We are already outside the outer fence. The big worry is a collapse."

"We have pushed along too quickly without enough timber for roof support. The autumn rains, if heavy, could cause collapse so we need to crack on. The prospect of a third winter stuck here being too awful to contemplate."

"So, we could go any day?"

"Indeed, but Colonel Strong has not yet given the word. I believe he wishes to be nearer the tree line. We must try to go before the snows arrive. Snow could give us too many problems."

"If we don't go soon, I'm climbing the fence," Peter answered.

The following week a game of Sevens was arranged outside hut six.

Peter was at his usual station as umpire standing as close to the gate as he could.

The guard on that afternoon was Walter. Peter began his customary out of the side of the mouth conversation, hoping to get a clue as to the nearest town or mountain village.

"Missed you. Have you had leave?" Peter asked.

"No, my friend. Another duty, guarding the harvest from thieves."

"A farm near here?" Peter picked up on this immediately.

Walter smiled, knowing exactly what Peter was about.

"I have brought you some ripe plums. I have put them in the corner of the wooden frame of the gate under the watch tower," he replied, ignoring Peter's question.

Peter was not surprised that Walter did not answer.

Walter's present of fresh fruit was fantastic.

"Thank you," he whispered, "what about the guards in the watch tower, won't they notice?"

Walter turned around and walked a little way up the fence and back looking up at the towers before replying.

"You are underneath the eyeline of this one and in the shadow of it. With the other one you should be fine. They will expect me to be watching. In any event the sun is now low to the west and in their eyes."

In September at this altitude, the days were pleasantly warm. Once the sun had gone down, the temperature dropped sharply.

The scene, apart from the Sevens game, which was being hotly contested, was one of tranquillity. The contrast between this beautiful weather heralding another harsh winter, did not allow Peter to relax.

It had been weeks since he had heard from Pen and months since hearing from Hal and his father. He was not looking forward to the long cold nights trapped in hut six with his thoughts and no real companionship.

Tommy was friendly but controlling.

Walter was different.

He was offering the friendship for which he longed. The present of the plums was food for his soul in addition to a change from a dull diet.

Cautious in the beginning, he edged backwards and sideways towards the plums nestling in the wooden framework.

He thought to himself that if he was spotted and shot it would solve his many problems.

Reaching out, he quickly grasped them and popped them into his pocket.

As he did, as if in response to this act, a siren began to wail.

Peter immediately flattened himself back to the wooden framework.

Armed guards started running from all directions to many shouted orders.

An officer ran up the slight slope to the inner gate.

"Guard, open up," he yelled at Walter.

Peter froze with his back to the fence expecting the worst.

The officer didn't see Peter in the shadows. Running by him he shouted orders to Walter.

"Get all prisoners into their hut then stay and guard hut six."

He then ushered several more men through the gate with similar orders.

All eyes were looking west to a where the guards were gathering between the forest and the fence shielding their eyes against the setting sun.

The inner gate was still open. Peter realised he was behind the officer's eyeline.

He looked down the slope to the outer gate house. The outer gate was also open as more soldiers were ushered through. Peter sidled along the fence then slipped through the inner gate and into the lean-to.

He was standing back in the shadows of the hut because he was open to view from below.

His face brushed the plumber's coat hanging there. He dodged behind it, his heart thumping.

The outer gate was still open with even more soldiers moving through and lining the fence.

Every eye was focusing west, against the setting sun.

That was all eyes but Peter's, who could only see the open outer gate. Reaching up he unhooked the plumber's overcoat and slipped into it. Donning the floppy hat, he took the plumber's bicycle, and resting a foot on the pedal he scooted down to the main gate.

Asking Peter why he did this might have brought the answer. 'At last I am alive and in charge of my own destiny.'

Peter in that moment could only see an open outer gate.

At the gate an officer was directing operations. A corporal and two guards were looking westwards towards the point of interest. The sun, rimming the treetops, cast long shadows over grass.

The shadows plus the sun in their eyes revealed little of what was happening.

A fresh line of soldiers arrived at the gate at the same time as Peter who was forced to stop.

The inevitable happened, one of the guards held out an arm keeping Peter back.

This was an automatic reaction because the guard was not looking at him.

"Was ist los?" Peter asked. This was the instinctive reaction of a mind trying to discover what was happening. He really wanted to know.

"Hau ap!" snarled the officer. (literally, 'Sling your hook.')

"Raus," added a corporal. Waving him away, the guard stood back. Peter immediately scooted out of the gate and mounting the bicycle properly he pedalled down the hill.

He expected to be shot down almost immediately.

After the first few hundred metres, the rock-hard muscles of expectation relaxed.

Adrenaline flowed. With the wind in his face, he was flying. He pedalled furiously and freewheeled downwards and onwards for almost half an hour. He left the forest, where the terrain opened into scrub and farmland.

The sun had just set on a dramatic day, the last of which was just showing in the western skies.

The moon was full, and the stars were sparkling brighter than crown jewels.

They enhanced Peter's sense of freedom. He stopped, not to admire the scenery but because he was brought to his senses by the change of terrain.

The first rush of emotion now passed, leaving him confused and with a banging headache.

He turned back instinctively towards the shelter of the trees. In the distance, he could hear sirens, sounds of pursuit. The terrain was wide open from there as the forest gave way to scrub and heath.

He turned back up the hill looking for cover.

A little way back up the road he stopped by a plantation of fir trees. Crossing the verge, he pushed the bicycle between two of the rows. He pushed until the bike would go no further.

Backing out of the 'tunnel', a broken branch slid up his trouser leg, breaking the skin. It dug into his flesh, a small piece breaking off under his skin as he dragged it free.

This wood splinter was difficult to remove until he was clear of the trees. Lifting his trouser leg, he removed it, spitting on his hand he then cleaned the wound as best he could.

The flashing lights of the pursuit vehicles forced him back under cover. He lay still until the sound of them faded. Crawling deeper into the trees, he found a little more space.

Once settled, Peter being Peter, tried planning his next moves. His head was still thumping, it was too difficult.

Breaking off several of the lower branches he swept together the carpet of pine needles to make a bed. The effort of the last minutes had left him exhausted and his headache worse.

He had now a raging thirst and no water. He flopped down and tried to gather his thoughts.

Gradually his heart rate slowed and he was able to control his breathing. Unable to think, he lay back, eyes closed, trying to clear his head.

How long he was in this state he had no idea. He spent some time trying to muster enough saliva to quench his thirst. His thigh felt damp reminding him about the plums. He reached into his pocket only to discover that they had been squashed.

He recovered enough flesh. The flesh tasted succulent and juicy. Not only did this quench his thirst, it rescued him from the state of panic which had overtaken him.

He then thought, 'At least I am free for now and must stay so as long as possible.'

How? That was the question he could not answer.

Eventually he gave up and pulled the plumber's coat around him. Sucking on a plum stone to keep his saliva running, he tried to sleep.

Questions, however, 'refused' to leave his mind.

He was not an easy sleeper.

The last two years trying to sleep each night heralded the beginning of a train of agonising thoughts.

He was now in a better place to formulate a plan.

Planning did not help him to catch his sleep. He did not do so until the early hours.

Chapter 49

Peter woke up much later than he intended. Instead of leaving under cover of darkness, as planned, he awoke to the sound of birdsong and a sun already climbing above the mountains to the east.

Slowly he inched out of the trees looking both ways to make sure that the road was clear.

Straightening and stretching he was reminded that his leg was more than sore. It was already throbbing with infection.

Keeping as close to the trees as possible he made his way down to the start of the open scrub land. His intention now was to travel east until he reached a water course then to follow this down to the Danube.

Leaving the forest behind he was met with an ethereal scene. Across the open scrub land, white mist patches lay in the hollows with scrub poking through.

A scattering of sunbeams shone through the trees on to the autumnal wildflowers. The scene enhanced by the beginnings of a heat shimmer.

Having no idea of the time he assumed it was mid-morning. He found the going rough, crossing winter marshland which was hardened by a prolonged dry summer. Walking was difficult, the terrain hard and undulating.

Thirsty, he searched for the plum stone to suck, without success.

How long it was before he came to an open ditch he didn't know. He knelt and cupped his hands but all it contained was a slimy pool of stagnant water.

Picking up a pebble he cleaned it as best as he could. He tried to suck it then spat it out. It was abhorrent.

His head was aching, as was his leg. If the army had turned up, he would have given in readily.

Turning back was not an option. Going forward into the unknown, without alternative.

Over to his right Peter could see a line of deciduous trees.

This was a change of scenery. All he could think of was the shade the trees would provide. Painfully, he hobbled towards them. This took longer than he imagined. By the time he reached them the thirst was causing him to croak.

Peter sat down in the shade trying to take his mind off this. He lifted his trouser leg.

The wound had been bleeding also it was suppurating.

Hearing voices nearby he hobbled beyond the trees to a hedgerow and looked over.

He could see several people dressed in dusky yellow overalls picking potatoes and loading them on to a horse driven cart.

Beyond this, to the right he could see a farmhouse. Painfully, he staggered down the hedge through a gap and along a worn path to the farm.

The door facing the yard was open. He limped to the open door to look in on a farm kitchen.

A handsome mature woman was busy cooking. Two young girls were attending to other tasks.

The smell of a stew drifted across from an iron pot atop a solid fuel cooker.

Peter's greater need now was for water. His presence in the doorway cut out the sunlight, his shadow spreading across the flagged floor.

The woman looked up. "Ja?"

"Wasser, bitte," Peter croaked.

The woman reached for a brown earthenware pot from a wooden dresser and filled it from an iron pump at the sink.

"Ingrid a chair, quickly," she ordered passing the water to Peter who drank greedily.

Taking the chair from the girl the woman placed it in the doorway.

"Take a seat."

Peter sat down gratefully.

Sofi Rensberg looked at this little man and gently removed his hat.

"Sleeping rough?" she asked.

Peter nodded.

She smiled. "Draft dodging?" This was more a statement than a question.

Peter objected more strongly than he would have with thought.

"No-no-no," he replied.

Sofi Rensberg concluded the opposite.

"Are you hungry?" she asked.

"Ja ich habe hunger," Peter said. The smell of the stew and years of sparse diet influenced his reply. Sofi noted the hard-edged pronunciation. Probably a Berlin accent, she thought.

This confirmed to her that he was indeed draft dodging.

Sofi Rensberg had no truck with the Nazis and the war which had robbed her of her son Joachim and her husband. It was a stupid war which was now dominating her life and farm.

Peter, conscious of his vulnerability, pulled the coat firmly around his uniform.

He needn't have worried because no one had noticed. Sofi was in no mood to hand him in.

She had heard stories of defectors travelling to northern Italy where sympathisers would hide and protect them.

This young man would have to cross Austria to do so. He did not look in a fit shape to cross the road.

She prepared him a sandwich of fresh bread and home cured ham along with a mug of cow's milk.

In the meantime, she was thinking of plans to help him. This young man was some mother's son.

She had not heard anything about her own son for three months, apart from a curt note saying he was missing.

Sofi could not help her son, but she could help this young man. She hoped and prayed someone would be as kind to Joachim.

"What say you help me get my potato crop in? You can sleep in the hay loft for a couple of nights."

Not only wishing to help him, she needed all the help she could to get the crop in before the frosts and to meet her quotas.

"Sorry, I must move on."

Peter, now fed and watered, was anxious to leave before they discovered who he was.

"At least one day's work. You owe me that. I will pay you. In addition, there will be food and a night in the hay loft. You could leave tomorrow, refreshed."

Peter did not answer but pulled his coat more closely around him.

"You will be safer out in the open dressed in overalls same as all the hands."

Peter looked up sharply. He liked this idea.

"Overalls?" he questioned.

"Across in the barn, choose a set to fit though you may need to roll up the sleeves and legs."

Sofi smiled encouragingly.

Sofi Rensberg felt empowered for a change to be doing something for this young man.

She wished for herself to escape the power of this suffocating regime which had destroyed her family, her settled good life and was dominating her present.

Peter accepted that he was in debt to this woman. Her idea had merit, but she wondered how she would react if she knew the truth.

Having no other plan, the day's food and an overnight rest was attractive. He weighed the chances of being picked up and concluded he stood a better chance here than on the open road.

Reaching the Danube was still the plan, but that could wait until the morrow.

"Overalls across in the barn you say?"

Sofi smiled. "Ingrid show ...' she hesitated and looked enquiringly at Peter.

"Dieter," he answered her unspoken question.

"Show Dieter where the overalls are kept and come straight back."

She knew Ingrid's tendency to hang around any male.

Peter limped across the yard and Sofi thought to herself, 'Shit, he's a wounded deserter.'

Then she decided this was even more reason to help him.

In the event of his arrest she would deny all knowledge.

Peter picked out a pair of overalls. Removing his hot surge uniform was a relief.

He then wrapped all, except the hat, in the overcoat hiding the bundle in one of the stalls.

Now fed and watered, he was feeling better.

At the head of the stalls an iron pump over a stone water trough 'beckoned'.

He pumped the handle and put his head under the flow. Lifting the leg of the overalls, he washed the wound as best he could, then returned to the farmhouse.

Sofi came to meet him and was encouraged by what she saw. Now in overalls and wearing a broad brimmed floppy hat, he could pass unnoticed.

"Report to the woman on the cart. Know this, if you give false names you will meet with the consequences. You have been warned." Peter crossed the field towards the pickers. An old woman looked down from the cart, sighed and picked up a clipboard. "Name?"

"Dieter."

"Shit, shell shocked, are we? Dieter who? Idiot." The old woman, dozing, resented being disturbed.

"Haering," Peter replied.

"HAERING." She spelled it out, looking up for confirmation. Peter nodded.

"It is hoped you pick better than you speak." Irmgard threw a basket at his feet.

The other pickers stopped momentarily appalled by the treatment of this young man who they assumed was a wounded soldier.

"Come on, get a move on!" Irmgard shouted.

An old man picked up the basket and handed it to Peter.

"Here son, you work with me and take the row alongside. Are you on five pfennig a basket?

I mean to say, in this heat, to be treated like dirt. Watch the woman, she'll cheat you if she can."

"Why the overalls?" Peter asked starting to pick.

"To stop pilfering, they spy on us all the time and send soldiers to watch that we don't.

If they see anyone picking without proper dress, there's trouble."

He straightened and spat into the soil.

"You'll notice there's no pockets, they'll not even let us have the odd potato."

Already the man had filled his basket, his mahogany-skinned bony hands clawing up the tubers, his arms pumping like steam pistons.

Peter was already beginning to realise he was not going to last the day.

The moment of being refreshed by shedding his surge trousers, overcoat and donning the lighter overalls was gone.

His stomach, unused to rich food, was already reacting to the ham.

The late September sun began to drain his strength. The headache had returned. His leg throbbed with the infection.

The old man didn't notice and continued his soliloquy of complaint.

"Frau Rensberg feeds us well or I wouldn't be doing this for just a few marks each day."

Peter could hear this tirade even though the man was already several metres ahead of him. Suddenly the old man stood up.

"See, there they are, snooping again."

Peter turned to see what looked like two policemen talking to Sofi Rensberg in the farmyard.

His heart missed a beat. He placed his basket on the ground and wiped his hands down his overalls. He was spent. No longer did he have the strength to resist. He felt ill and no longer cared.

The old man stood and joined him.

"Ach, there's a policeman with that inspector fellow, Rolf.

They might have been rumbled at last."

"Rumbled, who?"

"Frau Rensberg and that inspector. They've got a thing going and I don't mean just under the blankets. Cheating on her husband and him up at the Front," he snorted.

"Not just satisfied cheating the system. See, that policeman is checking up on us now. Time that they checked up on her."

The old man returned to his picking.

Peter looked towards the farmhouse. The policeman had walked over to the edge of the field and was looking across. Convinced the game was up Peter turned to face him. Feeling so ill, part of him was pleased that it was finally all over.

To his surprise the policeman touched his cap with his forefinger and returned to join his colleague.

Sofi Rensberg looked up and smiled when she saw Rolf in the doorway. He was the local quotas and inspection officer. She and Rolf had more than one mutually beneficial arrangement.

Quickly, she stepped outside the door closing it behind her. The girls she knew, would be all ears.

Her manner changed quickly, once she realised, he was accompanied by a police officer.

Her first thought was 'we have been rumbled.'

Rolf quickly put her at ease, or so he thought.

"We are looking for an escaped British prisoner of war," he announced thinking he was allaying Sofi's fears.

Sofi's heart missed a beat as she realised that she could be harbouring the very man.

The little man did appear to be a German citizen. The command of the language and the ease at which he understood and reacted pointed to this.

She thought quickly. If not careful, she was in severe trouble.

Rolf concerned with her reaction or lack of it asked, "You all right, Frau Rensberg?"

Sofi gathered her wits. "Thank God, I thought I was in trouble with my quotas."

"No," answered the policeman. "Have you seen a small man wearing a long dark coat, possibly riding a bicycle with a metal carrier on the back?"

Sofi now was in no doubt of her predicament. Maybe she would have been served better to confess the mistake, but, she shook her head slowly.

"No. I can't say that I have. When and where could I possibly notice anything? I'm working from dawn to dusk trying to harvest my crops. The chances of me getting the potato crop in before the frost and meeting my quotas are nil. No proper help, just three old men and a cripple."

Rolf avoided the implied complaint thinking it was a blind to quell any thoughts that they may be overfriendly.

"Frau Rensberg, I am here on other business not quotas. Believe me I understand your difficulties."

The policeman meanwhile left the two talking and walked to the edge of the field to survey the pickers.

Sofi, standing in the doorway prevented entry into the work room. Shielding the girls from any questioning, she watched anxiously as he did.

Rolf, now suspecting that Sofi was hiding something, raised an eyebrow in question.

The policeman returned. Rolf went to meet him.

"Frau Rensberg knows to be in touch if she suspects anything."

The policeman bowed slightly to Sofi. The two men left to continue their enquiries.

Sofi watched them leave then returned to the work room, her brain working overtime.

She needed to get the girls out of the way.

"You two, I want you to take lunch out to the pickers."

She handed them each a basket.

"Tell Irmgard the field will be finished by tomorrow night no matter what. While you are out there help with the picking to the end of the row before returning. Send that cripple back.

He is useless."

The girls removed their aprons and donned official smocks and left.

Working at the farm was a privilege. Many more were waiting to take their place.

Peter returned to the farmhouse to find the work room empty and no sign of the officials.

Not knowing what to expect, his head throbbing with shock and pain, he stood and waited.

A shout of 'in here' came through the open door.

Peter climbed up a single step then through the door which led into the farmhouse building proper. Sofi was inside a large living room sorting through some clothing on a wooden table.

"You conniving little shit. Where did you learn your language? In Berlin?"

Sofi spoke through gritted teeth not even taking the time to look up while searching.

Peter didn't answer, his head being full of questions, the foremost of these being.

'What happens now?'

As if hearing his thoughts, Sofi continued, "Get your clothes and your coat. Get out of those overalls and climb into these."

She held up a pair of Joachim's trousers and looked critically at him for a few seconds.

"Can you get into a 75 waist?"

Peter picked up on this and answered. "Maybe. I have lost a lot of weight."

Sofi came around and measured the leg length from the waist. Taking a pair of scissors, she cut a piece off each leg. Placing the scissors on the table with the trousers she continued to issue orders.

"Fetch your uniform and cut off all the buttons and other metals and put them in this bag and be quick about it or we are both dead."

Wondering why Sofi was helping him confused Peter.

He understood what she was about. Not why. Not only was he already in her debt, she was now, putting herself in greater danger. He wanted to thank her and apologise at the same time, but he was unable to find the words.

He stood frozen to the spot his temples banging.

"Move!" Sofi yelled.

Peter recovered his senses and hurriedly limped across to the barn and collected his bundle of clothes from the stalls. Returning, he carried out her bidding to instructions while she continued thinking out loud.

"Rolf suspects something and will be back to check on me. He dares not say a thing, because I will drag him down with me. The girls they are not fools. They'll keep quiet in front of me but once out of my hearing, who knows?"

She stopped what she was doing and looked at Peter.

"I want you out of my sight and off my farm quickly. Get into this outfit and out of the overalls, underwear. The lot."

She began thrusting his clothes into the solid fuel fire ramming them through the open enamel door with a poker.

Peter changed as she continued to work to destroy all evidence.

The replacement clothes fitted apart from the shirt sleeves which were too long. These he turned up. His heart was beating so hard, he could feel it in his chest and in his ears.

He was feeling sick and faint, just wanting to lie down.

Sofi thrust the bag of metal objects into his hand.

"Take this with you. Take a left at the hay barn and follow the field paths for about a kilometre.

You will come to a wooden jetty with a small rowing boat alongside.

Take the boat then follow the river down to the Danau. Once in mid-stream away from here, empty the contents of this bag into the water. Understood?"

Peter nodded finally finding his voice. "What about you?"

"Move, for God's sake. Move!" She shook him. "Now," she whispered.

"Please, you have never been here."

Following Sofi's directions Peter struggled on his way to the river jetty, stopping once to be sick.

He had to force himself onward, striving not to collapse.

Reaching the jetty, he fell into the boat and with a supreme effort he untied the rope.

The river's flow, typical of the late summer, was quite gentle. Peter feeling so ill, didn't even attempt to take the oars, passing out in the bottom of the boat.

The little craft floated on unmanned. Carried by the current, it drifted with the river's flow throughout the day towards the Danube.

Chapter 50

Alt Ulf or Ulfie Dumkof, as he was alternately known to the village children, was neither as old nor as dumb as he appeared.

Living with his blind widowed mother, he was caring, resourceful and sharp as a carpet tack.

So far, he had avoided being drafted into the army, which had befallen so many of his contemporaries. A survivor from the war which widowed his mother, his survival plan in this world had its roots in the trenches back in 1917.

Their home, an isolated woodman's cottage, was some way outside the village up against a newly planted forest; part of an Austrian government forestry plan begun in the 1920s.

The little house stood in the centre of a fire break clearing alongside a riverside track used by logging trucks when the river was too low to transport the timber by water.

The receiving wharf was at the junction where the river flowed into the Danau.

These timbers were to be loaded on to big river barges. Ulf occasionally worked as a labourer on this wharf. He sometimes worked on the shipbuilding and repair yard which lay alongside.

Otherwise, he mainly lived on his wits and the wild bounty of the region.

He fished upstream for brown trout and set traps for crayfish, rabbits, wood pigeon and other game. One of his most productive areas for crayfish was where the mountain river flowed into the Danau. The repeating wash from the huge river barges plus the spring floods had created the beginnings of a small island with a shallow channel between it and the east bank.

Trees and bushes overhung this channel from both sides. These shallows were favoured by the crayfish, and beneath these overhanging bushes, Ulf placed his traps.

These were pickle jars with holes punched through the metal caps. These jars were weighted with stones and baited with fish heads, bones and scraps then tied by the neck to the bushes.

This plan reliably provided him with a constant supply of crayfish.

This September morning, he arrived at these shallows just before dawn. Parting the branches to reach his traps, he discovered the body of a young boy.

Ulf first checked and found a pulse and signs of life.

He pulled the boy from under the branches then hoisted him over his shoulder in a fireman's lift. River water spouted out of the boy's mouth and ran down his back as he struggled up the bank on to the path. Placing the body head down on the slope of bank, Ulf applied pressure to his rib cage until he was sure that the lungs were free of river water, then heaved him back up to level ground to examine him. The victim had a contused head wound and a broken leg.

Ulf also discovered that it was not a boy but a small man. He straightened up and thought what next to do.

He did not wish to go to the police station just 300 metres or so up the street leading to the boat yard. Explanations as to why he was abroad wading in the river before dawn would lead the authorities to conclude, quite correctly, that he was out poaching. The inevitable prosecution would result in Ulf being drafted into the army.

It was common knowledge that men in their late fifties were already being conscripted.

The prospect of leaving his mother without support frightened him. Yet he could not just leave this stricken man.

Ulf picked him up and carried him on to the wharf then over to the emergency post which contained a life belt, a rope ladder and a direct telephone line to the police station.

Propping the limp frame against the unit, he lifted the telephone and cranked the handle.

Franz Mundt turned over in bed and moaned at the sound of the alarm bell and got up to answer. "Hello," he grunted.

"Help, please help." Ulf whispered hoarsely before letting the telephone fall to swing loosely from the unit. He then swiftly left the scene.

Franz smiled to himself at Ulf's crude attempt to disguise his voice. He both liked and trusted Ulf who presented no problems for the community.

Ulf's and Franz's view of morality and the law were not dissimilar.

The question of Ulf's poaching remained only in the back of his mind.

Ulf was no real trouble, robbing no one. In fact, the very opposite was true. He knew of beneficiaries who had received unsolicited gifts of rabbit, fish and pheasant also surplus vegetables.

Franz had not received any, but his old, widowed aunt had.

He dressed quickly and went to check the wharf finding, as he half expected, a casualty.

He immediately called the emergency services.

Chapter 51

It was several days before Peter came to anything like his normal senses.

He spent days spent drifting in and out of hallucinatory dreams.

Consciousness returned slowly with a sense of being warm and comfortable and cared for, which he enjoyed. Gradually he gained an appreciation of his surroundings.

His memory began, spasmodically, to return.

Meanwhile he eavesdropped on the medical discussions concerning him.

These were not good. Concussion, fever and an infected broken leg, about which the medics could do little except apply splints, dress daily and await the clearing of the infection.

This was a time of much confusion. How did he come to be here? What had caused his injuries?

Try as he may, he could not sort out who he was, let alone where he was.

An impression of Dieter freewheeling with the wind in his face to go and pick potatoes was gradually replaced by more accurate memories which were less than comforting.

On the fourth morning, the first of Peter's sensible memory, a nurse in the process of taking his temperature, noticed him looking at her. She smiled as she asked, "Hello, at last, Dieter. Feeling better?"

'Dieter?' Peter was still trying to sort out his thoughts.

"Is my name Dieter?" he asked still trying to come to terms with his situation.

The nurse looked at the thermometer.

"Temperature is normal at last."

She straightened his bed clothes. "Now don't you worry about a thing, just you rest for now."

After writing on his notes, the nurse left to report to the doctor.

There were few overt Austrian political attitudes in these difficult times other than National Socialism. The Nazis were largely, although not entirely, supported by the younger half of the population. Older heads were often split into two camps, one, the do nothing but stay neutral and hope the situation would resolve itself in good time.

Another faction, who without risk, were actively subversive when the opportunity presented itself.

A further much smaller group were actively working against the Nazis.

Information was frequently passed between these last two camps.

This hospital contained all these elements.

Frau Dr Elsa Weiskopf was occasionally drawn into the latter camp. Not from a proactive stance but mainly from a desire not to be part of a movement which she detested.

A few days earlier Elsa was the senior assessment and admission officer on the morning of the admission of patient 42/10178 crossed her desk. She read the papers carefully.

Nationality. Not known? Itinerant bargee? Broken tibia and fibula with infected wound. Concussion.

Lungs infected by ingested river water, and fever.

Elsa raised the telephone and after a moment's thought she replaced it. Her assistant looked up. "Who do we inform about that one?"

"No one for the time being," Elsa replied, "I doubt that he will last the night."

She placed the file into her pending box.

Chapter 52

'Gerda Weismann' called for the usual morning paper at the newsstand and caught her usual train to the clinic. She opened the paper to page two, column four to find written in pencil 'Lunch 12:30.'

At lunchtime she entered a small restaurant on a back street of the town and looked around before sitting at a small table for two. She was joined minutes later by an old man.

"Gruss Gott."

They exchanged greetings.

The real reason for their meeting was not discussed during the meal following which the gentleman paid for then moved through a curtain and up a single flight of stairs to a first-floor room.

Shortly afterwards Gerda followed him to the knowing looks of other diners.

The small room they entered was furnished simply with a small table, two chairs and a single bed.

Half an hour later they left by a rear entrance, separately.

That same evening a clinic closed its doors at 7.00 p.m. The staff were clear of the building by 7.15pm. Gerda and three others stayed behind to hold a 'practice' meeting.

Gerda finished her briefing and asked, "Any questions?"

"Could this be a trap?" she was asked.

"Yes, it could. The trouble is we have so little time."

"Why is this subject so important?" asked one.

"Why isn't the subject best left for the time being?" asked another.

She replied, "I can only say the subject is important and that time and timing is of the essence." Gerda was adamant. "Marshal your units. No. 1, your task is here." She passed to him a sealed envelope, followed by sealed orders to the others.

"You will be referred to by your individual numbers preceded by tomorrow's date and the time minus one hour and one minute that is of now 21.38. Can we now synchronise our watches? It is now 20.37 for the purpose of this project.

The coded times will be given via the usual route and will be your instruction to proceed immediately with your task. Once it is completed, disperse at once."

Gerda looked at each in turn. "Any questions?"

All three, familiar with this routine, left by separate entrances at separate times.

Chapter 53

Back in the P.O.W. camp Colonel Strong was holding a camp meeting in one of the huts. He said, "Our project Wind in the Willows as you know failed. I can't say just when, if at all, it will be resurrected. If any of you have any ideas as to where we can go or what we can do next, please contact Captain Davage and we will take it from there."

This statement was met with a wall of silence.

Realising that he could not leave it there, Charlie Strong cleared his throat and hoping that it would lift the assembly's spirits, said, "If it is of any consolation the project does not seem to have been a complete failure. The latest information we have is that Lt. Barnes is still at large and could be clean away."

Charlie Strong looked around the hut at the sea of disconsolate faces, conscious of the silence of disappointment and despair.

What he hoped for he didn't know. Perhaps knowing that at least one of them had escaped would really be some consolation. What he did know was that life was about to get very difficult for those left behind facing another winter.

There was no response. His words were met once more with ominous silence.

He added, "A measure of some sort of success I suppose."

The prolonged silence following was then broken by someone shouting at the back.

"Two and a half years of sweat digging a tunnel and failing. Then that little runt walks out of the fucking gate. Call that a measure of success?"

Another time, another place, the remark might have sparked laughter but not here.

The strange breathless silence continued as the comment rendered everyone including Charlie Strong speechless. The assembly waited for the colonel's reaction which should have been to find and discipline the culprit.

This reaction did not come. Time ticked by. Colonel Strong still couldn't find words.

Captain Tommy Davage realising that time had been suspended to the point of agony, took charge forcing himself to control his voice as he spoke.

"That will be all for now gentlemen, dismiss."

Then Tommy waited for the reprimand for taking the decision in the presence of the C. O. and three other senior officers.

Charlie Strong finally found his voice.

"Thank you, gentlemen, that *will* be all for now."

He emphasised '*that will*' leaving Tommy to understand that there would be consequences. The colonel turned to leave.

"Captain Davage. My room in five minutes."

Five minutes later Tommy knocked on the colonel's door.

Charlie wanted to thank Tommy for taking charge in the meeting. Protocol stood firmly in the way. He had already decided against disciplinary action. He wished to give the impression that he was reprimanding Tommy to the others especially Frances Etteridge, who was guaranteed to play everything by the book. Etteridge was certain to demand an example of the outspoken officer in the meeting.

Charlie answered Tommy's knock. "Enter."

Captain Davage did so and stood to attention.

Charlie fiddled with his empty pipe and tapped it on his desk.

"At ease. Tommy, we have to face it. Lt Barnes is not the measure of our success. His escape is more a measure of our failure. We now need to make the best of it. Certainly, it was Barnes's opportunism and nothing to do with us."

He paused and sighed.

"It's all we have. I don't want him to be returned here in chains. We need him out there.

We need him to succeed. Question is can we help?"

He tapped his pipe on the table as he thought.

"Tommy, I think it is time for a letter to Winifred, coded as usual."

He stood and began to pace.

"We must let the War Office know about Lt. Barnes; the nature of his escape and the failure of Wind in the Willows. It will be difficult, I know. Just do your best to fill them in. They have contacts in Switzerland I am certain. Maybe they can do something to assist Barnes."

"Will do, sir. Usual drill applying I take it?" Tommy stood back to attention.

"Yes, do your best. Thank you, Tommy. Dismiss."

Charlie Strong watched the door close behind Captain Davage, then threw his empty pipe at the wall.

It bounced back across the room to land at his feet.

Chapter 54

The doctor in charge of trauma and intensive care did not focus on the identity of admission 42/10798, only on his care and recovery. Now with the patient physically if not mentally improved, he needed to have him transferred to another ward. The infection in the leg wound, however, was preventing the doctor from ordering a plaster cast.

The orthopaedic ward was refusing to accept him until the infection was clear.

The question of the patient's identity had arisen. Frau Doctor Weiskopf was asking for a name.

All this he could do without not only because of his workload.

The trousers, removed when the patient arrived, had been crudely shortened.

The shirt was too large and turned up at the wrists. Whether it was pressure of work or deliberate obstruction, he'd had these clothes destroyed.

Making matters worse he had failed to record any of this.

"How is the little bargee today, nurse?" he asked.

"In and out of consciousness but improving Herr Doctor."

"Find out his name, nationality, age, etc. as soon as possible. You know the drill."

"Certainly, Herr Doctor."

Peter who had his eyes closed, listening to this exchange, knew that he would have to respond soon.

When the nurse questioned him, he answered.

"Where am I, what have I done?"

"We need to know your name so that we can contact your next of kin."

Peter, needing to know where he was, repeated, "Where am I?"

"You have had an accident and you are in hospital."

Peter closed his eyes and faked slipping back into a coma. He needed to think his next move.

The nurse reported back to the doctor that, in her opinion, the patient was faking loss of memory and that he should be treated as suspicious.

This left the doctor with a dilemma: to maintain silence or report these suspicions back to Frau Doctor Weiskopf.

Meanwhile Gerda was speaking for the first time in years with the nanny who had cared for Miriam Kessler before her escape to England.

"These are papers for an Irmgard Trossler. She is searching for her cousin who was reported missing in the conflict in Albania. This is a cover to allow you to visit a patient in the hospital. This patient is possibly Peter Barnes, one of the two who helped with Miriam Kessler's escape.

"If you recognise him, when you leave the hospital, carry these gloves. Do not wear them.

If you do not recognise him, then wear the gloves. If you think it might be Peter but are not sure, wear just one glove on your right hand.

"If this is Peter Barnes do not acknowledge that you know him. In fact, you will ***fail*** to recognise him as your cousin. Leave the hospital as instructed carrying your gloves only if you are sure it is Peter."

"You think that this patient really might be the Peter who helped rescue Miriam?" the woman asked.

Gerda replied, "We don't know that this person is Peter, only that it could be. We need you to confirm that it is him or not.

It could be a trap set by the Gestapo who, having caught him, are trying to get a bead on us."

"What about me if it is a trap? What happens to my children?

"Your papers check out, there ***is*** an Irmgard Trossler, whose cousin is missing. Your remit is to determine whether or not this patient is Peter, then leave as instructed and disappear."

Gerda was desperate to persuade her courier.

"You will be fine, also your children will be. I take it you are all well and settled?"

Gerda waited for the confirmation that she was on board. The woman still hesitated.

Gerda persisted. "You did promise to help if necessary."

"But the children," the woman interrupted.

Gerda leaned forward and pointed a finger at her.

"We kept our promise with those children. Remember this patient could be Peter Barnes.

The Peter who helped rescue Miriam. Should we not now rescue him?"

The implied threat worked. Gerda got the answer she needed.

"Who is this Kurt Jacobsen?"

"He is from Flensberg from the north, up against the Danish border. It is all in your brief and it all checks out. Learn it then destroy it. Take care and hurry. We have so little time."

In a dark smoke-filled office, the Special Services chief officer replaced the telephone and rang a bell which was answered promptly. The officer did not look up.

"Get me everything you've got on missing persons, deserters and draft dodgers. Then get over to the hospital and check on patient 42/10798."

The man clicked his heels, turned and left the office. He was equally curt issuing orders to a female assistant.

"Every file on deserters and missing persons on my desk now."

Then almost as an afterthought. "And get me a car."

Back at the hospital Frau Doctor Weiskopf was dealing with an application from a woman who wished to see 10798.

"And this Kurt Jacobsen is your cousin?" she asked.

The woman agreed. The doctor made a note.

"What causes you to think this might be him?"

"He is listed as missing in Albania. It could be that he is trying to return home."

"How did you learn about this patient?"

The woman produced a bulletin from a local shipping company giving basic details of the unidentified patient. The hospital had issued this information to the police also to the local shipping agencies as a matter of routine. Satisfied, Doctor Weiskopf signed the woman in then gave her a form.

"Fill this form in giving yours and this Kurt Jacobsen's details."

The doctor picked up the internal telephone and arranged for a nurse to escort 'Irmgard Trossler' to the ward.

The nurse pulled the curtain to reveal a sleeping Peter.

"Do you recognise him?"

The woman moved closer to Peter and studied his face which was damaged, bruised and swollen, it being years since she last saw him. She was not sure.

"It's difficult, he doesn't look the same."

Then realising that this might appear that she was saying yes, she quickly added, "No, I don't think it can be."

In truth, she could not be sure it was the Peter she remembered.

Peter, under the influence of a sleeping draft, became aware of her presence as in a dream.

He opened his eyes at the sound of her voice which was familiar.

As her face came into focus, he recognised her immediately and spoke her name.

"Ilsa, is that you?"

Ilsa /Irmgard straightened and stepped back saying at once, "No, no that is not Kurt. I am certain of that now. Sorry to have troubled you."

She quickly turned and left the hospital carrying her gloves.

Within the hour Frau Doctor Weiskopf was handing over all her paperwork on 10798 to an S.S. officer.

"This woman, calling herself Irmgard Trossler, almost certainly knew the patient whilst claiming that she didn't."

The officer looked up from the papers. "Are you sure?"

"All I can tell you is that he knew her and called her Ilsa," Doctor Weiskopf answered.

"And this she denied?" The officer thought for a moment. "You say he is sedated and very ill?" "Extremely ill."

The officer made notes before issuing orders.

"Keep him heavily sedated and report any change. Inform me immediately of any other visits."

Back in the office the commandant thumbed through the investigating officer's notes.

"What do you think? Is it worth pursuing?"

The S.S. officer clicked his heels.

"It is possible that this is Jacobsen. He was with a supply convoy which left the base in Macedonia to rendezvous with a parachute drop behind the Greek lines. They made a detour through Albania to circumvent the Greek defence. They didn't arrive. It is possible they were taken by Albanian guerrillas."

"Jacobsen might have escaped and is trying to return home. Is that what you are thinking?"

"Yes, Herr Colonel." The investigating officer was pleased with his theorising.

"Do I place him under surveillance until we know more?"

"Yes," the colonel answered. "Plain clothes surveillance and discreet though I doubt he is going anywhere."

The S. S. colonel then turned his attention to an overflowing in tray and the mountain of work awaiting his attention.

Chapter 55

At the hospital a private ambulance pulled up next to the mortuary.

In a co-ordinated move, two porters entered at the front.

They collected a trolley and made their way to the trauma ward and handed a signed form to the nurse in charge.

"42/10798 to X. Ray."

The nurse pointed out the bed. "Third cubicle on the left."

The porters rolled the trolley alongside and transferred Peter.

The nurse looked up from her notes, watched for a moment then reached out for the signed form. This appeared to be in order. She still watched and wondered as they left the ward.

After a moment's thought she lifted the phone and dialled, waiting impatiently for an answer.

"Frau Doctor is the amnesia patient to be X rayed?"

"Could be if the infection is clear. Why? Are you doubtful?"

"Firstly, the infection has not been cleared. Also, there are two porters. This is not usual unless one is in training. These are young men and fit."

The porters did not look to be genuine to the nurse. Porters were much older. There followed a short silence. The nurse persisted. "You did say Frau Doctor we are to keep watch."

"Stop them at once."

"They have already left the ward, Frau Doctor."

Frau Doctor Weiskopf replaced the receiver immediately noting the time on her work pad.

She then waited a full minute before picking up the internal address system microphone.

"This is an alert. Look out for two porters and a patient. They are to be detained. Stop all porter activity at once."

The bogus porters with Peter, completely covered by a white sheet, had already left by the rear entrance. Peter, placed into a coffin, was loaded into the ambulance which left at once.

This ambulance was now out on the main road travelling towards the east of the city.

The S.S. officer was in the process of reporting back when the colonel received a call from the hospital. It was some time before they had any idea of what or who they were looking for.

This mattered not at all, because the ambulance had already been abandoned in a back alley to be found a day later.

The S.S. colonel's first thoughts were 'who is this fugitive and why is he a target'?

The answer was in his overflowing in tray. All relevant information came to him via another source two days later.

He ordered roadblocks around the town and alerted the border controls. But all was to no avail.

Chapter 56

Adolf Richter, a reluctant hero, watched in silence while an old doctor examined Peter.

The doctor was not well pleased having been called out in the early hours of that morning.

It was a call which had led him into a very dangerous place.

"You do realise that he will need 24-hour nursing."

The doctor spoke without looking up.

Adolf looked across at his niece Sabina who was stood watching in the doorway.

He spread his arms in question. Sabina returned the gesture. Both appeared equally confused.

"Even so," the old doctor continued, "he will probably die."

He sounded the patient's chest before adding, "A spoonful of boiled water to be given hourly to him and the leg wound to be bathed gently with a mild saline solution."

The old doctor closed his bag and looked up.

"I'll not ask how he comes to be here. I will deny any involvement, nor will I return.

There's very little I can do anyway."

He shook hands with Adolf and stopping by Sabina, he looked her in the eyes and nodded.

"The rest is up to you. I shall not return."

He repeated making sure he was not going to be involved further.

Adolf waited until he had left before turning on Sabina.

"Stupid girl, what were you thinking?"

"Jan insisted. You did say you would help, uncle."

Adolf began to pace, his arms flapping like a wounded bird.

"What do I tell your Aunt Maria? If this gets out, we are all dead."

"Maria is here, so there's no need for telling."

Maria announced her arrival as she walked through to the stretcher trolley and looked at Peter.

"Who is this, Sabina?" she asked, looking at her niece.

"I don't know. Jan just brought him to our farm and said to bring him here."

"Then what?" Maria looked at Sabina who shrugged.

"He didn't say."

"Where is Jan now?"

Maria looked at Sabina, who again shrugged.

"Are you expecting to shrug away the responsibility for this young man?"

Maria's little disguised criticism was acid.

"I think they will be in touch. They can't just leave him."

Sabina's pleading tone and look betrayed the uncertainty.

Adolf, now sitting with his head in his hands, added, "If they do, we are dead, all of us. Even Lazlow." He looked up. "What do we tell Lazlow?"

"We don't," Maria answered. "This is not what we intended when we agreed to allow passage over the border through the farm. My guess is that they will be in touch and move him on quickly. Meanwhile we hide him in the cheese store."

She turned to Sabina. "Does your father know what is to happen?"

"I don't think so." Again, Sabina shrugged.

Maria studied her for almost a minute.

"We do as I suggest, hide him in the cheese store and wait events."

Peter, still heavily sedated, drifted in and out of a state of semi consciousness unable to differentiate between reality and dreams.

He seemed to be floating outside the gates of some great city whilst the elders discussed whether to allow him to enter the cheese store.

He uttered one word. "Please."

Maria placed her hand on his forehead.

"All right my son, we'll take care of you."

She turned to Sabina. "Cold compress girl, quickly. He's burning up."

"I ought to be getting back."

Maria bridled.

"You are going nowhere my girl. You stay here and nurse this young man. I will speak to Otto and we will come to an arrangement if he stays more than today."

The following morning Adolf, on the orders of his wife, was trying to hide the truth and his anxiety from Lazlow as they forked hay into the stalls.

Meanwhile, a tall rugged man walked up the dirt track leading to the farm.

Stopping halfway he leaned on the gate leading to a pasture which held several sheep, a donkey and a tethered goat. Slowly he filled his pipe and began to smoke.

He was a picture of contentment clearly enjoying the autumn sun.

Maria who was hanging out some washing left off immediately and went to the barn.

"Adolf, there's a fella watching the stock in the front pasture. Find out what he is about."

Rustling of stock was a major problem for all farmers. This was a first thought for them all.

Adolf and Lazlow stopped immediately and hurried out to check.

Chapter 57

Dorothy Price turned her coat collar up against a sharp east wind as she hurried home across the common.

The late October sun cast long shadows from trees and the statue in front of the war memorial.

This statue was backed by a curved white marble wall displaying the names of the fallen on burnished bronze plaques. All were fronted by three marble steps leading up to a viewing plinth.

The lone statue of a soldier, head bowed over reversed arms, stood in the centre. It was a stark reminder of the Great War.

Dorothy was particularly fond of this little park and the memorial gardens across the street from her home, No. 4 East Park Villas.

She sat down on the plinth. It was a place of quiet. The wall provided a shelter from the east wind; the evening sun reflecting warmth from the white marble.

Almost home, Dorothy was reluctant to cross the few yards to the cheerless Victorian terraced house with its high ceilings and pseudo Georgian windows. It was difficult to heat in autumn and winter even with a reasonable supply of coal.

Dorothy, often without coal and suffering from an unreliable gas supply, closed most rooms, apart from one small study, one bedroom and the kitchen.

She needed to sort out her mind.

Today had begun badly with her trying and failing to resolve an argument between Tolly and Samuel. This was all she needed before setting off to her job teaching 7 to 11 year old boys at the public school across the common.

Tolly was her sales manager and Samuel the works manager and cutter. That is if such titles were appropriate for the small tailoring and alteration shop behind the house which was reduced to two treadle sewing machines and just Samuel, Tolly, the two machinists and a cleaner who came in for just two hours at the end of each day.

Yesterday, Tolly had returned triumphant with a government order for 1,000 army desert camouflage uniforms and a suit length of quality wool worsted complete with bespoke measurements.

Samuel's reaction was not as Tolly expected. He was not thrilled by the prospect of cutting repetitive standards out of the same drab material.

The prospect of work, now in short supply, was to celebrate. The current order book was mostly alteration work to existing clothing.

This order was a substantial achievement for Tolly, with whom Samuel had been vying for the senior position ever since his arrival.

Tolly, in Samuel's mind, was a Jonny-cum-lately upstart, untrustworthy and too big for his boots.

Samuel, in Tolly's mind, was a pedantic, fusty old stick in the mud.

An element of truth existed in both cases, although with Tolly the claim untrustworthy was questionable in the non-legal mind. His view of morality was often at odds with legality.

That much was true. Tolly's intentions, however, were never ever dishonourable.

On the matter of Tolly's new order, Samuel probably knew why he reacted angrily.

He suspected the order was tainted by bribery. That the wool worsted suit length was of doubtful origin. He had no intention of being an accessory to Tolly's 'crime'.

Samuel's smouldering resentment of Tolly had burst into flame.

Dorothy had walked in on the argument prior to setting off for school.

Returning to sort this out after a momentous day of serious events, settling this petty squabble even though she had come to a decision, did not appeal.

She was tired, weary of the deprivation of good food, sleep from the constant raids on the docks and coping with two jobs.

Truth to tell she was lonely never having recovered from Margaret Firth's death.

The years since Tuss disappeared had been truly unfriendly.

Dorothy's mother and father had sailed for Canada in the summer of 1939 leaving Dorothy in charge of all their U.K. affairs.

These affairs, in addition to the house, included shares in Belle Amis, the bespoke tailoring shop in the town where Dorothy had been appointed a director.

Then there was the small tailoring and repair shop behind No. 4 East Park Villas.

These responsibilities were all unwished for.

Dorothy had also agreed in a sense of duty, to continue working as an occasional teacher.

The part time work arrangements originally agreed upon, were now being abused by an overstressed, understaffed headmaster.

That morning, walking through the house and out on to the common, she little realised that she was closing the door on her present life and that a new chapter was about to begin.

A still calm night had produced the first sharp frost of the autumn which adorned the trees, whitened the grass and sparkled in the sun on the tarmac like the jewels of Aladdin's cave.

Shadows of the trees spread deep across the common heralded the onset of winter.

Dorothy took a deep breath of clean fresh air hoping to clear her mind of the turmoil she had just left. Try as she might, her thoughts returned to the morning's fracas. What to do about these stupid, ridiculous men.

Dorothy was only vaguely aware of the young boy cycling furiously along the common towards her. He was wearing the distinctive green school blazer with gold piping and the flash black and gold badge of East Park School for Boys.

Scorning the use of brakes, the boy skidded broadside to a stop beside Dorothy, spraying water from the wheels.

His cheery greeting startled Dorothy out of her thoughts.

"Morning Miss, do you like my new bike?"

Dorothy recognised the freckled cheery countenance of Stuart Clyde Braintree-McColl known to all as Ginger.

"Hello, Stuart. What are you doing here?"

She was in no way surprised to learn he had a new bicycle, Stuart's father being the font of all procurement along the dockside. You named it; he found it (for a price).

Even in wartime anything seemed possible.

"It's got the latest Rollo-Bridges three speed gears," Ginger announced proudly.

"Stuart, the school is that way," said Dorothy pointing in the opposite direction from which he had arrived.

Stuart expertly let the bike slide to the ground catching the crossbar on his foot before lowering it.

"Yes Miss, but the man said it was urgent."

Stuart rummaged in his pocket.

"Which man is this Stuart and what is it that is so urgent?"

Dorothy liked and tolerated Stuart. He was always optimistic and cheerful.

"This letter, Miss."

He took a small crumpled buff envelope from his pocket and handed it over.

He began kicking at the grass as if looking for something.

"The man said be sure to tell you it was urgent and imp-imp ..." Stuart continued, while foraging the grass with his feet.

He stopped kicking and looked questioningly at Dorothy.

"Imperative?" she obliged.

"Yes, that's it, Miss, what you said."

He put a forefinger to his head as if it helped recover his memory.

"That you contact the authorities today. Oh, and he gave me a penny and said if I delivered the envelope and got the message right, you would give me another one."

In the middle of this speech he picked up his bike and began kicking at the grass once more.

Dorothy opened the envelope to find what appeared to be a standard telegraphic communication. At the same time as she was reading, she answered Stuart.

"That's as may be," she murmured. "We'll see."

Dorothy was now very thoughtful, Tolly, Samuel and the row forgotten.

She tried to make sense of the pasted wording which was confusing.

Her worries began when she read that the telegram was addressed to Pegasus, which was one of the call-signs the team had used to rescue the children from Austria.

Even more thought provoking, it was signed Helga.

This Helga could be Dieter's mother, whom she had not heard from for years.

There was now little doubt in her mind. She read the message for a second time.

It still did not make sense!

MERCURY TO PEGASUS BROKERS.
VEHICLE 140715 REG NO. PB 1418
DAMAGED AND IN NEUTRAL GARAGE.
NEEDS SPECIALIST ATTENTION AND
ASSISTANCE TO RECOVER AND RETURN.
DO YOU ACCEPT THE CHARGE?
HELGA.

Meanwhile Stuart walked alongside still kicking at the grass which irritated Dorothy.

"What *are* you doing Stuart? Need you?"

"I'm looking for shrapnel, Miss. I have found some smashing pieces."

He fished in his pocket.

"This piece is copper. Frithy says it's from an anti-aircraft shell nose cone, an' it must weigh half an ounce."

He began to calculate. "Forty pounds a ton that means over four pence a pound and that's a halfpenny an ounce."

Dorothy, half aware of Stuart's comments and puzzling what to do next, murmured.

"If only Stuart you would pay the same attention to your maths lessons."

"It's boring, Miss and in any case, who needs algebra anyway? Mi dad doesn't know any, an' he does all right," said Stuart, still kicking.

Dorothy stopped dead in her tracks. "Of course," she exclaimed.

"Cut along to school Stuart or you will be late for assembly."

"Mi penny, Miss? Do I get mi penny?"

"I said we'll see. Now cut along," replied Dorothy, a little more sharply than she would have done so normally.

Not understanding the message or why she had been singled out, yet realising that it was of significance, she stood undecided how to deal with it. She read the telegram again.

This was a cry for help from Mercury.

Stuart's delivered message was foremost in her mind.

The words imperative and authorities were mostly dominating. That could not mean Pegasus which was now disbanded.

It was natural that Helga would contact her in the U.K. now that Peter was a P.O.W.

The mysterious message via Stuart was that she should contact the authorities.

Which authority? After a minute or two of indecision, she turned towards the town and the underground station.

Authorities suggested the government. Accordingly, she decided to head for central London, the apex of all authority in the U.K.

Dorothy planned to contact Sir George Bridge Thompson, the only person she knew of in Whitehall. which was part of the highest authority.

Dorothy knew Sir George. She had met him on several occasions with Pamela with whom she had remained friendly since the meeting at Mim's solicitors. They had spent many happy weekends in St. Mary Upperford.

Pamela had been urging her to move in with her, away from the East End of London and the bombing. Her loyalty to her parents, the responsibility for their interests in London and her promise to the school all prevented her from accepting this extremely attractive offer.

Chapter 58

Arriving at Westminster, Dorothy was still undecided as to the best course of action.

Because she had no other ideas, she found her way to the Admiralty hoping that Sir George would be able to advise her. Her resolve, in the meantime began to fade.

The building was forbidding in the extreme, protected by sandbagged blast walls, armed guards and policemen, all suggesting that trivialities would not be tolerated.

She needed all her resolve to carry on.

Walking towards the entrance she hesitated then stopped. A policeman came across to ask what she wanted.

Dorothy's greatest fear was that she would not be taken seriously.

She explained to him the reasons for her presence.

The policeman listened then asked her to wait. No sign of misgivings and no further questions.

She was ordered not to move and take up a position in the centre of the main blast wall in full view of the armed guards.

Dorothy felt as though she was under arrest.

She huddled against the wall which offered little protection from a sharp north easterly wind. She waited for what seemed to be an age before the policeman returned.

"Open your bag, Miss." These were his first words when he returned.

Without a please or permission, he took it, searched it and returned it with a curt, "Follow me, Miss."

Dorothy now wished she hadn't started and wanted to abandon the mission.

It was now seeming to be a very flimsy reason to involve His Majesty's Government.

Inside the main hall she was met by a naval officer and a Wren. She was received politely and ushered into a side room.

The officer took her name and address and the details of her reasons for the approach.

All were carried out in an officious manner. Even the please and thank-yous appeared to Dorothy as officious as the orders were given.

The officer took notes of the telegram's content, then left without explanation. Another very long wait.

Time seemed to be drifting away with nothing happening during which the Wren stood silent as if she was on a parade ground avoiding eye contact and not speaking.

Dorothy felt compelled to complain.

"How long do I have to wait? Am I to see Sir George or not?"

"In good time, Miss."

Half an hour later Dorothy began to pace back and forwards across the floor of the office.

The Wren stood at ease, not moving. Dorothy wanted to scream. 'Why don't you do something? Why doesn't someone listen?'

About an hour later the officer returned. This time he was less officious.

"May I have the telegram please, Miss?" He read it again then looked up and with an apologetic smile asked,"Will you please submit to a body search?" He blushed and added, "By the Wren, of course."

With that he hurried from the room. Shortly afterwards the door opened.

Dorothy was confronted by a charming middle aged grey haired man in a smart grey lounge suit.

His vivid blue eyes 'locked' on to hers.

"Miss Price, how do you do."

Dorothy's hand was clasped warmly, a grasp that lingered longer than expected and the warmth of which seemed to flow through her arm and down to her toes.

His persona filled the room. Dorothy was surprised by this sudden presence.

More so by her own reaction, she could only stutter, "Hello."

"So sorry you have been kept waiting. Have you eaten? You must be starving."

He continued speaking without awaiting answers. Turning to the Wren, the man said:

"Tell the galley one extra for lunch and tea for two in the boss's room."

He stopped and smiled at the Wren. "Oh! and if you can, some biscuits, please."

The Wren sprang to attention and left.

The man nodded and smiled again while holding the door gesturing for Dorothy to leave with him. He then took the lead without another word.

Dorothy, confused by this 'onslaught', followed obediently.

The resentment which followed was maybe a residue of being treated with suspicion.

Dorothy was aware of losing control of her emotions. This was a new and disturbing experience.

The man in grey marched ahead without looking back except to open a swing door for Dorothy.

This led down some steps to a long dimly lit corridor. Dorothy waited at the bottom to receive a warm smile before following his lead along the passageway to a sparsely furnished room, just one large table and several chairs.

The man gestured for her to sit.

"Lunch may not be kosher, I'm afraid. There might be bully beef fritters and fried potatoes if you are lucky." he said accompanied by a charming smile.

To her continuing confusion Dorothy found herself waiting for this smile knowing she would have been hurt if he hadn't. The fact that he smiled at the Wren in the same way did not escape her.

This did not seem to matter.

Dorothy relieved that she was being taken seriously was still confused by the speed of events over the last minutes. The sea change in her emotional response to this charismatic male dominated.

Dorothy was confused by sensations she didn't recognise. It felt as though an electrical charge had invaded every part of her being whenever this man looked at her.

Desperately, she tried to resume control.

"What is the meaning of the telegram do you think?"

Dorothy was met by the smile and silence while he sorted some papers before looking up.

"Do you mind if I ask the questions?" He looked 'deep' into her eyes.

His piercing stare was such that she was once more silenced.

"Who is this Helga? Do you know him or her and if so, how do we make contact?"

"Her." Dorothy corrected him whilst feeling her answer was a small victory to know something the man did not. The man made a note, then asked, 'How come you know her?"

"She was a courier helping us to ferry refugee children out of Austria just before the Anschluss.

She is also a cousin of mine."

"She is Jewish." He made another note as if this was important.

"Where can we contact her? Do you have her address?"

"No, I last saw her in Zurich in 1938. This telegram is the only contact I have had since then."

He tapped on the table with his pencil.

"Why you? I wonder."

"I have no idea." Dorothy hoped that they would have the answers.

The man continued tapping on the table with the pencil, held between the first and third fingers. The noise was not unlike a woodpecker ferreting out a grub.

"Who else knows your call sign?"

"Pegasus?"

"Yes."

"Only me now."

"Ah! That explains that," the man said but offered no explanation as to what it explained.

The question and answer session continued amid more table rapping.

This tapping only stopped briefly to allow Dorothy to answer.

"Who do you think delivered this telegram? I don't mean the boy."

Dorothy was surprised how well he had been briefed. She thought to herself 'they are truly on to this, whatever this was'.

"I have no idea, sorry."

"Can you not think of any intermediary this Helga would use to contact you?"

After a short consideration, Dorothy began. "Maybe." Then she stopped.

"Please go on, Miss Price. Anything you can think of no matter how ridiculous."

"I am thinking the solicitors in London know of me and they would be in touch with Zurich and Helga. Surely, they would have contacted me directly not send mysterious telegrams. In any case, they don't know the call sign."

The man pushed a sheet of paper across to Dorothy.

"The name and address of these solicitors, please Miss Price."

Dorothy thought for a moment.

"It's been a while, but the name is Joubert and Joubert and they are somewhere on the Euston road in London if I remember correctly. Pen will know the address."

"Bridge-Thompson's daughter?" The man raised his eyebrows indicating this was both a question and a surprise that she knew Pen.

"Yes," replied Dorothy amid a feeling of slight triumph that she held some mysteries herself.

"Thank you, Miss Price." He collected his papers, indicating the interview was over.

"You have been of an immense help. Thank you again."

The man smiled the smile and stood up, indicating it was time to move.

The smile and approbation pinged through to the centre of her emotions.

She could barely trust her legs as she stood.

"Lunch time Miss Price. I believe our mysterious messengers trust in you was justified."

Dorothy glowed with pleasure.

He placed a hand on her arm and yet again his touch seemed like an electric shock causing her heart to miss a beat. Dorothy could barely breathe as she wondered what next.

The man looked at his watch.

"I must fly. Much to do, I must say. A Wren officer will host you for lunch and arrange a car to return you to your home."

Stopping briefly in the doorway, he smiled the smile and said, "Please be available tomorrow. We may need to talk again."

Then he was gone, leaving Dorothy still struggling to sort out her many emotions.

The Wren officer arrived to take her to lunch.

Chapter 59

Later that day, Dorothy, still confused but elated, stood in front of Harold Dewsnap, the school principal, explaining her absence.

"I am sorry, principal, but it was urgent. I had little time or choice to do anything differently and I am not able to tell you why. I shall need to take tomorrow off for the same reason."

Harold's day had not been good. He was in no mood to tolerate such nonsense.

He had to take lessons in her absence and learn via the school snitch, that Ginger McColl had delivered a secret letter to her that very morning. Entering the classroom for the maths lesson his first words had been. "McColl, come out here."

Harold Dewsnap refused to use the hyphenated name Braintree-McColl, deeming it to be pretentious. He considered McColl's father to be a common upstart only to be tolerated for the 12 guineas a term school fee.

"McColl, did you deliver a note to Miss Price this morning?"

"Yes sir, I gave her a secret letter," Ginger McColl proudly answered.

This was all Harold Dewsnap needed to know. Any fool could fill in the gaps.

There was no way that he could accept this anarchy.

Miss Price was now displaying a confidence and defiance he had not seen before.

He must nip this in the bud, or she would no longer be controllable.

He drew himself up to portray the necessary authority.

"Be here, on time, tomorrow or do not bother to return." He fixed her with his sternest gaze.

"That is an order."

Dorothy was on the verge of abandoning all protocol. The old Dorothy would have done so, the new didn't. Instead she looked at this pompous man and answered very correctly, "Very well, principal. I accept your decision."

Harold smiled, with more than a hint of triumph.

"I expect you to be here on time tomorrow."

"No, sorry principal, you misunderstand me. I meant I accept your decision to dismiss me."

Dorothy even managed not to return his smile.

Harold Dewsnap's jaw dropped as Miss Price turned and walked to the door.

She stopped and returned. Then she opened her purse and placed a penny on his desk.

"I owe Braintree-McColl a penny. Will you please see that he receives it with my thanks?"

All this had happened in the last ten hours.

In a trance, Dorothy sat on the steps of the war memorial and traced her way back through the day. There was no one thing she would change about it, even if she could.

About the fracas between Samuel and Tolly, she now knew what to do. A decision she found difficult that morning was no longer a problem. She was newly empowered by vision and now realised where she was and why and where she wished to be.

She could see what was wrong in her life and the way forward was now clear.

She barely noticed that the sun had dipped behind the houses over the road as she crossed over and into number 4 East Park Villas.

Down the hallway she could see that the door to the front room, normally closed, was ajar.

The long mirror by the hat stand reflected a fire burning in the grate. Someone was in there.

Not having had a delivery of coal for over a month, she was both surprised and nervous.

Several times over the winter supplies had failed or were late.

Once when the gas pressure failed, she spent nearly two weeks without hot water and was unable to make tea or hot food until Tolly 'found' a primus stove and a supply of paraffin.

Dorothy pushed the door fully open to reveal a blazing fire and a pile of sawn logs stacked neatly alongside.

Her nervousness evaporated. Delighted, she whispered, "Tolly" and went immediately to the kitchen where, as expected, Tolly was sitting at the table on which were two tins without labels and a bottle.

Tolly spread his hands.

"I've brought supper to apologise for this morning."

Dorothy smiled. "Thanks for the fire, Tolly. I suspect the wood has been taken from bomb sites."

She paused. "True?"

"No use to anyone just lying there."

Tolly stood and collected two glasses and a bottle opener from the kitchen dresser.

"But Tolly it's illegal, isn't it?"

Dorothy did not relish being an accessory after the deed.

"Maybe, but then the law is stupid," he said opening the bottle with a fizz and a flourish as if releasing a breath of common sense.

"Where's the harm in it. I ask you?"

"And the tins, Tolly?" Dorothy asked, clearly querying the origin of the canned food.

"Ah! They were a legitimate swap," he replied removing the key from the bottom of the smaller tin.

"Legitimate?"

"In my book, yes."

Tolly was a law unto himself. "Beans in the large tin, Spam in the small."

Dorothy was still in a state of surprise and wondered what else the day might bring.

"Spam?" she queried.

"Leviticus and Deuteronomy suspended for the duration," announced Tolly.

The key slipped as he removed over 2,000 years of tradition more easily than he removed the top of the Spam tin.

Dorothy could not help but like Tolly. His simplistic, common sense view of life reinforced her determination to take control of her own.

Besides which she was so glad of his company and the supper provided.

"Tolly, thank you for my supper and the firewood."

She paused, hesitating to return his favours with bad news.

"There is something I must tell you."

Dorothy took a deep breath and announced the decisions she had arrived at as this watershed day unfolded.

"I am leaving for St. Mary Upperford tomorrow and intend to stay there, at least for the foreseeable future. I am putting Samuel in charge of the shop."

She waited for his response, fully prepared to deal with whatever ensued.

"Will you promise to work with him, accept his direction, please?" she prompted.

Tolly poured out two glasses of brown ale.

"Thought you might, Miss. We are both sorry about the shindig earlier. Managed to get some brown ale." He continued as though they were discussing the weather.

Dorothy laughed with relief.

"Is it kosher?" she asked taking it from him.

"As the Spam, Miss. Cheers." He raised his glass. "All the best in St. Mary."

"Thank you, Tolly. You will both watch the house for me, won't you?"

"Of course, Miss. Can I move in?" Tolly asked, ever the opportunist.

Dorothy looked hard at him trying not to smile, amused by the speed at which he turned every situation to advantage. Yesterday she would have refused but today she answered, "I would be pleased if you would."

Chapter 60

Later that night, Dorothy opened the blackout curtains in her bedroom and looked out on a beautiful moonlit night remembering, with satisfaction, a day well spent. She was still curious as to meaning of the mysterious telegram.

It was turning very cold. Dorothy, reluctant to give up the day, pulled her dressing gown closely around her and continued to watch the changing scene as the familiar wail of the air raid sirens signalled the almost nightly raid on the docks.

Dorothy had no intention to take cover in the cold, damp cellar.

This was not unusual, even the fire watchers and wardens, who originally took cover in reinforced brick shelters, now only relied on their steel helmets as protection against falling shrapnel. Familiarity had dulled their initial fears.

This night the fire watchers and wardens stood in the open across the road watching.

Searchlights criss-crossed the sky as the anti-aircraft barrage began followed quickly by flashes and the crump of falling bombs and the rattle of falling masonry.

The familiar scene could be normally watched in relative safety from across the common.

Divorcing the mind from death and maiming had become surprisingly easy as the war progressed.

Time passed quickly in the bubble of relief at finally sorting out her disturbed life.

She watched the searchlights, the Moon, the stars and shell bursts competing for space in the skies.

Searchlights picked out a plane. Silvered and remote, it twisted and turned to escape the attention of the anti-aircraft gunners in a dance of death as the shells burst all around.

Dorothy felt just as separated from this as she did from her former life.

Slowly, she became aware of the long pulsating notes of a Dornier bomber's engines.

She smiled at this knowledge acquired from her pupils who were able to identify most aircraft merely by the sound of the engines.

Then she realised that something about this plane wasn't normal.

The fire watchers and wardens began to run towards the brick shelter. At one at the same time, she saw the plane. It was very low and heading in their direction.

Five hundred feet above the common a Dornier pilot was fighting with the controls as the plane spewed fuel and hydraulic fluid into the skies.

He ordered the crew to jettison the bombs and abandon the aircraft.

The crew was now left with the dilemma of falling with the bombs or staying with the aircraft.

The lottery was they were too low for the parachutes to fully open. Even if they did open, they would risk getting caught in the blast from their own bombs.

These bombs, because of the lack of height, may or may not explode.

Parachutes may or may not open in time to check their fall.

All were borderline in this lottery of life and death.

Dorothy, taking her cue from the fire watchers, ran into the alcove she used as a dressing room and flattened herself against the wall.

The stick of bombs straddled the park, the street and East Park Villas. The first narrowly missed the war memorial and exploded in the roadway, the second was a direct hit on No 4.

This bomb's spinner had not detached after being released too low. It did not explode.

Another landed in a street behind.

A brilliant white-blue light lit the room as the bomb on the street exploded.

A micro second later Dorothy was thrust violently against the wall. Her head smashed backwards. She was held there transfixed as the second bomb in the street behind exploded adding to the chaos.

Unable to breathe, move or even blink, she was vividly aware of the dressing table and wardrobe mirrors shattering into a thousand pieces before cascading in a bright sparkling 'waterfall'.

This was the last that she remembered.

Chapter 61

Adolf and Lazlow stood at the head of the driveway, pitchforks in evidence.

Rustling of stock was their greatest fear. This was the reason they kept the few animals left either in the front paddock where they were permanently in view or at night in the barn, even in the summer. Adolf motioned Lazlow to wait and made his way down to the paddock.

The man turned to face him and removed his pipe.

"Who's the big fellow?" he asked in German.

"Who are you and what is your business?" was Adolf's counter.

"The Englishman, is he still alive?" The man asked, ignoring Adolf's question.

He began to clean his pipe with a pocket knife tapping the residue out on the gate post.

Adolf's knees buckled. He had to jam his pitchfork down to steady himself.

"Careful," the man continued. "We are probably being watched."

Adolf could feel his pulse pounding in his throat and temples.

"Watched, by whom?" he croaked.

"The German Army amongst many. We have stirred up a hornets' nest. Half the army in this area on the orders of Berlin no less, are looking, probably on the orders of your namesake."

The man leaned casually back on the gate and began to fill his pipe.

He gave a practice suck before lighting up.

"The Serbs have also been recruited to help," he added between puffs.

Adolf was speechless with fear as the man continued.

"Does the big fellow know about this?" He nodded towards Lazlow.

"I take it he's your farm help?"

Adolf gathered himself and shook his head.

"No, just my wife and Sabina, my niece. Why Berlin and the Serbs?"

The man, again, ignored Adolf's question.

"Tell no one. Trust no one. A woman will be coming to assist, probably tonight around midnight. Keep watch but don't be surprised."

The stranger then asked, "Where are you keeping him? The Englishman. Don't point, just tell me."

"In-in the cheese store," Adolf stammered. "It-it's the building to your right f-facing.

We-we don't want a woman to help," Adolf protested. Surprising himself at the sound of his pleading, he gathered himself.

"We need him to be gone. When are you going to move him on?"

"Can't say when," the man answered. "The little Englishman is too ill to move. Where would we move him, if we could, is another question."

The man sat down on the bottom spar and continued to puff on his pipe.

This casual attitude irritated Adolf.

"When we agreed to help it was not intended that we be used as a sick depository. We need him to go and quickly," Adolf said, now sounding stronger.

"Needs must. We had to go to ground in a hurry. How else could we have concealed a sick man at such short notice?" The man ignored Adolf's pleading.

"You mean we are stuck with a fugitive on our farm while the Army and God knows who else are looking for him? Move him on please or else we are dead."

He took a shuddering breath before continuing to plead.

"Why is he so important? What is so different about this sick, injured man?"

Adolf tried and failed to disguise his agitation.

"Moving refugees through our farms is one thing. This, this we ***did not*** agree to."

Adolf's farm was one half of a much larger one owned by his grandfather. This larger farm straddled the now border between Austria and Slovenia. On the death of his grandfather the farm was divided between his two sons, Adolf's father inheriting the southern half and his uncle, Otto, the northern. After the Great War, the rearrangement of borders placed the farms in different countries.

Related, the two farmers had maintained the tracks between the two farms.

It now became a convenient unofficial route across the border.

"Sorry about this," the man countered. "The safest course is for him to stay put and for you to carry on as normal. We will arrange with Otto for Sabina to stay for the duration and this woman, who is coming, will carry most of the load. She should be here during the night and will take charge of nursing and medication."

The man leaned back on the gate and surveyed the area.

"Good spot here, isolated with good vision all round."

Adolf trembled with fear and rage at this man taking charge of his farm, his affairs, his life, gave out instructions. Adolf protested again, this time with real anger.

"Shit man, you can't do this. Our lives, the farm, everything."

His voice trailed away into the semblance of a pleading sob.

The man looked at Adolf.

"Calm yourself, it's done. Control your anger and think. If I walk away now, you'd be scuppered. Your best course is to trust us and help us get through this. If you do that, the chances of the German Army finding him are slim. We hear they are looking in the Italian sector right now.

Which is where we might have taken him. You must realise, he was and is too ill to go on."

Adolf stood speechless, shaking.

The emotion of the last 20 hours, contained until now, paralysed him.

Lazlow began to walk purposefully towards the two of them.

The man looked up.

"Your man is on his way and so am I. My advice is to tell him everything."

The stranger set off down the driveway then stopped, turned and spread his hands.

"He'll guess anyway, so trust him."

With this final shot, he walked swiftly to the road.

Adolf still shaking, watched him go.

Lazlow followed him off the farm before returning.

Maria, who was watching from the farmhouse, joined them as Lazlow returned.

"I'll sleep in the barn tonight with the stock," Lazlow suggested.

"What was that about Adolf?" Maria asked, ignoring Lazlow's suggestion He realised there was more to this than the rustling of stock.

Adolf didn't answer but stood, fist clenched, white faced and silent.

Maria turned him towards her and took his face in her hands.

"What is it Adolf? We need to know."

Adolf seemed incapable of answering. Maria tried again.

"Tell us, please."

Adolf took another shuddering breath and whispered, "They are not moving him. We are stuck with him."

Maria looked round sharply at Lazlow.

"Get Sabina and both of you come to the kitchen now. She is in the cheese store."

Turning to her husband she took his arm. "Come now, this needs to be sorted."

Lazlow, taciturn in nature, asked no questions and did her bidding.

Once all together in the kitchen Adolf managed to explain their predicament.

Maria went to the kitchen dresser then returned with a bottle and glasses.

She poured four measures of schnapps and joined them at the table.

"Gruss Gott," she said before turning to Lazlow.

"We are, clearly, dealing in death, Lazlow. Whether you are part of this or not is a question you need to answer."

She poured another measure of schnapps.

"If you choose to leave, join the partisans, you are free to go. You need have no part in this."

Lazlow drank his schnapps and nodded.

"Does that mean you will stay?"

"Depends."

Half an hour and several questions and drinks later Lazlow nodded, This time, he said, "I'm with you."

"Good," replied Maria, "now this is what will happen."

"You haven't asked me," said Sabina, interrupting and complaining.

Maria looked at her niece long and hard.

"You were instrumental in starting this. It is *you* that should be asking *us*. I will be talking to Otto to arrange for you to stay until everything is sorted. In the meantime, my girl you will nurse this young man with my help until this mystery woman arrives."

Maria began to pace.

"My guess is that he will die, in which case we will have to dispose of him. We can't stand on ceremony. Lazlow, will you prepare a grave at the back of the hay barn, please? And for now, we must carry on as normally as possible." She stopped and poured another schnapps.

Lazlow moved his hand over his glass.

"Enough." He growled before getting up and leaving.

Sabina pouting, protested. "It was Jan, not me. What else could I do?"

Maria took a great breath then sighed.

"You did the right thing probably. Jan and his colleagues would have been caught otherwise."

She moved around to sit with her niece and take her hands in hers.

"It was the right decision *but* with it comes responsibility. Now just go along and nurse the young man and I will speak to your father."

Sabina nodded and as she did a large tear splashed on to Maria's hands.

Chapter 62

Two nights later the promised help arrived. Sabina, asleep in the chair in the corner of the cheese store, woke up feeling cold. It was some moments before she realised that the window was open and that someone was moving about in the room.

She shrank down into the chair. As she did, a shadow crossed the window against the moonlight. "Hello, who's there?" she called.

"God Sabina, it stinks in here," the shadow answered.

Sabina, who had been told to expect a woman to help, was still thrown by the familiar manner of address and didn't answer at once.

"Come, give me a hand," Tanya ordered.

Sabina gathered her wits and jumped from the chair.

"Won't he catch pneumonia?" She protested about the open window. In the cold night air she was beginning to shiver.

"Doubt it," came the answer. "Got a mirror?" The shadow asked.

The stretcher trolley was up against the wall. Tanya was forced to stand in the way of the moonlight through the window.

"Whatever you do, don't switch on any lights."

Sabina could not see her face against the moonlight.

"Well? Mirror girl." Tanya let it be known that she expected immediate action.

"I shall have to go to the house to find one," Sabina answered grabbing her coat. She was confused yet pleased that help had finally arrived. She waited but as an answer didn't come, she set off.

"Keep to the shadows!" Tanya ordered as she left.

Sabina, complete with mirror, dutifully returned. Tanya issued the next order.

"Stand behind me and reflect the moonlight on to his leg."

After a couple of false moves Sabina finally managed to direct the light where it was needed.

While she did, Tanya stood statuesque. Sabina sensed her impatience, which did not help.

Tanya began to swab gently around the leg wound.

"When did you last clean this?"

Sabina flushed. "It's difficult by myself," she stammered.

Tanya didn't comment but took a broad leaf from a bag, smeared something from a small jar on to the shiny side and placed it over the wound. She then bandaged the leg.

She handed another leaf to Sabina and issued her the final order of their first encounter.

"Get to your bed. First thing tomorrow, return. On the way pick one of these leaves fresh from the hedgerow and collect as many spiders' webs as you can on the shiny side by passing the leaf through the webs and bring it to me."

Sabina was delighted to be able to go to bed and leave everything to this woman.

She queried nothing and left.

Maria awake and worrying, heard her niece go to her room. She climbed wearily out of bed and donned her house coat. She guessed the promised help had finally arrived. She wished to get all the news before Sabina slept, as sleep she would and soon.

Updated on events even to the strange request for the doctored broad leaf, Maria looked at the leaf which was on Sabina's bed side table. She said nothing and returned to her bed to a night of little rest. The next morning, she woke Sabina and reminded her about the strange request: to return to her duties with a fresh leaf 'doctored' with spiders' webs.

Sabina, waking in a bad mood, rushed her breakfast before going out to search for the leaf.

In the early morning sun, the webs glistened with dew and it was easy to see them on the hedges and grasses. Sabina took a strange delight in collecting the webs destroying them one by one and watching the spiders run or freeze in panic. Tanya saw her leave the farmhouse and went outside to watch. After a while when Sabina showed no intention of returning immediately, she called out, "Enough, bring it now."

Maria who was also watching, added, "Come on, girl."

Sabina returned as bid, followed by Maria who introduced herself to Tanya.

"Thank you for your presence. I am Maria, Adolf's wife."

Tanya, with the briefest of nods to Maria, took the leaf from Sabina and replaced the one she'd left on Peter's leg in the night.

Maria said, "You're that woman from the woods, aren't you?" She carefully avoided the title *witch*.

Without looking up Tanya expertly rolled Peter on to his side, folded the sheet underneath and rolled him the other way to clear and pulled it free before uttering her first words.

"I need clean bedding, please, also some ewe's milk. I have brought wild honey."

Maria looked as if she was going to say something to Tanya but instead mouthed 'Come,' to Sabina and picking up the soiled sheets left with Sabina following.

Once outside Maria put her arm around Sabina.

"Courage, my love. Take little notice of the Witch Woman, it is just her way and she will be a big help. Trust me. Come, I will get clean sheets."

Sabina who was feeling better for Maria's attention, thought for a moment.

"She will need feeding."

"Don't worry about food, my love we will manage. One thing is for sure, this woman will need to ask me first." Maria smiled at the thought.

Sabina returned with bedding to find Tanya crushing a white tablet between two spoons.

"Come Sabina and watch."

Sabina dutifully joined her. Tanya then stuck her fingertip in a jar of honey and dabbed it in the powdered tablet and parting Peter's teeth with her other hand, began to scrape the mixture on to the back of them. Peter began to cough.

"Excellent, a good reaction," Tanya said turning to Sabina. "Hold his head up so the bits don't drop into his throat."

After a short wait Tanya muttered. "He is not swallowing. I was hoping that he would."

She pondered a moment before asking, "Did Maria send the ewe's milk?"

When Sabina shook her head, Tanya added, "Bring me a cup half full of ewe's milk and half boiled water."

Sabina returned with the diluted milk and watched as Tanya added honey and stirred.

Lifting Peter's head, Tanya gently spooned a tiny amount into his mouth.

On the third spoonful Peter swallowed. Tanya smiled, lowered his head and turned to Sabina.

"Now we are making progress. Every five minutes I want you to give him three half teaspoons of this. Don't forget to raise his head while doing so. I am going to get some food and sleep. I will return in four hours. Call me if you have problems."

Without waiting for an answer, Tanya left.

Sabina dutifully carried out Tanya's instructions. In the minutes of waiting she looked out on the bright autumn scene through the small window. Peter didn't smell very nice and the open window was not letting in enough fresh air.

Eventually Sabina slipped outside the creamery around the building to stand with the sun on her face as she looked towards the wooded hills to her right.

She now wished she had joined the partisans and imagined herself with Jan, lying out in the sun in some clearing way up in the hills.

Four hours later Tanya returned to find that Peter had not only wet the bed but had vomited back some of the milk and that someone, she guessed Maria, had had the presence of mind to prop him on his side.

Back in London a P.P.S. knocked on the Prime Minister's door and handed him a communication from the Foreign Office. W.S.C. removed the cigar from his mouth and smiled.

"Good news, Prime Minister?"

"Could be, could be," the Prime Minister replied. "Tell S.O.E. I wish to be kept informed."

"About what specifically, Prime Minister?" The P.P.S. was eager to learn of the good news.

Churchill struck a pose pointing a well chewed unlit cigar.

"They seek him here, they seek him there; those Nazis seek him everywhere."

He paused before again pointing his cigar at the P.P.S. and continuing with a smile.

"And while they do so, they lack concentration on other, more important issues."

"A Scarlet Pimpernel, Prime Minister?"

"No, Private Secretary. A Houdini and a very convenient one."

Chapter 63

Tolly was in a carefree mood as he wheeled a coach-built pram across the common.

The autumn sun slanted shadows in front of him, highlighting the frost-covered grass and trees creating an early Christmas card scene.

This pram contained all his worldly goods. After many months of casual and inadequate lodgings, he was finally moving into a comfortable home.

This for the first time since his employers, Belle Amis Fashions building was fire-bombed and destroyed in 1940 along with his job and his grace and favour apartment.

A succession of bedsits on the dockside had been Tolly's lot ever since.

His only piece of good fortune was being offered work by Miss Dorothy who was now adding to this gesture by allowing him to move into her house.

To Tolly this was a palatial home. He couldn't wait to move in.

He was rudely jarred out of his reverie.

A schoolboy on a bicycle swerved around him before skidding to a stop, asking, "Is that Gibby's pram?"

Tolly nodded. "Yes. He died a week ago."

"He *is* dead then?"

Tolly irritated, raised his hand to the boy.

"Yes, still dead. Now bugger off."

"Thought so, we had heard something," the boy replied with a cheeky grin, then cycled on his way.

Tolly thought to himself how sad it was that someone's life can degenerate into a mere matter of casual interest. Folk pass by without seeming to notice their fellow souls crying and dying and using these traumas as mere gossip fodder.

It was as if they didn't exist.

Gibby, otherwise Harry Gibb, was an ex-docker who had fallen on hard times made significantly worse after the outbreak of the war.

Unable to work on the docks because of accidents and arthritis, Gibby 'acquired' a coach-built pram. This he converted into a carrier of small goods by fitting it with shelves and tiny drawers.

Over the years he struggled to build up business around the estates, selling ribbons, cottons, Silko, tape, packets of needles and pins, buttons, beef cubes, packets of children's sweets and lollipops. Came the war and his supply sources completely dried up.

Consequently, Gibby was unable to earn any kind of a living and had drifted into abject poverty.

Bombed out of his home, Tolly had moved into a succession of dockside bedsits.

The only accommodation available, Tolly's room was cold and cheerless.

He spent most winter evenings in the Ship and Tug hostelry.

Harry Gibb was an ever present in the pub sitting in the same corner with a glass of Old and Mild, which lasted all evening.

One evening last month Gibby was clearly ill with a deep chesty cough and running a temperature. The pub was busy, as usual. No one spoke to Gibby or sat near him.

They studiously avoided him.

Tolly was sitting with a glass of porter watching some regulars playing dominoes.

After a noisy bout of coughing from Gibby's corner, the four players stopped momentarily and looked across before resuming.

"Is Harry still sleeping rough?" asked one.

Another studied his dominoes and played his drop. "'appen." The reply.

This was all the interest shown that night within Tolly's hearing.

At closing time Tolly stood in the dark outside waiting to see where Gibby went.

Last to leave, Gibby was escorted to the door by the landlord.

The door was slammed shut and the bolts hammered home.

Harry Gibb sank down in the entry behind the ever-present pram. It was now empty save for a few pitiful belongings. Harry's only protection from the elements was the doorway and the facing sand bagged blast wall.

Later that week, in the early hours of one morning, Harry Gibb slipped quietly into the hall of the unremembered: a victim of the war as surely as the rear gunner of a downed Lancaster bomber. Just as vulnerable. One more life lost without edifice, bronze plaque. Nothing!

His only comfort was Tolly's gift of a bed for his final days.

Tolly's sole reward was the empty pram.

Tolly, sobered by the interruption, stared up at the common thinking how unfair life could be.

Walking on, he was jolted out of his thoughts yet again, this time by an army truck being driven across the common in the direction of East Park memorial gardens. It left a trail of black 'tram lines' in the frosted grass.

Tolly quickened his pace realising that the truck's route via the road must be blocked.

That the raid last night had reached this side of the common.

This precursor, however, did not prepare him for the shock he received as he approached East Park Villas.

The army truck was one of several parked up on the grass.

Armed soldiers disembarked. They were deployed along a rope barrier stretching from a lamp post to a tree on the common then back to another post then across to No. 1, isolating the block of four houses.

Tolly's jaw dropped as he surveyed a desolate scene.

Part of No 4's roof had collapsed, leaving a gaping hole.

The windows had been blown out. Apart from a few pieces of broken frame there was nothing. What remained of the front door was hanging diagonally across the jamb held by a single hinge.

A large shallow crater on the near pavement was evidence of the cause. A telegraph pole snapped off at the base was lying across the street resting on the steps of No 4.

The wires were stringing down from the houses like the beginnings of a spider's web.

The soldiers were now being deployed at intervals along the barrier ropes. They were all armed with rifles with fixed bayonets.

'Bit extreme,' thought Tolly.

His logical thought processes, suspended by the shock, then kicked in.

"Miss Dorothy," he gasped. He began to run towards No 4 only to be confronted by a Special Constable.

"Stay back please sir, there is an unexploded bomb in there."

"Miss Price. Is she all right?"

The constable looked to his notes. "Everyone has been accounted for, sir."

"Thank God, she's alive. Where is she? Where can I find her?"

The constable indicated an air raid warden standing with an army officer against the brick air raid shelter. "The warden has the detail, sir."

Tolly turned instantly to go to him only to be restrained by the constable.

"No nearer, sir. Remember there's an unexploded bomb," he ordered sticking out an arm.

The army officer began to walk in their direction followed by the warden.

"Here comes the warden you will be able to ask him."

The constable signalled to the warden that they wished to speak.

"Can I help?" asked the warden when he arrived.

"This gentleman is asking about the whereabouts of Miss Price of No 4."

The constable kept a restraining hand on Tolly's arm. Both officials were aware of the effects of anxiety on survivors. The warden flicked through his notes.

"I understand that Miss Price was not on the property overnight. Her bed and the bed in the cellar shelter have not been used. A search of the property found no signs of occupation."

Tolly was appalled and terrified at the same time.

"She *was* there. We had supper together only last night."

The warden made a note and aware that mistakes occur.

He didn't argue and suggested that Tolly contact the refugee control currently at East Park School, the Baptist chapel on Hale Street, the casualty clearing station, or the local hospital.

He listed all possibilities.

"Please just one more search of the house. She was there last night. I promise you."

"Sorry, sir it is far too dangerous."

Tolly surveyed a host of armed men guarding the site then looked down at the policeman's restraining arm.

Realising he was not going to make progress here, he protested again.

"You are making a mistake. She *was* there. Probably, still is."

The warden, used to distressed relatives' inability to accept the loss of loved ones, spread his arms in a gesture of futility, replied.

"I am sorry, sir." He turned and left.

Tolly's only hope now was that Miss Dorothy was at the school which was now a refugee centre.

He headed across the common towards the school at a run which was unsustainable for an older man. After a short while he stopped, gasping for breath.

The heavy gasping degenerated into sobbing as the enormity of the situation sank in.

In the distance, Gibby's pram was standing abandoned on the path.

The constable approached the pram. After checking the contents, Tolly's worldly goods, he sighed and wheeled it for safe keeping into the brick air raid shelter.

Meanwhile Samuel Solomons was returning from a futile search for Miss Dorothy at the school.

He was on his way back when he saw Tolly in his distress. Samuel realising what was happening ran to speak with him.

"I can't find her, and no one will listen," Samuel, distressed, continued.

"I think she is still somewhere in house. The word at the school is that she has run away with some man."

He looked towards the Villas. "She wouldn't do that, Miss Dorothy, not without telling us."

Tolly gathered his wits.

"She *was* in the house, Samuel. She's still in the house, but they won't let me go and check."

The two men stood looking towards the bomb site.

"What can we do? What can we do?"

Two schoolboys cycled alongside.

"They say there's a plane shot down. Do you know where it is, Mister?" the excited boys asked.

"Is it a Dornier?"

"Are there any prisoners?"

Both boys freed from school, now a refugee centre, were full of questions.

Tolly recovered a semblance of composure and thought what to do.

"Do you know Miss Price?"

"Yes sir, but she's left the school and run off with a mystery man to Brighton."

"I don't think that is true, boys. Mr. Solomons and I think she needs help."

He took a sixpence out of his pocket and held it up shining brightly in the morning sun.

"There's one of these each for you if you go to the Baptist chapel on Hale Street and the hospital. Check if Miss Price has been admitted or has been seen at either place."

The boys' eyes lit up. Sixpence was an awful lot of money to them.

"Shall we come back here, sir?"

"See the soldiers over there." Tolly pointed to the bomb site.

"Come to us there. Those soldiers will know about the German bomber.

If you find Miss Price and it's true. I'll make it a shilling."

The boys could hardly believe their luck and with a shout of. "Wilco, sir, over and out."

They cycled furiously away towards the chapel.

"Why did you do that?" asked Samuel. "We know she isn't there. She's in the house somewhere."

"*We* know," answered Tolly, "but the police and the army don't. I want independent witnesses to say that she's not accounted for. We need to get them to check the house again."

"What with an unexploded bomb in there and them thinking she's run off with some bloke?"

Samuel was not convinced. Tolly took him by both shoulders and shook him gently.

"We've got to do something. The warden took a note that Miss Dorothy and I had supper together last night. I think we've got an ally there."

Samuel looked shocked.

"You had supper together?"

Tolly waved his arms around as if he was trying to take flight.

"What does that matter? All he needs to know is that we did."

Samuel stared at Tolly then nodded.

"You were lying." This was a statement of realisation, not a question.

Tolly did not protest but after a moment's thought continued.

"What I need you to do is create a diversion and give me a chance to sneak by the guards."

"How do I do that?"

Samuel was trying to be helpful.

"I don't know. Ask questions, faint, start a fight."

In other circumstances Samuel would have thought the ideas ludicrous, today he accepted them without question. He nodded and the two of them started towards the bomb site.

Samuel was glad to be doing something, anything even to letting Tolly take charge.

Tolly, totally focused on forcing the issue, was trying to think how it could be done.

He could not come up with any ideas, try as he may.

"She's in there with that bomb. I just know it," Tolly gasped. "We've got to get in there."

"But how? The whole place is cordoned off and under guard," Samuel answered, also breathing hard. The pace and tension had taken its toll on the old men.

"What are we going to do?" he gasped.

"I don't know yet. Will you go along with me whatever?"

Tolly pleaded, stopping and bending down with hands on his knees, breathing heavily.

"Depends," Samuel gasped, in reply.

"Please?" Tolly pleaded.

Samuel also felt the strain and quietly began to sob.

"What *are* we going to do?" he asked yet again, once he was able to recover his voice.

"I don't know yet," Tolly replied.

"In which case I don't know either," said Samuel, in tears.

"For Miss Dorothy, please."

Samuel didn't answer. After a short while the two men straightened to survey the scene.

Even more soldiers, an ambulance and policemen had arrived.

An officer appeared from out of the air raid shelter which was being used as a temporary H.Q.

"How can we get past that lot? It's useless," Samuel moaned.

"We'll speak to that officer. That's the least we can do."

"What to say. What can we say?"

Tolly, tiring of Samuel's negativity, changed tack.

"You speak to him Samuel, you're good with words."

Samuel nodded.

"I'll think of something," he replied and began to walk towards the officer.

The policeman left the group and ran to cut Samuel off shouting.

"No further, sir. Wait right there."

Tolly had held his ground until then he noticed that all attention was centred on Samuel.

He made a run for No 4. The officer saw him and shouted an order.

"Guards! Stop and hold."

Tolly was stopped just feet from the barrier rope confronted by two armed soldiers.

Realising that he was beaten, Tolly sank to his knees and appeared to sob.

Another policeman, a regular from the dockside station recruited for the emergency by the East Park Station arrived and stood over Tolly.

"You are to come with me, sir. *You* are under arrest."

The arriving army officer arriving, heard this and said, "Give him a minute, constable, please. He is clearly distressed."

The policeman had taken out his notebook.

"I know this man, sir. He is under surveillance by my station. He is known to us as Tolly Thomas, also as Naphtali Tomaschenko, the British born son of Jewish immigrants who came over here in the last century. We suspect him of pilfering from bomb sites over at the docks."

Satisfied the policeman was in control, the officer returned to the path where he was organising a fresh exclusion zone.

Tolly continued to sob and fain distress while he peered through his fingers working out the best route to No 4.

Samuel, who had followed the policeman over, arrived on the scene crying.

"Please let him go, he's been bombed out three times."

The officer seeing Samuel shouted.

"What's that man doing? Get him back to the path, soldier. Move the exclusion zone tape back here."

Tolly observed that the soldier concerned was the one standing over him.

As he left, another guard alongside took his place, pre-empting Tolly's intention to make a second attempt.

Realising the game was up Tolly allowed himself a brief smile at Samuel's blatant lie.

It seemed that Samuel was human after all. The thought pleased him.

Tolly stood up and was about to make a plea to the officer for a further search of No 4 when several boy cyclists arrived at speed across the Common. They slid to a stop shouting.

"She's not at the chapel or the hospital, sir."

"What the hell!" the officer shouted.

"I ordered an exclusion zone. No one is to be allowed beyond the path. Get to it. Get these boys back to a safe distance."

Everyone shocked by this sudden incursion, focused on the boys.

The men guarding Tolly reacted to the officer's order and went to move them, leaving Tolly as they thought, in the hands of the policeman whose attentionwas also on the boys.

Tolly, belying his years, did a forward somersault over the rope.

Regaining his feet, he sprinted across the road, ran up the steps of No 3, vaulted the low wall on to No 4.

He ducked under the trailing wires and pushed at the stricken door which gave way.

Tolly crashed to the floor half blind with dust and effort.

He lay there gasping for breath trying to recover.

Almost a minute passed before he recovered. Scrambling to his knees he looked around.

The hall and staircase were almost clear except for an easily surmounted fallen hall stand, ceiling plaster, small debris and a few broken tiles. The doorway through to back of the house, however, was blocked by a partly collapsed wall.

Tolly, covered in dust, forced himself to his feet. Checking the front room was clear, he made his way upstairs to the front bedroom, Dorothy's room.

The roof was open to the skies, the sun streaming in. Shattered windows highlighted the devastation.

Tolly had been in many a bomb site but this was different. It was another world, another dimension. He turned as if in slow motion to the sound of shouted orders outside highlighting the eerie silence within.

Two single slivers of windowpane glass hung from the broken window frame angle. Held by sticky tape. They twisted slowly in the autumn breeze catching the sunlight.

They reminded Tolly of hanged men on a gibbet.

He turned back towards the hole in the floor and the shattered bed.

The bedclothes had been dragged through the gap. Snagged on the splintered floorboards, they hung down into the kitchen drawing attention to the bomb embedded in the floor.

The fins clearly in view, it was stuck between the kitchen floor and the cellar below.

Part of the bed frame lay collapsed on the floor. Down in the kitchen another part of the frame with the twisted wires of the bed springs still attached lay across the remains of the table. There was no sign of Miss Dorothy. What he expected to find that the search and rescue teams hadn't, Tolly had no idea. He had failed and no longer knew what to do.

Tolly's spirit left his body. He heard his scream. "Miss Dorothy."

His legs gave way and he sank to his knees once more sobbing. This time it was for real.

"Tolly, help, water please. I need water." Dorothy's voice was little more than a hoarse whisper.

Tolly, even in the depth of his distress, heard it.

He spun around and peered into the gloom of the alcove which contrasted with the bright sunshine pouring into the bedroom. His heart was pumping and the blood thundering in his ears.

The conflicting emotions of distress, elation and fear temporarily robbed him of coherent action.

It seemed to Tolly that he was without the power of movement.

His eyes adjusted to the gloom sufficiently for him to see that the main roof purlin had been split into two halves. One end was still attached to the gable while at the other, broken ends had crashed through the ceiling dragging other timbers and a large section of the heavily slatted Victorian plaster ceiling into the alcove.

This large piece of the ceiling plaster was pinned to the floor by the purlin's broken end.

Tolly unscrambled his brain and shouted. “Miss Dorothy, where are you?”

He was answered by faint rapping and scratching followed by what sounded like a failed attempt to cough. This seemed to come from under the section of plaster ceiling.

The slab of plaster was propped against the alcove wall. Tolly rose to his feet.

“Hold on Miss Dorothy, I’m coming.”

He went to the broken end of the purlin and tried to shift it off the slats.

The heavy Victorian timber remained fast.

He looked around, now wanting the army to arrive, but all was silent.

The scratching and choking sounds resumed giving Tolly an idea where she was.

The noises were coming from up against the alcove wall underneath the timbers and slatted plaster. Tolly peered underneath. There didn’t appear to be enough space for anyone to survive.

Tolly lay full length to peer beneath but could see nothing.

Ducking down he forced his head then body underneath and tried to heave the piece away with his shoulders but could not get enough leverage.

Dorothy coughed again. This time he felt her breath on his face.

With superhuman effort he heaved once more at the plaster. This time the slats cracked.

He threw the broken section back to reveal a ghost-like head covered in plaster dust.

It was in Dorothy’s hair, nose and ears, everywhere.

Dorothy’s eyes were only recognisable as two white lash-lined slits.

She was trying to breath, cough and cry all at the same time.

Tolly began to pick the bits of plaster out of her hair thinking how he could clear her nose and mouth without harming her.

Scarlet red streaks appeared copiously running down her face highlighted against the whiteness of her face.

“God, Miss, you’re bleeding,” Tolly gasped.

"*She* is not, sir. The blood is from you. *Your* hand is gashed."

Tolly turned and looked up into the face of the army officer.

Dorothy coughed again finally managing to croak. "Water."

Tolly looked around ignoring his wound. "I'll try the bathroom."

Dorothy had freed one arm and was reaching out, the arm waving around like a blind worm as she uttered incoherent noises. It was clear that she could not see and barely speak.

Tolly stood up to look for the water.

The officer put a restraining hand on him. "You stay with her, sir. I'll get help."

The officer marched to the window gap and shouted across to the N.C.O. anxiously watching from rope.

"Sergeant, at the double. Send a water bottle up here and alert the search and rescue team, also the medics. Get them up here now. Casualty critical, ***move***."

Chapter 64

The lady from the almoner's office looked down at Dorothy.

"Are we there, Miss Price? Are we paying attention?"

She tapped impatiently on her clipboard with her pencil.

"We need you to join us." The woman used the collective pronoun, even though there was no one else anywhere near the bed.

Dorothy's hearing was not good. The ringing in her head had not gone away nor could she see clearly. Nevertheless, she was acutely aware why this woman was there.

She was there to begin discharge proceedings. Dorothy was terrified.

She felt threatened and not just because of this woman's attitude.

She forced open her eyelids but could see little other than a blurred shape.

"Who are you, what do you want?" she asked trying desperately not to cry.

"We need you to sign for your emergency issues."

She opened an envelope and listed the contents as she removed them and placed them on Dorothy's locker.

"Emergency ration cards, points card, clothing coupons and an application form for permanent replacement of all documents and certificates lost."

"I can't see," Dorothy complained.

"They are all here. Get the ward sister to check for you and countersign both forms.

She knows the drill." The woman ploughed on regardless.

"I have no clothes. I've nothing to wear," Dorothy protested, now beginning to weep.

"There is an ample supply of donated clothing from which you can choose. It's all explained in this leaflet." The woman answered, cocooned in her self-importance.

Dorothy could have pointed out that she could not see to read the leaflet, instead she wailed.

"I have no knickers. I can't wear second-hand knickers."

Her cry rang clear throughout the ward.

Two beds away the consultant was on his morning round accompanied by the matron and the ward sister.

He looked up over his gold half rims at the commotion, as did everyone.

The matron uttered one word. "Sister."

The sister rustled in her starched uniform to the offending bedside and issued just one instruction to the startled woman. "Leave it Morrison, the papers are self-explanatory."

The woman offered a brief resistance. "Sister, I need a signature."

The sister spoke so quietly it was barely a whisper. "Out!"

This one word, however, held the venom of a snake.

The woman scuttled away.

Returning to do voluntary consultancy from retirement, Sir Desmond Hazel was in pretty good condition for his age.

He cut a comic figure in a Harris Tweed suit, which oozed class even though it looked as though it had been slept in. His enormous bald pate was surrounded by a half circle of wiry iron-grey hair.

This was matched by his eyebrows and moustache accentuating a red bulbous nose all of which seemed to be trying but failing to dwarf his piercing blue eyes.

These eyes now were focused on matron.

"Shall we?"

In accord, they moved to Dorothy's bed. The sister handed the chart to Sir Desmond who, after reading passed it back to matron saying, "Admitted Thursday, cleared for discharge today?"

He paused raising his eyebrows. "Premature, don't you think? I would have thought another day or so at the least. Who authorised this?"

Matron turned to the sister before she attempted a reply.

"Please continue the round, sister. Sir Desmond and I will catch you later."

Once sister had left, matron handed him a memo marked confidential.

Sir Desmond read it and with barely a twitch of his eyebrows, continued as though the past minute had not existed. Turning his attention to Dorothy, he asked, "Do you mind if I take a look?"

Dorothy, aware of the attention but still apprehensive, was calmed by the rich musical tones of this man's request which flowed like wine over her anxiety.

Sensing an ally, she pleaded.

"Please, ... I have no home and no one to go home to."

Sir Desmond looked at matron. "Perhaps a cup of sweet tea, matron?"

Matron did not answer but pursed her lips. Sir Desmond added, by way of justification:

"For the patient."

"There *is* no surplus of tea or sugar as I am sure you are aware, Sir Desmond," matron answered making it clear that she was not going to agree.

"I am well aware that it is rationed, matron, but perhaps an exception for this young lady?"

Matron raised her eyebrows and remained firm returning Sir Desmond's piercing stare.

"And take from whom Sir Desmond?" she asked, pausing for the briefest of moments.

"Now if you will excuse me, I must join sister. We are late with the morning rounds already."

The old gentleman watched her leave.

"Game set and match to matron I believe," he said glancing briefly at Dorothy's chart.

"Wouldn't you say so Miss Price?" He placed his hand on Dorothy's.

"Now if you don't mind, I will take a little look," he said taking a small pen light from his pocket. Peeling back her eyelids, he examined each eye before turning around and beckoning to a ward nurse.

"Everything is fine Miss Price, it is just a matter of time. Your vision will improve in a couple of days once you have completed the drops. Otherwise, I recommend bed rest and more bed rest."

He beckoned again to the nurse.

"Find out from the almoner's office please nurse, just who is calling for Miss Price. Tell Staff that Miss Price is not to leave without an approved escort."

Dorothy still was clinging to Sir Desmond's hand as he again glanced at her chart.

"Tell me, dear lady, are you the Miss Price reported on in the local newspaper last night?" "Newspaper? I don't know."

This was the first Dorothy had heard. The news took her mind off her immediate worries.

"It was under the heading Reluctant Hero. Some brave chap Tomo something,"

Sir Desmond explained.

"Tomoschenko,." Dorothy obliged now feeling more at ease.

The consultant smiled. "Tomoschenko? Interesting name, I suppose he is called Tommy or Tomo."

"No, we all call him Tolly."

The consultant chuckled. "Even better, Tolly Tomoschenko could be a compatriot of Bertie Wooster. Straight off the pages of P.G."

"Why *reluctant* hero?" Dorothy asked.

The consultant, having skilfully steered her mind away from her troubles, made an entry on the chart as he continued.

"Apparently he is dodging the limelight. Difficult to interview. One reporter who finally cornered him said that he was dismissed with a few choice words."

"That sounds like Tolly. So that is why he has not been to see me. I want to thank him. He saved my life."

Dorothy was feeling much better already.

Meanwhile, the nurse returned from her mission. Sir Desmond looked up.

"Yes, nurse."

"A Mrs Avery is escorting Miss Price at 3.00 p.m. Will she please leave by the rear entrance because there are reporters waiting outside, at the front?"

Dorothy burst into tears of relief. "Pamela, oh thank God."

"Ah a good cry, excellent. That will do more for your eyes than we can. If we try to remove the remaining grit, we could do more damage than good. If you will excuse me now Miss Price I must crack on."

As Sir Desmond walked away, he could be heard muttering to himself, "Tolly Tomoschenko, fascinating."

Chapter 65

Pamela Avery looked at her watch and sighed. It was almost 4.00 p.m.

The chances of them arriving back at St. Mary Upperford in daylight were beyond slim already.

She had been sitting in this dreary waiting room for over an hour. The clothes she had brought for Dorothy had been taken up ages ago. Still there was no sign or word of her friend.

A young woman entered bringing a package for Dorothy and asked her to pick up her friend in the Consultant No.4 waiting room.

Nothing about this visit seemed normal. The prospect of finally seeing her friend swept all her other emotions away.

Dorothy was in a wheelchair accompanied by a porter.

Pamela dropped to her knees and took her friend's hands in hers. Neither spoke for almost thirty seconds. Eventually through her tears, Pamela said, "Let's get you to your new home. I have waited so long for this."

Dorothy looked so frail and lost in the wheelchair. Pamela's desire to hug her was overwhelmed by fear of hurting her.

The porter, without waiting for a reasonable pause, ushered Pamela to her feet.

"Can we go now, Miss, out of the rear entrance?"

Pamela looked up at this man who seemed to carry much more authority than his station would suggest.

"Are you sure she is fit to be released? Why the rear entrance? That is even further away from the tube station. I doubt if she can walk that far."

The porter looked hard at Pamela.

"Please Miss, we need to get this patient home as soon as possible."

Pamela looked at him and was prepared to argue but there was something in his stare which persuaded her to keep quiet. She stood up and obediently followed him outside.

Meanwhile Dorothy seemed to have shrunk deeper into the wheelchair.

Pamela clung to her friend's hand even more firmly.

Once outside, a London taxi pulled up alongside. The back-seat passenger stepped out.

This man opened the door and without a word, along with the porter, helped Dorothy into the back. The man still holding the door, gestured to Pamela who, in a mixture of relief and confusion, climbed in. The man joined them in the back as the cab moved away swiftly.

At last, Dorothy and Pamela were able to hold, greet and console each other properly.

The man sat opposite on the tip-up seat. He opened a carrier box on the floor and removed a vacuum flask, two Bakelite cups and an invalid feeder cup.

Watching the two ladies he bided his time until they finally came to notice his presence.

Dorothy, relieved not to be just thrown out on to the street, was vaguely aware of why this might be. She had noticed there was something familiar about their fellow occupant even though her sight was blurred.

Pamela who had no such indications, was relieved to be free of the responsibility of seeing her sick friend home on public transport. But, she was full of questions.

Dorothy just accepted everything and childlike sank into the arms of Pamela preparing to sleep.

The man had part filled the invalid feeding cup and offered it to Pamela.

"Please Mrs Avery, persuade Miss Price to take some tea."

Pamela who was full of questions, asked the first. "Is that all this is, tea?"

"Yes, Mrs Avery, albeit very sweet tea. Proscribed medicine shall we say."

Pamela took the offered cup. "Who are you?"

"All will be revealed in good time Mrs Avery. Please, in the meantime trust me."

Pamela still looked uncertain, so he continued, "Miss Price and I have met before, briefly."

Dorothy now knew who he was. She had not fully recognised who he was. Her vision blurred, and he was out of uniform. It was she who next spoke.

"It's all right Pamela, I know him."

With that Pamela offered the spout to her friend who drank thirstily.

The man broke off two fingers of chocolate wafer biscuit and handed them to Pamela.

"Afternoon tea. It is time. There is tea and biscuits for you also Miss Avery. That is all I can offer just now. Explanations will follow in due course. Meantime we hope that you will nurse Miss Price back to health."

He pointed to a bag. "This contains supplies and necessary medication. A postman will deliver a package to your home tomorrow with more. If you need anything at all make your written requests to him. There is no need for you to leave Miss Price alone until she regains her health and confidence."

Dorothy who had been listening to the conversation, found the security she was seeking and fell asleep. A half-eaten chocolate finger slid on to the floor.

"Ah!" exclaimed the man. "That is not supposed to happen."

"Why not?" Pamela asked. "Who are you, what *are* you about?"

The man didn't answer but looked at his watch.

"Surely it is better for her to sleep the journey away?" Pamela made the point forcibly.

"You are right. I will wait until she wakes up or we get to your home. We have best part of two hours."

Pamela repeated her earlier question. "Who are you?"

To this the man repeated his earlier comment. "All will be revealed later."

"Later when?"

"After you have signed the Official Secrets Act."

The man looked across at Pamela who was now looking aghast.

"You see Mrs Avery," he explained, "Miss Price has provided us with some vital information.

We now need to have the answers to further questions and time is of the essence." He paused. "Please don't ask any more questions and assume that anything you hear and everything that has happened is secret. This is in the national interest."

Pamela was stunned, realising that there was probably a lot more to her friend than she had realised.

Dorothy woke up when the taxi pulled up outside Pamela's house. Pamela wrapped her cardigan around her friend's shoulders.

"Let's get you to bed, Pet."

The man held up a hand. "Just two questions Miss Price."

He checked that the taxi's door was locked.

Pamela bridled. "Have you no shame. Surely the priority is Dorothy's health."

"Please stay seated Mrs Avery and hear me out."

Pamela leaned forward and stared into this man's eyes.

"Why should we take notice of a stranger? We *don't know* you."

The man held up his hands. "Because a man's life is at stake. It *is* of national importance.

If you knew the detail you would not resist."

"Then just tell us." Pamela suddenly relaxed and sat back and sighed.

"I know, I know, all will be revealed in good time."

She knew in her heart of hearts that they would not have been able to manage the journey back home without this help. When she set out from St. Mary, she had no idea just how ill Dorothy was.

"Mrs Avery, we are counting on you to help us with Miss Price because she is our only contact with those with whom we need to open a dialogue. There was no logic in taking her out of hospital without your help. Miss Price's physical injuries are minimal. The best medicine now is rest and recuperation away from London in the quiet of this village with people who know her and care."

He turned and smiled at Dorothy who was sitting quietly listening. "May I?" he asked. Dorothy nodded her agreement.

The man reached for the flask and poured more tea into the invalid cup and passed it to Dorothy whose hands were shaking. Pamela took over being impatient to get her friend safely indoors even though she understood what the man was doing.

Dorothy waking with a foul dry mouth was grateful. The man waited while she finished drinking. "Ready Miss Price?" he asked. Dorothy nodded.

"When Pegasus contacted Mercury, how was this done?"

"Advert in *The Times'* personal column. P will meet M usual place, followed by time and date."

"Where?" the man asked as he made notes.

"In England, the Lyons corner House, Leicester Square."

"And in Austria?" The man asked making another note.

"Same in the Innsbruck Spiegel," Dorothy answered.

Pamela watched her friend closely. Her interest was no longer just in her health.

Without looking up, he continued, "and where?"

"A café behind the high street. There was a room upstairs."

"In Innsbruck, of course. You have been there?" he asked continuing to make notes.

Dorothy nodded. "Yes, but the venue changed regularly."

Dorothy paused and took another drink offered by Pamela who was now absorbed.

Continuing, Dorothy gave one further venue. "The main meetings were held in a clinic for sexually transmitted diseases along the river 12 kilometres to the west of the city."

The man finished his note, leant forward and kissed Dorothy's hand.

"Thank you, that will be all for now."

He released the car door, and the driver came around and opened it.

"Please ladies, the driver will bring the provisions. Oh!" He picked up the parcel which Pamela had placed on the seat. "Is this yours?" he asked.

"That was brought to me in the hospital. It is for Dorothy," replied Pamela holding out a hand.

The man held on to it.

"Do you know who it is from?"

Both ladies shook their heads.

"Do you mind if we check it over first?"

The man although smiling as he asked was making it clear that he was not going to part with the parcel. Dorothy and Pamela, more concerned with getting home, shook their heads.

Chapter 66

The following week in the late afternoon, Pamela, laying the table in the front room, saw Sir George Bridge Thompson crossing the Green towards them. She went to the front door to meet him with their traditional greeting. "Hilo, Sir George."

"Hilo, Pammy. How's the patient?"

"Recovering, coughing up dust, still little strained."

Pamela replied standing back for George to sweep in.

"Strange, did you say?"

"Yes, and that," Pamela answered. She and Sir George had their own ways of communicating.

Sir George was able to lose his pomp in her company, the over-the-top façade demanded by Amelia. Sir George looked around, lowering the boom in his voice.

"Where is she Pammy?"

"Out the back. I can't get her to come in and it is getting chilly."

"Sleeping all right?" Sir George asked. He was clearly on a mission. Pamela knew to wait his pleasure. She liked him and his way of coping with the awkward.

"Surprisingly well. She was still sleeping when I took Mim to Schule this morning."

"Still taking her.? I heard she decided to take herself." Sir George was a little surprised.

"Sometimes when it's fine, we like to walk by the river and talk. I get to know things especially just what I have missed by not having a daughter. It's usually when *Mim* wants to know something."

Sir George didn't speak for a while.

Used to his ways, Pamela waited for him to reveal the real reason for his visit.

Sir George walked into the kitchen and stood looking through the window at Dorothy.

The silence in the house was only broken by the ticking of the kitchen clock.

Eventually, Sir George asked. "You left her alone then? This morning."

"Good grief, Sir George, she knows her way around. She's a strong woman and she made it clear that she needs some space."

"Just stands there, does she?"

"For hours, sometimes." Pamela sounded wistful.

Sir George thought for a moment. "Perhaps we should get Horace Calderwood to look at her."

"I don't think so. I'll keep close watch. She just needs time."

They stood in the kitchen watching the lonely figure in the garden.

Their mood was matched by the gathering gloom and the measured ticking of the clock.

"Must have been hell," whispered Sir George eventually which jerked Pamela into action.

"I'll go get her."

Sir George placed his hand on her arm.

"In a minute, Pammy. Do you think she will be fit enough to come over tomorrow for a bit of a parley? Some chaps are coming from Whitehall for talks with Miss Price, yourself, Pen and Henry Steading."

"Hal! Why him?" asked Pamela, forgetting, for the moment, to ask at the same time, 'why me?'

"I haven't the faintest idea. I'm just the messenger boy."

Pamela again felt a sudden surge of warmth towards him and not for the first time that evening.

This left her confused and in a slight panic. She blushed and threw her arms into the air.

"What is all this about and why me?" aware that she was not just referring to the Whitehall meeting.

"I think that Dorothy knows but she's not saying." Pamela answered her own question, knowing more about her friend than did Sir George.

"Tomorrow Pammy, tomorrow eh! And get Miss Price in before she takes root. She will be covered in dew." Sir George headed for the door.

Pamela followed. "How's Lady Amelia coping with Mim? Without me there?"

Sir George stopped.

"Nothing said, but I guess all is tickety-boo. You know Mim, she could charm a bone from the jaws of a starving dog. Why do you ask?"

"I was thinking of taking Dorothy into Fernborough tomorrow morning to spend some of her clothing coupons. She needs more clothes. Get her out of the house, back into the bustle of life. A distraction. This constant thinking can't be helping her recovery."

"Good idea! Back into the mainstream of life. Be sure to get her back in time for the meeting."

With a final smile, he left Pamela sorting out her emotions.

Pamela waited to gather herself before going outside to join her friend.

Standing beside Dorothy in the garden she made no attempt to make conversation.

Dorothy broke the silence with a memory.

"On summer nights Tuss and I would stand outside on her balcony trying to see the stars.

It was never as sharp, never as clear. I can see more clearly here even with drops in my eyes.

This is so beautiful."

Pamela didn't answer so her friend continued.

"The moths and bats would be flitting around us while below a melee of revellers played and dined into the night. The two worlds side by side."

Again, there followed a long silence while Pamela waited for her to speak again, which she finally did.

"I miss her. I so miss Tuss. I wish now that I could now tell her that I understand." She paused.

"I really do now understand."

"Understand what Pet?"

"Why she got in with that man who ruined her. She was never the same. He took her child's life and hers. I thought it stupid and mad."

"And now you think differently?"

Dorothy nodded. "Never judge anyone until you have worn their moccasins for many moons,"

she whispered.

Pamela linked arms. "Why don't we go inside, and you can tell me all about it?"

Without waiting for an answer, she led Dorothy indoors.

"Shall we have supper now Pet, or do you just want to talk?"

"Talk please."

Pamela locked the door and drew the blackout curtains.

She switched on the standard lamp and set light to the already laid fire talking as she did.

"I do so miss leaving the curtains open and seeing all the friendly lights across the Green.

Now everything is so dark. So dark."

Suddenly she realised what she was saying. St. Mary Upperford had rarely seen a plane let alone heard the scream of a bomb and here she was complaining about the blackout.

"Oh! I'm so sorry, Pet. So sorry."

Dorothy didn't seem to notice.

"It is so beautiful here. I have been listening to a blackbird singing.

I had forgotten how lovely it can be at dusk with the sweet smells of the garden and the fields.

The soft wind on my cheek. I do thank you for letting me into your home."

Pamela felt ashamed.

"You were saying you now understood Tuss?" she added, quickly changing the subject.

The fire had caught, and the flames flickered on the walls.

"Could we just have the fire light please?"

Pamela switched off the standard lamp.

They sat quietly for a while, Pamela giving way to Dorothy's mood.

"Last week, before the bomb, I met a man. I was alone with him for a short while."

Dorothy began. Pamela sat forward.

Dorothy continued. "Something happened to me for the first time ever."

Pamela left her chair and sat beside her on the settee taking her hand.

"What happened?"

Dorothy shrugged.

"Nothing really but somehow I felt like Moses being shown the Promised Land."

Again, she was silent with no further explanation.

Pamela fished for the detail asking, "Moses wasn't allowed to go there so I guess neither did you. What then?"

"The air seemed to be full of electricity and I had this strange, excited feeling that invaded my throat and breastbone. I forgot why I was there. I was left with this massive uncontrollable emotion. Yet he just sat there in his ivory tower. It was as if there was a moat between us."

"And he wasn't going to let down the drawbridge?"

"No, but I tell you this. I was out of control. In other circumstances I am sure I would have swum the moat."

"Even though it was 'shark-infested'?" Pamela was intrigued. She needed the answer.

Dorothy sighed then gave a nervous laugh.

"Even so. Sorry about bothering you but I did need to talk about it. Thank you."

It was beginning to dawn on Pam that Dorothy was not just in shock from the bombing but from other matters.

"Is this what you were thinking about outside just now?"

Dorothy nodded.

"There was I thinking it was shell shock."

Dorothy looked up at Pamela.

"Is there a difference?" she asked.

Chapter 67

The British Restaurant was crowded. Pamela Avery was both amazed and resentful.

"How can people in large towns have access to this standard of food, off ration and for just five pence? In Bendesbury there's nothing like this."

She looked around in amazement. "Did you have these in London?"

"Yes, but this is the first time I have been in one."

"Why ever not? If there was one in Bendesbury I would be there regularly."

Dorothy waved her remaining buff tickets at Pamela. "Not without these you couldn't,"

she replied adding,"These are the first I have had. We wouldn't have these but for the courtesy of H.M.G.

I couldn't get them at East Park because I had access to the school canteen."

"Then where do we get them and how?" asked Pamela, the indignation raising the volume of her voice. Her complaint carried to a mature W.V.S. lady clearing empty plates.

She moved in and collected them with the friendly words,"Are these finished with, dearie?"

Without waiting for an answer, she swept the crockery on to the trolley while adding, "You can get them from your workplace or the council if you qualify."

It was the answer Pamela was seeking.

"Do all these people qualify?" Pamela asked, waving her arm around.

"Most of these are from out of town," she replied. "Delivery men and women bringing in supplies for the factories. They come from all over the country. Liverpool, Manchester, Birmingham,

Coventry, you name it. Some of these W.A.A.F. lasses over there-are here to fly new built Hurricanes out to who knows where. The chaps on the next table came down overnight from Glasgow. Come down regular. They all need to eat."

With that final offering, she moved on to the next table.

Pamela looked at her watch.

"We need to go Pet if we are to catch the one o'clock to St. Mary."

The bus station was crowded with service personnel and nurses in uniform who were given priority by the inspector.

"Are they allowed to do that? We will be lucky to board," said Pamela.

The queue was very orderly and accepted the situation.

"If you complain to the inspector the answer would be. 'Sorry, there's a war on'. It's the standard reply to everything nowadays."

As expected, the bus was full before they got near.

Pamela stood not knowing what to do.

"I should have known the bus would be busy, it is lunch hour. What now?

I promised Sir George and these men are coming from Whitehall."

Dorothy linked arms with her friend. "Whitehall, like all."

"What does that mean?" said Pamela. "We must telephone."

"Those pinstripe potentates all look the same in their underpants. They will probably be late themselves anyway and think on, they need us. I can't say I need them."

Pamela giggled. "You are good for me; but we really must telephone George."

"Let them wait. Besides we've still got clothing coupons to spend.

Last week I was like Gulliver. Tied down by a lot of little people. Then I had an epiphany.

In one day, I was able to cast off all my bonds. It will take a lot to tie me down ever again."

"You mean it really did take a bomb under you to get you here?" Pamela said, laughing.

"Strangely no, I had already decided. I made my first decisions earlier that day.

The bomb just gives me a convenient cover story."

"What was the trigger, if it wasn't the bomb?"

Pamela was fishing to find out more about the emotional encounter with a stranger.

"I don't know, possibly I suddenly understood Tuss and her problems. I suppose her death had been at the root of everything. I had never managed to recover properly."

Dorothy was clearly still seeking the reasons herself.

Chapter 68

It was three o' clock when finally dressed in a new outfit, Dorothy was ready to go to the meeting. She was still refusing to be hurried by Pamela.

They arrived almost at the same time as the Whitehall party, who entered by the side door off the Drovers Lane.

They moved into the library, a kind of second sitting room.

The room had been rearranged with the settee and chairs in a semi-circle facing a carved wooden fire surround. Stood with his back to this, was the man in grey.

Dorothy had imagined seeing him today without really believing it. She was astounded.

He arrived along with the officer who had escorted them from the hospital.

She gripped Pamela's arm who understanding, responded with "Steady, Pet."

There followed an order for all who wished to remain to sign the Official Secrets Act.

This without prior knowledge of any reason for so doing.

It was a case of sign and stay or leave the meeting. Curiosity won in the end.

Even Hal who claimed he was not bound by it being an American citizen, signed.

The man in grey's opening remarks brought a gasp of incredulity from the gathering.

If the subject had been mentioned beforehand it would have had all rushing to sign without argument.

He looked pointedly at each in the room, as he spoke.

"Each of you is involved and will be continue to be involved with the subject of an important and sensitive War Office project. We ask all to be on their guard against media involvement which will inevitably occur during this operation and one which may take some considerable time."

The man once more looked to each in turn. "This operation was not only approved by but initiated by the Prime Minister.

It concerns your husband, Mrs Barnes."

This prompted a plethora of questioning which forced the speaker to raise his hand and add, I will not, repeat, not be answering questions."

He paused, demanding silence.

"I am here to insist on your co-operation. In return I will give you all information as deemed necessary. Therefore, I ask you to keep quiet and to pay attention."

Once the room settled down, he continued.

"It is distinctly possible that William Joyce, Lord Haw-Haw as he is known, will broadcast that your husband Mrs Barnes, is dead." He paused for effect.

"Do not believe the rumours. Lt. Barnes is safe and in good hands. It suits the Nazis' purposes to spread these lies."

Again, it was necessary for him to hold up his hands and wait for the room to settle.

"After escaping from the P. O. W. camp where he was being held ..."

The man tried again to continue. There was a further wait until everyone took this in.

This took time. Meanwhile, he sat down and waited before quietly adding, "Look everyone we are trying to give you the best information we have. Please maintain silence until I have finished."

There was something in his manner which commanded silence. It was as though he had said.

'I **will** have quiet or you will hear nothing more.'

After looking at each in turn until he was sure he had their complete attention, he then resumed.

"The camp which held Lt. Barnes was a high security unit specially constructed to hold officers and significantly important prisoners. Somehow Lt Barnes achieved that which was thought impossible. We don't know quite how it was done, but Lt. Barnes **did** escape the camp."

The man waited to regain their attention before continuing.

"He made his way successfully over the border into another country. This was not without consequence. Lt. Barnes resurfaced with a broken leg in an Austrian hospital.

A resistance group, so far unexplained how they located him and were able to rescue him before the authorities identified him."

The man in grey had now got the measure of the situation and quickly learned the art of continuing his narrative with pauses for his audience to assimilate the revelations.

"In the ensuing days word of these remarkable escapes spread across Europe.

A plethora of anecdotes exploded after it was rumoured that he escaped their clutches from this hospital while under surveillance by the S.S.

If all this is true, twice escaping in as many weeks borders upon the miraculous.

Jokes and anecdotes spread quickly. An example being; This is an English take of the Czech version.

'They seek him here, they seek him there, those Nazis seek him everywhere, is he in heaven? No he's not well, he's having a kip in hospital. By the time the Nazis found out he was in their care, this invisible man was no longer there.'

"Here I need to repeat that this second escape had been successfully arranged and carried out by Austrian resistance. We have no idea how this was accomplished.

We do know where he is now. We are co-operating with Austrian friends and others to ensure his health and safety."

The man now had everyone's complete attention as he continued.

"The German high command is in disarray and at odds with a furious Berlin. Hitler is apoplectic. Compounding this, rumours are circulating that Lt. Barnes during the German advance into the Low Countries, held up an army column for many hours allowing units of the British Army to escape to the coast. This, although grossly exaggerated, has a basis in truth."

The man turned to Hal.

"A story which we believe you, Mr. Steading, are currently working on.

We have been in touch with your editorial staff who agree that we should be working on this together, sharing information. Eventually news of this action will be released, in your name of course, when advantageous to our plans."

"No one is supposed to know of this, not even my editor."

"He does now," replied the man in grey, adding, "We will share our knowledge Mr. Steading.

We have recently obtained a copy of a German communicate which confirms that Lt. Barnes did indeed hold up a German motorised column long enough for two of our army units to make their escape to the Dunkirk beaches.

"This column was heading to cut off our retreat at the Ypres road north. As a direct result of Barnes' action, this column was held up at a river crossing. Barnes blocked and defended the bridge for some hours allowing some British units to escape to the coast. We would like to hold this information until later. Rub salt in the Nazi wounds when the time is ripe."

The man paused again until the room settled.

"The German high command wish for this matter to be closed as it is disrupting their operations.

Hitler via Himmler is demanding Lt. Barnes's head on a plate.

Keeping this story running is both strategically useful and a morale boost for the occupied territories.

They are making up new jokes at the enemy's expense almost daily. We have a department in charge of a leaflet campaign to encourage them. Believe me this is **no small matter**.

Please, do not speak with anyone about this. The safety of Lt. Barnes may depend upon it.

Meantime Sir George will be your point of contact.

Be assured we will keep you informed through him of any developments."

The man then gathered his papers, nodded to his colleague and left with a curt.

"Thank you and good afternoon."

With the barest of acknowledgment to Sir George the two of them let themselves out by the side entrance and walked swiftly down the riverside path.

At Greensleeves the news had paralysed everyone with shock. The exceptions were Sir George and Dorothy, who had worked out the probabilities arising from the mysterious telegram.

Pen was demanding to know from her father more detail about Peter. Detail that he did not have. Pen ended crying and pleading to no avail.

The atmosphere created by this meeting was charged, more by desperate need for answers than anger. As question after question remained unanswered by Sir George, he was forced to either admit that he knew nothing more than his questioners or to pull rank.

He chose the latter. "Pen, will you and Hal join me in my study, NOW please?"

This he gave as an order which he hoped gave the impression that he was tied by legalities and not ignorance. His main interest was in speaking to his daughter about her association with Henry Steading. Astutely he had used the moment to his advantage, and as he left the room, he passed a package over to Dorothy.

"Yours, I believe, Miss Price."

Dorothy took it instinctively being more concerned about Pamela who was trembling.

Before she could ask Sir George what it was, he had left.

"You all right, Pam?"

"Of course, Pet."

Clearly, Pamela was not all right.

"Shall we go home?"

Pamela nodded and stood up straight away holding on to Dorothy's arm.

Now for protection. No longer to protect. The two friends made their way quickly back across the Green.

Once inside the house Pamela went straight through to the chair at the kitchen table and sat with folded arms across her body. Dorothy again asked if she was all right.

Pamela nodded her reply. Dorothy knew this was a lie and tried to change the mood.

"Sir George gave me this parcel and I have no idea what it is."

Pamela didn't answer as Dorothy hoped.

Instead Pamela spoke accusingly. "You knew what this meeting was about."

"I didn't *know*. I guessed what it could be about. That is not knowing."

Pamela looked up at her friend, her eyes brimming with tears.

"Peter's in great danger, isn't he? They are using him. Putting him in even greater danger."

Dorothy did not know what to say. Before she could gather her thoughts and answer, Pamela continued.

"It is all my fault."

Dorothy sat and tried to take Pam's hand, but both hands remained tight against her chest.

"How possibly could all this be your fault?"

In a voice, barely above a whisper such that Dorothy had to lean forward to hear, Pamela answered.

"Ah but it is, it *is all* my fault. Little do you know."

Nothing more was said for fully a minute. Dorothy could see Pamela shaking. Not just from the cold, it being distinctly chilly in the house.

Dorothy could not sit and watch Pam in torment.

She filled the kettle and lit the gas under it.

"I am going to make a pot of tea, light the fire in the room and we are going to talk this out however long it may take."

Half hour later, the fire was burning brightly.

Clouds had rolled in as dusk fell, rain and wind spattered and battered against the window.

Dorothy pulled the blackout blinds and the chintz curtains, closed the door and draft curtain.

She did so with demonstrable vigour as if battling to lock out the world.

She abandoned the use of the china tea service in favour of two large beakers laced with more than the usual one level teaspoon of sugar discipline.

She then joined Pamela on the settee in front of the fire.

Pamela was no longer trembling but sitting bolt upright, her arms clasped tight about her chest as if it was about to explode. Dorothy placed the beaker on the occasional table and waited for Pamela to speak, which she eventually did.

"I don't think Peter was a hero at that bridge," she said quietly.

"You don't?" The remark surprised Dorothy.

"He was trying to get himself killed."

Pamela paused before adding, "It would be his way of solving everyone's problems."

The long silence which followed forced Dorothy to ask.

"What makes you believe that?"

"I know him so well. Paul is my biological son, but I don't really know him like I do Peter."

She paused to think. "He is his father's son, keeps himself to himself. whereas Peter and me we are close. For six years I was all he had. We bonded in a way I never could do with Paul. Love him as I do."

Pamela was silent for what seemed an age before adding to Dorothy's astonishment.

"Peter was as good as my own child. That is until I fucked it all away."

Pamela began to sob quietly. Dorothy put her arms around her.

"Shush my love, it was not your fault. There are forces outside our control which dictate destinies."

Pamela shook her head violently.

"I should have told him about Paul from the beginning. When he found out, the shock was such that he didn't know what to do. He ran away to join the army. That's why it's my fault."

She took several deep breaths before continuing.

"I should not have turned a blind eye to him marrying Pen. He knew it was wrong. So did I.

He would have listened to me. Now he is in mortal danger. His father would have had Peter safe in a reserved occupation just as he has done with Paul."

Dorothy who had been trying to work out exactly what Pam was talking about, realised why Pamela was using language normally foreign to her nature. She said, "Peter's father is also Paul's? They are half-brothers?"

Pamela looked in surprise at her friend. "You didn't know? I thought everyone knew."

"No, no one told me."

"Everyone in the village does. Everyone knew back then, except Peter it seemed."

Pamela let out a huge sigh.

"Paul was conceived in a moment of madness which took over not just my life but everybody else's I then cared about."

She took time to compose herself before explaining.

"It was Peter's birthday. He was just six-years-old. His father didn't come home for his birthday party after promising faithfully to be there. When he did come it was late and he had been drinking."

Pamela gathered her memories.

"I was furious and shouted at him for the first time ever, and-and-and."

Pamela suddenly clapped her hand to her mouth as if to stop the words. Her memories and the tears began to flow. Eventually she managed to continue but in the tiniest of voices.

She gasped to breath, trying to control the sobbing.

"Richard just began to cry, to say sorry. It was so unlike him."

After taking a second or so to breathe Pamela struggled on, now with a little more control.

"It was then he told me he had been to the cemetery to his wife's grave who had died on that same date, in childbirth with Peter."

She gulped back her tears before continuing in the still tiny voice.

"I can only remember putting my arms around him to console him and somehow, somehow, Paul happened."

In the silence which followed the fire which had been burning brightly gradually faded then flared, spluttered and died leaving them facing a dull red glow.

How long they sat there neither knew. Dorothy wondered how to help. Her fear of offending her friend held her in check. She eventually stood and put another log on the fire.

It was some little while before the flames took hold. Before they did Dorothy took the poker, prodding at the log furiously hoping for inspiration.

Pamela appeared to shrink, holding her sides as she wept and shuddered.

Dorothy decided to try and rationalise the situation by saying, "From what little I know it seems to me that sometimes there are forces outside our control at work when it comes to sex."

Pamela didn't answer.

Desperate to fill the silence, Dorothy said, "The only reason I am not in trouble is my moment passed because temptation was locked away in his ivory tower. Had he lowered the drawbridge and raised the portcullis, who knows?"

Pamela suddenly spluttered into hysterical laughter.

This shocked Dorothy, she took also several seconds to realise what had happened.

She burst out laughing, joining Pamela.

"Sorry, did that sound pompous?" She shrieked, collapsing in a heap on the settee.

It was several minutes before any form of normality resumed.

Pamela wiped her eyes now reddened with crying and laughing.

"Thank you, pet. That's just what I needed. I was getting maudlin."

"Maudlin? What is that?"

"Sorry, pet. Self-centred, feeling sorry for myself." Pamela paused and began to giggle again.

"It was the thought of that 'cold fish' lowering his drawbridge and raising his portcullis.

It's the first time I've heard it called that."

This was the last time that evening that they were able to engage in sensible conversation without the interruption of explosive laughter. Any attempt at serious conversation was abandoned long before they went to their beds.

The next morning at breakfast the mood had changed again.

Pamela looked 'wrecked' after spending the night thinking, worrying about Peter and trawling through her past.

Dorothy made several attempts at conversation which were bounced 'out of court' by monosyllabic answers. It was clear to Dorothy that, whatever she said, was not going to improve the situation.

Dorothy decided to give Pamela some space. She put on her coat and walking shoes.

"I am off to Bendesbury to see the rabbi about starting at the Schule."

Pamela reacted positively for the first time that morning.

"Good idea. He did promise you a place." She hugged her.

"Sorry, I am a bear with a sore head I just need a bit of time. All I could think of during last night was Peter. He wasn't even seven before being shipped off to boarding school. Poor lamb. It destroyed him. Now he is in grave danger because of what I did over twenty years ago. I just know it."

Chapter 69

Peter tried to move, but couldn't.

He tried to scream "NO."

His lungs hurt as he strained to be heard.

His scream was like the squeak of a mouse as the trap closes.

Hurtling towards him out of a black tunnel, headlights glaring, came the infernal machine.

The sound of the engine reached a crescendo.

With a roar, it sped by him in a flash of lightning and into the distance only to spin around returning to repeat and repeat and repeat.

Each time he tried to dodge and cower. Each time it was in vain. He was held firm.

"Mother-rrr." He screamed.

From 'nowhere' she appeared and swept him up into her arms. He buried his face in her bosom.

"Ah, at last my little soldier, you are getting better."

Chuckling, Tanya replaced the penlight in her pocket.

"Prop him up on the pillows, Sabina."

Tanya held him to her while Sabina arranged the pillows.

"We can give you a good wash down now you are conscious."

"Can I go for now?" asked Sabina seizing the opportunity.

"Yes, but don't go far, I will need you to help wash him and change his bed. Just bring me a bowl of fresh water and a cloth. I will call you when I need you."

Tanya spent the next minutes sponging Peter's face and talking to him.

"Hello, anybody there?"

Peter's eyes were half closed. His pupils seemed to be responsive to her penlight, but he did not reply.

"Hello, little big man, answer me." His eyes opened wide then closed again.

"Answer me if you understand me," Tanya persisted.

"Try speaking German."

Tanya turned towards the speaker. Adolf was standing in the doorway.

"That might work."

Tanya shrugged with annoyance and muttered to herself "idiot." "Sorry, sorry, Adolf. I was speaking of myself not you."

Adolf, realising that he had made a positive contribution, afforded himself a little preening almost forgetting what he had come for.

"Heard he's now conscious. How long before you can ship him out?"

Tanya stopped attending to Peter and looked at him.

"Adolf, think! A broken leg with complications, a fever and in a coma for over a week.

The fever's now subsiding but will leave him weak and vulnerable. How in heaven's name can we think of moving him on right now?"

Adolf threw his head back against the door.

"Dear God, how long do we have to put up with this?"

Tanya turned her attention back to Peter.

"Three, possibly four months," she answered in a matter of fact voice avoiding looking towards him. Adolf continued to bang his head on the door.

"Please God, please no. We can't live like this. We just want to farm."

Tanya stood up and put her hand on his arm.

"By the time his leg heals he will be weaker than a new-born foal. Even with his undamaged leg he'd be unable to stand until his muscles are rebuilt. This whole process will take time."

Tanya was aware that Maria and Sabina had entered the creamery.

Sabina busied herself skimming the curds while Maria worked the cheese press.

Neither task was the reason for their presence.

Tanya raised her voice above that of the confidential and continued.

"We are just pawns in a much bigger game. You would be surprised who the main movers are. The opposing kings." She paused before continuing with added emphasis.

"It is a game *I* chose to join. *I do know* you did not but that no longer matters."

She looked towards the creamery.

"The collective next move is vital. One wrong choice and we are all lambs to the slaughter.

To be sure there will be a fair amount of bleating before we die."

The two women stopped what they were doing. Adolf who had been stood frozen in fear, eyes closed, protested.

"We are innocent. We never intended this."

"And you think the Gestapo will believe that?"

Maria moved quickly to Adolf's side and took his hand.

Tanya released the hold on his arm and took two steps away before turning and continuing.

"This farm is in a good position. The road curls around following the contours of the Wald with little connection to the many other farms and estates along its length.

"The German Army is not looking in this area yet. The word is that they have enlisted help from the Serbs. It would be easy for them to post a watcher up in the trees. There are at least 600 metres of open country before we could reach cover. The chances of us moving Peter without being seen is going to be difficult even if we had the means to do this in a suitable vehicle. The donkey cart you use to market your food will not do the job and anything other would be suspect." She looked at each in turn.

"So, he stays as long as it takes."

The frightened farmers froze for several dramatic seconds.

Maria pursed her lips, released her hand from Adolf's then gripped his arm and propelled him to the door. "Sabina, come!" she ordered. The three of them left for the farmhouse.

Tanya watched them go with mixed feelings. Having made the argument, she had no option other than leave them to their decisions.

She turned her attention back to Peter who appeared to be sleeping. This time, she spoke in German. "Hello there, my friend. Can you hear me?"

The response was almost immediate. He opened his eyes and looked around still unsure what was real or unreal. He was unable to connect anything current with the memory of cycling through a mountain forest towards snow-capped peaks, a star-studded sky and a full moon, with the wind in his face and a sense of freedom.

Now he was trapped in a tiny room with the smallest window.

He had the distinct impression that he had eaten cake which had caused him to shrink bodily, to shrink the world around him.

This gave him the belly ache and a huge depression.

He closed his eyes not wishing it to be true and drifted away.

In the distance Peter kept hearing this distant voice asking if he could hear while at the same time smothering his face in cold and wet.

"Get away from me!" he shouted.

His tormentor left him. He opened his eyes to check.

His vision spiralled back into the tiny room eventually focusing on two figures in the doorway speaking Jabberwocky. One was a woman, the other an old man with a large white moustache.

'Ah,' he thought, 'the Queen of Hearts and the Walrus.' His mind then spiralled back into oblivion.

The woman was there yet again talking, once more smothering his face in cold water. Peter flinched. "Steady on there, soldier." Tanya said.

"Where am I? Where is this?"

"Later, later, first you must eat and drink."

Tanya raised his head and held a cup to his lips.

The drink was warm and sweet. Peter gulped it down. Suddenly his stomach reacted.

Nauseous, he began to wretch. 'Consciousness' began to spin and spiral back down into the dark tunnel.

"Sabina, come quickly, please."

Tanya called to Sabina who was back skimming the curds next door. Adolf now working the press sighed.

"You'd best go, girl."

Sabina arrived just in time to see Peter throw up all over himself, the bed and Tanya.

She immediately began to strip him.

"The ewe's milk is still too rich. Must use more water next time. Sabina, clean bedding, warm water and a sponge quickly."

Sabina sighed and did as she was bid. More orders followed thick and fast.

"Hold the bad leg, lift and turn."

This was difficult because Peter was wet, floppy and covered in vomit and ewe's milk.

"My God, there's nothing to him and he stinks. This whole place stinks," gasped Sabina.

"I guess there was not much to him to begin with," replied Tanya gathering the dirty sheets and throwing them into the corner.

Peter stripped of all, including his dignity, unconscious, was propped against the wall on a chair.

He slumped to one side, head lolling. The image was of a skeletal like puppet.

His broken splinted leg spread wide. This strange, macabre scene revealed his masculinity which seemed to Sabina to be grossly out of proportion to the rest of him.

She was transfixed by his grotesque figure which mocked her altruistic decision to help him a little over one week ago.

She began to cry.

"No time for that my girl. Pass me the clean sheets so we can get soldier boy back into bed,"

snapped Tanya.

Sabina was still staring at Peter. The term 'soldier boy' appeared to be so ridiculous.

She began to snigger. Mucous from her nose splattered her face and, bawling like a baby, she ran from the room.

Tanya called out for Adolf. Already aware of the drama, he came at once.

Adolf helped Tanya wash, dress and get Peter back into bed. When this was achieved, Tanya sighed. “Sorry about that Adolf, I should have been more cautious with the ewe’s milk. Thank you for coming so promptly to my rescue. I could not have done it without you.”

Tanya chose her words carefully trying to draw Adolf psychologically back into a support role.

She need not have bothered for he was already ashamed of his earlier performance.

Boosted by logical argument from Maria and looking to make amends, he replied, “No problem. Anytime.” After a moment’s thought, he added, “There is just you, me and Sabina to cope isn’t there?”

Tanya nodded. “Yes, just we three.” She put her hand on his arm and looked into his face. “And you gave, give me the strength to deal with any emergency.”

“Then,” said Adolf, who was standing stiff and straight like an imperial guardsman, moustache bristling.

“We shall do it.”

Sabina returned, sent back by Maria.

Tanya held out her hand to her. Sabina ran forward and took it saying. “Sorry.”

Tanya then laid out her plans.

“We have much work to do to help this young man to recover and to keep him both safe and sane, also ourselves. It will be far from easy. Try and remember we are doing this for our country, and we are not alone. The support we have is far greater than you can imagine.

“Firstly, we must be sensible, keep this knowledge within the five of us and behave as normally as possible. To this end it will be best to keep Maria and Lazlow out of this.

"The bulk of the work will be done by me supported by Sabina. We will need to rebuild Peter's health and strength especially paying attention to his leg. We cannot hope to move him on until this is achieved."

Tanya turned to each in turn.

"You understand this will take months of dedication, don't you?"

Both uncle and niece hesitated wishing for the right of decision, now denied.

Adolf? He was desperate for a drink, his tongue 'clagging' to the roof of his mouth.

Sabina was trembling with indignation at being again driven into a corner.

Only the recent words of Aunt Maria explaining the consequences of failure prevented her from throwing a tantrum there and then. Both nodded in agreement.

"Good," said Tanya, "try and stay calm and sane. Equally we must plan to keep our patient sane, occupy his mind."

"How can we do that?" asked Sabina emphasising the 'we' as if this was ridiculous.

Tanya ignored this inference and continued.

"Peter is a linguist, speaking fluently German, French and Italian.

"I suggest we begin by speaking only in Slovene providing him with books in the language and also, in Serbo-Croat. These two languages will keep his mind active and may prove useful when we move him out through this area. Any books you can find in either language will be useful. Meanwhile I intend to provide the basic learning textbooks."

Chapter 70

By the following Christmas Peter was conversing easily in Slovene, reading a history of the Hapsburgs in Serbo-Croat and hopping about the small room with the aid of sticks, albeit with difficulty.

Adolf and Sabina gained in confidence as time went by and Maria was kept informed of all rumour as to the German Army's plans to locate Peter via Lazlow's trips to the markets.

This information she passed to Tanya but kept from her husband and niece.

She was not happy about this. Sensibly she acknowledged Tanya's advice keeping all information away from them.

Berlin kept up the pressure on the army to find Peter Barnes and the army did enough to appear obedient; but no more than was necessary by keeping disruptions to the minimum.

The resistance movements across the region, aided and abetted by Whitehall, renewed the ridiculing anecdotes constantly.

January brought a flurry of further activity. The German high command claimed that Lt. Barnes had been caught and killed. This report was accompanied by a photograph of a small unidentifiable figure hanging from a lamp post.

Lord Haw-Haw triumphantly announced his death to the listening public that same evening.

Back in Whitehall the man in grey was addressing a meeting of the combined services committee in one of the underground passage rooms during the now nightly air raid alert.

"As expected, the Nazis are claiming to have caught the subject of Operation Disrupt.

This is not true. He is alive, safe and well. The improvement in his condition has been maintained and the possibility of moving him on increases daily."

He passed a written copy over to one of the committee.

"This can be passed to Bridge-Thompson so he can inform the interested parties. The C in C wishes that this campaign be stepped up beginning with a rebuttal of the claim. The body hanging from a lamp post is that of a sixteen-year-old boy who was caught posting one of the partisan's propaganda leaflets. We may name him because everyone out there knows already."

The man in grey collected his papers and left.

The chairman of the meeting, a brigadier general, was preparing to close the meeting. He looked at his watch. "That special item concludes all scheduled business. It is getting late, so if there is nothing further, I will close the meeting."

A naval captain at the end of the table interjected.

"Is that it, sir? We have all been kept waiting for almost an hour for an announcement in which most of us have little interest. Who is this chap?" referring to the man in grey.

"We don't know his name. He is not one of us. He appears periodically dispensing orders with an authority that, as far as I am aware, has never been properly established."

The chairman smiled.

"I presume Nicholas that by 'not one of us,' you mean not a member of the armed services.

I can only say that this announcement today came directly from the Prime Minister.

This chap, as you call him, acts as his mouthpiece. He probably had to await the P.M.'s pleasure. Hence the delay. I can't think of a greater authority other than the King. Can you?"

This escalation of activity initiated by Whitehall was mirrored almost immediately by Berlin.

The conflict of opinion between the German Army command and Hitler on strategy was becoming extremely difficult to resolve. The loss of Tobruk in June had stretched the Afrika Korps' supply lines. Rommel was desperately short of equipment and reinforcements, Tobruk being the only close deep-water port. All was made worse by Hitler's obsessive attention to a lost cause at Stalingrad.

Himmler, on the instructions of Hitler and infuriated by the army's inability to capture Lt Barnes, took charge of the hunt and appointed a special team to find him.

The army command who had been unable to control Hitler's determination to maintain the Eastern Front against their advice of consolidation, were losing the argument to retreat to their own borders and defend the Fatherland. Their hope was to negotiate a ceasefire with the Soviets from a position of strength.

Late February, Lazlow returned from the market with a rumour that a new initiative to find Peter was underway focusing on the border between Austria and Slovenia. The plan reported was to section the border into twenty-kilometre units and for a co-ordinated search of all properties across each of them.

Chapter 11

Tanya received the news of this new search via Maria in the farmhouse kitchen during her break for her mid-day meal. Tanya barely stopped eating, though she did take a moment to say, "What kept them? Do we know where they plan to search?"

"No."

After finishing her meal Tanya looked at Maria and asked, "Do we know when?"

Maria shook her head. After a moment's thought, Tanya added, "We must obtain information about this search operation."

Maria, now clearing the table and clearly agitated, again shook her head.

"Then can you ask Mercury what they know or can find out? Meanwhile I will need to contact the partisans. Do you think that Adolf and Sabina can cope for 24 hours while we do that?"

Tanya smiled encouragingly as she asked, holding back on her desire to hurry.

"Adolf will know something is amiss." Maria pushed her hair back in frustration. "What can we do?"

"One thing we know is that we must move Peter and quickly. I must contact my people for instructions. We need to learn more about the German plans. Mercury is our best route. So?"

Tanya paused hoping for an answer from Maria, who showed little sign of agreeing.

"We have no option but to trust the two of them. Maria, try and think of a plausible reason to go and please keep it calm."

Tanya returned to her corner of the cheese store to take up her crocheting. Her mind was moving as quickly as her fingers. She had to break the news to Peter that she would be leaving him in the hands of Adolf and Sabina. In his state of mind, she knew from recent outbursts that he was on the edge of a breakdown. She would need to tread very carefully.

Peter was reading *A History of the Hapsburgs* and was nearly halfway through.

Tanya considered carefully what to say. Without looking up from her work, she asked "You're really into that book, Peter. Aren't you?"

Peter didn't look up either as he turned the page and muttered. "Yes, it's interesting."

Tanya crocheted a complete circle before adding, "And it's written in Serbo-Croat."

Tanya looked up and smiled.

"You really do have an amazing knack for languages."

Peter and Tanya had built up a rapport discussing literature, philosophy and other topics to pass the tedious hours. Peter, assuming this was Tanya opening up another discourse, replied. "All western languages are structured more or less the same. The Slavic are not so different. Once you have mastered the alphabet it is plain sailing."

Tanya began to laugh.

"I was just saying you really do have the knack. I was not looking to get a lecture."

Peter closed the book.

"I am sorry. It's this room, so small, gloomy and cold. Seriously, I am just longing for the sun on my face. If it wasn't for the books, I would probably walk out and surrender."

This reply gave Tanya a clue of how to approach telling Peter she was leaving.

"Speaking of cold, we are running short of gas oil for the heater. I must go and get some.

It will mean leaving you with Sabina. Are you all right with that?"

She waited for his reaction, which was as she expected.

"You are not thinking of leaving me with *Sabina*?"

Seeing his face convinced Tanya that she needed to more inventive.

"I didn't wish to raise your hopes. The real reason I am going, is to convince the partisans it is time to move you on." Thinking to herself, this was not really the lie she set out to tell.

Peter's reception of this was better than she had hoped.

Tanya went to see Maria to get her, Adolf and Sabina on board using the same economical 'truth' and omitting the information about the German Army's renewed search plans.

Adolf, but not Sabina, was buoyed by the news.

Sabina faced with the prospect of looking after Peter on her own for 24 hours without Tanya or even Maria on hand, rebelled.

"Why do you both have to go at the same time? Can't you, Aunt Maria go when Tanya gets back?"

"There is a very good reason, Sabina, it is only this once." Maria pleaded. "Please, you can manage." "Do I have to stay with him all night?" Sabina searched her mind for objections.

"It would be for the best, Sabina." It was Tanya who answered.

Sabina turned to her aunt. "All night. On my own? That's not right surely."

"You managed well enough for two days before Tanya arrived."

It was a dismissive answer from a stressed Maria. "Don't be difficult, Sabina. Just get on with it."

Tanya, horrified at this spat, worked hard to ensure that Sabina was placated before she left at sundown. Still unsure about her commitment or that of Adolf, Tanya was left with no option.

Forcing her mind to focus, she prepared to leave at sundown making sure that Peter was fed and had all kit and supplies within easy reach.

"Sabina is to watch over you for the next day or so until I return."

Peter didn't answer or give any indication that he had heard.

Tanya, making sure he understood what was to happen, repeated, "I am going now, and I might be some time."

"That's what Captain Oates said."

Tanya hesitated in the doorway then dismissed this comment which she did not understand.

She wondered once again about her patient's state of mind but only for a moment.

With no other choice she slipped quickly out of the store and into the night.

Maria served the evening meal then donned her coat announcing that she was leaving before turning to Sabina.

"We are relying on you to do the right thing. Don't let us down."

The two staried at each other. Neither blinked.

Maria turned on her heel and left leaving Sabina staring at the closing door.

Adolf and Lazlow watched this exchange. Adolf stood and went to the corner cupboard returning with a bottle of schnapps.

"Let's drink to a happy ending," he said pouring out two measures for Lazlow and himself.

"Don't I get one?" asked Sabina.

"Aren't you supposed to be with Peter?"

This rhetorical question from Adolf was intended to dismiss her.

Sabina went to the dresser, collected a glass and poured herself a very generous measure and sat down. Adolf was about to say something to Sabina but then changed his mind and decided not to and turned to Lazlow instead.

"Apricots," he announced, "wasp-damaged windfalls from last autumn. It has distilled beautifully. Carries a nice sting, don't you think?"

Lazlow nodded and offered his glass for a refill.

Sabina, again ignored, reached for the bottle only for Adolf to snatch it away from her.

"Too strong for you, girl. See to your duties."

Sabina threw her empty glass at the bottle. It bounced off the table and into the wall.

She stood for a long minute before flouncing out of the room.
"Girls!" said Adolf, "what can you do with them?"

Lazlow smiled. "Surely you don't need me to tell you," he said offering his glass for another refill. "This is good stuff. Best for years." He tossed the latest offering down his neck.

"That had better be it for me. This is vintage already," referring to the schnapps. "It carries quite a kick."

He shook hands with Adolf.

"Leave the stock and preparation of the back field to me tomorrow. You will have all on. I suggest you get an early night."

He watched as Adolf poured himself another measure.

Lazlow looked at Adolf.

"I would give that an early night, too."

Lazlow walked out leaving Adolf alone with the schnapps.

Chapter 72

Peter shivered from the cold and pulled the blanket closely around himself. The small oil heater had not been lit, neither had the oil lamp. He assumed it was because oil was in short supply.

It was one of the reasons for Tanya leaving. He waited for Sabina to appear to check with her.

In the meantime, he attempted to continue reading by the light of a small torch which was beginning to fade forcing him to switch it off and leaving him in the dark.

If Tanya had been there, they could have had one of their many conversations.

Conversations he really enjoyed. Left on his own to hope that Sabina would come was not a big problem. She was no company. He no longer needed help to get into bed. This he could now manage with difficulty. He still needed a new battery for his torch.

He switched it on again briefly only for it shine brightly then fade but not before he saw the shadowy figure of Sabina in the doorway.

"A new battery please, Sabina. I need to read and if there is enough oil, light the stove."

Sabina dutifully lit the stove and after a short search in the dark found a battery.

"What are you reading?" she asked as she stopped and leant over his shoulder.

The new battery lit the page.

"*A History of the Hapsburgs.* The book you lent to me. Thank you," Peter answered shrinking away from Sabina, who was leaning ever closer.

He quickly became aware of her intent.

Instant arousal of his latent sexuality followed swiftly. The emotional shock overwhelmed him.

Powerless and trapped, he was unable prevent it. 'Why didn't this happen with Pen?' was his first thought. There was no mistaking the primeval signals he was receiving, or his response.

Sabina leaned closer allowing her breasts to touch his cheek.

Peter, trapped in the small space between his chair and bed, panicked and threw back his arm knocking her away.

"Get off!" he shouted.

Sabina gasped and ran from the room.

Peter took a moment to recover before he reached for his sticks and hopped outside after her.

She was nowhere to be seen.

A sudden heavy splatter of hailstones drove him back indoors. He hopped painfully back to his bed, his bad leg throbbing.

Peter could not remember putting his bad leg to the floor in his panic to catch up with Sabina.

When he got back to his bed he screamed in frustration and hurled his sticks across the room.

Gradually settling down, he decided that the Sabina incident was not a massive problem other than facing her again. Even less of one probably than if she had stayed around.

He grimaced at the thought of what could have happened.

Peter began to get ready for bed. He checked that Tanya had left everything to hand, which she had. He then lay down to try to sleep which rarely came easily. This night was no exception with the pain in his leg and his inability to move freely. Finally, in the very early hours of the morning he did fall into a fitful sleep.

Chapter 73

Adolf was very late to his bed after an evening sitting alone fighting his fears and the desire to drink more than was sensible. Although not drunk he was sufficiently anaesthetised to sleep more soundly than he had of late. He woke much later than intended still suffering from the effects of the schnapps.

Lazlow, as reliable as ever, dealt with the stock. He was battling alone dragging the plough out of the barn into the daylight when Adolf found him.

"We will need to borrow a horse for the plough. The back field is rock hard. It's too hard to try to use the donkey or to use pick hoes."

Adolf threw his arms in the air in frustration not wishing to hear about further problems.

He turned and left without replying.

The farm horse and their last milking cow had been stolen last winter and were irreplaceable.

This was causing difficulties and Adolf was not the best at dealing with these situations.

Lazlow, used to Adolf's moods, took a moment to watch him leave knowing he had heard and he would apologise later.

"Neither wise men nor fools can work without tools," he murmured before continuing to check the plough.

Adolf returned to the farm kitchen looking for coffee to try and rid himself of the effects of last night's excesses. Lazlow had opened the range and the pot was bubbling away.

Adolf poured himself a cup of 'coffee' only to spit out the first mouthful; he couldn't get used to this brew of dried nettle leaves and roasted acorns.

Later that morning Adolf went into the creamery and the cheese storeroom looking for Sabina.

Peter appeared to be asleep and there was no sign of Sabina. He intended to check later to see if she had gone to her bed.

"Shit, lazy cow," he moaned as he returned to the barn to find Lazlow waiting.

"We need to call in Doc," said Lazlow. "The bearings on the wheel are worn and there's wobble. There is no way we can think of ploughing until it's repaired. Also, there is the beginning of a hairline crack in the plough share."

Adolf knew something had to be done quickly. They needed to plough in good time for the night frosts to do their work.

Doc, a travelling tinker who replaced broken pick hoes, arranged metal repairs with the smith.

The Doc would loan his horse for the ploughing. All this in exchange for produce.

Without a plough, there would be no produce and the farm could not survive with just the orchard and cheese production. Dairy produce was now being severely curtailed by the loss of his last milking cow.

"I'll get over to Otto's and see what can be arranged and how soon. Thank you."

Upset at the news, he was also aware that he had to make amends having been rude to Lazlow earlier. Outwardly, he was trying desperately to appear unflappable and wishing that Maria would return soon. He also wished that he had not drunk so much last night. Crossing the border to Otto's farm would give him the space that he needed.

It did not occur to him nor did he know that he was leaving Lazlow to cope alone.

Peter awoke to a call of nature around noon. He reached for the pee can to find it already full.

He reached for his sticks which had gone. They were laying where he had thrown them last night.

Placing his good leg on the floor, he considered the consequences of trying to hop across to retrieve them. Overestimating the strength of his 'good' leg without support of his sticks was the problem. Repeated trials to stand and balance without them ended in failure.

The call of nature was insisting on immediate action. He hauled in the top sheet from the bed and wound it into a ball like receptacle. He managed to relieve himself with the minimum of local damage. He then threw the soiled sheet into the doorway as far away from the stored cheeses as he could.

Immediate problem solved, Peter was still trapped in a cramped little world of indignity and depravation aggravated by the incident with Sabina.

Peter, not for the first time, was seriously considering suicide.

He banged his forehead violently several times upon the wall before falling back on the bed crying like a baby. Tears streaked down his face mingled with his blood flowing from a gaping wound.

Chapter 14

That night Tanya had made her way from the trees across the road and along the hedgerows around the back of the hay barn and into the creamery.

"I've brought the oil," she called announcing her arrival.

She continued talking as she went to check that the window was covered prior to lighting the oil lamp. "Where's Sabina? Has she looked after you well?"

Tanya was assuming Peter would be awake and listening.

Seeing little in the gloom and suspecting problems Tanya stopped and listened.

She struck a match and lifted the glass of the oil lamp while peering anxiously at Peter.

The match petered out before she got to light wick. It was enough to confirm her fears.

She lit the wick at the second attempt.

Tanya gasped. Peter's face was swollen and bloody. Swiftly she checked his pulse with the back of her hand against his neck. Peter rallied and took her hand.

"You came back," he said placing her hand against his cheek.

After reassuring him and settling him down Tanya freed herself and carried out a quick check of the room. She found the soiled sheet and collected the can of urine in silence. She knew now that her charge had been abandoned. Her brain was now working overtime thinking what could have happened.

"When did you last eat?"

"I'm not hungry."

"You must eat. I'll be back directly."

Tanya left for the house emptying the can in the hedgerow on her way. Stopping momentarily and feeling the weight of the soiled sheet in her hand she concluded that Peter had indeed been left to fend for himself. Where was everyone she was thinking as she entered the kitchen.

Adolf was there removing his boots. From his demeanour everything seemed to be normal.

"Where's Sabina?" Tanya asked.

Adolf threw his boots into the corner.

"Where's Maria?" was his riposte as he continued to complain.

"Shit, no food. I am starving. I can't live on bread and cheese."

"At least you have eaten. Peter has not eaten at all and no one has looked to him all day."

Adolf looked shocked. "I looked in at mid-day and he was asleep. Where's Sabina? That's her job. I've got a farm to run, practically single handed."

"Perhaps she's back with her family. Why would she do that? Leave Peter alone?"

"I was at Otto's this afternoon. She is not there." Adolf closed that line of thought.

Tanya began preparing vegetables for the pot.

"We'll manage without her, there is too much to do elsewhere."

Tanya forced her mind away from the blame game.

Adolf immediately showed interest. "Are you moving him on?"

"When we work out how to do it without being seen."

Adolf reached for the bottle which was still on the table where he left it last night.

"I might just have an idea that could work."

Thirty minutes later Maria returned to the farm to find Adolf and Tanya in discussion.

Tanya looked up when the door opened.

"Welcome back, Maria. What news?"

Maria removed her coat and hat and checked the broth on the stove before answering.

"Well, what *do* you know?" Adolf prompted.

Maria avoided the question asking, "Did Sabina manage all right?"

"Buggered off and left us high and dry. Where have you been? Are you working with them?"

Maria still didn't answer but turned and looked to Tanya.

"Adolf knows everything," Tanya replied to Maria's unspoken question.

"What news of the German plan?"

"No news as to the timing but it is clearly going ahead very soon. A crack S. S. unit moved in sometime in the last week followed by Austrian and Hungarian units. Then there's the Serbs.

We think they will be involved."

"Why all this to search for just one sick little man?" Adolf complained, adding, "You said *we*, Maria. Please tell me you are not part of the resistance?"

Maria continuing to stir the broth and didn't answer.

Tanya interjected.

"We are all part of the resistance, surely. This situation was initiated by this sick little man as you call him. His exploits were picked up by the people quickly and followed by the resistance movements across the continent. This project has been aided and abetted by the British. Interestingly, also by Nazi egotism against the advice of the military. It has taken on a life of its own. The British unsurprisingly have taken it up and run heavily with this."

"The British don't care about us. They are just using us, leaving us in greater danger."

Maria, grateful for the change in the direction of the conversation, picked up on Adolf's complaint. "We are where we are. Concentrate on the next move, Adolf. We can manage without Sabina which is perhaps a good thing. We need to move Peter soon, very soon, but how?"

"The partisans and a British unit in the hills are working on plans to move him into a hill camp.

We need to plan how to get him over into the cover of the trees where the partisans will take over. Adolf has given me an idea as to how this can be done," Tanya said turning to Maria.

"Maria, will you watch Peter for me? Cover me for tonight please?"

"You can't turn out again tonight," Maria protested. "When did you last sleep?"

"There's no alternative, I must go and now."

Chapter 75

Dorothy was happy. Dorothy was very happy. Happier than she had been for years.

The winter in St. Mary Upperford had been a very different winter from those she'd known in London just 40 some miles to the northeast. Dorothy could have been on another planet.

She had companionship, a job she had already grown to love, security and regular nights of uninterrupted sleep.

Today was a day stolen from spring, one of several days this February.

The weeping willows were already glowing with new leaf in the spring-like sunshine.

The river bank was festooned with snowdrop and crocus.

The 'icing on the cake' was that Mim, instead of returning home on the bus with her friends, had asked to walk home by the river with her.

Why? Dorothy had no idea, but she was enjoying the moment. She was more than content, despite feeling guilty about dropping everything to be here in this beautiful place.

This guilt was not caused by shedding responsibilities for her parents' affairs or those of East Park School. It was because of the handing of her duties over to Samuel and Tolly to whom she owed her life. A life which now was unbelievably good.

"Auntie Dorothy, the little fish have come to the edge of the river to say hello."

Mim's excited shout interrupted Dorothy's thoughts.

After running ahead, Mim was squatting down by the riverside near a weeping willow. Dorothy's first instinct was to shout, 'don't get your skirt dirty.' Instead, she smiled then changed her mind and stopped to take in the scene.

A feeling of warmth and satisfaction swept over her as the little girl stood and turned to face her. The sun reflecting off her white blouse and socks. Her shadow now stretched long behind her contrasting with the shimmering patterns cast by the sun's rays through the willows' trailing branches.

Without warning, Dorothy's satisfaction was overwhelmed by a great sadness.

As if reading Dorothy's thoughts Mim approached and asked, "Auntie Dorothy, did you know my real Mama and Papa?"

She presented a slightly comical sight, her hat tipped askew by the willows' cascade.

Mim was holding her head to one side as if to balance it.

Dorothy was taken aback by the suddenness and matter of fact delivery of the question.

"I'm sorry, Mim, I did not."

Immediately she worried that her reply had been too blunt.

Mim ran to Dorothy and took her hand. Dorothy gripped a little more tightly than normal as she fought to control her emotions. This sudden unusual flow of affection was as puzzling as it was delightful. They walked in silence for some while until Mim asked, "Did Mama Pen and Papa Yo know them?"

"No darling, Mama Pen and Papa Yo didn't."

Mim asked, "Where did they live?"

Dorothy stopped by a log seat. The sun had dried it enough for her to sit to gather her thoughts.

She was angry that she had not anticipated this when Mim asked to walk home with her.

She knew that for both their sakes this had to be dealt with there and then.

How much would a little girl remember? Three-year-olds' memories mostly recollect little.

Mim's memory, if any, was one of massive trauma.

Mim didn't sit down. She stood alongside and placed her arm around Dorothy's shoulders leaning her head against Dorothy's face. She gloried in the warmth of her touch but still failed to answer Mim's question.

"Where did Mama and Papa live?" Mim repeated the question, jolting Dorothy out of her jumbled thoughts.

"In Munich," Dorothy replied wondering where Mim was going in this quest.

"In Germany?" Mim persisted.

Dorothy began to fear how this would end as she answered. "Yes, in Germany."

Dorothy could almost feel Mim thinking. She was a bright girl and was probably more aware of her history than she was given credit for. She must have been talking with her friends.

"Why did those Nazis take my real Mamma and Papa?"

This was one of the questions Dorothy feared. She took Mim by her shoulders and turned her face towards hers.

"I don't know, darling. None of us know."

"They were not bad people, my Mamma and Poppa. Rabbi Greenberg said so and he doesn't fib." "No, my sweet, they were good people. They were very good people and very clever people.

Your Papa was a professor at the university. Your Mama was also very clever and brave."

Dorothy desperately searching her mind for positivity, added "It was your Mama's clever and brave thinking which allowed you to escape from these nasty people." Dorothy was pleased with this reply.

Mim was silent for a while before whispering, "They would have taken me as well."

Suddenly she brightened. "Then Mama sent for Papa Yo and he came and rescued me."

Dorothy smiled with relief. "I am sure that's true."

Mim's next outburst was delivered in one breath without the punctuation of pauses, the words tumbling out in a torrent of indignation.

"Then Beckie is wrong. She said it wasn't Papa Yo. It was you and in any case Papa Yo isn't my real Papa. I said **I know** then she said that Peter is my Papa now and that Papa Yo ...'

Mim was lost for words. So was Dorothy. Before Dorothy could think of a reply Mim added:

"Who is this Peter anyway? And Beckie is a cow."

Mim who had left Dorothy's side, kicked at a snowdrop. Immediately she stooped to try and straighten the broken stem.

Dusk arrived suddenly as the sun slipped behind clouds on the horizon. Dorothy took Mim's hand. "Come sweetheart, let's get you home, it is getting cold."

They walked in silence for some little while before Mim broke into Dorothy's thoughts asking:

"Why are the yellow crocuses all broken?"

"Because the sparrows and other birds peck them," answered a bemused Dorothy.

"Why? They don't peck the other colours, do they?"

"No darling, they don't and again, I don't know why."

To Dorothy's surprise Mim suddenly broke away running and skipping and spinning, her skirt billowing. That wasn't as bad as I feared, she thought.

As if in acknowledgement the sky brightened as the sun made a brief reappearance below the distant clouds. Dorothy looked at her watch.

"Gosh, Mim, look at the time, you'd best run straight home."

Mim returned and looked up at her.

"Who is Peter, Auntie Dorothy?"

"You know who he is Mim. Peter is Mama Pen's husband."

Dorothy answered promptly. She hoped firmly.

"Then why doesn't he live with us and why does Mama Pen go out with Papa Yo?"

Mim's directness pointed out the real reason for her request to walk with Dorothy.

"You know Peter is a prisoner of war and can't come home, as for Papa Yo, I am sorry Mim, that I can't answer."

Mim started to run across the Green stopping after a few yards to spin and billow her skirt.

"I think I can," she shouted before running on to repeat the manoeuvre.

"It's because Mama Pen loves him."

She disappeared through the gate into Greensleeves leaving Dorothy stunned.

Moments later Mim reappeared once more shouting.

"Papa Yo, I mean. She loves him."

"That's right, Mim. Tell the whole village, as if they don't already know," Dorothy muttered.

Chapter 76

Evenings now had been transformed from the most desolate to the favourite time of day for Dorothy. She sat on the settee with Pam in front of a blazing log fire listening to Variety Bandbox on the radio just chatting or sitting in silence after talking over the day.

The evening after Dorothy's traumatic walk with Mim produced bouts of silence broken by outbursts of considered discussion.

"Kids, eh," Pam offered apropos of Dorothy's talk with Mim.

"They are more resilient than we know. I guess they've been gossiping amongst themselves.

I wouldn't put it past them to goad Mim saying that Hal is not her father, and that Pen is a 'whatever' their parents are talking about."

Dorothy chuckled.

"I shouldn't laugh but it is the first time I've heard Pen called a whatever."

"I can't bring myself to say it."

"Sorry, Pam. I shouldn't have said anything, but I feel as though a weight has been lifted.

I am amazed just how matter of fact Mim was about it."

"Did she ask anything else about her real parents?"

"No, but she really wanted to know. I am glad that I was able to say something positive.

She accepted everything without further question which is just as well. I never really knew them."

"Peter maybe did," Pamela suggested. "He might well have met them. He knew Helga for some years."

Dorothy picked up on this. "You are right. Helga could be Mim's best connection to her past." Pamela got up and placed another log on a dying fire.

"I say, Pet, do you think the rabbi has been probing Mim about Hal and Pen?"

Dorothy didn't answer.

Aware that it was difficult territory for her friend, Pamela accepted that Dorothy was avoiding the question and changed the subject.

"Shall we have a pot of tea? I am not in a milk-at-bedtime mood," knowing Dorothy's preference for this.

"Can we spare it now the special rations are finished?"

"I think so, rations are seeming to go farther now there are two of us."

The phrase, 'there are two of us,' warmed Dorothy even more so than the log fire which stirred memories of arriving home not to an empty, cold cheerless house but to a blazing log fire and a tasty supper courtesy of Tolly.

"I am due time off Schule next week and I want to go into town," said Dorothy, reminded of her debt to Samuel and Tolly.

"Oh!" exclaimed Pamela surprised by this but also reluctant, almost frightened, to let Dorothy go anywhere, especially London. "Why?"

"I intend to give my shares in the tailoring business to Samuel and Tolly. Thank them properly and tidy up all the loose ends. After all I did leave in a bit of a hurry."

"Is that wise, Pet? Giving them all your shares, I mean."

Pamela's real objection was because she believed London to be dangerous.

"Probably not but then they did save my life."

Pamela shuddered remembering just how close it had been.

"Of course you must, Pet."

The following Wednesday Dorothy was met by her solicitor at Waterloo station who greeted her in his usual warm, ebullient manner.

"Hello Dorothy, my dear, how are you?"

"Very well, Harry, thank you. How are you?"

Dorothy looked in her purse for her rail ticket. She was desperate to avoid the usual kissing routine.

"Struggling against the slings and arrows you know," was Harry's glib reply.

'I bet,' thought Dorothy sarcastically flinching as Harry took her arm in a far too friendly manner as he ushered her along the platform.

"I have arranged for us to have a bite at a little place I know just off the Mile End Road. They do a nice lemon sole with new potatoes or, if you prefer it, brisket. How does that sound?"

Dorothy stopped and forcibly removed his arm.

"How come?"

"Ways and means, my dear, ways and means."

"I don't think so, Harry." Dorothy was thinking how much more profitable it would be for the police to spend some of the time they spent watching Tolly by looking elsewhere.

"Come on, old girl. Then we can sort things out over lunch so to speak."

"What is to sort Harry? It's sorted. Besides I need to get back." Dorothy was having none of this.

"I can have us there and back in a trice in the car."

Dorothy noted at once that Harry had already dismissed the idea of her visiting Samuel and Tolly in the East End. She was aghast at his arrogance.

"You have a car and petrol?"

"Gas, old girl. It is the latest. Come and see." Harry bowed in exaggerated manner.

Dorothy didn't move. The crowds of travellers were brushing by them much to the annoyance of Harry.

"We can't talk here my dear. Let's be away to the restaurant. We need somewhere where we can talk."

Dorothy refused to budge.

"Harry, don't bother. I don't need you to transfer shares. I will talk to a broker," Dorothy, stressed for the first time since she had left London. She just wished for everything to be settled and to return to St. Mary.

Harry finally got the message.

"Sorry, old girl if I have set off on the wrong foot."

"If, if," Dorothy almost shouted having little concern about the crowds around.

"Your mother" Harry began only to be interrupted by a now very angry Dorothy.

"Oh! I see, you have been in touch with dear Mama. Well, you can just get back to her and tell her that she no longer has any say in my life."

"I say old girl that is a bit strong. You don't wish her to cut you out of the will, do you?"

Dorothy took a deep breath and forced herself to stay calm *she* took *Harry's* arm and propelled him into the waiting room then, turning to face him whispered, "Tell Mama that I already have found my fortune and ask her to kindly keep hers. *Understood*?"

The quiet menace in her words were not lost on Harry.

"Sorry, old girl if I've got the wrong end of the stick."

"Indeed, you have Harry, indeed you have. Goodbye."

With this final shot Dorothy left him standing staring at the doorway long after she had left.

Two old ladies stopped their knitting to mouth in unison to each other. 'Lovers' tiff'.

That evening's 'end of day chat', was full of interest for Pamela who was anxious to hear, chapter and verse about Dorothy's day in London.

"You turned down a lemon sole and new potato lunch?" Pamela was both amused and intrigued.

"I'm afraid so."

"What did you do for lunch?"

"Pulled in my belt and went to see Papa's broker and it was all done and dusted inside an hour. I took the shares to Samuel and Tolly. They were delighted."

Dorothy smiled at her thoughts, enforced responsibilities being over.

"I bet they were, Pet. What do you get out of it? Nothing, absolutely nothing."

Pamela answered her own question.

"Ah!" Dorothy smiled. "That's where you are wrong, I did. I got two tins of mutton and vegetable stew, courtesy of Tolly. Labelless of course. I also got a great deal of satisfaction and a suitcase full of clothes, my own. Once more courtesy of Tolly and rescued from the house."

"From the house? I thought that was still out of bounds. Isn't that illegal?"

"Illegal to everyone but Tolly. His philosophy being, there is common law, statutory law and common sense. He chooses the latter. In other words, I hurt no one, risked no one and helped someone.

In fact observance of the law, in this case, would have deprived someone of their rightful dues." Dorothy spread her arms and hunched her shoulders in impersonation of Tolly, adding:

"So why not?"

"I like this Tolly."

"I suspect the dockside police do. There is somewhat of a love/hate relationship there. There is a story going the rounds that Tolly was at the Dockside Police Station being charged for illegally entering a bomb site to collect firewood."

She paused, adding, "I should say here that Tolly did not have an open fire in his bed sit."

"He was collecting for others?"

Dorothy nodded and continued. "The constable booking him was trying to explain the Emergency Act and Tolly said, 'Am I or am I not being charged with breaking and entering?'

The policeman gave him an old-fashioned look and asked the question.

'What if you had sprained your ankle and lain there starving to death with no one to find you?'

Tolly returned the old-fashioned look and is reported to have replied, 'Look, I have had Hitler and his henchmen lobbing chunks of metal at me day and night for the last three years and you try to suggest that I am in grave danger from an inanimate bomb site?

The desk sergeant, it is said, then smiled and interjected. 'Just book him, constable'."

Chapter 77

At breakfast the next morning, Pam was in one of her quieter moods, unusually quiet. Sensing that all was not well Dorothy looked across at her with more than a little concern. "Penny for them, Pam?"

"Oh!" replied Pamela jolted back into the present, "I was just thinking."

Having had another restless night, her thoughts were triggered by last week's conversations.

She was feeling tired, low and vulnerable and was attempting to disguise her emotions from Dorothy.

She tried to smile and change the subject.

"Lovely morning, will you be walking to school?"

Dorothy was not to be denied. "Come on Pammy, this is me. What's wrong?"

"Bugger!" Pam jumped up from the table, sided her plate to the draining board and stared out of the window fighting back the tears.

"Bloody jam! Why can't we get decent marmalade?"

She took a bite from the toast and hurled it into the washing up bowl.

Dorothy stood and went to join her friend and waited for the inevitable confessional.

It was a beautiful morning. The mist from the river drifted along the back field filling the hollows. Cattle were grazing, legs and heads immersed in the milky cotton wool flow. Their black and white patterned hides sharply picked out by the rising sun. The green dewdrop-lustred grass sparkling in the early morning sun contrasted with the white frosted shadows in the garden.

Eventually Pamela spoke.

"It is beautiful here and now you are here, I am no longer lonely. I am so fortunate, so why do I have this stone in my chest and a heavy gut?"

Dorothy opened her mouth to answer but no answer came to mind before Pam blurted out.

"I've let everyone down." Her tears began falling thick and fast.

Dorothy, lost for words, reached out to her only for Pam to pull away sharply.

Aware of these mood swings, Dorothy waited her time.

Pamela straightened her shoulders, dabbed her eyes and blew her nose then turned and apologised to Dorothy. "I am sorry, so sorry."

"It's all right, Pet," answered Dorothy adding hastily, "my love." realising that she had used her friend's term of endearment. She took her into her arms and waited until her friend composed herself.

It was some time before Pamela began to unburden herself.

"You have a lot of friends, don't you? Everyone, (meaning Mim) speaks to you," adding, after a pause:

"I've only got you."

Dorothy's first thoughts were, I've swapped one set of responsibilities for another. Somehow this was different. To be needed just for oneself alone. She stayed silent and waited for Pam's release of pain. This Pamela did haltingly, punctuated by deep shuddering sighs and sobs.

"Pen doesn't talk to me. She avoids me. I've nursed her and Mim. Yet it is you Mim talks to, not me. Peter, oh Peter, we parted on bad terms. I had let him down again. I will never even have chance to say I'm sorry."

"You can't say that. You can't possibly know that."

"I spent all last night praying for the chance to just to say sorry."

"You could write to him. That's it! You can at least send him a letter," Dorothy offered only for Pam to pull away.

"And send it where?" she asked. "Wherever he is, he is in great danger probably dying or even dead."

Dorothy opened her mouth to repeat, 'you can't know that.' She could not find the words probably because she didn't believe it herself. There was too much truth in what they knew.

There was no doubt the War Office was using Peter and that in their eyes he was as expendable as any other weapon of this awful war. Once his usefulness was exhausted, he would be abandoned. Words of comfort would not come to her. How long they stood without speaking Dorothy had little idea. She had the same overwhelming feeling of sadness and helplessness that she had felt when seeing the beautiful young Mim catching the sunlight only less than a week ago.

"Bloody war," she whispered to herself. Her voice was barely audible.

Pam heard her.

"It was not the war's fault. Peter would have been safe in a reserved occupation like my Paul, if I hadn't let him down."

Dorothy looked at the kitchen clock knowing that she was about to miss the bus to get to school in time. This made no difference and she sat at the table waiting for inspiration.

Without warning, Pamela set about siding the table and running water for the washing up as if the past minutes had not existed.

"If you don't get a move on you will be late for Schule."

Dorothy had Pam on her mind most of that day and when home time came, despite it being another lovely evening, she took the bus home rather than walk.

Uncertain just how Pam would be, she hurried up the Green. The moment she opened the door, she shouted, "Pam, I'm home. I've been thinking."

She continued talking as she removed her coat and shoes in the hallway, assuming that Pam was in the kitchen as usual.

"I think I will go over and see Pen tonight about Mim asking about her family. This needs to be dealt properly and it is only right that Pen knows, so that she can deal with it. What do you think?"

Dorothy entered the kitchen to find it empty.

"Where are you Pammy?"

"I am in the bedroom."

Dorothy went in to find Pam standing by the bed on which lay a suitcase alongside several of her outfits.

Not understanding, Dorothy sat on the bed and took Pam's hand.

"What is it my love?" she asked fearing the worst.

Pam sat down beside Dorothy and let out a huge sigh.

"Richard's dead and I have got to go to the funeral."

"Oh, my dear, I am sorry."

"Don't be, I'm not," snapped Pamela, immediately covering her face with her hands, adding in haste, "Oh! That was so rude. I didn't really mean it."

She got up and began to rearrange the clothes on the bed which were now a mess.

"I don't really know what I mean."

"What happened?" queried Dorothy, her first thoughts being an air raid.

"Heart attack, I think. Anyway, there's no inquest and the funeral will be sometime next week. That's what Amelia said."

Pam put her clothes in the suitcase then sat down with her friend. She was fighting against her emotions and trying to appear in control.

Dorothy, aware that her friend was struggling, changed the subject.

"Amelia came over, you *were* honoured."

"Yes, and she brought us some cheese. I don't know what to think."

"Cheese? Not flowers. How strange!."

"George has probably got a full cheese from somewhere otherwise we wouldn't have had a sniff."

"Ways and means," Dorothy observed.

Pamela changed the conversation back to her troubles.

"I am needed at the reading of the will. That's what is worrying me."

She paused, took Dorothy's hand and shared her troubles.

"You see this house belongs to Richard, not me. I don't know what is to happen. We could lose our home."

"Richard might have left it to you in his will."

"Or we could be thrown out of our home. I might lose the house and the monthly allowance Richard sends. I have no other income or provision."

"Nonsense, you wouldn't be told to attend a will reading to be told that I'm sure."

"You are right and a comfort as always." Pamela suddenly brightened.

"I thought we would have the McConachie's tonight with some of that cheese to follow. What say you?"

Chapter 78

The following week after Pamela had left to go to Sheffield for Richard's funeral, Dorothy arrived home after school to a cold and empty house.

For someone who had lived alone for the greater part of her adult life, it was a surprising shock.

Pamela, ever present, had provided something which Dorothy had never had before.

The calm unseasonable weather brought in its wake a thick mist and fog rolling down the river valley from Fernborough, blanketing out the sun and settling on the landscape in a chill early dusk.

The bus journey from Bendesbury had taken twice as long as usual.

Dorothy shivered her way across the Green.

In her mind, she was heading for the accustomed sanctuary.

She stood in the hallway with her coat half unbuttoned for some time before abandoning any idea of removing either that or her shoes. Hurrying into the kitchen she lit the gas under the kettle, which Pamela had filled and left ready. Returning to the lounge she discovered that Pamela had also laid the fire before leaving. There was even a box of matches in the hearth. Dorothy gratefully set the kindling alight and muttered, "Thank you, Pammy." These little touches of kindness left Dorothy feeling even more lonely.

The evenings waiting for Pamela's return followed a similar pattern with Dorothy wandering aimlessly around the bungalow from room to room unable to settle, listen to the radio or behave in the accustomed manner.

She sorted her recovered clothes then tidied and rearranged her wardrobe twice, once on the first evening and again on the last. In the process she came across the parcel received at the hospital. It was tucked away on the top shelf.

Not having looked at the contents properly, Dorothy opened it.

She knew that it contained lingerie and that it was a gift from an unknown. She had been in no state to show interest at the time, being quite ill. Pammy had probably put it up in the wardrobe and forgotten about it.

Opening one of two packets she took out a pair of silk cami-knickers. She held the silk against her cheek, talking to herself.

"They are beautiful."

Holding them in front of hers, she looked through the wardrobe mirror.

"Why not?" she murmured. She swiftly undressed donning them along with her best summer dress and a pair of court shoes.

She pirouetted trying to billow her skirt like Mim. Her dress clung tightly to her figure. This was not the intended effect, but Dorothy rather liked it. She spent time looking at her reflection, each and every way. Keeping the outfit on, she returned to the lounge only to return and primp several times before reluctantly undressing for bed.

The last thought as she snuggled down under the clothes was that she would wear them to school tomorrow. Smiling, she fell into the best night's sleep since Pamela had gone away.

"I'm home.," Pamela called out as she arrived late the following evening. and took off her coat and shoes, "And am I glad? The mist and fog are closing in."

Dorothy ran in from the kitchen and embraced her.

"Welcome home Pam, I have missed you. The kettle's on. I managed to see the lights of the bus. Well, how did it go?" she asked anxious to know everything.

"Not entirely bad news, we can have the bungalow," Pam was pleased to reply.

Dorothy gave a little squeal. "He left you the house?"

"Well, not exactly." Pam looked worried.

"What do you mean, not exactly?"

Pam's answer and her demeanour worried Dorothy.

"It's mine as long as I live. Some legal term which means it is mine until I die, then Paul gets it."

"And that worries you?"

"What happens to you if I die? You will lose your home, because this is now your home."

"Crikey, that's not a problem I'd be all right. In any case I wouldn't want to stay without you."

Dorothy embraced Pam.

"Without you, I would have no one."

The kettle began to whistle.

"I've made sandwiches with the cheese we have left. We can take them into the front room and you can tell me all about it," said Dorothy, changing the subject.

Sitting together in front of a blazing log fire Dorothy felt she was once more complete.

She was so pleased to have Pam home she could not stop talking.

"What do you mean just now saying you would have no one? You'd have Paul, Pen, Mim."

"No one who really cares," Pam interrupted. "Paul rarely talks to me, introduces me as 'my mother' but there's no warmth. Pen avoids me and Mim doesn't need me or talk anymore."

Dorothy moved on quickly trying to change Pam's mood.

"Nonsense, of course she does. What else Pammy? I want to hear it all."

"Richard's left me an annuity, not a lot but enough. The house and some properties go to Peter and this bungalow to Paul with all shares in the steel works. The rest is divided between Peter and Paul, some bits and pieces to his housekeeper and stuff I can't remember."

Pamela gabbled out this information in a dismissive manner.

Dorothy, aware that all was not well with her friend waited, knowing from experience that questioning would not provide answers. The long silence which followed was painful, but she tolerated this.

Eventually when Pam did speak, it was to complain.

"Sheffield was so cold, miserable and dirty. Full of smoke, broken buildings, bomb sites and piles of frozen dirty snow at the roadside alongside burnt out buildings and more piles of rubble. No one bothered with me, even at the church. They stood up saying all sort of nice things about Richard at the service, most of it untrue." She paused and rummaged in her handbag for a handkerchief.

"At the solicitors no one seemed to notice me, except for a brief moment when I was mentioned." She paused again and blew her nose.

"What did I get for Richard ruining my life? Losing Peter and my future? A pittance! He could at least have left me this house." Pam covered her eyes with both her hands and let out a huge sigh.

"Oh. I'm sorry, Pet. How have you been?"

"For someone who has lived alone for many years. I was so lonely and oh Pammy, I did miss you.

I did have a lot of time to think and tomorrow, I will be going to school."

Pam looked bewildered. "But you go to school every day."

"No, last week I went to Schule. Look Pammy, this is England not Bavaria. I have called it Schule all my life. Even when I was at a private school. No longer. This influence of dear Mama had to go and I'm getting rid. No longer will I be Mama's vassal."

"Good. You are sure there will be no regrets?"

"None at all. In fact, while you were away, I have been behaving like a young girl. I have been daydreaming, recovering my lost youth which was stolen from me. No longer Miss Responsible more Missy Frippery."

"And how did Missy Frippery behave?"

Dorothy stood, opened the buttons of her dress and slipped her arms free allowing her dress to fall revealing the camiknickers. She announced her emancipation with a "ta- dah".

Blood flooded up into Pamela's cheeks. By the time Dorothy realised anything was wrong Pam had jumped to her feet and was running out of the door flapping her arms as if surrounded by a swarm of bees.

Dorothy took only moments to gather herself and run after her only to discover an open front door and an empty hallway creepily seeping mist and fog.

She grabbed her coat from the peg and went to the door. In the blackout and fog she could see only for a few feet. There was no sign of Pamela. "Pammy," she shouted into the night, her voice echoing eerily in the fog.

Chapter 79

How long it was before Pamela came to anything like her senses, she had no idea, no concept where she was or why. 'Entombed' by the blackout and fog, terror and the cold night air was causing her to shake. She stumbled around trying to get her bearings but to no avail. Sobbing and confused, she staggered on. She tripped on the pavement edging and fell to her knees on a hard ridge.

Feeling around, it seemed to border a grass verge followed by a pavement. She rose to her feet.

Trembling and whimpering, she felt her way forward. Her outstretched hand caught a wooden upright. It was the wooden upright of the church lychgate. She recognised it. 'Why am I here?' was her first thought. Her memory of the last hours came flooding back. She screamed for help.

This scream, against the injustices of the years, the ungrateful and casual dealing by all but Dorothy, took on a surreal mantle.

Inside the lychgate were wooden seats on to which she fell. Whimpering, she tried desperately to think what she could do to get home to Dorothy; to apologise.

She tried to remember the layout of St. Mary's church and vicarage.

Not being a Catholic and a member, she had only seen this church from the street.

Father Michael Ryan was leaving the church at that moment having decided that there would be no one attending confessional that evening. He acknowledged that Mary Mahoney was correct in her forecast and that her attempts to persuade him not to turn out on such a night were soundly argued. He had ignored this advice and left. 'Duty calls,' were his parting words.

"My conscience is now clear, Mary Mahoney," he said out loud as he closed the church doors.

The clang of the closing doors was accompanied by a scream which turned his blood cold.

He stopped for moment before gathering himself and deciding that it was probably some animal in distress and there was nothing to be done.

He made his way along the path towards the rectory. He moved cautiously feeling the flags under his feet to find and reach the gate. The gate creaked as he opened it. It seemed to echo in the mist, a high-pitched note which continued repeating and repeating eerily.

"Michael, my boy, control yourself," he said, chastising his fear of the supernatural.

Listening intently, he realised that it could be human. Maybe someone in distress.

He decided that this needed to be investigated if only to prove to himself he was master of his psyche.

The sounds were coming from over by the Fernborough road. It wouldn't be safe to pick his way through the graveyard amongst the dead, he decided. Better to retrace his steps back along the paths. He set off feeling his way along the flags.

Pamela was half in this world and half in a world of confused fantasy. Desperate to return home to Dorothy and security, she was fighting with her reason to achieve this.

In fog all sounds carry far. This night they carried vividly to Father Michael Ryan, also back to Pamela. Father Michael felt his way forward cautiously towards the moaning.

The sound of his shoe leather on the paving stones carried forward moving ever closer.

Pamela's heart beating wildly held her breath and cowered into the corner.

Her whimpering increased in terror.

Father Michael, following the sounds of her, picked up on this. He realised that arriving out of the mist in his robe and cowl was not a good idea. He called out. "Michael Ryan here. Can I be of help?"

Chapter 80

Back at the rectory Mary Mahoney was true to form having finally settled the distressed Pamela with care and cocoa and dressed her grazed knee. She tried to find out what her problems were.

After the third time Pamela answered, 'I don't know' or 'I can't remember' to each question.

She raised her eyes to heaven. Father Michael sitting opposite said, "Leave it be, Mary."

"I just want to go home, please," pleaded Pamela.

Father Michael said, "Would you be lending your coat for Miss Avery, Mary? That is 'till I get back."

"You would not be thinking of turning out again tonight, Father."

"Just be getting the coat please Mary," said Father Michael, "it's only as far as the Green."

Mary was not going to give up without a fight.

"Father Michael, it's your senses you're in need of. How in heaven's name are you going to find your way in the blackout and fog?"

Father Michael smiled.

"In heaven's name, Mary Mahoney, I shall put my trust in St. Christopher and follow the Bendesbury road until I arrive at the bus shelter, then cross the road to the Green and follow the house gates counting as I go." He paused.

"Now do we get a lend of your coat or not?"

On the way Father Michael kept hold of Pamela's hand.

"It's No. 11 the Green, is it not?" he asked adding, "Don't you worry Miss Avery we'll soon have you home and safe."

This remark and the holding of the hand of this compassionate priest opened a floodgate of information and by the time they reached No 11, Father Michael had her life story and had a good idea why she had ended up in the lychgate in such a distressed state.

Refusing to enter the house, the priest waited for Mary's coat then retraced his steps back to the rectory deep in thought arriving safely.

This time it was more by good luck than good management or maybe the help of St Christopher.

Chapter 81

Tanya picked her way carefully through the trees, her heart thumping. She was unable to breath properly with the exhaustion and tension brought about by recent events.

Holding herself together in the presence of others was one thing. Now alone faced with another exhausting journey she struggled. A less strong and pragmatic character would have folded.

Unable to rest for the last twenty-four hours she had difficulty in thinking clearly.

She clung to the knowledge that she must contact Paurak quickly.

No one else would do. No one else could carry her message.

Tanya reached the meeting oak trembling and gasping with emotion.

She stood with her back to the tree trunk forcing herself to breathe deeply and control her limbs.

Settling herself, she cupped her hands and imitated the call of a night jar.

There was no answer.

The ominous silence began to get to her.

Had they been abandoned, she thought, knowing this did and could happen.

"Hello," she squeaked. The sound of her own voice so faint and tremulous, it shocked her.

The silence in the still night air was oppressive. The periodic screech of an owl did not help.

"Raise your hands and turn slowly!"

The order was given in a menacing whisper and was accompanied by a pressure in the small of her back. Tanya controlled her bladder and with immense effort she turned as instructed.

Under the cloudy sky and the shadows of the trees she could see very little.

She could just make out the shadowy hooded figure. This did not help her self-control.

Her training kicked in.

"The identifying call I gave. Answer. You must have heard. Identify yourself." Tanya spoke in Slovene.

"Whip?" The shadow spoke English.

"O-whil," Tanya replied in the same language.

"God, you frightened me." Tanya responded returning to her native language.

"Tanya?"

"Yes."

"Why are you back? I was told you only just left."

"I need to contact Paurak urgently. Take me to him at once."

"I don't know where he is. I can take you to the Forge. They perhaps will know.

It means four hours of mountain track. Can you manage the journey?"

"We must hurry. Try and do it in three."

The man removed his cloak and hood revealing a small figure with a heavy moustache.

He rolled his rifle in the cloak and stuffed it into a hollow trunk, speaking as he did.

"If we are stopped, we need a good story, but best sort it on the way."

This was not the same watcher who was there only four hours ago.

She asked no questions No one asked questions; nor did they refer to another other than by their given name or their profession. Least known, less to reveal under interrogation.

"If we are stopped, we are dead, whatever the story. Save your breath for the journey."

The nature of her intent was unmistakable. The watcher set off immediately.

After only a few hundred metres it was clear they were an ill-matched pair.

Tanya was unfit from months of inactivity incarcerated in a tiny cheese store. The last twenty-four hours of strenuous activity with no sleep and little food had taken their toll.

He young, fit, able, slight and nimble negotiated the mountain path with ease.

He paced himself so as not to overstretch Tanya.

Tanya was forced to rest frequently and to accept the watcher's help in difficult places.

She battled on, for how long she had no idea. She was hoping for their arrival around every corner. Around each corner she was disappointed. She became a determined 'auto woman,' unaware of anything other than the need to keep moving. There were many changes of level as the path undulated. The established routine was to accept the man's help. Even so, she lost footing her frequently. Her leg muscles becoming more and more tired and she suffered from frequent cramps. On one change of level with her vision impaired by a recurring red mist, she lost her both her footing and consciousness.

Tanya returned to semi awareness with her head banging repeatedly against a giant's chest. Confused and exhausted, she lapsed into oblivion.

Chapter 82

"First you must drink this and then eat." The smith encouraged Tanya awake.

Tanya was stirred by the aromas of a meat stew and fresh coffee and the voice of a bass baritone.

The smells reminded her of a happy childhood. Now rested and in her right mind she remembered her mission.

"I need to see Paurak urgently."

"First you drink, eat and sleep." The smith raised Tanya's head and placed a mug to her lips.

The aroma flooded her senses. It was warm, sweet and smelled of real coffee beans.

Her lips were sticky and crusty, her tongue like dry leather.

She took a huge draft of the coffee which was laced with some spirit.

Taking a breath Tanya returned to clear the mug.

The smith smiled then laid her head back on the pillow and filled a plate with stew and a piece of bread. Tanya sat up in anticipation as he handed her a spoon with the dish.

Tanya soon cleared this dish wiping it clean with the bread.

"Now sleep!" ordered the smith.

Chapter 83

Colonel Gunter Seitz, immaculately dressed in black uniform and mirror polished boots, strode into the assembly of army officers and faced his audience in silence for almost a minute.

Without warning, he slapped his swagger cane down on the lectern.

The 'crack' echoed around the hall like a pistol shot.

"This project so far has been a failure. A shambles."

The S.S. officer looked around the hall. "A disgrace."

He began to strut, stopping to point out each of the assembled officers, but not speaking.

The absence of words pierced the ego of everyone he pointed out, causing them to 'screw up' inside.

Returning to the lectern he struck his stick with force several times in time with his words.

"Tomorrow this will change. Tomorrow we will find this man."

'Find this man' being accompanied by the 'thwack-thwack-thwack' of the swagger stick on the lectern.

He turned to his fellow officer who had accompanied him into the hall.

"Herr Capitan."

An S.S. officer stepped forward. With a pointer he began indicating the starting point and finishing points along a displayed road map.

"This is the area we will be covering tomorrow from here to here. It's a distance of forty kilometres.

Each of you will have your task in a co-ordinated search of each farm, house or smallholding along a given sector of the border. The intention is to flush out the quarry who we believe has gone to ground after crossing somewhere along this stretch." He tapped the map with his stick.

"Each section will consist of a search unit for the farms and buildings. A stop and search unit on the main road. Each will be supported by observation units placed at vantage points along the route. Details are contained in the sealed orders to be issued as you leave.

The observation units will be connected by field telephone to motorcycle combinations and to central control by short wave radio. Any vehicle or movement along this route will be stopped, searched and the origin investigated. Each property along this length will be covered by sundown." The officer sprang to attention and raised his arm in salute. "Heil Hitler."

Gunter Seitz stepped forward.

"You will be issued with written orders which will be followed to the letter. Each unit will be in place and ready to begin at dawn. Heil Hitler."

Chapter 84

Four men sat around a table at the forge in conference speaking English. They included the smith, two partisans and a British officer in civilian clothes, referred to always only as 'the captain'.

"Tanya asleep?" asked a partisan.

"She'll probably not surface until this afternoon. She was exhausted when she arrived. She was clearly on the edge."

"We've asked too much, and she's finally cracked. She should have been informed about our plan. That's what you think isn't it?" The partisan taking charge didn't look up or wait for an answer as he continued to look at a map spread on the table.

"What do we do with her, send her home?" asked the captain.

The partisan continued to peruse the map and mark it in red pencil.

"No, her place could be watched. Keep her here to rest up and recover. She will be useful if we decide to keep the target here."

The partisan looked up, turned his pencil over and tapped the map leaving it in place.

"The Doc is here following his spring routine of calling at farms and smallholdings along the border. He probably stayed here overnight. He has been asked to proceed direct to the farm and will pick up the target sometime today."

The partisan reversed the pencil and began to circle points on the map.

"The Germans have set up roadblocks here, here and here. They stopped and searched Doc's wagon yesterday. This means that he is clearly in their sights. We have no option but to proceed with the plan because they are beginning a co-ordinated search today or tomorrow. He is to pick up and deliver the target to the stretcher team on this corner here. This is out of sight of the main road and the roadblock here."

The captain held up a hand.

"Hold it there, please! This sounds dangerous, too dangerous. Have we looked at all options?"

"There are no other options, captain. We go with this. I know it is dangerous. There is a less than a 50/ 50 chance of success but if the enemy is already charging the camp this is not the time to think they might die. We did not expect them to move so soon. Alternatives are not available.

Then there is the farm. If they find him at the farm that finishes them as our outlet, and they are dead."

"Do they know about this operation at the farm?" asked the Smith.

"Only the farm hand is in the know. He is co-operating following instructions given over to him at the last market day. He doesn't know the plan has been moved forward or exactly when the Doc is to arrive. The others know that something is to happen. Other than that, they know nothing.

We are working on a plan to take out the observation points. This should give about ten minutes to transfer the target to our people, but it is tight. Taking out other observers at the same time might help but we expect the Germans will be wise to double bluffs. We must be prepared for the worst outcome."

Later that night the partisan leader entered a clearing in the forest.

A motley bunch of armed men stood or squatted around chatting and smoking.

Taking up a central position he clapped his hands. The men stopped what they were doing stood and turned to face him.

"Message from Paurak that the situation is changed. The search area has been reduced to forty kilometres and goes ahead tomorrow.

This area covers the target and is split into search sectors by the German commandant. The target is in sector two, so we need to move quickly. Leaders, take up your positions as agreed marrying up with the German sectors one to six. The rest of you act as support with protection and diversionary tactics during the collection of the target. Otherwise proceed as laid down yesterday."

He paused before asking, "Any questions?"

The response was an immediate request for more information mostly the timing of the collection to which the answer was not known but to concentrate on sector two and the departure of the Doc and his wagon.

"It is a gypsy-type caravan. It is easy to identify. The German Army has been instructed to investigate all movement. It matters not that the Doc's wagon stands out, in fact it might have the opposite effect."

Chapter 85

The following morning the Doc turned the caravan on to the softer ground of Richter's farm drive. This was a relief from the repetitive ring of Bella's hooves on the metalled road which sounded like the bells of approaching doom. This plus the swing of her white fringed fetlocks had tended to hypnotically heighten the tension the Doc was feeling.

He had spent a restless night debating the question: was this single act in support of the partisans worth him risking his life? Seventy-one years on this earth was maybe his lot but he still felt young and active enough to continue to help his fellow countrymen through the jackboot years.

He had established a routine of helping his comrades survive by redistributing and bartering surplus farm products, providing seed and acting also as a repair service for farm equipment.

A qualified M.D, he was also a travelling health service.

All this and his life were now at risk. He did not mind the security of oblivion. He had no guarantee of a swift and painless passing. He took comfort from the cut throat razor in his pocket and a plan to slit his jugular, wrists or femoral arteries if caught.

Two German soldiers were high on the hill above the road with a clear view of the farm also the road below and the roads west and east and the junction curling back towards the Italian border allowing them to cover both routes.

Willie Volkman diligently reported to his motorcycle combination colleagues on the road below and to central control every ten minutes.

Meanwhile Josef Beck, his colleague, continued to complain that it had been a long cold morning.

The position they held was on a small promontory jutting out on the hillside, overlooking the farm. The hill and the forest around them shielded the watchers from the morning sun, providing no cheer for Willie who was suffering from cramp, the cold and an unhelpful and miserable colleague.

Nonetheless, he stuck to his task.

When the Doc's caravan appeared and turned into Richter's farm, he reported this immediately to central control to receive the information that the search unit was an hour away and to get the mobile unit to investigate and hold the situation. This he relayed to them.

Having done so, he felt safe in handing over to Josef.

"Josef, I need to pee. Takeover, will you?" he asked handing over the binoculars.

Josef who had been lying on his back warming his bones in a small patch of sunlight which had pierced the canopy, reluctantly took over.

Willie then disappeared into the trees. After ten minutes Josef cranked the handle of the field telephone but got no reply from the mobile unit who could now be seen turning into the farm.

He looked down at the Morse code signal to report no change to central control. Not sure whether he should report the arrival of the mobile unit at the farm, he called to Willie.

"Willie, will you call in to control. Your Morse is better than mine."

He watched as the motorcycle combination pulled into the front of the farmhouse.

"The sergeant has gone around to the rear and is out of sight," he called out.

Not hearing Willie answer, Josef lowered the binoculars, stood and turned to look towards the trees and down the barrel of a rifle. He turned back and looked briefly to where his automatic pistol lay, out of reach. He slowly raised his hands. The shadow of a garrotte then flashed across his eyes.

This scene was repeated in two other areas in co-ordinated attacks.

Within minutes the German central control realised that something was happening.

The reports came in. No contact with four, no contact with two, no contact with six. It was clear to Colonel Seitz that a co-ordinated attack was under way.

"Warn all units to be on the alert. They are moving him now. That is ***all*** units and pay attention to the areas where the observers are still in position. This could be a double bluff."

He issued orders stomping up and down the room like an overdressed clockwork mouse.

The officer in charge of the signal's unit, suppressed a smile. He secretly hoped this operation would end in failure. His morale was low and the arrival of this pompous overdressed, jack-booted, black, spangled decorated, uniformed buffoon had dealt a further severe blow to his wellbeing.

He was an older conscript with no wish to be involved in the Nazi ambitions. His presence in the army made him part of a destructive nonsense, something he had lectured against for years.

Nonetheless, he was bound to relay the latest information coming over the wires.

"Coming in from three, reports of a laden fruit and vegetable wagon heading west towards the Italian border," the officer reported.

"Who have we got?"

"No one, sir. The report was from three and it is already beyond them."

"Tell them to pursue and stop. What about sector two?"

"They are investigating the horse drawn caravan at the farm M and are currently out of contact." Seitz looked at the wall map.

"Farm M is at the junction where the road doubles back in a hairpin. Both routes lead to the Italian border. Contact all road-blocks and get the mobile at M to cover that junction."

The signals officer was aware that he could only contact unit two at M via short wave.

Because of the terrain, wireless contact was limited to high ground. The radio on the hill they already knew was now defunct.

He decided not to pass the information on to Seitz who should have been able to work this out for himself. In any event the information could result in him getting the blame.

He relayed the pursuit instruction to sector three and forgot the rest.

The colonel was stomping up and down the room.

"Shit, shit, incompetence. Two posted at each sector, how could they be taken out so easily?"

Chapter 86

Lazlow saw the caravan arriving and pulled the plough out to the front yard. He was waiting when the Doc arrived. After a brief word with him, Adolf left, leaving Lazlow to help the Doc dismantle the ploughshare axle and wheels. The Doc released Bella to graze.

"Take her round the back. The grazing is better there also that's the field we need to plough and cultivate."

The Doc unhooked a pick hoe from the wagon and led Bella round while Lazlow loaded the ploughshare, wheels and axle.

The field was not huge. It always amazed Doc how farmers managed a living on the narrow strip between the hills and the border. He swung the pick hoe three or four blows at the ground then returned to Lazlow.

"The ground is too hard, it should have been ploughed last back end. You will have to wait for the spring rains."

Neither mentioned the real reason for his early arrival even though Adolf was not there.

"That will be too late to plant for this year," Lazlow observed.

"Not for potatoes or root crop, I'll bring some seedling next time."

The Doc answered while at the same time he looked over Lazlow's shoulder.

"I believe we have company."

Lazlow turned to see a German Army motorcycle combination turning into the drive.

Instinctively, he reached out for the pick hoe which the Doc had propped against the wheel.

The Doc looked quizzically at Lazlow and with a slight shaking of his head indicated that this was a bad idea.

The rider and passenger quickly dismounted, neither announcing the reason for this visit.

After a quick survey of the situation the outrider said to his passenger, "Search the wagon and barns." Turning to the Doc, he asked, "Where's the horse?"

The Doc who was loading timber units from the plough straightened.

"Around the back in the pasture," he answered trying but failing not to sound curt and dismissive.

The soldier's face registered his displeasure but under orders to investigate and return to report urgently, he turned on his heels and walked around to the pasture to find Bella indeed contentedly grazing.

Meanwhile sector three's motorcycle combination was speeding westwards after the reported fruit wagon. This was a difficult road twisting and undulating making it impossible to maintain top speed. This was followed by sector three's search team led by an officer in a staff car who had almost caught up with them. Following the staff car and a little way behind was a fully manned and attendant army truck.

Up in the hills two partisans were making their way back to the agreed assembly point. They had seen the fruit and vegetable wagon pass by and could hear in the distance the sound of the pursuing units. Instinctively both flattened themselves to the hillside, training their rifles on the corner around which pursuing vehicles would come.

"Wait until they get alongside," one whispered to the other.

The combination burst into view. Both men followed it through their sights until it was alongside. Then each fired once. The first round ricocheted off the road surface, the second pierced the combination's fuel tank leaking gasoline on to the manifold.

The fuel flashed into flame engulfing rider and sidecar. The vehicle slewed across the road leaving a trail of burning gasoline then turned over on to its side in the drainage ditch.

The following staff car stopped before being ordered to drive on, encouraged by a bullet through the car's door. The following truck arrived, stopped and disgorged several soldiers who came under fire as they ran into the trees returning fire indiscriminately.

Debris showered down on to the partisans. A clamour of rooks scattered to the skies, their startled cries mingling with echoes reverberating up and down the valley.

From the ditch, a black plume curled up from the stricken combination as Vary lights arced over the scene.

Just around the bend, less than eight hundred metres from this scene, the pursuing staff car slowed to a stop. It failed to restart. A bullet passed through the driver's door and the car floor had ricocheted off the prop shaft into the chassis severing the fuel pipe.

The officer stepped from the vehicle and fired a Vary flare into the skies.

In the back pasture at farm M, the sergeant heard the fire fight and watched the Vary lights arc across skies. Both these flares were red which meant only one thing: all vehicles on the road to be stopped and held. Having decided that Doc's wagon was engaged in usual activities, nothing about the situation suggested anything otherwise. The horse removed from the shafts confirmed the visit was normal. He doubled back to his vehicle shouting for his colleague to join him waiting only a few seconds for him to leave the barn.

He saw the fruit and vegetable wagon turning down past his designated station at the road junction.

His colleague climbed aboard the sidecar. He opened the throttle almost pitching his passenger out on to the track.

Lazlow, who had finished loading the plough looked on.

"They might have said goodbye."

His relief at their leaving failed to obscure his sense of humour.

The Doc sized up everything in a flash.

"Get the target into the back of the wagon while I get Bella."

Lazlow entered the cheese store and collected the unsuspecting Peter.

He wrapped him in his bedding before lifting him as if he weighed even less than his sixty kilos.

Lazlow carried him to the wagon arriving at the same time as the Doc with Bella.

Neither spoke. Lazlow closed the canvas screens after loading Peter, who was acutely aware of what was happening. He co-operated without regard to all pain and discomfort.

Bundled unceremoniously on to the wooden floor, his only protection was the blanket he was wrapped in.

"Thanks for letting me know what is happening," he whispered as the screens closed.

Lazlow, already helping the Doc to strap Bella into the shafts, did not hear.

Up on the heights the partisan lowered the 'borrowed' German issue binoculars.

"Target loaded and ready to go," he called to his partner who immediately left to inform the snatch team waiting below.

The Doc set off, Bella's hooves thudding rhythmically to the beating of the Doc's heart.

Inside the wagon Peter clung desperately to one of the struts trying to mitigate the sway of the wagon over the rough track. He didn't mind the pain in his leg or the discomfort.

His whole being rejoiced in the release from the purgatory of months of incarceration in the tiny cheese store. What was about to happen he no longer cared about. He was excited, his nerves were tingling. He was 'alive' for the first time in an age.

The wagon made its way on to the metalled road, the thud of Bella's hooves replaced by the sharper sound of her iron-clad trot towards the junction of the roads.

There was no sign of the German motorcycle combination, now chasing the fruit and vegetable wagon down the valley road.

The Doc turned down this same road stopping as soon as the wagon was out of sight of the main route.

From the trees, half a dozen shadowy figures emerged.

Armed men also appeared and knelt at the side of the road monitoring the route north and south.

Two others carrying a stretcher followed and loaded Peter from out of the wagon, retreating into the trees followed by the guards.

The entire operation lasted little over one minute.

The Doc shook the reins and Bella's hooves rang out into the distance like church bells on a Sunday morning. There were no other sounds.

Colonel Seitz, cursing the inability of the signals officer to maintain wireless contact with all units, had taken to the road himself in a staff car. It reached the road junction, speeding after the fruit and vegetable wagon.

Three hundred metres around the first bend he ordered the driver to stop. He halted the following truck then paced back up the road followed dutifully by two officers.

Seitz stood looking at a steaming pile of horse manure. Bella, while waiting, had relieved herself of last night's hay.

"Look at this shit."

The two officers knew they were expected to respond but how?

They stood looking, feeling stupid, anxious about wasting time looking at a pile of shit.

"What do you see?"

The two officers each waited for the other one to answer. Both, in other circumstances, would have been quite capable of working out what the colonel was getting at. Here and now they were struck dumb by his power and presence. The silence lasted less than thirty seconds before the colonel slapped his boot in anger and screamed, "The shit is in a pile and steaming, not strewn along the road, meaning a horse was stationary here only minutes ago. Fan the men out and advance into and search in the trees ***now***.

"You, captain, take the staff car and run that fruit wagon down. On the way take note of the horse and wagon. It is clearly this tinker man who was at farm M. He is to be monitored constantly.

Don't detain him. I want daily reports of him, what he does, where he goes, who he meets.

Also, that farm is to be thoroughly searched today. Get that forest searched now. Find that man."

The men were already lined up. At a signal from the officer they entered the trees.

Chapter 87

Sir George Bridge Thompson looked over the top of his half rims at his wife who was sitting opposite reading a book. She had an embroidery ring, silks and needles on her lap and was listening to the radio.

"Mealie, old girl, are you listening to that wireless?" he asked wondering which of the three occupations were paramount.

"Obviously George, why else would I have it on?"

However, she sensed that George wanted to have a conversation which made for a refreshing change. Amelia didn't switch off the radio. She closed the book over her finger to mark the page and looked up.

Sir George opened the conversation with what he deemed to be important news only to be constantly interrupted by his prickly wife.

"*The Times* today have repeated Dickie Barnes's obituary alongside the detail of his will."

"Why on God's earth would they do that?"

"Services to the war effort and all that I suppose, but that is not the point."

"Then what is the point?" Amelia was clearly irritated by the subject.

"The point is my dear, he has left 2.94 million."

Sir George waited for the 'penny to drop', but he was disappointed.

"Three million pounds, good God, **that much** for a grubby little tool maker from the back streets of Sheffield. And not a penny for you, George. That's what you get for clinging to his coat tails all the years."

"Mealie, you are missing the point."

"The point is George," Amelia interrupted. "you threw away all our money on your stupid stocks and shares which left you clinging desperately to that upstart."

Sir George was now finding it difficult to control his temper, so he changed tack.

He could have countered with 'your father left you and your brother with debt, a huge demand for death duties', but instead he said, "The S.O.E. have news of Peter."

Amelia interrupted again.

"Enough, George! I have no wish to hear about that little runt."

Sir George finally exploded.

"Look here!"

That is as far as he got. The lights went out and the radio faded leaving them both in the dark with just the firelight flickering in George's half rims and hiding the anger in his eyes.

They sat for fully a minute whilst Sir George subdued his temper and Amelia adjusted her mind to the loss of all three of her distractions.

Candles plus matches were ready. Neither made any attempt to light them.

The firelight had a calming effect on both. George finally continued in a more reasoned manner.

"You know Mealie, old girl, you and I had a dream for Pen, but it was not her dream.

Nor was it Peter's."

He waited for Amelia's response but there wasn't one.

To Amelia, George's voice took on a disembodied, ethereal tone. She was fascinated by this and the firelight flickering on his half rims. This took away her indignation which returned rapidly as George continued.

"Pen and Peter did love each other," he paused before adding, "but not like that."

"Like what?" Amelia's scornful tone scythed through the darkness.

George now played what turned out to be a master card. It was as if some unseen director had called 'cut' and restarted the conversation.

"As ***we*** once were when we walked in the hills in Pennsylvania that wonderful summer on our honeymoon. We lay under a tall tree listening to nature's song not just out on the hills but in our hearts."

He sighed at the memory. George was keenly aware that he had Amelia's attention.

"No, Pen and Peter are more like sister and brother. It took the American fellow to teach her the difference," he continued. "She cares for this American so much more than she does Peter or his half of the inheritance."

As if someone had pressed button A on her coin box, 'the penny finally dropped'.

Amelia took only seconds to think this through.

"So, Peter is worth over a million?" She spoke slowly but forcefully.

"Exactly the point," Sir George almost shouted. "Pen is at this very moment talking to her friends about divorcing Peter. Desertion or something."

Amelia sat bolt upright.

"How do you know that, George?"

"Talk of the town, old girl. Talk of the town."

"Now what?" Amelia picked up on George's theme. George, she knew, was not given to idle gossip about his own daughter.

"Keep up, old girl, keep up. If she does get a divorce and her adultery is cited, Paul could challenge the will and end up with the lot. But if Peter dies, as he might well do very soon, as his widow ..." This is as far as he got. Amelia stood and left her book on the side table. The embroidery ring and silks slid from her lap. As she did so, the electricity returned. Amelia turned off the radio.

"I will be speaking to Pen. You George, get hold of that American and mark his card."

With Amelia at last on board, Sir George folded his newspaper.

Having successfully lit the blue touch paper he was preparing to retire to a safe distance.

He had anticipated Amelia taking charge but not his involvement with Henry Steading.

"Are we sure that is wise, old girl."

"Not only wise but prudent and essential, George. Just do it."

The electricity failed again. In the dark with just the firelight flickering on her face, Amelia was a formidable sight.

"Isn't it a bit late for that?"

"Just no divorce, no marriage until it is all settled or Peter ..." She hesitated. Even Amelia was unable to put her final thoughts into words.

"Well you know what I mean," she added lamely coming as near to being ashamed as she ever was.

Chapter 88

Pen came downstairs at 10 a.m. the following morning dressed in her auxiliary nurse's uniform.

Not looking forward to another gruelling 12-hour tour of duty. Lady Amelia who had been waiting impatiently in the lounge folded her *Telegraph* as soon as she heard Pen's footsteps on the stairs. "You're late," she called out expecting Pen to present herself in the lounge.

Pen, pretending not to hear, headed straight to the kitchen.

Twenty plus years of living with her mother had developed in her an instinct of just when and how to avoid Amelia.

Placing a slice of bread under the grill she steadfastly refused to turn around as she heard her mother follow her into the room and sit at the kitchen table.

Amelia looked 'daggers' at her daughter.

"I repeat, you're late."

This opening and her mother's oppressive presence did not help Pen's mood who thought to herself. 'What ever happened to good morning?' Aware that this heralded an unwished for opinion or more than likely, a flaming row, she was uncertain how to respond and didn't answer.

Pen turned her toast under the grill and waited for the next salvo which came as expected.

"Why you cannot rise at a decent hour and breakfast with us is beyond me."

Amelia managed an exaggerated sigh as she sat facing her daughter's back with a face which could be best described as appearing to be sucking a lemon.

Pen still did not reply but as her toast was done and she had little option but to join her mother at the table.

In silence, she spread some margarine on the toast and took a bite.

Her mother grimaced on her daughter's behalf.

"The butter is finished. If you arose at a decent hour you would have had your share."

Amelia registered a 'serves you right,' expression.

Pen realised that her mother was determined to have her way which probably meant a row would follow. She was Still wondering what it was all this was about, how she could deal with it and knowing she had to answer, Pen took another bite and said, "Actually, the margarine isn't bad. We are jolly fortunate to have spread at all."

Realising that this was a poor response, Pen added, "I was on duty until midnight and arrived home at 1.30 a.m. after walking from the station." Pen returned her mother's stare and raised her eyebrows in question.

"What time would you expect me to rise?"

"Speaking now with your mouth full. What other vulgar pitmatic habits are you picking up?"

Amelia said, looking up at the kitchen ceiling, adding, "After all we've done to try and bring you up as a lady?"

'Pitmatic'. Pen thought. Where did dear Mamma come across that expression? Probably from Pamela, she figured. At the same time Pen tried to muster a sense of humour. She tried desperately to keep her temper in check by imagining her mother wearing a coronet parading naked down the Bendesbury Road carrying a banner displaying, 'Death to all Pitmatics'.

Experience of years of controlling her anger in this manner counted for nothing this time.

Pen was not only tired and sick of being the one to keep the peace. She was just so tired, worn out by repetitive twelve hour shifts of duty, with only one day's respite before returning to six more nights of equally unsocial punishing hours on the alternative shift. One week off in thirteen was no compensation. Why she put herself through this purgatory only Pen knew.

This had been a continuing conflict between herself and her parents. This was dangerous territory. Even if she didn't have any answers, she was determined to see her war work through in the face of all opposition.

Amelia was struggling to keep her composure, control her disappointment. Her loss of control had manifested itself by causing her to appear even more haughty and disdainful.

She had spent the night alternating between a determination to approach her daughter's adultery with understanding and tact then flushing with anger in the knowledge that she and George had impoverished themselves to have her presented at court in the hope of a good marriage.

The dream had been overtaken by a rapidly changing world and her daughter's obsession with this common American. This was too much. Peter Barnes was not the catch she had hoped for, but at least he had money, now clearly in abundance.

Pen was about to throw this all away.

Pen was now even more confused and didn't understand just why her mother was so determined to pick a fight. She decided her best course of action was to leave for her work as soon as possible.

"I'm sorry, mother, I don't have time for this, this ..."

She hesitated, searching for a word. Baloney came to mind but constant association with her nursing colleagues and doctors took control and the word was transformed and she blurted "bollocks".

The silence thundered as the blood rushed into her cheeks.

All Pen needed now was to escape. Seconds stretched into an age before she jumped to her feet and made for the door.

This sparked Amelia into action who, being nearer the door, stood in Pen's way to prevent her leaving. Venomously, Amelia spat every syllable like a cobra.

"Such vulgarity, whilst you are under my roof Penelope you will adhere to my standards."

Then realising her purpose had been sidelined, she added, "I don't suppose you really are working all those hours; you are seeing that American."

Pen, at last, had an idea what this was all about. Struggling to hold back the tears, she was speechless and unable to respond.

Amelia, realising she had finally achieved the first of her targets to broach the subject of her daughter's adulterous relationship, then revealed her true purpose.

"If you don't take care you will lose your share of the Barnes's inheritance."

It was never her intention to put it so bluntly but at least it was out.

Pen somehow gathered herself. She managed to avoid the subject of Hal in her reply taking the argument back to her mother's former remark.

"Under your roof, mother. ***Your roof***. Might I remind you that the deeds to this house are in the hands of my ward's trustees of which I happen to be one. In addition to this, I am her guardian.

Therefore, as long as **you** are under what is technically **my** roof, you will keep your greedy nose out of mine and my ward's trough."

She thrust her mother roughly to one side and left the house slamming the door.

Chapter 89

Pamela Avery had just finished spooning the last of her rhubarb and apple puree sweetened with saccharine into jars, when an urgent hammering on the front door caused her to drop everything and hurry there still wiping her hands. Pam opened the door. Pen almost fell inside, obviously in great distress.

"Penny, my Pet, whatever is amiss?"

"Oh Pamela, Nanny Pammy. I've just had a ghastly row with Mamma." Pen grabbed on to Pamela.

"Your mother?" Pam's remark was not really a question more a reaction.

Pen nodded into Pam's cardigan.

"What about, my Pet?"

"I don't know," Pen answered, still confused, then corrected herself.

"Yes, I do, but why now?" She gasped and sobbed.

"Oh! Auntie Pam, I was horrible, just so horrible."

"I understand, Pet. And I suppose Amelia was all sweetness and light."

Pam hoped for a calmer response. It was becoming clear that this was serious. It was some while before Pam was able to calm Pen down. Finally, Pen with a huge shuddering sigh, then gave Pam a warm smile.

"Sorry Auntie Pam, I have no one else I can turn to and I've missed my train."

"There will be no trains for you today, Pet," said Pam still with her arms around Pen.

"Come into the room and I will light a nice fire, make a pot of tea and you can tell me all about it."

"What about the hospital?"

"Never mind about the hospital, Pet. A little later, when we are a bit happier, I will pop along to the telephone box and let them know you are sick. All right, Pet?"

Pam pulled her gently forward and kissed her gently on the forehead. Pen nodded and shivered.

Pamela put a match to the fire and busied herself off to the kitchen to put the kettle on feeling more alive than she had been all winter.

Over a cup of tea Pen recounted the whole sad story.

Pamela listened carefully and was silent for some time looking into the fire, thinking just how to respond. She stood up and went to the hearth and raked out the fire with the poker. She used it like a rapier as if she was fighting off demons stirring the remnants into flame.

She placed more logs on the fire then stood up very straight with her back to Pen, who watched and waited with increasing anxiety willing Pamela to say something.

After what seemed to be an age Pamela spoke.

"Are you still seeing Hal?" she asked and turned to look into Pen's eyes.

This look was not lost on Pen who lowered her head as she nodded.

"I love him," she answered, adding. "We love each other."

Pamela took a deep breath and replied, "I know, Pet. Thank you for being honest.

Question is what do we do now?"

To Pen that little word 'we' meant all the world. She was no longer alone.

"Thank you, Auntie Pam."

Pamela was irritated and at the same time confused. She wanted to hug Pen better and at the same time wanted to slap her. She still wished though to solve what was clearly a serious problem.

She was delighted to be asked and grateful to be involved.

This manifested in anger as she replied, "Please, cut out the Auntie Pam routine. If we are going to sort something out, we'd best get rid of the frills."

Pen jumped up from the settee and threw herself into Pam's arms on hearing only the words 'if we are to sort something out.'

"Oh Pam, thank you. I don't think of you as an aunt. I want to call you Mum even though I know it is wrong. It's you I turn to in trouble always. There's no one else. You are more my mother than Amelia ever was. She is more like a disapproving maiden aunt."

Pamela clung on to Pen in a daze as her whole body flooded with pleasure, so much so that she struggled to keep a grip on reality.

She managed to say, "I think plain Pam will do just fine."

"Can I come to you any time?" Pen stood back and took Pamela's hand.

Pam, unable to continue, nodded as Pen continued,"I used to be able to speak to Peter who would usually sort things out and make me laugh at the same time."

Pamela found her voice. "Yet, you don't love him?"

"Yes, I do. I really do but it is not the same. I wish I could explain."

"It is Henry Steading you really love?" This question was more rhetorical, Pam thinking through the situation as she continued. "And if you have been with him that is still adultery, you do know that?"

Pam looked deep into Pen's eyes. Pen flushed, looked away and nodded.

"I can't help myself."

What she then asked caused Pamela's eyebrows to almost lift from her face.

"Is it still adultery if Peter and me have never ...? She looked up, wide eyed and not completing the sentence.

"So you and Peter never ...?" Pamela began only for Pen to interrupt.

"It never seemed to be right."

She shook her head violently as if to force agreement out of Pam, who answered the question as much to herself as to Pen.

"Then you are not really married. You could have an annulment."

Pen didn't appear to take this in as she tumbled over her words to explain.

"You see it's just that with Peter we shared our thoughts and worries from being very small, lonely and frightened. He would make me laugh and sort things out. I always felt safe with him but with Hal ..." She paused for breath a before trying again. "Whereas with Hal ..."

Pamela realised that Pen needed help and gave it.

"I think I have got the message, Pet."

Pam waited, knowing that she would learn the most by staying silent.

"Peter had this way of seeing the truth in situations. He thought that Mama and Daddy were at best a little ridiculous and at worst pompous, overblown. A danger to themselves and others."

"Peter didn't like your parents?"

"I don't know, he certainly wasn't in awe of them. Not rude either. He showed the same respect as he did his father. None of this meant that he didn't know them. He warned me that his father was just using my parents and as soon as their usefulness was over, he would abandon them."

Pamela nodded. She knew that the only reason that Richard ever came to St. Mary was to see Paul. Richard Barnes's reconnection with Sir George after the war, was to access government defence contracts. Specifically, special steels for aircraft engine production.

He owed his life to the surgeon commander, but it was not gratitude which motivated the reconnection. Pamela's position with the Bridge Thompsons was arranged by Richard solely to protect his reputation and stay in touch with Paul.

The legacy from his will, such as it was, was acknowledgement of her bearing and raising his son. Otherwise she would have been ignored.

The Bridge Thompsons' need to acknowledge Richard Barnes interest was financially based.

Pamela knew enough of this story to know that Peter was calling it correctly.

"What to do now is the question?"

Pen didn't answer but looked anxiously at Pam.

Pamela answered her own question.

"If it was as bad as you say, and I don't doubt it, you can only go along with the truth. Correct me if you don't agree. Firstly, the only way you will ever sort any row out with Amelia is to apologise."

Pen looked pained and Pamela exchanged looks with Pen, raising a questioning eyebrow causing Pen to drop her gaze and nod. Pam continued.

"I know your mother provoked you but what you said and did was pretty bad. So, my Pet, let's hope that it not entirely unforgivable."

The tears were dripping off the end of Pen's nose. Pamela placed one finger under her chin and gently lifted her head to look into her eyes.

"Penny my love, I am afraid you must humbly ask for that forgiveness. That is if you really do wish to return to something like normal."

Pamela looked into Pen's eyes hoping for an acknowledgement but there was none.

"Secondly, you must tell your parents the truth about you and Henry Steading. Also tell them, politely and at the same time, that it is your affair. It is not open for discussion."

To this Pamela received a nod from Pen.

"Finally, tell them you do not have the slightest interest in Richard Barnes's money. In your opinion it can only bring unhappiness. Oh! And be sure to tell them you will house and care for them as long as that is needed."

Pen remained silent. As soon as Pam removed her finger from under her chin Pen immediately dropped her head. Pamela took her into her arms and whispered.

"That is all I have to offer, Pet."

Pam felt Pen nod into her bosom. For almost a minute they remained as such until Pam said:

"Two aspirins and a lie down in a darkened room is called for."

Knowing that she would need time to sort out her head, Pam led Pen into her bedroom and drew the curtains.

Throughout the past hour Pam was aware that they had re-enacted scenes from Pen's childhood.

Not being entirely comfortable with this. Pen, a grown woman, had accepted this without protest signifying the depth of her need.

As she entered the kitchen, Pam was shocked to see the time. It was now too late to buy fish from Sully, the local friendly, natural products entrepreneur. All fish plus any rabbit, pheasant and wood pigeon would now be gone. All would have been sold in minutes.

Sully's customers included the local magistrate's wife. His rise in stature from a poacher to valued provider of all things good, had been phenomenal.

Sully's own description of himself, delivered in a soft southern Irish accent was. 'Oim not at all what you t'ink. Oim the last of the Hunter Gatherers.'

Pam sighed and shrugged. It was to be a meatless, fishless meal that evening. With probably one extra mouth to feed, Pam set about producing meatless rissoles using mashed potato, breadcrumbs, caramelised onions, corn flour and a beef cube, leaving Pen to rest and come to terms with her problems.

Lost in her thoughts, Pamela again lost track of time. She was once more surprised to hear Dorothy call. "I'm home."

Pam hurried to the sink and washed her hands. Still drying them she followed Dorothy into the front room. Dorothy was sitting on the settee putting on her slippers.

"The house is nice and warm. Thank you."

Dorothy was looking at the fire grate and the remnants of the fire also at two small logs, all that was left of this morning's log pile.

"You remembered Friday early finish," she added, really meaning, 'what happened to all the logs?'

Pamela busily wiped her hands, wondering how to tell Dorothy of the day's events.

"Wasn't able to buy fish today. I am afraid tonight, it's just potato cakes and vegetables."

"No matter, we'll manage," Dorothy muttered, her mind elsewhere looking at the last flickering embers in the grate. She was about to ask, 'why the early fire?'

These thoughts were interrupted by an urgent banging on the window.

The urgency was such that they both ran to the door to find a very cross Mim.

She swept by the pair of them into the hallway shouting.

"There's no Mrs Emerson and Granny Thompson is sat on the settee with two suitcases not talking and there's no tea."

Mim spun around to face the two startled ladies with her legs splayed and hands on hips looking very cross indeed.

"Nanny Pam, why aren't you there anymore?"

Pam looked at Mim, trying hard not to smile.

"I thought you were a big girl now and no longer needed me."

"Well I do today, and I don't suppose you've got any jam?"

"As it happens, I might just be able to manage that," Pam replied lifting Mim bodily out of the way and going into the kitchen.

Pam wondered how she could tell Dorothy of the day's events now that Mim was there.

Both were following hot on her heels.

Pam was slicing a loaf. Dorothy standing behind Mim, mouthed the words, 'What is going on?'

To which Pam mouthed back, 'Tell you later.' She spread the slice with the still warm puree.

"Milk?" she asked Mim, pouring a glass without waiting for an answer.

Mim took a bite of the bread and spread and pulled a face.

"This is not proper jam."

"It's called puree, Mim," Pam explained. "I didn't have the sugar to make proper jam."

Mim pulled another face.

"I suppose it will have to do. What is the world coming to when one can't get proper jam?"

Dorothy mouthed over Mim's head. 'Manners.' Then she added loudly, "What is to be admired about we Jewish people is that we have learned to adapt to all situations. In fact, some manage to be more English than the English."

Pam mouthed back at Dorothy. 'Now who's being rude?' Both tried but failed to suppress the inevitable giggle.

"I don't see there is anything to laugh about. Grandad Thompson can get as much sugar as he likes. Why can't you?"

Pen appeared in the doorway.

"Mim, sweetie, what are you doing here?"

"Grannie Thompson is cross again and I had to come all the way across here for my tea." Unanswered questions were now getting in the way of normal conversation.

Pam and Pen were clearly uncomfortable.

Dorothy quickly realised her presence and that of Mim was an embarrassment.

She took Mim's hand.

"Why don't you and I go into the lounge and relight the fire?" she suggested, giving Mim a meaningful look. Seven-year-old girls were usually well equipped to read between the lines.

Mim was no exception. She gave an exaggerated shrug, pulled a face and went with Dorothy into the lounge. The door was then firmly closed. Once inside Mim tugged at Dorothy's sleeve.

"There's something well amiss going on. Shall we listen at the door?" she whispered.

Dorothy even though she was sorely tempted, replied, "I don't think that we should do that, do you?"

Once they had left the room Pam spoke her mind.

"I believe Pen my love, it is time for you to go and try and mend fences."

Pen nodded.

"Promise me you will come straight back if you need to."

Pen nodded yet again, grabbed her coat and left with a final hug.

"I promise. Thank you, Nanny Pam."

Pam went straight into the front room knowing that an explanation was needed.

"Only two logs and some kindling. What are we to do?" Dorothy asked.

"Never mind that. Mamma Pen and Grandma Thompson have fallen out. Mamma Pen has gone to try and make up with Grandma Thompson. Best, don't you think, that you should wait here for a while?"

Mim sat down on the settee and folded her arms.

"I've fallen out with Becky Swartz and no way will I make up. I'll not speak to her ever, ever again," she said, scowling.

Pam had realised there was little point in hiding the truth from Mim. Her reaction confirmed this.

Chapter 90

Pen met George coming across the Green. She peered through the gathering dusk.

"Is that you Daddy? You are home early."

Sir George called back. "Penny! Why aren't you at work?"

"You know why. Mother phoned you at work, didn't she? I am so sorry. I am just on my way to apologise."

Sir George took little notice of Pen's confession, other matters were on his mind. He sounded anxious.

"I can't find Mim, she is missing. I'm on my way to Pam's. She could be there."

"She *is* there Daddy, she's all right. Shall we go back? I need to mend fences with mother."

"This is all my fault, Pen. Truth is, I set this up last night with Amelia and ..."

He failed to complete the thought, until prompted by Pen.

"And?" she questioned.

"I've also had a bit of a to-do with Amelia."

"Mine was a little bit more than a to-do, Daddy. Let's get home, it's getting cold."

Pen had warmed towards her father. His concern for Mim's welfare, in the midst of all the other troubles, pleased her. Also, he was not in any way judgemental and quite vulnerable.

She put her arm through his and escorted him home. She was feeling much stronger now.

They entered the house and Pen could just make out her mother's silhouette.

She was sitting on the settee for all the world looking like one of the gargoyles carved around St. Mary's church.

She motioned to her father to wait then made her way into the room.

Pen drew the blackout curtains and switched on the standard lamp. She forced herself to face her mother.

"I wish to apologise mother for what I said and did. It was unforgivable. I am so sorry, really sorry." She bowed her head while speaking.

Amelia turned her head away reminding Pen of a slow worm she had seen on the path which froze in a similar position, trying to appear invisible.

Pen, then knelt, tried to take her mother's hand, which was snatched away.

"Please Mamma, forgive me."

With her head still exaggeratedly turned away Amelia stood, drew herself up to her full five-foot two inches. Her eyes avoiding all contact. She marched from the room brushing by her husband as if he did not exist.

Sir George, having watched Pen's valiant failed attempt to pacify her mother, made no attempt to intervene.

He went to his daughter and helped her up from her knees and on the settee.

Sitting beside her, he took her hand in his.

"She will come around," he paused before adding with emphasis, "eventually."

Pen, now beyond tears shook her head.

"Will she?"

The pale, yellow light of the standard lamp exaggerated the darkness of the fireplace, the fire having been neglected.

Pen shuddered with misery and the cold.

How long they sat in silence, neither knew nor cared. That is until George spoke.

"There's something else I've been thinking how to tell your mother."

That was all that was said. Time passed and neither spoke. Pen didn't register his words until much later.

"Something else?" she queried eventually, thinking what else could there be.

"I'm to lose my job."

This shocked Pen. "Why Daddy? You've been there years and there's a war on."

"That makes no difference. The War Office is moving my team into a combined services logistical unit and I am being sidelined. I have been offered admin posts in Scotland, Ireland or Dartmouth.

I am holding out for decent accommodation in married quarters. I will lose my Whitehall increments. Be left with just my surgeon commander's pay. Worse still, we would lose all our London and local contacts."

"Why not just retire and stay here with Mim and me?"

"What on just my pension?"

"Well, you won't have any other expenses and you will have free board and lodgings.

What about that?"

"Ah, but I would still have Amelia. She wants to move out immediately. Into a hotel and I don't mean the Drovers. If I could just wave a wand, get a taxi and a porter then book into the Savoy, I doubt that she would be satisfied."

"She'll come around in time."

"Sorry, Pen. She will never change. I will always be to blame."

"In which case Daddy tell her that it is your decision. Don't give her any options. You are going to be in the wrong, whatever the choice. So why not choose the one you prefer?"

Sir George looked thoughtful.

He imagined being alone week in week out with just Amelia, cut off from his family and from his contacts in the village. A life on his pension alone would not suit his wife but it would be worse to be separated from Mim, Pen and his home for the last twenty plus years. This, along with the loss of welcome supplements via Sully, did not add up to a good life. At this point he realised there was no sensible alternative. He turned to his daughter.

"Thank you Penny, I choose to remain here with you and Mim."

Pen squeezed his hand. "Good. Now let's go and pick up your granddaughter."

Chapter 91

The excitement of the sudden release from his incarceration had quickly disappeared.

A feeling of foreboding was beginning to rise in the pit of Peter's stomach.

Once more he was in the hands of the unknown. He longed for that euphoria he felt when he broke out from the prison camp to those brief hours of freedom.

Now he was clinging desperately to the sides of the stretcher surrounded by shadowy figures grunting and straining as they jolted him along the mountain track. Every 200 metres they were relieved by another four shadowy figures to follow the same routine.

The wind was knocked out of his body as the stretcher hit the floor of the forest to be immediately slid under a mess of last year's bracken. The dust from the dried-up fans filled his hair, his mouth and eyes. He coughed as he opened his mouth to complain only to be gagged by a huge hand over his face. He struggled to breathe trying to drag the hand clear.

"Quiet, laddie," A voice hissed in his ear.

What Peter already knew was that he was merely a weapon in the hands of those who wished to embarrass and disrupt the German high command and boost the morale of the occupied populace.

What Peter did not know, was the involvement the British.

He lay there trying not to cough but this very effort bounced off his now overfilled bladder which was not a matter for the consideration for his mentors at this time. A second bout of subdued coughing caused the hand to once more cover his mouth. The coughing exited through his nose splattering the hand with mucous. At the same time this forced urine from his bladder.

With a supreme effort born of desperation, Peter dragged the hand away.

"I need to pee," he whispered.

"Sorry laddie. It's pee your pants time or tie a knot in it," came the hushed reply.

Peter realising they were conversing in English, made to reply.

The hand was rapidly replaced as he felt the hot urine spurting despite his attempts to regain control. Miserable beyond words, he heard the pursuing army crashing through the trees and undergrowth sounding uncomfortably near.

All noise faded into the distance followed by an eerie silence broken only by the sound of the wind in the trees and the occasional cry of a bird.

After several minutes, the jolting, twisting journey recommenced.

Who they were, moved when they did, where they were going, remained a mystery.

After hours of clinging to the sides of the stretcher it was placed on the ground in silence but this time there was a hand on his shoulder.

"Where are we?" Peter asked.

"You have done well. We are leaving now." Peter realised that these conversations had been in English with someone with a familiar accent.

"You're English?"

"Nay laddie, I'm no English. Keep your insults for the enemy." This reply was accompanied by an amused chuckle as the man placed Peter's sticks alongside him on the stretcher.

Tired as he was, Peter still managed to smile. It was a smile which quickly faded. Insecurity kicked in as he heard the partisans moving swiftly away.

A short while later he was hoisted bodily from the stretcher by a giant of a man.

"Welcome Lt Barnes, we have food coffee and a warm bed waiting," he said speaking English.

“I stink,” Peter replied, aware that his soiled trousers made for unpleasant handling.

“I’m sorry,” said Peter, once more speaking in Slovene.

The man appeared not to notice. He didn’t reply nor speak again until they entered a wooden lean-to shelter.

“Warm dry clothes we have. First, you eat.” The man again spoke English.

“I think I would prefer to wash first,” Peter pleaded in Slovene.

“Food, drink and sleep are more important, washing will wait.” Once more, English was spoken seemingly ignoring the fact that Peter could speak in his own language.

With this statement, the dominance of the Smith began.

Chapter 92

Sleeping at the back of an open lean-to shelter was not a problem for Peter, it was a joy.

He so much preferred this to the cramped confinement of the last months.

Still sore of body, in this new environment his mind quickly began to heal, out in the open amongst the smell of pine needles, listening to the wind in the treetops, the dawn chorus and the myriad sounds and scents of the forest.

At the open side of the shelter there was a structure rather like an oversized beehive.

Peter could feel the warmth from it several feet away. He surveyed the pit which held this structure and smiled.

"Breakfast, Peter." The voice interrupted his thoughts. He turned on his sticks to see Tanya laying out food on the table in the lean-to.

Peter, constantly surprised by the events of the last days, was shocked by Tanya's sudden appearance. His reaction was gauche and sullen.

"You left and didn't return as you promised."

Immediately, Peter realised just how immature this was.

He struggled to recover his dignity. "Sorry." He muttered and hung his head. His embarrassment, complete. Tanya placed the last of the food on the table and went to Peter and took him in her arms. "I did promise, and I am sorry."

With this, Peter's embarrassment was complete and he burst into tears.

The Smith entered the clearing carrying a mechanical contraption which he placed on the floor in the lean-to, stood and observed and waited before deciding to intervene.

"Lt. Barnes, this is for you," he announced indicating towards the wooden framed unit.

Peter and Tanya split and turned to see what the Smith was talking about.

"What is it?" asked Tanya.

The Smith smiled. "I think Lt. Barnes is capable of working that out for himself."

Turning, he made his way back down the slope without further comment.

He returned later that morning with some twine and some steel pegs.

Peter was sitting alone on the wooden bench. Neither spoke at first.

The Smith aligned the machine to where Peter sat and pegged it to the floor. Peter placed his feet in the leather stirrups and began pushing against the tension springs.

"In your own time and don't overdo it at first. Now stand up, sir." The Smith ordered.

Peter did as he asked. The Smith measured from his armpit to the ground on both sides.

"I will make you crutches. They will be better for you to get around. We have less than six weeks to strengthen your legs before you are to move on. Meanwhile you are to watch the charcoal pit for me and check the net on the hour throughout the day."

He indicated the charcoal pit and the clay mound. "This one is maturing but it needs to be watched constantly. If you see the clay cracking or see any flame through the clay pack some more clay over the crack and seal it. If it breaks out at the top contact me at once down in the forge."

Peter nodded.

"I understand," he answered delighted to at last have a purpose.

"You mentioned a net I believe?"

"I will show you later when you have the crutches," The Smith replied and without further comment left.

Peter watched him go aware of a growing excitement in the pit of his stomach. The realisation that he was a part of a purposeful self-sufficient way of life was, for him, exhilarating.

During the next days, Peter quickly settled into a routine. The crutches arrived and proved to be a big improvement. Peter was now itching to learn more and even get involved in the forge.

The Smith would have none of that.

The net turned out to be a mesh-covered cap suspended on one edge by a stick which, when knocked away, trapped all underneath. This either happened accidentally or the stick to which a length of twine was attached, could be pulled away.

Often it was removed by a startled wood pigeon.

Peter quickly caught on to using the net. He refused to kill the trapped animals after watching the Smith who killed most with a flick of the wrist. As slick as a magician would produce a rabbit out of a hat, he took them out efficiently with the minimum of distress. Tanya then would pluck draw or skin them while still warm. They went straight into the pot with vegetables and edible forest fungi and natural herbs. One occasion the net trapped a squirrel. The Smith held it by the head, examined it then released into the nearest tree.

Peter enquired. "You don't eat squirrel then?"

The Smith replied. "We eat squirrel, rat, snake, all good food, but not next year's supply."

After four weeks, the improvement in Peter, physically and mentally, was marked. He lost most of the violent mood swings and was moving around the camp and the forest at speed on his crutches.

The Smith increased the level of his leg strengthening exercise.

"We have only two more weeks," he announced one morning.

"Why can't I stay here?" Peter pleaded, petulantly, sounding like a little boy.

The Smith didn't answer immediately. He examined the charcoal pit and closed off the top and emerged wiping his hands and looked down from his height at Peter.

"Two weeks," he replied quietly. "No more."

Peter's colour rose as he looked up at the huge man. If ever he felt the burden of his size it was now. This was not a new experience, but his ego was now trampled so deep into the clay.

To learn that these, some of his happiest days were to end, overwhelmed him.

He threw one of his crutches at the Smith who parried it easily.

Peter took the second crutch and wielding it like a hammer waded into the big man who caught hold of it, wrenched it free and threw it to one side observing, "You are standing without support. I don't think these are needed any more." Peter collapsed on to the ground and lay there gasping for breath trying to control his anger aware that even fully fit that he was never a match for the Smith.

"You are a metallurgist, are you not?" The Smith asked once Peter had regained some control.

Peter didn't answer at once but struggled to the lean-to upright and hauled himself to his feet.

He shrugged his shoulders.

"I know a little of this, why?"

"I could use a little help if you care to join me at the forge."

Peter spat into the pit. "Piss off, big man! Don't be so patronising."

The Smith replied, "Suit yourself." He then turned to walk down the slope taking care that Peter did not see the smile on his face.

Peter struggled to the table and sat with his head in his hands.

Tanya witnessed all. She quietly collected his crutches and placed them beside him then poured him a mug of coffee putting a consoling hand on his shoulder.

Peter looked up. "Oh! Tanya, I am so ashamed. I don't know what came over me, I'm sorry."

"The apology should be for the Smith. I think he intended to provoke you," she said taking his hand. "He either doesn't know or care what you have suffered over the last months with the succession of traumas. Your reaction was bizarre. I guess you wish to recover some dignity. An apology will go some way towards that."

Peter was staring down at the table. Try as she may, Tanya could not get Peter to look at her.

"Why can't I know the Smith's real name?"

Tanya was surprised by the irrelevance of his question. Taking him by his shoulders she shook him gently.

"Peter, I don't know his name nor he mine. You know me as Tanya but not my real name. Believe me, it's safer that way."

Peter steadfastly still refused to look at her.

"It seems that I no longer seem capable of thinking," he mumbled.

Tanya, after a moment's consideration, said, "I think you need a little time to yourself. I will leave you to your thoughts and see you at mid-day." With a sad thoughtful shaking of the head, she turned and left him alone.

Two hours later Tanya returned with Peter's lunch to find the shed empty and a note on the table. The note read, "I am going out into the forest. I might be some time."

Immediately Tanya was alarmed. She ran ran to the forge and showed the note to the Smith.

"I don't like this Tanya, we'd best inform Paurak straight away."

Chapter 93

Hours later Peter had still not returned. Two partisans, the Smith and an Englishman were talking down in the forge. The partisans and the Englishman were arguing.

The partisans had no wish to be involved with the search that the Englishman was proposing. "Enough," said one. "This little man is becoming a danger to our overall operation. I say we let him go."

The Englishman pursued his argument.

"I still have my orders and your agreement. If you wish to continue with British help and support, you will assist."

The first partisan considered this comment before replying.

"I want the S.S. out of my area and the reprisals on our people and the increased danger to my men to cease. While this man is at large we are in escalating danger. Enough is enough. I say we finish it now and leave this man to his fate."

"So, neither of you will help?" The Englishman looked at each in turn.

The second partisan considered before answering.

"We could, if he is found, move him further south into my area but it would take a week or two."

The first partisan shrugged. "That doesn't mean we lose the S.S. here."

"They are not omnipotent," replied the second partisan. "We will take them on."

The first speaker took a long look at this second man then slung his rifle over his shoulder and left without a further word.

The Englishman watched him leave until he melted into the forest. Knowing it was pointless to argue or comment, he turned to the other.

"We find Barnes first then move him out immediately. Scotty and your men are by now still ten kilometres away covering the trail west. The eastwards trail we must leave even though he is unpredictable. We meet up in Eagles Nest at 23.00 hours whether Barnes is found or not. I will take the trail leading from the forge and try and track him from this end."

The Smith spoke for the first time.

"Take Tanya along, she knows the trail well." Then turning to the partisan, he said, "I understand that if you find him, he and you will not return. In which case, I will clear this site."

This partisan also slung his rifle over his shoulder.

"You do that. We are out of here and returning to our camp. Smith, you are correct, it will safer for you to keep out of things for the time being."

The Smith followed Tanya and the Englishman up the slope.

"The note seemed to upset, you but why? What does it mean?"

The Englishman decided it was impossible to fully explain the enigmatic Barnes.

"It means Smith that we have misjudged his mental state and must look for him."

The Smith pondered for a moment.

"The note said he may be some time. Doesn't that mean that he intends to return?"

"No, smith it means exactly the opposite and that we must find him and quickly."

The Englishman then shook hands with the smith and turned to Tanya.

"Did Barnes take his crutches?" he asked. Tanya nodded.

"How long ago now?"

"About three and a half hours," Tanya replied, pointing out the indentations of Peter's crutches.

The Englishman thought for a few seconds.

"Say two to three kilometres an hour in this terrain maximum in his condition. That will put him about nine kilometres along. Let's hope that Scotty and the partisans are following this same trail.

In which case, they could intercept him within the next hour."

Chapter 94

Colonel Seitz of the S.S. addressed a group of officers in a small, smoke-filled room.

Seitz's face registered his distaste at the smell of tobacco. The offending officers immediately stubbed out their cigarettes. They need not have worried because the S.S. officer was in a good mood. After weeks of vain searching for Lt Barnes, he was in possession of priceless intelligence.

"Pay attention!" He looked around the room.

"You will be given sealed orders, a muster point and a time. You will be in position before opening the orders at the time given. All units will immediately move in on the co-ordinates therein."

He looked at each in turn as he spoke with menace.

"No guesses are to be made as to the purpose of this operation. You will not talk to anyone.

At the second timing, all will move in on the second co-ordinates, fully armed and ready for action. Every instruction is to be followed to the letter."

He looked around the room clearly pleased with his plan which in his opinion could not possibly fail.

"I will not be taking questions. You have your orders. Heil Hitler."

The smith, now alone at the forge, cleared the site of all traces of Peter then resumed his normal activities heating and reshaping pick hoes. Those which were destined for soft ground he quenched in a nearby tank. Others for harder ground, he re-heated the tips and left to cool naturally while he went to check the charcoal pit. Everything seemed fine.

He decided that he could break out the charcoal the following morning.

Stepping out of the pit he was surrounded by German soldiers who appeared in numbers out of the forest. There being no point in trying to escape, he stood and waited while they moved around searching.

A German officer in S.S. uniform appeared up the slope from the direction of the forge.

He marched up to the officer in charge.

"Nothing down at the forge, anything up here?"

"Nothing so far, sir," came the stiff reply accompanied by a click of the heels.

"Keep searching." The S.S. officer ordered turning and marching to the lean-to shed.

He stood over the leg-strengthening frame tapping it with his swagger stick.

He returned to face the smith who had not moved and was standing against the charcoal pit.

"Where is he?"

"Who?"

The S.S. officer strode around the pit. "You know who," he replied clicking his fingers at a nearby soldier pointing to his sub machine gun which the soldier handed over.

"What is this?" he asked the smith, indicating the cone with the gun barrel.

"Charcoal, it is needed for the forge," replied the smith looking the S.S. man up and down fully aware that this situation could have only one ending. He was trying to control his mind, forcing himself to think clearly. He was determined not to back off or show any fear.

"You're sure this contains charcoal?" The officer looked across the pit at this huge man who didn't seem to be intimidated by his presence.

The smith nodded. "I'm sure."

The officer squeezed the trigger firing several rounds into the cone which burst into flame, collapsing into the pit. Bullets passed within inches of the smith who did not flinch.

This annoyed the officer who then looked up and with a forced smile said, "It seems you are correct."

The smith didn't reply immediately but looked into the officer's eyes.

He smiled at the officer, who returned the smile. Neither spoke for several seconds.

Neither blinked. When the smith finally spoke, he made no attempt to disguise the contempt he felt for this pompous little man.

"You didn't need to do that. That charcoal has been rendered useless."

The smith stiffened all his muscles for the expected reaction. His wish was duly granted. The S.S. officer returned the smile which was hovering on the smith's lips as he replied, "I shouldn't worry, you will not be needing it." His smile broadened as he emptied the remainder of the magazine into the smith. He walked around the pit in silence as the searching soldiers froze in shock. Seitz, with his boot, pushed the smith's body, head downwards into the burning pit.

"Wreck this place; tear it apart," he screamed hurling the sub machine gun back at the soldier. He Turned on his heels and walked stiffly down the slope.

The officer in charge watched him go until he disappeared into the trees disguising his thoughts of just how Colonel Seitz would explain yet another failure to the high command.

He turned to his men.

"Continue to search into the forest, but stay in sight of your colleagues. No one is to go further than two hundred metres into the trees."

The smell of the burning body in the pit reached him as he spoke. He coughed and turned to his sergeant.

"Remove that body from the fire now."

The smith's body lay face down among the burning charcoal and broken clay. His long black hair and beard curled back to a crust in the heat in a blue haze giving off an acrid smell.

The officer then turned to his subaltern who was still frozen with a 'why' look on his face and resisted saying that this execution was the S.S.'s idea of being kind, snapping at him.

"Move lieutenant, get the search of the trees organised."

Chapter 95

Tanya stopped at the bank of a stream and pointed out the clear indentations of Peter's crutches. then ground out the marks with her heel before striding across.

Apart from here and the paths around the camp, Peter's trail was not obvious.

Under the trees, a carpet of pine needles did not register his passage.

"We are on the right track," she announced.

They had travelled less than a kilometre in the last half hour when they arrived at a fork in the trail. The Englishman sat with his back to a tree while Tanya searched for signs as to which track Peter had taken.

She kept control of her emotions as she searched along the up fork, anxious to find Peter before he did something silly.

After thirty or so metres she decided that there was no evidence of him taking the up track and returned to the Englishman.

The sharp crackle of a machine gun echoed from back up the trail, shortly followed by a longer burst.

The Englishman sprang to his feet. Both froze as the echoes of gunfire were replaced by the cries of startled birds. Tanya gathered her wits first and went to her companion.

"That was from the forge," she whispered.

The Englishman placed a hand on her arm.

"Can't be anywhere else. We've had a lucky escape, it seems."

"The smith," gasped Tanya and collapsed on to her knees.

The Englishman's head dropped for a second, he then looked up sharply.

"There must be a traitor in the camp."

He took Tanya's outstretched hand and hauled her to her feet.

"Barnes has escaped yet again which makes him even more valuable. We must find him."

"What about the smith?"

The Englishman shrugged. "Another casualty of this bloody war and think on this, we and Barnes would be goners but for his absconding. He seems to have an 'inbuilt antennae', aware for the moment to move."

An hour and half later and kilometres further down the track accompanied by countless breathless muttered 'bloody Houdini' and 'arrogant little swine' they were stopped in their tracks by the yakking call of a dog fox.

The Englishman answered with a like call; further answering calls immediately seemed to echo this.

"The forest is full of foxes. They must have found Barnes. Question is, alive or dead?" He sat down to rest. Tanya joined him and after a few moments' thought, she said, "He would hardly travel all that way to kill himself. If that was his intent, we would have found him some time ago."

Chapter 96

After Tanya had left him that morning, Peter sat for a long time with his head in his hands confused, embarrassed and wishing to die. He could see no way forward. They, whoever 'they' were, were going to move him on shortly. Taking a pencil and a piece of paper, he scribbled a quick note to Tanya.

In a strange way this amused him and made him feel better.

Whether or not at that point he really did intend to take off, he didn't know. He picked up the note and began to screw it up, then stopped and thought for a moment before throwing it back on to the table. Drinking the mug of cold coffee, he picked up his crutches and set off out of the camp.

At first the track was level and clear. He was able to move freely. He flew along revelling with the wind in his face and the sense of freedom. It was that feeling of self he had not felt since leaving the POW camp last autumn.

Entering the forest, the track was no longer level and the going became more and more difficult.

The pine needles on level ground cushioned the jar of his crutches. On uneven stretches they reduced the purchase and he slid about dangerously.

Struggling to move along the rough track took its toll on his strength and sliding to the floor, he sat trying to rethink what he was doing.

He didn't have a plan to know where he was going. The only thing he was certain of was that he would not return. Try as he may he could not think clearly. Around and around in his head the phrase 'I must escape,' returned.

He began to repeat the words out loud as if to drown out the only logical course of action open, which was to return. Out here the only certainty was death or capture.

Slowly, he formed a plan of action. This plan was to mirror the method the used when carrying him only weeks ago. This was to proceed two hundred metres stop, rest, and repeat.

For how long and to what purpose or destination seemed not to matter.

The effort and concentration eased his anxiety.

This routine, therapeutic in the beginning, began to drain his strength.

He came to a fork in the track and he took the lower route. He was overtaken by a need to find a less arduous track; a change of scene, perhaps a clearing with grass and flowers.

Somewhere away from the darkness, somewhere where he could see an expanse of sky.

He was in pretence that this was a logical plan. After about a kilometre the gradient downwards increased sharply. He lost balance pitching forward on to his face.

The fall winded him and he lay moaning in frustration until he lost consciousness.

He lay there drifting in and out of a weird, oppressive world. He was hallucinating that he was a bird fluttering trying to get away from an enormous black cat. At each attempt to escape more feathers were torn from his tail until he was surrounded by clouds of them drifting about his person obscuring his view.

It was there the partisan scout found him. He cupped his hands and imitated the cry of a startled dog fox. The scout sat alongside Peter, his back to a tree and his rifle across his knees and waited. Every minute or so he put his fingers in his mouth and issued a piercing whistle.

Other members of the search party gradually appeared out from the trees and lined the track squatting or sitting.

From among them a tall, angular figure strolled up the track, his rifle casually held by the muzzle and lodged on his right shoulder. He arrived and stood over Peter.

"So here you are! You ungrateful, little turd," he muttered and kneeling on one knee left his rifle on the ground. He turned Peter over. What he saw dissipated his anger.

"You poor, wee sod. I guess you are not yet fit to join in with the Gay Gordons.

I've scraped better than you off my shoe when walking the streets of Coatbridge."

He handed his rifle to the nearest partisan, Peter's crutches to another.

Gently and easily he placed Peter across his broad shoulders in a fireman's lift and returned down the track, followed by the partisans.

Chapter 97

Pen left the hospital and headed for Fleet Street to the offices of the United Overseas Press Services. She waited at the commissionaire's desk in the hallway while the commissionaire, resplendent in full dress uniform, was seeing a VIP. to a waiting car. Pen sat back on his desk and peered up the staircase hoping to see Hal even though she was aware that this was unlikely.

"Miss Penelope, what brings you here at this hour?" the commissionaire asked, even though he knew why. Used now to these frequent visits, he smiled knowingly as he moved to his accustomed place behind his desk. He did not sit, in deference to the visitor, acknowledging her connections despite her nurse's uniform.

"Bit of a favour, Ron. Ask Hal to call me, please." Pen placed a friendly hand on his arm and gave him her sweetest smile. "I don't suppose he is around right now?"

"No, Miss Penelope. There's a bit of a flap on and the place is a ghost town. Just a few editors and that's it. I have no idea of the whereabouts of Mr. Steading."

He liked Miss Penelope but was under orders not to give any information to anyone.

This Pen was also aware of, so she gave his arm a little squeeze.

"I understand Ron. Just do your best for me please."

The following night Pen arrived home to find her father alone in the lounge listening to the radio.

"Hi, daddy. Still not talking?" she enquired, sitting down and removing her shoes.

Sir George gave a wan smile. "No Penny, sad to say, but at least I have unfettered access to the wireless. Oh! by the way, 'phone message for you ... Lyons corner house. You know where. You know when."

"Sounds like a cue for a song by Vera Lynn," said Pen going back out into the hallway and shouting through the doorway whilst putting her cloak on the hallstand.

"Was it from Hal?" she asked looking up the stairs expecting Amelia to be up there in her room.

"It was Hal of course. Have you brought him up to date?" Sir George replied with equal volume.

"No, that's why I have asked to meet him." Pen continued to shout up the stairs.

"I just wish I could get in touch with Peter. He would know what to do. If only it were possible."

It was Mim who responded from the top of the stairs appearing in her pyjamas.

"Is Papa Yo coming home Mama Pen?" She leaned over the balustrade.

"Will he be staying, this time?"

Pen shot back into the room and mouthed to her father, 'How does she know?' Then she returned to the bottom of the stairs hesitantly replying, "I don't know Mim, possibly soon. Now back to bed please young lady."

Mim ran back along the landing, spreading her arms in imitation of an aeroplane screaming.

"Yip-yip yippee."

Pen returned to her father her arms spread in amazement eyes wide open mouthing, 'How?'

Sir George began to chuckle. "If Amelia didn't know before, she certainly does now."

Pen who was still standing in the doorway said, "I'm for some cocoa daddy, will you join me?"

"Please," said George who was starved of family moments.

"Good, then we can have a good yarn before bed."

Cocoa in place, father and daughter sat together on the settee. Sir George sighed.

"You know, Penny." He started to say something but didn't finish. He got up and closed the door, it being still slightly ajar. Pen carrying two beakers had only been able to kick it part closed.

"I have never been happier."

"You mean not talking to mummy?" Pen asked, looking quizzical.

"No! I didn't mean that."

"Then why close the door?"

"Well there is that I suppose, not wanting her to know but that isn't all."

"You *are* scared she might start talking to you again?" Pen giggled.

Sir George began to shake trying not to laugh. "No, stop Penny, please. This is serious."

Both tried to control themselves. Pen took a drink of cocoa to hide the smile which was lurking around her mouth only to snigger into the beaker splattering both herself and her father with cocoa. Choking and spluttering, she placed her beaker on the floor. Both fell about laughing.

Sir George's self-control broke resulting in a series of loud guffaws interspaced with shushes though who he was trying to silence was not clear. A modicum of decorum was achieved although not without a great effort. The laughter remained however, bubbling under the surface.

Sir George said, "Seriously, Penny, it is not what you think."

Pen didn't dare to try and respond. Sensibly she allowed her father to continue.

"It's just that everything is now out in the open. No hypocrisy. All out on the mat and ..."

Sir George paused then speaking with feeling and not a little emotion. "It is such a relief."

Pen didn't answer this last statement, this serving to finally sober her.

"I'm on a month's notice. I have no responsibilities, arrive late, and take deliciously long lunches at my club."

"They serve lunches. What about ration books? Yours is still here."

"Least said soonest mended," he replied laying a forefinger alongside his nose.

Although Pen was not familiar with the gesture, she knew precisely what was meant and thought. 'How unfair!'

"Furthermore, I do not defer to Amelia about anything. Life is bliss, sheer bliss."

"If only?" Pen asked, detecting in this last statement a lack of enthusiasm.

"If only Amelia could be happy and join in." Sir George gave his daughter a weak, humourless smile and patted her hand. Suddenly he stood up with exaggerated energy.

Still this is not going to win the war is it, old girl?"

"That's what you say to mummy. I'm your daughter. Remember?" She chided, a little disappointed that the Colonel Blimp, as Auntie Pam calls his pompous outbursts, reappeared.

Still she wished to keep her 'newfound daddy' unsullied.

"Sorry old- err Penny, my love." He stuttered. "Time to hit the hay, what?"

Chapter 98

Meeting with Hal at Lyons Corner House was for Pen a salutary experience on more than one level. Hal was waiting at their usual table for her when she arrived breathless and confused.

She was excited, longing to see him, desperate to talk to him. She had had a difficult morning unable to concentrate rehearsing what to say and how to say it. She had been making mistakes on the ward, forgetful. crossing Sister on more than one occasion. This was not a good idea because she needed permission of leave for an hour at lunchtime.

An uncomfortable standoff existed between Sister and this semi-trained auxiliary who was of the gentry. Both were aware of the other's position respecting the strange demands of this war where these different 'stations' still existed.

What she expected of this meeting was unreal. Pen was behaving like a little girl living a fairy tale. She was full of plans for their future together.

Her first thought was 'I hoped for somewhere less public.'

Hal's greeting was pleasant and polite but to Pen he appeared too formal. Before she could speak, a waitress appeared.

"I am sorry, sir, madame, the supplier has not arrived. Probably 'cos of the raid last night. There's no tea or coffee, if you can call it that. We can offer Oxo or Bovril, reconstituted milk or water."

She stood, pencil poised.

"And lunch? Are you serving lunch?"

"Dried egg omelette with chips or potato cakes. Unless you have points. Also toast and spread."

Hal pulled a face. "Spread! I guess you don't mean butter?"

"No sir, but I'm told it's all right." The waitress looked away avoiding Hal's response.

Clearly, she was used to receiving unwelcome comments.

Hal looked across at Pen and smiled. "Bovril or Oxo?"

Pen wished to talk privately and was irritated by the presence of the waitress. This girl had served them on occasions previously and was, in Pen's mind, showing an unhealthy interest in their affairs. "Bovril," she answered and looked out of the window avoiding even the basic pleasantries.

"Then I guess it's Bovril for two and we will skip lunch, thank you." Hal smiled as he answered the waitress who returned the smile over one shoulder as she left. Hal looked at Pen.

"What are you wanting to talk about so urgently?"

"It can wait Hal until that waitress serves the drinks."

Pen waited to reply until the waitress was out of hearing.

"You got away O.K.?" Hal asked aware that Pen was nervous.

"I have officially one hour."

"Officially one hour! What does that mean?" Hal said smiling, trying to relax her, adding, "Will you be able to eat at all?" Hal was aware that he had refused food offered.

"The girls will save me something. Anyway, I am not hungry," Pen replied as the waitress returned with the Bovril. Both waited until she'd left the table then both spoke at once.

"Why the urgency?" asked Hal. At the same time Pen announced, "I have told daddy and Amelia."

Pen's statement confused Hal.

His response was silence for many seconds.

"Told them what?" he asked eventually.

"About us." Pen's look emphasised her words.

Hal took a little time to register what she had said.

"Everything?"

Pen nodded. Hal let out a low whistle and sat back.

"Jumping Jehoshaphat. What did they say?"

"Daddy is all right. He knew already so did Amelia but she ..."

Pen shrugged her shoulders and looked pained.

Hal reached out and took her hand and asked, "Why?" Meaning why did you confess.

"You have not fallen out with your mother I hope."

"I haven't," Pen replied emphasising the 'I'.

Hal nodded. “But she of course ...” He didn’t finish the thought.

Pen waited anxious to get to the point of marriage but struggled to find the words.

“Also, I’m divorcing Peter.”

Hal’s face registered shock so Pen hastened to add “I am even told I can even get my marriage annulled.”

Hal withdrew his hand and jumped to his feet. “**No**!” he exclaimed.

“Sit down please, Hal people are watching,” Pen whispered.

Hal sat down shaking his head then stood up again and walked around the back of the chair waving his palm at Pen as if trying to erase the last minute.

The waitress and a colleague suspended service and watched from the shadows, as did others from their tables. All eyes were upon them.

Pen searched her mind what to do. This was not working out the way she had hoped.

“Steady Hal, sit down, please,” she whispered.

Hal sat down again shaking his head. “This is so unfair.”

“What is unfair, Hal? Being in love yet not free to marry?”

Hal thought for a moment before answering.

“We’ll talk about this another time, but I guess I won’t change my mind.”

“We can’t possibly talk here, and I must get back.” She paused before suggesting, “What say Mini Ha Ha Bridge at three p.m. next Sunday?”

Hal, aware of all the attention, nodded. At least they would have privacy and he would have time to think.

Pen stood up looking at her watch.

“I must go, darling. Please don’t be sad. It is the truth. Think about it.”

Hal just nodded. The diners and the waitresses watched as Pen left.

All eyes then turned back to the lonely figure sat at the table.

Hal was still sitting there when the waitress came to collect the untouched cups.

"You finished, sir?"

Hal nodded.

"Well, there's a pity," she said as she left the bill on the table, "and you barely started."

Chapter 99

Sunday dawned with blustery winds and sharp showers of hail and sleet scudding across St. Mary Upperford which did not clear all day.

Pen willed the clock around to the appointed time. Sundays or for that matter any days off just now, were not the most pleasant of times. The disturbing memory of her meeting with Hal hung around her waking thoughts and throughout each broken night.

Pen arrived at the bridge early. When she turned off the lane into the cricket field, she could see Hal there waiting. She broke into a run, willing Hal to turn around and acknowledge her as she waved, leaving go of her coat which flapped wildly in the wind gusting down the river.

Her skirt was plastered back against her legs and the wet grass caused to her slide to a standstill and grasp the handrail in shock.

Hal stood looking down at the bouncing spray-flecked waters seemingly indifferent to Pen's arrival. He was impervious to the weather nor did he react when she took his arm.

All the words, everything she had planned to say stuck in her throat.

She released Hal's arm and stood in silence, the wind tearing at her clothes and hair.

"We can't do it Pen." Hal finally broke his silence.

"Why not, Hal? What would be different?"

"This is Peter we are talking about, remember?" He turned at long last to face her.

Encouraged by this, she took hold of him.

"Isn't it more honest to acknowledge our relationship. Accept the truth. Tell the truth?" She remembered at least part of her rehearsed speech.

The look he gave her conveyed the pain he felt, his face streaked with rain.

"Peter is in desperate circumstances and unable to speak for himself."

"I have tried to contact him, but it is hopeless," Pen countered.

"Then we wait."

Hal's rapier-like responses were hurting.

"Peter left me and walked out to make space for us. Remember?"

"We still wait," came the stubborn rejoinder.

Hal felt in his pocket and passed Pen a paper.

"What is this?" she asked sounding just like her mother. Her fears of what it contained scrambled her thoughts causing her to sound curt and dismissive.

"Read it, please. It is my draft article for *The Post*."

Pen held the paper which was difficult to read being wet and flapping in the wind. She managed to read. 'Your correspondent has been involved in reporting the conflict with Nazi Germany. Now dear old Uncle Sam has decreed that it is necessary to formalise this''

The wind gusted tearing at the now damp paper. It broke free from Pen's grasp and flew down on to the water to be swept away down river.

Pen looked up at Hal. "What does it mean?"

"What it says," Hal answered. "I am being drafted into the Army Press Corps."

Pen was stunned. "Are you going to appeal?" she asked before realising the truth and adding in shock, "you've volunteered, haven't you?"

"I am finished with dodging issues."

"Isn't that exactly what you are doing now? Dodging the issue?"

"Our being married is not the issue now, Pen. Protocol ***is***, to say little of propriety on all counts."

His jaw set, he added, "We wait." Hal pushed his hair back from his face and turned around to face the wind.

"You are sounding so pompous and self-righteous as if you belong in this little backwater of, of ..." She hesitated, adding "of nosey intrusive biddies." The wind and rain carried her voice way from Hal. It was as though everyone even the elements were conspiring against her.

She began to cry in her frustration. Hal took her by the arms trying to pull her towards him.

Pen pushed him away and turned her back. Hal bent down and spoke directly into her ear.

"I love you and want to be married but if we do so now, that marriage will always be tainted.

We don't want that. Please try and understand."

Pen didn't answer but stood buffeted by a violent gust accompanied by a scudding heavy shower. She stood quietly sobbing.

Hal again took her arm. "Come, I will see you home."

Pen shook Hal's hands away. "Go, just GO," she said through clenched teeth.

Hal stood behind her shielding her from the wind and tried to take her in his arms once more only to be shrugged away yet again. Hal kissed her hair then turned away and crossed over to the lane towards the Green stopping twice to look back wondering, whether or not, it would be better to let everything go. Finally, he decided that his presence was too much of an aggravation.

They both needed time to think.

He turned up his collar as he hurried towards the Green and the bus shelter.

Chapter 100

Sir George was fast asleep in his favourite armchair after lunch. The *Sunday Times* was covering his face. The headline, AFRIKA CORPS FORCED BACK TO THE TUNISIAN BORDER trembled violently under a barrage of snores.

Mim, looking for something to do on a wet Sunday afternoon, walked in on this 'desolate for a child' scene. She let out an exaggerated sigh, loud enough she hoped to awaken Grandad Thompson, but to no avail. Climbing on to the settee in the bay window she looked out on to the garden and began to hum loudly. When this didn't work either she let out an even louder sigh, again to no avail.

Looking out on to the covered paved front terrace she watched the wind bouncing the border's daffodils and noticed that a vortex had marshalled last year's leaves into a skittering whirlpool.

She imagined these to be a circle of mice doing a conga. It was then that Mim looked up to see Hal crossing the Green towards the bus shelter.

She began to scream. "Papa Yo, Papa Yo, I'm here," as she hammered on the window with the palms of her hands.

Sir George was catapulted into consciousness. He was spluttering and waving his arms like a drowning man surfacing for the third time. "What, what?" He looked around for the source of this disturbance. Mim continued to scream and shout and hammer on the window.

"Mim sweetheart, don't do that you will wake Grandma." He pleaded in vain.

"Stop him, please Grandad. Stop Papa Yo from leaving. He promised." Mim squealed.

Sir George's brain was still recovering from the shock. He was having great difficulty in coming to terms with Mim's world. He decided that he needed help to sort this.

"Where's Mama Pen, Mim?"

"She went out to meet Papa Yo. Stop him Grandad, please."

Mim continued to pull on Sir George's sleeve.

"Where did Mama Pen go?" he asked hurrying into the hall and collecting his hat and coat from the hallstand, his brain finally taking in that some sort of mini crisis was afoot.

"Stop him, please Grandad." Mim had thrown open the door and was pointing down the Green after Steading who was walking towards the bus shelter.

Sir George lifted Mim out of his way as the gusting wind blew down the hall and removed his hat. He thought to himself, 'Steading leaving for the bus. That is a good sign'.

Meanwhile he tried to reassure Mim.

"Wait here sweetheart, Mama Pen and I will do something. I promise."

What they would do he had not the first idea as he stepped hatless out into the wind and rain.

He had enough information from Mim's reaction to know that Steading had come from the cricket field. 'The pavilion,' he muttered to himself as he struggled to fasten his coat in the wind and at the same time open and close the side gate into the lane.

He reached the pavilion to find no sign of Pen or of them being there. Before he could start to worry, he spotted her tiny figure leaning over the footbridge rail. He began to run across the field towards her. His coat, still not fastened, was flapping in the wind.

Fortunately, because of the weather, none of the villagers were there to witness Sir George's version of a sprint which had more resemblance to a fat man riding a trotting seaside donkey than any sprinter. He bounded and bobbled to arrive with barely enough breath to gasp.

"Penny my love, what on earth are you doing out here?"

This he managed leaving out the intended 'in this ghastly weather,' because of shortage of breath.

Pen turned from the rail and threw her arms around Sir George.

"Oh, Daddy! I have made a mess of everything," she cried as another blustery shower drowned out her words adding to Sir George's utter confusion.

"We can't talk here," he shouted trying vainly to wipe the tears and rain from his daughter's eyes adding, "come over to the pavilion then we can talk."

Placing his arm around her waist he propelled Pen across the field and on to the pavilion veranda which provided some shelter from the elements.

Sweeping the debris from one of the forms he sat Pen down with himself to the windward side and turned her face towards his. "Now Penny, from the beginning, please?"

"He won't. He just refuses." She sobbed.

"Won't what?"

"Marry me. He wants to wait." Pen gasped in reply.

Sir George was by now coming to some sort of understanding, sufficiently for him to feel a glow of satisfaction at this news. With a degree of self-control, he nodded gravely.

"Makes sense," he answered taking care not to sound triumphant.

"No, it doesn't Daddy. If he loved me, he would want to."

"But you **are** married. Married to Peter or have you forgotten?"

Pen began to shake in frustration. "I can get a divorce for desertion, but Hal won't hear of it."

Sir George took a moment. Not only did he have an inherent dislike of Americans and all things pertaining, this American was interfering with all their plans and his daughter's marriage.

Worse still, with her inheritance.

Hal Steading did not behave according to type, being quiet, polite and not at all fitting George's impression of a brash American. All this made for a very difficult situation because Penny was clearly deeply in love with him.

He realised this needed a subtle hand. He tried his best but, after all, he was a naval officer not a diplomat. Sir George shuddered against the unpleasant wind and struggled to make a sensible rejoinder. "Did he just storm off?" he asked eventually.

"No. I told him to go and he went," she wailed.

This was all too much for Sir George who could not even turn to Amelia. She would surely know what to do. The wind and rain were not helping. He still needed Pen to help explain things to Mim. He was acutely aware that he had made a promise to his granddaughter.

It was a promise he was determined to keep. What to do, he thought, difficult as it was to even think, let alone talk in the circumstances.

"Let's go to Pamela's. We at least then can talk in comfort," he suggested surprising himself by this obvious solution.

"Why can't we go home? I'd sooner go home," Pen replied without any real conviction.

Home was not the happiest of places. The idea of talking to Pamela did not appeal either.

Pen was aware that Auntie Pammy had this disconcerting habit of forcing her to acknowledge the truth.

"Trouble is Penny," Sir George confessed, "I promised Mim that when we got back, that you and I would explain everything. She will be waiting for us right now."

"Explain what?" Pen was confused.

"Why Steading didn't call and went back to town."

"She saw him?"

"Yes, crossing the Green. She got upset and began calling to him with that silly name, Papa Yo or something. She also said that HE promised her."

"I did say Hal might be coming but I didn't promise." Pen was now getting upset about Mim and her promise.

"No Pen. Mim said ***he*** promised. Do you know what she means?"

Pen thought for a moment. "No, but Dorothy might."

"Then it's to Pamela's next and we'd best go around the back way. Mim will be looking out for us."

Pamela was furiously beating a bowl of eggs in the kitchen when they knocked on the back door. "Get the door please, Pet. That will be Sully with the pheasant and my hands are all messy."

Dorothy, who was reading a recipe from Mrs Beaton at the table went to the door and ushered in the bedraggled cold and wet Sir George and Pen.

"Good grief, you look like a pair of drowned rats. What on earth is the matter?" Dorothy exclaimed. Pamela almost threw the mixing bowl on to the table as she wiped her hands and passed them both a kitchen towel.

"Don't panic. Nothing serious," said Sir George wiping his face.

"We just want to talk please, Nanny Pam," Pen added pushing wet hair away from her face.

Pamela analysed the problem with near accuracy within a split second.

"Oh! I see. Just to talk. What say you get out of those wet things before you catch your death?"

Then turning to Dorothy, she said "I think we'd best light the lounge fire. What say you Pet? Sir George, why don't you give Dorothy a hand."

Pam waited for Dorothy and Sir George to leave the room which they did at once.

Sir George was pleased to hand over responsibility.

Pam then looked to Pen.

"Sit yourself down, Pet. I think a cup of hot Bovril for you, young lady?"

Beef tea would not have been Pen's first choice right now, but as Nanny Pam was clearly not taking any prisoners, she just nodded.

Pam filled the kettle before returning to beat the eggs.

She made a conscious decision to do so, in order to appear to be in control, while she discovered the crux of the present crisis.

"Now Pet, in your own time and with as little emotion as you can muster," Pam said beating rhythmically at the bowl of eggs.

Pen finally got to the point where she told Hal to go and he did go.

The kettle had boiled, and the Bovril was in Pen's hands.

She was grateful for the warmth seeping through her wet gloves into her body.

Pam stopped beating. "Hal went when you told him to, did he?"

Pen nodded clinging even more tightly on to the hot mug.

Pam picked up the bowl and began to beat once more. "What was it you expected him to do then Pet?" she asked ceasing the beating and looking questioningly at Pen.

Pen didn't reply but her resentful look said it all.

"Well?" said Pam insisting on an answer whisk held motionless above the bowl as if to emphasise the question.

Pen pouted. "Well not to go. *Not just like that.*"

Pam once more began to beat the eggs which now seemed to have become a central prop to her strategy. "Love is patient, love is kind ..." She began.

"Please no ... NO." Don't start preaching to me now." Pen almost screamed.

Pam placed the bowl on the table and drew a chair up to Pen.

"Drink your Bovril, Pet." She paused and smiled placing a finger gently under Pen's chin and lifted her head which was almost buried in her chest.

"Would you be so good as to answer a couple of questions, Pet?"

Pen nodded and drank some Bovril as asked. The warmth spread into her small frame.

Despite her original opposition to Pam's questioning she was comforted that her former nanny and now mentor, was taking charge.

"What do you think Peter would say? What do you think that he would advise?"

Pen put down her Bovril and spread her arms wide and pumped them for emphasis.

"It was Peter who walked out."

She was interrupted by Pam raising her forefinger to silence her.

"That is no longer the question. What would he think the reaction of the village gossips would be or for that matter the whole village, your family and friends would be?"

"Peter understood, he always did, always will." Pen was not going to give in easily.

"Yes, Peter always did understand but that also is not the question. Which is, who else would?"

She paused.

"Anyone?" Pam paused yet again before asking,"what sort of a marriage would you have in those circumstances?"

Pen's mouth began to open and close like a fish out of water.

Pam stood and made another cup of hot Bovril.

"I'd best take a hot drink to your father before he catches his death."

She got as far as the door then stopped as if she had just thought of another question.

"Do you think that might be why Hal wishes to wait?"

Pam raised her eyebrows to Pen before leaving and closing the door.

The fire had already caught. Sir George was bending forward trying to warm his hands when Pam passed him the hot drink.

"Thank you, Pam, I'm beginning to feel better already. How's it going with Penny?"

"I'm glad you are here. I have a question which you might be able to answer."

Pamela ignored George's question, speaking casually as if there was no crisis.

"Well of course, if I can."

Sir George was surprised by the change of emphasis.

"I went to Sully this morning to try and get a rabbit for the Sunday lunch, but he didn't have one. He sold me some eggs and offered to let me have a pheasant but not before next Thursday, which is a bit late for Sunday lunch. So, it's omelettes for us today. These eggs, however, are only about half size. I suppose they will be all right to use?"

Sir George had stiffened when he heard Pam mention the pheasant.

"A pheasant you say, who is this chap Sully?" Sir George pretended not to know of him.

"Just a useful contact," Pam answered, "I suppose you still have yours."

"Maybe. I think Bendesbury would be interested to learn about your Mr. Sully."

"I rather think Sir George, Lord Bendesbury knows all about him." Pamela smiled almost winking letting Sir George know she was aware of his little charade.

"Perhaps you will come and check these eggs for me."

She turned back towards the kitchen. Sir George following as bid.

Pam showed Sir George the eggshells, watched by a surprised Pen who was wondering what was going on.

"Just as I thought. They are pheasants' eggs. Bendesbury will be furious."

Pamela enjoyed playing on her former employer's indignation.

"Sully says they are not viable, the birds being fooled by the early warm spell."

"And I suppose the pheasant had dropped dead from shock when it turned cold."

Sir George caught Pamela's smile.

"You are having me on, aren't you?" he said relaxing and returning her smile.

Pen interrupted the discussion.

"Daddy, Nanny Pam," she said plaintively, as if to say. 'I am still here.'

"Of course, Pet." Pam responded. "Sorry, Pet. Your father and I both think that you should write to Henry Steading. Tell him that you will wait for him, however long that it takes."

Pen's mouth dropped open. She had no words.

At this same time Sir George felt Pam nudge him rather forcibly.

Playing bumps-a-daisy, with a former nanny was not Sir George's idea of decorum.

It took several seconds for him to respond.

"Oh! My word, yes, er. Steading will need your support now that he's been, er, called up,"

Sir George replied dutifully. He turned to Pamela intending to bring up Mim's question.

"There is another problem," he began, only to be interrupted.

"Not just now Sir George. Why don't you ask Dorothy if she can help?"

Pamela signalled that she wished to be left alone with Pen.

Only months ago, he would have had apoplexy at being so dismissed. His life had taken so many blows and fall backs. 'Colonel Blimp' had finally been deflated. He no longer cared.

In fact, he was already enjoying the tranquillity of a non-entity. Sir George obediently left.

Pamela waited for him to leave before going to Pen and taking her into her arms.

She didn't speak. Pam just held her until her sobs subsided.

She gave Pen a large white handkerchief which she magically produced from her apron pocket.

"Oh! Nanny Pam, please don't think that I am fool."

Pen dabbed her eyes then added, not in any manner that was accusing, "You did tell me to follow my heart."

"Heart and head are all too often uneasy bedfellows. At no time did I say that following your heart would be pain free."

Pen blew her nose. "I can wait," she nodded. "I promise."

Pamela somehow had managed this difficult situation perfectly. She was pleased, proud and more than a little surprised.

"Once you are home, write to your man and tell him and while you are doing so, write to Peter." Pamela, now comfortable in the role, continued, "Your father still has contacts in Whitehall. Give the letter to him and ask him to do the best he can."

"Do you think they can reach Peter?"

"One thing is for certain Pet, they can't if you don't write." Pamela kissed Pen on the forehead and whispered, "If I wanted something this badly, I would put a message in a bottle and throw it into the river rather than sit and weep."

She stood and held out her hand to Pen. Together they went to join the others.

Sir George was in conversation with Dorothy when they entered the room.

"Ready to go, Daddy?" Pen asked.

"I am asking Dorothy if she knows anything about Steading's promise to Mim.

Mim is distraught. She is genuinely upset."

Pamela picked up on this.

"Mim upset? About what?"

"She saw Steading leaving for the bus and insisted that he had made a promise to stay, presumably in St. Mary, but where or who with we have no idea. Mim was adamant. Dorothy seems to think it harks back to when they left Austria. That a contact in Switzerland may know what this is about."

"Or Munich. Her parents perhaps," Dorothy suggested.

Pamela looked at Pen. "Has she said anything to you, Pet?"

Pen shook her head. "No, but she has always looked to Hal to be her father for some reason, never Peter. She calls Hal, Papa Yo. There is clearly a strong bond between them."

"That's the name she called after him today and I for my sins promised to do something, but what? We thought you ladies would perhaps have some ideas." Sir George looked to Pamela, having already asked Dorothy.

Pamela was once more the centre of attention, no longer an afterthought. Even her former employer now turned to her. She searched her mind for the answer to maintain this new status.

"What have we got? A seven-year-old hanging on to a dream, a damaged child so we need to tread carefully," she answered, while thinking to herself 'this won't do Pet. Stating the obvious.'

"Yes," added Sir George. "We still don't know what to say and I did promise Mim."

Pam noticed his distress. "You really do love the child, don't you?"

Sir George nodded.

"And Mim loves you?"

"I hope so," said the old man.

Pam surprised herself by once more dealing with Sir George as she had Peter, Pen, Paul and Mim. Immediately she was embarrassed. Pen saved her blushes by answering for her father.

"Yes, Mim loves her Grandad and trusts him," adding, "as I do."

Sir George was flushed with pleasure at this. To be fair, he had not taken offence at Pamela's familiarity. Pam took strength from these vibes.

"Then I suggest that you tell her the truth as much as you know of it. I suspect she knows more than you anyway. That which she doesn't, she has managed to fill in the gaps by talking to her school friends." Pam paused and looked at each in turn.

"The whole truth. All you know," she added with authority.

"To a seven-year-old?" Pen asked, clearly not convinced.

Sir George nodded. "This will not be easy, but we will try."

He turned to his daughter.

"Nanny Pam is right. No more nonsense. Let's do it."

Not having answers, George decided this would have to do.

Pamela and Dorothy watched father and daughter arm in arm crossing the Green towards their home.

The clouds parted for the briefest of moments bathing the scene in bright gold.

Pamela took Dorothy's arm and squeezed it as they looked to each other and smiled.

Chapter 101

The partisans broke through the tree line and into the sunlight. They moved in small groups in a diagonal line up the steep incline towards a distant peak. Large rocks, outcrops and shrubs strewn across the terrain provided cover as they moved swiftly, picking their way carefully between each cover point. They stopped to catch their breath as they sheltered behind each rock or outcrop.

Travelling as quickly as the terrain would allow, they moved in sequence. Assuring that only one unit was in the open at any time. Peter reached for his crutches and made to stand only to be restrained by Scotty.

"Nay so fast, laddie. We go last."

Peter patronised, despite his military training recognising the logic behind the procedure.

Part of him accepted this logic. This was swamped by his anger. No matter how he strove, all direction along with his destiny, remained in the hands of others.

"When do we go and where to?" he hissed.

"In good time," answered Scotty then realising Peter was angry and needed a reason, added, "We will go last otherwise we would slow everyone following."

This explanation further aggravated Peter.

"You Neanderthal. I am not an idiot. Is all this palaver necessary? The Germans would be mad to venture up here."

Scotty let this anger wash over him.

"I was told that you are an intelligence officer, Lt. Barnes," he replied rolling on to his back enjoying the sun after the gloom of the trees.

He was also enjoying winding up this annoying, conceited little man.

"Then answer this, Scotty. What is the point of this palaver? Why not cross after dark and avoid spotter planes?"

Scotty ignored this question and took another tack. This exchange was helping him to pass the time until they got the signal to move.

"Because I was brought up in Scotland, it doesn't change my blood. I am a Croat to my fingernails.

I think like a Croat." This boast was not as true as he made it sound.

He intended to imply that he understood all that was happening.

Scotty was in the middle of his fourth tour in Yugoslavia although he would never admit it.

He was relieved to be able to interact with someone from his own culture.

Peter would never be the ideal companion but having someone of his own rank with whom to bait and banter was a welcome relief. The last few days had passed better for Peter's presence.

"That is not an answer, Scotty. Whether you consider yourself to be a Scot or a Croat, the question is the same."

Before they could continue the English captain interrupted.

"Follow me when I signal. One station at a time," he ordered before moving up and across to the nearest outcrop.

He waited for the next station to clear before moving on to it. Turning, he signalled to Scotty to move.

Scotty took Peter's crutches in one hand and held out the other to support him up the rocky path. Peter refused his help. He climbed painfully after Scotty up the steep gradient to the first station taking what seemed an age.

"Fucking hell, Peter. This will nay do. Yea'll have to let me carry you."

Peter, sat with his back to the rock nursing his aching leg, did not answer, nor did he react when the captain signalled them on once more.

"Hold this!" Scotty passed Peter one of his crutches then draped him across his shoulders.

Scotty struggled his way to the next station, using Peter's other crutch to help push on upwards.

It was some while before Scotty could regain his breath. Peter was embarrassed by his inabilities and the indignity. His powers of self-determination were nil.

He slumped against the outcrop, in powerless and humiliating silence.

The signal to move came all too soon. Scotty reached out for Peter's hand.

Peter moved away turning his back.

"For fuck's sake, Peter, you've got to help me."

"You can go. I'm staying here."

"Och! Come on laddie, don't be daft. It's suicide to stay."

"Promise," Peter replied. He had had enough. He now wanted out.

Scotty looked at this stubborn somewhat pathetic, ridiculous little man and curbed his temper.

"Look Peter, we are holding everyone up. Are you coming?"

"In a word, no." Peter shuffled a yard further away causing a small avalanche of stones.

Scotty took one hard look at Peter.

"You selfish, little bastard," he whispered through his teeth. Without a backward glance he moved up to the next station where the English captain was waiting.

"What's with Barnes, his leg giving trouble?" asked the captain.

Scotty spat into the dust. "More like his fucking ego Sassy. He refuses to shift. I cannae manage unless he co-operates. That little idiot would have us both down into the trees along with half this mountain."

Peter looked around at the terrain. The beds of rivulet tracks formed by the melting snows snaked down towards a large shrub partly flattened. almost torn from its roots.

He smiled and took up a small stone and tossed it down the slope creating another small avalanche. The English captain watched in disbelief.

"Idiot," he whispered, "why on earth would he do that?" He turned to his colleague.

"Have you been winding him up Scotty? You know he is a head case. How important he is."

"Oh yes, so you keep telling me. All because this pathetic Crumpelstiltskin is spinning gold because he accidentally got up Hitler's nose. Well I've got news for you Sassy. He's getting up my nose and," Scotty raised his rifle and pointed it at Peter, "if he wants a fucking avalanche, I'll give him one."

"That's enough Scotty. I don't know just what's gone on between you two, but I'll deal with him from now on. You Scotty make your way back to camp and that is an order."

"All yours, sir." Scotty replied, leaving immediately, delighted to be free of the responsibility.

The captain watched Scotty out of sight then gingerly made his way back down to Peter and sat alongside him.

"The leg bad, Peter? Do you need a hand?"

Peter didn't answer but pulled his legs up against his butt almost glorying in the pain this caused and dropped his head on to his knees. His whole attitude exuded stubbornness.

"We need to move on. Please." The captain pleaded being aware that an order would not produce the desired co-operation. Peter still did not answer.

The captain searched his mind for the right motivation.

"You do realise that you are making a dangerous situation even more so."

Peter neither moved nor gave any indication of moving.

The captain tried again.

"Are you aware just how many people have, and are, risking their lives to get you out and safe?"

This finally got an answer.

"Did anyone think to ask me if I wanted any of this?" was his sullen retort.

The English captain, if that was really his rank, clearly outranked Scotty and therefore Peter.

He thought hard and long of giving Peter an order to move before deciding not to do so.

"We, none of us asked to be involved, Peter. I was conscripted. Scotty volunteered.

He was safe in a reserved occupation and almost fifty years old, but he volunteered to return to the land of his forebears. I was co-opted into the S.O.E. No one asked me."

The captain waited but there was no response. Peter remained silent and obdurate.

He decided to try and shock Peter into a positive response.

"You could have killed us all when you started that avalanche. You would be surprised how little it takes."

At last, Peter answered.

"That's why we were all dodging from cover to cover in broad daylight to minimise any damage. Scotty thought I couldn't work that one out," he answered barely raising his head.

The English captain, flushed with anger, had great difficulty in controlling his temper.

He thought hard and long before speaking. When he did, he spoke quietly in a manner tinged with amazement.

"The smith gave his life, died to get you here and ***you*** think an insult to your intelligence is important? Is that what you are saying?"

Peter took only seconds to register what the captain had just said.

His head lifted. He turned to face the captain.

"The smith dead?" he asked, clearly shocked.

"The Boche shot him and threw him into the charcoal pit and left him to burn."

The captain was in no mood to spare Peter's feelings.

"God. I am sorry. I had no idea."

"I was going to spare you that, but you are leaving me no other option."

The captain waited for Peter's response. Peter sat silently looking down into the trees.

The captain took a deep breath before continuing.

"In the chaos of this ghastly war I am not important. The smith was not important, nor are you alone of much use. Collectively, we can do something to help bring an end to this conflict. This cannot be just about you. You can and will destroy all our efforts if you so choose."

He paused before adding with emphasis, "And the smith will have died for nothing."

Peter still had not answered. He continued to stare down at the distant trees.

"The German Army cannot break us easily be it the S.S. or whoever. *You* can and without your co-operation *you* will."

The captain extended his hand to Peter who looked at it for what seemed to the Captain an age before it was taken. He helped Peter to his feet.

"Come Lt. Barnes let's join the others."

Chapter 102

The partisan hideaway camp proved to be a natural fortress complete with a series of caves. Some were natural, some dug out in past centuries. A natural fortress, it was protected on three sides by steep cliffs overlooking wide expanses of hillside stretching down some six hundred metres to the tree line. The sole access was the steep angled rough pathway across the eastern approach, only accessible by foot and prone to sudden avalanches.

The partisans had turned potential avalanches into an offensive asset by building several artificially triggered rock piles at strategic points along the slopes.

Peter was housed separately in what was little more than an open fissure giving scant protection from the cold nights. The open face was to the south, protecting him from the coldest winds.

The isolation did not worry him, nor did it concern him that the captain left him to arrange his recovery programme and to take charge of his personal welfare.

The captain was clearly not pleased with Peter's attitude nor the British obsession with him: the using of him as a weapon and totally prepared as he may be to obey orders by the high command. The English captain had all the evidence necessary to assume that this policy was being dictated directly from Whitehall.

This and Peter's attitude did not oblige him, in his judgement, to issue any special favours.

Peter used the days to continue his convalescence and to strengthen his weak leg.

The only movements available were either up or down the slope or to traverse east to west.

He found the going difficult at first having lost one of his crutches probably on the hillside somewhere. Much of the terrain sloped. There was little that was level.

This turned out not to be crucial. He quickly discovered that travelling westwards along towards that cliff was relatively easy where the track sloped downwards. This suited his now shortened right leg. Returning, he needed the steadying use of the remaining crutch.

Sometimes he would return part of the distance by walking backwards using the crutch, but not always successfully.

It was a source of amusement to the partisans.

The concentration on this activity, as with other activities recently, became an obsession.

Food was in short supply. It was issued as daily rations. Peter, not turning up to eat for the first days, was an empty gesture. Food was then brought in by a partisan who was not receptive to Peter's attempts at conversation.

Water was to help yourself from the afternoon's issue of melting snows for drinking and washing. Coffee was an extra and depended on the favour of the possessor. This was not Peter.

Peter, being Peter, he did without.

The days passed without incident. One morning Sparks, the wireless operator, went to the west cliff edge and lowered a rope. Minutes later he hauled it back up with a canvas satchel attached.

He quickly recoiled the rope hurrying back to the captain in his cave and handing it over.

Sparks stood to attention. The captain looked up and smiled.

"At last. At ease, thank you, Sparks. I hope there is something here for you."

The captain thumbed through the contents of several brown envelopes all with O.H.M.S. and two larger ones and one other white envelope.

"No, sorry Sparks."

He looked up at the young man as he spoke. Sparks shrugged, stood to attention and left.

The captain opened the white envelope and read the contents. As he did so he became aware that someone else had entered and was stood by the hessian curtain. Without looking up he answered the unspoken question.

"Sorry Scotty, nothing I'm afraid."

Scotty didn't answer for some seconds, then sprang to attention, then about turned, to leave.

It was an attitude so far removed from his usual casual manner. This set the alarm bells ringing.

"Don't go, Scotty. I may need to talk to you."

Marking time and awaiting mail which came usually with orders was always difficult.

More so when in isolation, as were the three Britons.

The level of expectancy rose as each scheduled delivery of mail approached.

The anticipation triggered when the call came during the night, this message delivered by tape transmission by the weekly plane from Benghazi passing over exchanging taped communications.

The captain knew words of consolation would not be well received. He needed to give Scotty another focus immediately to stop him leaving to brood.

He ripped open one of the two larger envelopes and examined the contents.

"Bloody hell, Scotty these are all for Lt. Barnes."

He perused each envelope in turn.

"One from his wife and three from solicitors."

There was another envelope marked O.H.M.S. addressed to Y.O.S.S. 01c.

"At last Scotty, somebody loves us."

He waved the envelope at Scotty indicating that he also had not received any personal mail.

Scotty sat down and sighed before speaking. Thankfully for the captain, he reassumed his normal informal irreverent manner.

"You can stuff those official buff envelopes. If we ever make it out of here alive Sassy, I shall never ever open another. They are all bad news."

The captain slit open he envelope and read earnestly for several minutes finally looking Scotty straight in the eye whilst taking a small box camera out of the bag placing it on the table.

"Brace yourself, Scotty. We've been ordered to anoint a hero."

He began to fill his pipe. Try as he may he failed to resist shaking his head.

Scotty waited for a follow up, which did not arrive. The captain made a few practice sucks on his pipe then emptied it and refilled it again. Scotty was used now to his ways and knew the captain was stuck for words. Scotty thought and for sought for answers while watching his boss fiddling with his pipe. Then the penny dropped.

"God! You are not referring to that conceited little shit I hope."

"The Military Cross, no less."

Held up by the pin, ribbon and bronze cross, the captain dangled it in front of his colleague then passed over a couple of sheets of typed notes.

Scotty passed them straight back as if they were hot.

"No, leave me out of it Sassy. I want no part of this."

The captain assumed formality.

"Orders Lt. direct from the Prime Minister's office via C.I.G.S. I am to give the citation.

The ceremony is to be photographed. Therefore, I need a photographer and that leaves only you."

He tapped the box camera with his pipe stem.

"Fuck off," Scotty replied as he got up to leave.

"Sit down, Scotty! That is an order. There is to be no discussion."

The captain rarely regretted allowing Scotty's informality in the circumstances.

He needed now to pull rank. He returned the documents to Scotty, slapping them forcibly against his shoulder.

"You will have read this and will have understood the content before I return. I am now going to pay a visit to Lt. Barnes."

Collecting the rest of Peter's mail, he then left leaving Scotty holding the typed script.

Peter was on his back stretching his legs up against the fissure wall when the captain arrived and nodded his approval. It pleased him that Peter was beginning to co-operate.

Peter forced himself upright.

"How's it coming?" asked the captain.

"Pretty well," Peter answered hesitating. "By the way, what do I call you? You clearly outrank Scotty and me that makes you at least a captain but that as much as I know."

The captain didn't answer so Peter continued.

"The Englishman and the English captain are both clumsy and ..."

Peter left the remainder of his question unspoken. Aware that Scotty acknowledged this officer on one level but on another, it was lax to the point of gross familiarity.

He could not use Scotty's term Sassy. Feeling envious of this, he wished somehow to adopt a similar stance. He liked this man and wished to please him, even be friendly.

"Sir, will do," the captain answered, his mind elsewhere. He finally lit his thrice-filled pipe and sat down signalling Peter to join him. He took a puff then wafted away the resultant blue cloud being aware that Peter was a non-smoker.

"There's no easy way to play this," he began wafting away another blue cloud.

"There are letters for you."

Peter sat up straight.

The captain raised his hand as if to stop Peter's thoughts saying, "There is not much good news." He paused and took a few puffs on his pipe.

"I have been asked to judge how much to tell you and when."

Peter stood up then sat back down. What he expected he didn't know.

Hoping to hear about Pen and Hal was maybe part of this.

Before he could gather his thoughts, he spoke his mind.

"Pen's all right, isn't she?" he asked. Then, as if countermanding this question, added, "Just tell me all. I am not a child."

The captain didn't continue for some seconds, so Peter added,"Please sir, what's happened?"

Realising that he had allowed a position to arise where secrets would present a greater danger, he sense that this unfortunate officer might struggle. He, being isolated, vulnerable and on the edge of a massive breakdown. But the captain decided to hold nothing back.

"First off, your father is dead." He waved away another cloud thinking to himself. 'Just how crass was that?'

Peter showed little emotion. "When?"

The captain fiddled with his pipe and forced himself to look Peter in the eye.

"Some little while ago." He cleared his throat. "We have only just been informed."

Peter was silent which made the captain feel even more uncomfortable.

"There's more bad news, I'm afraid." The captain ventured again, clearing his throat, again.

"Your wife is asking for a divorce."

Peter still didn't answer and stared straight ahead apparently still unmoved.

This continued for over a minute and despite clearing his throat yet again the captain still had great difficulty in speaking.

"Look Peter, it's all here in this correspondence. May I suggest you read them in chronological order. Should you wish to talk, or I can help in any way, come to my place."

"What's to talk about?" said Peter not moving a muscle.

"The War Office read all my correspondence and withhold personal information without consideration. My feelings count for nothing."

The captain, lost for words, dropped the letters on to the box serving as a table.

He put his hand on Peter's shoulder and left. He took comfort by the fact that Peter did not shrug him off.

Outside, he stood for a short while breathing deeply in the fresh mountain air trying to wash his thoughts out of his mind and trying not to say them out loud.

'Whatever are Whitehall thinking of? What is this agenda for?' He wished he had someone with whom he could discuss, someone with whom he could let off some steam. It was the unfairness of the random bullet paling into insignificance by the insidious intrigue of the powers that be.

His thoughts were shattered by Scotty.

"Is this true, sir?" he said holding out the papers.

The captain stared down into the forest and nodded. Scotty whistled.

"That weedy ...?" He shook his head. "When I first saw him, he couldn't hold his own water.

How the hell did he hold up a German column single handed?"

"It's true, Scotty, you read the citation. Everything has been corroborated independently."

"I bet he's real smug and can't wait to crow."

The pair looked down into the distance together as if searching for a missing answer.

"I haven't told him yet." The captain broke a long silence.

"Why not?"

The captain scraped around his pipe bowl with a penknife and tapped the residue out on the heel of his boot and began to refill it and didn't answer.

"He couldn't have Sassy. He's a wreck."

Still the captain didn't answer. "I mean, can you believe it?" Scotty persisted.

The captain took a few practice sucks and re-lit his pipe and took a few puffs.

Scotty stared at him willing him to answer. Eventually he did.

"We know he has escaped the Bosch on more than one occasion, so he's no fool.

In addition, according to legend, he survived toxaemia, a badly broken leg and spent months incarcerated in a nine by six cheese store." He turned at last to face Scotty.

"Now I've had to tell him his father is dead and his wife is asking for a divorce."

The captain took a few more puffs on his pipe.

"Just think, Scotty. How many chaps would stand up to this?"

He paused again before adding, "I didn't tell him about the citation Scotty because it didn't seem to be the right moment."

Neither spoke for quite some time until Scotty whispered, "I would have gone scatty."

The captain removed his pipe and gave his colleague a meaningful look.

"I reckon he has Scotty. I reckon he has." The captain turned on his heels and left.

Chapter 103

The following day Peter paid his first call on the captain asking for writing materials and asked if it was possible to send letters.

The captain searched and provided Peter with a pencil and three sheets of writing paper and one official looking buff envelope. The captain asked no questions and said nothing beyond saying:

"All returns come through me."

He didn't enter into any further conversation. He debated in his mind, whether or not this was the right time to mention the award of the Military Cross. He was thinking perhaps, that the plethora of bad news and the freshness of disappointments would swamp its effect. Maybe, given the state of his mind, it could cause an adverse reaction. Once more he decided to leave it.

The captain was hovering between sympathy and irritation with this disturbed little man, having already decided it was better to keep this association on a strictly professional level.

Twenty-four hours later, Peter still hadn't written the answer to Pen's letter. He was struggling to find the right words and was down to his last usable sheet of writing paper.

Leaving this emotional turmoil behind, he concentrated on recovering his mobility focusing on leg strengthening and travelling east to west and back across the escarpment.

This was to the entertainment, jeers and cheers of the assembled partisans, all of which he ignored.

It was a beautiful afternoon with bright sunshine and very little wind, other than that created by the updraft from the warming escarpment counteracting the downdraft from the peaks.

Everyone was outside. A casual observer may have thought that the sunshine was the draw.

Sharper minds would have noted that all eyes were frequently drawn away from Peter's efforts to the western horizon.

The captain and the partisan leader sat together on one of the level patches of grass dotted around the barren landscape.

Scotty and Sparks were sitting on a rock a short distance away.

Sparks was the first to stand and shield his eyes looking towards the south west.

Scotty, the captain and the partisan leader followed suit.

Sparks went over to man his wireless transmission unit.

All was silent but for the sound of Peter's boots and crutch as he fought his way across towards the west cliff. The absence of cat calls and jeers caused Peter to stop.

He looked around for the reason and then to the south west where the rest were looking.

A moving dot, in the distance, which could have been mistaken for a bird, was the centre of attention.

This dot gradually took shape accompanied by the hum of the engines.

Peter expected to take cover but no one else moved. This aroused his interest.

He looked closer at the plane. It did not resemble a war plane.

It was a two engine over wing monoplane of the type which was familiar to the Greek islands and the Aegean as an island hopper.

The plane finally arrived over the west cliff then banked around climbing at an angle up the hillside over the assembled crowd.

The plane released three dark objects from beneath the fuselage. Immediately, they were steadied by small parachutes.

Peter sank to the ground and watched, noting that no one moved until the objects hit, bounced and slid to a standstill. All but Peter and Sparks ran to stabilise the packages.

Sparks pressed the transmission button on the tape unit. The punched tape immediately transmitted over one thousand words of the captain's weekly report in less than ten seconds.

Within minutes, Peter was left alone in the open watching the plane disappear into the distant empty sky.

He shook off a feeling of loss by smacking his stick at the rock alongside then forced his mind to evaluate what was happening.

This made sense to Peter once he had thought about it. He quickly worked out what and why. Somehow this event served to make Peter feel even more isolated, if that was possible.

He sat thinking, unwilling to resume his obsessive journeying.

The arrival of the obvious, be it tobacco, coffee or whatever, meant nothing, beyond emphasising his isolation. He was the only one among so many who was denied the excitement of the day.

In the captain's quarters Scotty was incensed; barely stopping short of mutiny.

He was arguing with his superior officer.

"What a fucking pantomime. We, the sitting ducks, are not allowed to take flight.

We are ordered to dress up and perform this farce. Do you really expect me to inform that tiny twat of this load of bollocks?"

He indicated two officers' dress uniforms hanging behind the captain.

"Are you going to accept this while Gerry is probably preparing this very moment to bomb the shit out of us?"

"SOE has asked us to move within 24 hours which suggests an attack is not imminent. That gives us time Scotty. Are you sure you are not just arguing against the ceremony?"

The captain kept his composure.

"Why wait at all? One bomb anywhere near and we could be buried alive, Sassy. I say we move now." Scotty paced the floor pushing his hair from his eyes then returned and placed his hands on the captain's table and stared into his face.

"Och! Sassy please, let's be away. Now."

The captain, silent and thoughtful, allowed Scotty's storm to blow out before lighting his pipe and waving away the smoke, as if to dispel Scotty's objections.

"We have to wait until dark, Scotty. We can't risk moving in daylight now that the Boche know our whereabouts. Just do it for me Scotty." He paused. "Please."

He was aware that giving an order would be necessary for him to act according to the book.

Equally he was aware that the authors of the book probably had never worn the 'boots of espionage' for a fourth tour behind enemy lines where capture meant more than incarceration and a probable worse death than that of facing a firing squad.

This was Scotty, a dedicated courageous, reliable friend, trusted in all circumstances.

The captain watched as Scotty paced the small cave. He allowed him all the time he needed.

"Please, Scotty. He has to be told."

Scotty, also aware the captain could give him an order, sighed and shuffled sloppily to attention, turned and left.

Peter was still sat in the same spot on the escarpment staring into the distance.

Scotty arrived and just sat next to him. For several minutes neither spoke.

Scotty eventually took a tin of cigarettes from his pocket and offered one to Peter who just stared at him disbelieving. Scotty shrugged, took one for himself and lit it.

"Is it true you held up a Gerry-motorised column single handed for two hours?"

Peter froze solid, giving the appearance of someone turned to stone. He didn't answer.

Nearly three years had passed. This was history. It now seemed unreal.

Inside his head he was having difficulty with coming to terms with his own memories.

He had difficulty in even remembering the incident. It seemed so long ago.

It was part of a distant dream that he now struggled to piece together.

Furthermore, he couldn't understand just how Scotty knew of this, or anyone else for that matter.

"I can't believe it possible, so I am not surprised you don't have an answer," Scotty said flicking his cigarette down the slope as if to cast out the thought.

"I think a narrow bridge and a burning truck had something to do with it."

Peter broke silence, as much talking to himself as answering Scotty.

Scotty turned to Peter. "It says in the citation you alone with a Bren gun held them at bay for two hours allowing time for several units to avoid capture."

This was news to Peter who turned to face Scotty.

"It allowed some units through, did it?"

"You didn't know?"

Peter shook his head, thinking to himself that it was something to hold on to if true.

Scotty now began to realise there was more to this man than he first thought and found it easier to deliver his message.

"I have been asked to tell you that you have been awarded the Military Cross."

"Bollocks," replied Peter both angry and surprised. Disbelieving and thinking that Scotty was winding him up, he resorted to language normally foreign to his nature. No other retort seeming to fit.

Scotty now looked at Peter in a different light.

"I am not kidding, laddie. It's true and the captain is to give the citation. We are to hold the ceremony here on the escarpment and I am to be your photographer."

"You can stuff all that. I want none of this."

Peter struggled to get to his feet and to escape.

Confused, Peter was now certain Scotty was sending him up.

Scotty reached out with a helping hand which was waved away.

Peter shuffled painfully across the terrain at for him a surprising speed. His single crutch created a series of small avalanches. He disappeared into his crevice like a frightened lizard.

Scotty followed watching closely in case he fell, then followed.

"May I sit please?" Scotty asked sitting beside Peter.

Peter irritated, moved away. "I don't think we have anything left to say."

"Maybe not but as I am under orders to take part in your citation, we should discuss."

"You talk as if I accept and that it is to be a formal occasion. How can that be, out here?"

Peter was still thinking that Scotty was sending him up. Part of him recognised the truth behind this, Scotty having no other way to know anything of the event.

"Full dress uniforms were dropped into here by that plane today. They are hanging in the captain's quarters at this very moment to remove any creases."

Scotty's answer sounded bizarre.

Peter scoffed. "Get serious! You will be saying they dropped an electric iron and an electricity supply next."

Scotty realising how this must sound, sharply changed tack.

"I find it hard to believe that you alone could possibly hold up an armed motorised column for two hours."

"I have already told you that a narrow bridge and a burning truck had something to do with that," Peter retorted, not wishing this to continue.

"Still it was still a bloody brave thing to achieve with just a Bren gun. Why not just accept due recognition?"

Peter realised that Scotty was serious and searched his memory, shuddered, then sighed.

"Scotty, I am not disputing what happened. It is not the what. It's the why."

"It was a critical point. That's the why. They needed to be stopped and you stopped them."

Scotty suggested.

"That's not the why," said Peter emphasising the 'why'. He continued his thinking out loud. "Was that bravery, or was I just desperate to leave this world?"

It seemed as if Peter was asking the question of himself. Scotty looked perplexed.

Peter added, "I think I was trying get myself killed. That was probably the why."

He was surprising himself with his recollections which were new and painful.

Peter did not wish to dwell any longer on the subject.

Scotty thought for some seconds before replying.

"Look, laddie, your action maybe was tinged with a desire to cop out. According to the citation, it was innovative, intelligent and brave. I've read the whole paper and what you accomplished. Whatever the reason it was impressive."

He held out his hand. "So, 1700 hrs before sunset. Agreed?"

Peter drew his legs up into his body slewing away from Scotty, placing his hands over his ears.

Scotty stood and looked at Peter for fully ten seconds before mouthing silently at the foetal figure on the bed, words which would have shocked the most liberal of lip readers and left.

"No dice, I'm afraid Sassy." Scotty reported back.

Once Scotty had recounted the whole story the captain went through the motions of his thinking pipe drill.

"What to do then, Scotty? We are under orders to carry this out today, dropping off the camera and photos in the post box. If Barnes won't co-operate, where do we go?"

"There is only one route left, Sassy. A direct order. Tell him to present himself dressed in his monkey suit at 1700 hrs or else face a charge of mutiny."

The captain nodded. "You are right as usual Scotty. That will give him good reason to co-operate which, hopefully, he will."

"Then can we get the fuck out of here?"

"Yes Scotty, but with pre-conditions which will affect you I'm afraid, about which I will tell you later." The captain meanwhile was changing into his dress uniform top and Sam Browne, speaking as he did. "We are splitting the band into three groups with all the latest partisan intake being the last to leave. They are to be sent back home. Sparks and I will be the first and second groups to leave.

We all have different orders and routes. Today's drop included a ten-metre rope ladder.

We will climb down over the west cliff into the clump of larch, which serves as a post office.

We'll leave the camera and photographs there."

The captain buckled on his Sam Browne and turned to Scotty.

"How do I look?"

Scotty retorted. "Who in C.I.G.S. choreographed this palaver and why?"

He didn't wait for an answer before asking another question.

"And you've left out the knobs on bit for me. When do I go?"

"Ah well there's the rub. Barnes will not be able to manage the rope ladder.

Someone will have to take him across 'avalanche alley' at night with all that it entails. Get him to the meeting oak, roadside, before dawn."

The captain reached up and collected the other uniform. Smiling, he slapped Scotty on the shoulder. "Meanwhile I have the more difficult task of changing Barnes's mind."

Without looking round, he left to speak to Peter with these parting orders, "Gather the partisans and assemble them outside. Bring the box camera and be ready for action in thirty minutes."

Peter persuaded/ordered was on parade looking anything but the part of a hero or that of a serving British officer. Unkempt hair and an unruly beard dominated.

The uniform size, diligently researched and checked against Peter's records before despatch, had taken no account of the ravages of the last years. Scotty, waiting to take the photographs, hovered between being furious at being ordered to take part in this pantomime and wanting to laugh.

He was only restrained by the presence of amused partisans.

"It doesn't look very authentic, sir." He addressed the captain who looked smarter and tidier than one would expect in the circumstances.

The captain didn't acknowledge this, ordering Scotty, "Take one from the rear of Barnes showing the western aspect then one from behind me showing the eastern."

“Showing the Germans exactly where we are captain?”

The captain looked at Scotty and nodded adding, “I will skip all the formalities just take the photos as would appear as if so. Then we can pack up and out of here as soon as it is dark enough.”

After all was finished, he replied to Scotty’s earlier comment.

“On the contrary Scotty, the S.S. already know our position therefore it will look authentic.

The German high command will go over the photos with a fine-tooth comb.

This will be a bonus and confirm their intelligence. Peter’s appearance will be more or less as expected. Also, our ability to manage a ceremony in full dress uniform behind their lines will really get up their nose.” He paused and allowed himself to smile, before resuming a serious note.

“How the Bosch found this place is the worrying part. There is possibly a spy in the camp which is why P and I are sending all the latest partisan intake out of the escarpment and back to their homes.”

He stopped outside his cave and added one further set of orders.

“When Sparks has sent the confirmation out, help him pack the essentials then get Barnes and Sparks organised and ready to ship out leaving the generator behind.”

Chapter 104

Nightfall and Scotty peered down the slope of avalanche alley from the escarpment.

Seeing little, he waited for his eyes to adjust to what little light there was.

The cliff jutted out from the mountain like a badly fitted shelf with a drop of a few feet increasing to a much deeper drop at the eastern edge. The southern and western cliffs varyied from thirty feet to one hundred feet.

The night was cloudless in the first quarter of the moon.

This and the stars provided all the light there was. Once his eyes had adjusted, Scotty stepped out and turned to Peter, taking from him his remaining crutch.

"You've got everything you need with you I trust?" Scotty asked, hoisting him on to his shoulders in a fireman's lift.

Peter, after a brief vision of an unfinished letter to Pen, left on the rocky ledge weighted down by the Military Cross. He answered, "Yes."

His weight, almost one hundred and thirty pounds when he was taken from the farm, had dwindled to little over one hundred in the past weeks.

Using Peter's crutch with his right hand Scotty steadied his way down the rough track not stopping at all on this occasion until he reached the tree line, creating a significant number of small avalanches. Scotty and Peter sat trying to recover from the journey. Peter was sore to his ribs.

The downhill jolt had been an ordeal.

Peter was overjoyed to be moving off the barren escarpment where there were few diversions.

There had been little food and only a trickle of water over the last weeks.

Sweating, despite the cold night air, both were dehydrated and very thirsty.

Scotty led the way to a track alongside a mountain beck where they drank their fill of ice-cold water.

"Thank you, Scotty." Peter acknowledged once he recovered.

"That was a big ask for you. I am most grateful."

Scotty looked at Peter almost rudely retorting, so unused as he was to courtesy from Peter.

He threw Peter's crutch to him and turned back down the forest track without comment.

Peter took the point that this was the last of being carried, followed as best he could with just the one crutch. The diligent, obsessive exercise on the escarpment had clearly improved his mobility. Scotty slowed his pace, waiting when necessary and taking account of Peter's struggles.

The harsh climate of the escarpment melted away as they entered the forest gloom.

How far they descended they couldn't tell. The temperature rose steadily as they did.

They arrived at the meeting oak without incident.

Exhausted but exultant that he made the rest of the journey without help, Peter sat under the oak in the darkness. The air was filled with scents of the forest, spring and pine needles.

He flooded with pleasure. A feeling, so strange, he couldn't quite understand.

The warmth of it flowed throughout his body. Exhausted but contented, he lay back counting the pain pulses, throbbing in his leg and fell into the first real sleep since leaving the forge.

Chapter 105

Peter woke to the smell of wood smoke and an awareness that he was in strange company.

He raised himself on one elbow and looked around for Scotty. There was no sign of him ever being there. The cold and barren depravation of yesterday's morning had been replaced by the sweet perfume of springtime. It was as if he had slipped through a curtain into a new world.

The sun was already pleasantly warm. Above in the branches new leaves were unfurling, appearing to have burst forth overnight.

He sat up. In the background a bay horse was grazing on the lush spring grass verge.

Behind this horse stood a cross between a brightly painted gypsy caravan and a covered wagon. This he might have recognised but didn't. An old man was cooking over an open fire, pouring olive oil into a pan into which he sliced some mushrooms or fungi.

Peter fascinated, watched. In no way was he alarmed even though he had no idea who the old man was. The man took a large knife from his belt. Picking up the saucepan, he used this knife to strain water off the boiled rice into a large enamel jug. Once drained, he emptied the rice into the frying pan along with the flesh from two trout which had been roasting on sticks over the fire.

Peter watched as he scraped the flesh from the bones, then put the heads, tails and bones into the same enamel jug into which he had strained the rice water.

"Did you catch the fish yourself?" Peter asked, speaking his thoughts out loud.

The old man looked up and smiled through a tobacco-stained moustache and beard.

"Good morning, young sir." He greeted Peter in English.

Peter was even more certain now that he was in a time slip.

"Not this time," the old man said, answering Peter's question about the trout.

"These were bartered for potatoes, vegetables and sharpening of knives."

He tossed the contents of the pan and returned it to the fire.

Peter, starved of fresh food, watched the preparations with great anticipation.

His hopes rose as the old man emptied the contents of the pan on to two enamel plates, then cutting two chunks of bread from a loaf, joined Peter handing him a share of breakfast, leaving a pan of water on the now vacant fire.

The old man began to eat with his fingers.

Peter, unused to this simple habit, looked down at his hands which were filthy.

He pushed his unruly and matted facial hair from his mouth.

Hungry as he was, his overwhelming emotion was a desperation to wash and shave.

Personal hygiene on the escarpment had been low premium. With little or no water, it was of little consequence. Now, it was paramount.

The old man looked up momentarily then felt into an inside pocket removing a spoon, passing it to Peter without comment. He then resumed his breakfast.

"Thank you," said Peter still hesitating, staring at a gross reflection in the bright spoon.

"You can call me Doc," the old man said spitting rice with his speech.

"Thank you, Doc," replied Peter. He forced the distorted, ugly reflection in the spoon out of his mind and began to eat reverently, perhaps the most delicious breakfast of his life.

The Doc wiped his plate clean with the last of his bread before going to the wagon and returning with tins out of one he spooned several measures into the pan on the fire adding several more from a second.

He stood stroking his moustache and beard into shape before going back to the wagon returning the cans. He stopped to pat Bella on the flank.

He unhooked two enamel mugs from inside the wagon into which he poured the contents of the pan with scant regard to straining out the coffee grounds.

All this, without a word.

Peter had no need to ask what he was doing from the minute the Doc spooned the contents into the pan. The smell of coffee drifting across the morning breeze triggered a host of memories. Memories of childhood, awaking to the smell of coffee, of hurrying downstairs and hoping for acknowledgement from his father.

Richard, sober in the mornings, was approachable, sometimes almost friendly, a mood which dissipated with the passing of the day.

The coffee was surprisingly good given the manner it was brewed.

By the end of that morning Peter was already comfortable with this old man of few words and surprising habits. Awareness of his unkempt hair and lack of personal hygiene was all that was preventing him from lapsing into a state of euphoria.

The packing of the wagon and the harnessing of Bella had been completed without haste and little effort. The mare refused to move until the Doc emptied the strained contents of the jug into a bucket. This Bella cleared before answering the Doc's click of the tongue to amble slowly into the road, heading south.

About noon the Doc took a track through a gap in the forest. This track ran alongside a stream leading to a small clear mountain pool. The Doc leaned back to the inside of the wagon and retrieved a towel. After a little more rummaging, he produced a large tablet of green soap. Giving these to Peter, he offered a hand down before uttering his first words for over an hour.

"I am making a visit and will be back in two hours."

The Doc hoisted himself back on to the wagon and was away with couple of clicks of the tongue. Peter, aware of his body odour, had been sitting as far away as he could from the Doc for the morning's journey. He needed no further instruction.

He quickly undressed and bathed then washed his clothes, laying them on a rock to dry in the sun.

Peter sensing freedom as he lay back in this same sun, smiling at his first reaction as the Doc drove away, which was to run after him and cry 'can I come with you'?

The Doc returned as promised, to find Peter bathed and dressed in newly washed clothes which were steaming from the heat of his body and the sun.

Without a word, he reached down and helped Peter up on to the wagon.

Then he turned back along the track towards the road.

Peter, left alone with his thoughts, had stacked up the questions in his mind.

Having learned from Tanya and the others that questions were generally received with hostility, he kept quiet.

Normally it was his nature not to engage in trivial conversation but these silences in the circumstances, much as Peter trusted this man, were unsettling.

The Doc surprised Peter mid-afternoon by speaking. He had just snorted snuff from the back of his hand and caught Peter's questioning look. He wiped his nose and mouth with a large spotted handkerchief then straightened his moustaches.

"Animals have more sense than humans," he suddenly announced.

"We imbibe foreign matter with ne'er a thought." He sniffed loudly and spat over the side on to the road.

Peter thought to himself, 'what brought that on?' but did not reply.

Nor did the Doc add anything further for fully ten minutes.

In the meantime, Peter's mind drifted in and out of many subjects, confusing himself with a host of unspoken questions.

He cleared his mind and replaced his thoughts by playing a 'game' of who could stay silent the longest.

"Take Bella." The Doc eventually continued his previous comment as if no time had passed at all. "She wouldn't move this morning until she got a share of the fish stock."

Peter, without realising it, had been transported out of his oppressed and imprisoned mind and body into the Doc's strange but tranquil world. He had truly stepped through a 'curtain into another place' on this spring day. He felt compelled to speak.

"Why fish stock?"

The Doc took another pinch of snuff, snorted and repeated his earlier performance, as if to exorcise his actions. Eventually, he answered Peter.

"Who knows, animals seem to. Bella is a grand old lady who will do anything I ask."

He cleared his throat and spat again into the road.

"But if she needs something, she will let me know."

The sound of Bella's hooves on the road, measured and constant, seemed to emphasise the Doc's comment. After several minutes he continued,"Cattle eat mud, dogs, grass. Surely for good reason."

He paused again to take even more snuff in what now was an established ritual.

Doc finished his thought.

"We fill our bodies with rubbish for no sensible reason. Animals don't do that."

He cleared his throat yet again and spat once more into the road.

"Of that I am certain."

That evening the Doc visited yet another farm, leaving Peter alone.

Returning, he removed Bella's harness leaving her to graze before lighting a fire and cooking a stew of meat and vegetables. Peter sat and watched. For the second time in months he was looking forward to a meal, the first meal since breakfast.

Afterwards the Doc stood up and momentarily placed a gentle hand on Peter's head in an obvious gesture of affection. Peter's emotions welled up as he tried and failed to stem the flood of tears. The following days followed this pattern.

This simple routine gently eased the anger from Peter's soul.

At sundown on the fourth day the Doc swung the wagon to the left on to a track which led to a clearing alongside a tree-lined river. After the meal, Peter, now feeling that he was valued for himself, assisted with Bella and the chores. He fitted comfortably into the daily pattern of life.

After the evening meal they were washing the utensils and dishes in the river.

Peter finally asked one of the many unspoken questions.

"Are you really a doctor?"

"Medical college in London, a spell at St Jude's Hospital, then I was a G.P. in Pimlico for ten or more years," the Doc answered as he washed his hands, face and beard in the stream, adding, "It was where I learned to speak English."

This discussion was sharply interrupted by a night jar's call.

The Doc stood up and left without the usual drying and combing of his beard and moustache, saying as he left, "Excuse me, Peter, I have a call of nature."

Peter watched him leave keenly aware that these sudden responses didn't seem natural.

The Doc had claimed a weak bladder as a cause for these sudden disappearances.

The call of the night bird had preceded this excuse on at least one other occasion.

Peter was not fooled.

Ten minutes passed. The Doc had not returned. This being much longer than usual, it unsettled Peter.

He washed and dried the pans and plates returning them to the wagon carrying them in his left hand as he limped across on his crutch to stow them. He stood a while talking to Bella, patting her flanks in the same way as would the Doc.

"What is our dear friend up to old girl?"

He picked up some peel of the turnip used for the meal which the Doc had carefully stored away in a hessian bag, offering this to Bella in an absent-minded gesture.

The mare raised her head, snorted and shook her head. Peter dropped the peel back into the bag.

"Neither do I, old girl. I have good idea who he might be meeting."

The slight tremor in his gut arrived in his voice as the comfort zone of the last few days disappeared. Looking around he imagined danger in every shadow.

The river was bordered to the south by a high grass and shrub-strewn bank. This had been built to prevent river water overflowing into the fields and flooding the farms and small holdings to the south. diverting the river at flood time. The excess water redirected into a substantial drainage ditch away from the culvert where the river flowed under the road and down the rift valley to the Adriatic.

This drainage ditch ran alongside the road to the south with irrigation channels at intervals at right-angles.

This flood bank, the trees and bushes had held them safe from prying eyes.

The bank and trees however restricted vision further than a few metres in any direction.

Peter, reluctant to enter the bushes, needed to find somewhere where he could see and search for the Doc. He looked up at the bank debating whether he had the strength to make it to the top.

The scattering of mature bushes would provide holds to pull himself up.

The Doc had been gone far longer than a call of nature would allow.

This decided Peter. The bank was three to four metres high. To Peter, it was mountainous.

He threw himself forward at the first available shrub.

Hanging on with left hand, he reached out with his right to the next losing control on his crutch which slid back down out of reach.

Peter had an idea who the Doc had gone to meet. Asked what he was going to do next, he would not have had an answer. He only felt that something was badly wrong.

He frantically pulled, heaved and scrambled without resting until he reached the top.

He lay across this with his hands gripping the tufts on the opposite slope gasping with relief as if his problems were over.

After recovering his breath, he began to look around. The wooded area to the north revealed little.

To the south a star shone brightly in the early night sky. This stars'brightness 'reached' into his inner soul, consuming his attention. Peter focussed on this and this alone, gradually calming down.

He drew his left leg up then manhandled his right alongside until he was then sitting atop the bank. Keeping his eyes firmly fixed on this star and the surrounding night sky, trying to forget the pain in his leg.

Strangely, the fears arising from the Doc's sudden departure, no longer figured.

The star grew in importance. He wondered at the vastness of space and what peace might accompany his death.

A more logical Peter would have been thinking to escape. If he followed the river down through the mountains to the sea, he might achieve the freedom he yearned.

This thought didn't even enter his head. He just sat, for how long he didn't know or care.

"Get your heed down, laddie. You're sat up there like a fucking clay pigeon."

Scotty's frantic whisper barely penetrated Peter's reverie.

Not responding, Peter appeared not to hear. He kept staring ahead.

Scotty tried again.

"Peter, I'm down here. Come down and join me. **Don't go back**."

This last phrase came in as a louder whisper.

Peter still did not respond.

Below in the camp a German army patrol appeared from out of the trees.

They surrounded Bella and the wagon. An officer issued a sharp word of command.

The men then searched inside the wagon and around the site.

Peter turned to look back down. He tried to stand, but without his crutch, he failed.

Scotty at that very moment grabbed Peter's leg, pulling him down the south side of the bank.

Peter cried out in pain. At this same moment the officer found Peter's crutch and ordered his men to search the trees.

Scotty gagged Peter with his hand, the pair rolling and sliding down to the bottom.

Scotty's rifle slid down after them. It stopped halfway down, caught by a bush.

Peter kicked with his good leg, scratched then punched until Scotty was forced to use both hands to hold him down.

"Fucking hell, Peter. You'll get us both killed."

Peter, red in the face and in great pain from his injured leg, began to cry.

"The Doc and Bella, I can't leave them."

Scotty looked around for somewhere to hide. A small brick building towards the end of the flood bank seemed to offer the only solution. He picked up Peter and carried him there.

It housed the sluice controlling the flow of river water into the drainage channel at flood times. Another sluice controlled the irrigation channels.

Both lay in the hut recovering. Peter was still crying.

Scotty felt dreadful. "Peter, Peter laddie. The best chance for the Doc is for you not to be discovered. Without you there will be no evidence against him."

Peter thought that Scotty was lying but decided to lay low just in case it was true.

Scotty, for his part, had no doubts the Doc was dead meat as was his horse.

He weighed up their chances.

"We wait here Pete until dawn. I will recover my rifle at first light then make an assessment.

If all is clear, we cross the road into the forest and away."

Peter didn't answer but curled up in the other corner.

Scotty had yet to learn that their escape route across the road had been blocked.

Chapter 106

To the west, up in the forest a scout made his way back into the partisan camp and reported to the English captain and a committee of leaders.

"What news?" asked one. "Why the delay?"

The scout squatted breathing deeply.

"The Doc's been taken, so have our cover patrol. Also, German troops are stationed along the road at 10 metre intervals. I had to travel south for a kilometre before I could work my way through."

"What about Barnes and Scotty?" asked the captain.

"No news. Scotty left the team before the rest were captured. Why or where to I have no idea.

I shadowed the others until they were picked up. I assume the Germans got Barnes along with the Doc and that Scotty's in the clear for now."

"What chances of a rescuing the team and finding Scotty?" asked the captain.

The scout shook his head. "Scotty is out there to the wrong side of the cordon. I saw more troops unloading and spreading out to the south. I had to move quickly to get through."

P who had not so far spoken, nodded to the captain who was filling his pipe for the second time and both stood up and began to leave. The Professor, or Gold as he was alternately known, protested.

"You are not leaving? We have yet to decide what to do."

P stopped as he was leaving with the captain, turned and replied.

"What's to do Professor? The German Army is on its territory and in numbers.

You know the rule. We don't venture out there overtly. They have the area surrounded. We can only leave Scotty and anyone else to their own initiatives."

With that P and the captain left the group while the rest of the committee were left to argue and discuss possible action. Most agreed that the German plan was to await daylight then close the 'net' collecting all within.

Away from the committee and any listening ears, P and the captain reassessed the position.

It was now clear to both that the German intelligence had an informant in the partisan camp.

"Are you thinking what I am?" the captain asked.

P smiled. "Probably not. My interest is not the same as you British. We have lost at least three probably four good men. The chance of their rescue is nil. All in my opinion for a lost cause."

The captain didn't answer at once. He lit his pipe and leaned back against a tree.

Peter and Scotty, primarily Scotty, were the subjects of his concern. His arguments for further co-operation simply to help them were so thin as to be non-existent.

He blew a cloud of blue smoke into the air.

"I was referring to the informant in your ranks. The loss of your good men is down to him not the British. The German command have lined the road for, shall we say, four kilometres north to south. Let us assume that they don't know that we are aware. In which case they will think there is no need to watch their backs. They can't possibly know your scout has slipped through their cordon.

Furthermore, the informant in our midst, whoever he is, is in no position to warn them."

The captain paused before adding, "So, we are in command."

P studied for a moment. "To do what?"

"Perhaps unmask a traitor or failing that, exact revenge."

The captain blew another puff of blue smoke into the air. "Revenge for the loss of your men."

The Captain walked up to P and slapped him on the back.

"With their backs to the forest those Boche will be sitting ducks."

P nodded but before answering looked into the captain's eyes for some seconds.

"I am wondering why Scotty left the patrol. Was he under orders?"

He was clearly thinking Scotty was possibly the mole. Claiming affinity to Croatia did not mean necessarily loyalty to the partisans.

The captain didn't answer as it was now clear with the unrelated question from P, that he had made his point. It was clear to P that a revenge opportunity would be good tactics.

The idea that the enemy were unaware and vulnerable appealed, moreover knowledge that the informant was powerless to warn them, had registered.

Chapter 107

In the sluice hut Scotty was thinking how they could cross to the forest and safety and whether he should carry Peter or not. Unaware that the road was to be lined with soldiers, he continued to plan. He went outside to select a suitable stick to replace Peter's lost crutch.

He took time selecting a suitable one, cutting it from the bush with just an army knife.

This he took back to the sluice hut and began to trim and cut to size.

The sky began to lighten. Scotty was not sure whether Peter was sleeping.

He had not moved for almost an hour. He put the stick down and decided to go and find his rifle. This, in the emerging daylight, he did easily.

Having retrieved his rifle, Scotty scrambled up to the top of the bank to reconnoitre.

Scotty surveyed the scene. In the early morning mist, the way across to the forest looked to be clear.

The German officer in charge of the section covering the culvert and the flood prevention bank now had enough light to study the photograph issued during the night.

This had been taken from leaflets dropped from the air the previous day.

It was of a British officer in an oversize uniform, bearded and bent. Looking very strange, the little man was receiving a medal. The caption read, 'Target to be taken alive.' Alongside this was an artist impression of what the target might look like out of uniform.

These were the only images of the target the officer had seen.

One hour later, out of the morning mist appeared a biblical looking figure, bent and hobbling towards them with the aid of a long stick.

The officer did a double take. He took the photo/sketch from his pocket. He studied for a second or two, then stood and issued an order.

"Two men, you and you, come with me the rest of you act as cover."

The three made their way towards the little man.

In his mind the officer was already receiving the accolades for the capture of this man who was the prime target of the last months.

Sadly, these were his last thoughts.

Scotty had his binoculars focused on the woods to the north of the bank when the fusillade of shots rang out. He spun around in time to see the three men fall.

Peter was standing in full view halfway across towards the drainage ditch.

"Shit! Oh! Fucking hell, Peter."

Training his binoculars on the ditch, Scotty saw a line of German soldiers spin around and duck behind the drainage ditch wall for cover returning fire in a massive fire fight.

Unable to see the attackers hidden in the forest the Bosch were firing blindly into the trees from where they were being cut down unmercifully. It was payback time for years of oppression.

Scotty grabbed his rifle and began picking the Germans off methodically.

The German lines were well and truly broken. They were lined up like ducks in a shooting gallery.

Pinned down, they were taking what shelter they could behind the drainage ditch wall which was the only cover available.

They were unable to lift their heads without being met with a fusillade of fire.

Splattered with blood, bone slivers protruding from wounds, they flattened themselves in the ditch which still left them open to attack by Scotty who had hoisted himself on to the very top of the bank. This left him in full view of the culvert soldiers, but their attention was on the forest.

In the chaos, it was a long journey for the Germans to realise that they were being attacked from the flood bank. A unit further away from the main fire fight eventually noticed.

They returned fire with all weapons.

A burst of automatic fire hit alongside Scotty's head. Shattered stone splinters and soil shrapnel caught him in the face.

Scotty parted company with his rifle. He rolled and slid to a stop under a bush, out of sight of all except for an old farm hand who had been out working nearby.

The old farm hand had taken shelter from the fire fight under a hand cart. Using this hand cart for protection, he made his way to the sluice housing just below where Scotty had fallen.

He slipped inside the building for cover. His heart was thumping as he peered out from the hut planning his next move. This was to recover Scotty's rifle and get involved.

The German soldiers, in an impossible position, were crawling away, escaping along the ditch.

The old man checked that the valves to the irrigation channels were fully closed.

The river was now in spring flood, its flow boosted by melting snows.

He opened the valve wide diverting the flow of the river into the drainage ditch. The river water thundered down the trough in a tidal wave.

The flood water hit the bodies and crawling men, piling them living, dead, dying and wounded into a dam forcing the water into the fields one side and on to the road the other.

Those who were still alive and able were forced to lift their heads above the water, only to be cut back down.

Bodies slammed against an army truck, piling underneath. The river water swirled across the road, creating an even greater flood. The stricken soldiers floated around this truck. Some wounded were waving their arms frantically as they were swept away.

P called a ceasefire. Having made the point, he needed to conserve ammunition.

The Germans were in full retreat. Those to the north of the culvert sprinted out of range, those to the south, dead, dying and defenceless.

The captain, feeling sick with anxiety, had seen the sniper on the bank fall.

He was sure this was Scotty. It could not be anyone else.

After a brief check that the main danger was passed, he braced himself and issued an order.

"Come with me, Sparks."

The pair set off towards the flood bank.

Peter could be seen sitting between the bank and the culvert surrounded by flood water.

He was untouched physically nor seemingly emotionally.

Stepping over the broken bodies of the dead and dying, the captain, followed by Sparks, forced their way forward. Crossing the flooded trench Sparks saw an arm waving from beneath the water. He stopped and grabbed it, trying to pull the head clear of the water.

"Leave him Sparks and help me with Lt. Barnes and Scotty," The captain ordered, aware that they were in the open and easy targets.

Sparks was heaving at the arm of a very young soldier. He appeared to be little more than a boy. Sparks slipped on to his back in the mud. The captain helped him to his feet, then pulled him away breaking his grip on the boy's arm.

Sparks pulled back still looking and reaching towards the young soldier who slipped back into the drain crying, "Hilfe. Hilfe."

His head submerged leaving a vivid memory of the terror in his eyes.

Sparks heaved himself free then slipped again in the water and mud.

"Move, Sparks!" the captain ordered dragging him back to his feet.

He was aware that they were still an open target and was anxious to reach Scotty.

While this was all going on the old man was returning with the rifle leading Scotty by the hand.

He helped Scotty on to his hand cart. He reached the sluice housing and turned off the diversion valve, then began wheeling Scotty towards the culvert.

The captain reached Peter and hauled him to his feet. Unresponsive, he followed zombie-like with the support of a very distressed, very confused Sparks.

The captain ran forward leaving Sparks to deal with Peter.

He had seen the old man with Scotty and was focused on reaching them.

He gasped when he got close enough and saw Scotty's face, bloodied and unrecognisable.

"You O.K. Scotty?" the captain called out.

Scotty recognised the captain's voice and replied with surprising calmness.

"Sure thing. I am looking forward to a wee spell back home, Sassy."

Relieved, the captain answered, "Yes, Scotty, I will arrange it at once."

Reaching out, he grabbed Scotty's hand.

"Then you'll be able to see Elspeth and the grandchildren."

Scotty, emotionless until this moment, wailed.

"Sassy, I'm blind. I'm fucking blind."

Chapter 108

Back in the trees once more the captain looked around for help. The forest was empty with only debris, cartridge cases, the smell of cordite and split trees the only evidence that the partisans had been there.

He beckoned to Sparks and ordered, "Take Lt. Barnes in hand. I will deal with Scotty."

Sparks ignored him. He was standing looking back towards where he had tried to help the young soldier.

The captain tapped him on the shoulder. "Time to move, Sparks."

"To do what, sir?"

"We need to move sharpish before the Bosch return."

"Sir, what can we do?" Sparks asked still looking towards the piles of dead and dying.

"Get out of here at the double," came the sharp reply.

He tried to sound confident and in control as he informed the others.

"We are to return to our last camp site."

Sparks clearly was having problems which troubled the captain.

A smart operator in telegraphy and a conscript, Sparks had been co-opted by the SOE.

His Morse expertise paramount. He had been shipped behind enemy lines without basic training or even proper briefing of what the posting entailed.

Sparks was just twenty and had never been trained for combat. He had been fast tracked by the M.O.D. by-passing the accepted training.

He was excellent in his comfort zone with headphones and a Morse key.

Here, he was way out of his depth.

In vain, the captain felt in his pocket for his pipe. His last memory of it was before the first shots were fired. Confused, aware of an equally confused and questioning Sparks plus two disabled men, he needed all his strength to stop his hands from trembling. There was not the time and space to sort out his mind. With a supreme effort he controlled his emotions and gave this very young man his orders.

"I am placing you corporal, in charge of Lt. Barnes' welfare. See to it that he doesn't stray and arrives safely with us at the previous camp."

"W-what, sir?" Sparks stammered. Meaning why me? What is happening?

The look on Sparks' face registered, alerting the captain to the fact that he was suffering from severe shock. Having only seconds to make a judgement, he held his hands rigidly to his sides not knowing quite what to do with them. He decided not to issue another order.

"Please Sparks, I need your help. There are only the two of us."

"Fuck off, Sassy, just 'cos I can't see does not make me non-compos-mentis.

Sparks, give me your hand and follow the captain."

Scotty gave the order which the captain, in his view, had shirked.

The silence which followed underlined the captain's dilemma.

Scotty sighed.

"Och! Sassy, court martial me when we get back but let's get the fuck out of here."

Peter took Scotty's arm, much to Sparks' relief and Scotty's surprise.

"I'll look out for Scotty, Sparks," he said quietly.

Severe shocks such as this often send some mad. Others, however, as it appeared, could be driven sane. Peter's demeanour had miraculously changed from the sullen and introspective.

Peter was now Scotty's eyes. Scotty acted as Peter's crutch.

The stick Scotty cut in the night had floated away in the flood.

None of this took the captain's mind away from the last ghastly hour. His only plan was to lead a pitiful looking, muddied and wet trio back towards the last partisan camp.

Repeated apologies from Peter specifically to Scotty were ignored until this rebuttal.

"We are all victims of circumstance, laddie. Ye are not to be thinking that my injuries are any way related to any one individual action."

The awkward silences fell away and led to breathless exchanges between the two which not only helped them heave their broken bodies up the sloping track but also helped the captain through the next two hours.

It was an imperative to take many stops on the way occasioned by Scotty's injuries, Peter's leg and the effects of shock upon them all.

This caused the captain to think.

Scotty, he knew well and would be O. K. His main difficulty was deciding whether Lt Barnes, now behaving normally, was really mentally disturbed or just plain insubordinate.

Four exhausted, tattered men arrived at the partisans' last camp. Their wet, muddy clothes had dried like boards adding to their feeling of desolation in an unyielding world.

The camp was deserted with little sign that the partisans had ever been there.

The captain, his mind in turmoil, tried to sort out the present thinking how to plan Scotty's repatriation and also deal with Lt Barnes. All this was impossible without Sparks' radio kit which was missing. He hoped that the partisans had taken this for safe keeping and maybe find them sooner rather than later, to return it.

Someone, anyone to return, with or without, would be a blessing.

Meanwhile he needed to deal with two, possibly three sick men with no food or drink and no protection. The partisans would not be looking for them at the forest edge.

There was no point in staying or returning there. That would be the last place they would look.

That is if they were looking at all.

He looked around at each of the others. Peter was trying to tend to Scotty's wounds.

Sparks was sitting hunched up and trembling against a tree.

The captain forced himself to go and speak. "You all right, Sparks?"

"Why?" Sparks turned to look at the captain. This clearly was the plea of a badly shocked man.

"I know, son. This war is horrible."

The captain sat beside him, still feeling automatically for his pipe.

"Not the war, sir. That young soldier was drowning. We should have saved him."

"It was an enemy soldier," the captain began, only to be interrupted by Sparks.

"It! Sir?" The look on his face was of disbelief.

"He was just a boy. We are not animals, sir. He needed help."

"If he couldn't raise himself, Sparks, he probably had a broken back. Probably would have died anyway. We need to forget it."

The captain tried to shake off his own feelings.

Sparks sat for almost a minute then without speaking, moved across to the other side of the clearing.

It was another hit on the captain's morale which was already teetering near to collapse.

Despite his comment of the need to forget, the incident of the young soldier preyed on his mind.

No longer did he wish to carry the responsibility of this mission.

The trembling he felt inside was beginning to force itself into his limbs.

He reached yet again for his pipe in the desperate hope that it had miraculously returned to his pocket.

A blackbird in the tree above chose that moment to bridge the forest's silence.

The evensong contrasted vividly with the captain's memories of the day, knowing that the carnage had been his idea and that he had ordered Sparks to leave a young man to drown. The death of this helpless boy and the wholesale slaughter of so many men would stay with him for the rest of his life.

Chapter 109

"Looking for this?" P handed the captain his pipe who, without speaking, took it and promptly filled the pipe bowl then handed the pouch to P to do the same all with little outward surprise or comment on P's sudden appearance out from the trees.

The captain's soul, however, flooded with warmth in the presence of another one who, maybe, understood. Neither spoke until both pipes were lit.

P then asked, "Have you recovered yet?"

"No, I don't suppose I ever will."

"How's Scotty? We saw him taken down." P looked towards Scotty and Peter.

"Scotty's lost his sight. It might be temporary. I need to get him home as soon as possible."

The captain hastened to bring up the repatriation of Scotty.

P then ignored the Scotty problem.

"The radio and other kit are back in the goatherd's hut," answering the captain's other unspoken question. "I've broken up the band into much smaller, more mobile and independent sections who will keep on the move. We have no facility for casualties and are sending them to safe places.

The German high command will be out for revenge. We still have no idea who or where their informant is."

He took some time sorting and a relighting of his pipe before continuing.

"I am sorry, but you are on your own for now. I will not risk any more of my men. We will deal with Scotty later."

"Lt. Barnes, what of him?" the captain asked.

"Put simply, he is not a priority, now that we have today's victory to our credit. This will play well with our people's morale." P immediately closed off that enquiry.

"So, what am I supposed to do?" the captain asked. Receiving no response, he added, "I will need help to move Scotty to a suitable landing strip."

P nodded and thought before answering.

"That we can do in time, but we have no room for cripples. I am afraid your Lt. Barnes has outstayed his welcome. We have left your sleeping bags and food in the hut with the radio equipment."

P stood and offered his hand. The captain struggled to his feet and took it, knowing that argument was useless.

"We'll catch up with you once we and you are sorted," said P who turned to go then stopped adding:

"We need new supplies of ammunition and other things." He meant medical supplies, coffee and tobacco. P was acknowledging that co-operation was still alive, on his terms.

He paused once more and looked up at the distant peak as if for inspiration before speaking further.

"Lt. Barnes I will give thought to, but no promises."

P then slipped back into the forest as swiftly and silently as he had arrived.

Chapter 110

The captain was sitting outside the goatherd's hut at dawn on a second night without sleep. He looked back over the trees at a lightening sky and wondered what to do with the approaching day: How to contact the S.O.E. tell them of their predicament. Thinking whether or not to suggest to them that he was no longer fit for purpose.

Radio contact had yet to be made. Sparks had prepared the tapes for transmission at the first sight of the contact aircraft but how would this aircraft know where to find them?

Would its flight path ever be near enough to transmit?

Sparks had refused to re-punch the tape and argued that he wasn't sure about the battery level.

Use for non-transmission purposes may drain this, leaving them without power.

The generator and transformer having been left on the escarpment.

The captain only partly understood the technicalities, but knew that this equipment's capability to intercept and transmit signals was limited. He was frustrated that he was unable to contact Benghazi direct or even his British counterparts in Slovenia.

He was unable to contact anyone and was annoyed by Sparks' covert insubordination.

He was angry with himself for loss of control and losing his temper, unfairly, with Sparks.

He was aware that this anger had its roots in Sparks' attempt to rescue the young soldier.

A desperate flailing arm he could have dealt with. The memories of the boy's cries for help and frightened eyes as he sank out of sight was a very different matter. This would not let him rest.

Out of contact with everyone with little food and two unfit men he had no alternative but to sit tight and pray that P would act soon to help.

Over the horizon, silhouetted against the sky as if in answer to this prayer, appeared two figures leading horses. They were coming from the north east not from the west from where he was hoping for contact from the partisans. The captain jumped to his feet and moved up on to the mountain track intending to intercept.

The leading figure, a woman, began waving to him.

"Tanya," he gasped and swallowing a sob of relief, he hurried to meet her, but resisting the urge to run.

Tanya, despite the captain's efforts to control his emotions, was alerted to his psychological state. She stopped and opened her arms in welcome. The captain was not fooled either, recognising the maternal gesture for exactly what it was. He stopped in his tracks.

All this before they both went to meet each other to formally shake hands.

The captain looked past Tanya to her companion, an adolescent boy.

Tanya answered his unspoken question.

"We are to follow the original plan with Peter. The boy will now take over from me.

I am to accompany you and the wireless equipment."

The captain, now being used to the procedures, would normally not have questioned anything, but anxiety decreed otherwise. He asked,"Are we to part company with Barnes?"

Later that morning they did part company. Peter left with the youth back in the direction from which he and Tanya had come. Tanya and the rest took the track to the west.

Peter, once more bound to the will of unseen hands and reliant upon a young boy, was forced to ride on a mule which was neither easy nor comfortable.

Peter twisted around anxiously looking for Tanya and party until they were out of sight.

She had persuaded him to defy his own instincts. Trust himself to this youth.

The order from the captain after argument and pleading from Scotty, had left Peter no option but to obey.

Peter initially exploded in anger until Tanya calmed him.

Once he was quiet enough to listen, she took him by the wrists and said, "We are all pawns, with few choices but if we are to win the game, each of us must accept our roles. The path is being planned by the master. We can only move one place at a time until the game is up. It is this way, or we all lose."

Holding him by the wrist was really a ploy to check on Peter, who she suspected was running a temperature. She placed a hand on his face to confirm her suspicion.

Peter did not receive either well, replying angrily in an uncharacteristic manner, especially to Tanya:

"Piss off with your fancy philosophy. I just wish to leave the game. Why can't you all just leave me to die?" He thrust her hand forcefully away.

The captain intervened, "Because you are helping protect others who do not wish to die. Tanya is right, we must stay together, stay true."

Taking Tanya's lead, he was trying persuasion in place of orders.

In truth, he just wished to rid himself of this obstreperous little man.

Tanya added, "When you leave, as leave you must, you carry me and my hopes with you.

One of those hopes Peter is that we will meet again." She smiled and took his hand. "Very soon."

This time Peter accepted even to allowing Tanya to check his pulse.

Peter didn't reply, withdrawing into himself, still listening to Tanya's gentle persuasion.

Most of the other arguments and orders from the captain and Scotty, he closed his ears to.

At one Scotty comment, "we all want away home," he wanted to respond by saying, 'at least you have a home to go to'. Peter, being Peter, remained silent, for fear of breaking down.

Peter's memories of the past days were spasmodic and confused. He was aware of the major events, aware of his part in the slaughter only days ago.

Tanya went outside to the youth who was sitting with his back to the shelter, sucking a straw and gave him last minute instructions and a package.

Going back inside, she returned with Peter and marshalled the others.

The youth lifted Peter on to the mule's back showing a remarkable strength for a young man.

Then he began leading the mule down the track into the rift, back towards the river.

The track was undulating pitching Peter forward frequently on to the mule's neck.

The smell of the animal and the swaying motion brought on nausea which closed out and replaced all his previous troubles.

Of all the many ordeals Peter had recently suffered, this was the worst.

The jagged rocks of the downward slope threatened with every jolt of the mule.

How lost track of how long he hung on as he spiralled into a maelstrom of pain.

Peter struggled back into confused consciousness. He was wrapped in a blanket, naked and stinking of vomit. He was lying on the banks of the river.

The youth was in the shallows washing Peter's clothes, pinning each garment down in the faster flows with heavy stones.

Peter sat up, then lay back down immediately. The world around him began to spin.

Out of the maelstrom the youth appeared. He lifted Peter's head placed a yellow tablet on his tongue and offered water from a bottle. Peter drank thirstily, swallowing the medicine.

The youth laid Peter's head back on to a canvas pack which was doubling as a pillow.

The spinning sensation intensified. Frantically he reached out to the youth watching from above.

This desperate clutching failed. Spinning round and round he was sucked into to a black hole.

Chapter 111

He awoke from a deep sleep with the warm afternoon sun on his face.

Peter covered his eyes against the bright glare.

He took a while to adjust his mind to where he was and why.

He sat up, shading his eyes and looked around. The youth was attending to a pan of boiling rice.

Behind, on the rocks were several items of Peter's apparel drying in the sun.

His trousers were drying separately on a short line. The shredded ends flapped in the wind blowing down the valley; a tattered metaphor for Peter's life.

The youth did not acknowledge Peter. He went about his business of gutting a pheasant then washing it by the river's edge before placing the carcass into a canvas bag and hanging it from a tree on the shady side.

He placed several small eggs into the pan of boiling water before putting another pan on to the fire, adding olive oil then the offal. This activity caused Peter to remember the Doc, a memory that he had snuffed out of his mind for the last few days. He began to weep silently, trying to hide his distress from the boy. Despite a great effort to subdue his emotions, he was overwhelmed by grief. Between sobs, he let out a series of pathetic moans while holding his sides.

The youth seemed not to notice. He went about draining the rice. He broke the softly boiled eggs into the pan before adding this to the pan of oil and frying offal.

This he shared, serving this without comment.

Peter took his, unable to speak, even to thank the boy. He managed the weakest of smiles and a nod of his head.

The boy began to eat using the fingers of his right hand in the same manner of the Doc.

Peter began to eat the warm rice wishing not to offend his benefactor.

The food tasted of egg yolk and offal. Peter threw up.

He retched and retched hurting his already empty stomach fetching up a mere spot or two of bile.

The youth put down his dish. He locked his arms around Peter's stomach until he settled.

Then he laid him on his back and removed the blanket revealing a naked skeletal body, strangely mottled. Ghostly white skin contrasted with a patchwork of dark brown where he had been exposed to the sun.

Turning Peter over he searched his body.

Peter was too weak to object and lay like a pathetic, homeless puppy.

The youth went to one of his packs to return with a piece of thin twine which he looped over a dark blob nestling in the crease between Peter's right buttock and the top of his leg then pulled the loop tight until the tick dropped off. Then he stamped it into the ground.

Peter managed to thank him in Slovene.

The youth smiled and nodded while examining Peter's body until he was sure he had no further parasites.

He then returned to finish his meal. Then he ate Peter's leavings.

Collecting Peter's clothes, he returned and spoke for the first time.

"Dress, please. We are late, we must hurry, or we will miss the tide."

He poured the remaining water on the fire then repacked the mule bringing from the packs a pick hoe with which he covered the embers of the fire with soil.

Wrapping a shivering Peter in the blanket, he lifted him on to the mule.

Peter wanted to know the boy's name. To ask if he was Tanya's son but he felt too ill to speak. Patronised by a youth who took liberties with him, he lay roped precariously to the packs along the animal's back.

They set off at a steady pace. The path alongside the river was mostly of grass, a gentle slope almost level at times.

The journeying was now less violent. This would have been tolerable to a normal Peter. Now he moaned and gasped at every jolting step. Disorientated, his brain drifted in and out of reality.

In a technicolour dream he hammered on a door which collapsed. He was pitched forward violently rafting down rapids, bouncing off rocks until finally sliding over a waterfall into a maelstrom and disappearing into a dark hole. He reached out to May Sheppard whose hand he could not quite reach. He was lost, drifting down and down, surrounded by black feathers which clogged his nose and mouth stopping him from breathing.

The boy heard Peter's choking struggle to breathe. He stopped to check.

He turned Peter's face away from the mule's mane. Then with a cloth wetted from a water bottle sponged his face before trying and failing to get Peter to take some tablets and a drink.

Peter being tied face down, this was impossible.

The youth untied the rope and lowered the limp body on to the riverbank. As he did so Peter kicked and lashed out. The boy lost his grip and Peter fell heavily.

Sitting down alongside Peter, he took a swig of water before trying and failing again to get him to either drink or take more tablets. Sighing, he picked Peter up, impatiently throwing him over the mule's back and set off once more. This time Peter was draped over the mule's back, arms and legs. Inevitably, he slid off again on to the grass.

The youth, having already seen the beach and the sea, unstrapped a satchel.

Slinging this over his shoulder he walked on alone leaving the mule and Peter where he had fallen.

The mule went to drink from the river. Peter lay isolated like discarded rubbish.

The only movement was a pathetic flapping of the tattered remains of his clothes in the breeze flowing down the river valley.

Down this valley towards the sea a small man emptied a small fish into a large bottle while a pair of egrets watched nearby. Seeing the youth, he turned and waited for him to arrive wiping his hands.

Arriving the youth dropped the satchel without comment. The man screwed the top on the bottle and waded ashore and picked up the satchel, emptied it and searched through it, placing back each item, with the exceptions of a pack of tobacco and one other package.

"What is this?" he asked, holding up the other package.

"Medication," the boy answered, speaking for the first time since arriving.

"Who for?" the man asked, there being no sign of anyone else. The youth pointed back up the valley and began to return from where he had come, expecting the man to follow, which he did.

"Problems?" the man asked adding catching up with him.

"I have missed the best of the tide. Where is this cargo?"

The boy did not answer any of the man's questions. He just pointed to the ragged bundle lying in the shadow of a mule.

"What would I want with, do with a horse?"

"Your cargo's on the ground alongside."

The two walked on in silence to where Peter was lying. The man looked down.

"He's got a fever and is lame. I must go now. I'm late," the boy announced.

The man considered then asked, "Is that it? No information? No instructions?"

The boy shook his head. "I've delivered him as instructed."

The man sucked his teeth.

"Paurak's message said vital cargo for safe storage. Do you know who this is?"

The youth heaved himself aboard the mule, saying over his shoulder, "No. Does the second hand stop to ask the balance wheel where to next?"

With this remark he set off back up the track.

The man watched him leave. He smiled and shook his head then turned to pick Peter up in a fireman's lift. Holding on to one arm and a leg he returned to the beach. Lowering Peter on to the ground, the limp body slid out of his hands landing heavily.

Peter was once more under the butterfly bush in his dreams, afraid of what was lurking outside. Pamela pulled away the trailing branches and reached out with her hand and smiled.

Peter took her hand whereupon, he was dragged out and thrown over the wall into the trees.

The man stroked his beard thinking. He went to the pool returning with water in cupped hands.

He began dripping this on to Peter's face. He read the instructions on the packet of tablets, then shook his head, putting the tablets back into the satchel returning to continue fishing in the pool.

Half an hour later Peter woke up in confusion unable to sense reality from delusion.

The sky was clear and blue. The evening sun was warm and pleasant. Peter, with a raging thirst, raised himself on to his elbow and shielded his eyes against the brightness which troubled him.

Two white birds crossed his vision. The egrets coasted into the waters of a dammed river pool to fish. If it was not for the fire in his throat and a throbbing head, he could have been in heaven. Unsure where he was or what was happening Peter forced himself upright into a sitting position. There was no sign of the boy or his mule. To his left the Adriatic tide swept with a gentle hush, hush on to a golden beach. Further up this beach away from the tide a small boat leaned on its side. A half-raised sail flapped in the evening breeze.

To his right the river stretched and sparkled away back up the ravine.

Ahead the water was dammed to create a pool which overflowed a crude bank into rivulets down towards the sea.

Peter dragged himself painfully to the edge of the pool and cupping his hands began to drink greedily.

"You are late. We have less than two hours before the tide turns."

A disembodied voice came from above. Peter looked up to see a hairy face dominated by a huge smile and vivid blue eyes.

"Sorry, I was taken ill," Peter replied to a small man not much bigger than himself.

The man offered a huge hand.

"Attila."

A surprised Peter, taking his hand, replied, "Peter."

"Well Peter, shall we set off without further delay?"

Instead of moving towards the boat, as Peter expected, he waded into the pool collecting a large bottle.

The two egrets took off and circled his head before settling back to the water.

The sea appeared to be part of a channel which ran between the coast and a series of mountainous islands several kilometres out in the Adriatic. Peter watched as Attila stowed the bottle. He dragged the boat into the surf before returning with a boat hook for Peter to use as an assist.

He collected the satchel and the pack of English brand tobacco.

"Come, my friend." Attila held out a hand to help him to his feet. Peter followed him for a few steps before sliding back into a faint.

Attila picked him up once more and loaded him gently into the prow of the boat.

Raising the sail, Atilla steered the little craft out into the straights and to the south along the coast.

Peter briefly woke then, rocked by the familiar motion of the boat, slept on.

Two hours sailing was all Attila could manage before the wind dropped. The boat slowed and stopped. The little craft began drifting back up the channel.

Attila released the sail and took the oars from the rests. Singing in time to his rowing, he headed for the mainland shore.

Peter woke to a gold tinged twilight. The sun was setting behind the mountains. It was still light enough to see the tree-lined sands ahead. He was cold and his arm was numb from sleeping on it. Otherwise he was feeling much better, not just physically but mentally.

The emerging moon's reflection was lucent on the gentle swell. Attila's soft light baritone voice accompanied the swish of the oars and the cries of the sea birds circling around the boat.

Charmed by the scene, Peter sat rubbing his arm. He was further encouraged by the white of Attila's teeth as he smiled.

"Supper time, my friend. Mother wind has retired for the night and the tide is sucking us back to our beginnings."

"Why?" asked Peter, still sorting out his confusion and garbled memory of the last twenty-four hours. This question was not directed at any specific subject.

Attila answered the obvious.

"It is the time. The sun sets. The land cools. Mother wind takes a moment of stillness to bless the day. When the tide ebbs, a strong current flowing north stops all progress. We cannot proceed further tonight without using the outboard and I have only enough diesel for emergencies."

Peter, still aching from illness and the cramped space in the unusual craft, looked around him. "Strange little sailing boat."

Attila looked over his shoulder as they approached the beach.

"Customised for these waters, short stow able mast and shallow draught."

He gave a final heave on the oars. "Built by my grandfather and perfect."

"Perfect," echoed Peter. "I belong here."

Chapter 112

The boat slid on to the shore. Attila jumped out into water of very little surf, a mere gentle lapping of the shore. With one huge hand, he held the prow and with the other helped Peter step out and stand unsteadily in the surf holding on to the boat.

The beach area was contained in a small cove ringed by trees and bushes.

There was a small shelter formed by bent saplings woven into an arbour. This shelter was to the left of the cove facing south. The arbour had been set some time ago and recently maintained.

Attila handed Peter the boat hook and he hobbled ashore to wait patiently for instructions from this caring, gentle and interesting man who after dragging the boat ashore began to unload.

"What can I do?"

Attila looked at Peter and smiled.

"You are looking better. What was it? Tick fever?

Peter shrugged. "I don't know."

Attila returned to Peter's earlier question.

"Dry pieces of driftwood, small to medium size would be useful."

He continued unhooking the sail. This he carried up to the arbour draping it over the top, tying it down.

Peter began to look around the beach above the tide line, to show that he was capable.

More so than Attila's first impression of him. Peter was feeling better.

Somewhere in his senses he felt this moment was going to be good. It was the same feeling as he had sensed with the Doc.

He no longer felt sad about the Doc. All previous emotions were swamped by an intense excitement. His leg agony, headache and leather like tongue faded into insignificance.

Supper under the stars in front of a driftwood fire, was of conger eel with freshly picked green lipped mussels served with crisp fried seaweed. To collect the mussels Attila pulled on a rope to beach a section of an old wreck. From the timbers he picked the choicest mussels and returned the wreck with its cluster of molluscs to the water.

"The eel was too greedy and would not let go of the lobster in my trap so instead of having supper, he is supper," he announced on his return.

Nothing further was said until they finished eating. Peter expected Attila to light a pipe, but he didn't. Not uncomfortable with silence, Peter relaxed although his mind was full of questions.

Later sensing that Attila was in a mood to talk, he asked, "Those songs you sang I didn't recognise the language?"

"Hungarian," Attila replied.

"You speak Hungarian?"

"No. I know only a little. The songs I learned from my grandfather who was Hungarian.

I was born in Austria to an Austrian mother. My parents sent me down here to live with my grandfather for safety during the troubles before the big war and I stayed.

I learned the ways of the sea from him. The songs he sang always when the boat answered the call of the wind and tide."

Atilla washed the pans out in the sea and scoured them with sand and stowed them, returning to continue his story to an attentive Peter.

"I will never return north; life is not good there. Here the sea provides. It is gentle mostly and I have developed a sense of how to use her when she can be kind and when she can be cruel.

The sea is a good partner. More predictable than a wife."

Attila smiled as he spoke. As well he might. I would smile, thought Peter, envying this life.

His excitement since waking in the boat to a way of new life was undiminished.

Once more he was Peterkin on his coral island.

This excitement kept him awake until the early hours. A rain shower pattering on the sail-covered arbour lulled him to a deep sleep.

All too soon he was disturbed by Attila removing the sail. Peter sat up and looked around.

Everything had been cleared away and stowed.

He watched Attila reattaching the sail to the mast. He then recovered the bottle of freshwater fish from out of the sea to stow it in the boat.

This amazing little man did nothing without purpose.

This gave Peter something to think about.

He reached out for the boat hook, but it was gone from where he had left it last night.

Attila was using it to hoist the sail, Peter watching this consummate performance with interest and more than a little envy.

Attila returned to the arbour, handing the boat hook to Peter.

"Come my friend, Mother wind is calling, and Father tide is arriving on schedule."

Minutes later the boat was heeling over to a steady wind and making good progress on the rising tide. Peter in the prow relived the sensation of freedom that he remembered when coxing the eights at Cambridge. Sadly, without the same control.

The waters spread before him in full vista with mountains right and left. Attila was singing, the sea birds circling and calling, the wind in the rigging whistling and tapping.

Peter noticed a bright star still twinkling in defiance of the lightening skies and his spirits soared.

Peter though was still weak and sore from bouncing on a mule and the fever.

Tired and weak he was compelled to curl up in the bottom of the boat and allowed it to rock him to sleep.

He awoke later to a warm, soporific calm. The boat swayed gently to Attila's song. Sea birds were circling and crying as he hauled in a lobster trap and a night line.

Peter sat up; the wind had dropped. The boat slewed to and fro, as Attila pulled in his pots.

He had moored the prow to a buoy. The boat mirrored the pull of the now ebbing tide.

Attila emptied the trap into the bottom of the boat. Singing softly, he began to sort the catch throwing the smallest over the side. Some would be snapped up by dive-bombing black capped gulls.

A little gull snatched a morsel from right under Peter's nose and took off pursued by others.

Attila stowed the catch in the rear locker, baited the trap with the remains of last night's supper then lowered it back down into the sea.

The boat rocked gently, and the sail began to slap.

"My friend, the eel will no doubt return my lobster to me on my next trip," said Attila speaking for the first time. "Mother wind is returning so, with the ebb current now in our favour, we could make anchor by sundown or even earlier."

Chapter 113

Pen ran up the station escalator and out into the gloom of black-out Britain. She was late and her heart pounding. She clutched this telegram in her pocket.

PRESS OFFICE 21.00 TONITE. PLEASE.

The telegram was not signed but it had to be from Hal, who else? She had not seen him since he had left her in the wind and rain at Mini Ha Ha Bridge.

Hal had answered her letters and had written more letters afterwards, almost weekly. His letters however were strained and unnatural. Devoid of any semblance of affection.

Pen ached in every fibre of her being to hold him. She had reproached herself daily and night about the manner of their parting, replaying the moment again and again.

Thinking how to play it differently.

Pen, late and knowing the offices would be closed, expected Hal to be there on the platform to meet her. In the crowd on the platform she could not see him. The street quickly emptied as the last commuters hurried home.

Across the street Pen could just make out the shadow of a lone figure of a man seemingly waiting and began to run towards him then stopped, unsure.

The street was now almost deserted, everyone hurrying on their way home.

Many more were already down in the underground station, in shelters and off the streets in anticipation of the nightly air raid.

Unusually, the air raid warning had not yet sounded.

A young woman on the streets alone in the blackout was not a good idea. Moments passed as she thought what to do. Her need to see Hal was such that she forced herself forward.

"You all right, Miss? Where are you heading? Shouldn't you be home or down in the shelter?"

the air raid warden asked.

Hal appeared from out the subway shouting to Pen. He sprinted across the road and wrapped his arms around her.

"Thank God, I thought I'd missed you."

Hal had been on the arrival platform when he saw Pen alight but was unable to reach her.

His way through was blocked by the crowds settling down on the platform for the night and the many passengers leaving by the narrow space left on the platform.

Seeing Pen leaving by the lower exit, he tried to cut her off through the next exit.

His way was then blocked by more people arriving with their bedding and passengers leaving and by the W.V.S. tea trolley travelling in the opposite direction.

Pen spun around and clung to Hal as sirens began to wail.

"I can't do this anymore Pen," Hal whispered.

The siren's undulating moaning wail matched Pen's sobs of relief.

"Sorry I'm late," she said, her face buried in Hal's chest, adding, "Emergency admissions and I couldn't get away."

Hal gently lifted her face to kiss her.

"No matter, you're here now. Sorry for the short notice. We were only told this morning to clear the decks and be ready to move. We guess we're for shipping out pretty damn quick."

Pen looked up at him in shock.

"Where?" she asked instinctively, knowing full well that he could not answer.

Hal didn't know, although the kit issued left little room for doubt.

"When?" asked Pen, changing the question. Another question she knew she shouldn't be asking.

"I don't know. Soon, I guess. I shouldn't be here now. I'm A.W.O.L. and must be back before dawn ... the guys are covering for me."

Pen could see the searchlights criss-crossing the skies behind Hal's head followed immediately by anti-aircraft shell bursts. The warning siren had now faded and was replaced by the crack and thump of the guns and the menacing sound of the bomber's engines throbbing.

The warden who had retired to the fire watchers' post on top of a nearby bank shouted down.

"You two take cover NOW!"

Shrapnel from the ack-ack shells was already spattering down on to the roofs and streets.

"We'd best move," urged Hal.

As if to emphasise the urgency, this suggestion was accompanied by the scream-crack-flash and the reverberating shock after shock of a stick of bombs followed by the clattering of falling masonry. Holding hands, they ran around the corner into the next street arriving at the entrance to a hotel opposite the press offices. In the dark passageway between the sandbagged blast wall and the hotel entrance Hal stopped and turned Pen towards him.

Pen raised her face to receive the expected kiss. Hal held her at arm's length.

"Before we go in Pen, I must tell you that I have booked a double room. Are you O. K. with that?

I need to know first."

Pen nodded frantically and kissed him passionately making sure her message reached the centre of Hal's soul.

Pen felt unusually nervous for someone familiar with constant air raids.

This was not only the repetitive rattle of the doors and windows rattling to the many explosions. She knew now that they were entering a fresh relationship, hopefully, an honest and open one.

All this and the bombing seemed to echo eerily around her as they entered the hotel foyer.

The noise of the air raid diminished as the heavily curtained sets of doors swung to behind them. The boarded, heavy draped windows muffled the harsh racket although everything still shook in response to a mobile anti-aircraft gun moving up and down the street to a background of throbbing bomber engines and the scream of falling bombs.

The only light in the foyer came from a single shaded desk lamp on the reception desk which flickered with each vibration. A darkened room was to their right. A central unlit staircase rose between the reception and to the left, two glass doors were propped open emitting a pale-yellow glow from a smoke-filled bar. This was the only other illumination.

At the tables were a scattering of customers plus three British Army privates who were drinking at the bar.

Not one seemed to take account of the raid. The laughter and conversation continued unabated. No one appeared to acknowledge the falling bombs.

Pen stood, not understanding her conflicting emotions. The elation that at last she and Hal were being honest about their passionate attraction, opposed her trepidations of the strangeness of her surroundings and of what the next hours and years would entail.

All this coupled with the knowledge that Hal was about enter dangers unknown.

Hal stepped up to the desk and tapped the bell. Pen followed and took Hal's arm, her heart beating. A portly little man appeared from a room behind the desk, a grey moustache contrasted against his smooth skin which gave the impression that he was much younger than his 66 years.

He wore a bowler hat a black frock coat with a contrasting dusky yellow waistcoat over pinstriped trousers, patent leather shoes and buttoned spats.

Had they fitted and matched he would not have been out of place at the Savoy.

Hal smiled. "We are already booked in. Any chance of a meal, Wilfred?"

"Evenin' Mr. Steading we heard you had been called up," Wilfred replied tipping his bowler to Pen. "Madame," he said emphasising 'Madame' and looking pointedly at the rings on her left hand.

Pen reached across and linked both hands around Hal's arm hiding the rings from view.

Wilfred then attended to Hal's question.

"Sorry Mr. Steading, sir. The kitchen closes at 7.00 p.m. last orders at 6.30."

Hal seemed not to notice Wilfred's disapproval of their presence together.

"Perhaps some coffee and a plate of sandwiches, Wilfred?"

It would normally have been at this point Wilfred would have introduced the question of ration books and points. However, he had been forcibly made aware by the hotel manageress of the hotel's connection with the American press office and the advantages of this.

Wilfred swallowed his disapproval and replied, "Very well, sir, I will have a word with Madame. Perhaps you will wait in the bar."

He walked stiffly back through the door behind the desk.

Hal wrapped his arm around Pen's waist. She was now trembling with the noise of the bombardment which had intensified. This was aggravated by the humiliation, her conscience and the disapproval of Wilfred combining to destroy this, her often dreamed of moment.

Pen had spent her shift cleaning and caring for a six-year-old girl rescued from under the rubble of her home. The little girl had been constantly asking for her Mam.

Her mother had not been found, alive or dead, by the time Pen had left the hospital.

Most dead and critically injured pulled from the same row of houses had yet to be identified.

The casual attitude and a string of vulgar jokes issuing from the bar seemed out of place.

It was as if the falling bombs were of no concern.

All Pen wanted was to be alone with Hal.

In the kitchen, a mature woman dressed in a smart suit and immaculately coiffured, issued orders. "Only the best available, chef and Wilfred. The tray is to be taken up to the honeymoon suite with real coffee in the best china."

Wilfred's face registered disapproval and Maude noticed.

"No arguments Wilfred, you are to be on your best behaviour."

The little man shrugged. "Mint Imperial to me Madame."

Though immaterial it clearly was not.

Maude never was quite sure how to deal with Wilfred's obvious insolence.

He, being one of a very few who were willing to man the hotel during air raids, this stood between her and his dismissal.

There was a growing and significant band of clientele who preferred to risk the bombing and stay comfortable rather than take shelter. Maude needed staff to deal with them.

She gave Wilfred a long piercing stare before leaving the kitchen and left it at that.

Wilfred watched her leave before lifting his eyes to heaven.

"Would you Adam and Eve it? Just 'cos the Yankee press boys dolly up tins of bully beef, spam, coffee and a couple of hundred Lucky Strikes a week, they think they can swank in and steal our girls."

Wilfred was marching up and down the kitchen, his face flushed.

Several near explosions accompanied this tirade which he seemed not to notice.

The chef expertly pulled a tea cloth over the sandwiches he was preparing and waited until the dust and plaster particles stopped falling from above.

"That lot was a bit too close, Wilf," he said before carrying on preparing.

Wilfred thrust his face in the chef's.

"Don't you care?"

Wilfred was clearly resentful of the chef's apparent compliance.

The chef looked up and smiled. "Nope, I just cooks and serves."

Wilfred continued his rant.

"So it's tickety-boo that this Yank is nicking one of our country's hero's wife," he spluttered.

"And him a jumped-up colonial. Three months ago, he was a civvy reporter and now, now he's a three pipper. A captain no less. The likes of me was shot at, shelled, bombed and gassed for four years. Three of them waiting for that lot to turn up and I barely made sergeant."

The chef cut the sandwiches into neat triangles.

"Different world, Wilf," he said setting a tray with two double damask napkins neatly folded. This simple action seemed to inflame Wilfred even more.

"So, it's all right with you that for a can or two of spam or bully beef and some coffee, you are prepared to doff your cap and say thank you Mr. Yankee Doodle. Corn in egg wipe. Please take your pick of our youth. Deflower our young girls and steal our wives?"

The chef handed him the tray. "All ready, Wilf. On your way."

He added, with a smile, "Give 'em my love."

In the bar, the three private soldiers were becoming even more bawdy to the encouragement of the room. They began reciting, in turn, a typical Englishman, Irishman, Scotsman jokey pokey monologue.

The third offering of this 'monologue', was delivered in an almost passable Scottish accent.

"Then the Scotsman took to the start and raising a caber sized bar of thirrrrteen and a haaalf inches, placed upon it a half pint of old and mild, a randy old goat and a packet of the only cigarettes W D and H O Wills Wild Woodbines and careeerred around the arena thirrrrty-three and one thirrrd times. Thus beating the record by one haaalf inch. One packet of the ownleee cigarettes and one thirrrrd of one time arrround the arrreena."

This brought applause and comment from the room and colleagues ... very bawdy comment. "What a cock up." "I bet he wasn't as good at tossing his caber as you Bert." "Piss off, Padre," etc.

Hal now embarrassed, suggested to Pen that they return to wait in the foyer to which Pen replied:

"I'm not a nun, Hal. I now recognise these soldiers. They visit the hospital regularly as part of the R.I.P. unit."

This unit of the British Army was known under several different adopted names. Mostly they referred to themselves as the three R's: Recovery, Re-calibration and Return.

"You know them Pen?" Hal was surprised.

"And I like them." Pen replied. "They are real heroes doing a real job. Two of them were at the hospital today."

The two had brought in the little six-year-old along with others dug out from the same row of houses. Pen loved them for what they did, gruesome though it was.

It was dangerous work. This unit were called in on rescue work when unexploded bombs were present also unstable buildings.

In addition to rescuing the living, they recovered the dead. Too often this involved unconnected body parts. If possible, they identified them and returned these remains, such as they were, to the next of kin. There was no pretence in these men. No playing a part. They were real heroes doing a real and important job. If this was how they relaxed; so be it.

Besides, Pen found the monologues amusing and distracting as did the rest of the room.

"R.I.P.?" asked Hal. "At the hospital? What's that all about?"

"Tell you later," Pen replied as Maude arrived at their table with the key to the bridal suite.

"Coffee and sandwiches will be served in your room directly, Hal," said Maude smiling at Pen.

"Thank you, Maude, this is ..." Hal started to introduce Pen only to be interrupted by Maude.

"I guess that this is the Hon Penelope we've heard so much about."

Pen shocked, turned to Hal. "They know about us?"

"Oh dear," said Maude, "I have spoken out of turn. Think about it, my dear. An affair in a press office across the road from the bar the boys frequent, is never going to be secret for long.

We all wish you well. You just take care and be happy."

Hal quickly filled the following silence with, "Can I pay you now Maude? I must leave in the early hours, before dawn."

Maude smiled and patted his hand. "Consider it to be my present for the wedding you may never have." Maude blew them a kiss as she left saying, "Good night and God bless."

She got as far as the doors then returned saying with great feeling, "Just be sure to come back to us soon. Please."

These final remarks thundered in Pen's ears reminding her of the dangers which came with Hal's posting.

Later, at last lying in his arms she reached out and pushed the packet Hal had placed on the bedside table on to the floor and whispered.

"Please try and leave me with something of yourself, right now."

Chapter 114

Peter was glowing with pleasure steering the lively little craft which was scudding through the water, pulled by the afternoon onshore wind and the ebbtide current.

The sun was high above and Attila was heaving tight on the sail rope and leaning out board to counter the tilt. His teeth gleaming as he grinned in pleasure. The wind 'combed' his beard, gulls wheeled and chased; constant companions of the little craft.

Rarely did he have a crewman to allow him to take this advantage of the conditions, Peter being a competent helmsman.

The channel was no more than a kilometre at the widest and the adjacent island not as mountainous as the mainland. For almost half an hour the conditions were perfect for fast sailing.

All too soon Peter felt the pull on the rudder as they left the narrow island channel and the ebb current pulled toward the open Adriatic.

Peter steered towards the mainland coast.

Attila signalled for him to steer further away.

Of course, thought Peter, the ebb tide will expose dangerous rocks some below the surface.

The onshore wind moderated, the boat settled back into a more usual position rather like a middle-aged man after trying to recapture his youthful past, finally accepting those days were long gone.

Attila having been sat on rim leaning out, hooked the sail and left control entirely to Peter and stood rubbing his buttocks.

"That was good I enjoyed it." He smiled and sat centrally.

"You really are a good helmsman, Peter."

Peter glowed, still exhilarated by the run. For the first time in years he felt life was worth living.

He settled back as did Attila and the gulls mostly wheeled away save two or three who coasted alongside as the little craft sailed smoothly in the constant wind.

Peter got to imagining a new life crewing for Attila, fishing daily and living off the land with no connection to his past life. He felt good.

Attila eventually signalled to Peter that he wished to take over.

"Just two more traps and we head for home," he announced taking the tiller, settling on the rear seat steering toward the mainland coast.

Peter, part of him reluctant to let go yet tired and aching from sitting on the hard board, lay down and curled around the mast on his left side to shield his painful leg.

Out of the wind, warmed by the sun and lulled by Attila songs he dreamily watched the drifting gulls wheeling white against the blue sky and once more slept.

Chapter 115

The boat rocked violently. Peter's head connected with someone's kneecap. He sat up and found himself looking up into the face of a young girl. She was bent over rubbing her knee where it had collided with his head after she jumped into the boat the moment her brother tied the little craft up at a small wooden jetty.

"Who are you?" she asked Peter in an accusing tone and questioning his right to be there.

Attila who was also securing the boat to the jetty with the help of the teenage boy answered.

"This gentleman Marineska, I suspect is the famous, Houdini British officer hero the German Army has been looking for."

Mari looked hard at Peter and pulled a face then looked up at Attila.

"Are you sure?"

Attila turned to Peter now sitting in the boat in a state of utter confusion.

"I am sure Peter will tell us who he is in his own time."

Peter ignored this remark and pulled himself to his feet with the help of the mast. He looked around trying to make sense of this awakening.

Marineska immediately climbed out of the boat. She stood for a moment looking in disbelief at Peter. Pulling another face, she turned and stomped up the path by the river towards a row of three cottages.

"Mari, there are nets and traps to repair," Attila called after her.

The boy meanwhile leaned out from the jetty and took hold of the mast with one hand and held the other hand out to Peter.

"I am Jarny, sir. May I help you out?"

Peter took the hand. The grip was strong and Jarny almost lifted Peter on to the jetty.

"I apologise for my sister, sir. She is very young."

Peter stood a little unsteadily looking into the smiling face of a very handsome youth.

Still holding on to Jarny's hand he introduced himself.

"Thank you. I am Peter."

Feeling unsteady he continued to hold on to Jarny while looking around.

On the same side of the river was a boathouse and a warehouse building.

Up along a riverside path were three stone cottages tucked underneath a sharply rising bank of the heavily wooded hillside. Goats were tethered spaced apart just below the tree line.

One large Billy goat was standing atop one of the many rocks on the hillside: A miniature Monarch of the Glen.

Across on the other side of the river were the remains of two cottages almost buried by a landslide which completely blocked the river valley, leaving just the three remaining cottages and the boat house intact. The warehouse was now derelict and cannibalised.

The river dammed into a lake behind the landslide which flowed over this bank in a series of waterfalls back into the riverbed and on into the sea.

On either side of the river this bank was lined with cultivated terraces. Several of these were already in healthy growth of vegetables, evidence of an organised self-sufficient community.

The evening sun shone directly into the ravine lighting up all in a golden glow.

This was clearly a demi paradise. So engrossed was Peter that he failed to notice that Svetka, Jarny's mother, had joined them accompanied by a sullen Marineska.

"Peter, this is Svetka." Attila introduced her.

"Pleased to meet you, Peter. Please come to the house, I have food prepared."

Svetka smiled at Peter who found himself looking at a mature woman with a weather-lined face and greying hair.

Attila turned to the children.

"Jarny and Mari, empty today's catch and bring them to the house for your mother to sort. Then check the traps and lines are in good repair for tomorrow."

The two almost clicked their heels and stood to attention before going about these tasks.

They approached the house, now in twilight, the sun having sunk behind the island mountain across the straits. Peter, thinking out loud and knowing there was certain to be a lake caused by the river backing up behind the landslip, asked, "Are there fish in the lake?"

Attila recognising Peter's question was one of many he might ask but which he did not wish to answer. He did so with care.

"The sea is easier and less dangerous avoiding all movement from the outside. The only other safe route in here is via the mountain path. This is difficult but safe from prying eyes. Not the riverside where the Germans can watch and follow."

Attila and Peter spent the night in the boathouse.

Attila fell asleep almost immediately, leaving Peter's many questions unanswered.

Excitement pulsed through his veins. Peter was hoping to stay with this community.

To be part of it and, after the war return to live out his life here.

Exhausted though he was, sleep did not arrive for hours.

Maybe he had slept or was at the point of sleeping, when Attila's urgent whisper jarred him awake. "Peter, now is the time to move. The tide is rising, and the wind set fair."

Peter was warm and desperately in need of rest. The cold air which poured down the mountain like a waterfall was flooding through the gaps in the old wooden boathouse. He turned away and pulled the blanket tight around him and moaned.

"Must we? I hoped to stay for a while," meaning I want to stay here for all time.

Attila rapped the side of the bed frame with the broom handle he had brought for Peter.

"Your presence is too dangerous for the settlement. There is no connection currently with the resistance even if the Germans find it. They could reach us coming down the ravine or following me off the sea. If they discovered you here ..."

Attila didn't complete the sentence but rapped again on the bed frame.

"Peter, please move there is such a narrow safe window of time and tide for a safe arrival at your destination. An island which is secure. I promise it is perfect for you to live out the war."

Seconds past before Peter sat up and accepted the coffee Attila was offering.

He shuddered against the cold and the thought of setting sail into the dark night and drank the coffee.

"I can settle then?" he asked handing back the empty cup.

"For the rest of your life. Your choice."

Chapter 116

Shortly after the little boat slipped smartly out on to the straits at a fair rate of knots.

Peter clung to the mast as it heeled over thrust by a sharp constant wind.

Darkness enveloped Peter trapped at the mercy of wind, the tide and Attila.

The spray from the prow frequently accentuating his discomfort.

Gradually the wind lessened and the skies to the east lightened. The sun rose behind the mountain and the sea moderated as the tide began to turn.

Attila began to tack into the wind towards a large island now looming above them.

The sun appearing from behind the mainland mountain gave a much clearer view of their destination. At first, from a distance, in the morning mist the island looked like a mountain which had been thrust straight out of the sea. It looked to be forested down to the shoreline but as they came closer, Peter could see the undulating cliffs, some as high as forty metres. As they approached, the rocky coast became clearer.

Peter who had been silent for the last hour, shivered with the cold.

Attila was also silent and concentrating which all added to the grimness of the journey. The song filled, sun ridden happy hours of only yesterday seemed light years away.

Cold, aching, longing to rest, Peter could not see a landing place.

His hopes of an early arrival faded.

"I can't see a landing place," he complained.

"You will on the next tack," Attila replied breaking his silence.

He had made this trip often but he never took it for granted. It needed absolute concentration and judgement. It demanded setting sail on a rising tide and timing to arrive with enough water for a safe landing in his shallow draught-little craft.

If the wind failed him, as it could in high summer, he returned or waited for the next tide.

It was safe enough at night if he made it across with timing to have enough light to pick his way through the offshore rocks when he arrived.

The early morning wind was invariably off the land, conversely off the sea later in the day.

Safety depended on his seamanship, judging every stage of the journey truly.

Today Attila got it right and they were as good as there. He relaxed and began to sing.

Tacking south west, aligning with an offshore rock then switching back up the channel.

Attila stopped singing and turned to Peter with a huge smile on his face. He pointed towards the shoreline. Peter searched the terrain and eventually he saw some signs of cultivation and building.

This had been hidden behind a promontory on the northern tack.

A break in the trees and shrubs revealed ruined buildings below an olive grove and terracing reaching almost to the cliff edge. The terraces were separated centrally by a mountain stream which billowed out over the cliff edge on to the shore and into the sea.

This was a south-eastern facing, water-etched ravine. Peter could see that the terracing was being currently farmed and tended.

He could not see any way to access this from the beach or for that matter see a building which appeared habitable.

"How and where do we land? That cliff must be fifty feet high at least."

"Certainly not there or else that settlement would not exist."

Attila then tacked back south as if in response.

"This settlement dates from the 17th century. Farmers were forced to farm away from the western coast to avoid the frequent pirate raids. When these raids ceased, they returned to the coastal strip.

This site has been derelict since the end of the 19th century except for one farmer, nicknamed the Hermit who died in the 1920s."

Attila let loose the sail and took to the oars to cover the last 200 metres to the shore.

They were still at least one mile away from this settlement by sea.

Peter looked at the shore as they approached. There seemed not to be an easy exit from the beach with no recognisable path up the steep banks, cliff falls and landslips hemming in a very small shallow cove.

The little boat slid on to the sandy stretch Attila had aimed for.

He leaped out and in time with incoming swell began to heave the boat up the beach.

Peter, partly out of shame at his inability to assist, his embarrassment at adding to Attila's load by staying in the boat and partly because of his automatic reaction as a former eights crewman, scrambled over the stern and into the surf. He lost his footing falling flat on his back.

He lay gasping and taking in water as he tried and failed to regain his feet.

Attila swiftly reached him and carried him ashore then left him to recover while he secured the boat and unloaded the bottle of fish, a canvas satchel and a basket.

Peter only a few days ago would have been angry and frustrated at his inability to move freely.

This day he just lay still and wept quietly. Attila finished unloading and securing.

He stood and looked at Peter and shook his head sadly.

Attila hauled Peter up on to his feet then holding him tight in a fireman's lift, climbed up the nearby cliff fall with the agility of a mountain goat up and on to a rough path.

Peter hurting from the jolting, his leg throbbing, gasped at every footfall for the next four hundred metres until Attila had to rest. Even Peter's mere one hundred pounds was too much.

The two men lay gasping on a grassy spot. The effort and the climbing had caused the sun to steam the wet from their clothes.

"Sorry," gasped Peter.

Attila didn't answer but slapped him on the shoulder and squeezed. He was hoping to build some resilience into his frail frame. Then Attila fell back and rested.

After a few minutes this resilient little man sat up and repeated the shoulder squeeze.

"Wait here my friend, I must get those fish out of the sun."

Attila set off back down the track. Peter in a daze of exhaustion watched him leave then collapsed.

Attila gently shook Peter awake.

"Peter, are you all right for me to leave you? I am leaving the fish behind this shrub in the shade and will be back inside two hours. Moving into the shade yourself might be a good idea."

Peter looked up and nodded his agreement even though he had not fully understood what Attila was asking. He only wished to be left to sleep.

Two hours later Attila returned with a donkey harnessed into a sledge to find Peter in the same place still sleeping.

Twenty minutes later Attila had managed to wake him up, equip him with two crude crutches and load the fish, satchel and basket on to the sledge.

"Just a little over a kilometre of flat track Peter and you are at last there. Then you can rest as long as you wish."

Peter still longing for sleep and his head, nose and lips sunburned and sore, forced himself upright and followed Attila wearily along the track.

This track was bordered by flowering shrubs and wildflowers, white, yellow, pink and blue blossoms. Bright gold, pink and blue flowers were peeping from the grass verges.

The air was sweet and fresh with perfumes of the pine forest.

Peter frequently turned his face into a cooling breeze from off the sea.

Brimstone yellow, brown and blue butterflies were everywhere.

He stopped again and again to rest and to soak in the atmosphere.

When he did, Attila waited with him.

Peter was enchanted but found it difficult to believe that this beautiful island was to be his home.

"Am I really to be staying here?"

Attila nodded and smiled.

"Here you will be safe and have time to recover fully."

This reply was enough to give Peter the strength to continue.

The track began to dip down and away to Peter's right. He struggled to keep upright.

The crude crutches didn't have hand holds and didn't grip the soil.

He slid to the floor and sat there feeling helpless.

Attila's huge hand and smile rescued him from this moment of despair.

Once more he lifted him and carried him to a nearby rock in the shade of a tall pine.

This time Peter felt loved and cared for and was glad to rest his head on Attila's shoulder, no longer resentful.

"Rest here Peter," said Attila as he gently sat Peter down against the rock.

"I must release the fish. I will return shortly."

Peter watched with interest as Attila led the donkey away, taking a path along to where Peter could see an olive grove and some almond trees in blossom.

Shortly after he set off, Attila passed another track leading downhill to the right, disappearing behind a large crag. A further track led down to and around a small lake formed behind a dam wall on which there were two stone pillars placed centrally.

Peter could see a mountain stream flowing down into this dam then out through a channel between the pillars. It flowed down between the terraces over the cliff into the sea.

The bank in front of the dam wall was planted with fruit trees, all in blossom.

Peter, charmed by the entire scene, barely noticed the throbbing pain in his leg, nor a large heavily patterned snake slither from under the rock on which he was sitting, taste the air around his leg then return into the shadows.

He watched as Attila emptied the fish into the dam. There must be habitation other than the three ruined houses below the olive grove. Peter searched for any such habitation but try as he may, any housing, if it existed at all, was not within his sight line. Yet the evidence was that the terraced farmland was well tended.

Attila returned with the donkey and emptied the dregs of the bottle on to the ground along with some dead fish, unhooked the sledge and tethered the donkey in the shade of the pine tree.

He stood and looked at Peter for a few seconds.

"Ready, Peter? This is it. Your new home just a hundred metres down the track. Try and make it on your own, please."

Peter noted something in Attila's look. He had previously not considered anything other than arrival until that moment. He recalled Marineska's face when she first set eyes on him last night.

He began to run his fingers through a mass of matted hair and beard.

Attila was aware that Peter's acceptance as a potential help on the farm assumed that he would be able bodied. Attila was keen that Peter arrived without help.

The path curling down to the right and behind the crag was graduated with a single step, every ten metres.

The slope being gentle, hopefully Peter could do this.

Peter summoned up all his remaining strength, taking great care to stop every so often to ensure his grip on the crutches was sound. Around the bend they moved into the shadow of the overhang. Peter was glad to be out of the sun's glare. He had to stop until his sight adjusted.

His eyes were drawn first to the cream white blossom of a tree at the back of a stone patio on which stood a wooden table with forms each side. Aside this stood three small figures.

The tallest, wearing a large floppy brimmed hat, was to the rear of the little bent figure of a man with a white beard. At the head of the line was a little bird-like woman in a black dress with a white lace collar and wearing a white apron.

The scene reminded Peter of the Capodimonte figurines in his father's house.

This scene was brilliantly backed by the blue sea, the mainland mountains shimmering in the distance.

Under the pine tree the donkey stamped and brayed as the snake reappeared to taste the air.

The snake located and swallowed the dead fish before returning under the rock.

To Peter's left he could see the arc of cultivated terraces still in bright sunlight. Immediately below the shadow of the rock was already creeping across the near terraces towards the stream.

The whole impression was that of an amphitheatre centred around this mountain stream.

A focal point was an old gnarled olive tree on the edge of this stream where the flow disappeared over the cliff.

Attila waited patiently for Peter to move, stopping when he stopped. They reached the level of the patio. Peter drew himself upright aware that he did not present a very convincing picture.

The little woman spoke.

"You are welcome, sir. Sorry, we have no wine."

Peter's first thought was 'what a strange greeting and why did she mention wine?'

The little woman looked at Attila before continuing.

"Please join us. Share our meal."

Peter who was reminded of house servants greeting the return of a master, shook hands with each in turn repeating his name as he did so, 'Peter.'

This was answered by each giving their name. "Maria," then "Josef." When he came to the girl, she all but curtsied as she whispered. "Helena." She touched Peter's offered hand and bowed her head obscuring her face behind her hair and the brim of the floppy hat.

The wooden table was set out with jugs of water, bread, cheese, eggs, olives, olive oil, fruit and vegetables. Adding to this simple fare Attila produced a bottle of wine. Reaching down again into his satchel, he placed two bags on the table, one of coffee beans and the other rice.

Atilla then kissed Maria on both cheeks.

"Thank you, Attila." Maria nodded her approval.

"Now we have all we need. Please sit and eat."

She gestured to Peter then helped Josef to sit at the table. Josef stumbled and caught his foot. At no time did he take his eyes off Atilla.

Attila smiled and delved one last time into the satchel and produced a packet slapping it down on the table announcing, "and finally tobacco."

Josef banged a gnarled hand on the table several times.

"Thank you, thank you Attila," he shouted. "Helena, my pipe."

Maria looked at Josef but spoke to Helena.

"Helena, sit down, take your place and serve our guests please. Your father will wait until after we have eaten."

She spoke softly without for a moment taking her eyes off Josef's face who began to fidget.

"Of course, of course afterwards," he replied slapping his face, suggesting he had been bitten by a mosquito.

Maria clasped her hands and bowed her head.

"Father, we welcome our guests and ask that you bless all our endeavours so that we may be worthy of this food and all your bounty. Amen."

She reached out for the wine adding softly. "Helena, hat."

Helena dutifully removed her hat revealing momentarily bright brown eyes set in a nutbrown face before she dropped her head, her features hidden behind a mass of hair.

Peter noticed little other than her eyes. He turned to his hosts.

"Sorry for my looks. I should wash."

Maria studied Peter for a few seconds before speaking.

"You need food and rest first my son. The world will not cease to turn if you don't wash."

She smiled at Peter. "The Lord does not judge us by the dirt on our skins."

She nodded to Helena who rose from the table and entered a small stone built house tucked underneath the cliff overhang.

"The long hot summer last year dried up the stream and we barely had enough water to drink by September, let alone wash so we know son, we know." Maria repeated yet again. "We know,"

in the faintest of whispers.

Helena returned with a jug and bowl which she positioned at Peter's feet then half-filled the bowl from the jug and hurried back to her seat.

"Water we have this year, but sorry no soap," Maria said pouring the wine.

Peter, unsure what to do, bent and washed his hands then looked around for something on which to dry them.

"To good friends and fine wine.," said Maria raising her glass to a chorus of 'Good health.'

Peter had little option but to abandon his search for a cloth.

Later that evening as twilight fell, stars began to prick their light into view against a dark velvet sky.

The coffee was roasted and drunk, Josef's pipe lit and smoked.

Fireflies flew their patterns over the terraces and Peter was at last able to engage with Helena to see her face which was full of character with eyes like jewels and a ready smile.

She looked older than he first thought, her sun-bleached hair hiding flecks of grey.

He wanted to know all about her and the farm. She was only too pleased to oblige.

Helena, now more relaxed, displayed an intelligence mixed with a bashful demeanour more aligned to that of a young girl. Peter who had resisted the urge to apologise again for his appearance was even more conscious of his body odour when Helena, smelling of almond oil, moved to sit by him. He flinched. Helena seemed not to notice as they engaged in deep conversation unaware that they were not engaging with the others.

Maria who had begun collecting the pots, glasses and empty wine bottle stopped momentarily and looked at the two of them. "Helena," she said quietly raising her eyebrows then turned and walked back into the house.

Helena's head dropped, her hair hiding her face once more.

She looked up and smiled at Peter before standing to obey.

"Thank you for the talk," she said as she left.

Attila, who had been speaking with Josef, came over to Peter's side of the table.

"Peter, I have to leave shortly to catch the tide. I will try and find some fresh clothes for you the next time I come."

He smiled and took Peter's hand.

"If you sit on the top terrace you will be able to bathe in the stream, meanwhile."

Attila spread his hands and shrugged as if to say I have done my best, the rest is up to you.

"Now I must say my goodbyes to Maria."

Peter thanked him warmly.

He then sat looking at the soft night scene, the dancing fireflies and listening to the hush of the stream as Attila and Josef left him to his thoughts.

Shortly afterwards the trio came out to say farewell to Attila.

They watched him until he left their sight around the crag. Returning, they saw Peter asleep with his head on the table.

"Make space in your room for our guest and your father, Helena. You will sleep with me this night." Maria looked at the sleeping Peter.

"He has been to hell and back. We must nurse him gently and hope that he heals in time for the harvest.

Chapter 117

Stanislaw Vittek tapped urgently on the back window of the house.

Raula grabbed a kitchen knife and stood to one side and shouted through the window.

"Who's there?"

"Let me in please, Raula."

"Stanislaw." She gasped and ran to the door and threw back the bolts then threw herself into her husband's arms. "Where have you been, are you staying? Oh, thank God!"

For almost a minute they just held on to each other. Stanislaw started to tremble.

"What is it? Are the Germans after you?"

She pushed him away.

"God! You have not led them here."

"No, I am just glad to be back." He lied.

Raula knew straight away this was an evasion.

"Where have you been, we heard nothing for months?"

Stanislaw avoided Raula's eyes and the question.

"How are the kids?" he asked instead.

Now Raula knew for certain he was avoiding something and that something was serious.

She began to squeeze this out of him.

"I wondered how long it would take for you to ask about them."

Raula was aware he had not even enquired about her welfare. This was priority in her thoughts. Raula deliberately didn't answer his question but watched her husband as if assessing a stranger.

Stanislaw began to pace.

"Any food?" he asked.

Raula turned her back and walked to the stove and opened a flue.

Her mind was chewing over her worries like a dog with a bone. She opened a second flue and placed a saucepan on the fire throwing in a cupful of half boiled rice.

"Rice, beans and peppers, it will have to be."

Raula returned to the table and began chopping the peppers all the time watching Stanislaw pacing.

"You could have had fish stew if you had come earlier."

She was aware that whenever she dropped her gaze to chop, he looked at her.

When she looked up, he looked away.

He said nothing for a while and Raula continued to chop. Stanislaw stopped pacing and asked:

"Fish? From where?"

Raula could have said from the beach or anywhere. Instead she replied, "Attila left some." She knew full well that Stanislaw did not like Attila.

She was prepared to needle him. She was resentful that after months of absence he turned up lying and evading her questions. She no longer *knew* the father of her children. No longer trusted him.

The following seconds were filled with Raula's furious chopping.

Raula, aware that Stanislaw had turned his back, stopped chopping and looked at him then turned as she strained the rice emptying it into a bowl with the peppers and beans.

"And what exactly does Attila get by return?" Stanislaw asked. He was still turned away from the wife he had not seen for months.

Raula looked at his back.

"Nothing from you for months, not a word, no money, no food. How do you think me and the kids survive?" Raula paused before adding, "Why are you back now? Now without warning?"

She paused, determined to get the truth out of him.

"You appear suddenly in the middle of the night for what? To see me and your children? I think not."

Stanislaw shuffled his feet as he turned.

"There is an informer in the camp, and I have been sent home until further notice."

Raula considered this for a moment. "Why you especially?"

Stanislaw shrugged. "Because I'm a Serb."

"Nonsense, why?" Raula repeated the question.

Again, Stanislaw looked uncomfortable confirming Raula's suspicions that he was hiding something. "Well?" She stopped what she was doing and went over to face him.

Stanislaw tried to turn away but Raula grabbed his arm.

He failed to look her in the face and muttered, "It's true we have been dispersed until further notice."

"And that is all?"

Stanislaw's voice dropped to the barest of whispers. "Three of the group were on patrol. They were captured by the German Army who had been tipped off."

Raula let go of Stanislaw and thought for a moment.

"As I thought! It's not because you are a Serb."

She grabbed him again. "And Stefan? Is he back too?"

"Three of them, didn't return." Stanislaw's head dropped.

He pulled away going to the window.

Raula followed him turned him around. She lifted his face in her hands.

"Oh God! Stefan was one of them? Please say he wasn't."

She shook him. "Answer me?"

Stanislaw turned his head away again. "The Germans ..." He began.

Raula's hands flew to her face.

"Oh God! Oh God! What can I tell Svetka and the kids?"

Stanislaw sat down at the table, his head in his hands. Then, he pulled the bowl of food to himself and began to eat.

Raula stood watching unable to believe what she was seeing.

She did not know that he had not eaten for days.

"Any bread?" he asked.

Raula looked at him for some seconds then turned and left slamming the door.

Chapter 118

The windowless room was lit by a single central bulb and sparsely furnished with a single desk and two chairs. At this desk sat the man in grey his vivid blue eyes fixed on the door which opened to admit a senior naval officer in uniform.

"Sorry old chap. Got held up." The officer spoke as he entered breathlessly.

The man in grey didn't answer but gestured for the officer to sit then pushed a sheet of paper towards him. The officer read then looked up puzzled.

"Is this a joke?"

The man in grey tapped the paper with his pencil.

"From the boss himself. A priority order signed by him."

The officer studied the note again.

"W.S. not the First Lord, why?"

"It's the boss's project. He has taken a personal interest from the beginning. The First Lord is in the know." The man in grey then added, "This is for your eyes only."

The officer interrupted. "You are aware that this order clashes with Husky.

I thought that the target was settled and safe so why? We need all units for Husky."

The man in grey didn't answer but just raised his eyebrows.

The officer stood and threw the note back on the desk.

"You would have thought he had learned something after fucking it up at Gallipoli."

He stood breathing heavily. The man in grey folded the note and handed it back to the officer.

"The boss is adamant. You will be receiving sealed orders directly. You are to tell no one. Not one soul," he added emphatically ...

The officer continued his protest.

"So! We are being asked to take our eye off the ball. If he thinks this really is important, why can't it wait until after Husky when there is no clash?"

The man in grey did not answer and began sorting some papers indicating that the meeting was over. The officer was furious dropping his hands on the desk as he leaned as near to the man in grey as he could.

"You are not Lord God almighty. You are just an errand boy. We are being ordered about by you and we have no official notification of who you are and on whose authority."

The man in grey placed his finger on the officer's lips and said quietly, "On the very highest authority."

The officer pulled his head away then spun around and marched out slamming the door.

Chapter 119

It was turned 9.00 p.m. when shadow from the rock reached to where Peter was still working on the far terrace. Now cooler, he removed his hat. Being too large for him it kept dropping over his eyes. It had been a long hot day relieved only by the sea breeze.

Peter stopped and stretched flexing his right leg which had not yet regained the strength needed for these demanding days. Only his stubbornness preventing him from resting.

Maria and Helena were setting out the evening meal.

"Helena, go bring Peter in, he must be exhausted."

Maria stopped laying out the food and watched her daughter while she crossed the stream towards Peter.

"Don't build your hopes my daughter, that young man has problems," she muttered to herself.

"What's that Maria?" asked Josef cupping his hand to his ear.

"Peter. He is working too hard. I've sent Helena to bring him in." Maria lifted her voice.

"Peter, good man. I think Helena likes him. Hard worker." Josef was sucking on his empty pipe.

"You managed to work that one out. Perhaps you are not as daft as I thought."

Maria resumed laying out the food adding, "She must take care." She banged the olive oil and lemon juice in place on the table.

"He might be the only ship in port, but it strikes me he could be holed below the water line."

Josef, cupping his ear, again asked, "What are you talking about?"

"I was saying we could do with a bottle of wine," Maria answered raising her voice again.

"And some tobacco." Josef looked forlornly at his empty pipe. "When is Attila coming again?"

"If we only knew. If we only knew."

Peter returned with Helena and sat opposite Maria who poured him a glass of water ignoring for once that Helena was sitting a little too close.

"Enough now, Peter. Just because the days are long that mustn't mean working the whole time."

"I was about to come in."

Maria passed him a dish of roast vegetables and chicken.

"You do too much. Eat and rest."

Peter liked being cared for especially by Helena who trimmed his hair and beard and also mended his clothes. With Maria he sensed her hostility even though there was never an overt word or move. "How did you manage last year with just the three of you?"

Peter was trying to build a better relationship because he loved his life here and wished to stay.

He was even hoping to return permanently after the war.

"Josef was well to begin with but as the year progressed without rain after an unusually dry winter the stream ran dry, followed by the reservoir. We were without water for irrigation, the stock and ourselves. When Josef got the fever, there was a crisis."

Maria looked out to sea. "If it hadn't been for Attila, we would have had to abandon this place and return to the west coast."

"How do, did you, contact Attila?"

"By signal flag on the olive tree at the edge of the cliff." Maria pointed to it.

"It was several days before Attila saw it but then he brought water and medicines knowing it was one or the other, probably. We hauled this up on a rope slung over that branch bent to a right angle by the winds down the straight."

Maria paused nodding at the memory.

"It is the only time I wished for water not wine. After that he brought ten litres every week or so until the rains returned. Then, we had to restock the reservoir with fish to keep down the mosquitoes."

"That's less than two litres a day for everything. How did you manage with the three of you and the stock?"

"We did somehow manage with just that and goat's milk." Maria laughed.

"The goats were a godsend. They would survive in Hades."

Helena returned with fruit and goat's milk.

Maria again laughed this time in embarrassment. "Goat's milk again right on cue."

"Sorry, it is this or water until Attila brings coffee or wine."

Peter didn't answer but it wasn't the lack of wine or coffee that concerned him in any way but because he was deep in thought staring across at the hillside.

"Up there behind the olive grove there is a stretch which could be planted with vines.

Then we could have our own wine. It is in the sun most of the day. It is still in sunshine now although the shadow of the rock has been across the terraces for almost an hour. I reckon that would be ideal."

Maria smiled at the thought and replied, "Thank you, Peter but it would be an awful lot of extra work I don't see how we could manage that even if we had the vines."

"Peter and I could give it a try. I wouldn't mind the extra work. Attila could bring us some vines, or we could bring some back from the west coast this autumn when we take and sell the surplus fruit and vegetables."

Maria frowned irritated by her daughter's childish enthusiasm. She was aware that Helena was frequently trying as hard to get Peter on his own as she was trying to keep them apart.

"Nonsense, Helena. You forget Peter will not be here forever or even until the autumn."

Helena flushed bright red, jumped up and ran down the hillside towards the cliff.

Peter stood up. "I'd best go to her."

Maria skipped around the table in time to place a hand on his arm.

"Don't concern yourself. Leave her to sulk and return in her own time."

Peter was aware of the conflict between Maria and Helena which had been going on from almost the first days. Helena's attention to his every need he loved. He owed so much to her help in his recovery in those difficult first weeks. He hesitated, not wishing to arouse any friction.

Taking Maria's hand, he said, "Trust me Maria. I will not let you or Helena down."

Without waiting for an answer he stepped off the patio and hurried down after Helena.

This image did nothing for Maria, although he was now moving relatively freely. The hip hop dipping to his right looked grotesque.

"Hardly Prince Charming," She remarked drily.

"What's that?" Josef asked cupping his ear.

"Our Helena is making a fool of herself. Dreaming impossible dreams."

Maria snorted. "Just look at them."

Josef turned to look at Maria and Josef watched until Peter reached Helena and took her hand.

Maria snorted again. "Look at them, Josef. A pair of fools."

Josef stood for a moment alongside. "What do you mean impossible? He seems a nice man and a hard worker and Helena is thirty-years-old."

"I am worried for her."

Josef again shrugged. "I'm away inside to sit comfortably," he said rubbing his backside.

"Those forms are hard." He shuffled into the house.

Maria continued speaking her thoughts out loud as if Josef was still there.

"I am also worried for us. What will we do if they both go to England as Helena wants?"

Peter, before reaching Helena, stopped to give himself time to think what to say.

Meanwhile Helena sat on the bottom terrace holding her hands over her face.

Peter moved over and sat alongside taking her hands.

"I am sorry about that. I was trying to help, not cause trouble."

Helena sat staring out to sea. "Is what my mother says true?"

Peter took care with his answer.

"It's true I am a serving soldier," he said quietly, his brain working overtime, trying to sort his mind out. He was desperate to stay to make a life here, a life with Helena but knowing it was never going to be that simple.

"This is a horrible war."

Peter continued to hold her hand unable to think what to say or how to find words of comfort.

Then his hitherto unacknowledged logic wormed its way out of his subconscious and finally broke surface.

"I may be ordered to leave. In any event I will need to go back to England sooner or later.

There is much to sort out."

Peter turned to face her taking her head and turning it towards him.

"I promise you I will return. I must." He paused before adding with emphasis, "I want to."

Helena brightened. "I could come with you, come to England. You could teach me the language," she said, her eyes shining through the tears.

Peter was shocked. The thought that she would even think about leaving her home.

This beautiful place where only a few months ago, broken in mind body and spirit, he had limped down into another world to become at last the Peterkin of his dreams.

Thinking quickly, Peter answered, "I am sorry that is not possible until after the war. Also, there will remain the question of Maria and Josef. What will happen to them?"

He was a little too forceful in his handling, his inner thoughts being why would she wish to leave this place?

Helena's reaction was shock.

"I am thirty-years-old, think about it? Trapped here with one visit to the west coast every autumn. That has been my life. My brother left before the war and returned just once three years ago. No one stood in his way."

She pulled away from him and ran to the cliff edge. Peter hobbled after her and caught her. "Whatever happens I will return," he shouted over the noise of the stream hitting the cliff side and crashing on to the beach. Gently, he walked her away from the noise talking to her trying to console her.

"I promise you this that once the war is over, I will sort out my problems in England and return." Helena pulled away yet again.

"What are these problems? Why can't I come with you?"

Peter took her by the shoulders. "Please be patient. It is complicated and as soon as I am free ..."

He intended to go on and say, then we can travel the world.

Helena wrenched her hands free and covered her face.

"I knew it. You are married," she cried turning and running back up to the house leaving Peter without the chance to explain.

Chapter 120

Adolf Hitler, head jutting, eyes bulging, stared at the officer standing stiffly in front of him trying to avoid his stare. An aide standing some paces behind looked distinctly uncomfortable.

Hitler let out an explosive 'Hah' and began to stomp up and down the room.

"Excuses, always excuses! The world is laughing at us and what do you do?"

He stopped and screamed, his spittle and breath clouding the officer's glasses because his face was so close.

"Nothing! Excuses! More excuses."

Hitler stood a mere 30 centimetres from the officer's nose. He was almost standing on the poor man's toes and he had great difficulty in holding himself steady.

Nothing was said for a long time. To the officer the silence seemed to be even more oppressive than the rant. Hitler's bulging-eyed stare pierced his brain. He screwed his toes up inside his boots and clenched his teeth, trapping the reply he was dying to make.

Eventually, unable to hold his tongue a moment longer, he blurted, "Council wish you to know, Mein Fuehrer, that the British are ..."

That was as far as he got. Hitler screamed. "Get out!"

The field marshal sat with his head in his hands and without looking up said to the demoralised general, "Just do as the Fuehrer asks."

The general began to object only to be interrupted by the field marshal.

"Friedrich, it doesn't matter anymore, whatever we do now. Just do as he asks and do it tactically. For the time being, do everything he asks and do it correctly."

He paused and stood up and walked over to face the picture of Hitler hanging on his wall.

"Image is everything, Friedrich. We need to uphold that until we are ready."

Chapter 121

The July sun was almost setting behind the hill. The heat shimmer from the eastern terraces contrasted sharply with the cooler western. Peter and Helena were harvesting and preparing for replanting. They sheltered in the shadow of the hill moving across in time with the setting sun.

Maria stopped laying out the table from time to time to watch her daughter who had now moved from Peter's side back up the terraces to begin diverting the streams flow along the terraces which were now out of the sun. She did this methodically by moving each stone block forty-five degrees. "What are you looking at?" Josef asked.

"I am wondering what to do about Helena," Maria replied.

Josef sucked on his empty pipe. "What about her?"

"Surely you've noticed." Maria stopped what she was doing and sat by her husband.

"Noticed what?" he asked without removing his pipe which was beginning to bubble as he sucked over the saliva which had run down on to the empty bowl.

Maria couldn't make out whether or not the whistle which accompanied his sucking was from the pipe or from his chest. She reached out and removed the pipe and wiped the spittle from his mouth then turned the pipe over, flicked it several times to remove the moisture, wiped it and handed it back.

"What?" Josef repeated continuing to suck on his pipe.

"When is Attila coming?"

Maria lifted her eyes to heaven in silent prayer.

"Soon I hope or there could be trouble."

Josef removed his pipe. "Trouble, what trouble?"

He and Maria looked out at the scene; Helena was working up the top and Peter over to the east and near the bottom.

"Oh Josef, they've been circling each other like cats for days now."

Josef continued to survey the scene.

"They are nowhere near each other."

Maria sighed. "Are you blind? She is after him and he knows it."

Josef scratched his head. "Strange way of showing it."

Maria was desperate for Josef to understand. "We must do something."

Josef realised Maria was upset and turned to face her. "What?"

Maria tried once more. "She is after him. Unfortunately for her, as she is thinking now, that he is the only apple on the tree."

Josef was about to say we don't have apple trees when the penny dropped.

"Oh! I see but she is a long way from the tree." He nodded gravely rather pleased with his answer. Maria sighed and got up and stood at the edge of the paving arms folded.

"Where's Attila. Why isn't he coming?"

"What has this to do with Attila coming?" asked Josef looking at his empty pipe.

"I am hoping he is coming to move Peter on."

"Pity, he's a good worker."

"He is a good man but like that branch on the olive tree he has been misshapen by the winds of fate. Our daughter is a good Catholic, Josef, but nature is nature and her biological clock is ticking.

When that second hand reaches high noon," she paused before adding, "well, flesh is flesh.

Josef struggled to make sense of what Maria had just said.

The silence dragged on until he grasped the gist of Maria's concern.

"You are frightened that Helena is going to take a bite of the apple."

He was even more proud of this answer than he was concerned for his daughter.

To be fair he liked Peter and wished to keep him. He reached out and took an olive. After removing the flesh, he chose to keep sucking the stone instead of his pipe.

"A bite is one thing Josef." She paused and let out a huge sigh.

"But I am afraid she intends to swallow the pip."

Josef's pleasure at understanding what was being discussed disappeared. He spat the olive stone out.

"I don't understand what we are talking about. What has all this to do with Attila coming?"

Maria looked out on the scene as the July sun began to dip behind the hill, bathing the terraces in an ethereal glow. She turned to finish preparing the evening meal.

"Don't worry about it, Josef. Just hope that Attila comes soon."

Chapter 122

The following evening Maria's wish was granted. Attila appeared with the usual satchel bulging even heavier than usual.

Maria was on the terrace talking with Peter, having had no response speaking to Helena.

She was appealing to his better nature not to destroy their lives.

Seeing Attila, she crossed herself and offered a silent prayer that he had come to move Peter on. Peter sat down. He was expecting, even sensing, that the moment was coming when he would have to go. Part of him was still hoping that whichever way this war ended, he could stay.

Part of him wanted to resolve his problems back in England.

Helena had made her way back up from where she was working.

As she drew level, he could see the pain and fear in her eyes. Clearly, she was having similar thoughts.

Peter seeing Maria returning with Attila, whispered urgently to her, "If I am to go, I will be back, that I promise you. I belong here."

Tears started to roll down Helena's cheeks.

Peter had to hold himself in check as Attila arrived with Maria.

"Good to see you Attila," he lied. "We didn't see you coming."

"Came in from the south," Attila answered as he opened his satchel and produced two bottles of wine. "This is much as I can manage."

He gave the impression that his journey to the south was just to collect these.

He then added rice and coffee beans and two packs of tobacco.

"Thank you for everything."

Peter and Helena looked at each other, now certain of the reason for his visit.

Attila then produced a lobster and a bag of mussels.

"I thought a special meal tonight as a thank you to all."

Helena ran into the house. Maria picked up the sea food and followed.

"Thank you," Maria said over her shoulder as she followed her daughter.

Attila was more than a little puzzled by Maria's sudden departure. He watched her go then turned to Peter.

"What's that about?"

Peter tried but failed to make light of it.

"I suppose they have gone to prepare dinner."

Attila gave Peter a nod after looking at Josef who was happily filling his pipe.

"Shall we take a walk?"

The two of them strolled down to the cliff edge.

Peter waited until out of earshot then asked straight out, "When is it to be?"

"Tonight," Attila answered. "We are to meet on the beach at the southern tip of the island at 23.30 hrs. Rendezvous is at high tide, 01.00 hrs. We will set sail from a beach which is five hundred metres further south along the path from where we first landed. Come alone."

"So soon? We expected more warning."

"We?" queried Attila. "Is there something going on between you and Helena?"

Peter didn't answer but walked on in silence. Attila did not pursue this further.

"I only got my orders late yesterday hence the short notice."

Peter did not respond but looked out across the straits and the distant mainland.

Attila guessed that something was going on between Peter and Helena.

"Is there a problem, Peter? You are not trying to pull out on us, are you?"

Peter took several seconds to answer.

"Whatever problems there are, I will sort them out. I need to return to England to do so."

There was something in the manner of his answer and his bearing which was different.

This was a new Peter that Attila was seeing. Someone sure of himself.

"23.30hrs. at the beach then," Attila said, adding, "You are sure you can find your way there?"

"No problem. I will be there."

Peter turned and hobbled back up the terraces to the house followed by Attila.

After dinner Josef sat under the olive tree in a cloud of blue smoke, enjoying the last of the day.

The lovely evening and the excellent food had passed all by, but him, all including Attila. All were preoccupied. Conversation was awkward and limited.

Maria apologised to Attila.

"Thank you for the food and wine. I am so sorry I didn't mean to be rude. Please forgive me."

Peter and Helena ate little and tasted less. Even Maria left her glass of wine untouched.

Helena got up, left the table and made her way down to the Cliffside.

Maria rose as if to follow but Peter put a restraining hand on her arm and stepped from the terrace. Maria ran after him. "Please, Peter," she pleaded.

Peter nodded then followed Helena down to the tree by the cliff.

Maria stood where Peter had left, watching. Attila rose and walked over to stand next to her.

"Thank you, Maria. You have all been brilliant. It cannot have been easy."

Attila took both Maria's hands in his.

"Be assured we will continue to watch over you."

When Maria did not respond, he continued. "I am sorry, I must go now."

Attila shook hands with them both and left them still watching the two at the cliff's edge.

They watched for some time until the twilight turned to dusk.

Josef knocked out his pipe and collected his sticks. "Come inside Maria. The day is over."

Maria reluctantly turned to follow. "He's finally going tonight Josef so hopefully that is that."

Peter and Helena began to walk up the terraces towards the olive grove up on the hill.

Maria and Josef stopped to watch them go. Josef looked at his wife.

"Come, Maria, there's little to be done and there's an end to it."

Maria took his arm in a sudden show of affection.

"I always knew that the apple would prove too sweet."

Peter was aware of Helena's intentions from first setting off towards the olive grove. He followed, a willing, yet frightened 'lamb to the slaughter'.

He was attracted to Helena from the first but could not comprehend that this attraction could possibly be returned. He only knew that despite all this, Helena wanted him.

That she wanted him now.

Out of the corner of her eye Helena saw Maria and Josef go into the house.

Immediately she took Peter's hand and drew him to a nearby bush.

Mesmerised, Peter allowed himself to be drawn gently on to the grass behind.

Perhaps he thought that if he did not initiate, he could keep his integrity.

Helena began to gently direct his hands to her bosom. Peter nervously took his hands away.

She unbuttoned her dress baring her breasts.

Peter, still hesitant, saw the desire in her erect nipples on her white skin.

Helena wanted him to caress her breasts.

Peter just stared.

"You can touch. I won't break," she said lifting her hips clear of the grass and hitching her skirt above her waist and then laying back and spreading her thighs.

Peter, in a state of shock, was unsure what he should do next.

She unbuttoned his trousers and pulled them down. His natural instincts finally took charge. The odour of her desire which earlier had caused him to swell now consumed his senses.

She drew his hands to her body and her silken skin, then to the soft yearning centre of her need as she took him in, wrapping her legs round his back, locking her ankles behind his butting hips.

It was all over in seconds. Peter fell back gasping, unable to clear the red mist from his eyes.

Helena turned and lay on top of him stroking his hair and beard, kissing his eyes.

The minutes past, Peter gradually returned to 'sanity'.

Over Helena's shoulder the crescent moon and stars shone brighter than he could remember.

The smell of the pines and flowers were sharper than ever.

He should feel guilty he thought, but he didn't. Instead there was an immense feeling of relief and fulfilment. Even triumph.

Gradually at Helena's prompting he was once more a slave to her urgency. This time he managed, with Helena's help, to satisfy her need to be sure and his desire to be more aware.

Chapter 123

Peter negotiated the cliff path well in the dark. The journey passed so quickly. His thoughts on Helena and the past hour now loomed 'magical'. He was consumed with a wonderful sense of belonging, triumph, fulfilment and a fierce desire to sort his life out; to return to Helena as soon as he could.

He arrived at the beach in good time to find Attila waiting. Peter was jolted out of his reverie into the reality of what faced them in the coming hours. For the first time he had a real sense of fear.

At last he had something to lose other than just his life.

The boat was up on the beach, the mast and sail stowed and the oars set in the rowlocks.

Attila was tossing pebbles at a stick propped in the sand. Peter stood and watched.

Momentarily his tension eased to see Attila playing a children's game.

Attila looked up. "It helps to pass the time while you said your goodbyes."

Peter ignored this and observed, "You've taken the mast down."

"Yes," Attila replied. "Are you fit enough to row?"

"I'm a little out of practice but yes. I think so."

"Good," Attila answered, "the tide is not yet up and the currents between the islands are unpredictable. I will steer while you do so. We are in good time, so we'd best set off now and hole up on a nearby sandbank."

He went to the boat and returned with canvas trousers, a cotton shirt, a woollen sweater, socks and canvas shoes, all regulation Royal Navy submariner apparel.

"Leave your clothes behind."

Peter, glad of the new clothes, accepted readily.

"I am guessing the rendezvous is with a submarine."

Attila did not answer.

Around 00.15 hrs. Attila steered the boat up on to the beach of a small island. It was little more at full tide than a small sand-bank. It was bare but for a bunch of marron grass on top of a single dune.

"This it?" Peter asked, surprised.

"Yes, my dear friend, but it looks like we may have company."

Attila took a spyglass from his locker and handed it to Peter.

"Go to the top of that mound and see if you can identify what those two vessels between this sand bank and the next island."

Attila turned his boat around facing it out to sea.

A few minutes later Peter slid back down the dune.

"Well, my friend?"

Peter was breathing heavily, more so than the short journey up and down a small dune warranted.

"E-boats. German M.T.B.'s. here in the Adriatic. Two of them anchored to the west of the larger island." He gasped, his heart thumping and stomach churning.

Attila was silent.

Peter tried to recover some composure and think clearly what this meant.

Attila was stunned, thinking how anyone could have known about the plan other than himself.

He knew there were the only three in the know: Paurak, the professor and the English captain.

Attila right now was faced with a problem of what to do.

He was hoping that the submarine captain would approach from the open sea and would see the ambush then abort. If not, what then?

Unbeknown to him but already known to the German high command who had received word that the submarine two days ago landed a small party of two ratings and two Royal Engineer sappers on a coastal inlet a few kilometres further south.

The submarine captain had issued 'silent orders' and waited on the straits bottom until today. The submarine was already approaching the meeting point along the eastern side of the island along the straits.

Attila, without a word, passed the tie-up rope to Peter and reached out for the spyglass then climbed to the top of the dune and scanned the sea on the open side. He looked at both vessels and noticed a brief signal light from the leading S-Boat.

Attila thought for a second or two. This was clearly an answer to a signal from the larger island.

It could not be anything else. Attila slid back down the sand dune and went to the edge of the surf training the spyglass down the straights just as the moon appeared from behind a cloud. Instinctively he focused on a cloud of sea gulls flying north tracking something.

He scanned the waters beneath them. The distance lessened. The vee drag on the surface from the submarine's periscope was soon clearly visible.

Attila realised that unless the submarine surfaced, they would have no chance of survival against the S-boats. In such a confined area one depth charge would crush them.

On the surface, they would at least have a chance of fighting back.

There was little or no time to warn them. He had to try.

Peter watched in shock as Attila leaped into his little craft without a word.

Peter got to his feet intending to join him.

The outboard motor spluttered to life and Attila shot away into the night leaving Peter stranded watching helplessly.

Simultaneously the E-boats' engines started up. The vessels swept through the narrow channel between the island and the sandbank where Peter stood.

The leading boat arced north, the other to the south.

Peter stood in the surf and watched and listened helplessly. Over the noise of the E-boats he heard distinct metallic staccato sounds coming from the straits.

Attila knew that he needed somehow to persuade the submarine captain to surface at once.

He had no time to explain to Peter let alone ask him to join him on such a dangerous errand.

Once under way he stood up from the locker. With his free hand he took out a metal cooking pot and ladle. Steering the boat towards the periscope he let go of the tiller and held the pot over the water striking it with the ladle. Three sharp taps followed three heavier ones repeating this sequence.

He repeated this twice more before the E-boat approaching from the north opened fire with cannon and machine gun.

Attila opened the throttle to full power and threw himself into the bottom of the boat losing his cooking implements into the sea. The little boat sped on its way, the tiller unattended.

Fortunately, it was quickly out of the range of the E- boat's forward mounted weapons.

The E-boat released a single depth charge and wheeled away westward immediately.

Peter who was still standing in the surf watched helplessly as a huge plume of water and debris shot skywards. He couldn't believe that the use of depth charges in relatively shallow water was safe or feasible even for the aggressor.

Peter, unable to move from the shock of sudden events, just stared.

A second plume rocketed skywards from the second E-boat.

Peter was hit by a huge wave, sweeping him off his feet and into the sea.

Fighting against the swirling waters he surfaced but had barely time to take a breath before being hit by a second tidal wave.

Losing track of his bearings and barely conscious he struggled to survive.

He was cast back on to the sandbank by a combination of deflected water off the next island and the water's natural return. Gasping and confused, he lay down on the sand to recover.

Meanwhile the stricken submarines' debris bobbed in the turbulence. A large oil slick spread across the water. Peter took a little time to struggle back on to his feet. He looked across the strait towards the mainland. There was no sign of Attila or his little craft.

Peter, streaming sea water, his clothes clinging, struggled to the top of the dune past stranded wriggling fish and crustaceans. There was still no sign of Attila or the E-boats.

Down below a black and white wader flapped feebly in the surf among dead and dying fish, flotsam and seaweed. Peter felt their pain, their death throes, and shuddered.

Out in the straights the water now appeared strangely smooth and silent in the moonlight.

The oil slick had spread highlighting clumps of debris and struggling creatures.

Peter strained his eyes still looking for signs of Attila and his boat.

He saw nothing.

Peter sat wondering what to do next. His very next thought was 'I must return to Helena and the farm.'

Thoughts of what had happened to Attila disappeared from his mind.

Even the dramatic loss of a submarine no longer registered. Planning how to return to Helena was now everything.

He realised that to do so he would have to swim back to the beach where less than two hours ago he had embarked with Attila. There was no other choice.

Best await low tide, he thought, wishing he had paid more attention to the tide's timings.

The Navy sweater was soaking, heavy and uncomfortable. He removed this and the one remaining sock and shoe which had stayed with him. Feeling free of unwanted weight, Peter slid back down the dune. There was nowhere to dry himself or his remaining clothes. Everywhere was damp, even the air. He began to shiver with cold and shock. He struggled to his feet as he began to hobble around the little island in the now strange dipping gate, trying to get warm.

Faint sounds began to invade the curious silence of the last minutes. This became louder and more persistent as time passed. To Peter this sounded like a host of demons arriving.

The noise rose to a crescendo as thousands of gulls, eagles and other birds of prey swarmed on to the scene. Peter stopped amazed at the sight of them fighting and settling in thousands covering the waters of the straits in a white haze reflected by an impervious moon.

Little changed as he shivered the time away, walking around the sandbank. He longed for low tide, dawn and the sun, the sandbank growing as the tide ebbed.

The flow of dead fish and debris gathered pace in the channel, floating past the sandbank.

The current swept all out towards the open sea. Peter worked out that when this flow slowed and stopped it would signal low tide. Any riptide currents would then cease.

Not only was it safer to wait but nearer to his now island home. The flows would slowly reverse and he would no longer be in danger of being swept out into the open sea.

The receding tide gradually enlarged the sandbank into a sizeable island, each circuit of it taking more time.

Hours later when the movement of the debris slowed to a stop Peter waded into the water and made his bid for home and freedom.

For a good distance, he was able to walk and bounce along the sea floor. This he maintained until the trapped air in the canvas regulation issue navy trousers billowed up into a ring around the tied waist band lifting his feet clear of the sand. He then struck out for the distant shore, leaving the sweater, one sock and one shoe as the only evidence that he was ever there.

Chapter 124

Dorothy Price stood in the square at the head of Bendesbury Park watching the children in the playground. Mim was twisting and spinning around on a swing to the amusement of her friends in a melee of exaggerated excitement. That level of excitement was only generated by schoolchildren at the start of the long summer holiday.

Dorothy was in no rush. She was looking forward to a leisurely stroll back home along the riverbank.

She didn't expect Mim to join her. She just needed to know if she would be wanting her tea.

More often, than not, Mim chose to spend time with Pam and herself.

Greensleeves was less animated than a morgue at midnight, Mama Pen was at work, Amelia in permanent sulk mode upstairs and Grandad George reading *The Times*, listening to the Third Programme or sleeping with the newspaper over his face.

This was no place for an eight-year-old.

Nanny Pam's was now Mim's escape.

Pam was even thinking about asking for the lion's share of Mim's ration book.

Dorothy sighed with pleasure. She was free from stress and now, far away from the sound and fury of the war. The prospect of weeks of free time beckoning, life could not be better.

Slowly she became aware of a young woman watching her from a short distance.

Dorothy turned to face her. She was a pupil from the upper school.

She was smart and beautiful in a gingham dress over which she wore the school blazer sporting an enamel badge bearing the single word Prefect.

Dorothy raised her eyebrows and smiled. "Hello, can I help you?"

The girl blushed and took a step forward and gave the vaguest semblance of a curtsy.

The school uniform did little to disguise the fact that she was already a beautiful young woman.

Dorothy was about to ask if they knew each other when the girl rushed forward and threw her arms about Dorothy and gasped.

"I just needed to say thank you, Miss Price."

The young woman blushed bright red then backed away. She gave another semi curtsy and turned to rejoin a small group of older girls who were watching everything.

Dorothy took a little time to search through her memory but could not recall having met this girl before.

Nonetheless, her heart swelled with happiness.

Happy thoughts were interrupted by Mim's sharp tug on her sleeve.

"Who's that girl, Auntie Dorothy?" Mim stood back hands on her hips her chin jutting.

"And why did she hug you?"

"I don't know who she is. I don't remember her."

Dorothy, well versed in Mim's non-verbal communication, added,"I really don't, Mim. It could be years ago when we met. She could have been a very little girl then, nearly as small as you were."

Mim cocked her head to one side and screwed up her features. She thought for a moment before she answered.

"I must have been very, very tiny when you and Papa Yo rescued me."

Then she smiled. "It doesn't matter anyway because I can come to you any time, can't I?"

Dorothy laughed and hugged her. "Of course, sweetheart. Any time."

Mim stood back and struck another pose.

"Are we having a special tea today to celebrate the holidays?" she added with the familiar pleading look.

"That should be all right with Nanny Pammy, shouldn't it?"

Mim, aware of the problem of sharing rations, was unashamedly using the presence of their love.

"We should never doubt that for one moment, Mim. Not one single moment."

Dorothy smiled as she smoothed away Mim's false anxiety.

"Good. See you."

In a trice, Mim was gone.

Dorothy, in a state of reverie and satisfaction with how her life had turned out, was nearly halfway to St. Mary without realising it. She would probably have made it all the way back in her dream bubble but for seeing Pen sat on a log seat staring into the river.

Dorothy wondered whether or not to invade Pen's space, so intense was her demeanour.

Eventually obeying an instinct, she decided to sit alongside in silence.

No questions or greeting. She was just presenting opportunity.

Pen continued staring at the water where a weeping willow's branches trailed patterns in the water and a shoal of tiny fish flashed silver as they startled away with the sudden appearance of Dorothy's shadow.

Pen was pleased to have someone to sit with. Someone who would not be judgmental.

Not knowing where to start, she appreciated that Dorothy did not question or even greet her.

This gave her thinking time as to what to say.

Pen knew that once Dorothy knew her secret, so would Pamela.

Pen also knew that she should talk with Nanny Pam first.

Dorothy, however, would present an easier route to confession.

Pen eventually decided to be economical with the truth answering the unspoken question.

"I have just been to see the doctor.".

"You are pregnant?" This was more statement than question. Dorothy, delighted, took hold and hugged Pen.

Pen gasped in surprise. "How do you know?"

"Pamela guessed when you came over last week. We were waiting for you to tell us."

Pen had gone to Pam to tell her but was unable to find the words to do so. She flunked it and left. This very afternoon sat on the seat before Dorothy arrived, she was trying to sum up the courage to try again. To think of anyone else who might help. Dorothy's arrival was the answer to a prayer.

"How did Pamela know?"

"Mother's instinct I suppose," replied Dorothy taking Pen's hand and clasping it between hers.

Pen looked troubled.

"But Pamela isn't my mother." Pen's whisper was more regret than protest.

"Maybe not biologically but in every other conceivable way she most certainly is," Dorothy said taking Pen's face between her hands.

It was Pen's turn to return Dorothy's embrace.

"Oh! thank you, thank you."

Dorothy and Pen continued to hold each other.

"I guess you went to Bendesbury rather than your own doctor, to keep it secret. Not to announce it to the *Bugle* or the St. Mary Mafia."

Pen gave a little wry, little, humourless laugh.

"Now I have to tell Nanny Pam. Then I suppose my parents."

Dorothy hugged a little more tightly. "At least Mim will be excited."

Pen pulled away and looked shocked.

"I haven't given Mim much thought. How do I tell her? How do you think she will take it?"

Dorothy shook both Pen's hands as if trying to pump up her courage.

"Best brace yourself for the onslaught because once Mim knows, so will the world."

"Do you think I should keep it from her then?"

Dorothy laughed. "No chance, it's unavoidable. She will pick it up quicker than a magnet picks up iron filings. The Government could save thousands on training for espionage.

All they need do is employ a couple of eight-year-olds from my school. Come, let's both go and tell Pamela."

Dorothy smiled encouragement and linked arms as they walked on in the afternoon sun.

Pen was grateful for the support.

Pamela was less warm receiving confirmation of that which she had suspected for some while.

She did not speak immediately but leaned silently over the kitchen sink and stared out of the window.

"How far on?" she asked eventually.

"Eleven weeks," Pen answered.

She stood in the kitchen doorway, head bowed, her hands clasped in front.

Dorothy stood behind in quiet support.

"That's from the doctor?" Pam's questions rapped out. There was reprimand in every syllable.

Pen clicked her heels together in shock at the sharpness of the question and answered.

"Yes, but I already knew."

Pamela let out a huge sigh.

"I don't suppose I need ask who the father is?"

She continued to wipe and polish the cutlery while at the same time continuing to stare out of the window.

Pen didn't answer. The silence dragged on for what seemed to be an eternity until Pamela ceased to polish a knife now burnished warm by the intensity, asking, "What news of Peter?"

Pen jumped as if she had been shot and Dorothy reached out and took Pen's shoulders as if to say I am still here with you. Pen didn't answer so Pamela rapped out the question again.

"I asked what news of Peter?"

Pen stepped back, Dorothy leaned forward and whispered.

"It will work out Pen, don't worry."

Pamela spun around and for the first time in this conversation looked Pen in the eye.

Pen looked up and whispered. "Nothing, we've heard nothing for weeks."

Pamela shook her head sadly. "Does Hal know?"

Pen again looked down and shuffled her feet before stammering.

"No, I thought you might help me ..." Pen's voice faded to nothing as her chin dropped on to her chest as she looked down at the floor.

Pamela swallowed her disappointment that this news had not, as she had often hoped, come from Peter and Pen. With a great effort she controlled her anger. She realised that if she didn't help Pen now, her future and that of the unborn child could be damaged.

If she didn't support her, no one else would; certainly not Amelia.

Pamela turned again to look out of the window and grasped the edges of the sink determined not to cross the kitchen and shake the life out of Pen's womb.

After what seemed another age Pam turned and said quietly, in a softer tone, "First thing, Pen you must write and let Hal know."

Relieved, Pen nodded. Dorothy in the shadows behind smiled in relief as Pamela continued.

"First, we must tell the family. George and Amelia first and then Miriam."

Pen's relief was obvious. "We?"

"Of course. I will be there."

"Thank you, Nanny Pam." Pen started forward in relief followed by Dorothy to be stopped in their tracks by a sharp reply.

"Don't you dare thank me yet."

Pam paused before adding with menace, "That, believe me, is the easy bit."

"The hard bit being?" asked a relieved Dorothy speaking for the first time.

Pamela leaned back on the sink.

"Dealing with the local gossip. The ridicule that will come thick and fast.

The Women's Guild will have a field day. Your child will be called a bastard.

You might have to move away unless you can cope with that and much more."

Pen tried to defend her position. "The baby won't be illegitimate. I'm still married."

"Married or not it will not make one jot of difference to the gossips who know full well that you cannot get pregnant by correspondence course."

Pamela paused and took a deep breath before letting this out audibly before asking, "Then there's your father and Amelia. Do you think you can handle that? How do you think they will deal with the fall out?"

Tears began to roll down Pen's cheeks. "I don't know Nanny Pammy," she sobbed.

"Then you should have thought." Pam turned again to look out of the window.

"Dear God, how could you be so stupid, so, so careless?"

"It wasn't an accident Nanny Pammy. It was just that I thought that I might never ever see him again."

Pam turned around and flew across the kitchen and gathered Pen up in her arms.

"Oh, dear God! Preserve us."

"Amen," echoed Dorothy.

Chapter 125

In later years, Svetka, a light sleeper, sat up in bed startled by the crackle of gunfire echoing through the night. Her first thoughts were for the safety of her children.

Suddenly all was silent. The echoes faded into the hills. All seemed so strangely quiet.

Outside in the moonlight even the usual night sounds stopped.

She put on her shoes and coat and went to look out of the window and saw nothing untoward.

All seemed normal.

The glow of an oil lamp then appeared from Raula and Stanislaw's window showing that they also were awake. The cottage and the world outside appeared to shift fractionally and shudder.

This was quickly followed by the thump of an explosion.

Svetka ran to Marineska's room to find her fast asleep. She stood for a minute watching, making sure Mari had not been disturbed.

Svetka started down the stairs intending to look outside when the house was shaken by a second explosion. She slid down on to the steps holding on to the walls so as not to tumble all the way down.

Yarny, half-dressed, came to the top of the stairs accompanied by Marineska's screaming and crying. "Mama, I'm frightened."

Svetka ran back up the stairs. Yarny stood back to let her pass, then grabbed her arm.

"Mum, you are to stay here with Mari. Understood?"

Svetka looked into the eyes of her son, accepting that he was no longer a boy and nodded agreement. "Just take care, my son."

This transformation from protected to protector hit Svetka in the pit of her stomach. She instinctively reached out after her boy.

Mother and daughter watched from the top of the stairs as Yarny left the house. Svetka recovered her breath. "Love you, son."

Marineska buried her head in Svetka's coat.

Yarny rounded Attila's boathouse and on to the beach looking south.

Stanislaw had already waded a hundred metres out to look northwards around the promontory and was returning.

Yarny felt instinctively that the explosions and firing had come from the south.

He had noted ripples flowing up the river even though the tide was beginning turn.

Raula joined him. "See anything?"

Yarny shook his head. "Nothing."

Stanislaw returned. "Anything?" Raula asked her husband.

Stanislaw shook his head.

"Just dead fish and birds. The waters covered out there."

"I must get back to the kids." Raula turned to go.

"Might as well join you. Whatever it was, it's over now."

"Nothing to be done until daylight."

The three turned by Attila's boathouse to see the women and children stood together in a group outside. Stanislaw crossed-waved his hands across his face, palms outwards signalling. 'Nothing.' The noise from the gathering birds rose to a crescendo as Yarny joined his mother and sister now standing outside.

"Whatever that was it is over now. Nothing to be done until daylight then perhaps we can find out more," he announced repeating Stanislaw's comment.

Only Marineska slept at all afterwards.

At first light Svetka and Yarny stepped outside. The noise of the birds was deafening.

"I don't know how Marineska can sleep through this noise. I had best wake her to say we are going out to see if we can collect some of the dead fish."

Stanislaw and Raula were already returning with laden baskets.

"Any wiser?" Yarny asked.

"Chaos! Wade out into the water for the good fish. The tide has not yet turned. Above the tide line the fish are already damaged. There are rats, cats, jackals. We saw two bears lower down just before full light. No danger, most of them are away now," replied Raula adding, "Will you help Stanislaw to find the drying frames in Attila's hut later?"

"Any sign yet of Attila?" Yarny asked.

Raula almost on her doorstep stopped and returned to Yarny.

"Yes! Where is Attila? He must have heard. Why hasn't he come back?" Raula asked looking anxiously out to sea. Stanislaw had already disappeared into their cottage.

Yarny started running towards the beach turning. He shouted, "Tell mum I am out looking for Attila please, Raula."

"Oh God, Attila. Where is he?" muttered Raula as she hurried back home.

"Stanislaw, what about Attila?" she shouted as she walked into the house.

Stanislaw was already washing and gutting fish over the stone sink in the corner.

He didn't even stop what he was doing or look up.

"Raul!" he ordered.

"Gut the rest of this fish and I will go find the drying frames."

Raula stood and glared at her husband as he dried his hands. "And Attila?"

Stanislaw wanted to reply, 'Fuck Attila,' but he didn't.

"Attila can show us where he has put the drying frames, that is if he ever turns up.

Missing, as usual," he muttered to himself as he left the house.

Stanislaw's opinion of Attila was that he was no patriot but an opportunist ingratiating himself with gifts of fish and lobster whilst he carried on with his idyllic life untouched by the war.

Yarny searched vainly for signs of Attila or his boat among the chaos of the dead and still dying. Some still flapped feebly along the shoreline having escaped the now sated predators, to die slowly, struggling in the surf. Another time Yarny would have ended their misery.

Today his concentration was elsewhere.

He had already guessed that, involved in the incident or not, Attila was out there somewhere and probably in need of help. Otherwise for sure he would have returned at once to check on the community.

He was nowhere to be seen which could only mean one thing, that he must found and quickly.

Eventually his attention was drawn to a regular line of Gulls perched on some floating debris out in the straits. He ran into the water wading, forcing his body through the water.

The gulls flew away and circled around to settle elsewhere.

Yarny returned with, not a mast as he first thought, but an oar which he examined thoughtfully as he returned to where Svetka, Marineska and Raula waited anxiously.

"What is it?" Svetka shouted. Yarny didn't answer or even acknowledge them at all.

"He's stupid rude." A disgruntled Marineska moaned. She was still smarting from her mother insistence she come out and search with Raula and herself. She was tired and had not had breakfast.

Yarny arrived and kept turning the oar over and over still not speaking.

"What is it Yarny?" Raula asked.

"An oar." Marineska answered testily only to be shaken quiet by Svetka.

Yarny answered Marineska.

"You are right, Mari but has this come from Attila's boat?"

He turned it over and showed her. He was not just being kind and was aware his sister often noticed things that others did not. Marineska looked at it.

"It looks like it, why?"

"Because if it is, we must try to find Attila and quickly, Mari. Will you help?"

Marineska nodded furiously. "Why?" she asked yet again worried and wondering what this was about.

Yarny turned the oar over again and ran his finger over a fresh groove running at a slight angle along the length towards the blade.

"What is that son?"

"I am guessing that this has been struck a glancing blow by a bullet. See how it runs a little way along and splinters the wood where it bounced off and left."

The three gathered around and looked, "What do you think that means?" asked Raula.

"I am guessing, but it looks to me that the oars were stowed when the boat was fired on."

He looked at his mother. "That would be the firing we heard."

The two women looked at each other saying almost together, "Attila?"

The rest of their thoughts remained unspoken.

"If I am right, we must find him and quickly."

Marineska had run towards a small black and white wader flapping feebly at the tide's edge only to pick it up then drop it and wipe her hands on her dress. "Ugh!"

She turned her head sharply away looking south. Anywhere but at the bird. She turned and ran back to Svetka and buried her head in her bosom. Svetka looked back from where Marineska had come wondering what had upset her. She screwed her eyes against the heat shimmer and mist rising.

"Yarny, I think I can see a boat to the south. It could be Attila's but there is no mast.

If the oars were stowed surely the mast would be raised."

Yarny didn't answer but began running towards the boat followed by the others.

It was Attila's boat. No other craft like it existed to Yarny's knowledge.

It was empty and slewing to and fro on the gentle incoming tide.

Yarny walked slowly around it looking for damage. At first sight, there seemed to be little to be seen. Certainly, no bullet holes. Maybe the oar did not belong but where was Attila?

The outboard motor was attached, the throttle fully open.

He walked and waded around it once more stopping at the prow which had sand and leaves sticking to it. A broken twig was forced through a gap in the planking. Looking into the boat it was full of water. He was still looking and thinking when Svetka and the others arrived.

"It is Attila's," said Marineska announcing the obvious.

"What are you looking at?" Svetka enquired.

Yarny did not answer at once but examined the prow again then turned around and looked to the forest fringing the shoreline.

"What are you thinking?" pleaded Svetka. "Share your thoughts, please."

"I am still guessing but Attila was using the outboard motor. It was open at full throttle so there was an emergency. He would not use it otherwise. The mast is stowed and locked, so he was first rowing then engaged the motor when whatever happened, happened."

He walked back to the front of the boat to look once more and placed his finger on the sand-covered damaged prow.

"It hit the tree bank at speed, but why?"

Svetka understood Yarny needed time to think and knew if anyone could solve the problem, he could. She curbed the urge to plead again and reached out to Raula who immediately grasped her hand and squeezed encouragement.

Yarny walked to the tree line then walked thirty metres to the south.

He could see little other evidence than the forest edge was littered with debris, dead fish and other creatures. Fresh seaweed was hanging from the lower branches. He picked some from a branch before returning to do the same inspection to the north.

Svetka could not hold herself in any longer.

"Tell us what we can do, son, please?" Her voice trembled with panic.

Yarny ran back to them.

"Mum, Raula, Mari, we must search in the trees. Attila's boat hit the tree bank at speed.

Spread up and down the beach and look for signs where it did."

"Won't Attila be near the boat?" Marineska asked.

"No Mari, the boat could have floated some distance away in the night. Use those sharp eyes of yours please."

Raula and Yarny moved south and Svetka and Marineska north. They were less than three minutes into the search when Marineska plunged into the trees to reappear shortly pulling out the other oar. Yarny ran over beckoning to the others.

"Well done Mari."

"What now?" asked Raula and Svetka.

Yarny deliberated while pacing up and down.

"Line up four metres apart and search into the trees."

Stopping, he took Marineska by her shoulders.

"You stay here please Mari and mark the spot where you found the oar."

Yarny jammed the oar into the sand.

"How far in?" asked Svetka looking at the thick forest.

"To where the debris and dead creatures finish, look high and low, even above head level."

Svetka and Raula looked at each other.

"Go with Yarny, please," Svetka begged Raula, who was spreading her arms in question.

The three of them moved into the trees together. It took a minute to adjust to the darkness after the July sun. They were stumbling over in the undergrowth which hampered all movement.

Yarny realised that maybe they were too far apart. They were not able to see each other.

He was wondering whether to ask them to move in closer so that they might miss clues.

He was about to suggest this when Svetka screamed.

Unable to move over to her quickly because of the density of the trees and the tangled undergrowth, both he and Raula had to fight their way back to the beach.

Breathlessly, they re-entered at the same point as Svetka.

They arrived to find Svetka picking crabs out of Attila's beard. His face was battered and bloodied and covered with seaweed, sand and debris.

He was crumpled at the base of a large tree like a rag doll, showing no sign of life.

Svetka shuddered as she picked a small crab out of Attila's open mouth.

"Is he alive?" cried Raula.

"I don't know," sobbed Svetka. The others were not able to get close because of Svetka and the dense undergrowth.

"We must get him out on to the beach. I will get Attila's boat sail."

Yarny shouted to Marineska, "Mari, is the sail still in the boat?"

Together, the brother and sister carried the folded sail. Marineska was crying all the time asking Yarny repeatedly, "Is Attila dead? Please don't let him be dead."

Her brother answered, "I don't know Mari just help me get him out of there."

Finally, after a difficult struggle, Attila was carried out wrapped in the sail then laid on the sands. Svetka was still desperately clearing his face and beard which was a matted mess of blood, sand and debris. The youth gently moved his mother aside to check Attila's pulse.

The two women and Marineska waited anxiously. Mari clasped her hands in supplication as her brother turned Attila's head to one side and placed the back of his fingers on his neck.

Yarny's hands were trembling from stress and effort. He sat back, took several deep breaths and composed himself before repeating the test for a pulse.

Stanislaw and the others arrived and realising what was happening, stood waiting.

The silence was shredded by mocking cries of the many gulls.

Slowly, Yarny began to nod his head then more vigorously he turned and smiled.

"Yes, let's get him home quickly."

Everyone burst into action and gathered around the shrouded figure of Attila.

"How? By the boat?" asked Raula, "that would be easiest and quickest."

It had been so difficult getting Attila out from the trees once they had freed him from the tangle of broken branches and debris. They wrapped him tightly in the sail and dragged and carried him out by which time they were exhausted.

Floating him back to the settlement seemed to be the easiest solution.

"I have left the other oar up the beach and I am not sure that the boat is waterproof," said Yarny. Stanislaw interrupted for the first time. He was feeling sore that he had allowed a fourteen-year-old boy to take charge so far.

"The boat is floating now. We can take turns to wade and push it and if it does sink then we will have to carry him."

"Yes, and we can all take turns," the others chorused.

From that moment Stanislaw, boosted by the support, took charge, successfully returning Attila to the settlement.

Yarny, Svetka and Marineska, drained by the effort, trauma and events, helped each other back along the beach. Marineska repeated the same question over and over.

"Are you sure Attila is alive?"

Only her brother was sure. Svetka was not daring even to hope at this stage.

Once back, Svetka asked for Attila to be taken up to her bedroom.

In the very small house, a bed downstairs would be too difficult.

Stanislaw and Raula helped get the sick man upstairs leaving Svetka and her son to cope.

"I don't think he's still alive," Stanislaw whispered to Raula as they returned downstairs adding:

"and even if he was is, carrying him upstairs will have no doubt finished him off."

Raula glared at her husband.

Marineska, who had heard what he had said, ran upstairs to her mother.

Raula didn't speak for some time, she just stood in shock.

Stanislaw searched vainly for words to apologise. Eventually Raula found her voice.

"Go fetch some of that fish and I will prepare lunch for all ... no one has eaten yet."

Later that day Raula waited outside with trays of gutted and salted fish to receive the drying frames from Stanislaw and Yarny. The hope was to get the maximum of drying time before nightfall.

Yarny was the first to return. The pair of them set about cleaning the frame to receive the fish.

"How is Attila? Has he regained consciousness?" Raula asked.

Yarny straightened and shook his head.

"It doesn't look good. Mum has not left him alone, she keeps trying to clean him, to get the blood and filth out of his beard.

"We have no idea of the extent of his injuries let alone how to deal with it if we knew.

I have pleaded with Mum to take care in case he has spinal or brain damage.

I don't know what else to do."

"What do you think happened and how did you work out where to look for him?"

Raula looked up from hanging the slit fish over the slats as Yarny passed them to her.

"I guessed."

"That was a lot more than a guess and if we hadn't found him, he would have been food for the jackals and rats by now."

Raula had watched Yarny that morning working out where to look. She could almost hear his brain working. She was having none of his modesty. Boy still he may be, but he had a special air about him beyond his years. She had listened all day to her husband trying to belittle Yarny's acumen in finding Attila claiming it was luck. Raula knew this was far from the truth.

"Please Yarny, you worked it out. It was no guess."

Yarny passed the last of the fish.

"When I was little back at our real home, not here, and before the Nazis came, we had a bath and I would slide my butt to and fro across its bottom. The water would build into a huge wave much to the annoyance of Mum when it sloshed over the end of the bath. I remembered this. That plus that twig through the prow of the boat which gave me another clue.

"When Mari found the oar, I knew then roughly where Attila might be, simple. Good night Raula I must go and relieve Mum now."

Raula watched him go little the wiser for that explanation.

Chapter 126

Two naval ratings stood to attention in front of the English captain.

"At ease lads, sit down you must be shattered. I have arranged for food and coffee."

The two sat and waited.

"What happens now, sir?" asked one.

"I need your names, rank and number. In fact, I will take them now," replied the captain.

They both jumped to attention.

"Relax lads, just your details please. Skip the formalities for now."

"C.P.O. Smithson 651," announced one. The other added, "S.M. Wellbeck 201, sir."

"Thank you we will advise the War Office of your position. Thanks for the supplies and the bag by the way." The captain nodded towards a canvas bag on his right.

"What happens, sir, if we cannot return to unit?" asked the C.P.O.

"Let's be optimistic and say your commander is lying doggo and knows that you were cut off by the German Army. In which case we will be returning you when appropriate. One thing more, lads, do any of your crew have the same or a similar name to yourselves?"

"No, sir." Again, they came to attention. The captain smiled.

"Good, now go and ask Sparks to find some grub and arrange quarters for you, then send him in."

The men about turned and left.

Minutes later Sparks arrived.

"Yes, captain?"

Contact between the two men had been minimal for months and only then on formal occasions.

Losing Scotty was a source of regret. Sparks was another loss for the captain.

"Tape the following, usual code, minimal information just three letters and numbers. Any problems with quarters and equipment let me know."

"Something amiss, sir?"

The captain resisted a smile of relief at this almost normal question.

"Let's hope not Sparks, let's hope not." The captain reached for his pipe and filled it.

There was clearly something not right. He lit his pipe and blew the smoke in the air.

"Contact P and say no news this end of Harvest Moon. Any news from your courier?"

"There is something amiss then, sir?"

The captain considered for a moment before deciding to answer.

"Those two navy lads are stranded. The rendezvous and collection didn't happen.

Make them as comfortable as possible please."

He realised that Sparks, knowing the position, did not represent a danger. He welcomed the chance of a semblance of normality.

"Those other two lads, sir. Them as passed through with these navy lads. If they return, we will have problems."

Clearly Sparks knew something was seriously wrong and was fishing for information.

Sparks had probably worked out that the other two in civilian clothes were specialists on a mission.

The captain considered this question for some seconds. Normally he would have cut Sparks short and told him nothing. He puffed on his pipe for seconds before answering.

"You know as much as I do, Sparks. I just do as asked, without question."

He sucked in more nicotine but was savouring this contact more than the tobacco.

Just to have a near normal association with Sparks was a relief. Their relationship had not healed fully from the incident at the river sluice.

"And I doubt we will see those other two back here."

The captain looked down at the papers on the table signalling that the meeting was over.

Sparks did not retire as he normally did. He was clearly reluctant to leave. The captain looked up from what he was doing, which was an ancient *Times* crossword.

"Yes, Sparks was there something else?"

Sparks, aware he was breaking a primary rule of not leaving the company of a superior officer, stubbornly stood his ground.

"Yes, sir. Lt. Scotty, is he going to be replaced?"

The captain leaned back and sighed. "I do hope so Sparks. The likes of Scotty are difficult to find.

I will however keep you informed."

Sparks turned and left, albeit a little reluctantly. He had more questions. The main one was:

'Can I be returned home to Blighty please?'

Sparks left only to return almost immediately. The captain, now irritated, looked up.

"Yes, Sparks?"

"Tanya's boy, sir, outside. He's brought a sealed communicate."

The captain opened the sealed envelope and read. He looked up sharply.

"Sparks, according to Paurak, the Allies have landed in Sicily and gained a foothold."

He jumped up and went to shake Sparks' hand. Then he thought better of it.

"Get those navy lads in here. I still have some Slovenian brandy. Time for celebration."

Chapter 127

Raula came again into Svetka's to prepare an evening meal just as she had for the last two evenings. "Any change, Yarny?" She asked her now usual question. Yarny shook his head.

"No, Mum has cut a lot Attila's beard away to get rid of the blood. She was determined to clean him when she found a beetle crawling on his face." He went to the door and said as he walked out quickly to avoid Raula seeing his distress, "He might never regain consciousness. He could be brain damaged."

Raula looked towards him and sighed as she started the meal.

After the meal in which Svetka had refused to join them, not being willing to leave Attila to come and eat.

Worried about her, Raula asked,"What do we do about Svetka?"

"Nothing," replied Svetka from the dark.

"Attila is awake and wants to speak with Stanislaw urgently."

Raula jumped to her feet to find Svetka leaning on the wall at the bottom of the stairs crying with relief.

"Attila also wants a pencil and paper. Have we got any?"

Chapter 128

The Captain startled awake, confused after a night of celebration, drinking. He had been shaken out of his first fitful sleep by Sparks.

"Sorry, sir it's one of the goofers outside. He's is in a state. Sorry, sir," he repeated.

"I didn't know what else to do."

Sparks was worried that he might have misunderstood the man.

"Send him in Sparks."

Stanislaw was in a sweat from the humid night lower down and the effort of climbing up to the camp.

"Paurak?" he gasped.

The captain spread his hands. "Not here."

Stanislaw was clearly upset.

Sparks turned to leave.

"Stay please, Sparks. You may be able to help interpret."

This was one of the times that the captain sorely missed Scotty.

Stanislaw was near exhaustion, that was clear. He had no idea where Paurak would be if not here. He handed the captain a small folded sheet of paper which the captain read. He then looked to Sparks.

"Has Tanya's boy left yet?"

"Don't know, sir."

"Then make sure he doesn't. No, send him to me. Also get this man some water please."

The captain indicated for Stanislaw to sit down.

"No interpretation needed sir?" asked Sparks, returning with the water.

The captain shook his head and began hurriedly to dress as Sparks left, confused.

He was dying to know what this was about.

The captain opened the satchel holding the delivery of supplies. He took out a block of chocolate and gave this to Stanislaw who thanked him in Serbo-Croat and then said, "Attila." He smacked his head then each of his arms letting both swing loose, as if he had no control.

The captain understood and searched his vocabulary to ask.

"You take me to Attila, please." The captain used his pointing finger to convey meaning.

He then searched his memory for the Serbo-Croat, then resorted to German. "Schnell."

Stanislaw nodded and answered in kind. "Ja."

Sparks returned with Tanya's boy.

The captain scribbled a note and put this in an envelope along with the note Stanislaw brought, sealed it and gave it to the boy ordering, "Paurak. Schnell" He slapped the palm with the other hand and swept it up into a Nazi type salute, a gesture which Stanislaw copied.

"Ja, Schnell."

The captain reached into the bag for another block of chocolate which he gave to the boy who bowed, turned and ran.

Before noon that day the captain dropped down into the settlement with a very tired Stanislaw who introduced him to Attila.

Svetka stood to one side but did not leave the room.

"You speak English? I assume it was you who wrote the note," asked the captain of the sick man.

Attila looked down at his arm slings then nodded towards Svetka.

"Svetka wrote to my instructions."

"She speaks English?" The captain was thinking of asking her to leave the room then realised if she had written the note, she was already in possession of vital information.

Attila answered quickly and firmly. "No. I dictated one letter at a time. Neither understand English, so we can speak openly."

The captain offered Attila a fill of tobacco from the pouch embarrassing himself, realising that Attila even if a smoker, was incapable of using his hands.

"What are your injuries?"

Attila shrugged. "I don't know."

The captain nodded. "Whatever. You need attention and quickly. I have contacted Paurak so we will see." He took his pipe out for the third time, then replaced it.

Attila smiled. "Smoke if you will, captain."

Relieved, the captain began at once to fill his pipe.

"Tell me, in your own words just what happened with Harvest Moon."

Afterwards the captain leaned back.

"You are sure they were German S-boats?"

"Your man Lt Barnes was certain."

"Do you think Barnes could have possibly survived?"

"It's unlikely. If he was washed off the sandbank by the shock wave as he probably was, the rip current would have taken him out to sea."

The captain considered this for some seconds.

"Just to be sure. Can this be confirmed? Is there anyone who can search the sandbank?"

"My boat is not safe even for such a short journey I am told."

The captain stood up to leave.

"The only positive to come from this is we are now certain who the mole is. Thank you, Attila. We will be in touch."

He was thinking the two ratings stranded from Harvest Moon had come ashore in a dingy.

Maybe they could check the sandbanks for evidence now that it was clear their collection rendezvous was off the map.

The following day, Attila confirmed that the sweater, shoe and sock were those he had given to Peter. Stanislaw returned with the two naval ratings to report to the English captain who cast the evidence into the far corner of the tent, sighed and lit his pipe.

Chapter 129

The commander was in a bad mood, worse he was furious, as were all his men.

He had been ordered by the First Lord to attend an urgent meeting. Did the powers that be know what they were doing?

Men were dying. We're being lost by sheer stupidity. His work was now being interfered with by this summons,without due warning or any briefing.

'Do the fools know what they are doing?' he repeated to himself. He was prepared for battle.

He was being led by an aide along the underground passage from Whitehall to meet, as he thought, the First Lord. This passageway he had been aware of for some little time. It had several offices along it all with non-descript doors. The passage he guessed ran underground across the square towards parliament.

The only occupied office that he knew anything about was the one at the bottom of the steps leading down from his department. This office was used frequently by the man in grey.

The aide stopped at one of the many doors and pressed a bell. A lamp above the door immediately shone red. The aide saluted the commander.

"Sir, I will leave you now. Please wait, you may enter when the lamp turns green."

He then did a smart turn to the right and returned down the corridor and out of sight leaving a bemused, confused and very angry commander in the dim silent corridor with only the memory of the aide's receding footsteps echoing to eerie silence.

This did nothing for the commander's blood pressure. He was unused to being kept waiting and told what to do by juniors. This anger built as time passed.

He was beginning to feel that he was the victim of a hoax when the light turned green.

The imperious order through the door "come" did not help.

The commander entered ready to do battle.

The room smelled of stale cigar smoke.

Smaller than he imagined and dressed in a dark blue siren suit an unlit cigar in hand, sat an old man. Tired, grey of complexion and sparse of hair. None of this fitted in with the popular view.

The only sign of opulence was a cut glass brandy goblet. The commander was struck dumb.

His anger dispersed as his gaze was met by a pair of large, watery, sad eyes.

"Brandy, commander?" The old man enquired.

Only moments before, the commander's answer would have been a little disguised and critical.

'With respect, sir, it is not yet noon.' Instead he replied with, "Thank you, sir, I would, if you don't mind, like to keep a clear head."

In truth, he couldn't quite come to terms with what was happening.

The old man leaned back in his chair and for a moment or two his eyes twinkled.

"Helps me to think."

His smile was short lived. He looked down at the end of the well chewed cigar as he spoke in the now familiar manner.

"You know commander this war will only be won." He paused.

"We shall only triumph over this evil by outwitting and out-thinking the Nazis."

He fixed the commander with an intense gaze for several uncomfortable seconds.

The commander's brain was in a whirl wondering why he was there. He was trying to think what this could be about. Why he was here. Above all, is he talking to me and 'is this really him'?

The P.M. continued in the manner so familiar.

"The power of thought outweighs the arc of the shell, out-paces the speed of the bullet."

He paused again before leaning forward before delivering a final phrase "or the thud of a depth charge." The arrogance and indignation of only a short while ago dissipated with the realisation that this speech which could have been delivered to a packed House of Commons was a reprimand meant solely for him.

He now knew why he was there and just why he had been summoned. In a red mist of he sensed this powerful voice, forcing its way into the marrow of his bones.

The P.M. continued, "The mouse, commander, can see no further than the next clod. The hawk sees better, a much greater scene."

He swirled the brandy in his glass before he delivered the punch line. "However."

He took a sip of brandy. "The eagle sees the far side of the mountain."

He looked down once more at the end of his cigar for long enough to make sure his words resonated. The commander's discomfort mounted with every second.

"We have not slept properly for weeks."

The statesman was suddenly replaced by the old man. He shook his head sadly.

"I seem to have lost the knack."

A long following silence served to emphasise the massive responsibility carried on seemingly frail shoulders. The commander was by now completely dominated. He waited not knowing what to say or do.

Finally, the P.M. took another sip of brandy and continued.

"Not very far from here we have assembled a team of the finest brains, most of whom do not know one end of a rifle from the other."

He swirled the brandy yet again then continued.

"Those few who gave their all, also gave us time to think. Now these assembled brains are the most powerful weapons imaginable and will be, without a shadow of any doubt, the reason we prevail ... and prevail we shall."

He took another pause followed by another sip of brandy. The commander, now even more than uncomfortable, wished himself far away.

Struck dumb, the commander could only try and hold his limbs still and listen as the P.M. continued.

"A few days ago, we finally set foot in occupied Europe." The P.M. paused.

"At the same time as many were dying in the sea and on the beaches, we lost some gallant Italian partisans who destroyed vital stores of fuel and ammunition in Slovenia." He paused again.

"We also lost gallant submariners in these vital hours to German E-boats active in the Adriatic when those E-boats would have better served their cause off the coast of Sicily as would the crack S.S. unit deployed on this very same operation."

The P.M. stood and turned aside and placed both hands on the small of his back.

"I have been sitting too long," he complained.

Suddenly he spun around on his feet with surprising speed for an old man.

"Therefore, commander, it is never helpful to look at a single operation in isolation."

"You." The P.M. left the word 'hanging in the air' for emphasis, before starting once again.

"*You*, commander, are in charge of combined services operations and logistics."

He leant forward, hands on hips, square jaw jutting and repeated with emphasis.

"Combined services."

He held this position for almost twenty seconds before reclaiming his chair, his cigar and brandy. Not raising his eyes, he continued to examine the end of the cigar.

"In a few short months we could be embarking on the final assault in Northern Europe which will demand the focus of all. To this end I implore you to get a hold upon your team, and together."

He paused. "And it is only together that we shall achieve the final victory."

Once more he considered the chewed end of his cigar for even longer.

"Many thousands will die." He frowned as he continued.

"We have no power. No one has the power to decide which husband, whose mother's son that will be," The P.M. sighed, "or how many more will die because I have made the wrong choice."

He suddenly looked up with the now enormously sad eyes.

"I have and will continue to get it wrong sometimes." He paused yet again, gathering his strength. "The intention is what matters. Life is and always will be a series of corrections. War is no different. Can you say in all honesty that you are infallible?"

He waited, eyebrows raised in question, for what seemed an age.

Suddenly he relaxed and turned away.

"I know and will remember constantly to my eternal cost that I am not."

He turned back to face the commander.

There followed a prolonged sad stare which tore at the commander's soul until he felt he should kneel to apologise. Sitting back down, the P.M. finally lit the cigar. He smiled through the blue haze.

"Thank you, commander. I know you and your team will not fail us when the time comes."

It was several seconds before the Commander realised that his ordeal was over.

That he had been dismissed.

Speechless he saluted, holding his position long enough to signify respect and left.

It seemed a long, long lonely way back down the long corridor. He was so preoccupied with his thoughts he didn't notice the aide was standing in front of the stairs up to his department.

From the aide's position it was clear he was there to guard the door.

The commander reached the end and noticed the end office door was ajar. The message was clear. He was expected to call and see the man in grey.

The commander was spent and in no mood to continue his discomfort. He just wanted to return to his desk to hide, also to think.

The aide nodded and the man in grey appeared and opened the door for the commander to enter. "Tea and biscuits please, Lieutenant." He ordered from the aide as he closed the door.

The office was better furnished than the P.M.'s with two armchairs and a coffee table to one side. "Take a seat Commander." He said indicating one of the easy chairs.

Some minutes passed and neither spoke. Eventually the man stood, collected a couple of glasses and a bottle of whisky.

The commander was not prepared to talk and in no mood to accept a friendly gesture.

He refused the offer of a glass with a wave of the hand. The man in grey shrugged and poured himself a couple of fingers and sat back.

"You survived then?"

The commander replied keeping his voice steady.

"You knew and didn't warn me. Tell me who."

The man in grey raised his hand, interrupting.

"It was my belief that you were best off not knowing. Thinking about it."

After a moment's thought the Commander said, "I think I might take you up on that whisky."

The man in grey passed the bottle and glass and sat back again.

The commander helped himself to a very stiff ration and downed it in one.

"I am still angry about the loss of those men on a stupid exercise. Just lads. Our lads. Some we knew. Sacrificed for what?" He poured another whisky.

"Tell me, Henry. Are you still assuming that the main object of the exercise was to deliver rations and repatriate Barnes?" The man in grey made his point, mollifying this by using the commander's Christian name.

The commander took time to examine this question. He was already feeling foolish, because he wasn't able to think of an answer acceptable to himself, let alone the man.

"Something so trivial?" the man in grey continued.

The look on Henry's face caused him to stand up and say. "Sorry, sorry."

This was the first time Henry had seen this man lose his *savoir faire*. "Sorry."

The man sat down. Henry, destroyed by the morning's events, felt unable to move on to face his responsibilities. Two comments of that morning stuck, 'something so trivial' and Churchill's, 'gallant Italian partisans destroying vital stocks of fuel and ammunition in Slovenia.' Why did the P.M. point that out?

"Henry?" The man dragged the commander out of his thoughts.

"The reason I called you in is because it is almost certain that Lt Barnes was lost, died along with the crew of the sub. We have enough evidence to announce that he is missing presumed killed.

Because of his high profile in the media it will be picked up quickly. This story could break any time. We don't wish that Mrs Barnes, Lady Amelia and Sir George learn by way of the newspapers or by telegram."

Henry stared into the distance then reached out for the whisky bottle. The man placed his hand over the bottle. "Please, no more."

Henry sighed and sat back. "You want me to go and tell them before tonight's papers arrive?"

"That would be an excellent idea. Thank you, Henry."

The man didn't pass on the knowledge that an appreciation and obituary had been issued already via the press office. He passed over an official looking envelope.

"This covers all and includes a copy of the intended obituary. These are file copies, so read now please."

Henry read and tossed the copies back along the coffee table realising just how much he was being manoeuvred. He was becoming irritated by the man's 'dear Henry old chap' attitude.

"There is so little in there that is true. They were crushed as an elephant would crush an egg without any chance to respond."

Henry stood up to leave.

The man picked up the copies.

"This is not an application for the priesthood, Henry. Just do it."

He waited until Henry reached the door to comment further.

"Commander, we are not doing this without purpose. Time is running out for the big one and you are clearly the man for the job, but we are worried a about some of your team.

They give the impression of Oxbridge chums arranging a varsity match at Twickers.

Do what you need to do. Whatever it takes, whatever the cost. You have mine and the P.M.'s full support."

The man walked with Henry to the door.

"Just sort it, please."

Chapter 130

Henry sat at his desk in the main office and tried to get his head together.

Henry's desk had just one screen each side. The rest of the office was open plan with the different units spaced out. Navy, Army and Air Force worked together, segregated into logistics, supplies, action/analysis and forward planning units.

All were aware that something was brewing and were pretending to work but listening for any clues as to what Henry had learned from the rumoured meeting with the First Lord.

Henry reached for the telephone and dialled. Immediately he was aware of the collective reaction. He closed his hand over the speaker and lowered his voice. Sir George answered.

"Henry here, George, will you and Lady Amelia be able receive me later today?"

After a short conversation, inaudible to the others, Henry replaced the receiver and surveyed the office. All eyes were down. All appeared to be concentrating on their tasks.

Taking a deep breath, the commander walked around his desk and in his best parade ground voice addressed them.

"Gentlemen, I am convening a meeting in the conference room at 13.30 hrs. I suggest you take lunch now and be back in good time."

Len Redmile who was in charge of forward planning co-ordination broke the stunned silence.

"13.30 hrs. sir? Mid-lunch hour and short notice? Some of us have other plans in place."

The commander looked across but didn't answer. He thought carefully about how to reply. He was already beginning to understand why and what this morning's sessions were about. Another voice piped up.

"We don't normally return until at least two pip emma ..."

Another voice added, "If then."

A ripple of laughter followed. This and other voiced comments faded to a whisper as the commander turned towards the sound.

Henry didn't speak for at least twenty seconds then he repeated,"13.30 hrs. prompt please, gentlemen. Bring with you all up to date info on all projects especially the latest detail on personnel carriers, landing craft, gliders, support aircraft, a list of trained operators and training beaches so far confirmed as available."

An army subaltern sprang to attention. "Permission to speak, sir?"

The commander nodded in his direction.

"I don't think I can do that sir and get lunch." He looked at his watch. "In less than one hour. Sir."

The Commander looked around. "Does that go for all of you?"

"Yes, sir," they chorused.

"Just do it," the commander replied, adding, "And may I suggest if you think this harsh, that you take the same lunch break as your colleagues in Italy currently liberating Reggio. That is if they have any break at all and are still alive to take one." He paused, taking a tip from the P.M.

"For those of you who are not sufficiently on top of the job and who miss lunch, this order comes from me, not from the First Lord."

The Commander returned to his desk and tried not to look at the confusion around the office.

He thumbed through the schedules and dates and made notes. Meanwhile out in the office some sort of order began to appear. Some left the office others began to organise their response.

His attention was drawn by a slight cough followed by, "Henry old ..."

The voice faded as the young officer rephrased. "Permission to speak, sir.".

"Yes, Lt. Peat?" Henry was warming to his task. Already feeling better.

The young man looked straight ahead over the commander's head with his one good eye.

"I have had a look at Weymouth beaches, but it seems that the Yanks have claimed them.

Can something be done about it? He said angrily, 'After all, they are our beaches."

The commander was already even more understanding the reason for his trials this morning, more aware of his responsibilities. Feeling ashamed yet trying not to take this out on the staff.

"Could it be Lt. Peat, that our American friends are smarter than us?"

Henry repeated Peat's question, then answered it. "Can anything be done about it?

Yes, it can, but that will require that we all step up to the plate. Sharpen our act."

Henry raised his voice and looked around the office.

"Conference room 13.30 sharp gentlemen, prompt."

He then left to take a breath of fresh air.

Chapter 131

"That is the house, driver. The big detached with the green tiles at the head of the crescent."

Henry reached for his papers.

Sir George stood in the bay window watching for Henry's arrival at the appointed hour.

Amelia, in one of her rare visits to the lounge, was sitting in her usual chair, 'under sufferance', embroidering.

"I have no idea why it is that I am needed, George," she complained, although she was bursting to learn what this was all about, hoping, perhaps, for the recall of George to Whitehall.

"Furthermore, you invited him for coffee. You know full well we have none."

In her mind, her husband was the architect of all their problems opting for retirement with no more extras like coffee and lamb chops from the city. He had conveniently forgotten that such items would not be available in Dartmouth.

"They're here," announced Sir George from the window.

"I will get Emerson to make tea. Also, I must make sure it is made in the best china and not the brown pot." Lady Amelia put down her embroidery and left.

Sir George noted with some satisfaction the village was aware. Curtains were twitching up and down the Green with the arrival of this chauffeur-driven limousine. He straightened his tie and went to the door to greet their guest.

In his stomach, the 'butterflies' swarmed at the prospect of this meeting. Despite his latest resolve, 'Colonel Blimp' re-emerged.

"My dear chap, delighted to meet you again."

Henry was relieved to be received cordially by the man he had so recently replaced.

He shook hands warmly.

"Good to see you, Sir George. Can my driver come in and have a drink? It's roasting in the car."

Henry did not wish to allow Sir George's neighbours access to his man.

"Of course. If he goes through into the kitchen Emily will take care of him."

Sir George took the opportunity to look over Henry's shoulder to see if those same neighbours were taking note.

Henry signalled to his driver to come in. This was just as well because some of the more shameless watchers were already at their garden gates.

Sir George showed his guest into the lounge and offered him a seat.

Henry looked around. "I was hoping Mrs Barnes and Lady Amelia would be joining us?"

Sir George was taken aback at the mention of Pen. He was hoping that Henry was going to offer him an escape from this retirement. He had not considered Pen's involvement until now.

He heard himself stammering. "Oh, sorry Pen's working at the hospital."

This Henry already knew having checked before he set off.

"Amelia is arranging some tea. She will be with us directly." Sir George's voice faltered as his brain re-processed the reason for this sudden visit. He replayed in his head his hesitant response and blushed at this and the memory of his crass hopes of a recall.

Henry concerned about George, was about to go to him when Lady Amelia swept back into the room.

"So sorry Rear Admiral not to receive you. I was arranging tea." She looked across at George.

"Coffee I am afraid is currently off the menu."

Henry's attention was temporarily diverted from his concern at Sir George's problems which were manifest.

"How do you do Lady Amelia?" He opened his briefcase and produced a brown paper bag.

"Real coffee and ersatz Garibaldis, by way of apology for this sudden intrusion."

Amelia looked across at her husband and replied, "Thank you, Rear Admiral, so kind," emphasising, "so thoughtful."

Emily knocked on the door and entered wheeling in the tea trolley.

"Thank you, Emerson, that will be all. Please make yourself comfortable, Rear Admiral."

She sat ramrod straight and waved an imperious hand towards a chair.

All this George heard to the background of his thoughts, memories of Peter, a serious little boy lost arriving for the long summer holidays. Looking on, never competing for Pamela's attention with Paul while Pen did so, using all her feminine wiles. Pen turned to Peter for solace when rejected.

He turned to her as sibling family,the only 'real' family he had.

This had led Amelia, Richard and himself to assume that Pen and Peter were meant for each other. Blinded by the lure of money.

George was now aware of his part in the failed destinies of both Peter and his daughter.

It was now being brought to an ugly head by the news which he now fully expected. Out of the mists of his many thoughts he heard Henry addressing him.

"The Garibaldis aren't that bad George considering the lack of sugar and fat. I am guessing the currants are dried elderberry. Note though, they are definitely non-dunkable."

"What please is the reason for this sudden visit, Henry?"

George was anxious to cut through the small talk; to stop Amelia's gushing hopes of a magical recall to Whitehall.

"Bearer of sad news, the worst I am afraid. We are so sorry."

Henry swallowed and struggled to keep George in vision, aware that he had already guessed.

"We wished to give you the opportunity to break this to Mrs Barnes before it gets out in the newspapers or perhaps even on the radio tonight."

He reached again into his briefcase and produced the envelope passing this on to George.

'How can I tell Pen?' was George's first thought as he opened it.

The import of this news finally penetrated Amelia's brain.

"Peter Barnes, dead?" she whispered.

She placed the cup and saucer on the coffee table and sat back ramrod straight. Her lips pursed into a thin red line as she waved away the communicate offered by George.

"There is a copy of the obituary issued via the press office. If there is anything either of you wish to add Lady Amelia."

Henry's offer was also waved away immediately by Amelia who stood up.

Henry jumped to his feet. Amelia drew herself up to her full 5ft 2ins. Thank you for your concern Rear Admiral, please be so kind and excuse me."

She held her poise and composure until she was outside the door. Then she put her head in her hands on the lower staircase bannister for several seconds, took several deep breaths and disappeared up the stairs.

"Perhaps I should leave now George if you will excuse me," the commander suggested.

"Must you go, Henry? Give me something for Pen, please. The how, the when. You know the sort of thing?"

Henry was now anxious to leave, having delivered the awful news.

Realising that George was struggling, he answered, "Well, of course."

Sir George offered his hand. He was both in need of a touch of humanity and to escape the 'shrapnel' of Amelia's reaction.

"Please can we take a walk? I need some air."

Henry gripped George's hand.

"Good idea, we all need a moment. Perhaps a walk by the river?"

Sir George led the way out of the side gate and down the lane by the cricket ground.

Much had changed since that eventful match on August Bank Holiday. The score box was derelict, the grass unkempt, the paint peeling off the pavilion and sightscreens. The neat white boundary lines and picket fence were gone. Nothing was left which remotely resembled that idyllic world.

Sir George was absorbed in his thoughts when he was not apologising for Amelia promoting Henry to a Rear Admiral. This on another occasion would have been a source of some amusement.

George's head finally cleared when they reached the footbridge over the ford.

"This is where Pen comes when she is troubled."

Henry looked down along the river. The rippled surface bathed in the evening sunshine.

Sunbeams pierced the trailing branches of the weeping willows creating diapason patterns on the green bankside. The gentle river breeze, cooling and welcome.

"I can now understand why you chose to take retirement and to stay in St. Mary. It is beautiful."

"It no longer works for me I am afraid." George laughed awkwardly. "In fact, I was flattering myself that you were coming over to offer me a job. An escape route."

An awkward silence ensued which George hastily attempted to fill.

"Is what happened to Peter as quoted all true? No flannel?"

Sir George looked Henry in the eye.

"All true. There is very little doubt that he could not have survived the action."

"Tell me, George," he continued, "we have a reliable witness who says that Peter identified the two M.T.B.'s involved in the action as German E-boats. How much credit would you give to Peter's abilities in that respect?"

Sir George reacted with surprise. "E- boats in the Med?"

"Adriatic. Amounts to the same thing," Henry answered. "Takes some believing."

"If Peter said they were, it is certainly worth serious consideration."

Several minutes passed while neither spoke. George was now embarrassed because of his ill-disguised plea for a return to Whitehall.

Meanwhile Henry stared down into the bouncing waters and nodding as if to agree with his thinking. Henry eventually gave voice to his thoughts.

"Do you know Connie Peat's boy, Timothy? His grandfather Bertie Peat was at Jutland.

Captained one of the cruisers?"

"No, Henry, can't say as I do. Where's this going?"

"Well, I knew Connie before the war. We have a bit of history. Nothing heavy and we are still good friends."

George had not the first idea where this was leading but he had a good feeling about it as Henry continued.

"Well, Tim is Connie's son. He's got a bit of a wonky eye, picked it up at Dunkirk or some place or other. Anyway, he turns up on my watch. Desk job and all that."

Henry sighed and looked up.

"Trouble is he's got a bit of a wonky brain too. A clear case of who you know, not what."

He continued to look at the bouncing waters. "Too young really, too nice. Gets pushed around and has lost a couple of good venues to the Americans."

Henry continued nodding away to the water.

He turned and took a long look at George, much to Sir George's embarrassment.

"You did say you would take anything?" he asked eventually.

Sir George started, almost springing to attention.

"Too true Henry, old boy. Too true." He almost shouted.

George had not the first idea what Henry was on about. Then again, he didn't care.

"Would mean a lot of travel. Of course, you would have a car and driver. Best you work from the club up west. Wouldn't do to have the car swanning in and out of St. Mary."

Henry was clearly thinking out the plan and talking it through out loud. He paused between each thought.

Sir George could only just stop himself between thoughts from shouting out, 'Yes, please.' He waited until Henry had finished and asked “Wouldn’t you have to get this all cleared first?” Fear and logic took over.

Henry shook his head slowly.

“Already got it cleared at the highest level and I do mean the highest.”

Sir George managed to make his next question sound almost casual.

“When would this project start?”

“At once. We are already behind schedule. Would that be a problem?”

Ignoring that salary, expenses and conditions had not been discussed Sir George smiled and attempted humour.

“No problem. Could this wait until tomorrow?”

Henry had no thought for humour.

“I will sort the detail immediately. Ask you up for briefings as soon as that is done.”

He nodded again vigorously at the water as if to acknowledge the inspiration.

“Your title, Sir George Bridge-Thompson Bart will be a great asset. Councils love a Sir.”

Sir George still had no idea what he was being asked to take on.

He didn’t care.

Chapter 132

Watching the official car leave the Green was to Sir George like watching his new belief disappear leaving him lonely and insecure.

The watchers from the gates one by one returned to their homes leaving him isolated and wondering what to do. Pamela Avery and Dorothy watched from the front room window.

"What was that all about?" asked Dorothy.

"I have no idea what that can be about, Pet," Pam replied although the opposite was true.

In her chest, the stone of fear had returned. She knew that if she opened the front door George would accept her unspoken invitation and call only if it was good news.

Deep down, Pam knew that he wouldn't accept her invitation today.

The door remained closed. If what she feared was true, George would wait until Pen returned home and not call as was his habit.

Pamela went into the kitchen and put on an apron and oven gloves. She took all the shelves out of the oven and began to clean furiously.

Dorothy watched from the doorway then decided not to question her and returned to see George still standing there at the head of the Green.

Amelia watched from the upstairs window waiting for George to return but he didn't.

Sir George was now dreading Pen's return. He also knew that a return to the house was going to be unpleasant. Even if he told Amelia about the Whitehall offer, the questioning would be incessant. Having accepted probably a junior position and not negotiated anything. He had no answers for her. Normally he would have headed for Pamela's but that was 'out' until Pen returned and that could be another hour.

Eventually he walked down towards Bendesbury by the riverside path and out of sight of the Green.

A confused and lonely figure, he sat waiting for 7.45 and Pen's arrival from town.

He was not entirely alone in this vigil.

Amelia remained in the window watching. Pamela kept an eye on the kitchen clock.

Dorothy, asking no questions, sat in the front room helping Mim with her homework which was difficult as all windows were open and the noise of children playing outside filtered through constantly.

When the limousine had appeared and stopped at Greensleeves, Pam had clapped her hand to her mouth and gasped. "Oh God. Peter." She ran into the kitchen. This was proving both a distraction and in a strange way a help with Mim's homework question.

"What is all this with Nanny Pammy and Peter, Auntie Dorothy?" Mim asked.

Dorothy didn't answer but told her to take no notice and carry on with her homework.

Mim's homework title was, Family Connections. A Beloved Child has Many Names.

The teacher's instruction was to write 200 words about family connections.

This was part of a lesson on culture and tradition. This was a problem for Mim who said:

"I have no proper family, Miss."

In reply the teacher asked, "Who first called you Mim, when your given name is Miriam?"

When Mim replied she didn't know, the teacher said that there was a connection even if no one remembered when or why. She was to think about it.

Mim asked Aunt Dorothy what to do and write. Dorothy kept the answer simple.

"Mim is a diminutive version of Miriam and was probably your mother's affectionate name for you." This pleased Mim. "And I still have my real Mama's name for me even now."

Little did either know that it was Peggy Firth who called her Mim on Zurich station platform at their first meeting and it had stuck.

That mattered little. Mim was happy. She had this connection to her mother or, so she thought.

Pam and Dorothy waited, as did most of the Green's neighbours, windows open listening for the 7.30 bus from Fernborough Station.

At the appointed hour George got up and moved to the head of the Green.

The bus was on time and stopped.

Pen was the only passenger alighting at St. Mary. She walked up the centre of the Green then broke into a run instinctively when she saw her father waiting for her before stopping just as abruptly. George did not move. Normally he would have marched in soldierly fashion to greet her.

Pen slowly sank to her knees on the grass. The *Evening Standard* fell out of her grasp on to the ground, the headline screaming ..." ALLIES CAPTURE REGGIO. Establish a bridgehead on the Italian mainland."

Pen had fallen asleep on the train and had not opened the paper.

Out of the corner of her eye she was aware that Pam had come to the front door.

Her father began to run towards her, a beloved comical bouncing figure.

Another time she would have laughed. Tonight, she cried.

"Please Daddy, not Hal. Not Peter."

George helped Pen regain her feet. "Sorry, Penny my love. It's Peter."

"Not dead, Daddy. Please not dead." Pen was relieved that it was not Hal but devastated at the news of Peter. She felt sick with guilt.

"I am afraid so, Penny," answered George as Pam arrived and gathered Pen into her arms.

"I guessed, George. I had already guessed."

The watching neighbours now were now in no doubt.

"Fool. You utter fool, George," muttered Amelia still looking from the window.

"Making a spectacle in front of the neighbourhood. Why could you not wait until she was inside?" George, Pen and Pam, arms linked, walked slowly up the Green watched in silence by all.

Even the children stopped playing. Amelia snorted and moved away from the window.

Pen broke free as they approached the front gate and backed towards the lane.

"Are you not coming in?" asked George. Pen continued to back away shaking her head.

"Just leave me. Please, Daddy. Just leave me." She turned around and began to walk quickly then began running down the lane.

George making to follow was restrained by Pamela.

"Leave her, George. She needs time alone."

Pam looked at his sad tortured face almost forgetting her own trauma.

"Would you prefer to come back to mine?"

George just shook his head. Pam realised he was in no fit state to be left on his own.

"Why don't we take a walk by the river?" was all she could offer.

Gently, she steered him away from Drovers Lane across the Green toward the riverside path.

They walked slowly, arms linked, until they were out of sight watched by all including Amelia who had been pacing to and fro between the door and the window listening for George and Pen to return. She stopped pacing and watched Pam and George disappear then placed her hand over her mouth stifling a whimper.

Amelia went to sit in her usual corner where she spent her afternoons at a small occasional table reading or embroidering. She picked up her work and sat staring into space, the stitched floral picture remaining half completed. The radio was still playing in the background with the announcer speaking over dramatic music. 'From the falling leaves collection by Ivan Bunin. How sad. How quickly did it fade?'

Amelia reached out and switched off the radio.

She stood, smoothed her dress, repaired her make up at the gilt mirror and went downstairs.

Chapter 133

Pamela and George walked slowly along the riverbank until a row of weeping willow masked them from the Green. They sat together on a log seat. Neither spoke as they sat staring at the river.

George was the first to break the long silence.

"I am so sorry, Pammy. Are you all right?"

Pamela shook her head.

"Not really, although I didn't ever expect Peter to return."

"You didn't?" George asked although showing little surprise himself.

Pam continued in a tired, small voice.

"My regret is that I never had chance to make things right again between us.

We wasted so many years. Then just when things seemed to be getting better, I messed up.

My pain is that now I will never have the chance to make it right, apologise."

Pam brushed away a tear. "I knew the moment that limo stopped outside yours. No one knows my pain. That pain of parting is not dulled by the passage of time. I have ached every hour from that day when Peter walked out. Every knock of the door, every ring of the bell, I hoped. Every day, every night I have cried." The tears began to flow freely.

George passed her a large white handkerchief. Pam covered her face with it.

The silence which followed became more and more oppressive. Neither spoke.

George stared at the water sparkling by and full of life.

Across the other side of the river rhododendrons and azalea blazed red, orange and gold contrasting with their mood.

George kept looking anxiously back up the river. Eventually, he stood up then sat down again.

"Pammy, are you sure Pen will be all right? What if she has gone back home? I don't know what to do. I don't want to go home but I can't leave Pen alone not now."

Pam recognised then just how desperate George was and with a great effort she drew on every ounce of courage. She was half aware that things were not all right with the Bridge-Thompsons.

Not just how bad it was.

Pam gave a half-hearted chuckle. She was trying to lift the mood, but irony dominated.

"You know, George. I have it on the best authority that you and I are having an affair."

Sir George turned towards Pam astonished. "Really?"

"It's all over the village." Pam replied, pleased she had shaken him out of the black place.

It was George's turn to give a humourless chuckle. "No one has told me."

"It is too dangerous for you to stay at mine. So, it is home to Amelia or under the stars."

Pam knew as she spoke this was no joke.

Sir George earlier had considered whether he could afford to go and stay in the club in town, but this was now out of the question. Desperate to change the subject, he confided in his friend.

"Pammy, no one else will know of this yet, certainly not Amelia."

George did his best to sound positive.

It was a mood which had disappeared the moment Henry's car left the Green.

"I have the chance to return to work. Back to the firm at Whitehall but how can I leave Pen just now?"

"What will Amelia say?"

"I no longer care. I plan to stay at the club pro-temp."

Pam took George's arm. "Take it, George. I will look to Pen and Mim. In fact, Mim is with Dorothy right now."

Sir George sighed. "You don't know how bad things are Pammy. Amelia will not compromise.

She cannot accept that we no longer own Greensleeves and are guests. Amelia and Pen are at daggers drawn permanently. Leave them alone for a second and they are fighting like Kilkenny cats."

"Maybe you should rent a place in town until something is sorted."

"Tried that one, Pammy but Amelia won't accept that which we can afford. Loss of standing and all that."

Pam thought for a while before asking, "George, is this job important? I don't mean just for you?"

"No doubt, otherwise, they would not have asked me."

"Then go, leave Pen and Amelia to fight to the death if needs be. Pen is a grown woman.

She will sort this out for herself. If she needs help, I will be there for her. Trust me."

Chapter 134

Pen stood on Mini Ha Ha Bridge staring at the water. In her heart, so much pain and guilt.

In a strange way she felt justified. Both blessed and cursed.

Out of the corner of her eye she became aware of Amelia marching by the cricket field just as she had done five years ago.

Pen knew at once what this was about and what she must do.

She turned to face her mother who now stood at the head of the footbridge with hands on hips.

"Clever girl, you have managed now to ruin everything for me. I will never be able to show my face in this village again. Haven't you just fallen on your feet? Inherited a fortune and, now, free to marry that man who has ruined all our lives."

Amelia stood flushed with anger. "I just hope you can live with yourself."

Pen walked towards her mother and looked down from the steps at the tiny bundle of fury.

She replied very quietly but firmly.

"Marry him, mother? That I will and as soon as it is possible. If that doesn't suit you, you can pack your bags, take what is yours and go."

Chapter 135

The night was dark but clear with just the barest sliver of a moon. Lit only by this and starlight.

Two shadowy figures made their way gingerly down the landslip terracing towards the small settlement and harbour. Stanislaw took Mario's arm to steady him.

"Ah! Sacramento, Aah!" Mario gasped.

"Sorry Mario, I forgot." Stanislaw apologised.

He spoke only Serbo-Croat and Mario, Italian. This journey was proving difficult.

Mario, fit and nimble from the waist down, was severely handicapped above the waist.

His attempt to return with colleagues to his home to Trieste had to be abandoned lest his condition and the source of his injuries gave away the rest of his party to a searching German Army.

Leading Mario around the back of the cottage Stanislaw tapped on the kitchen window several times with increasing urgency. Raula eventually opened it slightly. "Stanislaw?"

"Yes, open up please, Raula."

She slid back the bolts and opened the kitchen door and let him in. Surprised that he had someone with him, Raula lit the oil lamp. The dim glow revealed the stranger to be a dark, athletic man who offered a bandaged hand. "Ciao."

Raula looked to Stanislaw to introduce this guest. Stanislaw removed his backpack but didn't seem to notice or care. The man pointed to his chest with two heavily bandaged hands.

"Mario. Ciao."

Realising that communication was going to be difficult, Raula asked Stanislaw "Who is this and why is he here?"

"Mario is an Italian compatriot. He's here to stay the night."

"And where is Mario going to sleep?"

"On the floor," Stanislaw replied, placing two kitchen chairs on their side each side of a rag rug.

"On a stone floor?"

"He can only sleep face down," replied Stanislaw, as if this answered the question.

He placed a cushion at the head of the rug and unrolled a blanket from his backpack.

Raula looked at Mario wishing to ask if this was all right with him but did not have the language.

She noticed that he did not look at all well for all his charm. Even in the dim light of the oil lamp she could see that he was trembling with shock, a fever or fatigue.

Stanislaw shook out the blanket and motioned Mario to lie down. Painfully, unable to use his hands easily, he dropped to his knees on the rug letting out a gasp of pain.

"For God's sake, help him Stanislaw."

"I can't. I don't know how."

Fool, thought Raula, moving forward to help the poor man only to be stopped by her husband. "Leave him, Raula." A strange smell and the urgency in Stanislaw's voice stopped her.

Mario flopped forward on to his face like a rag doll. Fortunately, his head hit the cushion.

Stanislaw draped another blanket over the chairs to make a tent-like cover.

"Grazi," Mario said, moaning as he spoke.

"What's he doing here?" whispered Raula. "He should be in hospital."

"It is only for tonight."

"Then what?"

"Attila will know." Stanislaw put his arm around his wife. "Let's go to bed."

Raula pulled away. "Stanislaw, you bring a sick stranger in the night and leave him to sleep on the stone floor. We can't just leave him. What is this with Attila? How on earth is another sick man going to help?"

"There is the rug. What else can we do?" replying to the earlier observation about the stone floor. He walked towards the door.

Raula, desperate not to allow him just to leave the sick man on the floor, asked. "Have you eaten?"

"We're fine Raula, come to bed." He stood holding the door open.

"He needs to drink," said Raula picking up a jug and filling a mug.

Stanislaw moved back into the kitchen. "What's that? Not milk, I hope."

Raula looked at Stanislaw with that look that only wives have for their husbands.

"In July, you fool? Milk is best left in the goat. It's water."

She placed the mug next to Mario so he could reach it easily. She caught her breath, stood up and shuddered.

"He smells of smoke and diesel, he smells putrid. He is suffering from shock. He should drink."

"You can't force him Raula, leave him and come to bed."

Raula followed her husband out, all the while looking back over her shoulder.

"I am not sure," she said clearly reluctant to leave a sick man alone.

Raula found it impossible to sleep with the knowledge of Mario lying in pain.

She got up several times to check on him.

The first time she got up, Raula discovered Mario had drunk the water. She refilled the mug and after assuring herself that he was sleeping, went back to her bed. Finally, she slept.

Raula was still the first to wake in the morning. She went straight to check on Mario to find him still sleeping and that he had taken more water.

The smell in the room was not at all pleasant. Stepping around the makeshift tent bed, she opened the window then the front door to allow the cooler mountain air to flow through the house, before she lit the kitchen fire. After dropping some rice into the saucepan on the fire hob, she turned to go out to milk the goat. The fire crackled and burst into flame. Mario stirred and raised his head.

"Feuer. Zu fil." He gasped and tried to get up.

It took seconds for Raula to realise that Mario was trying and failing to rise.

She pulled back the blanket from over the chairs and gasped. In the daylight, the full extent of Mario's problem turned her stomach.

His back was a festering mass of burn, covered in peeling skin or fabric. She couldn't see which. His head at the rear was a matted crust of burned hair, a huge weeping scab.

He had struggled thus far to his knees but was not able to get to his feet.

"Oh, dear God! Raula ran to him.

Mario raised one arm, whether for protection or not, Raula couldn't tell.

He began to fall back down. Raula knelt and placed her arms under his armpits. Bracing herself, it took a tremendous effort to get him to his feet.

The shock of seeing his torment plus the smell of him at close quarters was even worse than last night. He had urinated on the rug. It was so awful.

Raula's senses started to swim. She turned her head and held her breath. Somehow, Raula made it to the front door. Gasping, she found it difficult to keep still.

Gradually she regained control of her senses. The sickness now replaced anger at Stanislaw bringing this problem to their house, then sleeping on as if it did not exist.

She paced up and down the path several times before running to Svetka's.

The door was open. Svetka was inside preparing breakfast.

The moment she saw Raula she dropped what she was doing and ran to her.

"Raula, what on earth is wrong?"

Svetka was unable to get a coherent answer from Raula's distressed garbled pleading. Svetka tried for some minutes struggling to understand. Mario appeared and leaned on the door jamb facing it exposing his back. It was only then that Svetka understood.

Svetka went to him immediately followed by a distressed Raula. Seeing his injuries, she gasped. "Oh! You poor, dear man."

Mario, on hearing her voice, turned to face her and reached out with his bandaged hands as if to plead for help. Svetka turned to Raula.

"Get Yarny at once, tell him to bring my first aid kit and be sure the scissors are in there."

Mario was getting some relief from the cool mountain air and through the house. Svetka went to the river and wet the cloth she was carrying. She began to bathe Mario's face. He raised his hands indicating he needed them to be seen to and even in the fresh air they stank.

Yarny arrived with the kit and scissors. Svetka could see that the damage was confined to the backs of Mario's hands. The material was sticking and appeared to be woven into his skin, as with his back. She began to slit the bandages up each palm.

Meanwhile, two figures were making their way down to the path.

Svetka began carefully to remove the bandage layer by layer from one hand.

The newcomers, a woman and a boy stopped. The boy left some luggage on the path then returned up the slope. The woman continued down to where the group were gathered outside the house. Svetka had got to the point where the remaining bandage was stubbornly sticking to Mario's skin.

"Leave it at that!" ordered Tanya.

Svetka turned to see a mature woman looking critically at Mario.

"This is clearly not Attila," Tanya murmured signalling Mario to turn around.

He did as bid like a naughty boy who had been playing with matches.

Svetka noted that the woman's reaction was clinical and divorced emotionally, unlike that of herself and Raula. Having reached an impasse with the stuck bandage she gladly stood back.

After several minutes Tanya turned to Yarny. "Young man, collect my bags." She pointed back to where the bags lay at the foot of the terraces. "Then find me a chair and bring all to the beach against that building there." Tanya indicated Attila's boathouse.

No one questioned Tanya or argued. All were glad to hand over Mario's problems to this stranger.

Tanya indicated to Mario to accompany her to the beach.

"I'll bring a chair," said Svetka.

"And a shirt or pyjama top," added Tanya.

On the way down, Tanya said, "I am here to assess Attila. Where can I find him?"

It was Raula who answered. "He's with Svetka. She has gone for a chair and a shirt."

Mario was coping well with walking down to the beach. He had the instinct to know that he was in the hands of someone who could really help.

Minutes later Yarny and Svetka arrived with the chair, Tanya's bags and one of Stefan's shirts to discover that Tanya and Raula were out in the sea. They were lowering Mario gently into a sitting position. Svetka joined Yarny and they watched them lower Mario into the water.

Leaning right back into the sea, Mario let out a moan of relief.

Keeping his head above water left no alternative but for Tanya but to place her hand under his head.

Raula stood for a moment or two before realising that she was no longer needed and waded ashore. Stanislaw came out of the house and threw a saucepan into the river yelling at the same time for Raula.

"Oh God, the rice and the saucepan," she cried running up the path.

Svetka looked up the river after Raula then at Yarny.

"Seek out Attila's camp beds, son, the canvas ones. They are in the back of his workshop.

This poor man and this woman can sleep in the boathouse for the time being."

She watched her son go before muttering to herself. "That's if she intends to stay."

Tanya left Mario floating on his back in the shallows and returned to the beach.

"He is more comfortable in the water which is good and after a good soak in salt water we can then begin to dress his wounds."

She arranged the chair on the sand and found a pair of scissors. She then placed the shirt over the chair back and slit it up the back. Svetka, although surprised, did not object.

Tanya removed one half of the shirt then took some tape, needles and cotton from her bag and cut the tape into short lengths. She then began to sew a length of tape on to the shirt.

"Attila's injuries, what are they?"

Svetka, knowing that she was there primarily to check on Attila, was non-committal.

"Difficult to tell, it's early days."

Tanya finished the first tape then took the other half of the shirt off the chair and offered it to Svetka.

"Do you mind?" She passed tape and a needle to Svetka. "I don't wish to leave him too long in the water. Ten cm. spacing, please."

"Do you really think you can help Mario?" Svetka took the tape and began to sew.

"Yes, but his morale and determination are the key. He has made the journey from Slovenia down here with these injuries. I have no idea how. A man with that determination and courage can achieve almost anything."

"From Slovenia? Really? How do you know that?"

"From his injuries." Tanya smiled. "Of course, you are so isolated here. You won't know. Mario, an Italian with burn injuries. He must have been part of the team which blew up a fuel and arms store up there. The Germans were storing vital supplies in caves at Postojna. These supplies were to cover for both the Adriatic and Italian coasts in the event of invasion of either."

Svetka was about to ask for more detail especially about Italians fighting against the Axis when Mario called out. At the same time Raula returned.

Tanya waded out immediately and helped him ashore.

"He lasted well, the sea water is cooling at first, but later with the salt it tends to feel almost as bad as the burn. He seems to understand what to do, which is good as I don't speak Italian."

Raula spoke up. "I am sure he spoke German this morning. I had forgotten that what with everything else happening. I meant to mention it to Attila."

"He could be from the Germanic north," said Tanya. She turned to Mario.

"Deutsch spreche?" she asked. Mario shook the sodden bandage from his right hand and held it out for rebandaging. Smiling at last, he answered, "Das fuhlt sich besser. Danke."

One hour later Mario's wounds were dressed. Tanya had clipped carefully around the matted hair and removed the blackened crust revealing an angry wound. All this had taken much time. In the process, by question and answer, she learned much.

"That's about all we can do for now," said Tanya. "I now need to see Attila and not just about his injuries."

Chapter 136

Attila listened to Tanya's take on Mario which she gave while examining him.

"You are sure he is not a plant. A German attempt to infiltrate?"

Tanya nodded. "Northern Italians speak German as readily as Slovenians and western Hungarian folk. I am not worried. He would not announce that he spoke German so readily if he was a spy."

"Still takes a lot of believing. Travelling so far with such injuries undetected."

Tanya then queried something else which concerned her.

"You say Paurak knew nothing of the sabotage of the caves?"

Attila shook his head. "No one knew."

Tanya raised her eyebrows in surprise then returned to Attila's problems.

"You have broken your right collar bone and wrist. The left arm is just bruising and sprain. I am going to put a figure of eight bandage round to pull your shoulders back. The collar bone and wrist will heal in weeks if you stay quiet."

She began winding a broad linen bandage looping this under and around the arms in a figure of eight while carrying on a conversation.

"The British must have organised the operation, yet they did not involve us. They didn't tell even Paurak. Why?" Attila asked between gasps of pain.

"They don't trust us or involved another partisan group nearer the scene in which case we didn't need to know."

She put her knee in between Attila's shoulders and heaved the bandage tight.

Attila gasped. "They trusted Italian partisans ... not us."

He was trying to keep his mind active to take away the discomfort of Tanya winding and pulling adding, "I still think it's unlikely that Mario could have made it this far south."

"From what I could gather, remember he is a sick man. He travelled south hidden in the cabin overhead toolbox of a railway engine aided by a Slovenian train driver."

She gave a final heave and added, "Do you believe it?" Tanya was also trying to divert Attila's mind.

"It was a troop train full of Axis men." She fastened off the bandages. "Also, there are rumours that two British Army explosive experts passed through this English officer's camp before the attack." Tanya collected her bag. "There, that's you fixed."

Attila sighed with relief. "The English captain knew but didn't tell us."

He shook his head. "I must think about this."

"The English captain knew we had a mole remember," Tanya reminded Attila.

"I will call to see you daily. I must stay with and help Mario. He is really tough. He must be to have made it with second degree burns. The next 24 hours will be critical."

She got as far as the door then added, "Mario must have had help from Slovenian resistance and the British. Talk to Stanislaw. It was he who brought him in last night."

Later that evening after sunset Tanya let Mario bathe in the sea once more.

Afterwards, Yarny was watching her dressing Mario's wounds.

"You are clearly a very clever woman, Tanya. Are you a doctor?"

"You are clearly a very clever young man. Always watching and learning."

Tanya fed the shirt over Mario's arms from the front and fastened the tapes at the back.

"Mario, now you must sleep and tomorrow and each day you must bathe in the sea.

Keep out of the sun. That means bathing after sundown."

The two conversed in German. Tanya repeated this in Serbo-Croat for Yarny's benefit.

Mario understood enough to wonder why she was confiding in the boy.

"Are you leaving me?"

"I don't intend to. I may have to. If so, hopefully, I will be back quickly."

Tanya turned to Yarny and placed an affectionate hand on his arm.

"Please will you ask Stanislaw to meet Attila and me at your house in half an hour? Please also, go to the trees at the top of the landslip, there will be a canvas bag hanging there. Bring anything inside back to your mother's."

Later when Tanya was checking on Attila's condition and bandages, she continued the discussion. "The British knew there was a mole in the camp? We can understand why we were kept in the dark."

"I have been thinking about that. Maybe I am fantasising being stuck here."

Attila was finding the tight bandaging difficult to get used to.

Tanya was checking that his blood circulation was not a problem and was pleased to take Attila's mind off his problems.

"Why don't you fantasise out loud and see what I think?"

Attila jumped at the chance to discuss his worries. This sudden 'invasion' of outsiders into this sanctuary was worrying: The English captain and the two Britons who returned with Peter's clothing. Now Mario. They were all unknown quantities.

It was a situation he had always tried to avoid. This applied to Stanislaw who had returned without warning. Stanislaw had now brought in Mario without asking. Who was Stanislaw now working with was also a question.

"If the British knew there was a mole, the English captain had suspicions.

Why did they proceed with the operation to pick up Peter, risking both him and the submarine? They informed us of that operation but did not mention the sabotaging of the caves."

Tanya replaced the bandage on Attila's right arm including a splint to immobilise his wrist.

"That would mean they deliberately risked the submarine, your life and Peter's. Would they do that?"

No, maybe I am hallucinating. They wouldn't risk the sub. Maybe Peter and me, but not a submarine."

"They wouldn't know about the S-boats being in these waters."

"I could be correct. Peter and I were expendable. Peter having as good as outlived his usefulness and me, well ..." Attila didn't complete the thought as Svetka shouted upstairs.

"Raula is here, she says Stanislaw has left and she doesn't know where."

Raula had been crying and was still clearly upset when Yarny arrived. He told his mother.

Svetka knew what the problem was even before Raula uttered the words.

"Stanislaw has gone. We had a blazing row and he left this morning. Now Attila wants to speak with him. I don't know what to say."

Back upstairs, Attila and Tanya heard this news.

"Stanislaw has information about Mario if nothing else," Attila emphasised, "and he has been recently in touch regularly with the British camp. I sent him there myself."

Tanya took time to think and didn't speak as she continued to check Attila's bandages.

Attila struggled with all the confusion which was crowding his mind.

"I feel so guilty about leaving Peter stranded and defenceless on that sandbank. He would not have had a chance. I didn't have time to think."

Attila shook his head. "Maybe I am just looking for excuses."

"I don't have you down as a guilt carrier, Attila. In any event you are clearly not to blame, if you are right about the timings of the landings. The sabotage of the cave stores and the incident with the S- boats stacks up with your theories. The fault, if there is any, lies with the British."

Yarny shouted up the stairs.

"Tanya, there was a rabbit and a pheasant in the canvas bag."

"Good. You can rest easy, Attila. We have an alternative food supply."

Chapter 137

Food did become a problem in the autumn, although the terraces cropped well.

The supply of rice and grains via Attila's contact with the British and others ceased as did the regular supply of sea food.

The partisans, including Tanya's boy and the British attachment, moved back into Slovenia.

The salted and dried fish failed to compensate. Most of this was unpleasant and didn't keep. Yarny and Marineska gathered crustaceans and seaweed from the shallows. Yarny was prevented by Svetka and Attila from taking Attila's boat out because it was still in need of repair.

With Mario and Tanya, extra mouths to feed, something needed to be done.

After a violent November storm Svetka and Raula went out to check on the goats and the terrace plants. Most of the crop was still in the ground but had been washed away as was most of the soil and a lot of the retaining stones.

Down by the beach Attila checked on the boathouse and his boat which had been washed out to sea from where it had been beached then back into the shallows lower down the coast by the incoming tide. It had been dragged ashore by Yarny who had been out early to check the night lines.

Attila was checking for further damage. Mario who had been in the sea for his early morning therapy joined him. "Is she O.K?" he asked in German.

"It is full of water, mostly rainwater I hope," Attila answered in the same language.

Mario examined the timbers at the prow.

"She is in need of repair here." Mario pointed out the damage. "We need to remove the prow-timbers, replace and caulk." He looked down at his hands.

"But my hands are still stiff. My fingers won't move easily. Tanya says I must swim."

Mario mimed the breaststroke. "Like this. Then maybe I can repair. But until ..." He spread his arms in a gesture of futility.

"You know about shipbuilding?"

"I have a build and repair yard in Trieste." Mario gestured again. "But how do I get home?"

Attila although used to routine maintenance had not carried out this level of repair before, asked, "Could you, me and Yarny manage this together now that my strength is returning?"

Mario considered for a moment.

"We have not the proper tools. Do you have clamps? If so then when we are a little stronger, maybe. For now, I am useless."

"I was hoping to sail again soon. We need more sea food. Also, I am worried about some friends of mine. If this storm has done this to us, they will have been hit as badly if not worse.

I have news also which they should hear." Attila looked out across the straits.

"The days are getting short. I need to go soon."

The community's problems did not end there for Attila. They could also do with other supplies such as fruit and olive oil from the island farm.

Attila's first concern was not the lack olive oil or anything else, but the need to move Mario on.

He liked Mario. He was an asset to the community, but he was walking forensic evidence of the settlement's involvement with the partisans, the British and the cave sabotage.

Mario took another look at the prow. "Maybe if just we clean and caulk." He rocked his hand in a maybe/maybe not gesture. "Not good for heavy weather."

Chapter 138

Pen looked out across the Green from her bedroom window as she rolled on her black stockings getting ready to go on shift. A telegram boy cycled into view making his way up towards Greensleeves.

Pen's heart began to thump. She struggled to find her dressing gown through a red mist.

Losing all control and with scant regard for her condition, she hurtled down the stairs two at a time arriving at the front door just managing to fasten her dressing gown before the boy rang the bell.

Unable to speak, Pen took the small familiar envelope and ripped it open to read.

72 HOUR FURLOUGH.
ANY CHANCE OF A SPECIAL LICENCE.
ARRIVING FRIDAY A.M.
HAL.

At first, Pen could not focus. The words appeared to melt and swim around the page.

Her eyes cleared to read the telegram again, to be certain she was not dreaming.

She collapsed on to the hall carpet sobbing with relief, revealing much of her white flesh and black stockings to the consternation of a young boy. Pen then squealed with relief and excitement.

A huge sigh released her earlier terror. She took a moment to compose herself.

"Sorry, please wait," she said closing the door on him. She hurried into the kitchen, returning with a sixpence, borrowed from Emily. Shedding her dressing gown, she replaced it with her coat. This she buttoned tightly then put on her shoes and opened the door on the boy.

"Thank you. Thank you, happy news."

She gave the boy the sixpence and followed him out on to the Green and headed straight for Pamela's at a run.

Amelia put down the paper she was reading. She heard Pen tumble down the stairs and went to look through the window. She saw nothing. Then she heard Pen squeal and later watched her run across to Pamela's. Amelia thumped on the bedroom floor with a stick. Receiving no response, she went to the head of the stairs. "Emerson, are you there?" she called. Then she rapped her stick on the balustrade. "Emerson," she called again, expecting Emerson to come at once.

Some little while passed before Amelia, who was not in the best of moods, marched down to the kitchen to discover Emily sweeping the floor.

"Emerson, did you not hear me knocking?"

Emily ignored her and continued to sweep thinking to herself, 'I think the whole village heard you.'

Amelia was now irritated beyond measure. She was aware that Emily most likely knew of the content of the telegram. "Look at me whilst I speak."

Emerson, without looking up, replied.

"I have neither time nor reason to stop. Some of us have work to do."

Amelia, now purple in the face, slapped her stick on the table.

"You can forget work, Emerson. You are dismissed as of now."

Emily finally stopped sweeping and turned to face Amelia. Leaning on the brush handle she looked the little woman in the face.

"I shall wait and see what Pen says about that. Meanwhile I will be considering whether I wish to stay." She propped her broom in the corner and sat down to pour herself a cup of tea.

Chapter 139

Pam opened the door and Pen almost fell into the hall.

"Careful, Pet," gasped a surprised Pamela. "You have more than just yourself to think about now."

Pen grabbed hold of Pam and held on tight.

"Nanny Pammy, he's coming this Friday. He wants me to get a special licence."

Pamela pushed Pen away looking into her flushed face.

"I don't suppose I need to second guess who?"

Pen was disappointed with Pam's reaction. She wanted so much for her to share her joy. It was clear, however, that this was not so. Pen hung her head.

"I haven't forgotten Peter and I never will." She looked up into Pam's face.

"You do know that, don't you?"

Pam sighed, "I do know, Pet but so soon after Peter's death, it will not sit well with the village."

"I know but Hal has only got 72 hours and we might not get another chance before."

Pen didn't finish the thought, so Pam interjected.

"Maybe not, Pet, but you and Mim are settled. Mim is the legal owner of the house. She is settled and happy in school. You will have to live in this village with the decision. It won't be pretty."

"I understand. I'll live with it," Pen said defiantly, determined not to be dissuaded.

"And Mim, what about her?"

"I will ask her," Pen replied, knowing what her answer would be.

Pamela also knew the answer and changed her argument.

"You will need to give three weeks' notice even to get a special licence."

"Fourteen days now and I have already taken one out and over two weeks ago."

Pen was fighting for Pam's approval. Without this she would have nothing, no one.

"What about Hal? Doesn't he also need to sign?"

Pen thought about this and panicked. "I should go and see the registrar, don't you think?"

Pam felt Pen's panic and took her hands in hers.

"If you are determined, I'll back you all the way. Whatever happens know this, I will be here for you." Pen grabbed Pam once more and buried her face in her bosom.

"I love you Nanny Pammy, I really love you." She drew her face away from Pam's chest and looked up, "and I really did love Peter."

Pam took a moment to gather herself. "What about your shift, Pet, should I ring in sick for you?"

"No thank you, Pam, Matron has put me on cover shift only, with permission to go in or not at my discretion."

"Matron knows?"

"Couldn't keep the secret for ever. The sooner everyone knows the better. That's if they didn't know already."

Pam shook her head. "How times change, I was hidden away like a criminal."

It was Pen's turn to take Pam's hands. "I am really happy with my lot and to share this with you." Pen kissed Pam. "Now I must go and get changed to go to Bendesbury."

"Take my tip, Pen, go in your uniform."

Amelia saw Pen returning and was waiting for her when she entered the house.

"Emerson has gone too far this time, Penelope I insist that she be dismissed at once."

Amelia, as was her style, stood blocking Pen's way. Pen made to walk by, but her mother again blocked her path.

Pen sidestepped her to get to the stairs. "I haven't got time for this, mother."

All Pen could think of was getting to Bendesbury and the registry office.

Amelia followed Pen up the stairs. "Is it not time for your train yet and what was that telegram about?" Amelia demanded attention. "Hear me out, Penelope."

Pen entered her room and through a half-closed door said, "Sorry mother, I need to dress."

She closed the door. Amelia stood outside knocking on it with her stick.

"At least you could have the common decency to tell me what is in the telegram."

Realising she was being unfair, Pen in a hurry to dress, answered.

"Hal is coming this weekend on a 72-hour pass."

Amelia, surprised by this, didn't speak for several seconds, then the full import dawned.

"Where will he be staying? Avery hasn't the space."

Pen hadn't thought. The question caused her to take time to think. He could stay at the Drovers was her first thought. She fastened the final button on her uniform, donned her cloak and cap then opened the door by which time she had her answer ready.

"As you point out, mother, Pamela doesn't have the space so her old room here is no longer in use. He will stay here."

Once more she had to push past her mother. Pen was halfway downstairs by the time before Amelia took this in.

"I refuse to stay under the same roof as that American."

To Amelia being an American was sufficient to qualify as being persona non grata.

Pen's patience was nearing the end. She tried to reason but with a thinly disguised threat.

"Please be sensible, mother. Where could you go?"

Emily appeared from the kitchen wearing her hat and coat.

"I am sorry, Pen. I can't stay here any longer. I would normally work the week out to give you chance to find someone else, but Lady Amelia leaves me with no option."

The emphasis Emily uttered the word 'Lady' left nothing to the imagination regarding her opinion.

Before Pen could protest Emily was gone carrying with her a lovely piece of juicy gossip.

Pen was left staring at the front door closing behind her.

"Well done, mother, you don't believe in making life easy for anyone. Do you?"

Pen hurried to the door intending to leave before she really lost her temper.

She stopped just long enough to say, "As Emily won't be here, you will be good enough to look after Miriam when she comes home."

"I most certainly will not," Amelia retorted, "I am leaving. You have made it impossible for me to stay."

Pen tried to swallow her angry retort. She looked at her mother, now a tiny remnant of the person she once knew. She shook her head.

"Really, mother. Where can you go? Who else on God's earth, other than me, would have you?"

Chapter 140

Pen decided to walk to Bendesbury by the river to calm down. She focused on her real purpose for that day. She struggled at first to dismiss the memory of the morning's battle with her mother.

Gradually the pleasant September morning burst through with the swallows flitting to and fro across the water and a light breeze patterning the willows as they whitened with its caress. The late morning sun highlighting Virginia creeper on house walls across the river, now glowing brilliant red, all served to finally restore her sense of proportion and focus on the day's task.

Amelia stood in the hallway alone. The house now feeling big and empty. How she wished that she had not driven Emerson away.

She desperately needed George. Where was he now when she needed him?

Slowly a tear squeezed out of one eye. She wiped it away with an impatient gesture and reached for the telephone. She straightened her back and dialled George's Whitehall number.

The answer came quickly.

"Reception, can I help you?"

"I wish to speak urgently with Sir George Bridge-Thompson."

"Who is calling please?"

"This is Amelia Bridge-Thompson."

"Sorry, Lady Amelia, personal calls are not allowed."

"Young woman, this is important, connect me at once."

Amelia tapped her stick on the floor in frustration. The telephonist closed off the connection.

"We've got a right one here Joycie, a right Lady Muck."

"Who is it Dolly? Do you want me to have a word?" Dolly nodded and reopened the line.

"Thank you for holding Madame my supervisor will be with you directly."

Before Amelia could speak, she closed the connection once more.

"It's Lady Amelia, Georgie Porgie's wife. Will you have a word, Joycie? Tell her to get lost."

Joyce reopened the line. "Good morning, Madame, may I be of assistance?"

"I need to speak with my husband urgently, put me through at once."

"Certainly Madame, I will make an immediate request for him to contact you forthwith."

Joyce used her 'cut glars' accent as she called it. She closed the line once more cutting of any repost.

"Bollocks, you silly old fart."

"Thanks, Joycie, I had best put a request in the internal mail though for Georgie Porky pudding and pies to ring her."

Pen arrived at the registry office in Bendesbury well settled and determined to get a result.

The registrar, a wise old campaigner, was temporarily underemployed. September, unlike January, had few deaths and even fewer births and marriages. War parted couples no longer producing the usual workload.

"Hello again, Mrs. Barnes. Mrs. Calthrop tells me that you wish to marry Captain Henry Steading next Saturday."

"Yes please, if we can. Hal has just 72 hours leave."

The registrar looked through his papers. "We have no death certificate or record of your husband's passing, which does give me a problem."

Pen passed over a piece of newspaper. "There is an obituary in *The Times*."

The registrar read, then looked up in surprise. "This is dated July less than two months ago."

Pen nodded. Her mouth was dry. This was not going well at all.

"I know this looks awful, but Peter left me in 1938, shortly after we married. You can see from the obituary he was a prisoner of war from 1940."

"And you have not cohabited since 1938?"

Pen shook her head. "No."

The registrar went to the door and called to Mrs. Calthrop. "Any reply from War Office records, please?"

He returned to his desk and read through his notes and papers. This took some time and did little to sooth Pen's nerves.

He had two submissions, one an objection on moral grounds against the granting of the licence which was still relevant and another which made astonishing claims in support.

The registrar then consulted his manual for some minutes before looking at Pen for some further seconds. What he saw was a young woman from a known titled family in the uniform of a nursing auxiliary which in no way squared with the derogatory claims on the one hand, yet, on the other, supported the claims of the supporter. All this time he had kept a finger in the manual as a bookmark. He gave a nervous cough, then asked, "May I ask if a third party is involved?" He coughed again. "Who will be affected by my decision, so to speak?"

Pen had intended to use her pregnancy in a last plea if all else failed, took a moment to realise what he was saying. She looked down avoiding his gaze. Blushing, she answered, "It is not the only reason we wish to marry."

"Please forgive the question Mrs. Barnes. I have no wish to pry, but the 1872 Act does give me room to use my discretion in such cases." He had his head in his hands and appeared to be thinking.

The letter of objection had given him the reason to ask the question about Pen's pregnancy.

He smiled at the thought that the intent to destroy, cleared the way for him to accept.

A tap on the door preceded Mrs. Calthrop's entrance to announce that the War Office had confirmed that Lt. P. R. Barnes was listed as killed in action and that Pen was his widow. Confirmation of which would be in the post that night.

The registrar raised an eyebrow thinking, 'How unusual for the War Office to be so co-operative'.

"On your way to work, Mrs. Barnes?" he asked eyeing Pen's uniform.

Pen shook her head and answered truthfully. "No, I was dressing for work when this telegram arrived." She took the telegram from her pocket showing it to him.

"I have matron's permission to work as and when because of my condition."

The Registrar held up a hand. "Enough, Mrs. Barnes. I will need a medical certificate, confirmation of your condition and Captain Steading's signature before 11 a.m. on Friday. Saturday at 3.00 p.m. is now provisionally reserved for your marriage to Captain Steading."

Chapter 141

Amelia waited and waited for George to return her call. She felt lonely for the first time, even though she had chosen a solitary lifestyle. Now the house echoed empty. No Emerson to bring her morning coffee or to annoy her using that infernal Hoover machine. Just silence. A silence filled with her daughter's last words spoken this morning. 'Really mother where will you go, who on God's earth will have you other than me.'

She swept everything off the small table, book, embroidery and newspaper and stumped downstairs to the telephone.

'After all we have done for her', she thought, 'to be repaid with contempt. Miriam's money and the money she had inherited from Peter's death made no difference. Pen refusing to employ decent servants. Relying on just one insolent daily. We deserve better.'

She arrived at the telephone and dialled Upperford Cars who answered promptly.

"Amelia Bridge-Thompson, I need a car a soon as possible."

"Certainly, Lady Amelia, where to?" came the polite answer. Amelia immediately began to feel better, at last proper civility. "London, Westminster."

She didn't have the first idea of the cost, nor did she have any money. Perhaps she imagined George would see to it or she could just charge it.

There followed a short silence before the question, "and the reason for the trip ma'am?"

"Reason, reason, what do you mean reason?"

"Lady Amelia, is your journey really necessary?" came the standard reply to such questioning.

"What sort of a question is that, of course, why else would I ask?"

Amelia was now really irritated.

The owner, well versed in explaining, answered. "Well ma'am, Westminster is a long way and we have only a limited allocation of petrol and gas. If you can show that your journey is essential, we reclaim the fuel used."

Amelia thought for a moment, discarding her first reply, 'Of course my journey is essential,' changing it to, "What might qualify?"

"Urgent matters such as an imminent birth journey to hospital, ma'am. That sort of journey."

Amelia, much as she wished to order/demand the service, realised that she had no valid reason and needed to ask. "Then what do you suggest I can do?"

"Sorry, ma'am, I can only suggest the bus to Fernborough railway station. There are regular services." There followed a long silence, so he finally said, "So sorry I can't be of help, ma'am."

Receiving no reply, he replaced the receiver.

Amelia stood in the hallway with the telephone still in her hand unable to comprehend.

The world as she knew it no longer existed. Chaos and lassitude everywhere.

George had not returned her call. She knew only one thing for sure, she no longer belonged.

She could not stay in this house which was no longer hers.

She must seek out George at his club and discuss once more the question of that flat in London. Fifteen minutes later, nosey neighbours saw Amelia doing something she had never ever before contemplated. She had raided the cash box in George' study removing its entire content, seven shillings and six pence and was walking down the Green to catch a bus.

Chapter 142

Pen stepped out of the registry office into the September sunshine. The baby kicked several times.

The square was bathed in gold. She felt good. Suddenly she realised that she was hungry, starving.

She had not eaten since last night. She decided to treat herself. She had one British Restaurant ticket which she had been saving in case she got another to share. This now was so unlikely because of a more settled scene in London and her new circumstances.

This and a shopping trip afterwards, then she would wait for Mim to leave school and walk home with her. This was more attractive than returning home to resume hostilities with her mother.

After all she had something now to celebrate even if this meant celebrating on her own.

Four o'clock arrived and she waited outside the school for Mim looking forward to giving her the news. True to form, Mim and her friends were the first out into the square talking and giggling. Mim did not notice Pen until she called to her. Mim ran to her.

"Mama Pen, what are you doing here?"

"I've got news. Hal is coming on Friday."

Pen at last, was able to share the good news with someone who felt the same as she.

Mim stood stock still for a second before spinning like a top then stopping and asking.

"How long for?"

"Just the weekend I'm afraid."

Mim's friends were taking all this in and Pen was aware of it.

Mim stood, legs apart, head cocked to one side in the now familiar pose.

"You're getting married."

Pen was totally unprepared for this intuitive, wish fulfilled statement. Her intention to tell Mim in private, was scuppered. Out of the corner of her eye she was aware of Mim's friends running for the school bus armed with the news. She had little time to recover her wits before Dorothy arrived.

"Hi Pen, what are you doing here?"

Before Pen could answer Mim grabbed Dorothy's hand.

"Auntie Dorothy, Papa Yo is coming this week and, and, and ..." Pen took Mim's arm, squeezing and shaking her. Mim stopped speaking and looked up, worried. Pen tried to sound calm.

"I thought we could walk back home together when we can talk in private."

"Sorry Mama Pen, have I said something wrong?"

Pen hugged her. "No, my darling, just the right thing at the wrong time."

The three of them walked hand in hand to the bridge turning on to the riverside walk. As soon as they were out of sight of the square, Mim looked up to Pen.

"Sorry Mama Pen, but you did say I was right. Permission to scream now?"

"Scream away, my darling." Pen laughed. She was so very happy.

Mim threw her hat in the air and ran spinning and screaming into the middle distance.

Dorothy picked up Mim's hat. "Is this about what I am thinking? Hoping?"

"It is," Pen replied, "I want to run about shout and scream, except."

"Except what? Amelia?" Dorothy identified the problem immediately.

Pen nodded and looked wistful "I am afraid so."

"You have told her of course?" Dorothy was angling for detail.

"No. I didn't get chance. We had already fallen out when she knew that Hal was coming."

Dorothy took Pen's arm. "Never mind, we will get through this together. Don't let Amelia influence you."

After a moment's pause Dorothy added, "Don't, whatever you do, give in to emotional blackmail. My mother took my young life away. By the time I took control, it was too late."

Mim came running back and pirouetted in front of them, "and I will be bridesmaid."

Pen, who had not got around to thinking of this, was shocked.

"Oh! Mim, I don't know, sweetie. We have only five days and no coupons."

Mim's disappointment was painful to see and both women bent to console.

Dorothy straightened. "I think I have an idea."

She smiled at Mim. "We shall have to see."

"We'll see," squealed Mim, "that means yes's's's's's." She squealed again and before chancing any argument, she was running up the path towards home. Pen squeezed Dorothy's arm. "Don't worry if it doesn't work out. Take no notice of Mim's attempt to blackmail us. I'll talk her round."

"We may not have to. Is it O.K. if I use your telephone?"

"Of course." Pen was intrigued.

"If this works, consider it to be part of my wedding present," continued Dorothy still deep in thought.

What is this idea? I am both fascinated and too frightened to be delighted. Do tell."

"Well, it is just an idea of course, no guarantees."

Pen realised Dorothy didn't wish to say more. "So now we pray. Do we?"

They walked on in silence each lost in thought. It was Dorothy who first broke their reverie.

"When I see Mim, happy and excited like today, I remember Tuss. Her determination to save those children from the Nazis. It gives me comfort knowing that her life had such purpose. That she achieved so much."

Pen was shocked by Dorothy's unexpected thought.

"I just wish I had known her," Pen replied, politely if just a little confused and still thinking of Mim's mythical bridesmaid's dress.

"You do know her." Dorothy answered. "Mim's presence is also her presence, as far as I'm concerned, she is with me every day. Mim has changed your life beyond measure. You do know Tuss, she is also part of you."

Pen confused changed the subject. "I wonder where Mim is. She's just disappeared?"

"She will have gone ahead to tell Pam and not just about the wedding. I am sure the bridesmaids dress will take pride of place. That really will put me under pressure."

Sure enough, Mim and Pam were waiting for them at the head of the Green.

"I've already got all the news, Pet, especially about the bridesmaid's dress."

Pam turned to Dorothy. "How come Fairy Godmother?"

"Now I really am worried," Dorothy replied. "How come you ask? Well a wing and a prayer plus one telephone call." She crossed her fingers on both hands.

"And clothing coupons?" Pamela raised her eyebrows in question to her friend suggesting that she was attempting the impossible. "In five days?"

Mim who had been listening intently grabbed hold of Dorothy's hand.

"Make the call now please, Auntie Dorothy."

Mim pulled her running and laughing towards the house.

By the time Pam and Pen arrived at Greensleeves, Dorothy was in mid conversation on the telephone. "And how is business, Samuel?"

The three others stood around trying to make sense of the one-sided conversation.

"Oh! Samuel I am so sorry. Just you hang in there until this war is over."

Mim began to fidget and look worried. Pam took her hand and squeezed. She was still thinking her friend was on an impossible mission.

"Well, Samuel there is good news and bad news. The good news is that I have a creative order for you. The bad news is I have no coupons and it is needed by Friday next. A bridesmaid's dress."

Dorothy listened, then spoke again. "You will have a word with Tolly?"

Dorothy turned to the anxious Mim.

"Samuel is going to have a word with Tolly. If anyone can find a way around this, he can.

If Tolly finds the material, Samuel will produce something fantastic."

After an anxious silence Dorothy answered. "Parachute silk? Yes, perfect."

She again placed her hand over the receiver. "White silk dress all right?" she asked the excited little girl, who was already nodding.

"And knickers, Auntie Dorothy. I can't be wearing school knickers."

"Right then, Samuel. A white silk dress and pants for Friday next." Dorothy turned to Pen.

"Tape measure, please."

Chapter 143

The one-armed receptionist at the Pelican Country Club knocked on the door of the secretary's office and entered.

"Commander Bridge-Thompson's wife is asking to drop anchor, sir."

"Lady Amelia?"

"Yes, sir."

"Have we taken a booking?"

"No, sir. She just arrived without so much as an up periscope."

The secretary took a deep breath then let it out with a sigh.

"Well, all right. Insist on cash and ration card up front."

"That's the trouble, sir, she doesn't seem to have anything left in her locker. I don't mean just purse and ration book."

"Hold hard, Matlo, take care. Sir George's wife must be treated with the utmost respect at all times." The secretary was worried he had given the wrong impression. He tapped the desk with his pencil.

"You do know, Williams, that Sir George was at Jutland, gave a cracking show. Though injured he carried on regardless. Take care of Lady Amelia. Stow her in the galley. Tell her I will be along shortly."

He picked up the telephone. "Purser, what have you got on Sir George, Commander Bridge-Thompson? I mean personal. Not paid for by the M.O.D. Up to date, warts and all."

He stood and paced his office shaking his head.

The receptionist returned the secretary stopped pacing.

"Yes, what now man?" He was clearly irritated.

The Matlo sprang to attention shocked by the sharpness of the question.

"Lady Amelia has ordered tea and sandwiches Sir."

"Sorry, Williams." The secretary sighed and apologised.

“Well, all right. I suppose we can stretch to tea and cucumber sandwiches.”

Later armed with the latest information from the purser, he picked up the ‘phone again and dialled.

Henry was reading a report from Sir George when this call came through.

“Combs, stats and logs. Henry Duckenfield.”

“The Pelican here, sir. Is the Commander Sir George Bridge-Thompson with you?”

Henry continued to read the report. “Not at this moment. Is this priority?” he asked, sensing the anxiety in the secretary’s voice.

Henry listened for at least half a minute to the secretary before asking, “The Lady Amelia is there, with you?” Then he listened again, placing the report to one side. “Quite right, secretary. Please entertain her a little longer until I can arrange to have her collected.”

Henry replaced the receiver and sat thinking before dialling out again. He tapped his fingers waiting for the answer which came eventually with an imperious, “Constance Peat.”

“Connie, how are you?”

“Henry? Is that really you?” The lady sounded delighted.

“I thought I’d make a quick call to check on your welfare. How are things, really?”

“Not good, Henry. I’m lonely. Bloody lonely.”

“What with a house full of servants?”

“You know what I mean Henry.” Connie gave an exaggerated sigh.

“Herbert neglecting you?” Henry astutely reminding Connie of her married status.

“Buggered off somewhere. Again.” Connie repeated the exaggerated sigh.

Henry ignored the second sigh and quickly moved on to the matter in hand.

“Connie, seriously. I am in need of a favour. A big one.”

Connie didn’t answer but put her hand over the mouthpiece and muttered a word or two which would embarrass Old Nick. Then in her sweetest tone she asked “How big? Henry, darling.”

Henry knew he was pushing it, so ignored Connie's jibe and asked, "You remember George Bridge-Thompson?"

"Vaguely."

"Well, his Lady wife has turned up at the Pelican. A bit short on rations, confused and looking for George who is away on H.M.B."

"Oh! I see. Same excuse as Bertie." Connie immediately engaged sympathetically.

"No, no, Connie, this is pucker. Really important. George is away for at least a couple of nights.

I am needing someone to give her a berth for a night or two."

"When you say short on rations, you don't mean round the twist?"

"No, Connie, on a different planet, stuck in the 1930s. Thinks Hitler's harmless and the servants are subversive."

"Got one of them right, Henry," Connie said placing her hand over the speaker while she considered Henry's request.

"You still there Connie old girl?" Henry asked anxiously.

"That's my hopes for the reason you are calling out of the porthole," she replied pausing again.

Henry waited patiently. Connie didn't keep him long.

"Tell you what, Henry, I will give her a night or two if you promise to come up and see me some time. It could be fun."

Henry smiled with relief. "Thanks, Connie, you are a star and as a bonus I will send Tim over with her. I will need him back tomorrow. He could stay overnight. See you."

Henry replaced the receiver and bellowed. "Lt. Peat, to me at the double."

Tim Peat hurried to Henry's desk. "Sir."

"Some decent reading. Interesting reading, Peat. Sir George's latest report on the beaches procured. Put away the *Beano* and the *Dandy*, read, inwardly digest and learn. Liaise with army assault training and navy landing craft chaps." Henry handed over George's latest report.

"Then I have another task for you. Get yourself a staff car. Hare over to the Pelican, see the secretary and pick up Commander Sir George's wife, Lady Amelia. Ferry her over to your mother's.

It is all arranged. Oh! and you can stay overnight." Henry noted Tim's smile.

"Don't you dare make a jolly of it. I need you back here tomorrow morning sharp. Don't take that report off the bridge, not even to read on your way to the Pelican."

Tim, delighted with the task, sprang to attention and saluted, "sir."

His enthusiasm echoed down the office and everyone looked up.

Henry was shocked. "Bloody hell, Tim, too much. Far too much. Give my love to your mother."

Chapter 144

The following Friday Pen looked anxiously along the carriages as the London train pulled in to Fernborough. The alighting passengers were jumping off the train before it had stopped.

Pen was buffeted by them as they jostled through the exit to get to the front of the queue for the bus. To her delight and relief, she saw Hal bringing up the rear.

Hal grabbed her in a bear hug. She was forced to speak through compressed lips cutting short an intended prolonged kiss.

"Quick, darling!" She grabbed his hand and ran from the station platform dragging a very confused Hal behind her to the waiting queue for the bus.

"Hey, hey where's the fire? What gives, sweetheart?"

"Tell you when we get on the bus."

The driver and conductor put out their cigarettes.

"All uniforms, please," announced the conductor. Several soldiers, sailors and airmen and women walked to the front of the queue followed by Pen dragging a still confused and reluctant Hal.

They sat towards the rear as the saloon began to fill up with the rest of the queue.

The aisle was filled with strap-hanging standing passengers.

The bus left the station leaving a dozen or so people behind. Hal, realising the reason for Pen's strange behaviour, looked back at the disappointed few, feeling guilty.

"No need to ask why you are in uniform today," Hal, said, thinking to himself this was not the reunion he had hoped for.

"Sorry about this. I know it feels like cheating, but we have an appointment at the registrar's office at 11 a.m."

Hal squeezed her hand. "Are we all set?"

"Yes, 3.00 p.m. tomorrow."

"And this morning? What is this for?" Hal was anxious to know all was in hand.

"For you to sign your life away. Paradoxically, I think it is called, 'a declaration of freedom'."

Pen paused before adding, "to marry."

Ignoring the public display, they kissed.

"I too feel so mean Hal, but we daren't miss the appointment."

After signing and receiving final confirmation that their marriage could go ahead, Pen and Hal walked back to St. Mary along the river path scarcely believing that their dream was now within reach.

"We've got the house to ourselves that is if Mim can be persuaded to stay with Pam."

"What about Sir George and Lady Amelia? Your Mom will not be too pleased about me staying."

"Daddy has been recalled to Whitehall and they are both in London right now."

"Your Ma and Pa will be here for the wedding though?"

This was another question Pen didn't wish to answer.

"Too short notice, I doubt that they will make it."

This was the best answer she could think of. This, plus the knowledge that village disapproval could become a demonstration on the day, was tearing the heart out of their reunion.

Hal, sensing the tension, avoided asking more questions.

Chapter 145

They arrived at Greensleeves to step over the weekend's *Bugle* lying on the mat with the headline obscured. It read: 'THE RESCUER RETURNS TO MARRY.'

The narrative detailed Henry Steading's part in the escape from Austria of 39 Jewish children in 1938. One of the children rescued, Miriam Kessler is to be bridesmaid to the bride, The Hon Penelope, daughter of a local dignitaries Sir George and Lady Bridge-Thompson.

There followed the *Bugle's* version of the rescue.

This headline however was not overlooked by the organisers of a 'Yank Go Home' protest.

They retired to the pub leaving the placards discarded on the floor.

Pamela was waiting for Pen and Hal with a cooked lunch of roast rabbit, potatoes and vegetables. Sully provided the rabbits which were plentiful and easily caught at harvest time.

After lunch Hal thanked Pamela then took a Moonpenny from a vase and stripped the leaves leaving two opposing remnants of them. He threaded a gold wedding ring up the stem, passing the leaf stubs which now held the ring from slipping off. He then gave the flower to Pamela and asked, "Will you be both witness and ring carrier tomorrow, please."

Pamela understanding only too well what Hal meant, nodded and kissed them both.

After taking a little time to recover her composure Pam asked, "Have you seen the headline in *The Bugle,* Hal? Looks like you are viewed as a celebrity now."

Saturday morning dawned to clear, blue skies. Hal and Pen were already up and dressed having been woken early by Mim who was lying on the settee having cried herself back to sleep after failing to persuade Mama Pen to let her go across to Nanny Pam's to make sure that Auntie Dorothy had got her dress.

Hal was making eggy toast. Pen looked in vain for George's stash of real coffee which she knew existed.

"I can't find it, I'm afraid," she finally admitted. "It will have to be tea. I'm sorry."

"O.K. by me."

"You're sure?"

Hal smiled and gathered her into his arms. "I'm sure."

Breakfast over, they cleared up together. Mim was still fast asleep.

Hal and Pen stood in the window watching the shadows shorten and the dew disperse.

"I am afraid it is bus to Bendesbury and a walk back along the river path afterwards. Hardly hail the conquering hero or the arrival of the Queen of Sheba."

Pen sighed, feeling sad that she had not heard from her father.

Hal, sensing this sadness, avoided asking again about Pen's parents.

"O.K. by me. Looks to be a beautiful day for the walk back. I am sure looking forward to walking back as Mr. and Mrs Steading."

Taking Pen in his arms, he whispered in her hair, "When this war is over, we will have a fantastic church wedding in New England with Ma and Pa, yours, bridesmaids, the whole wagon train."

"Would you agree to having a page boy?" Pen whispered in return.

Hal spun Pen around. "Could be twins, one of each, plus Mim."

She lifted her face for his kiss.

The letter box clicked open and shut. "Daddy," she gasped, wriggling free she ran to the mat.

"What gives with your Pa?" Hal followed her into the hall.

The question both he and she had been avoiding even though they knew it had to be answered.

Pen was already ripping open the envelope.

"My mother and I have fallen out." Pen answered as she began to read.

"Over me and our marriage?" Hal turned away in frustration. "Jeez I am so sorry."

"Don't be, its better this way, believe me."

"What about Sir George?"

Pen raised a finger to his lips while she read.

Darling Pen,

My heart will be with you today, as it is every day. Your mother is still not well as you know.
Take care, give my good wishes to Henry Steading. Tell him I expect him to take good care of you and our grandchild. I plan to see you all as often as possible of that you can be sure.
Your wedding gift is under the kitchen range hood. Underneath there is a ledge, on this ledge is a key (to the extreme right) to all my secrets. (The cellar cupboard.) All you find in there are now yours.

All my Love always. George xxxx

Pen looked up at Hal. "Daddy's not coming," she sighed. "Somehow I just knew he wouldn't."

She passed the letter to Hal. In a sudden show of brightness Pen grabbed Hal's hand and ran into the kitchen. "Let's see our wedding present."

She quickly found the key and dragging Hal after her, descended into the cellar.

The door to the cellar cupboard opened to reveal a cash box, some bottles and clasp top jar of coffee beans.

"The coffee," exclaimed Pen in triumph. "Let's get this lot upstairs."

Together they carried the contents up into the daylight. Pen did a quick check to see that Mim was still sleeping.

"Typical! Awake half the night then fast asleep when it matters."

"There are two bottles of champagne," said Hal who was reading the labels at the window, "a half bottle of brandy and a nearly empty bottle of single malt. I guess it is too late to roast some of the beans."

"Not for the wedding breakfast. I will get to it." Pen collected the jar of beans.

"What's in the cash box?"

"Who's this woman coming in the gate?" Hal asked looking out of the window.

"It will be Dorothy with Mim's dress," Pen answered from the hall.

"It's not Dorothy, she's a stranger." Hal shouted back. Pen returned in time to answer the door to Emily Emerson.

"I thought you might need a little help today, Pen." Emily smiled. "Consider it to be my wedding present. What fine fare have you got for the feast?"

"Would you believe chicken," Pen replied smiling, delighted to have Emily back if only for the day. Emily removed her hat.

"I hear her Ladyship has left," she said trying to peer into the lounge to where she had seen Hal in the bay window.

"You heard right," Pen answered avoiding the subject quickly by adding.

"Come and meet Hal, he's in the lounge."

A delighted Emily swept into the room and introduced herself.

"Hello Capt. Steading, I'm Emily, here to give a hand." She offered her hand which Hal took readily.

"And you needn't worry about demonstrations, there won't be none. That article in *The Bugle* has blown their plans clean out of the water. On behalf of all those kiddies, captain, thank you."

"You are very welcome," answered a surprised and confused Hal.

"Doesn't sound very American, does he?" Emily whispered to Pen as they moved into the kitchen. "Leave the beans, I'll see them roasted." Emily was continuing to talk as she busied about her tasks as if she had never left.

"I was telling the captain there is to be no demonstration and if it suits, I could come back to work."

"Thank you, Emily, it suits me fine." Suddenly Pen felt that everything was going to be all right.

The demonstration by villagers appeared to have been abandoned thanks to *The Bugle* and the weather was perfect.

Pen went to join Hal at the window just in time to see Dorothy crossing the Green with Mim's dress as the smell of roasting coffee beans filled the house with memories of yesteryear.

The cash box held no cash although Pen remembered it once contained several sovereigns and half sovereigns. Now there were just several Victorian brooches, little else.

The time flew by and the girls were scrambling to be ready in time to catch the 2.15 bus.

Hal, standing in the bay, looked up from the many times he had looked at his watch to see an open landau turn into the Green pulled by a single prancing white horse.

He did a double take then shouted, "Hey guys, there's a Cinderella coach arriving. I kid you not."

Mim tumbled down the stairs losing one of her white ballet shoes on the way.

The shoes, from Pen's childhood ballet days, were a little too big. The delay had been caused by Mim refusing to wear her everyday shoes. The finding of the ballet shoes, the cleaning, whitening and packing the toes with newspaper took time. Pen chose the front page of last night's *Bugle* to do this.

Mim retrieved the lost shoe and hopped down the remaining stairs.

Landing with a bang, she ran into the lounge and when she saw the 'coach' and horse she began to squeal.

Pen, who at first dismissed Hal's shout as a wind up, went to the window and gasped. She was unable to believe her eyes.

Front doors from all around opened and folk were appearing at their garden gates.

Freda was one of the first. Her jaw dropped and she returned inside and removed the 'Yank Go Home' poster from her front window.

The landau stopped outside the gate. The coachman, in full livery, sat resplendent but unmoving. Pamela hearing Mim tumbling down the stairs, went to Pen's room.

"Everything allright, Pet?"

Pen didn't answer, she was still trying to comprehend.

"Sounded like a wildebeest stampede," said Pam. Just at that moment Mim caught her second breath and began to squeal again. Pam recognised the squeals as delight and added, "Sounds like one of them has been caught. What's that all about?" Pen finally re-engaged her brain and tongue. "Come to the window Nanny Pam and see."

It was as if she needed confirmation that she was not dreaming.

Dorothy entered talking as she came and pinning a carnation to her dress.

"We are going to miss that bus," she said as she joined the others in the window. A casual observer could be forgiven for thinking that for the next thirty seconds time had been suspended.

Only Mim's excited screaming and shouting destroyed the illusion.

A small group of lunchtime drinkers were enjoying the late September sunshine outside the Stagecoach Inn on the Bendesbury Turnpike, when the landau appeared in the distance.

It did not take long for them to realise it was not just any horse and cart.

They all moved to the roadside to cheer and jeer as it went by.

Edna stubbed out her Woodbine and moved to join them. She stopped and returned to retrieve a half-finished glass of ale from the rickety wooden table.

"One rule for the sodding rich and another for us poor buggers," she announced to all.

Mim, sitting on Pam's knee, waved excitedly to the crowd as the landau swept by.

This 'reception committee' was a minor precursor to their entry into Bendesbury square.

A crowd of school children were waiting to cheer. Shoppers left the shops, children left the playground and those passing through stayed to watch.

Mim made the most of the moment. Unfazed, she stood waving to the crowd while the coachman opened the door and lowered the steps. She held out her dress with her left hand and took the coachman's offered hand to descend in the elegant manner of the lady seen in a recent film.

The four adults sat still trying to work out what was afoot. It was Pamela who spoke up first.

"What are the school children doing here? Is this your doing, Dorothy?"

Dorothy shook her head. "This is all news to me, how come? No, no, no," she repeated.

Mim remembered that she was not the star of the moment. She tried but failed to stand quietly by.

She was aware that she was the best dressed of the bridal party in her white silk gown with scalloped panels flowing like petals to mid-calf, slash neck trimmed in pink, a broad matching pink sash and white ballet shoes. She carried a posy of pink and white carnations.

Pen, by contrast, was dressed in a plain navy suit, white blouse, a small corsage pinned to her lapel with an antique brooch. A wide brimmed white hat with a matching navy coloured ribbon side bow completed her outfit. Tolly should have been there to advise her that she could have applied for extra clothing coupons with the signature of a vicar or registrar.

Hal alighted from the coach followed by the ladies.

The wedding party, (with the exception of Mim) were confused and self-conscious as they entered the registry office through a crowd of interested bystanders.

Pen's hopes for a quiet, anonymous wedding and a leisurely romantic walk home with her new husband by the river path had disappeared with the arrival of the landau.

She clung to Hal. She just wanted to scream, 'NO.'

When the landau arrived at the last minute she was confused and driven by Mim's excitement. Passing the jeering crowd on the turnpike, it was then she realised all was lost.

Given her time over again she would have refused ... but how?

Inside the registry office she managed to settle and persuade herself that the crowds would disperse by the time they left. If there had been a rear entrance, she would have pleaded to use it.

Pamela who was carrying the ring on the flower stem felt this representation of Peter's presence keenly and her tears flowed freely throughout the simple ceremony.

Their day of shocks was not over. They walked out into the sunshine into the public glare of the local and national press. Two rows of identically dressed school children lined the route from the doorway to the waiting landau.

Pen gasped and nearly fainted. Pamela, recovering from her emotional involvement, was first to realise Pen was having trouble. The others were too shocked.

Pamela moved quickly alongside, took her arm, and whispered,"Now is the time, Pet to show your metlle. Ten minutes and it will all be over. Trust me."

The little party 'froze' on the step. Down the centre of this guard of honour a young girl/woman began to walk. She carried a scroll in her hand. Dorothy recognised her immediately.

She remembered the self-conscious curtsy and the prefect badge.

Today the curtsy was deep and correct.

She was holding an unfurled scroll. She began to speak in a clear strong voice.

"On behalf of myself and the 38 other children you helped walk to freedom, we thank you and wish you a long and happy life." She paused, coughed and took a little time to control her emotion.

She continued to speak, her voice gradually fading.

"May you be aware for the rest of your life of the great gift you have bestowed upon us. The named children on this scroll, their children and grandchildren, know that you have changed for the better countless lives you will never ... nev ...” Her voice faded and stopped, she lost her poise and stepped forward thrusting the scroll towards Hal then bent and kissed his hand and held it briefly to her cheek. She curtseyed again, this time less than perfectly. Turning around she began to walk then run back down the rows of children.

Pen was recovering now that she was no longer the centre of attention. She stepped back as one of the girls lining the route hissed.

“Mim, you are supposed follow her down the line. She should have said ‘please follow me’.”

Applauded all the way, they managed to arrive at the Landau where Lords Bendesbury, Benjamin, the rabbi and the press waited.

Pamela hung on to Pen’s other arm continually whispering in Pen’s ear.

“Be strong, Pet, be strong.”

The speeches droned on and on and Pen found this more and more difficult.

Then there were the photographs and reporters asking questions of Hal, who recovered to handle the situation well.

Mim was loving it all especially when she was asked to pose for photographs.

Hal stepped forward and faced the crowd. He raised both hands to quieten the applause.

“Please, we must go. Before we do, please know I was not alone in the saving of these children. There were many helpers and one very special friend without whom we would not have succeeded.”

He paused to make sure the reporters were paying attention.

“That friend was Lt. Peter Barnes. In 1940, he was awarded the Military Cross for taking on the enemy single handed, delaying their advance and allowing many more to escape to Dunkirk and safety.” Hal paused again. “It hurts me to tell you that he was killed on active service only a few short weeks ago again fighting this very evil which targets babies. He was hugely instrumental.”

He paused again.

"Then there was the very special Miss Dorothy Price, here today." He took her hand.

"She and her team of ladies successfully carried out this and other rescues."

Pen found this difficult, even though every word was true it seemed to her tortured mind that Hal had prepared this speech. He appeared to be part of this conspiracy which had stolen her day.

The gods were punishing her for daring to defy them in her pursuit of happiness.

The journey back to St. Mary was bad, but not as bad as Pen feared The Stagecoach Inn was closed and apart from one or two pedestrians, they saw only a few people.

Even the Green was quiet, the usual Saturday afternoon families playing and picnicking on the grass were missing.

Not that any of this helped. Even Hal and Dorothy, who handled it well so far, were badly disturbed and strangely silent.

Mim was disappointed with the lack of attention away from the town.

They all arrived at Greensleeves feeling flat.

Pamela whispered to Hal. "Look to Pen, she's hurting."

Pen had left the lounge and was removing her hat in the hallway.

Hal followed and put his arms around her. "Sorry kid, someone has stolen our day."

Pen stiffened. "You seemed to be enjoying the limelight."

"Hey, hey, sweetheart, none of this was my doing. Would you have me not reply, not mention Peter Dorothy and the gang?" He tried to turn her round to face him.

"You still managed to sound as pompous as those silly men."

She wriggled free and fled into the kitchen.

Hal made to follow only to be stopped by Pam. "Leave her Hal, give her time."

Emily Emmerson came up from the cellar to find Pen crying in the corner of the kitchen.

"What is it Penny, lovey." She put down the ice bucket and sped across to her taking her in her arms.

"It's all gone wrong Emily and it was going to be so lovely. Hal was so distant, and I know Pamela is still cross about me and him." Pen buried her face in Emily's bosom.

Emily let her stay for a short while before pushing her to arm's length.

"So, your day wasn't your day and it was everyone else's."

Emily shook Pen gently in time with her words as she said.

"Show me a Bride who got her own way on the day which is laughingly called the bride's day and I'll show you my ..." Emily didn't finish the sentence thinking better of it, saying instead, "No bride gets all their own way my pretty. No one bride ever did. No one bride ever will."

Pen sniffed. "I didn't want much, just to marry Hal and walk back home by the river. It wasn't much to ask for, was it?"

Emily took out a hankie and wiped Pen's eyes.

"Well you got the first bit and ..." Emily began until Pen interrupted.

"But they couldn't wait to snatch him away and he, he let them."

"Don't you think it was better than the 'Yank Go Home' demonstration that was planned?

Think on, when this war is over you can have a big, big beautiful wedding in America or wherever and really do what ***you*** want." What Emily thought and didn't say was. 'If you think you will get all your own way even then you are deluded. There will be a mother or female relative trying to relive their dreams'.

Encouraged and comforted by Emily, Pen began to settle down. Emily sat her at the table and put the kettle on, then took it off again. "You are a bit low on tea, lovey what about a coffee?"

"I should be going back to the lounge."

"Tell you what, lovey, let them come and find you. You just sit a while."

Emily poured the coffees. "And we can talk or not."

"I'm sorry, Emily, I don't know why I am like this."

Emily sat down and took Pen's hands in hers. "You've had a big, big week."

She hesitated and corrected herself. "In no less than one week, you arranged for your marriage and succeeded in marrying your man and survived a whole heap of envy from a tribe of hypocrites."

Emily sat back and took a drink. She was enjoying this moment, the luxury of real coffee and helping Pen. She was hoping to keep this job which was better than anything else on offer.

"Lord knows Captain Steading is the right man for you."

Emily noticed that Pen was hanging on to her every word. "Working miracles takes it out on you. Now go my lovely and make peace with your man and make the most of what time is left.

Pen nodded and stood to go. "Thank you, Emily, I am feeling much better now."

Emily followed her to the door, not wishing to relinquish this moment.

"How your wedding went is not important. How your marriage goes is.

Stow your pride and fears, go give yourself to your man. If I were you, I would not waste one precious second."

Emily, very proud of these final words, went back to savour the rest of her coffee and her moment of power.

Chapter 146

Pamela, after persuading Hal to give Pen some space, engaged him in conversation to prevent him 'ducking under her guard'. This was difficult because he spent his time looking past Pamela at the lounge door.

Dorothy, ever sensitive, took Mim upstairs to put her posy in a vase, leaving Pam and Hal alone.

"Thank you for your speech to the press including Peter, making them aware of his part in everything. Mim does not realise how important Peter's part was in not only getting her over the border but setting her up here to live the life she now has." She sighed.

"How is it that people continually get things wrong?" With this comment Pam finally got Hal's attention.

"Pen and me, we are permanently strapped into a guilt buggy," he suddenly announced.

Pam, surprised by this sudden turn, didn't respond. She waited for Hal to continue which he eventually did.

"We cannot choose our emotions. They choose us. If we try to deny them, they don't go away.

They ferment inside and destroy us. I have tried to live without Pen but the pain of that was worse than the guilt. Problem is we now have to live with this guilt for the rest of our lives."

Pamela was shocked into silence. Her resentment melted into understanding.

Hal stood and walked to the window and looked out.

"I knew this shadow would curse us when I tried to break with Pen."

He didn't continue for some seconds. "What are we to do?" he suddenly asked.

Pam didn't know whether the question was directed at her or the gods. In the silence following she adjusted her mind to this new understanding.

"Maybe, Hal, we all need some form of closure for Peter's death. You have no Peter to ask for forgiveness or his blessing. I have no Peter to bury."

Hal didn't answer but continued to look out of the window for over a minute before quietly recalling his friendship with Peter. He was clearly thinking over what Pamela had just suggested.

"When Pete and I had something on our minds in Cambridge, we would go to the river.

We first met on a bridge over the Cam. Pete had a problem. I was just enjoying the cool of the night and watching the lights reflecting in the ripples. They had a kind of rhythm."

Hal didn't say another word for what seemed an age.

Pamela, listening intently, willed him to continue. Hal turned and came back to the chair and sat.

"I began to recite some verse. Just one line, 'If I could choose a world to be.' And that was it!

Pete turned to me and broke his silence. 'I don't recognise that,' he said.

So, I gave with 'This royal throne of kings.' He replied, 'This sceptred isle,' I said. 'This seat of Mars.' Pete corrected me with 'This earth of majesty.' That was it, we clicked."

Hal recognised that he had Pam's attention and suspected her need to hear.

He sat back and sighed at his memories.

"Pete had this encyclopaedic memory. Whatever quote anyone gave he could pick up on and continue. I guess we were just soul buddies from the start."

"Even to sharing Pen?"

"Ah! therein lies the rub." Hal gave a humourless laugh. "Pete would like that one."

"You had something on your mind talking just now when looking out the window. Would you like to share it?"

"Have you still got the flower we gave you?" Hal answered her question with a question.

Pam knew immediately where he was coming from. "In a vase in the dining room."

"What say we go this evening to the footbridge by the ford, have a kinda service? Each say a few words and drop the flower into the water?"

"Didn't you do that for Dorothy's friend who disappeared off the ferry?"

Hal remembered the fiasco that whole weekend turned out to be.

"Yes, but this will be different. The river is where Pete would go, where he would be. I even have a quote of his from somewhere which I know would feel right."

The door flew open and Pen ran across to Hal and threw herself into his arms.

A much wiser Pamela smiled and left the lounge wiping away a tear.

Chapter 147

The sun was rimming the horizon. The quiet of the evening was broken only by the hush of the waters over the ford and a blackbird's evensong carrying far on the September evening mist.

The little wedding party walked in silence down the lane, across the cricket field to the footbridge each carrying a flower.

Silently, they lined the rail. No one spoke for a long minute.

Hal took from his pocket a small slip of paper and read from this accompanied by the sound of the river and the blackbird. "We remember Peter, Margaret Firth and Miriam's mother and father Professor and Frau Kessler." Hal paused to be sure that he had not forgotten anyone, then spoke these words.

"The petals of our lives fall,
Unbidden, into living waters,
Bounce briefly over life's pebbles,
Circle softly in the eddies of memory,
Fade into the seas. To rise again as
Vapour to shroud the distant hills
Become a dewdrop on a rose or
The breath of a child writing its name
On a brief window of time."

One by one they dropped the flowers into the river. The evening breeze ruffled the leaves of the weeping willow which blazed white in the fast fading sun's rays.

The party silently turned and made their way back, Pen with her head laid against Hal's chest,

Pam and Dorothy walking slowly behind followed by Mim.

Mim suddenly ran back to the edge of the field to pick an armful of moonpennies, dandelions, buttercups and daisies.

Pam and Dorothy stopped to watch as Mim returned to the footbridge and tossed them into the water. She remained poised, arms raised and fingers splayed.

Mim, holding the pose, watched the flowers drift down river to disappear into the evening mist rising from the surface.

She turned in her white bridesmaid's dress, startling white against the twilight.

She held the skirt out wide in both hands and skipped back along the planking and jumped down the steps on to the grass, her skirt ballooning. She did a couple of pirouettes to try and hold this effect then ran back to Pamela and Dorothy who were waiting.

Chapter 148

The setting sun stretched the shadow from the old olive tree on to the terrace until it resembled a monster. The fingers reached down towards where Peter and Helena were sitting in the shade of the south cliff enjoying the evening air after the day's work.

Josef spat out an olive stone which landed at his wife's feet, breaking her thoughts as she stood on the edge of the patio watching her daughter and Peter. "Dirty crow," Maria said.

Normally she would have turned to give her husband the steely eye but tonight her gaze did not waver from the couple down below.

"It makes a change from sucking an empty pipe. Good crop this year might as well enjoy them," Josef replied and despite this comment he returned to sucking on the empty pipe.

Maria took her time responding eventually replying thoughtfully.

"Speaking of pointless activity, you had best move back into my bed tonight."

She continued to watch Peter and Helena.

Josef failed to pick up on this. "What are you talking about?"

Maria still didn't turn around to answer but continued watching Helena and Peter.

"Well Josef, we will be cropping more than just olives next year."

Josef was now really confused. "All this because I spat out an olive pip."

Josef was used to Maria talking in riddles, which he ignored, however, something was telling him this was different.

"It's the indiscriminate sowing of seeds which bothers me."

Josef sucked on his pipe trying his best to keep in touch.

"Take that olive tree on the cliff edge, it shouldn't be there, should it? That was probably spat out hundreds of years ago."

"Or sown in some goat's crap and casually trodden in by its hind leg as it left," Maria added wryly.

With Maria's last comment Josef gave up and looked forlornly at his empty pipe.

"Do you think Attila is really dead?"

Maria finally turned and looked sadly at her husband.

"Yes Josef, still dead. Keep sucking your empty pipe."

Josef suddenly spotted a flaw in Maria's thinking.

"If I move back in with you where will Helena or Peter sleep?"

"Peter will sleep the back with Helena."

"You've changed your tune."

Maria finally came to sit with her husband. "Well, my dear Josef. Our daughter, it seems, has not been sucking on an empty pipe." She took his hand. "So, there is no point anymore, is there?"

Chapter 149

Three kilometres away across the straits. Attila and Mario had spent the day repairing and cleaning the timbers of Attila's boat. The bending, reassembling and refixing the prow had defeated them. Neither had recovered the full use of their hands and arms. Neither they nor Yarny were strong enough. The light was already fading, the days now shortening. Attila was impatient and under pressure to move Mario to safety away from the settlement.

The Germans were redoubling their efforts to locate this man, who was walking evidence of his crime.

The three of them sat on the wooden jetty resting from the day's labours. Tanya joined them and inspected the unsprung timbers. "Still no nearer relaunch?"

"None of us have the strength and dexterity yet," Attila replied.

"Keep trying anyway, it is good therapy for both of you. Don't try too hard but build slowly. Soon your strength will return."

It was late November when Mario and Attila with Yarny's help finally managed to reassemble the prow in a fashion which was, hopefully, watertight. Mario insisted then that they wait for calm seas before proving the repair, November and December being particularly stormy. Daylight hours and the high tide rarely coincided. This along with the weather's unpredictability, was too dangerous a 'cocktail'.

Paurak now had moved away north. The German Army had by and large been withdrawn to fight the Allies in Italy.

Attila decided to wait for the spring and for better weather and the longer daylight hours.

He could only hope that Maria, Josef and Helena were all right.

Mario's transfer and the news of Peter's death would have to wait.

There followed one of the worst winters in living memory and by early March the damage to the terraces and the houses bore witness on both sides of the straits. Maria and Josef were weary, Helena was heavy with her child. All three depended upon Peter more and more.

Peter thrived on the challenges but Maria, forced into working on the farm by Helena's condition, was less than happy.

"Trust this to happen," she said struggling to replace a large terrace-retaining stone, one of the many washed away along with the soil. She gave up struggling and sat down on the stone and began to sob. Peter hurried across to her.

"Leave it to me, Maria. Go back to the house, I will cope."

"We need help," Maria said between sobs. "The sets and seeds should have been planted and the seeds germinating by now."

Peter gently drew Maria to her feet. "Do as I ask please. Today is sunny and warm. Go back to the house and open all the windows and doors. That will help the house dry out."

Maria was not to be consoled. She had grown to love and rely on Peter over the long winter.

Small and crippled he may be, but he was a tower of strength. Peter, by contrast, had finally found his place in life. Battling with the elements to protect and nurture his new family gave him peace and purpose.

Maria sighed. "There is still the roof to repair."

Peter had tried to explain, unsuccessfully it seemed, that the roof did not need repairing.

This was difficult to explain away when water was pouring down the bedroom walls down into the ground floor.

The north wind was hitting the cliff side creating an updraft between it and the house wall.

This updraft carried the rain up the wall and under the eaves then over the top of the walls into the house. Peter now fluent in every day Serbo-Croat, struggled to explain, not being in possession of the necessary technical language. It was doubtful that Maria and Helena would have understood anyway. Josef, more and more 'away with the fairies', was of little help.

Peter ignored Maria's cry about the roof and took her into his arms and said, "Leave all to me. I will start today to plant the east terraces which are still usable. There will enough produce then for us, although little left to sell in the town but as the road west is no longer open that is no bad thing."

Maria began to feel better, "Please don't leave us, Peter."

Maria getting older, was tired of having to shoulder all burdens. Her strength had been sapped by the unusually long and harsh winter and an increasingly demanding Josef.

She was now more than ready to hand over.

"I am going nowhere. I belong here with Helena, Josef and you."

"You have a wife in England."

"I will have to go to England eventually to sort out my life. I promise to return quickly."

Peter held Maria at arm's length and looked into her eyes.

"I have money, big money back there some of which I will bring back. We will build that vineyard and winery. You will then have all the wine you wish."

Maria smiled at last. "You are good man, Peter. I will pray for you." She turned to go then stopped, crossed herself and added, "I will also pray for help. We do need help whatever you say."

Chapter 150

Across the straits on this same day Attila had risen early aware the tide was rising towards full. The weather was set fair. He decided that it would be a good day to prove the boat.

Mario and Tanya were already awake and joined Attila. "Today?" they both asked.

"Today," Attila replied. Together they rolled the boat into the river alongside the jetty to await the tide backing up the creek and raised the mast.

"I am thinking to risk the journey across to the island if the boat survives the trial."

Mario, aware of his uncomfortable position in the settlement and anxious to start his journey back home, was enthusiastic. "The boat is good for calm seas. Let's go."

Tanya, no longer a permanent fixture and planning to leave the settlement for good later in the week, agreed.

"Just keep your wounds covered particularly the head when at sea. Do not underestimate the power of the sun."

Attila had another agenda which was to carry on and sail to the west of the island to a boatyard where the repairs could be completed. Taking Yarny with them was also part of his plan.

This was to ensure that a second person could know the destination, to navigate and negotiate the rocky coast to arrive safely at the island's eastern landing site. This he had arranged with Svetka and Yarny. Attila had needed all his powers to persuade Svetka to allow both her men, as she saw it, on the water together in a suspect craft.

Attila returned to the house to advise them that today was the day.

"We sail within the hour. The sooner the better," Attila announced.

Svetka argued briefly. "Take care please. Do you need food?" were her final words. Yarny could not wait to be away not least to be finally free of the ghastly winter and all the work needed to recover the damaged terraces.

They left the jetty with Yarny at the tiller, Attila on the sail and Mario in the prow checking for any leakage. Soon all nervousness passed as the little craft behaved well making good progress in the early light winds. As far as all were concerned the proving was over.

"Let's go for it." Attila shouted. The sun quickly warmed the land. The wind picked up.

Attila was once more in his element.

"Tack with the second highest peak of the island as your central marker until you see a lone olive tree on the cliff edge beside a waterfall on to the beach," he shouted to Yarny.

There is no better feeling on God's earth than to sail freely in constant winds on a sunny day followed by the gulls dipping, weaving and calling around the boat.

The little craft was behaving perfectly. Attila began to sing. Yarny whooped with joy.

Mario laughed, tying the white piece of linen protection more tightly under his chin, the wind threatening to blow it away.

"You look like a woman," Yarny shouted, laughing, "you look beautiful."

"Better than having a head looking like a baboon's arse," Mario shouted back.

Quickly, all three of them were laughing.

A gull called, ka-ka-ka-ka, yuk, yuk, yuk, seemingly in response. This had them laughing even more. Free at last on the water, free of the shackles of winter; the three of them were euphoric.

Attila began to sing.

'Follow the day. Follow the wind
Take me along. Sing me your song
Take me back home. Where I belong.'

His light baritone was carried by an onshore breeze to the island. Mario and Yarny picked up on the folk tune and Attila's translation from the Hungarian. Soon all three were singing as one.

Across on the island Maria had plated some food and filled a fresh jug of water for Peter who was planting on the lower reaches of the eastern terraces.

"Peter, take a break and eat, please."

Peter stood and stretched, thanked Maria and walked to the usual place on the cliff edge to wash his hands in the stream. He sat in the shade of the olive tree, pleased to rest in the cool on an unusually warm March day.

Maria sat with him, "Peter, when do you plan to go back to England?"

Peter after drinking from the bottle poured the remaining water over his head. He took a bite of goat's milk cheese. "Who knows," he answered throwing some scraps to the chickens which had followed Maria and the food. They were clucking and gathering around his feet.

Maria, now used to Peter and his curt and monosyllabic answers, hoped that more might follow and waited. Peter finished his meal without further comment and got up to start work.

Maria, disappointed, stood. Being the same size as Peter, she looked him straight in the eyes raising her eyebrows in 'continuance' of her question.

Peter understood. "When will this war be over?" he countered.

Maria thought briefly. 'I hope it doesn't end then.' She didn't really wish this. She only wished to keep Peter. She also wished for Helena to be married and in her words 'made respectable'.

Unable to reconcile these emotions, she shrugged and gathered the plate and debris.

She turned to leave with the chickens following.

'Follow the Day
Follow the wind.'

The chorus of the song wafted faintly on the breeze to the island.

"Quiet please," Peter said, more to the clucking birds than Maria, cupping his hands to his ears. Maria stopped and returned. "What is it Peter."

"Quiet please," Peter repeated cupping one ear and shielding his eyes from the sun with his free hand and looking out to sea.

Maria could also hear the faintest sound of singing and wanted to ask what it was. She peered out to sea, but her old eyes could see little against the heat shimmer.

Peter spoke just one word. "Attila?"

"Attila?" echoed Maria. "Could it be?"

Peter turned to look at Maria and suddenly grabbed her in a bear hug and spun her around.

"That is Attila's song. That is his translation from the Hungarian. It can't be anyone else.

It can only be Attila. He has others with him by the sound of things."

Peter began to hurry back up the terraces dragging an astonished Maria.

"Helena, Josef, its Attila, he's alive, he is coming. He is coming at last," he shouted.

Attila ceased to sing and focused on the olive tree. He reached for his spyglass.

"Yarny, when we are in line with that rock to our right, swing south parallel to the shore for five hundred metres until we are in line with the other large rock ahead then swing right and head straight for the shore."

All this time his focus did not stray from the tree. "There are four of them," he muttered to himself. He dropped the spyglass and waved back. "That must be Peter. But it can't be."

Yarny turned to look over his shoulder to see what Attila and Mario were seeing.

Attila felt the boat swerve as Yarny lost the tiller. "Hold your line!" Attila shouted.

"Keep in line with the big rock, remember the submerged inshore rocks." He reached down again for the spyglass, but Mario had already claimed it and was taking in the scene of his future abode.

"Piero," Mario said, "that could be Piero." He handed the spyglass back to Attila.

"The little man," he repeated, "could be Piero."

"That, beyond doubt is Peter Barnes," said Attila he lowered the spyglass.

"Peter survived, impossible," he muttered. "He has more lives than a cat."

Meanwhile Yarny concentrated on staying in line. Attila was watching and called.

"Turn directly inshore and hold your line, avoid those strips of white water. Pass between them."

Once ashore and the boat secured, Attila explained again the details of how to arrive safely pointing out and repeating the salient features.

They climbed to cliff path and stopped for breath.

"You mention Piero, do you know Peter?" Attila asked Mario. He was thinking that Piero was the Italian for Peter.

"No, no, Piero was with me at the caves. He was behind me when the big explosion flared up the passageway. He took most of the blast and saved me from the worst. My friends carried me out. Piero was left." Mario crossed himself.

The trio resumed their journey through the flowers and shrubs covered with butterflies and bees. "Bella, bella, bellissimo," Mario kept repeating.

They stopped to rest on a rock in the shade of a larch.

"I shall leave you both on the next tide and sail round to the west coast port boat repair yard and return once the repairs are complete," said Attila. He then turned to Yarny.

"Please stay and help, son. I will return for you. How long that will be, I cannot say."

At the farm the ravages of the savage winter went unnoticed in the euphoria of the reunion and introductions. Mario was the first to comment. He assessed the damage and causes accurately. He endeared himself instantly with Maria by prefacing each suggestion.

'What needs to be done is' and 'What we must do.'

Josef hovered around Attila and Peter who were explaining to each other what happened that night when they both 'cheated' death.

Helena sat and smiled contentedly with her hands clasped over her swelling belly. She was holding the future, her reason to be alive.

Attila looked beyond Josef, noticing Helena. He went over followed by an anxious Josef.

Attila looked at Helena carefully avoiding her condition. He spread his hands smiling, unable to find the right words. Helena smiled back at him.

"My father is hoping for tobacco."

Attila didn't wish to disappoint Josef but realised it could not be left.

"Josef, I am sorry, I bring nothing but myself. The supplies of coffee, rice, wine and tobacco are no longer available. My movement has been limited. The British have moved out of the area."

He spread his hands. "We are no longer in contact."

He took the old man by the shoulders.

"I am going on to the west coast. Maybe I will find tobacco there. If so, it will be yours."

Attila returned ten days later to discover that the eastern terraces were planted.

Peter and Yarny had made a start with repairing the western side terraces.

Mario, more engineer than farmer, was well underway in rebuilding one of the derelict houses to the east just below the olive grove where Pietro Josef was conceived.

Attila brought much needed supplies.

Josef had his tobacco, Maria had wine and Helena baby clothes. The evening meal with wine was full of conversation, questions and conviviality. There was a new optimism.

"How Attila did you get baby clothes to say nothing of the wine and tobacco?" asked Helena.

"I worked in the market while waiting for completion of the repairs."

"Baby clothes stall?"

"Fish," Attila answered, "paid part in fish, perfect for bartering."

Attila and Yarny left a much happier farm the following day.

Pietro Josef was born on time in April and Papa Peter and Uncle Mario became a formidable team. By the end of summer, they had rebuilt the house on the eastern slope. Peter and Helena had moved in. Mario was properly housed for the winter in the second bedroom of Maria and Josef's house.

Helena helped on the terraces with Pietro strapped to her back only occasionally yielding to her mother's pleas to have him.

Attila and sometimes Yarny visited the island with fish and crustaceans for barter, returning with olives, figs and almonds, sometimes live chickens. The co-operation between the two settlements became even more important once contact with the British ended. The association with the partisans ended, leaving the mainland settlement isolated. The farm was also isolated, the road to the west coast port remaining closed. It was of little interest to anyone other than the farm.

After the olive harvest Attila and Mario took surplus olives and produce by sea to the west coast and returning with wine and tobacco.

The winter was mild, the weather making recompense for past cruelty. Peter and Mario cleared the ground for the planned vineyard. They redesigned the irrigation system to service the vineyard and the terraces. The spring planting was completed ahead of schedule.

In early summer Attila brought news of the Normandy landings which relieved the frustration of the stalemate in Italy.

They had no immediate knowledge of what was happening on the Eastern Front, little news having filtered through. They only learned of this when they visited the west coast port.

Early in 1945 it was already clear to all that a plan was needed for Mario to return to his home in Trieste. Maria and Helena were aware that Peter could soon be able to return to England.

He needed to sort out his affairs, hopefully then to return to settle with them. Both women wished this to happen being concerned for their futures. They managed to avoid the subject mostly, but it was clearly not a peaceful time. Helena closed off her mind better than Maria.

When Attila and Yarny came in February after the winter break, they brought with them vines to start the vineyard, also maps and charts and a plan for the repatriation of Mario via the sea.

Isolated and immune from the realities of the war, it was easy for all but Maria to close their minds to all but the immediate. It was as if the rest of the world did not exist. Mario settled apart from often in the dead of night when he frequently relived the trauma of the caves, the loss of Piero and the confused and tortuous escape from the Germans.

In the daylight he managed mostly to keep busy and to shut out these memories.

After Attila's return with his plans, Peter and Helena were having to face the fact that Peter needed to return to England to confirm his divorce and claim his inheritance.

Attila's plan was to sail direct to Italy by following the coast to Trieste.

Both Mario and Peter were surprised. They had not even considered returning via the sea.

Attila counselled against their ideas of an overland return warning that any attempt to return through Croatia and Slovenia would be dangerous. The German Army there was all but non-existent. The different cultures, drawn together by a common enemy, were already breaking up into their different factions and turning on each other.

Attila pointed out that they could carry more food and have guaranteed transport in the boat.

None of these would be certain via other routes. Convinced, they laid their plans.

Maria had other concerns on her mind. Listening to the men reinforced her fears.

"If Peter and Mario leave together what happens with us and the farm?" she asked.

A silence followed. None of the planners had considered the farm and what would happen to the rest of the family. It was Peter who answered first.

"The planting and preparatory work will be done. I plan to return for the harvest."

Maria scoffed. "As usual, Peter, you talk the easy game. We all know that life will not always pan out as we hope."

Attila leaned across to Yarny. "Would you stay here until I return, please?

"What about Mum and Mari, won't they need me?"

"I think Svetka will stay in the settlement for now. She didn't feel safe when she was home last.

She will wait for me to return. Raula and family are also staying put for the time being."

Attila was planning to stay on the coast which was his home for nearly forty years.

Svetka insisted that because of Marineska's schooling, she must return home once the troubles were over.

Keeping Yarny on the coast was another of Attila's hopes. Yarny didn't answer so Helena spoke up.

"With most of the heavy work done and the new irrigation system working well, what little needs to be done I'll do. That is if you, mother, will look to Pietro Josef."

At the end of April the German command in Italy surrendered. This was followed in early May by the surrender of Donitz to Montgomery on Luneburg Heath. The Berlin commander surrendered to the Soviets and the smaller Axis states surrendered one by one.

The war was finally over leaving Europe in a state of unimaginable chaos.

Millions of displaced people and army deserters especially those many nationalities conscripted into the Axis forces, struggled to survive. Abandoned, they clogged the routes east and west as they tried to return home. Others were searching to find lost loved ones or just wandering, confused and unaided. The failure of the Yalta conference to resolve the many complex issues facing the changed face of Europe suggested the situation was unmanageable in the short term.

Meanwhile the separate armed forces of the West and the Soviets tried to establish dominance prior to the later Potsdam conference.

Jewish people, traumatised and decimated but ever resourceful, headed for the coastal ports to try and relocate back in their perceived safe homeland in Palestine. Progress was blocked by a confused and stressed British Government trying to deal with the responsibilities of a Palestinian Protectorate and the demands of occupation and a broken economy.

With no established Government anywhere on the continent outside Vichy France and the Iberian Peninsula, anarchy ruled the days. British and American forces tried to police on a regional basis while at the same time deal with over 1, 500,000 prisoners of war and the countless who had been displaced. Marshal Tito battled to re-establish the former Yugoslavia in the face of a resumption of hostilities between the different factions.

Mass murder, assassinations and pillage proved Attila's forecast that a journey through Croatia and Slovenia would be difficult and dangerous.

On the island farm all was peace and tranquillity. They were completely unaware of the trauma that was Europe. Peter completed the stone terrace in front of the rebuild house complete with wooden table. The house faced south across the river. There was no olive tree otherwise the house would have been a mirror image of Maria's and Josef's.

Mario looked daily for signs of Attila's coming to ferry him home.

In mid-June Attila obtained the diesel he needed for him to feel confident to attempt the voyage to Trieste. He arrived at the island farm provisioned and ready for the trip.

Peter forced himself to accept that he needed to sort out his affairs in England. He wished to remain on the farm where he had spent his happiest years.

Within a day or two the three men agreed plans and completed provisioning the boat. They decided to sail on the next morning's tide.

Peter and Helena sat out on the newly paved terrace, Pietro Josef asleep in a box by their sides. Helena trimmed Peter's hair and beard. "I don't want to go," Peter sighed.

"I don't want you to go either. Are you sure that you must?"

"I must get an annulment or a divorce then we can marry and be a proper family. Apart from that I have money, good money which will set the farm and the vineyard on to a sound basis."

"It doesn't work like that here. Divorce is not allowed."

"Annulment is though. We must try if only for Pietro and our future."

Helena, silent then began to cry softly. "Mother says I must be prepared that you may never return."

Peter took her hand.

"I was born for this place. Until I set foot on this farm I was lost. How could I not return to you, Pietro and my only home?"

They spent the remainder of the night not sleeping. They stayed outside holding each other until Attila arrived in the early hours to announce it was time to go.

Peter kissed the sleeping Pietro. He took Helena in his arms one final time that night. "Believe," he whispered. "Watch the sunset every night until I return and know that I will return as surely as that sun returns to start the new day."

The three voyagers disappeared over the ridge watched by Helena and Maria. Peter hardly dare turn around to wave even at the last moment. They finally vanished into the darkness.

Chapter 151

The voyage to Trieste took all of twelve days. The winds were too light during the day for sailing and the high summer sun was too much for all and unbearable for Mario. They sailed mostly in the evenings picking up the onshore winds sometimes in the early morning.

Three weary travellers arrived at the private jetty to Mario's boat repair yard hoping to land and rest up. This was not to be. The boatyard and jetty were crammed with refugees.

They were sitting or sleeping on the jetty even to the very edge.

"What do we do? This is not safe. Better not to tie up here," said Attila.

Mario didn't answer. He and Peter just stared in disbelief at the mass of shredded humanity.

"I am not going in there. I can't risk my boat."

Attila tacked along the coast for a little way and back. The crowds seemed to be everywhere.

"Where can we land? There is nowhere." Attila was not willing to risk his boat.

"Land at my jetty, it will be all right."

"I can't risk my boat. It is my everything. Do we need to land here? Try to think of somewhere else." Mario knew that all landing places would be the same but was desperate to get home.

"They will not be violent. The boatyard doesn't matter, it is rented so it's the landlord's problem. It's the papers. I must have my papers from the office safe."

"What papers? Are they important?" Attila was still not willing to risk his boat. The people on the jetty were paying too close attention to his little craft.

“Piero’s and my identity papers and seamen’s certificates. I must have them. Without them I am nothing. We were told to carry nothing of identity when we left for the caves.”

“Is there another landing possibility anywhere nearby?

He wanted to land and rest, but he could not risk losing his little craft.

The little boat drifted as the three sat and thought now watched by a growing crowd on the jetty.

“If we go to any other place it will be the same. I was warned of the refugee problems before we left but I never imagined this.”

“This is Trieste, a magnet for all seeking a new life, a new world or even a reason to live.”

Mario shrugged his shoulders, “What can they do.” He studied the people for a while.

Women and children started appearing from within the main boathouse.

“What can they do?” he repeated. Then feeling a little ridiculous he removed his head dress preferring to reveal his scars. Mario was now getting desperate and was forced into a decision.

“You stay at a safe distance, Attila. Peter and I will swim. It is only a short way and we can wade most of the way. Come, the sea is warm but not as warm as me,” he added with a forced smile.

Mario looked intently at Peter who was still unable to take in the scene they faced.

“Piero, you can swim yes?”

Peter wondering what was happening, answered. “Yes, but is it safe?”

Mario spread his arms, “We have nothing to steal so we must thank Attila and let him sail back home and to safety.”

Without waiting for Peter’s answer, he embraced Attila, forcing the issue.

“Thank you, my friend for everything. Stay safe and you go now on your way. I wish you a safe journey home and for the future calm seas and a following wind for the rest of your life.”

Peter felt they just couldn’t leave Attila just like this after all he had done.

"What will you do?"

Attila was pleased that Mario had resolved the impasse. He smiled encouragement at Peter.

"I will take my time returning. I hope to see you back at the farm before too long."

"Won't Svetka be worried? You've been away for over two weeks already."

Peter was still reluctant to summarily leave, and still sought to find another way.

"Svetka will return to her home village for Marineska's schooling," said Attila adding:

"me? I belong on the water," Answering Peter's unspoken question.

Attila shook Peter's hand. "Now go with Mario and hurry back to where *you* belong."

Mario jumped into the sea to be followed by the very reluctant Peter.

Together they waded to the boatyard slipway. They turned and waved to a relieved Attila who returned the wave before sailing back out to sea.

Two very tattered, strange looking men, skin burned almost black and beards bleached by the same sun, climbed up on to the jetty assisted by a mainly passive and curious audience. Steaming in the climbing sun they walked into the main boathouse trailing sea water across to an office in the corner. Mario led the way as interested and curious onlookers watched them closely.

The door to the office had been forced. Inside on the floor they found a very nervous woman sat on a heap of sacking cradling a newly born baby. "Ciao signora, Ciao bambino," said Mario.

He smiled at the Nativity-like scene and blew them a kiss before removing a key from around his neck. Opening a wall safe, he took out some papers and stuffed them in his shirt. He then took out a cash box, removed the lira inside and threw a handful of notes to the watching crowd. Whilst they fought over them, he tucked more lira up the nursing mother's blouse sleeve and placed his hand on the baby's head and repeated, "Ciao bambino."

He dropped the empty cash box on the floor and walked out. Peter followed.

Outside on the street Mario took out his papers from his still damp shirt and held them over his scarred scalp protecting the bright pink new skin and to dry out any damp.

Walking quickly away with Peter dipping and hobbling tried to keep pace, he headed for his family home and safety.

"Did you have to give all your cash away?"

"You will discover my friend that money is useless. If there is no food, no shops open, no goods, what can it buy? It got us out of the yard without problems. Just keep going. Let's get away from here."

The watching crowd in another time or another place might have laughed at these strange two men literally steaming up the road.

Not here! They watched in silence, then returned to the shelter of the buildings.

"We go now to my home and stay with my people," Mario said breathlessly.

For all his apparent camaraderie, discovering the boat yard destroyed had upset him. Peter, also severely disturbed, hobbled after him in silence.

Mario arrived at the end of the street where his family lived to find it closed off.

The way was barricaded. Two trucks, sideways on, bonnet to bonnet, blocked the entrance.

Armed men stood guard vetting all who came and left. They did not recognise Mario and tried to turn them away at first. When they realised who he was, they embraced him.

He was feted as the returning hero.

Peter, an outsider, was held outside of the barrier until Mario shouted.

"And my hero friend Piero he has been with me all the way."

Peter, with his limp and heavily scarred face, was accepted without further question.

In the comparative calm of the street Mario hammered on the locked door of his family home.

A neighbour heard and came with the key to the house to explain the house was empty.

"The partisans came and took your family away in case the Germans came for reprisal. What you achieved was feted on the streets of Trieste. It alerted the German Army directing them here."

"Where are they now? They could come home. The war is over."

The neighbour spread his hands. "Who knows?" he answered and shrugged.

He had no answers. No one did.

Inside the house there was no food, no electricity and no water. Nothing! Whatever there had been of value had gone. Probably looted. Mario stood unable to comprehend.

"What do we do?" Peter asked. Mario tried the hot water tap and didn't answer.

A trickle of water came from the tank. Mario immediately closed the tap to conserve what little water there might be. Then he began to open any cupboard doors which were not already open.

He then ran up the stairs. Peter stood where he was and waited not knowing what else to do. Mario returned down the stairs.

"There is bedding and clothes they have taken, mostly food and valuables. We can sleep but not eat or even drink," Mario announced sitting down to recover and think. It was not long before his natural positivity returned.

"We have the papers and I have other family in the town." He tapped his chest indicating that he had the answers to their problems. "At sea we have food and shelter away from this chaos."

The only water they had was from the hot water tank and little of that. The feed tank was empty. They had no food, nothing. Mario returned to the barricades to be told there was little or no food to be had. The fields and gardens had been stripped of all produce even to the unripe fruit. Shops were closed to the general public. The whole immediate area was flooded with refugees. Food supplies were dangerously low and only regular customers were being served by arrangement.

He returned empty handed to Peter and explained, "We go to sea. We have no option."

"What about me. What do I do? I must contact the British Army or the Consul but, where are they?" Peter asked hoping that Mario had answers.

Mario did have answers but not the ones Peter was seeking.

"The British Army, that is if they are still here, could be anywhere dealing with this crisis. And if they are here, do you really think they will listen to you with no papers and no identification.

As for a consul there is none and there will probably be no consul for months."

Mario looked Peter in the eye. "Here you have no chance and we have papers."

He tapped his pocket. He took out one set and held the papers in Peter's face.

"You are now Piero Bellini, ship's engineer."

"That is fraud. I am not an engineer."

Mario took Peter by the shoulders. "Peter my friend. Here we are nothing. This is not your home farm. Even my friends do not have food for us. We have no water. We have nothing. Here we are nothing. But I do have family. I have uncles and cousins in this port and in Valetta. We go to the docks. I will get us berths on the ferry to Malta and from there a commission for you to sail to England. This is the only answer. Here we will starve and you will never return to your family."

"I am not an engineer."

"You know Attila's engine. It is the same on a ship: pistons, cylinders, seals and shafts, only bigger."

Peter had done preliminary engineering in his father's plants as part of his training. He knew what Mario was saying to be true. He searched his mind for another solution but could not find one.

Mario sighed. "We sleep here tonight. Tomorrow we see my uncle."

Mario looked at Peter and then down at himself. "But not like this. I will find clothes for us."

Peter, aware of his tattered image, searched his mind as to how to get out of this dilemma and began to seriously consider Mario's plan. "I would need to look very different for anyone to take me on and I would have to get rid of this beard."

Mario looked at his little friend and said, "We will need to change your clothes, but you don't need to get rid of your beard. Just your halo."

Mario went upstairs and left Peter sitting in the gloom of the shuttered house with just the one open door letting in the only source of light.

Chapter 152

In Malta with the help of Mario's cousin, Peter, posing as Piero Bellini, signed on as second engineer on the S. S. Rossini bound for Southampton via Gibraltar transporting British troops and equipment. Registered in Palermo, the ship's remit was to repatriate Italian prisoners of war by return. The vessel commissioned by the British made Peter even more aware of his crime.

When the ship finally docked at Southampton it was a huge relief. What Peter intended to do was to disappear as Piero and resurrect Peter. Then return to St. Mary Upperford to re-establish his existence. This, even though he had signed for the ship's return to Valetta via Palermo.

Without funds Peter was relieved to learn they would be paid for the outward journey. It was enough to more than cover the three nights ashore awaiting the turnaround. This pay was in lira which was only exchangeable in the Seamen's Union.

Peter immediately asked to exchange lira for sterling. The officer gave Peter a chit, advising that a local bank teller attended the Seamen's Union at 11 a.m. each weekday. He would exchange the lira. Peter assumed that this would mean all his money, but the chit was only for two days which legally restricted the exchange to eight shillings, four shillings for each full day ashore.

The teller was helpful giving Peter a form to apply for a visa, the issue of which would allow him to cover all lira if he qualified.

Peter took the eight shillings and sat staring forlornly at the visa application.

He would have to lie not just about his identity but also the reason for his visit. Even if he confessed his crimes this would not help. He was trapped not only in his lie, but in the port of Southampton. He was uncomfortable, unlikely to achieve anything and his journeying would be futile. Worse it could end with a criminal record. None of this would help Helena, Pietro and the farm.

All he now wished for was to be back on the farm with his family.

His crime grew and grew in his mind. He could have made a mistake at sea with loss of life. If only he could return to the uncomplicated life he had left behind only a few weeks ago, he would make a very different decision.

"Problems, matey?"

Peter looked up to discover he was being observed by a friendly mature man of maybe sixty years. "You could say that."

"Oh! You speak English, that's a start," the man observed. "Are you having problems with the form?"

"Who are you?"

"Seamen's Union rep."

"Ah, thank you," Peter replied thinking quickly. "I don't think I can get a visa. In any event, I just don't have enough time. Time, I don't have."

"How much time do you have?"

"Just 48 hours."

"To go where?"

Peter was pleased with his answers and the way the conversation was going.

"Fernborough. Can I get there direct from here by rail from here?"

The man took a railway guide from his reefer jacket.

"Let's see, Fernborough." The man murmured thumbing through the guide. "On the hour weekdays until 10 a.m. then every two hours until four. Stops at every cow on the line."

"And the fare?" Peter enquired, aware that he had only eight shillings.

"Four shillings single, Seven and six, return," The man answered looking quizzically at Peter, who was now working out what to do. He could make it with a single fare or a return though the return would leave him without money for food. Having opted to be paid he was not included in the 'in port' crew. He needed it for today and probably tomorrow. If Pen was up in Derbyshire, as she could well be, he could be stranded.

Meanwhile the union man who was watching closely, interrupted his thoughts.

"Don't even think about it, matey. The authorities are looking out for the likes of you. You will be arrested and shipped back here before you know it. You stick out like a sore thumb."

"What do you mean?"

"Continentals, P.O.W.'s, they are being rounded up all over the country. Of course, they want to stay or come here. Who wouldn't? Isn't that what your ship is here for to return the likes of you?"

"About my looks I mean?"

The union man laughed. "When did you last look in a mirror, matey?"

Looking in mirrors was never top on Peter's agenda. Since his accident he actively had avoided this. Helena had trimmed his hair and beard. Peter had never bothered. It had not occurred to him to even think about it. Now the six weeks after his leaving the farm had made their mark.

Peter went at once to the washroom. He could not believe the image he saw reflected in the mirror. He took a tepid shower and 'combed' his hair and beard with his fingertips.

Peter's idea of grooming was to wash his head each morning, towel dry and to push his fingers through his hair and beard. The shower did little to improve his image.

In the union bar he enquired from the barman about the nearest barber and the cost of a shave and haircut.

"Two bob at least for that lot," Was the answer.

Two shillings Peter could not afford, so he bought a cheese sandwich and headed for the railway station with just the price of his railway ticket and four pence change.

Peter did his best to avoid all authority. He was constantly reminded of his appearance by the looks from other passengers. He had with him his seaman's papers, or rather Piero Bellini's, in case he was picked up.

Arriving at Fernborough was a relief. Peter waited in the station toilets for the platform to clear before leaving a little later avoiding the ticket collector and the bus passengers.

He then headed for the river path and the two-mile walk to St. Mary.

Nervous, tired and hungry, having eaten just one cheese sandwich since breakfast, he made his way along the river path stopping occasionally to drink from the river or to pick the few ripest blackberries from the hedgerow.

Chapter 153

Hal was on extended leave having been seconded to the East Coast Press London office pending his release from the Army Press Corps. Commuting from St. Mary to London according to demand, he was taking a free day. Hal was living the dream of family life in the village with Henry IV, now 16 months old, toddling, speaking his first words, a little brother or sister on the way. Life could not be better.

At breakfast that morning Hal picked Henry out of his high chair.

"Hey little fellah, what say we go picnic by the river this afternoon?"

Mim jumped to her feet and despite her ten years climbed on Hal's other knee.

"Yes, yes, yes please, Papa. Can Auntie Pam and Dorothy come too?"

Pen laughed. "Do you think I could have a say in this?"

Mim shot off Hal's knee, transferring herself to Pen putting her arms around her neck.

"O.K. Mama Pen, what do you say?" she drawled.

"I say you have been watching too many American films."

"About the picnic? Silly Mama Pen."

"Oh all right. I say, yes, yes, yes let's do that. Mim get dressed then go see what Auntie Pam and Auntie Dorothy say."

Came the afternoon they made their way to their favourite spot by the ford where the children could paddle in the shallow water in safety.

"Are we sure we have everything?" asked Pen as they walked down the lane.

"Not quite everything," answered Pam, "Dorothy and I have saved our rations. We have made a sponge cake. It is just out of the oven and cooling. I will nip back later to get it."

It was a beautiful afternoon by the river with the children paddling watched over by Pam and Dorothy.

They tried fishing for tiddlers to much laughter and no success. Hal and Pen relaxed and talked plans now they had sold the big house in Derbyshire. Pen had no use for it. All they needed to keep were the riverside properties with the rents handled by local agents.

"Then we can settle here until Mim comes of age and throws us out," said Pen.

"Sounds good to me."

"What, Mim throwing us out?" Pen laughed and threw herself on Hal, who grabbed her and holding on tight rolled over right up to the bank's edge threatening to roll into the river.

Pen screamed. "Please no, please," as they teetered on the edge.

Mim ran out of the water and threw herself across them screaming in unison with Pen.

Pam ran with Henry and held him feet dripping water on to all of them.

Exhausted with the merriment they flopped all five of them on the grass.

"We might as well have fallen in the river," gasped Pen.

"I'm hungry," Hal said. "Where's that food? Let's eat."

Chapter 154

Peter left the suburbs of Fernborough and the last of the houses backing on to the river. As he rounded a bend in the river, he caught sight of the northern end of the footbridge over the ford.

His pace slowed and his pulses quickened as he began to think for the first time seriously how he would approach Pen and for that matter Pamela. Up to this moment he had only concentrated on the travelling and getting here.

Now, within this hour, he would have to reveal a violent truth. The question of a financial settlement was the easy bit; the marriage annulment more difficult. How would Pen feel being suddenly confronted by her 'dead' husband?

Less than half a mile away the picnickers were in merry mood.

Pen and Hal vied for which word Henry would say next.

Hal pointed Henry in Pen's direction. "Mama. Go to Mama."

The little boy toddled across to Pen and held a well chewed rusk to his mother.

"Ta." Little Henry spoke clearly.

Pen turned him around and pointed to Hal. "Go to Papa, darling."

Henry toddled dutifully back to Hal and pushed the rusk into Hal's face. "Ta." He repeated.

Hal fell back laughing. "Ta! What the heck does that mean? What went wrong with Papa?"

Pen trying her best to sound serious, answered.

"Henry must learn manners as a priority. Manners maketh the man."

"Manners maketh! Jeepers Pen, what is this?" Hal was now shrieking with laughter.

"You know what I mean, you idiot. I am determined to raise Henry in a proper manner."

"Thus spaketh the Hon. Penelope Bridge-Thompson. Might I remind the now Mrs Steading that her world has changed," replied Hal with equal mock gravity.

"Am I wrong for trying to teach our son manners?" Pen threw herself on Hal and rubbed noses with him. Hal rolled over and grabbed Pen holding her over the water.

"What was that you just called me?"

"An idiot." Pen defied him.

"What's this?" asked a laughing Pamela who was putting on her shoes after paddling with the children.

"Pen figures that I am an idiot, so it's in the river or an apology."

Pamela smiled. "Well, just you two remember that Pen is with child. I am away to fetch the sponge cake. Have your fun but take care."

Peter, recognising their voices from afar, was using a weeping willow to shield his approach.

He had been watching for some minutes, his heart thumping.

Mim he recognised even though she had grown so much.

Pen and Hal seemed to be different people. Not matching his memories.

He felt so different about them and himself. He no longer needed them.

What he really wanted was to be back on the farm with Helena and Pietro.

He resented the fates forcing them apart, taunting him with this scene.

Yet he was married to this woman who bore little resemblance to his memory of her.

Dorothy came out of the water with the little boy. He was the image of Hal.

Peter at long last began to assess what he was seeing. What this really meant.

The boy was at least 16 months maybe older. Then Pamela saying to be careful of Pen's unborn child. 'Hal and Pen are married? They must be,' he thought.

They had to be told about his survival. Maybe this would help with the annulment or severance.

But at what cost? Hesitating would not help anyone, he decided.

He owed nothing to either really and if that little boy is at least a year and a half he was conceived before his reported death.

Peter took a deep breath, pushed aside the trailing branches and stepped out into the sunlight.

"Any more sandwiches please, Papa?"

"Nanny Pammy's famous jammies." Hal offered Mim the packet.

Mim took one and began to go to Pen when she saw Peter staring.

"Papa, there's a strange little man watching us." She ran back to Hal.

Hal looked across assuming the strange little hairy figure was probably an Italian P.O.W. one of the many wishing to stay in Britain avoiding being returned home.

"I guess he's hungry Mim. Take him a sandwich." Hal offered the packet again to her.

Mim shuddered. "No please, Papa. I don't like him."

Little Henry toddled up to Hal's offered sandwich and took it.

"Take that to the bum little man," said Hal pointing, ignoring Pen's furious shaking of her head and mouthed. 'No.'

Little Henry toddled across to Peter to the amused gaze of Hal.

"Ta," he said and held up the sandwich in his little chubby hand.

Peter automatically took the sandwich. His spirit seemed to leave his body and stand aside watching. He clearly heard his answer. "Grazi."

Confused and in a panic, he hobbled, bobbled away towards the Drover's Lane.

He turned his head away to avoid being recognised.

Amazed and at the same time furious about his lame response, he was in complete daze.

He approached the Green aiming in his confused state to go to Pamela's. His instinct was to take his problems to her. It was then that Pamela suddenly appeared in front of him carrying a sponge cake. Both stood transfixed looking at each other.

Peter's already traumatised brain turned another somersault.

"Pamela," he gasped, "I am so sorry. Please forgive me."

Pamela's eyes popped. She and the sponge cake fell on to the Green.

Peter dropped to his knees alongside. "I am so sorry. Please forgive me." He pleaded again.

Out of the corner of his eye he saw a figure enter the Green from the Bendesbury river path.

Peter got to his feet. He was confused as to what next to do. He needed time to think.

This before confronting Pamela again or anyone else. Wishing he had stayed on the farm, he hurried on his way down to the Fernborough road. His only thought being to get away.

To think what to do next and clear his head which was banging.

When Pamela came to, she was no longer looking at Peter but at Father Michael Ryan.

"There now, Miss Avery. Just be taking your time," he said gently.

"Where's Peter?" Pam asked.

"Peter? There is no one else here Miss Avery. You must have fainted."

Pam tried to sit up. Michael Ryan stood and began to pick up the sponge cake which had broken into two pieces, He arranged the two bits back on the plate.

"Your cake looks to have survived although broken, it looks lovely. I suppose it will still eat."

Pamela struggled to a sitting position and looked anxiously around.

"Peter was here. Where has he gone?" She struggled to her feet. Still looking all around, she sobbed.

"He was here. Really here. I saw him. He spoke to me. Honest."

"I didn't see anyone. Only you."

The priest regretted the remark almost as soon as he made it. From Pam's distress, he realised that he was dealing with a very sensitive situation.

"Which way do you think he went?" Father Michael added hastily.

"I don't know but he was here. I heard him. He spoke to me. I heard him," Pamela repeated and sobbed while turning around in confusion.

Father Michael pretended to look around. "Do you think he went on to the cricket field?" he asked, adding, "Shall we be going to look together?"

Pamela stopped, stood very still, looking for all the world to be frozen to the spot.

Father Michael was caught by this stillness, the silence and the atmosphere of this sudden isolation. It was as if the Lord had ordered the world at large to back off.

In that moment, the priest felt a presence of, if not the Holy Spirit, possibly a moment when his priesthood would really become meaningful.

It was not that he believed or didn't believe Pamela. He felt somehow that his input would change significantly the happenings of this day.

He couldn't explain why he thought that even to himself.

Pamela said quietly, speaking to herself as if she was answering a question.

"I think I leave well alone. I will go home. I need to talk and think."

Father Michael followed her across the Green and into her home and kitchen.

Not a word passed. He didn't ask permission nor ask if she could spare the tea that he was about to make.

Pamela meanwhile sat at the table with her head in her hands.

Without any prompting Pamela began to speak about Peter and their early life.

Father Michael had heard some of this before. About Peter's insecurity, a little boy 'deserted', sent away, when she became pregnant with Paul. The whole sad story poured out yet again.

The priest sat at the table opposite with his back to the light. They sat and drank their tea in silence until Pamela suddenly looked Father Michael in the eyes.

"Could I have imagined this this afternoon? Am I going mad?"

Father Michael considered for a moment. "Would you tell me exactly what happened, please?"

Pamela took a long drink of tea and composed herself then took a deep breath before answering.

"I was carrying the sponge cake over to the river side to where we are picnicking.

I was thinking about Peter. How he would hang around when I was making a cake hoping to scrape out the mixing bowl once the cakes were in the oven. He loved that moment and so did I."

Pamela stopped speaking to blow her nose. "I miss that always and I missed it today."

She dabbed her eyes.

"I saw this little man coming towards me up the lane. Somehow, he reminded me of Peter. My first thought was that he was just some tramp or vagrant. He had his head turned to one side towards the hedge, obviously not wanting to be seen bobbing along with a funny limp.

This attracted my attention. Even though he looked strange there was something about him that was Peter. Even though I knew it couldn't be him. I was drawn towards him and as ..."

Pam swallowed composed herself again then repeated, "... and as we came together."

Pamela stopped speaking unable to get the words out. Father Michael sat and waited for her to compose herself yet again until she finally managed to whisper. "He turned into Peter and said ..."

Pamela stopped and nodded her head as if confirming her words.

"He said. 'I am sorry Pamela. Please forgive me'."

She continued to nod her head then broke down into uncontrollable sobbing.

It was a long, long time before she calmed down enough to say to Father Michael, "You do think I am mad, don't you?" Pamela gave a long, loud sigh. "I am so sorry."

The front door opened, and Dorothy shouted.

"Pammy, are you O.K. we were wondering where you were?"

Pam pulled herself together and replied. "In here, Pet."

Dorothy popped her head around the door. "There you are. We were getting concerned."

"I am sorry, Pet. I dropped the cake and the vicar kindly helped me."

Father Michael stood and took the cake to Dorothy. "It will still eat I'm sure."

"Kind of you, Pet. Tell the others I will be along presently." Pamela tried her best to sound normal. Dorothy stopped in the doorway, looking as if she was going to ask a question, then said:

"Don't worry, it's only a cake, Pammy."

Dorothy knew full well that this was not just about the cake. She knew also that Pam would tell all in her own good time just why the Catholic priest was in their kitchen.

This interruption sobered Pam. She went to the hall mirror and began to repair her makeup. Father Michael followed thinking perhaps he should go. Yet still he thought he needed to do more. That there was more unfinished business.

"I am sorry, Father this is the second time you've rescued me. Thank you."

She did her best to sound normal although still confused.

"I must go, people might be talking," he smiled, "and for the record, Miss Avery, I do not think you are mad. I believe you." He put on his hat and walked to the door.

"There is more to this life than either you or I ever dreamed of. That includes Peter's appearance today."

Pamela checked her hair in the mirror. "That's as maybe Father, but I must get back."

Father Michael stopped on the front garden path and squatted to look at the edging of London Pride, blocking Pamela's way to the gate as she left to return to her friends.

"I love your front garden with the roses," he said.

"And this beautifully marked little flower standing so proud and unnoticed by most."

Pamela, impatient to get back to the others, tried to pass.

The priest stood up, still blocking her path.

"You know Miss Avery there are a myriad of beautiful designs in nature. Artists over the centuries have endeavoured to capture their magnificence on canvas and yet."

He stood and fixed Pamela with his earnest grey eyes.

"To my recollection I cannot think of one, not even one design of man, that is memorable or even vaguely comparable. Humankind so far can only copy a pitiful few of nature's brilliant creations. People pass these miracles by every day, even foolish enough to explain their existence as an accident of evolution."

Pamela tried to push by him. Walking to the gate with her, he opened it and stood back tipping his hat. "Now that Miss Avery, really is mad."

By this time Pamela, beginning to feel very uncomfortable, left hurrying away.

Father Michael stood watching her leave whispering to himself, "What was all that about you idiot?"

He left for the rectory, still with this strange unignorable feeling that his mission for the day was far from over and trying to think why.

Chapter 155

Peter, totally confused, had little idea where to go except anywhere to hide and think.

Pamela's fainting and the arrival of Father Michael on to the Green panicked him sending him hob-bobbling down towards the Fernborough road. He cursed the unguarded moment and his meeting of Pamela before he had time to think and unscramble his mind.

He instinctively turned left towards Fernborough, away from the Green.

Two women were coming towards him on the same side of the road. They were vaguely familiar.

Nervously, Peter veered sharply across to the opposite side.

Freda and Edna could not help but notice this strange apparition hob-bobbling across the road.

They stood and watched as Peter dodged inside the lychgate of St. Mary's Church.

Peter knew that if Pamela and these women were to compare notes, it would open a ghastly can of worms. He was still unsure what to do with all his new knowledge.

He curled up in a corner, turning his face away waiting for them to pass. This they did but only after having a good look at his back. Continuing down the road they turned frequently to finally see him scurry thorough the churchyard and into the church.

Edna stopped. "Freda I'm off to warn the vicar." she said turning back.

"And I'm away to take my washing in," replied Freda. The two ladies hurried on their different ways.

Inside, the church was cool, silent and dark, serving to calm Peter down. He sat in one of the pews and tried to think.

He was still there much later when Father Michael arrived later that evening.

Edna had been to the rectory to warn about a tramp hanging about the church and to lock up the silver. Since then the priest had put in an hour or so of research from the local press. He had also quizzed Mary Mahoney who was his ever-present contact for the latest village gossip.

All St. Mary Upperford's recent history, being a small community, was common knowledge but as Michael Ryan knew, gossip and truth were all too frequently strangers.

Father Michael entered his church hoping that the reported tramp was still there. A quick look around confirmed his presence in the centre towards the front.

Peter heard the door open and clang to, the echoes sniggering away to be replaced by ringing echoes of footfalls. He welcomed this sudden invasion of what had become an oppressive and unproductive silence. He had thought his mind to a standstill.

Peter did not look around but was aware that the incomer was sitting right behind him.

Father Michael bowed his head and whispered a familiar prayer "God be in my ears and in my hearing. God be in my mind and my understanding."

Not knowing whether or not the man was praying, the priest stayed silent and waited.

Peter broke the silence. "I am at an impasse."

"Have you prayed?" Michael Ryan was relieved to hear him speak.

"No, just thinking," came the prompt reply. Peter was desperate to talk.

"Thinking can be a prayer when you are seeking the way."

Peter considered this for a short while before speaking again.

"Where there is conflict between the truth and a lie, the truth being cruel, and the lie involving less hurt. How can prayer help?"

"It might help, whereas I can't. Sometimes though it helps to share. I am here to listen."

Peter again considered before deciding he would like another opinion.

"I'm at a fork on my journey. If I choose honesty it will hurt a little family. Probably ruin the rest of their lives."

"And if you are not honest, does that mean lie?"

"They will be as happy as they are now, but I will be living a lie and breaking my word to others."

The priest nodded and didn't reply immediately. He had no answer. After some consideration he said, "In which case prayer is of little use and you will be judged on your action by wiser minds than mine."

This answer frustrated Peter. "Which is exactly where I was before you came in."

"Can I enquire as to how this problem has arisen?" Michael Ryan needed more information.

"Apparently because I have been listed as killed in action and no one bothered to let me know."

"And your resurrection is now the problem?"

Peter didn't answer. He was still frustrated that the discussion had not helped.

"Are you hungry?" Father Michael asked in a moment of inspiration.

"Yes," came the instant reply.

"Have you anywhere to stay tonight."

"No." This reply was equally quick.

Michael Ryan stood and placed both hands on Peter's shoulders.

"You have now. Let's talk some more over supper."

Chapter 156

Mary Mahoney was not best pleased. She flounced in and out of the rectory dining room grumbling out loud as she did so.

"Typical man, no thought for the airing of the bed." She plonked dishes of rabbit stew and vegetables on the table, "and as for food, not one thought either. It is only by providence, the promiscuity of rabbits and my nephew Sully that we have food at all." She stood and glared at Father Michael. "You expect me always to be working miracles."

Michael Ryan suppressed the smile which was only a whisker away from the feigned apologetic countenance he presented.

Peter, having ascended from a position of having nothing, to having a room, a bath and a bed for the night was now being presented with a feast. He was humbled to a position where he could barely speak these words. "Thank you so much for this and everything I am so grateful for such, such love." Mary was at the point of being really offended, then looking into this little man's eyes, recognised the absolute sincerity behind the words.

"Oh! To be sure young man, it's a pleasure." She paused and looked at Michael, adding, "to serve a real gentleman."

Michael Ryan watched Mary leave before reacting.

"Mary is an absolute treasure, but I suggest we wait until she is away home before any serious talking begins."

He smiled encouragingly at Peter. "Now let's eat and enjoy this bounty from the Good Lord."

He bowed his head, said grace, adding the prayer he had used earlier in the church, rewording 'my' with 'our.'

"God be in our minds and in our understanding."

Later, once they had the house to themselves, Peter told his story right up to the moment when Pam fainted. Father

Michael was able to fill in the many blanks from the encounters he had had with Miss Avery and Mary's retelling of the village rumours.

"You were totally isolated and had no idea of your reported demise or have any contact with the outside world?"

"None whatsoever until Attila finally came to the island. Even then I still was not able to contact the authorities. Essentially, we were still in hiding from the German Army. Attila and the partisans in Croatia had lost contact with the British."

Peter got up and walked over to the window which was open to let in the cool night air. He looked out into the night as if searching for inspiration.

"When I saw Hal, Pen and the family this afternoon, it did not take long to work out what had happened. Thinking what to do about it? Well that was and still is the question."

Peter seemed to struggle with his next point making several false starts.

Michael Ryan was content to wait whilst Peter continued to look out of the window and sigh.

"One thing keeps bugging me is that little boy of theirs was walking and talking."

He began drumming with his fingers on the window ledge.

"He is either a prodigy or he was conceived over two years ago."

He stopped drumming and stared out of the window. "This bothers me."

"Why?"

"It gives me good reason to announce my existence, claim my inheritance."

"And are you wishing to be doing that?" said Father Michael feeling that the moment of decision was approaching.

Peter didn't answer directly.

"I have promised money to Helena and Maria. They need money to sustain the farm and start a new venture of growing vines and making wine."

"Another reason to claim and I suppose your father wished for you to have this money?" suggested Father Michael.

Peter turned and looked directly at the priest, "I would give all the momey for just one year, one month or even one week of my father's attention."

Peter appeared to be waiting for the priest's reaction.

"All I ever got was one brief, moment. The barest glimpse of what could have been my father and then he was drunk. I never wished for his money, only his love."

"Will you claim the money? After all it is yours."

Father Michael waited for the answer, but Peter turned back to look once more through the window. The silence dragged on and still he waited.

"What's stopping you, Peter? You were hours in the church thinking. Is it that you don't wish to destroy that little girl's world after she was torn from her family by the Nazis?"

Meanwhile, Peter looked out into the night.

The slice of watermelon moon looked unreal against the skies. The stars twinkling reminded him of the fireflies back on the farm. Peter was feeling homesick.

"It's beautiful," Peter suddenly said, thinking primarily of the farm.

"What is?"

"The sky, the world, nature everything ... except." Peter paused.

"Except what?"

"Man." Peter spat his reply with a puff of venom.

"We can be beautiful too."

Peter didn't answer for nearly a minute. Father Michael waited for his reply.

"The little boy was beautiful." Peter smiled at the memory. "I, ugly, unkempt even menacing."

He paused again. "Still he came to me and gave me his sandwich."

There was an even longer pause. Father Michael waited remaining silent until Peter finally spoke.

"That little boy doesn't deserve to be a bastard."

Father Michael, at last, was able to seize a chance to break the impasse. He stood, smiled and invited Peter to join him. "Come Peter, let's away to our beds. I do believe you have made your decision."

Chapter 157

Deep River, Connecticut settled to the calm of the evening. That day and the town had been arrayed in their very best. It would have been a perfect day for a wedding. Everything was just as any bride would have hoped. Helena was hoping the weather would hold until tomorrow.

Helena Bellini was living her dream of finally visiting America. She had wished for this throughout her teenage years. Now at last she was not only visiting, she was staying. She was to marry Steed the following day.

Steed and Helena had met earlier that summer while he was holidaying on the Dalmatian coast with three friends. They were cruising the Adriatic and the Mediterranean.

Helena, tomorrow, would set off on the road to Providence on her honeymoon to consummate not only her marriage but her every hope and dream.

Her great grandmother after whom she was named had said to her as a small child, "If the world does not open up to you, then you need to open up to it. Create your own dream. Sometimes fate needs a helping hand. If I had not done so I would never have held you in my arms. Remember that, my sweet. Promise me that you will."

Helena looked up at the skies and whispered, "This is what you meant Grandmamma, isn't it?"

Last July Helena was a waitress in one of the hotels along the coast where she worked each summer before returning to her home island for the winter.

Speaking good English, she had no difficulty in finding a job.

She looked forward to each summer because she was able to use and hone her English.

Also, she was saving her wages and tips towards her dream of visiting America.

Helena adored observing the interaction between guests and the frequent inclusion of herself in the badinage; the visitor's subtle use of language; the various nuances for each situation.

The way that they delved into literature to decorate a point, especially the Americans whose easy inclusive camaraderie had the edge over the British who generally accepted the service of the waitress but not their presence.

It was in such a situation that she and Steed first became aware of the chemistry.

Having been served drinks by Helena, Steed, in a toast, said. "Come, fill the cup what boots it to repeat how time is slipping underneath our feet."

"Bit heavy that, Steed. What's that about?" said Waz.

"Eat drink and be merry for tonight we may dine with Pluto. Eh, Steed?" added Arnie.

"Now you are taking the mickey," replied Waz.

Each of the foursome, were jostling for the attention of the pretty waitress.

Forget the trash Guys." Said Joey, "Here's to the pretty waitress who wonders what the heck we are talking about."

The four turned towards Helena as one and raised their glasses saying in unison.

"To?"

"Helena," she replied smiling. Her eyes fixed upon Steed. Eager to impress, she completed the Khayyam quatrain. "Unborn tomorrow and dead yesterday, why fret of them if today be sweet."

Steed impressed, observed, "Great knowledge and you speak excellent English."

"My family all do, always have. It is a second language for us."

Both Helena and Steed were trying to impress.

Arnie, taking note of this, interrupted. "What's the toast then guys?"

"To Helena," they chorused laughing. She smiled happily and turned to go, aware that the head waiter was watching.

An instantly 'magnetised,' Steed searched his mind for an excuse to keep her.

"Do you have a local wine, say something special to this area?"

Helena,m equally attracted, returned. "I can try and find out but most of the local wines come from a co-operative." She turned again to leave then hesitated then, once more returned and without any depth of thought said, "My grandfather has a small vineyard which produces superb wine."

"Well bring it on," they all chorused.

Helena blushed and stuttered. "Silly of me, sorry, there is none here; it doesn't leave the island."

Aware of her embarrassment, Steed asked seriously, "This wine, does it have a name?"

"Hamadryades Par-role," she answered. There followed a short silence broken by Steed.

"Strange name. Why Parole? Why not Hamadryades Spirit. A Hamadryade is the spirit of the tree isn't it?" He asked. Helena, who aware the head waiter was still watching, collected a glass from across the table leaning close to Steed and whispered, "Tell you all later after my shift at 12.30 a.m." Blushing at the forwardness which seemed outside her control, she quickly left the table. The quartet watched her leave. Arnie leaned across the table and stage whispered, "Steed, I think you have just been given a ticket to ride."

He paused before adding, "She said 12.30." He paused. "Pity, the ship sails at ten."

The three of them roared with laughter.

Joey, the thoughtful one of the group, finished his drink, looked at his watch, stood and said, "Seriously guys, we really should push on. The last packet leaves in less than an hour."

Waz swallowed his drink. "Yup let's git. Tomorrow we see Venice and die."

"That's Naples you jerk. The other side of Italy."

Steed did not move or react as normal to any of this banter but sat looking to where Helena had left. Waz nudged Arnie. "I guess Steed's left the planet."

Arnie recognising this was perhaps just a little bit serious, tried to get through.

"Hey Steed, dude, get a hold of the reins we've got a boat to catch."

Steed looked up but made no effort to move.

"Sorry guys, something happened there. I need time to think."

"We don't have time, buddy." Arnie pleaded with him.

Joey added, "Steed, while you are circling the planet Venus, we're missing the sailing."

Steed still did not move. "Seriously guys, I mean it,"

Joey shrugged. "Come on fellas, Steed has lost the plot. He can follow."

"Yes, go on I can catch up with you in Gib. or Southampton."

Arnie was still reluctant to leave, looked at his watch.

"Come on, Steed. You can't really mean to stay."

"Yes, I do Arnie. There is a tide in the affairs of man ..." Steed began but he got no further because Arnie slapped the table. "Steed, wake up. This is no time to be listening to a five-hundred-year old Englishman whispering in your ear."

Arnie began to leave walking backwards, still pleading. "Come on Steed, this is stupid."

"Sorry Arnie, it's something my Great Grandpa once said whispering in my ear right now."

Arnie stopped, spreading his arms. "And Great Grandpa is saying?"

"When 'it' happens, you might only get one chance. Be sure and take it."

Arnie threw his arms in the air in frustration. "And what is this 'it'?"

Joey returned and grabbed Arnie. "Come leave him, we can still make it."

The two of them turned and ran. "Best of luck, Steed. See you, buddy."

Steed watched them leave and whispered,"We must take the current when it serves or lose our ventures." He was not the slightest bit worried. So sure, was he, that it was the right move. In any case he was bored with the demands of the tour company's routine and the 'nothing new' of it. Same drinks, same artificial destinations.

No getting to know the real folk and customs. It was all becoming so false. It needed to change.

At least that what he was telling himself.

Almost one hour later Steed was still sat staring into his beer waiting for 12.30.

Helena appeared dressed to leave, carrying a holdall.

Steed delighted to see her so soon, stood and motioned her to sit with him.

"Where are the others?" she asked.

"Back on the cruise ship. I thought you said 12.30."

"Plans changed. I've been dismissed." She smiled as she spoke.

Steed was shocked. "Jeez I'm sorry. I guess that was my fault."

"Don't be and it wasn't." Helena laughed, "I was already on a second warning for talking and not serving." She paused then said reassuringly, "I'm glad truly I am." She instinctively placed her hand on his. Steed feeling the 'electricity' surge through his body, took hold of her hand.

"Do you feel it too?"

Helena nodded yet tried to remove her hand. Steed's grip tightened.

"What do you feel?" He looked deep into her eyes. Helena surprised herself with an audible intake of breath and took a little while to answer. She was unsure where this was going.

She was surprised at her openness with someone who only hours ago was a stranger.

She had dreamed of the possibility of being swept off her feet and carried off to America.

Now it could be happening. She was not certain of her own motives. Steed waited for her to answer.

Finally, she did. "I don't know, maybe."

"For me it was just it." Steed was in no doubt. "I've let the cruise ship leave without me."

"It?" Helena repeated, questioning what 'it' meant.

Steed nodded, "It just hit me POW right to my soul centre, as if it was always meant to be."

They sat quietly thinking and watching the lights of the cruise ship out in the bay.

Presently, Helena asked, "You were really on that ship and you let it go without you?"

"Sure did."

Helena couldn't find a response; she didn't quite know what to think.

"Why Hamadryades Parole?" Steed suddenly asked.

This broke the spell which seemed to have been cast on Helena. She laughed.

"What a strange question. I haven't the first idea."

"You did promise to tell me," Steed prompted.

"I did, didn't I? Sorry, it was just a ruse to keep you interested."

"Thank you for that."

For a long time, they just sat enjoying each other's company watching the world go by.

The ship leaving the docks.

"What will you do now?"

Helena shrugged. "Get another job, I think. What will you do?"

"I figured I might visit your island in search of this Hamadryades Parole."

His answer was prompt and definite indicating that he was not fooling.

Helena was taken aback. It was not as though this was not part of her sub plot. She was beginning to feel the chemistry from this earnest, handsome American. Still she managed to remain cautious. "That would take two ferries and an eight-kilometre uphill hike and permission from Grandpa Pietro."

Steed was not to be denied. "I'll risk it if you will."

Helena, now warming to the idea, replied, "On condition that you take me on a reciprocal trip to America."

“I’m in.” Steed was equally prompt and definite with this answer adding, “That is if Grandpa Pietro is willing to sell me a bottle.”

“There is only one way to find out.” Helena finally relaxed against Steed.

Chapter 158

Which was why Helena with her mother were watching Steed and Grandpa Pietro on the terrace across the stream to the east. "Do you think I am doing the right thing, Momma?"

Her mother crocheting, showing little sign of the importance of the question, replied, "I have given you your moral compass girl. When you fly the nest and in which direction is down to you." She paused and took her daughter's hand.

"I will say this. If you ask the question, you are rightfully considering what you are doing. That I like. You will have worries. It is a big step, but it is one which we all need to take. That is if we are to grow. So, do it and trust to providence."

Helena smiled knowing that her mother approved.

Across at the other terrace Steed was slightly mellow. His mind encompassed by the content of the now empty bottle of Hamadryade's Par-role, asked, "Can I keep the bottle or at least, the label?"

"I will give you a label, it is easier carried," Pietro replied.

"Thank you." Steed turned the bottle over in his hands. "And you don't know why the name?"

"No, my father refused to answer me when I asked. It remains a mystery."

Steed continued to study the label. He looked up at the olive tree on the cliff edge.

He looked at a facsimile of the tree on the label.

Somewhere inside his head he felt the need to find the answer.

"This picture is a facsimileof that olive tree plus there's an acorn, an olive and a grape in that order hanging from that crooked horizontal branch. What's that about?"

He looked at Pietro who spread his arms and shrugged away the question.

Steed smiled and continued to look at the label. "And this quatrain of Khayyam's underneath intrigues me. You say that it used in a traditional blessing of the new wine each year?"

Pietro nodded but didn't speak.

Steed had the feeling that he knew more than he was prepared to say.

Steed continued his muse. "There is sure a hidden message here."

He paused, still thinking.

"This is similar to a ritual my family perform when on holiday in New England about this time."

"Really, what is this?"

'Pietro is prepared to talk but not about the wine's message,' Steed observed to himself.

He began to answer.

"We link arms and say. 'If I could choose a world to be ...'

He hesitated while still looking intently at the bottle. Quickly he changed tack.

"No, I much prefer the Khayyam," he continued, now reading from the label this familiar quatrain:

"Ah love! Would not you and I with fate conspire
To grasp this sorry scheme of things entire
Would not we shatter it to bits and then
Re-mould it nearer to the Heart's Desire."

The author

Frederick Munn was born in 1928 in a one-bedroom tenement in Sheffield and attended Firth Park Grammar School. He has had many jobs, including a book salesman, vacuum cleaner salesman, an engineering clerk, Steel Buyer and a self-employed entrepreneur. He is the third son in a political family including two Lord Mayors and a junior Minister. He chooses to be apolitical, an observer describing himself as a "chancer" and a "romancer" fed on an early diet of AA Milne and Kipling and his mind was formed into that of a natural storyteller. He likes to write, read, watch and learn. Each day being the unopened present that it is. This is his first novel. He lives in Bristol, married over 60 years to Brenda. They have one son, Jonathan Paul and two Granddaughters, Juliette and Lydia.